# REALMS OF DARKNESS

# REALMS OF DARKNESS

INTRODUCED BY
## CHRISTOPHER LEE

EDITED BY
## MARY DANBY

This edition published in Great Britain
in 1985 by

Octopus Books Limited
59 Grosvenor Street
London W1

in collaboration with

William Heinemann Limited
10 Upper Grosvenor Street
London W1

and

Martin Secker & Warburg Limited
54 Poland Street
London W1

ISBN 0 86273 2441

Printed and bound in Great Britain by Collins, Glasgow

# Contents

# Contents

# Introduction

From 1947 when I began my career as an actor until 1957 I had spent, I suppose, about one fifth of my acting time in sinister roles, but one tends to forget that so popular is this element of human make-up (I mean social and psychological make-up, not cosmetic, important as this is) that connection with it tends to fix a person forever in the public mind as one of the legion of the damned. Let me illustrate.

Some years after *Dracula* was first screened, I was living with my wife Gitte in Switzerland and working mainly in Italy. We were going home after I had played a couple of roles in that country such as the noble father of a brood of lesbian vampires (in a film loosely tied to *Carmilla*, by the great Irish author of supernatural stories Sheridan Le Fanu), and another as something called *Count Drago* in a film set in a whole castleful of living dead – and late at night on the road between Milan and Stresa we had a tyre blow.

Now Gitte was heavily pregnant, and I told her to stay put while I went to fetch help. A few seconds later I fell twenty feet down into a cutting made for a new road, and covered with mud and sand, I tottered through fields of turnips and jettisoned rubbish and by turns made my way towards some lights about half a mile away. I fetched up panting, by a solitary building by a telephone pole. An Alsatian appeared in the window, in full voice, then his owner shouting, 'Who's there?' I explained and asked to use the phone. When he opened the door he immediately took a whole pace back, goggling. I knew I must look somewhat undesirable, covered in slime, but I wasn't prepared for his extreme reaction. He uttered a piercing shriek, cried '*E lui*' ('It's him.') – and fainted. It turned out that he had confused me with the dreaded Count, and thought it would not be long before he joined the ranks of the undead.

Now far be it from me to disown my long past association with the Count, for the byways of that area of nocturnal frights, casements overlooking unfathomable abysses and messages from the dark side of the moon. It has paid the rent, and it has been fun as well as work, and fine artists like Peter Cushing and Boris Karloff have become my friends. But I have to recognize, from an enthusiasm for macabre stories that began in boyhood and is still with me, that there are limits to what films can do. If you want the authentic *frisson*, the dawn of apprehension rising on the naked crags of malice and evil, you have to go back to written texts, to the stories as the authors first imagined them.

And what a lot of them there are to choose from! My first affinities in the field were discovered through being interviewed for a place at Eton by that great master of the ghost story, M. R. James and later at school being read to by that prolific story-teller E. F. Benson. And in spite of having been Count Dracula, I am just as thrilled and chilled by a finely-spun yarn as anybody else, and delighted to be shown the way to different varieties of short, sharp shock by practitioners who became my friends, like Robert Bloch and Ray Bradbury in America, and Dennis Wheatley who was almost a neighbour when we lived for some years in the same quiet London square.

It is sometimes said by killjoys that the authors of macabre stories should be locked up in the horrid cages of their own invention and sunk in the sea, but the truth is that quite apart from the fact that almost every great European author, whatever his general preoccupations, has tried his hand with a ghost story, those I have known were excellent, civilized companions, and certainties one day to sing among choirs of angels. Of course, I wouldn't say that either Edgar Allan Poe, or that strange figure Ambrose Bierce was exactly sociable, but every craft has its loners.

Exploring the field, one is glad to discover that it is immense, apparently without fences, and that the skill and versatility in the short story which have always been such a strong feature of both British and American writing show no signs of diminishing. It's a pleasure to point out to those who think that supernatural stories are always portly and quaint in manner and style, that in this anthology are featured many modern writers, like Roald Dahl, Stephen King and Paul Theroux – all let us hope full of stories and novels for the future.

The problem for the modern writer eager to work out the more disturbing emotions burning at the back of his mind, and who wants to test him or herself against the best of the occult, black magic, horror, the weird and the gruesome, as exemplified in this excellently catholic range of stories, is that the reader is not willing to give him, as he would in another age, the benefit of accepting the tale from the outset. There is, of course, a fairly long tradition of narrators on the defensive, foreseeing trouble from sceptics in the audience, but today he has to marshal his arguments and his theatrical props to erect a barricade of plausibility against attacks from every quarter of science and technology. Actually the position was very plainly and straightforwardly stated by a character in a story called 'The Judge's House' by Bram Stoker, that figures in this anthology. The speaker is a cleaning woman, discussing with the protagonist the rumours of evil concerning the house he has just taken:

'I'll tell you what it is, sir,' she said, 'bogies is all kinds and sorts of things – except bogies! Rats and mice, and beetles, and creaky doors, and loose slates, and broken panes, and stiff drawer handles that stay out when you pull them and then fall down in the middle of the night. Look at the wainscot of the room! It is old – hundreds of years old! Do you think there's no rats and beetles there? And do you imagine, sir, that you won't see none of them? Rats is bogies, I tell you, and bogies is rats; and don't you get to think anything else!'

But what if in the middle of the night you are persuaded that the right-enough rat is nevertheless a reincarnated bogie? Like a boxer, the writer must go for his opponent at the first inkling of uncertainty. And whatever you may think of the strangeness of the situations the contributors to this volume make, they all have that intrinsic and essential gift of wanting to paralyse the audience with the sheer excitement of their extraordinary invention.

Now the quotation above comes from a story by the man who wrote *Dracula*, which is where I came in. But before leaving again with a deep obeisance to the editor for her taste, arcane knowledge and labours for such a prodigious volume, I must add a couple of slight observations.

The story Dracula first appeared in book form in 1914 in a Stoker collection called *Dracula's Guest* and was originally intended to be an extra chapter in the book *Dracula* however Mrs Stoker talked her husband out of it. Thirteen years later a special edition of a thousand numbered copies was distributed to the audience at the 250th night of the play of Dracula. Each recipient, as he opened the book, was startled by a black bat that flew out, powered by elastic. It's interesting to note, incidentally, that merchandising stunts of this kind are not as modern as some disenchanted people feel.

It is difficult for an actor who has appeared in so many grim legends and shivery fantasies, and who has been killed more than any other actor alive (if I may so put it), to end on an upbeat note. But the volume before you enables me to do that, not only because of its manifest bulk, but because it makes a wonderfully rich sampler for talents of all kinds spread over centuries. Almost every author represented here has a body of work worth investigating, if you decide you like the example of it now being offered you.

But whether the rat is a bogie, or the bogie is a rat, is something between you and each individual author. If, on the other hand, any bats should fly out of this book – you have been warned!

# Denton's Death

## *Martin Amis*

Suddenly Denton realized that there would be three of them, that they
would come after dark, that their leader would have his own key, and
that they would be calm and deliberate, confident that they had all the
time they needed to do what had to be done. He knew that they would
be courtly, deferential, urbane – whatever state he happened to be in
when they arrived – and that he would be allowed to make himself
comfortable, perhaps even offered a cigarette to smoke first. He never
seriously doubted that he would warm to and admire all three at once,
and wish only that he could have been their friend. He knew that they
used a machine. As if prompted by some special hindsight, Denton
thought often and poignantly about the moment when the leader would
consent to take his hand as the machine began to work. He knew that
they were out there already, seeing people, making telephone calls; and
he knew that they must be very expensive.

At first, he took a lively, even rather self-important interest in the
question of who had hired the men and their machine. Who would
bother to do this to him? There was his brother, a huge exhausted man
whom Denton had never liked or disliked or felt close to or threatened
by in any way: they had quarrelled recently over the allotment of their
dead mother's goods, and Denton had in fact managed to secure a few
worthless extras at his brother's expense; but this was just one more
reason why his brother could never afford to do this to him. There was
a man at the office whose life Denton had probably ruined: having
bullied his friend into assisting him with a routine office theft, Denton
told all to his superiors, claiming that he had used duplicity merely to
test his colleague (Denton's firm not only dismissed the man – they also,
to Denton's mild alarm, successfully prosecuted him for fraud); but
someone whose life you could ruin so easily wouldn't have the determination to do this to him. And there were a few women still out on the
edges of his life, women he had mistreated as thoroughly as he dared, all
of whom had seemed to revel in his frustrations, thrill to his regrets,
laugh at his losses: he had heard that one of them was about to marry
somebody very rich, or at any rate somebody sufficiently rich to hire the

three men; but she had never cared about him enough to want to do this to him.

Within a few days, however, the question of who had hired them abruptly ceased to concern Denton. He could muster no strong views on the subject; it was all done now, anyway. Denton moved slowly through the two rooms of his half-converted flatlet, becalmed, listless, his mind as vacant as the dust-whorled window panes and the shrilly pictureless walls. Nothing bored him any more. All day he wandered silently through the flat, not paying for it (no payment seemed to be seriously expected), not going to his office more than once or twice a week and then not at all (and no one there seemed to mind; they were tactful and remote like understanding relatives), and not thinking about who had hired the three men and their machine. He had a little money, enough for milk and certain elementary foods. Denton had been an anorexic in his youth because he hated the idea of becoming old and big. Now his stomach had rediscovered that ripe, sentimental tenseness, and he usually vomited briskly after taking solids.

He sat all day in his empty living-room, thinking about his childhood. It seemed to him that all his life he had been tumbling away from his happiness as a young boy, tumbling away to the insecurity and disappointment of his later years, when gradually, as if through some smug consensus, people stopped liking him and he stopped liking them. Whatever happened to me? thought Denton. Sometimes he would get a repeated image of himself at the age of six or seven, running for the school bus, a satchel clutched to his side, his face fresh and unanxious – and suddenly Denton would lean forward and sob huskily into his hands, and stand up after a while, and make tea perhaps, and gaze out at the complicated goings-on in the square, feeling drunk and wise. Denton thanked whoever had hired the three men to do this to him; never before had he felt so alive.

Later still, his mind gave itself up entirely to the coming of the men and their machine, and his childhood vanished along with all the other bits of his life. Facelessly, Denton 'rationalized' his kitchen supplies, importing a variety of dried milk and wide-spectrum baby foods, so that, if necessary, he should never have to leave the flat again. With the unsmiling dourness of an adolescent Denton decided to stop washing his clothes and to stop washing his body. Every morning subtracted clearness from the window panes; he left the dry, belching heaters on day and night; his two rooms became soupy and affectless, like derelict conservatories in summer thunder. Once, on an impulse, Denton jerked open the stiff living-room window. The outdoors tingled hatefully, as if the air were full of steel. He shut the window and returned to his chair by the fire, where he sat with no expression on his face until it was time to go to bed.

At night, exultant and wounding dreams thrilled and tormented him. He wept on scarlet beaches, the waves climbing in front of him until they hid the sun. He saw cities crumble, mountains slide away, continents crack. He steered a dying world out into the friendly heat of space. He held planets in his hands. Denton staggered down terminal arcades, watched by familiar, hooded figures in dark doorways. Little flying girls with jagged predatory teeth swung through the air towards him at impossible, meandering speed. He came across his younger self in distress and brought him food but an eagle stole it. Often Denton awoke stretched diagonally across the bed, his cheeks wet with exhausted tears.

When would they come? What would their machine be like? Denton thought about the arrival of the three men with the gentle hopelessness of a long-separated lover: the knock at his door, the peaceful and reassuring smiles, the bed, the request for a cigarette, the offer of the leader's hand, the machine. Denton imagined the moment as a painless mood-swing, a simple transference from one state to another, like waking up or going to sleep or suddenly realizing something. Above all he relished the thought of that soothing handclasp as the machine started to work, a ladder-rung, a final handhold as life poured away and death began.

What would his death be like? Denton's mind saw emblem books, bestiaries. Nothing and a purple hum. Deceit. An abandoned play-ground. Hurtful dreams. Failure. The feeling that people want to get rid of you. The process of dying repeated for ever. 'What will my death be like?' he thought – and knew at once, with abrupt certainty, that it would be just like his life: different in form, perhaps, but nothing new, the same balance of bearables, the same.

Late that night Denton opened his eyes and they were there. Two of them stood in the backlit doorway of his bedroom, their postures heavy with the task they had come to do. Behind them, next door, he could hear the third man preparing the machine; shadows filled the yellow ceiling. Denton sat up quickly, half-attempting to straighten his hair and clothes. 'Is it you?' he asked.

'Yes,' said the leader, 'we're here again.' He looked round the room. 'And *aren't* you a dirty boy.'

'Oh don't tell me that,' said Denton, '– not now.' He felt an onrush of shame and self-pity, saw himself as they saw him, an old tramp in a dirty room, afraid to die. Denton lapsed into tears as they moved forward – it seemed the only way left to express his defencelessness. 'Nearly there,' one of them called fruitily through the door. Then all three were upon him. They hauled him from his bed and pushed him into the living-room. They began to strap him with leather belts to an upright chair, handling him throughout like army doctors with a patient they knew to be difficult. It was all very fast. 'A cigarette – please,' said Denton. 'We haven't got all night, you know,' the leader whispered: 'You do know that.'

The machine was ready. It was a black box with a red light and two chromium switches; it made a faraway rumble; from the near side came a glistening, flesh-coloured tube, ending in what looked like a small pink gas-mask or a boxer's mouthpiece. 'Open wide,' said the leader. Denton struggled weakly. They held his nose. 'Tomorrow it'll be a thing of the past,' said the leader, 'finished ... in just ... a couple of minutes.' He parted Denton's clenched lips with his fingers. The soft mouthpiece slithered in over his front teeth – it seemed *alive*, searching out its own grip with knowing fleshy surfaces. A plunging, nauseous, inside-out suction began to gather within his chest, as if each corpuscle were being marshalled for abrupt and concerted movement. The hand! Denton stiffened. With hopeless anger he fought for the leader's attention, tumescing his eyes and squeezing thin final noises up from deep in his throat. As the pressure massed hugely inside his chest, he bent and flexed his wrists, straining hard against the leather bands. Something was tickling his heart with thick strong fingers. He was grappling with unconsciousness in dark water. He was dying alone. 'All right,' one of them said as his body slackened, 'he's ready.' Denton opened his eyes for the last time. The leader was staring closely at his face. Denton had no strength; he frowned sadly. The leader understood almost at once, smiling like the father of a nervous child. 'Oh yes,' he said. 'About now Denton always likes a hand.' Denton heard the second switch click and he felt a long rope being tugged out through his mouth.

The leader held his hand firmly as life poured away, and Denton's death began.

Suddenly Denton realized that there would be three of them, that they would come after dark, that their leader would have his own key, and that they would be calm and deliberate, confident that they had all the time they needed to do what had to be done. At first, he took a lively, even rather self-important interest in the question of who had hired the men and their machine. Within a few days, however, the question of who had hired them abruptly ceased to concern Denton. He sat all day in his empty living-room, thinking about his childhood. Later still, his mind gave itself up entirely to the coming of the men and their machine, and his childhood vanished along with all the other bits of his life. At night, exultant and wounding dreams thrilled and tormented him. When would they come? What would his death be like? Late that night Denton opened his eyes and they were there, 'Yes,' said the leader, 'we're here again.' 'Oh don't tell me that,' said Denton, ' – not now.' The machine was ready. The leader held his hand firmly as life poured away, and Denton's death began.

# In the Slaughteryard

## *Anonymous*

'You seem to have had a lively time of it, Jeaffreson; at all events you've got something to show for *your* night's adventure,' said the President of the Adventurers' Club, pointing to the bandaged hand of Mr Horace Jeaffreson.

'Yes,' replied that gentleman, 'I've got something to remember last night by; but I've got something more to show than this bandaged hand that you all stare at so curiously.' And then Horace Jeaffreson rose, drew himself up to his full height of six feet one, and exhibited the left side of his closely-buttoned, well-fitting frock-coat. 'I should like you to notice that,' he said, pointing to a straight, clean cut in the cloth, just on a level with the region of the heart. 'When you've heard what I've got to tell, you'll acknowledge that I had a pretty narrow squeak of it last night; three inches more, and it would have been all up with H.J. I don't regret it a bit, because I believe that I have been the means of ridding the world of a monster. Time alone will prove whether my supposition is correct,' and then Mr Horace Jeaffreson shuddered. 'Before I begin the history of my adventures, there are two objects that I must submit to your inspection; they are in that little parcel that I have laid upon the mantelpiece. Perhaps as my left hand is disabled, you won't mind undoing the parcel, Mr President.'

He laid a long, narrow parcel upon the table, and the President proceeded to open it. The contents consisted of a policeman's truncheon – branded H 1839 – and a long, narrow-bladed, double-edged knife, having an ebony handle, which was cut in criss-cross ridges. There were stains of blood upon the truncheon, and the knife appeared to have been dipped in a red transparent varnish, of the nature of which there could be no doubt.

'Those are the exhibits,' said Horace Jeaffreson. 'The slit in my coat, my wounded hand, that truncheon and that bloodstained knife, and a copy of the morning paper, are all the proofs I have to give you that my adventure of last night was not a hideous nightmare dream, or a wildly improbable yarn.

'I must confess that when I placed my forefinger haphazard upon the map last night, and found that fate had given me Whitechapel as my hunting-ground, I was considerably disgusted. I left this place bound for the heart of sordid London, the home of vice, of misery, and crime. Until last night I knew nothing whatever about the East End of London. I've never been bitten with the desire to do even the smallest bit of "slumming". I'm sorry enough for the poor. I'd do all I can to help them in the way of subscribing, and that sort of thing, you know; but actual poverty in the flesh I confess to fighting shy of – it's a weakness I own, but, so to say, poverty, crass poverty, offends my nostrils. I'm not a snob, but that's the truth. However, I was in for it; I had got to pass the night in Whitechapel for the sake of what might turn up. A good deal turned up, and a good deal more than I had bargained for.

'"Shall I wait for you, sir?" said the cabman, as he pulled up his hansom at the corner of Osborne Street. "I'm game to wait, sir, if you won't be long."

'But I dismissed him. "I shall be here for several hours, my man," I said.

'"You know best, sir," said the cabman: "everyone to his taste. You'd better keep yer weather-eye open, sir, anyhow; for the side streets ain't over and above safe about here. If I were you, sir, I'd get a 'copper' to show me round." And then the man thanked me for a liberal fare, and flicking his horse, drove off.

'But I had come to Whitechapel to seek adventure, something was bound to turn up, and, as a modern Don Quixote, I determined to take my chance alone; for it wasn't under the protecting wing of a member of the Force that I was likely to come across any very stirring novelty.

'I wandered about the dirty, badly-lighted streets, and I marvelled at the teeming hundreds who thronged the principal thoroughfares. I don't think that ever in my life before I had seen so many hungry, hopeless-looking, anxious-looking people crowded together. They all seemed to be hurrying either to the public-house or from the public-house. Nobody offered to molest me. I'm a fairly big man, and with the exception of having my pockets attempted some half-dozen times, I met with no annoyance of any kind. As twelve o'clock struck an extraordinary change came over the neighbourhood; the doors of the public-houses were closed, and, save in the larger thoroughfares, the whole miserable quarter seemed to become suddenly silent and deserted. I had succeeded in losing myself at least half a dozen times; but go where I would, turn where I might, two things struck me – first, the extraordinary number of policemen about; second, the frightened way in which men and women, particularly the homeless wanderers of the night, of both sexes, regarded me. Belated wayfarers would step aside out of my path, and stare at me, as though with dread. Some, more timorous than the rest, would even cross the road at my approach; or, avoiding me, start off at a run or at a shambling trot. It puzzled me at first. Why on earth should the poverty-stricken rabble, who had the misfortune to live in this wretched neighbourhood, be afraid of a man, or appear to be afraid of a man who had a decent coat to his back?

'The side streets, as I say, were almost absolutely deserted, save for infrequent policemen who gave me goodnight, or gazed at me suspiciously. I was wandering aimlessly along, when my curiosity was suddenly aroused by a powerful, acrid, and peculiar odour. "Without doubt," said I to myself, "that is the nastiest stench it has ever been my misfortune to smell in the whole course of my life." "Stench" is a Johnsonian word, and very expressive; it's the only word to convey any idea of the nastiness of the mixed odours that assailed my nostrils. "I will follow my nose," I said to myself, and I turned down a narrow lane, a short lane, lit by a single gas-lamp. "It gets worse and worse," I thought, "and it can't be far off, whatever it is." It was so bad that I actually had to hold my nose.

'At that moment I ran into the arms of a policeman, who appeared to spring suddenly out of the earth.

'"I'm sure I beg your pardon," I said to the man.

"Don't mention it, sir," replied the policeman briskly and there was something of a countryman's drawl in the young man's voice. "Been and lost yourself, sir, I suppose?" he continued.

'"Well, not exactly," I replied. "The fact is, I wandered down here to see where the smell came from."

'"You've come to the right shop, sir," said the policeman, with a smile; "it's a regular devil's kitchen they've got going on down here, it's just a knacker's, sir, that's what it is; and they make glue, and size, and cat's-meat, and patent manure. It isn't a trade that most people would hanker for," said the young policeman with a smile. 'They are in a very large way of business, sir, are Melmoth Brothers; it might be worth your while, sir, to take a look round; you'll find the night-watchman inside, sir, and he'd be pleased to show you over the place for a trifle; and it's worth seeing is Melmoth Brothers."'

'"I'll take your advice, and have a look at the place," I answered. "There seems to be a great number of police about tonight, my man," I said.

'"Well, yes, sir," replied the constable, "you see the scare down here gets worse and worse; and the people here are just afraid of their own shadows after midnight; the wonder to my mind is, sir, that we haven't dropped onto him long ago."

'Then all at once it dawned upon me why it was that men and women had turned aside from me in fear; then I saw why it was that the place seemed a perfect ants'-nest of police. The great scare was at its height: the last atrocity had been committed only four days before.

'"Why, bless my heart, sir," cried the young policeman confidentially, "one might come upon him red-handed at any moment. I only wish it was my luck to come across him, sir," he added. "Lor bless ye, sir," the young policeman went on, "he'll be a pulling it off just once too often, one of these nights."

'"Well, I suppose he helps to keep you awake,' I said with a smile, for want of something better to say.

'"Keep me awake, sir!" said the man solemnly; "I don't suppose there's a single constable in the whole H Division as thinks of aught else. Why, sir, he haunts me like; and do you know, sir – " and the man's voice suddenly dropped to a very low whisper – "I do think as how I saw him;" and then he gave a sigh. "I was standing, sir, just where I was when I popped out on you, a hiding-up like; it was more than a month ago, and there was a woman standing crying, leaning on that very post, sir, by Melmoth Brothers' gate, with just a thin ragged shawl, sir, drawn over her head. She was down upon her luck, I suppose, you see, sir – and there was a heavyish fog on at the time – when stealing up out of the fog behind where the poor thing was standing, sir, sobbing and crying for all the world just like a hungry child, I saw something brown noiselessly stealing up towards the woman; she had her back to it, sir – and she never moved. I could just make out the stooping figure of a man, who came swiftly forward with noiseless footsteps, crouching along in the deep shadow of yonder wall. I rubbed my eyes to see if I was awake or dreaming; and, as the crouching figure rapidly advanced, I saw that it was a man in a long close-fitting brown coat of common tweed. He'd got a black billycock jammed down over his eyes, and a red cotton comforter that hid his face; and in his *left* hand, which he held behind him, sir, was something that now and again glittered in the light of that lamp up there. I loosed my truncheon, sir, and I stood back as quiet as a mouse, for I guessed who I'd got to deal with. Whoever he was, he meant murder, and that was clear – murder and worse. All of a sudden, sir, he turned and ran back into the fog, and I after him as hard as I could pelt; and then he disappeared just as if he'd sunk through the earth. I blew my whistle, sir, and I reported what I'd seen at the station, and the superintendent – he just reprimanded me, that's what he did.

'"'1839, I don't believe a word of it,' said he; and he didn't.

'"But I *did* see him, sir, all the same; and if I get the chance," said the man bitterly, "I'll put my mark on him."

'"Well, policeman," I said, "I hope you may, for your sake," and then I forced a shilling on him. "I'll go and have a look round at Melmoth Brothers' place," I said. I gave the young policeman goodnight, and I crossed the road and walked through the open gateway into a large yard, from whence proceeded the atrocious odour that poisoned the neighbourhood.

'The place was on a slope, it was paved with small round stones, and was triangular in shape; a high wall at the end by which I had entered formed the base of the triangle, and one side of the narrow lane in which I had left the young policeman. There was a sort of shed or shelter of corrugated iron running along this wall, and under the shed I could indistinctly see the figures of horses and other animals, evidently secured, in a long row. All down one side of the boundary wall of the great yard which sloped from the lane towards the point of the triangle, I saw a number of furnace doors, five and twenty of them at least; they appeared to be let into a long wall of masonry of the most solid description, and they presented an extraordinary appearance, giving one the idea of the hulk of a mysterious ship, burnt well-nigh to the water's edge, through whose closed ports the fire, which was slowly consuming her, might be plainly seen. The curious similitude to a burning hulk was rendered still more striking by the fact that, above the low wall in which the furnace doors were set, there was a heavy cloud of dense white steam that hung suspended above what seemed like the burning hull of the great phantom ship. There wasn't a breath of air last night, you know, to stir that reeking cloud of fetid steam; and the young summer moon shone down upon it bright and clear, making the heaped piles of steaming vapour look like great clouds of fleecy whiteness. The place was silent as the grave itself, save for a soft bubbling sound as of some thick fluid that perpetually boiled and simmered, and the occasional movement of one of the tethered animals. The wall opposite the row of furnaces, which formed the other side of the triangle, had a number of stout iron rings set in it some four feet apart, and looked, for all the world, like some old wharf from which the sea had long ago receded. At the apex of the triangle, where the walls nearly met, were a pair of heavy double doors of wood, which were well-nigh covered with stains and splashes of dazzling whiteness; and the ground in front of them was stained white too, as though milk, or whitewash, had been spilled, for several feet.

'There were great wooden blocks and huge benches standing about in the great paved yard; and I noted a couple of solid gallowslike structures, from each of which depended an iron pulley, holding a chain and a great iron hook. I noted, too, as a strange thing, that though the ground was paved with rounded stones – and, as you know, it was a dry night and early summer – yet in many places there were puddles of dark mud, and the ground there was wet and slippery.

'But what struck me as the strangest thing of all in this weird and dreadful place, were the numerous horses lying about in every direction, apparently sleeping soundly; but as I stared at them, brilliantly lighted up as they were by the rays of the clear bright moon, I saw that they were not sleeping beasts at all – that they were not old and worn-out animals calmly sleeping in happy ignorance of the fate that waited them on the morrow – but by their strange stiffened and gruesome attitudes, I perceived that the creatures were already dead.

'I'm no longer a child, I have no illusions, and I am not easily frightened; but I felt a terrible sense of oppression come over me in this dreadful place. I began to feel as a little one feels when he is thrust, for the first time in his life, into a dark room by a thoughtless nurse. But I had come out of curiosity to see the place; I had expressed my intention of doing so to Constable 1839 of the H Division; so I made up my mind to go through with it. I would see what there was to be seen, I would learn something about the mysterious trade of Melmoth Brothers; and as a preliminary I proceeded to light my briar-root, so as, if possible, to get rid to some extent of the numerous diabolical smells of the place by the fragrant odour of Murray's mixture.

'And then, when I had lighted my pipe, I was startled by a hoarse voice that suddenly croaked out—"Make yourself at home, guvnor; don't stand on no sort o' ceremony, for you look a gentleman, you does; a real gentleman, a chap what always has the price of a pint in his pocket, and wouldn't grudge the loan of a bit of baccy to a pore old chap as is down on his luck."

'I turned to the place from whence the voice proceeded. It was a strange-looking creature that had addressed me. He was an old man with a pointed grey beard, who sat upon a bench of massive timber covered with dreadful stains. The bright moon lighted up his face, and I could see his features as clearly as though I saw them by the light of day. He was clad in a long linen jerkin of coarse stuff, reaching nearly to his heels; but its colour was no longer white – the garment was red, reddened by awful smears and splashes from head to foot. The figure wore a pair of heavy jack-boots, with wooden soles, nigh upon an inch thick, to which the uppers were riveted with nails of copper; those great boots of his made me sick to look at them. But the strangest thing of all in the dreadful costume of the grim figure was the head-dress, which was a close-fitting wig of knitted grey wool; very similar, in appearance at all events, to the undress wig worn by the Lord High Chancellor of England – that wig, that once sacred wig, which Mr George Grossmith has taught us to look upon with that familiarity which breeds contempt. The wig was tied beneath the pointed beard by a string. I noticed that round the figure's waist was a leathern strap, from which hung a sort of black pouch; from the top of this projected, so as to be ready to his hand, the hafts of several knives of divers sorts and sizes. The face was lean, haggard, and wrinkled; fierce ferrety eyes sparkled beneath long shaggy grey eyebrows; and the toothless jaws of the old man and his pointed grey beard seemed to wag convulsively as in suppressed amusement. And then Macaulay's lines ran through my mind –

> 'To the mouth of some dark lair,
> Where growling low, a fierce old bear
> Lies amidst bones and blood.'

'"Haw-haw! guv'nor," he said, "you might think as I was one o' these murderers. I ain't the kind of cove as a young woman would care to meet of a summer night, nor any sort of night for the matter of that, am I? Haw-haw! But the houses is closed, guv'nor, worse luck; and I'm dreadful dry."

'"You talk as if you'd been drinking, my man," I said.

'"That's where you're wrong, guv'nor. Why, bless me if I've touched a drop of drink for six mortal days; but tomorrow's pay-day, and tomorrow night, guv'nor – tomorrow night I'll make up for it. And so you've come to look round, eh? You're the fust swell as I ever seed in this here blooming yard as had the pluck."

'And then I began to question him about the details of the hideous business of Melmoth Brothers.

'"They brings 'em in, guv'nor, mostly irregular," said the old man; "they brings 'em in dead, and chucks 'em down anywhere, just as you see; and they brings 'em in alive, and we ties 'em up and feeds 'em proper, and gives 'em water, according to the Act; and then we just turns 'em into size and glue, or various special lines, or cat's-meat, or patent manure, or superphosphate, as the case may be. We boils 'em all down within twenty-four hours. Haw-haw!" cried the dreadful old man in almost fiendish glee. "There ain't much left of 'em when *we've* done with 'em, except the smell. Haw-haw! Why, bless ye, there's nigh on half a dozen cab ranks a simmering in them there boilers," and he pointed to the furnace fires.

'And then the old man led me past the great row of furnace doors, and down the yard to the very end; and then we reached the two low wooden gates that stood at the lower end of the sloping yard. He pushed back one of the splashed and whitened doors with a great iron fork, and propped it open; then he flung open the door of the end furnace, which threw a lurid light into a low, vaulted, brick-work chamber within. I saw that the floor of the chamber consisted of a vast leaden cistern, and that some fluid, on whose surface was a thick white scum, filled it, and gave forth a strangely acrid and, at the same time, pungent odour.

'"This 'ere," said the old man, "is where we make the superphosphate; there's several tons of the strongest vitriol in this here place; we filled up fresh today, guv'nor. If I was to shove you into that there vat, you'd just melt up for all the world like a lump of sugar in a glass of hot toddy; and you'd come out superphosphate, guv'nor, when they drors the vat. Haw-haw! Seein's believin', they say; just you look here. This here barrer's full of fresh horses' bones; they've been piled nigh on two days. They're bones, you see, real bones, without a bit of flesh on them. You just stand back, guv'nor, lest you get splashed and spiles yer clothes. Haw-haw!''

'I did as I was bid. And then the old man suddenly shot the barrow full of white bones into the steaming vat.

'"There, guv'nor," he said, with another diabolical laugh, as the fluid in the cistern of the great arched chamber hissed and bubbled. 'They *wos* bones; they're superphosphate by this time. There ain't no more to show ye, guv'nor," said the old man with a leer, as he stretched out his hand.

'I placed a half-crown in it.

'"I knowed ye was a gentleman," he said. "It's a hot night, guv'nor, and I'm dreadful droughty; but I do know where a drink's to be had at any hour, when you've got the ready, and I'll be off to get one.'

'"You've forgotten to shut the furnace door, my man,' I said.

'"Thank ye, guv'nor, but I did it a purpose; the boiler above it's to be drored tomorrow."

'"Aren't you afraid that if you leave the place something may be stolen?"

'"Lor, guv'nor," said the old man with a laugh, "you're the fust as has showed his nose inside of Melmoth Brothers' premises after dark, except the chaps as works here. Haw-haw! they durstn't, guv'nor, come into this place; they calls it the Devil's Cookshop hereabouts," and taking the iron fork up, the whitened wooden door swung back into its place, and hid the mass of seething vitriol from my view.

'Then, without a word, the old man in his heavy wooden-soled boots clattered out of the place, leaving me alone upon the premises of Melmoth Brothers.

'For several minutes I stood and gazed around me upon the strange weird scene of horror, when suddenly I heard a sound in the lane without, a sound as of a half-stifled shriek of agony. I hurried out into the lane at once. I looked up and down it, *and fancied that I saw a dark brown shadow* suddenly disappear within an archway. I walked hurriedly towards the archway. There was nothing. And now I heard a low voice cry in choking accents, "Help!" Then there was a groan. At that instant I stumbled over something which lay half in, half out of the entrance of a court. It was the body of a man. I stooped over him – it was the young policeman. I recognized his face instantly.

'"I'm glad you've come, sir," said the poor fellow, in failing accents. "He's put the hat on me, sir. He stabbed me from behind, and I'm choking, sir. But I saw him plain this time; it *was* him, sir, the man with the brown tweed coat and the red comforter. Don't you move, sir," said the dying man, in a still lower whisper; "*I see him, sir*; I see him now, stooping and peeping round the archway. If you move, sir, he'll twig you and he'll slope. Oh, God!" sobbed the poor young constable, and he gave a shudder. He was dead.

'Still leaning over the body of the dead man, I tried to collect my thoughts, for, my friends, I don't mind confessing to you, for the first time in my life, since I was a child, I was really afraid. An awful deadly fear – a fear of I know not what – had come upon me. I trembled in every limb, my hair grew wet with sweat, and I could hear – yes, I could hear – the actual beating of my own heart, as though it were a sledge-hammer. I was alone – alone and unarmed, two hours after midnight, in this dreadful place, with – well, I had no doubt with whom. No, not unarmed. I placed my hand upon the truncheon-case of the dead man. I gripped that truncheon which is now lying upon the table, and in an instant my courage came back to me. Then, still stooping over the body of the murdered man, I slowly – very slowly – turned my head. There was the man, the murderer, the wretch who had been so accurately described to me, the crouching figure in the brown tweed coat, with the red cotton comforter loosely wound round his neck. In his left hand there was something long and bright and keen that glittered in the soft moonlight of the silent summer night.

'And I saw his face, his dreadful face, the face that will haunt me to my dying day.

'It wasn't a bit like the descriptions. Mr Stewart Cumberland's vision of "The Man" differed in every possible particular from the being whom I watched from under the dark shadow of the entry of the court, as he stood glaring at me in the moonlight, like a hungry tiger prepared to spring. The man had long, crisp-looking locks of tangled hair, which hung on either side of his face. There was no difficulty in studying him; the features were clearly, even brilliantly illuminated, both by the bright moonlight and by the one street-lamp, which chanced to be above his head; even the humidity of his fierce black eyes and of his cruel teeth was plainly apparent; there wasn't a single detail of the dreadful face that escaped me. I'm not going to describe it, it was too awful, and words would fail me. I'll tell you why I'll not describe it in a moment.

'Have you ever seen a horse with a very tight bearing-rein on? Of course you have. Well, just as the horse throws his head about in uneasy torture, and champing his bit flings forth great flecks of foam, so did the man I was watching – watching with the hunter's eye, watching as a wild and noxious beast that I was hoping anon to slay – so did his jaws, I say, champ and gnash and mumble savagely and throw forth great flecks of white froth. The creature literally foamed at the mouth, for this dreadful thirst for blood was evidently, as yet, unsatiated. The eyes were those of a madman, or of a hunted beast driven to bay. I have no doubt, no shadow of doubt, in my own mind, that he – the man in the brown coat – was a savage maniac, a person wholly irresponsible for his actions.

'And now I'll tell you why I'm not going to describe that dreadful face of his, because, as I have told you, words would fail me. Give free rein to your fancy, let your imagination loose, and they will fail to convey to your mind one tittle of the loathsome horror of those features. The face was scarred in every direction – the mouth –

'Bah! I need say no more, the man was a leper. I have been in the Southern Seas, and I know – I know what a leper is like.

'But I hadn't much time for meditation. I was alone with the dead man and his murderer: as likely as not, if the man in the brown coat should escape me, *I* might be accused of the crime; the very fact of my being possessed of the dead man's truncheon would be looked on as a damning proof. Gripping the truncheon I rushed out upon the living horror. I would have shouted for assistance, but, why I cannot tell, my voice died away as to a whisper within my breast. It wasn't fear for I rushed upon him fully determined to either take or slay the dreadful thing that wore the ghastly semblance of a man. I rushed upon him, I say, and struck furiously at him with the heavy staff. But he eluded me.

'Noiselessly and swiftly, without even breaking the silence of the night, just as a snake slinks into its hole, the creature dived suddenly beneath my arm, and with an activity that astounded me, passed as though he were without substance (for I heard no sound of footfalls) through the great open gates that formed the entry to the premises of Melmoth Brothers. As he passed under my outstretched arm he must have stabbed through my thin overcoat, and as you see,' said Horace Jeaffreson, pointing to the cut in his frock-coat, 'an inch or two more, and H.J. wouldn't have been among you to eat his breakfast and spin his yarn. The slash in the overcoat I wore last night, my friends, has a trace of bloodstains on it – but it was not *my* blood.

'"Now," thought I, "I've got him," his very flight filled me with determination, and I resolved to take him alive if possible, for I felt that he was delivered into my hand, and I was determined that he should not escape me; rather than that, I would knock him on the head with as little compunction as I would kill a mad dog.

'As these thoughts passed through my mind, I sped after the murderer of the unfortunate policeman. I gained upon him rapidly, I was within three yards of him, when we reached the middle of the great knacker's yard; and then he attempted to dodge me round a sort of huge chopping-block that stood there.

'"If you don't surrender, by God I'll kill you," I shouted.

'He never answered me, he only mowed and gibbered as he fled, threatening me at the same time with the knife that he held in his hand.

'I vaulted the block, and flung myself upon him; and I struck at him savagely and caught him across the forehead with the truncheon; and suddenly uttering a sort of cry as of an animal in pain, he stabbed me through the hand and turned and fled once more, I after him. At the moment I didn't even know that I had been stabbed. I gained upon him, but he reached the bottom of the yard, and turned in front of the low whitened doors and stopped and stood at bay – crouching, knife in hand, in the strong light thrown out by the open furnace door, as though about to spring. Blood was streaming over his face from the wound I had given him upon his forehead, and it half blinded him; and ever and anon he tried to clear his eyes of it with the cuff of his right hand. His face and figure glowed red and unearthly in the firelight.

'I wasn't afraid of him now; I advanced on him.

'Suddenly he sprang forward. I stepped back and hit him over the knuckles of his raised left hand, in which glittered the knife you see upon that table. I struck with all my might, and the knife fell from his nerveless grasp.

'He rushed back with wonderful agility. The white and rotting doors rolled open on their hinges. I saw him fall backwards with a splash into the mass of froth now coloured by the firelight with a pinky glow.

'He disappeared.

'And then, horror of horrors, I saw the dreadful form rise once more, and cling for an instant to the low edge of the great leaden tank, and make its one last struggle for existence: and then it sank beneath the fuming waves, never to rise again.

'That's all I have to tell. I picked up the knife and secured it, with the truncheon, about my person, as best I could.

'I'm glad that I avenged the death of the poor fellow whom I only knew as 1839 H. I shall be happier still if, as I believe, through my humble instrumentality, the awful outrages at the East End of London have ended.

'I got to my chambers in the Albany by three in the morning; then I sent for the nearest doctor to dress my hand. It's not a serious cut, but I had bled like a pig.

'I bought the morning paper on my way here; it gives the details of the murder of Constable 1839 of the H Division by an unknown hand; and it mentions that the murderer appears to have possessed himself of the truncheon of his victim. You see he was stabbed through the great vessels of the lungs.

'I have no further remarks to make, except that I don't believe we shall hear any more of Jack the Ripper. Of one thing I am perfectly certain, that I shall not visit Whitechapel again in a hurry.'

# The Dead Man of Varley Grange

*Anonymous*

'Hallo, Jack! Where are you off to? Going down to the governor's place for Christmas?'

Jack Darent, who was in my old regiment, stood drawing on his doeskin gloves upon the 23rd of December the year before last. He was equipped in a long ulster and top hat, and a hansom, already loaded with a gun-case and portmanteau, stood awaiting him. He had a tall, strong figure, a fair, fresh-looking face, and the merriest blue eyes in the world. He held a cigarette between his lips, and late as was the season of the year there was a flower in his buttonhole. When did I ever see handsome Jack Darent and he did not look well dressed and well fed and jaunty? As I ran up the steps of the Club he turned round and laughed merrily.

'My dear fellow, do I look the sort of man to be victimized at a family Christmas meeting? Do you know the kind of business they have at home? Three maiden aunts and a bachelor uncle, my eldest brother and his insipid wife, and all my sister's six noisy children at dinner. Church twice a day, and snapdragon between the services! No, thank you! I have a great affection for my old parents, but you don't catch me going in for that sort of national festival!'

'You irreverent ruffian!' I replied, laughing. 'Ah, if you were a married man . . .'

'Ah, if I were a married man!' replied Captain Darent with something that was almost a sigh, and then lowering his voice, he said hurriedly, 'How is Miss Lester, Fred?'

'My sister is quite well, thank you,' I answered with becoming gravity; and it was not without a spice of malice that I added, 'She has been going to a great many balls and enjoying herself very much.'

Captain Darent looked profoundly miserable.

'I don't see how a poor fellow in a marching regiment, a younger son too, with nothing in the future to look to, is ever to marry nowadays,' he said almost savagely; 'when girls, too, are used to so much luxury and extravagance that they can't live without it. Matrimony is at a deadlock in this century, Fred, chiefly owing to the price of butcher's meat and bonnets. In fifty years' time it will become extinct and the country be depopulated. But I must be off, old man, or I shall miss my train.'

'You have never told me where you are going to, Jack.'

'Oh, I am going to stay with old Henderson, in Westernshire; he has taken a furnished house, with some first-rate pheasant shooting, for a year. There are seven of us going – all bachelors, and all kindred spirits. We shall shoot all day and smoke half the night. Think what you have lost, old fellow, by becoming a Benedick!'

'In Westernshire, is it?' I inquired. 'Whereabouts is this place, and what is the name of it? For I am a Westernshire man by birth myself, and I know every place in the county.'

'Oh, it's a tumbledown sort of old house, I believe,' answered Jack carelessly. 'Gables and twisted chimneys outside, and uncomfortable spindle-legged furniture inside – you know the sort of thing; but the shooting is capital, Henderson says, and we must put up with our quarters. He has taken his French cook down, and plenty of liquor, so I've no doubt we shan't starve.'

'Well, but what is the name of it?' I persisted, with a growing interest in the subject.

'Let me see,' referring to a letter he pulled out of his pocket. 'Oh, here it is – Varley Grange.'

'Varley Grange!' I repeated, aghast. 'Why, it has not been inhabited for years.'

'I believe not,' answered Jack unconcernedly. 'The shooting has been let separately; but Henderson took a fancy to the house too and thought it would do for him, furniture and all, just as it is. My dear Fred, what are you looking so solemnly at me for?'

'Jack, let me entreat of you not to go to this place,' I said, laying my hands on his arm.

'Not go! Why, Lester, you must be mad! Why on earth shouldn't I go there?'

'There are stories – uncomfortable things said of that house.' I had not the moral courage to say, 'It is haunted,' and I felt myself how weak and childish was my attempt to deter him from his intended visit; only – I knew all about Varley Grange.

I think handsome Jack Darent thought privately that I was slightly out of my senses, for I am sure I looked unaccountably upset and dismayed by the mention of the name of the house that Mr Henderson had taken.

'I dare say it's cold and draughty and infested with rats and mice,' he said laughingly; 'and I have no doubt the creature-comforts will not be equal to Queen's Gate; but I stand pledged to go now, and I must be off this very minute, so have no time, old fellow, to inquire into the meaning of your sensational warning. Goodbye, and . . . and remember me to the ladies.'

He ran down the steps and jumped into the hansom.

'Write to me if you have time!' I cried out after him; but I don't think he heard me in the rattle of the departing cab. He nodded and smiled at me and was swiftly whirled out of sight.

As for me, I walked slowly back to my comfortable house in Queen's Gate. There was my wife presiding at the little five o'clock tea-table, our two fat, pink and white little children tumbling about upon the hearthrug amongst dolls and bricks, and two utterly spoilt and over-fed pugs; and my sister Bella – who, between ourselves, was the prettiest as well as dearest girl in all London – sitting on the floor in her handsome brown, velvet gown, resigning herself gracefully to be trampled upon by the dogs, and to have her hair pulled by the babies.

'Why, Fred, you look as if you had heard bad news,' said my wife, looking up anxiously as I entered.

'I don't know that I have heard of anything very bad; I have just seen Jack Darent off for Christmas,' I said, turning instinctively towards my sister. He was a poor man and a younger son, and of course a very bad match for the beautiful Miss Lester; but for all that I had an inkling that Bella was not quite indifferent to her brother's friend.

'Oh!' says that hypocrite. 'Shall I give you a cup of tea, Fred!'

It is wonderful how women can control their faces and pretend not to care a straw when they hear the name of their lover mentioned. I think Bella overdid it, she looked so supremely indifferent.

'Where on earth do you suppose he is going to stay, Bella?'

'Who? Oh, Captain Darent! How should I possibly know where he is going? Archie, pet, please don't poke the doll's head quite down Ponto's throat; I know he will bite it off if you do.'

This last observation was addressed to my son and heir.

'Well, I think you will be surprised when you hear: he is going to Westernshire, to stay at Varley Grange.'

'*What!*' No doubt about her interest in the subject now! Miss Lester turned as white as her collar and sprang to her feet impetuously, scattering dogs, babies and toys in all directions away from her skirts as she rose.

'You cannot mean it, Fred! Varley Grange, why, it has not been inhabited for ten years; and the last time – Oh, do you remember those poor people who took it? What a terrible story it has!' She shuddered.

'Well, it is taken now,' I said, 'by a man I know, called Henderson – a bachelor; he has asked down a party of men for a week's shooting, and Jack Darent is one of them.'

'For Heaven's sake prevent him from going!' cried Bella, clasping her hands.

'My dear, he is gone!'

'Oh, then write to him – telegraph – tell him to come back!' she urged breathlessly.

'I am afraid it is no use,' I said gravely. 'He would not come back; he would not believe me; he would think I was mad.'

'Did you tell him anything?' she asked faintly.

'No, I had not time. I did say a word or two, but he began to laugh.'

'Yes, that is how it always is!' she said distractedly. 'People laugh and pooh-pooh the whole thing, and then they go there and see for themselves, and it is too late!'

She was so thoroughly upset that she left the room. My wife turned to me in astonishment; not being a Westernshire woman, she was not well up in the traditions of that venerable county.

'What on earth does it all mean, Fred?' she asked me in amazement. 'What is the matter with Bella, and why is she so distressed that Captain Darent is going to stay at that particular house?'

'It is said to be haunted, and . . .'

'You don't mean to say you believe in such rubbish, Fred?' interrupted my wife sternly, with a side-glance of apprehension at our first-born, who, needless to say, stood by, all eyes and ears, drinking in every word of the conversation of his elders.

'I never know what I believe or what I don't believe,' I answered gravely. 'All I can say is that there are very singular traditions about that house, and that a great many credible witnesses have seen a very strange thing there, and that a great many disasters have happened to the persons who have seen it.'

'What has been seen, Fred? Pray tell me the story! Wait, I think I will send the children away.'

My wife rang the bell for the nurse, and as soon as the little ones had been taken from the room she turned to me again.

'I don't believe in ghosts or any such rubbish one bit, but I should like to hear your story.'

'The story is vague enough,' I answered.

'In the old days Varley Grange belonged to the ancient family of Varley, now completely extinct. There was, some hundred years ago, a daughter, famed for her beauty and her fascination. She wanted to marry a poor, penniless squire, who loved her devotedly. Her brother, Dennis Varley, the new owner of Varley Grange, refused his consent and shut his sister up in the nunnery that used to stand outside his park gates – there are a few ruins of it left still. The poor nun broke her vows and ran away in the night with her lover. But her brother pursued her and brought her back with him. The lover escaped, but the lord of Varley murdered his sister under his own roof, swearing that no scion of his race should live to disgrace and dishonour his ancient name.

'Ever since that day Dennis Varley's spirit cannot rest in its grave – he wanders about the old house at night time, and those who have seen him are numberless. Now and then the pale, shadowy form of a nun flits across the old hall, or along the gloomy passages, and when both strange shapes are seen thus together misfortune and illness, and even death, is sure to pursue the luckless man who has seen them, with remorseless cruelty.'

'I wonder you believe in such rubbish,' says my wife at the conclusion of my tale.

I shrug my shoulders and answer nothing, for who are so obstinate as those who persist in disbelieving everything that they cannot understand?

It was little more than a week later that, walking by myself along Pall Mall one afternoon, I suddenly came upon Jack Darent walking towards me.

'Hallo, Jack! Back again? Why, man, how odd you look!'

There was a change in the man that I was instantly aware of. His frank, careless face looked clouded and anxious, and the merry smile was missing from his handsome countenance.

'Come into the Club, Fred,' he said, taking me by the arm. 'I have something to say to you.'

He drew me into a corner of the Club smoking-room.

'You were quite right. I wish to Heaven I had never gone to that house.'

'You mean – have you seen anything?' I inquired eagerly.

'I have seen *everything*,' he answered with a shudder. 'They say one dies within a year –'

'My dear fellow, don't be so upset about it,' I interrupted; I was quite distressed to see how thoroughly the man had altered.

'Let me tell you about it, Fred.'

He drew his chair close to mine and told me his story, pretty nearly in the following words:

'You remember the day I went down you had kept me talking at the Club door; I had a race to catch the train; however, I just did it. I found the other fellows all waiting for me. There was Charlie Wells, the two Harfords, old Colonel Riddell, who is such a crack shot, two fellows in the Guards, both pretty fair, a man called Thompson, a barrister, Henderson and myself – eight of us in all. We had a remarkably lively journey down, as you may imagine, and reached Varley Grange in the highest possible spirits. We all slept like tops that night.

The next day we were out from eleven till dusk among the coverts, and a better day's shooting I never enjoyed in the whole course of my life, the birds literally swarmed. We bagged a hundred and thirty brace. We were all pretty well tired when we got home, and did full justice to a very good dinner and first-class Perrier-Jouet. After dinner we adjourned to the hall to smoke. This hall is quite the feature of the house. It is large and bright, panelled half-way up with sombre old oak, and vaulted with heavy carved oaken rafters. At the farther end runs a gallery, into which opened the door of my bedroom, and shut off from the rest of the passages by a swing door at either end.

'Well, all we fellows sat up there smoking and drinking brandy and soda, and jawing, you know – as men always do when they are together – about sport of all kinds, hunting and shooting and salmon-fishing; and I assure you not one of us had a thought in our heads beyond relating some wonderful incident of a long shot or big fence by which we could each cap the last speaker's experiences. We were just, I recollect, listening to a long story of the old Colonel's, about his experiences among bisons in Cachemire, when suddenly one of us – I can't remember who it was – gave a sort of shout and started to his feet, pointing up to the gallery behind us. We all turned round, and there – I give you my word of honour, Lester – stood a man leaning over the rail of the gallery, staring down upon us.

'We all saw him. Every one of us. Eight of us, remember. He stood there full ten seconds, looking down with horrible glittering eyes at us. He had a long tawny beard, and his hands, that were crossed together before him, were nothing but skin and bone. But it was his face that was so unspeakably dreadful. It was livid – the face of a dead man!'

'How was he dressed?'

'I could not see; he wore some kind of a black cloak over his shoulders, I think, but the lower part of his figure was hidden behind the railings. Well, we all stood perfectly speechless for, as I said, about ten seconds; and then the figure moved, backing slowly into the door of the room behind him, which stood open. It was the door of my bedroom! As soon as he had disappeared our senses seemed to return to us. There was a general rush for the staircase, and, as you may imagine, there was not a corner of the house that was left unsearched; my bedroom especially was ransacked in every part of it. But all in vain; there was not the slightest trace to be found of any living being. You may suppose that not one of us slept that night. We lighted every candle and lamp we could lay hands upon and sat up till daylight, but nothing more was seen.

The next morning, at breakfast, Henderson, who seemed very much annoyed by the whole thing, begged us not to speak of it any more. He said that he had been told, before he had taken the house, that it was supposed to be haunted; but, not being a believer in such childish follies, he had paid but little attention to the rumour. He did not, however, want it talked about, because of the servants, who would be so easily frightened. He was quite certain he said, that the figure we had seen last night must be somebody dressed up to practise a trick upon us, and he recommended us all to bring our guns down loaded after dinner, but meanwhile to forget the startling apparition as far as we could.

'We, of course, readily agreed to do as he wished, although I do not think that one of us imagined for a moment that any amount of dressing-up would be able to simulate the awful countenance that we had all of us seen too plainly. It would have taken a Hare or an Arthur Cecil, with all the theatrical applicances known only to those two talented actors, to have 'made-up' the face, that was literally that of a corpse. Such a person could not be amongst us – actually in the house – without our knowledge.

'We had another good day's shooting, and by degrees the fresh air and exercise and the excitement of the sport obliterated the impression of what we had seen in some measure from the minds of most of us. That evening we all appeared in the hall after dinner with our loaded guns beside us; but, although we sat up till the small hours and looked frequently up at the gallery at the end of the hall, nothing at all disturbed us that night.

'Two nights thus went by and nothing further was seen of the gentleman with the tawny beard. What with the good company, the good cheer and the pheasants, we had pretty well forgotten all about him.

'We were sitting as usual upon the third night, with our pipes and our cigars; a pleasant glow from the bright wood fire in the great chimney lighted up the old hall, and shed a genial warmth about us; when suddenly it seemed to me as if there came a breath of cold, chill air behind me, such as one feels when going down into some damp, cold vault or cellar.

'A strong shiver shook me from head to foot. Before even I saw it I *knew* that it was there.

'It leant over the railing of the gallery and looked down at us all just as it had done before. There was no change in the attitude, no alteration in the fixed, malignant glare in those stony, lifeless eyes; no movement in the white and bloodless features. Below, amongst the eight of us gathered there, there arose a panic of terror. Eight strong, healthy, well-educated nineteenth-century Englishmen, and yet I am not ashamed to say that we were paralysed with fear. Then one, more quickly recovering his senses than the rest, caught at his gun, that leant against the wide chimney-corner, and fired.

'The hall was filled with smoke, but as it cleared away every one of us could see the figure of our supernatural visitant slowly backing, as he had done on the previous occasion, into the chamber behind him, with something like a sardonic smile of scornful derision upon his horrible, death-like face.

'The next morning it is a singular and remarkable fact that four out of the eight of us received by the morning post – so they stated – letters of importance which called them up to town by the very first train! One man's mother was ill, another had to consult his lawyer, whilst pressing engagements, to which they could assign no definite name, called away the other two.

'There were left in the house that day but four of us – Wells, Bob Harford, our host, and myself. A sort of dogged determination not to be worsted by a scare of this kind kept us still there. The morning light brought a return of common sense and natural courage to us. We could manage to laugh over last night's terrors whilst discussing our bacon and kidneys and hot coffee over the late breakfast in the pleasant morning-room, with the sunshine streaming cheerily in through the diamond-paned windows.

'"It *must* be a delusion of our brains," said one.

'"Our host's champagne," suggested another.

'"A well-organized hoax," opined a third.

'"I will tell you what we will do," said our host. "Now that those other fellows have all gone – and I suppose we don't any of us believe much in those elaborate family reasons which have so unaccountably summoned them away – we four will sit up regularly night after night and watch for this thing, whatever it may be. I do not believe in ghosts. However, this morning I have taken the trouble to go out before breakfast to see the Rector of the parish, an old gentleman who is well up in all the traditions of the neighbourhood, and I have learnt from him the whole of the supposed story of our friend of the tawny beard, which, if you will, I will relate to you."

'Henderson then proceeded to tell us the tradition concerning the Dennis Varley who murdered his sister, the nun – a story which I will not repeat to you, Lester, as I see you know it already.

'The clergyman had furthermore told him that the figure of the murdered nun was also sometimes seen in the same gallery, but that this was a very rare occurrence. When both the murderer and his victim are seen together, terrible misfortunes are sure to assail the unfortunate living man who sees them; and if the nun's face is revealed, death within the year is the doom of the ill-fated person who has seen it.

'"Of course," concluded our host, "I consider all these stories to be absolutely childish. At the same time I cannot help thinking that some human agency – probably a gang of thieves or housebreakers – is at work, and that we shall probably be able to unearth an organized system of villainy by which the rogues, presuming on the credulity of the persons who have inhabited the place, have been able to plant themselves securely among some secret passages and hidden rooms in the house, and have carried on their depredations undiscovered and unsuspected. Now, will all of you help me to unravel this mystery?"

'We all promised readily to do so. It is astonishing how brave we felt at eleven o'clock in the morning; what an amount of pluck and courage each man professed himself to be endued with; how lightly we jested about the "old boy with the beard", and what jokes we cracked about the murdered nun!

'"She would show her face oftener if she was good-looking. No fear of her looking at Bob Harford, he was too ugly. It was Jack Darent who was the showman of the party; she'd be sure to make straight for him if she could, he was always run after by the women," and so on, till we were all laughing loudly and heartily over our own witticisms. That was eleven o'clock in the morning.

'At eleven o'clock at night we could have given a very different report of ourselves.

'At eleven o'clock at night each man took up his appointed post in solemn and somewhat depressed silence.

'The plan of our campaign had been carefully organized by our host. Each man was posted separately with about thirty yards between them, so that no optical delusion, such as an effect of firelight upon the oak panelling, nor any reflection from the circular mirror over the chimney-piece, should be able to deceive more than one of us. Our host fixed himself in the very centre of the hall, facing the gallery at the end; Wells took up his position half-way up the short, straight flight of steps; Harford was at the top of the stairs upon the gallery itself; I was opposite to him at the further end. In this manner, whenever the figure – ghost or burglar – should appear, it must necessarily be between two of us, and be seen from both the right and the left side. We were prepared to believe that one amongst us might be deceived by his senses or by his imagination, but it was clear that two persons could not see the same object from a different point of view and be simultaneously deluded by any effect of light or any optical hallucination.

'Each man was provided with a loaded revolver, a brandy and soda and a sufficient stock of pipes or cigars to last him through the night. We took up our positions at eleven o'clock exactly, and waited.

'At first we were all four very silent and, as I have said before, slightly depressed; but as the hour wore away and nothing was seen or heard we began to talk to each other. Talking, however, was rather a difficulty.

To begin with, we had to shout – at least we in the gallery had to shout to Henderson, down in the hall; and though Harford and Wells could converse quite comfortably, I, not being able to see the latter at all from my end of the gallery, had to pass my remarks to him second-hand through Harford, who amused himself in mis-stating every intelligent remark that I entrusted him with; added to which natural impediments to the "flow of the soul", the elements thought fit to create such a hullabaloo without that conversation was rendered still further a work of difficulty.

'I never remember such a night in all my life. The rain came down in torrents; the wind howled and shrieked wildly amongst the tall chimneys and the bare elm trees without. Every now and then there was a lull, and then, again and again, a long sobbing moan came swirling round and round the house, for all the world like the cry of a human being in agony. It was a night to make one shudder, and thank Heaven for a roof over one's head.

'We all sat on at our separate posts hour after hour, listening to the wind and talking at intervals; but as the time wore on insensibly we became less and less talkative, and a sort of depression crept over us.

'At last we relapsed into a profound silence; then suddenly there came upon us all that chill blast of air, like a breath from a charnel-house, that we had experienced before, and almost simultaneously a hoarse cry broke from Henderson in the body of the hall below, and from Wells half-way up the stairs. Harford and I sprang to our feet, and we too saw it.

'The dead man was slowly coming up the stairs. He passed silently up with a sort of still, gliding motion, within a few inches of poor Wells, who shrank back, white with terror, against the wall. Henderson rushed wildly up the staircase in pursuit, whilst Harford and I, up on the gallery, fell instinctively back at his approach.

'He passed between us.

'We saw the glitter of his sightless eyes – the shrivelled skin upon his withered face – the mouth that fell away, like the mouth of a corpse, beneath his tawny beard. We felt the cold death-like blast that came with him, and the sickening horror of his terrible presence. Ah! can I ever forget it?'

With a strong shudder Jack Darent buried his face in his hands, and seemed too much overcome for some minutes to be able to proceed.

'My dear fellow, are you *sure?*' I said in an awe-struck whisper.

He lifted his head.

'Forgive me, Lester; the whole business has shaken my nerves so thoroughly that I have not yet been able to get over it. But I have not yet told you the worst.'

'Good Heavens – is there worse?' I ejaculated.

He nodded.

'No sooner,' he continued, 'had this awful creature passed us than Harford clutched at my arm and pointed to the farther end of the gallery.

'"Look!" he cried hoarsely, "the nun!"'

'There, coming towards us from the opposite direction, was the veiled figure of a nun.

'There were the long, flowing black and white garments – the gleam of the crucifix at her neck – the jangle of her rosary-beads from her waist; but her face was hidden.

'A sort of desperation seized me. With a violent effort over myself, I went towards this fresh apparition.

'"It *must* be a hoax," I said to myself, and there was a half-formed intention in my mind of wrenching aside the flowing draperies and of seeing for myself who and what it was. I strode towards the figure – I stood – within half a yard of it. The nun raised her head slowly – and, Lester – *I saw her face!*'

There was a moment's silence.

'What was it like, Jack?' I asked him presently.

He shook his head.

'That I can never tell to any living creature.'

'Was it so horrible?'

He nodded assent, shuddering.

'And what happened next?'

'I believe I fainted. At all events I remembered nothing further. They made me go to the vicarage next day. I was so knocked over by it all – I was quite ill. I could not have stayed in the house. I stopped there all yesterday, and I got up to town this morning. I wish to Heaven I had taken your advice, old man, and had never gone to the horrible house.'

'I wish you had, Jack,' I answered fervently.

'Do you know that I shall die within the year?' he asked me presently.

I tried to pooh-pooh it.

'My dear fellow, don't take the thing so seriously as all that. Whatever may be the meaning of these horrible apparitions, there can be nothing but an old wives' fable in *that* saying. Why on earth should you die – you of all people, a great strong fellow with a constitution of iron? You don't look much like dying!'

'For all that I shall die. I cannot tell you why I am so certain – but I know that it will be so,' he answered in a low voice. 'And some terrible misfortune will happen to Harford – the other two never saw her – it is he and I who are doomed.'

A year has passed away. Last summer fashionable society rang for a week or more with the tale of poor Bob Harford's misfortune. The girl whom he was engaged to and to whom he was devotedly attached – young, beautiful and wealthy – ran away on the eve of her wedding-day with a drinking, swindling villain who had been turned out of ever so many clubs and tabooed for ages by every respectable man in town, and who had nothing but a handsome face and a fascinating manner to recommend him, and who by dint of these had succeeded in gaining a complete ascendancy over the fickle heart of poor Bob's lovely fiancée. As to Harford, he sold out and went off to the backwoods of Canada, and has never been heard of since.

And what of Jack Darent? Poor, handsome Jack, with his tall figure and his bright, happy face, and the merry blue eyes that had wiled Bella Lester's heart away! Alas! far away in Southern Africa, poor Jack Darent lies in an unknown grave – slain by a Zulu assegai on the fatal plain of Isandula!

And Bella goes about clad in sable garments, heavy-eyed and stricken with sore grief. A widow in heart, if not in name.

# Footsteps Invisible

## *Robert Arthur*

The night was dark, and violent with storm. Rain beat down as if from an angry heaven, and beneath its force all the noises of a metropolis blended oddly, so that to Jorman they sounded like the muted grumble of the city itself.

He himself was comfortable enough, however. The little box-sized news-stand beside the subway entrance was tight against the rain.

The window that he kept open to hear prospective customers, take in change and pass out papers let in a wet chill, but a tiny oil heater in one corner gave out a glow of warmth that beat it back.

A midget radio shrilled sweetly, and Foxfire, his toy wire-haired terrier, snored at his feet.

Jorman reached up and switched the radio off. There were times when it gave him pleasure. But more often he preferred to listen to life itself, as it poured past his stand like a river.

Tonight, though, even Times Square was deserted to the storm gods. Jorman listened and could not hear a single footstep, though his inner time sense – re-enforced by a radio announcement a moment before – told him it was barely half-past twelve.

He lit a pipe and puffed contentedly.

After a moment he lifted his head. Footsteps were approaching: slow, measured, familiar footsteps. They paused in front of his stand momentarily, and he smiled.

'Hello, Clancy,' he greeted the cop on the beat. 'A nice night for ducks.'

'If I only had web feet,' the big officer grumbled, ''twould suit me fine. You're a funny one, now, staying out so late on a night like this, and not a customer in sight.'

'I like it.' Jorman grinned. 'Like to listen to the storm. Makes my imagination work.'

'Mine, too,' Clancy grunted. 'But the only thing it can imagine is my own apartment, with a hot tub and a hot drink waitin'. Arrgh!'

He shook himself, and with a goodnight tramped onward.

Jorman heard the officer's footsteps diminish. There was silence for a while, save for the rush of the rain and the occasional splashing whir of a cab sloshing past. Then he heard more steps.

This time they came towards him from the side street, and he listened intently to them, head cocked a little to one side.

They were – he searched for the right word – well, odd. *Shuffle-shuffle*, as if made by large feet encased in sneakers, and they slid along the pavement for a few inches with each step. *Shuffle-shuffle – shuffle-shuffle*, they came towards him slowly, hesitantly, as if the walker were pausing every few feet to look about him.

Jorman wondered whether the approaching man could be a cripple. A clubfoot, perhaps, dragging one foot with each step. For a moment he had the absurd thought that the sounds were made by four feet, not two; but he dismissed it with a smile and listened more closely.

The footsteps were passing him now, and though the rain made it hard to distinguish clearly, he had the impression that each shuffling step was accompanied by a slight clicking noise.

As he was trying to hear more distinctly, Foxfire woke from his slumbers. Jorman felt the little dog move at his feet, then heard the animal growling deep in its chest. He reached down and found Foxfire huddled against his shoe, tail tucked under, hair bristling.

'Quiet, boy!' he whispered. 'I'm trying to hear.'

Foxfire quieted. Jorman held his muzzle and listened. The footsteps of the stranger had shuffled past him to the corner. There they paused, as if in irresolution. Then they turned south on Seventh Avenue, and after a moment were engulfed in the storm noise.

Jorman released his hold on his dog and rubbed his chin perplexedly, wondering what there could have been about the pedestrian's scent to arouse Foxfire so.

For a moment Jorman sat very still, his pipe clenched in his hand. Then with a rush of relief he heard Clancy's returning tramp. The cop came up and stopped, and Jorman did not wait for him to speak. He leaned out of his little window.

'Clancy,' he asked, trying to keep the excitement out of his voice, 'what does that fellow look like down the block there – the one heading south on Seventh? He ought to be about in the middle of the block.'

'Huh?' Clancy said. 'I don't see any guy. Somebody snitch a paper?'

'No.' Jorman shook his head. 'I was just curious. You say there isn't anyone –'

'Not in sight,' the cop told him. 'Must have turned in some place. You and me have this town to ourselves tonight. Well, be good. I got to try some more doors.'

He sloshed away, the rain pattering audibly off his broad, rubber-coated back, and Jorman settled back into his chair chuckling to himself. It was funny what tricks sounds played on you, especially in the rain.

He relit his dead pipe and was thinking of shutting up for the night when his last customer of the evening approached. This time he recognized the steps. It was a source of pride to him – and of revenue as well – that he could call most of his regulars by name if they came up when the street wasn't too crowded.

This one, though he didn't come often and had never come before at night, was easy. The step was a firm, decisive one. *Click* – that was the heel coming down – *slap* – that was the sole being planted firmly. *Click-slap* – the other foot. Simple. He could have distinguished it in a crowd.

'Good morning, Sir Andrew,' Jorman said pleasantly as the steps came up to his stand. '*Times?*'

'Thanks.' It was a typically British voice that answered. 'Know me, do you?'

'Oh, yes.' Jorman grinned. It was usually a source of mystification to his customers that he knew their names. But names were not too hard to learn, if the owners of them lived or worked near by. 'A bellhop from your hotel was buying a paper last time you stopped. When you'd gone on, he told me who you were.'

'That easy, eh?' Sir Andrew Carraden exclaimed. 'Don't know as I like it so much, though, being kept track of. Prefer to lose myself these days. Had enough of notoriety in the past.'

'Had plenty of it four years ago, I suppose,' Jorman suggested. 'I followed the newspaper accounts of your tomb-hunting expedition. Interesting work, archaeology. Always wished I could poke around in the past that way, sometime.'

'Don't!' The word was sharp. 'Take my advice and stay snug and cosy in the present. The past is an uncomfortable place. Sometimes you peer into it and then spend the rest of your life trying to get away from it. And – But I mustn't stop here chatting. Not in this storm. Here's your money. No, here on the counter...'

And then, as Jorman fumbled for and found the pennies, Sir Andrew Carraden exclaimed again.

'I say!' he said. 'I'm sorry.'

'Perfectly all right,' Jorman told him. 'It pleases me when people don't notice. A lot don't, you know, in spite of the sign.'

'Blind newsdealer,' Sir Andrew Carraden read the little placard tacked to the stand. 'I say –'

'Wounded in the war,' Jorman told him. 'Sight failed progressively. Went entirely a couple of years ago. So I took up this. But I don't mind. Compensations, you know. Amazing what a lot a man can hear when he listens. But you're going to ask me how I knew you, aren't you? By your footsteps. They're very recognizable. Sort of a *click-slap, click-slap.*'

His customer was silent for a moment. Jorman was about to ask whether anything was wrong when the Englishman spoke.

'Look. I' – and his tone took on an almost hungry eagerness – 'I've got to talk to somebody, or blow my top. I mean, go barmy. Completely mad. Maybe I am, already. I don't know. You – you might have a few minutes to spare? You might be willing to keep me company for an hour? I – it might not be too dull.'

Jorman hesitated in answering. Not because he intended to refuse – the urgency in the man's voice was unmistakable – but there was something of a hunted tone in Sir Andrew Carraden's voice that aroused Jorman's curiosity.

It was absurd – but Jorman's ears were seldom wrong. The Englishman, the archaeologist whose name had been so prominent a few years back, was a hunted man. Perhaps a desperate man. A fugitive – from what?

Jorman did not try to guess. He nodded.

'I have time,' he agreed.

He bent down and picked up Foxfire, attached the leash, threw an old ulster over his shoulders and turned down his bright gasoline lantern. With Foxfire straining at the leash, he swung up his racks and padlocked the stand.

'This way,' Sir Andrew Carraden said at his side. 'Not half a block. Like to take my arm?'

'Thanks.' Jorman touched the other's elbow. The touch told him what he remembered from photographs in the papers he had seen, years back. The Britisher was a big man. Not the kind to fear anything. Yet now he was afraid.

The bowed their heads to the somewhat lessened rain and walked the short distance to the hotel.

They turned into the lobby, their heels loud on marble. Jorman knew the place: the Hotel Russet. Respectable, but a bit run down.

As they passed the desk, a sleepy clerk called out.

'Oh, pardon me. There's a message here for you. From the manager. Relative to some work we've been doing –'

'Thanks, thanks,' Jorman's companion answered impatiently, and Jorman heard paper stuffed into a pocket. 'Here's the elevator. Step up just a bit.'

They had been seated in easy chairs for some minutes, pipes going, hot drinks in front of them, before Sir Andrew Carraden made any further reference to the thing that was obviously on his mind.

The room they were in was fairly spacious, judging from the reverberations of their voices, and since it seemed to be a sitting-room, probably was joined to a bedroom beyond. Foxfire slumbering at Jorman's feet, they had been talking of inconsequentials – when the Englishman interrupted himself abruptly.

'Jorman,' he said, 'I'm a desperate man. I'm being hunted.'

Jorman heard coffee splash as an unsteady hand let the cup rattle against the saucer.

'I guessed so,' he confessed. 'It was in your voice. The police?'

Sir Andrew Carraden laughed, a harsh, explosive sound.

'Your ears *are* sharp,' he said. 'The police? I wish it were! No. By a – a personal enemy.'

'Then couldn't the police –' Jorman began. The other cut him short.

'No! They can't help me. Nobody in this world can help me. And God have mercy on me, nobody in the next!'

Jorman passed over the emphatic exclamation.

'But surely –'

'Take my word for it, I'm on my own,' Sir Andrew Carraden told him, his voice grim. 'This is a – feud, you might say. And I'm the hunted one. I've done a lot of hunting in my day, and now I know the other side of it. It's not pleasant.'

Jorman sipped at his drink.

'You – this enemy. He's been after you long?'

'Three years.' The Englishman's voice was low, a bit unsteady. In his mind Jorman could see the big man leaning forward, arm braced against knee, face set in grim lines.

'It began one night in London. A rainy night like this. I was runing over some clay tablets that were waiting deciphering. Part of the loot from the tomb of Tut-Ankh-Tothet. The one the stories in the papers you referred to were about.

'I'd been working pretty hard. I knocked off for a pipe and stood at the window looking out. Then I heard it.'

'Heard it?'

'Heard him.' Carraden corrected himself swiftly. 'Heard *him* hunting for me. Heard his footsteps –'

'Footsteps?'

'Yes. In the pitch-black night. Heard him tramping back and forth as he tried to locate me. Then he picked up my trail and came up the garden path.'

Sir Andrew paused, and Jorman heard the coffee cup being raised again.

'My dog, a Great Dane, scented him. It was frightened, poor beast, and with reason. But it tried to attack. He tore the dog to pieces on my own doorstep. I couldn't see the fight, but I could hear. The beast held him up long enough for me to run for it. Out the back door, into the storm.

'There was a stream half a mile away. I made for that, plunged into it, floated two miles down, went ashore, picked up a ride to London. Next morning I left London on a freighter for Australia before he could pick up my trail again.'

Jorman heard the archaeologist draw a deep breath.

'It took him six months to get on to me again, up in the Australian gold country. Again I heard him in time. I got away on a horse as he was forcing his way into my cabin, caught a cargo plane for Melbourne, took a fast boat to Shanghai. But I didn't stay there long.'

'Why not?' Jorman asked. He fancied that Carraden had shuddered slightly.

'Too much like his own country. Conditions were – favourable for him in the Orient. Unfavourable for me. I had a hunch. I hurried on to Manila and took a plane for the States there. Got a letter later from an old Chinese servant that *he* arrived the next night.'

Jorman sipped slowly at his coffee, his brow knitted. He did not doubt the man's sincerity, but the story *was* a bit puzzling.

'This fellow, this enemy of yours,' he commented slowly, 'you said the Orient was too much like his own country. I assume you mean Egypt.'

'Yes. He comes from Egypt. I incurred his – well, his enemity there.'

'He's a native then? An Egyptian native?'

Carraden hesitated, seeming to choose his words.

'Well, yes,' he said finally. 'In a way you might call him a native of Egypt. Though, strictly speaking, he comes from another – another country. One less well known.'

'But,' Jorman persisted, 'I should think that you, a man of wealth, would have all kinds of recourse against a native, no matter where he might be from. After all, the man is bound to be conspicuous, and ought to be easy to pick up. I know you said the police could not help you, but have you tried? And how in the world does the fellow follow you so persistently? From London to Australia to Shanghai – that's a thin trail to run down.'

'I know you're puzzled,' the other told him. 'But take my word for it, the police are no good. This chap – well, he just isn't conspicuous, that's all. He moves mostly by night. But even so he can go anywhere.

'He has – well, methods. And as for following me, he has his own ways of doing that, too. He's persistent. So awfully, awfully persistent. That's the horror of it: that blind, stubborn persistence with which he keeps on my trail.'

Jorman was silent. Then he shook his head.

'I admit you've got me curious,' he told Carraden. 'I can see easily enough there are some things you don't want to tell me. I suppose the reason he's hunting you so doggedly is one of them.'

'Right,' the Anglishman admitted. 'It was while the expedition was digging out old Tut-Ankh-Tothet. It was something I did. A law I violated. A law I was aware of, but – well, I went ahead anyway.

'You see, there were some things we found buried with old Tothet the press didn't hear of. Some papyri, some clay tablets. And off the main tomb a smaller one . . .

'Well, I can't tell you more. I violated an ancient law, then got panicky and tried to escape the consequences. In doing so, I ran afoul of this – this fellow. And brought him down on my neck. If you don't mind –'

There was a desperate note in his host's voice. Jorman nodded.

'Certainly,' he agreed. 'I'll drop the subject. After all, it's your business. You've never tried to ambush the fellow and have it out with him, I suppose?'

He imagined Carraden shaking his head.

'No use,' the other said shortly. 'My only safety is in flight. So I've kept running. When I got to 'Frisco, I thought I was safe for a while. But this time he was on my heels almost at once. I heard him coming up the street for me late one foggy night. I got out the back door and ran for it. Got away to the Canadian plains.

'I planted myself out in the middle of nowhere, on a great, rolling grassy plain with no neighbour for miles. Where no one would even think of me, much less speak to me or utter my name. I was safe there almost a year. But in the end it was – well, almost a mistake.'

Carraden put down his cup with a clatter. Jorman imagined it was because the cup had almost slipped from shaking fingers.

'You see, out there on the prairie, there were no footsteps. This time he came at night, as usual, and he was almost on me before I was aware of it. And my horse was lame. I got away. But it was a near thing. Nearer than I like to remember. . . .

'So I came to New York. I've been here since, in the very heart of the city. It's the best place of all to hide. Among people. So many millions crossing and recrossing my path muddy up my trail, confuse the scent –'

'Confuse the scent?' Jorman exclaimed.

Carraden coughed. 'Said more than I meant to, that time,' he admitted. 'Yes, it's true. He scents me out. In part, at least.

'It's hard to explain. Call it the intangible evidences of my passage.'

'I see.' The man's voice pleaded so for belief that Jorman nodded, though he was far from seeing.

'I've been here almost a year now,' the Englishman told him. 'Almost twelve months with no sign of him. I've been cautious; man, how cautious I've been! Lying in my burrow like a terrified rabbit.

'Most of that time I've been right here, close to Times Square, where a million people a day cut my trail. I've huddled in my two rooms here – there's a bedroom beyond – going out only by day. He is usually most active at night. In the day people confuse him. It's the lonely reaches of the late hours he likes best. And it's during them I huddle here, listening wakefully. . . .

'Except on stormy nights like this. Storms make his job more difficult. The rain washes away my scent, the confusion of the winds and the raging of the elements dissipate my more intangible trail. That's why I ventured out tonight.

'Some day, even here, he'll find me,' Sir Andrew Carraden said continuing, his voice tight with strain. 'I'm prepared. I'll hear him coming – I hope – and as he forces this door, I'll get out through the other one, the one in the bedroom, and get away. I early learned the folly of holing up in a burrow with only one exit. Now I always have at least one emergency doorway.

'Believe me, man, it's a ghastly existence. The lying awake in the quiet hours of the night, listening, listening for him; the clutch at the heart, the sitting bolt upright, the constant and continuing terror –'

Carraden did not finish his sentence. He was silent for several minutes, fighting, Jorman imagined, for self-control. Then the springs of his easy chair squeaked as he leaned forward.

'Look,' the Englishman said then, in such desperate earnestness that his voice trembled a bit. 'You must wonder whether I just brought you up here to tell you this tale. I didn't. I had a purpose. I told you the story to see how you reacted. And I'm satisfied. Anyway, you didn't openly disbelieve me; and if you think I'm crazy, maybe you'll humour me anyway. I have a proposition to make.'

Jorman sat up a bit straighter.

'Yes?' he asked, his face expressing uncertainty. 'What –'

'What kind of proposition?' Carraden finished the sentence for him. 'This. That you help me out by listening for him.'

Jorman jerked his head up involuntary, so that if he had not been blind he would have been staring into the other's face.

'Listen for your enemy?'

'Yes,' the Englishman told him, voice hoarse. 'Listen for his approach. Like a sentinel. An outpost. Look, man, you're down there in your little stand every evening from six on, I've noticed. You stay until late at night. You're posted there not fifty yards from this hotel.

'When he comes, he'll go by you. He's bound to have cast about a bit, to unravel the trail – double back and forth like a hunting dog, you know, until he gets it straightened out.

'He may go by three or four times before he's sure. You have a keen ear. If he goes by while you're on the job, you're bound to hear him.'

Carraden's voice quickened, became desperately persuasive.

'And if you do, you can let me know. I'll instruct the doorman to come over if you signal. Or you can leave your stand and come up here; you can make it easily enough, only fifty paces. But somehow you must warn me. Say you will, man!'

Jorman hesitated in his answer. Sir Andrew mistook his silence.

'If you're frightened,' he said, 'there's no need to be. He won't attack you. Only me.'

'That part's all right,' Jorman told him honestly. 'What you've told me isn't altogether clear, and – I'll be frank – I'm not absolutely sure whether you're sane or not. But I wouldn't mind listening for you. Only, don't you see, I wouldn't have any way of recognizing your enemy's step.'

Carraden gave a little whistling sigh that he checked at once.

'Good man!' The exclamation was quiet, but his voice showed relief. 'Just so you'll do it. That last bit is easy enough. I've heard him several times. I can imitate his step for you, I think. There's only one thing worrying me.

'He – not everyone can hear him. But I'm counting on your blindness to give your ears the extra sensitivity – No matter. We have to have a go at it. Give me a moment.'

Jorman sat in silence and waited. The rain, beating against the panes of two windows, was distinctly lessening. Somewhere distant a fire siren wailed, a banshee sound.

Carraden was making a few tentative scrapings, with his hands or his feet, on the floor.

'Got it!' he announced. 'I've put a bedroom slipper on each hand. It's a noise like this.'

With the soft-soled slippers, he made a noise like the shuffle of a large bare foot – a double sound, *shuffle-shuffle*, followed by a pause, then repeated.

'If you're extra keen,' he announced, 'you can hear a faint click or scratch at each step. But –'

Then Jorman heard him sit up straight, knew Carraden was staring at his face.

'What is it, man?' the Englishman cried in alarm. 'What's wrong?'

Jorman sat very tense, his fingers gripping the arms of his chair.

'Sir Andrew,' he whispered, his lips stiff, 'Sir Andrew! I've already heard those footsteps. An hour ago in the rain he went by my stand.'

In the long silence that followed, Jorman could guess how the blood was draining from the other man's ruddy face, how the knuckles of his hands clenched.

'Tonight?' Carraden asked then, his voice harsh and so low that Jorman could hardly hear him. 'Tonight, man?'

'Just a few minutes before you came by,' Jorman blurted. 'I heard footsteps – *his* steps – shuffling by. The dog woke up and whimpered. They approached me slowly, pausing, then going on.'

The Englishman breathed, 'Go on, man! What then?'

'They turned. He went down Seventh Avenue, going south.'

Sir Andrew Carraden leaped to his feet, paced across the room, wheeled, came back.

'He's tracked me down at last!' he said in a tight voice, from which a note of hysteria was not far absent. 'I've got to go. Tonight. Now. You say he's turned south?'

Jorman nodded.

'But that means nothing.' Carraden spoke swiftly, as if thinking out loud. 'He'll find he's lost the track. He'll turn back. And since he passed, I've made a fresh trail. The rain may not have washed it quite away. He may have picked it up. He may be coming up those stairs now. Where's my bag? My passport? My money? All in my bureau. Excuse me. Sit tight.'

Jorman heard a door flung open, heard the man rush into the adjoining bedroom, heard a tight bureau drawer squeal.

Then Carraden's footsteps again. A moment after, a bolt on a door pulled back. Then the door itself rattled. A pause, and it rattled again, urgently. Once again, this time violently. Jorman could hear Carraden's loud breathing in the silence that followed.

'The door won't open!' There was an edge of fear in the Englishman's voice as he called out. 'There's a key or something in the lock. From the outside.'

He came back into the sitting-room with a rush, paused beside Jorman.

'That message!' The words came through Carraden's teeth. 'The one the bloody clerk handed me. I wonder if –'

Paper ripped, rattled. Sir Andrew Carraden began to curse.

'The fool!' he almost sobbed. 'Oh, the bloody, bloody fool. "Dear sir" ' – Carraden's voice was shaking now – ' ' "redecoration of the corridor on the north side of your suite necessitated our opening your door this afternoon to facilitate the painting of it. In closing and locking it, a key inadvertently jammed in the lock, and we could not at once extricate it. Our locksmith will repair your lock promptly in the morning. Trusting you will not be inconvenienced –'

'God deliver us from fools!' Sir Andrew gasped. 'Luckily there's still time to get out this way. Come on, man, don't sit there. I'll show you down. But we must hurry, hurry.'

Jorman heard the other man's teeth chattering faintly together in the excess of emotion that was shaking him, felt the muscular quivering of near-panic in the big man as he put out his hand and took Sir Andrew's arm to help himself rise. And then, as he was about to lift himself, his fingers clamped tight about the Englishman's writ.

'Carraden!' he whispered. 'Carraden! *Listen!*'

The other asked no question. Jorman felt the quivering muscles beneath his fingers tense. And a silence that was like a hand squeezing them breathless seemed to envelop the room. There was not even the faint, distant sound of traffic to break it.

Then they both heard it. In the hallway, coming towards the door. The faint padding sound of shuffling footsteps. . . .

It was Foxfire, whimpering piteously at their feet, that broke the spell momentarily holding them.

'He' – Carraden's word was a gasp – 'he's out there!'

He left Joman's side. Jorman heard him shoving with desperate strength at something heavy. Castors squeaked. Some piece of furniture tipped over and fell with a crash against the inside of the door.

'There!' Carraden groaned. 'The desk. And the door's bolted. That'll hold him a moment. Sit tight, man. Hold the pup. He'll ignore you. It's me he wants. I've got to get that other door open before he can come through.'

His footsteps raced away into the bedroom. Jorman sat where he was, Foxfire under his arm, so tense that his muscles ached from sheer fright.

In the bedroom there was a crash, as of a man plunging against a closed door that stubbornly would not give. But above the noise from the bedroom, Jorman could hear the barricaded door – the door beyond which *he* was – start to give.

Nails screamed as they came forth from wood. Hinges groaned. And the whole mass – door, lintels, desk – moved inward an inch or so. A pause, and then the terrible, inexorable pressure from the other side came again. With a vast rending the door gave way and crashed inward over the barricading furniture.

And in the echoes of the crash he heard the almost soundless *shuffle-shuffle* of feet crossing the room towards the bedroom.

In the bedroom Sir Andrew Carradden's effort to force the jammed door ceased suddenly. Then the Englishman screamed, an animal cry of pure terror from which all intelligence was gone. The window in the bedroom crashed up with a violence that shattered the glass.

After that there was silence for a moment, until Jorman's acute hearing caught, from the street outside and five floors down, the sound of an object striking the pavement.

Sir Andrew Carraden had jumped....

Somehow Jorman found the strength to stumble to his feet. He dashed straight forward towards the door, and fell over the wreckage of it. Hurt, but not feeling it, he scrambled up again and stumbled into the hall and down the corridor.

Somehow his questing hands found a door that was sheathed in metal, and he thrust it open. Beyond were banisters. Stairs. By the sense of feel he rushed down recklessly.

How many minutes it took to reach the lobby, to feel his way blindly past the startled desk clerk out to the street, he did not know. Or whether he had got down before *he* had.

Once outside on the wet pavement, cool night air on his cheek, he paused, his breath coming in sobbing gasps. And as he stood there, footsteps, shuffling footsteps, passed close by him from behind and turned westward.

Then Jorman heard and astounding thing. He heard Sir Andrew Carraden's footsteps also, a dozen yards distant, hurrying away from him.

Sir Andrew Carraden had leaped five floors. And still could walk....

No, run. For the tempo of the man's steps was increasing. He was trotting now. Now running. And behind the running footsteps of Carraden were *his* steps, moving more swiftly, too, something scratching loudly on the concrete each time he brought a foot down.

'Sir Andrew!' Jorman called loudly, senselessly. 'Sir An –'

Then he stumbled and almost fell, trying to follow. Behind him the desk clerk came hurrying up. He exclaimed something in shocked tones, but Jorman did not even hear him. He was bending down, his hand exploring the object over which he had stumbled.

'Listen!' Jorman gasped with a dry mouth to the desk clerk, jittering above him. 'Tell me quick! I've got to know. What did the man look like who followed me out of the hotel just now?'

'F-followed you?' the clerk stuttered. 'Nobody f-followed you. Nobody but you has gone in or out in the last hu-half hour. Listen, why did he do it? Why did he jump?'

Jorman did not answer him.

'Dear God,' he was whispering, and in a way it was a prayer. 'Oh, dear God!'

His hand was touching the dead body of Andrew Carraden, lying broken and bloody on the pavement.

But his ears still heard those footsteps of pursued and pursuer, far down the block, racing away until not even he could make them out any longer.

# The Potter's Art

## *Denys Val Baker*

Mrs Bartholomew had good taste, there was no doubt about that. It was evident in her whole background: the almost regal nature of her large Georgian house in London, the impressive variety of the various *objets d'art* which adorned every room – and also, to be fair, in the exquisite flair with which the good lady dressed her own formidable personage. Slim and elegant and soignée, with bold sensual features crowned by a rather magnificent sweep of raven dark hair that conspired to reduce the effect of her forty years – yes, it had to be admitted that here was a woman, fundamentally hard and shrewd and acquisitive, who still managed to project an image of allure and glittering beauty. Few people, that is men, found themselves able to resist Mrs Bartholomew: she always got her own way, if not by one means then by another.

Ever since the early demise of her late, very wealthy husband, an event which she had cogently foreseen when she married him, Mrs Bartholomew had been free to devote herself entirely to her favourite hobby of seeking out works of art. It was a pastime at which she had become increasingly expert, and one which she divided strictly into two categories. First, there were works of art of the inanimate or what might be termed real estate kind – these she collected and kept. And then there were works of art of a more lively, fleshly nature, which she also collected, consumed – and then discarded.

In this way the beautiful Mrs Bartholomew had picked her way through a surprisingly varied selection of painters, sculptors, writers, actors and so forth. But she had never had a real, live potter before. Indeed, the thought probably would never have occurred to her. Pottery, yes – upon her Chippendale writing bureau there stood a much prized Ming vase: on the mantelpiece of her drawing room two very rare Dresden shepherdesses: scattered about the house a number of other valuable pots including, for Mrs Bartholomew was nothing if she was not up-to-date, a Bernard Leach and a Lucie Rie.

But potters themselves – Mrs Bartholomew had not really spared them a thought. Until that fateful afternoon when, wandering through the cobbled streets of a tiny Cornish fishing village, she came upon the dark-haired lad in blue jeans and sweater, bent intently over an old potter's kick-wheel. His name was a very long Cornish one which began with the syllable, Pen, and ever afterwards Mrs Bartholomew called him just that – Pen. Somehow she felt it struck just the right note of impending intimacy.

Mrs Bartholomew found her Pen almost accidentally, at the far end of a long, low fish-cellar which she might have passed by if she had not heard the whirring sound of the kick-wheel in action. Intrigued, she stepped down the stone steps and into the semi-gloom of the interior, relieved a little at the far end where a small window let in some afternoon sunshine. By this vague light she saw outlined the shadowy shape of what at first seemed a young boy, bent forward and engrossed, indeed seemingly welded to the movement of the wheel. On approaching closer Mrs Bartholomew saw that it was not a young boy but a young man – a powerfully built young man wearing an open-necked shirt behind which could be sensed the ripple of strong muscles. And this positive and virile being was not so much welded into the rhythm of the wheel but, more interestingly, directing its mood and movement.

What immediately seized Mrs Bartholomew's attention – then, and as it happened forever more – was what the whole thing was really all about: the young man's sinewy sun-bronzed hands, hovering delicately over the small, spinning cast-iron wheel – hovering and then suddenly plunging forward and enveloping, with impressive confidence, the whirling lump of raw red clay. While Mrs Bartholomew watched, spellbound, the wheel whirled round faster and faster, the hands increased their subterranean pressure, fingers alive with tension, and at last, subtly, the ball of clay began to take shape and life of its own . . . at first spreading out messily, then miraculously assembling into some sort of order and form – at last rising, like the phoenix, into cylindrical triumph. Higher and higher the column rose, until it even began to tremble so that Mrs Bartholomew held her breath in anguish . . . but all was well: the expert touch was eased slightly, the cylinder returned to its former, more solid shape . . . and all at once, so abruptly that Mrs Bartholomew gave a gasp of surprise, the wheel stopped moving, and there was the clay, virgin pure, a definite, living shape.

It was then that the young potter turned around, and Mrs Bartholomew was pleasantly surprised to see a dark, almost Spanish type of face, sullen and handsome and crowned by a mop of curly dark hair – the whole completed, now, by an engagingly youthful grin. This, Mrs Bartholomew decided, was going to be quite interesting. She moved more into the young man's line of vision, draped herself decoratively over a low bench, and smiled brilliantly.

'You must,' she said softly, 'be very clever. I mean to handle the clay like that.' She paused, and then said warmly. 'Please go on ... I like to watch.' She gave a pearly laugh, opening her wide mouth, showing white teeth, and the tip of a rapacious tongue. 'I think it's fascinating – absolutely fascinating.'

Mrs Bartholomew, always an opportunist, altered her holiday plan. Instead of travelling about Cornwall she took a room in the local hotel and spent most of her time in the little fish-cellar, watching Pen at work. He didn't seem to mind: indeed, why should he have done? He was, she surmised, flattered by her elegant presence, perhaps even a little awed. All the same, she judged, he was no fool, no country bumpkin ... no, that was made pretty clear by the shrewd way he appraised her sometimes, the almost impudent gloss of his smile.

To do her justice, Mrs Bartholomew really was fascinated by the potter's art. She loved the way the inanimate red clay was taken hold of, pushed and pummelled, slapped down on the wheel – and all at once, as if by magic, transformed from something dead into something incredibly alive. And above all, she liked to watch the way Pen did it – the way his strong, sensuous hands splayed out purposefully, applying pressure here, now there, touching delicately one part, stabbing fiercely into another. Yes, it was really the hands that fascinated most of all, Mrs Bartholomew had to admit. They seemed in a way to become almost apart, an entity in their own right, those hands: young, strong, meaning-ful – indeed, beautiful. And day after day she found herself strangely content to come and sit in a corner of the cellar, just watching and waiting ... for those hands to spring into life, to seize upon the clay, claw it into being – and, in the end, it often seemed, consummate it.

It would have been interesting to have known what Pen made of it all in those early days: that thoughts crossed that untroubled young mind. Perhaps they were none, for he was – as Mrs Bartholomew herself would have been the first to admit – very much a creature of the moment, very much a physical being. You did not really feel that the intellect was a strong point. And after all, did that really matter? Not really, reflected Mrs Bartholomew, as day after day she sat and watched, the tip of her red tongue poking out, her lips drawn back in vicarious delight, her eyes fixed bright and burning upon the endless restless movements of those hands. Yes, she had never before realized how interesting the potter's art could be.

As for Pen, his feelings remained, as you might say, incognite. He acknowledged Mrs Bartholomew's somewhat unusual interest with appropriate appreciation: he answered her questions politely, sometimes animatedly, no matter how probing they sometimes seemed: he was ever ready to demonstrate for her every aspect of the fascinating potter's art ... and when finally, unable to contain herself any longer, Mrs Bartholomew leaned forward and seized the two, by now beloved hands in her own and pressed them sensually against her own throbbing breast – well, Pen showed himself as surprisingly able to cope with the ensuing and inevitable developments: indeed, delightfully so.

Now that, most pleasurably, she had succeeded in making her point, establishing the routine so to speak, Mrs Bartholomew was full of her usual ambitious plans. Pen must not stay in this dingy hole, in this remote village, a moment longer – he must bring himself and his potter's art into the full limelight. She would set him up in a pottery of his own, no expense spared, in the heart of fashionable London. What's more, she would see to it that his work became properly appreciated by the people who really mattered. She'd organize an exhibition of his work. And invite all the critics. And ... and ...

It was true that in her single-mindedness Mrs Bartholomew had not exactly appreciated how complicated the removal of a pottery might be: that there were other items besides the potter and his wheel. It might, alas, have been in her own interest to have paid more attention now when, with surprising vehemence, Pen explained how strongly he felt about the other processes of pottery – and in particular, the ultimate art of glazing. 'It's the glazing, you see, that makes the pot ... why, it's an art in itself. And that's really what spurs a potter on. All my life, I've been seeking a glaze that would be unique, my own creation – just perfect.'

He looked at her with sudden earnestness to which, unhappily, she was impervious, and repeated, slowly.

'Imagine – my own glaze, something quite unique.'

'Yes, yes, dear boy. Mmmh. You'll have plenty of time for all that when you're set up in London.'

Well, to give her her due, Mrs Bartholomew did the boy proud, not only converting a large section of her house into a full-scale professional pottery, but installing all the most modern equipment – including, wonder of wonders, possibly the largest studio kiln which Pen had ever seen.

'Why – it's big enough to live in!' he said jocularly, in reality hiding a faint sense of irritation. It was, after all, preposterous to buy a kiln of that size for a single potter. Why it would take him weeks, months even, to accumulate enough stock for a single firing.

All the same, he wasn't one to look a gift horse in the face. He did really care about his art, except that in his eyes it was, more mundanely, a craft, and he really did welcome the opportunity to experiment and expand. What's more his work did have a definite quality about it which perhaps in the remoteness of a Cornish fishing village might have passed unseen – but which now, under the umbrella of Mrs Bartholomew's formidable patronage, soon began to attract attention. Indeed, before long Pen's pottery was definitely a with-it item on the ever changing panorama of London art life.

Perhaps out of a certain gratitude to his benefactress Pen endeavoured to repay her for her assistance in the manner to which she was obviously most accustomed . . . but truth to tell he found it increasingly exhausting and, sad to say, even displeasing. The fact was that not only was Mrs Bartholomew without any of the native earthiness which Pen really appreciated, but she was, he had to admit, a good deal older than he had imagined – a very good deal older. And somehow, as time went on and his own success obviated more and more the need for her support, this factor began to loom larger and larger, so that he was hard put to it to hide his unwillingness, and even, finally his disgust.

It was no doubt most unfortunate that around this time, in response to the obvious hard facts of a potter's life, equipped with a very large kiln, Pen took on an assistant . . . and that assistant happened to be a young girl student by the name of Miranda. If Mrs Bartholomew had not by now been so completely obsessed by her relationship with the young potter and his tantalizing hands she might have done well to ponder on the significance of the appearance of the buxom, fleshly and youthful damsel – and above all upon the fact that she was a pottery enthusiast, with the same all-consuming interest in the craft as Pen himself.

As it was, Mrs Bartholomew continued upon her imperious, selfish and self-centred way, as she had done all through her life . . . with the inevitable result that might be expected. Her protégé's patience turned to impatience, his tolerance to intolerance, his acceptance to rejection.

What really clinched things was the exciting discovery of a true compatibility between himself and Miranda. Not only did they find real physical pleasure in each other's company, not only did her quicksilver mental powers seem to rejuvenate his own rather sleepy ones – but, incredibly, they had the same all-pervading interest. And not only that, but like himself Miranda appreciated the supreme challenge of finding the perfect glaze. Together they could work for it in complete harmony.

Unfortunately for herself Mrs Bartholomew could not bear to allow this. Coming upon the two of them in an unmistakably compromising position one day she flew into a rage and ordered the girl out of the house. As she departed in tears, an ominous, dark glowering look appeared upon Pen's face – a look that should have filled Mrs Bartholomew with apprehension, had she not been so consumed by her own rage. Like the rest of the Cornish race, Pen was slow to rouse, hard to appease.

That evening Pen had planned a firing of his large kiln. Unusually, as the evening progressed, he was to be found removing rows of finished pots out of the kiln. At last they were all out, and the huge kiln stood quite empty. For a while Pen stood back, eyeing the kiln speculatively: then he went across and checked the instruments. Only when he was quite satisfied that everything was working did he go to the door and call out, in a soft, almost wheedling voice, for Mrs Bartholomew.

She – who had been wandering aimlessly about the house, regretting her spleen, miserably haunted by memories of those exquisite hands and all the pleasure they could inflict upon her sensual being – came running at once.

'What is it, my dear? Oh, I'm so glad you called – do let's be friends again.'

'Yes, of course,' said Pen softly. 'Friends again. Here, come and see what I've been doing. I've something that will interest you, I think.'

He then escorted the unsuspecting Mrs Bartholomew into the pottery workroom and carefully locked the door after him. Exactly what happened immediately afterwards is a matter for conjecture. Let us hope, out of generosity, that at least Pen granted Mrs Bartholomew once more the pleasure of a last luxurious caress of those beloved hands ... But that much apart, the next somewhat grimmer development was that he neatly stunned the lady, trussed her up in a most undignified fashion, and, not without a good deal of huffing and puffing lifted her up and placed her into the large potter's kiln. Then he firmly closed the door, bunged up the eye-socket – and switched on the kiln.

There is no need to dwell on the less pleasant side of the next few hours. Things that had to be done and disposed of were done and disposed of: but a certain important residue was not disposed of, but carefully gathered in a deep pottery urn ... and later, after certain excited experiments, mixed with various other chemical ingredients to produce a most unusual glaze. In due course the excited Pen applied this to a number of test pots and placed them in the kiln for a firing.

Some time later, arm round his beloved Miranda, he stood holding open the doors of the kiln, staring in reverent wonder at what was revealed. The pots shone bright and metallic, aglow with a mysterious sheen never before seen.

'Why, look,' cried out the girl. 'What a marvellous glaze. Blood-red – why, it's fantastic.' She turned and looked at him marvellingly. 'Why, it must be unique.'

For a moment Pen did not speak. He tok a cloth and picked up one of the pots, holding it up to the light so that it shone and sparkled like – like something alive. For a moment, almost sadly, he wished that Mrs Bartholomew was there to share the triumph: he hoped, at least, wherever she was she might have some sort of appreciation of what had happened. After all, it was most certainly due to her. What a pity – what a pity that the glaze was going to be in very such short supply. Ah well: he sighed, and turned to the girl beside him, looking forward amiably to the pleasurable future together.

'Yes, indeed,' he said. 'It's unique.'

# The Thing in the Hall

## *E. F. Benson*

The following pages are the account given me by Dr Assheton of the Thing in the Hall. I took notes, as copious as my quickness of hand allowed me, from his dictation, and subsequently read to him this narrative in its transcribed and connected form. This was on the day before his death, which indeed probably occurred within an hour after I had left him, and, as readers of inquests and such atrocious literature may remember, I had to give evidence before the coroner's jury. Only a week before Dr Assheton had to give similar evidence, but as a medical expert, with regard to the death of his friend, Louis Fielder, which occurred in a manner identical with his own. As a specialist, he said he believed that his friend had committed suicide while of unsound mind, and the verdict was brought in accordingly. But in the inquest held over Dr Assheton's body, though the verdict eventually returned was the same, there was more room for doubt. For I was bound to state that only shortly before his death, I read what follows to him; that he corrected me with extreme precision on a few points of detail, that he seemed perfectly himself, and that at the end he used these words:

'I am quite certain as a brain specialist that I am completely sane, and that these things happened not merely in my imagination but in the external world. If I had to give evidence again about poor Louis, I should be compelled to take a different line. Please put that down at the end of your account, or at the beginning, if it arranges itself better so.'

There will be a few words I must add at the end of this story, and a few words of explanation must precede it. Briefly, they are these.

Francis Assheton and Louis Fielder were up at Cambridge together, and there formed the friendship that lasted nearly till their death. In general attributes no two men could have been less alike, for while Dr Assheton had become at the age of thirty-five the first and final authority on his subject, which was the functions and diseases of the brain, Louis Fielder at the same age was still on the threshold of achievement. Assheton, apparently without any brilliance at all, had by careful and incessant work arrived at the top of his profession, while Fielder, brilliant at school, brilliant at college and brilliant ever afterwards, had never done anything.

He was too eager, so it seemed to his friends, to set about the dreary work of patient investigation and logical deductions; he was for ever guessing and prying, and striking out luminous ideas, which he left burning so to speak, to illumine the work of others. But at bottom, the two men had this compelling interest in common, namely, an insatiable curiosity after the unknown, perhaps the most potent bond yet devised between the solitary units that make up the race of man. Both – till the end – were absolutely fearless, and Dr Assheton would sit by the bedside of the man stricken with bubonic plague to note the gradual surge of the tide of disease to the reasoning faculty with the same absorption as Fielder would study X-rays one week, flying machines the next, and spiritualism the third. The rest of the story, I think, explains itself – or does not quite do so. This, anyhow, is what I read to Dr Assheton, being the connected narrative of what he had himself told me. It is he, of course, who speaks.

After I returned from Paris, where I had studied under Charcot, I set up practice at home. The general doctrine of hypnotism, suggestion, and cure by such means had been accepted even in London by this time, and, owing to a few papers I had written on the subject, together with my foreign diplomas, I found that I was a busy man almost as soon as I had arrived in town. Louis Fielder had his ideas about how I should make my debut (for he has ideas on every subject, and all of them original), and entreated me to come and live not in the stronghold of doctors, 'Chloroform Square', as he called it, but down in Chelsea, where there was a house vacant next his own.

'Who cares where a doctor lives,' he said, 'so long as he cures people? Besides, you don't believe in old methods; why believe in old localities? Oh, there is an atmosphere of painless death in Chloroform Square! Come and make people live instead! And on most evenings I shall have so much to tell you; I can't "drop in" across half London.'

Now if you have been abroad for five years, it is a great deal to know that you have any intimate friend at all still left in the metropolis, and, as Louis said, to have that intimate friend next door is an excellent reason for going next door. Above all, I remembered from Cambridge days, what Louis's 'dropping in' meant. Towards bedtime, when work was over, there would come a rapid step on the landing, and for an hour, or two hours, he would gush with ideas. He simply diffused life, which is ideas, wherever he went. He fed one's brain, which is the one thing which matters. Most people who are ill, are ill because their brain is starving, and the body rebels, and gets lumbago or cancer. That is the chief doctrine of my work such as it has been. All bodily disease springs from the brain. It is merely the brain that has to be fed and rested and exercised properly to make the body absolutely healthy, and immune from all disease. But when the brain is affected, it is as useful to pour medicines down the sink, as make your patient swallow them, unless – and this is a paramount limitation – unless he believes in them.

I said something of the kind to Louis one night, when, at the end of a busy day, I had dined with him. We were sitting over coffee in the hall, or so it is called, where he takes his meals. Outside, his house is just like mine, and ten thousand other small houses in London, but on entering instead of finding a narrow passage with a door on one side, leading into the dining-room, which again communicates with a small back room called 'the study', he has had the sense to eliminate all unnecessary walls, and consequently the whole ground floor of his house is one room, with stairs leading up to the first floor. Study, dining-room and passage have been knocked into one; you enter a big room from the front door. The only drawback is that the postman makes loud noises close to you, as you dine, and just as I made these commonplace observations to him about the effect of the brain on the body and the senses, there came a loud rap, somewhere close to me, that was startling.

'You ought to muffle your knocker,' I said, 'anyhow during the time of meals.'

Louis leaned back and laughed.

'There isn't a knocker,' he said. 'You were startled a week ago, and said the same thing. So I took the knocker off. The letters slide in now. But you heard a knock, did you?'

'Didn't you?' said I.

'Why, certainly. But it wasn't the postman. It was the Thing. I don't know what it is. That makes it so interesting.'

Now if there is one thing that the hypnotist, the believer in unexplained influences, detests and despises, it is the whole root-notion of spiritualism. Drugs are not more opposed to his belief than the exploded, discredited idea of the influence of spirits on our lives. And both are discredited for the same reason; it is easy to understand how brain can act on brain, just as it is easy to understand how body can act on body, so that there is no more difficulty in the reception of the idea that the strong mind can direct the weak one, than there is in the fact of a wrestler of greater strength overcoming one of less. But that spirits should rap at furniture and divert the course of events is as absurd as administering phosphorus to strengthen the brain. That was what I thought then.

However, I felt sure it was the postman, and instantly rose and went to the door. There were no letters in the box, and I opened the door.

The postman was just ascending the steps. He gave the letters into my hand.

Louis was sipping his coffee when I came back to the table.

'Have you ever tried table-turning?' he asked. 'It's rather odd.'

'No, and I have not tried violet-leaves as a cure for cancer,' I said.

'Oh, try everything,' he said. 'I know that that is your plan, just as it is mine. All these years that you have been away, you have tried all sorts of things, first with no faith, then with just a little faith, and finally with mountain-moving faith. Why, you didn't believe in hypnotism at all when you went to Paris.'

He rang the bell as he spoke, and his servant came up and cleared the table. While this was being done we strolled about the room, looking at prints, with applause for a Bartolozzi that Louis had bought in the New Cut, and dead silence over a 'Perdita' which he acquired at considerable cost. Then he sat down again at the table on which we had dined. It was round, and mahogany – heavy, with a central foot divided into claws.

'Try its weight,' he said; 'see if you can push it about.'

So I held the edge of it in my hands, and found that I could just move it. But that was all; it required the exercise of a good deal of strength to stir it.

'Now put your hands on the top of it,' he said, 'and see what you can do.'

I could not do anything; my fingers merely slipped about on it. But I protested at the idea of spending the evening thus.

'I would much sooner play chess or noughts and crosses with you,' I said, 'or even talk about politics, than turn tables. You won't mean to push, nor shall I, but we shall push without meaning to.'

Louis nodded.

'Just a minute,' he said, 'let us both put our fingers only on the top of the table and push for all we are worth, from right to left.'

We pushed. At least I pushed, and I observed his fingernails. From pink they grew to white, because of the pressure he exercised. So I must assume he pushed too. Once, as we tried this, the table creaked. But it did not move.

Then there came a quick peremptory rap, not I thought on the front door, but somewhere in the room.

'It's the Thing,' said he.

Today, as I speak to you, I suppose it was. But on that evening it seemed only like a challenge. I wanted to demonstrate its absurdity.

'For five years, on and off, I've been studying rank spiritualism,' he said. 'I haven't told you before, because I wanted to lay before you certain phenomena, which I can't explain, but which now seem to me

to be at my command. You shall see and hear, and then decide if you
will help me.'

'And in order to let me see better, you are proposing to put out the
lights,' I said.

'Yes; you will see why.'

'I am here as a sceptic,' said I.

'Scep away,' said he.

Next moment the room was in darkness, except for a very faint glow
of firelight. The window-curtains were thick, and no street-illumination
penetrated them, and the familiar, cheerful sounds of pedestrians and
wheeled traffic came in muffled. I was at the side of the table towards
the door; Louis was opposite me, for I could see his figure dimly
silhouetted against the glow from the smouldering fire.

'Put your hands on the table,' he said, 'quite lightly, and – how shall
I say it? – expect.'

Still protesting in spirit, I expected. I could hear his breathing rather
quickened, and it seemed to me odd that anybody could find excitement
in standing in the dark over a large mahogany table, expecting. Then –
through my finger-tips, laid lightly on the table, there began to come a
faint vibration, like nothing so much as the vibration through the handle
of a kettle when water is beginning to boil inside it. This got gradually
more pronounced and violent till it was like the throbbing of a motor
car. It seemed to give off a low humming note. Then quite suddenly the
table seemed to slip from under my fingers and began very slowly to
revolve.

'Keep your hands on it and move with it,' said Louis, and as he spoke
I saw his silhouette pass away from in front of the fire, moving as the
table moved.

For some moments there was silence, and we continued, rather
absurdly, to circle round keeping step, so to speak, with the table. Then
Louis spoke again, and his voice was trembling with excitement.

'Are you there?' he said.

There was no reply, of course, and he asked it again. This time there
came a rap like that which I had thought during dinner to be the
postman. But whether it was that the room was dark, or that despite
myself I felt rather excited too, it seemed to me now to be far louder than
before. Also it appeared to come neither from here nor there, but to be
diffused through the room.

Then the curious revolving of the table ceased, but the intense, violent
throbbing continued. My eyes were fixed on it, though owing to the
darkness I could see nothing, when quite suddenly a little speck of light
moved across it, so that for an instant I saw my own hands. Then came
another and another, like the spark of matches struck in the dark, or like

fire-flies crossing the dusk in southern gardens. Then came another knock of shattering loudness, and the throbbing of the table ceased, and the lights vanished.

Such were the phenomena at the first séance at which I was present, but Fielder, it must be remembered, had been studying, 'expecting', he called it, for some years. To adopt spiritualistic language (which at that time I was very far from doing), he was the medium, I merely the observer, and all the phenomena I had seen that night were habitually produced or witnessed by him. I make this limitation since he told me that certain of them now appeared to be outside his own control altogether. The knockings would come when his mind, as far as he knew, was entirely occupied in other matters, and sometimes he had even been awakened out of sleep by them. The lights were also independent of his volition.

Now my theory at the time was that all these things were purely subjective in him, and that what he expressed by saying that they were out of his control, meant that they had become fixed and rooted in the unconscious self, of which we know so little, but which, more and more, we see to play so enormous a part in the life of man. In fact, it is not too much to say that the vast majority of our deeds spring, apparently without volition, from this unconscious self. All hearing is the unconscious exercise of the aural nerve, all seeing of the optic, all walking, all ordinary movement seem to be done without the exercise of will on our part. Nay more, should we take to some new form of progression, skating, for instance, the beginner will learn with falls and difficulty the outside edge, but within a few hours of his having learned his balance on it, he will give no more thought to what he learned so short a time ago as an acrobatic feat, than he gives to the placing of one foot before the other.

But to the brain specialist all this was intensely interesting, and to the student of hypnotism, as I was, even more so, for (such was the conclusion I came to after this first séance), the fact that I saw and heard just what Louis saw and heard was an exhibition of thought-transference which in all my experience in the Charcot-schools I had never seen surpassed, if indeed rivalled. I knew that I was myself extremely sensitive to suggestion, and my part in it this evening I believed to be purely that of the receiver of suggestions so vivid that I visualized and heard these phenomena which existed only in the brain of my friend.

We talked over what had occurred upstairs. His view was that the Thing was trying to communicate with us. According to him it was the Thing that moved the table and tapped, and made us see streaks of light.

'Yes, but the Thing,' I interrupted, 'what do you mean? Is it a great-uncle – oh, I have seen so many relatives appear at séances, and heard so many of their dreadful platitudes – or what is it? A spirit? Whose spirit?'

Louis was sitting opposite to me, and on the little table before us there was an electric light. Looking at him I saw the pupil of his eye suddenly dilate. To a medical man – provided that some violent change in the light is not the cause of the dilation – that meant only one thing, terror.

But it quickly resumed its normal proportion again.

Then he got up, and stood in front of the fire.

'No, I don't think it is great-uncle anybody,' he said. 'I don't know, as I told you, what the Thing is. But if you ask me what my conjecture is, it is that the Thing is an Elemental.'

'And pray explain further. What is an Elemental?'

Once again his eye dilated.

'It will take two minutes,' he said. 'But, listen. There are good things in this world, are there not, and bad things? Cancer, I take it, is bad, and – and fresh air is good; honesty is good, lying is bad. Impulses of some sort direct both sides, and some power suggests the impulses. Well, I went into this spiritualistic business impartially. I learned to "expect", to throw open the door into the soul, and I said, "Anyone may come in." And I think Something has applied for admission, the Thing that tapped and turned the table and struck matches, as you saw, across it. Now the control of the evil principle in the world is in the hands of a power which entrusts its errands to the things which I call Elementals. Oh, they have been seen; I doubt not that they will be seen again. I did not, and do not, ask good spirits to come in. I don't want "The Church's one foundation" played on a musical box. Nor do I *want* an Elemental. I only threw open the door. I believe the Thing has come into my house, and is establishing communication with me. Oh, I want to go the whole hog. What is it? In the name of Satan, if necessary, what is it? I just want to know.'

What followed I thought then might easily be an invention of the imagination, but what I believed to have happened was this. A piano with music on it was standing at the far end of the room by the door, and a sudden draught entered the room, so strong that the leaves turned. Next the draught troubled a vase of daffodils, and the yellow heads nodded. Then it reached the candles that stood close to us, and they fluttered, burning blue and low. Then it reached me, and the draught was cold, and stirred my hair. Then it eddied, so to speak, and went across to Louis, and his hair also moved, as I could see. Then it went downwards towards the fire, and flames suddenly started up in its path, blown upwards. The rug by the fireplace flapped also.

'Funny, wasn't it?' he asked.

'And has the Elemental gone up the chimney?' said I.

'Oh, no,' said he, 'the Thing only passed us.'

Then suddenly he pointed at the wall just behind my chair, and his voice cracked as he spoke.

'Look, what's that?' he said. 'There on the wall.'

Considerably startled, I turned in the direction of his shaking finger. The wall was pale grey in tone, and sharp-cut against it was a shadow that, as I looked, moved. It was like the shadow of some enormous slug, legless and fat, some two feet high by about four feet long. Only at one end of it was a head shaped like the head of a seal, with open mouth and panting tongue.

Then even as I looked it faded, and from somewhere close at hand there sounded another of those shattering knocks.

For a moment after there was silence between us, and horror was thick as snow in the air. But, somehow, neither Louis nor I was frightened for more than one moment. The whole thing was so absorbingly interesting.

'That's what I mean by its being outside my control,' he said. 'I said I was ready for any – any visitor to come in, and by God, we've got a beauty.'

Now I was still, even in spite of the appearance of this shadow, quite convinced that I was only taking observations of a most curious case of disordered brain accompanied by the most vivid and remarkable thought-transference. I believed that I had not seen a slug-like shadow at all, but that Louis had visualized this dreadful creature so intensely that I saw what he saw. I found also that his spiritualistic trash-books, which I thought a truer nomenclature than text-books, mentioned this as a common form for Elementals to take. He on the other hand was more firmly convinced than ever that we were dealing not with a subjective but an objective phenomenon.

For the next six months or so we sat constantly, but made no further progress, nor did the Thing or its shadow appear again, and I began to feel that we were really wasting time. Then it occurred to me to get in a so-called medium, induce hypnotic sleep, and see if we could learn anything further. This we did, sitting as before round the dining-room table. The room was not quite dark, and I could see sufficiently clearly what happened.

The medium, a young man, sat between Louis and myself, and without the slightest difficulty I put him into a light hypnotic sleep. Instantly there came a series of the most terrific raps, and across the table there slid something more palpable than a shadow, with a faint luminance about it, as if the surface of it was smouldering. At the moment the medium's face became contorted to a mask of hellish terror; mouth and eyes were both open, and the eyes were focused on something close to him. The Thing waving its head came closer and closer to him, and reached out towards his throat. Then with a yell of panic, and warding off this horror with his hands, the medium sprang up, but It had already caught hold, and for the moment he could not get free. Then simultaneously Louis and I went to his aid, and my hands touched something cold and slimy. But pull as we could, we could not get it away. There was no firm handhold to be taken; it was as if one tried to grasp slimy fur, and the touch of it was horrible, unclean, like a leper. Then, in a sort of despair, though I still could not believe that the horror was real, for it must be a vision of diseased imagination, I remembered that the switch of the four electric lights was close to my hand. I turned them all on.

There on the floor lay the medium; Louis was kneeling by him with a face of wet paper, but there was nothing else there. Only the collar of the medium was crumpled and torn, and on his throat were two scratches that bled.

The medium was still in hypnotic sleep, and I woke him. He felt at his collar, put his hand to his throat and found it bleeding, but, as I expected, knew nothing whatever of what had passed. We told him that there had been an unusual manifestation, and he had, while in sleep, wrestled with something. We had got the result we wished for, and were much obliged to him.

I never saw him again. A week after that he died of blood-poisoning.

From that evening dates the second stage of this adventure. The Thing had materialized (I use again spiritualistic language which I still did not use at the time). The huge slug, the Elemental, manifested itself no longer by knocks and waltzing tables, nor yet by shadows. It was there in a form that could be seen and felt. But it still – this was my strong point – was only a thing of twilight; the sudden kindling of the electric light had shown us that there was nothing there. In this struggle perhaps the medium had clutched his own throat, perhaps I had grasped Louis's sleeve, he mine. But though I said these things to myself, I am not sure that I believed them in the same way that I believe the sun will rise tomorrow.

Now as a student of brain-functions and a student in hypnotic affairs, I ought perhaps to have steadily and unremittingly pursued this extraordinary series of phenomena. But I had my practice to attend to, and I found that with the best will in the world I could think of nothing else except the occurrence in the hall next door. So I refused to take part in any further séance with Louis. I had another reason also.

For the last four or five months he was becoming depraved. I have been no prude or Puritan in my own life, and I hope I have not turned a pharisaical shoulder on sinners. But in all branches of life and morals, Louis had become infamous. He was turned out of a club for cheating at cards, and narrated the event to me with gusto. He had become cruel; he tortured his cat to death; he had become bestial. I used to shudder as I passed his house, expecting I knew not what fiendish thing to be looking at me from the window.

Then came a night only a week ago, when I was awakened by an awful cry, swelling and falling and rising again. It came from next door. I ran downstairs in my pyjamas, and out into the street. The policeman on the beat had heard it too, and it came from the hall of Louis's house, the window of which was open. Together we burst the door in. You know what we found. The screaming had ceased but a moment before, but he was dead already. Both jugulars were severed, torn.

It was dawn, early and dusky, when I got back to my house next door. Even as I went in something seemed to push by me, something soft and slimy. It could not be Louis's imagination this time. Since then I have seen glimpses of it every evening. I am awakened at night by tappings, and in the shadows in the corner of my room there sits something more substantial than a shadow.

Within an hour of my leaving Dr Assheton, the quiet street was once more aroused by cries of terror and agony. He was already dead, and in no other manner than his friend, when they got into the house.

# The Boarded Window

## Ambrose Bierce

In 1830, only a few miles away from what is now the great city of
Cincinnati, lay an immense and almost unbroken forest. The whole
region was sparsely settled by people of the frontier – restless souls who
no sooner had hewn fairly habitable homes out of the wilderness and
attained to that degree of prosperity which to-day we should call
indigence than, impelled by some mysterious impulse of their nature,
they abandoned all and pushed farther westward, to encounter new
perils and privations in the effort to regain the meagre comforts which
they had voluntarily renounced. Many of them had already forsaken
that region for the remoter settlements, but among those remaining was
one who had been of those first arriving. He lived alone in a house of
logs surrounded on all sides by the great forest, of whose gloom and
silence he seemed a part, for no one had ever known him to smile nor
speak a needless word. His simple wants were supplied by the sale or
barter of skins of wild animals in the river town, for not a thing did he
grow upon the land which, if needful, he might have claimed by right
of undisturbed possession.  There were evidences of 'improvement' – a
few acres of ground immediately about the house had once been cleared
of its trees, the decayed stumps of which were half concealed by the new
growth that had been suffered to repair the ravage wrought by the axe.
Apparently the man's zeal for agriculture had burned with a failing
flame, expiring in penitential ashes.

The little log house, with its chimney of sticks, its roof of warping
clapboards weighted with traversing poles and its 'chinking' of clay, had
a single door and, directly opposite, a window. The latter, however, was
boarded up – nobody could remember a time when it was not. And none
knew why it was so closed; certainly not because of the occupant's dislike
of light and air, for on those rare occasions when a hunter had passed
that lonely spot the recluse had commonly been seen sunning himself on
his doorstep if heaven had provided sunshine for his need. I fancy there
are few persons living to-day who ever knew the secret of that window,
but I am one, as you shall see.

The man's name was said to be Murlock. He was apparently seventy

years old, actually about fifty. Something besides years had had a hand
in his aging. His hair and long, full beard were white, his grey, lustreless
eyes sunken, his face singularly seamed with wrinkles which appeared
to belong to two intersecting systems. In figure he was tall and spare,
with a stoop of the shoulders – a burden bearer. I never saw him; these
particulars I learned from my grandfather, from whom also I got the
man's story when I was a lad. He had known him when living near by
in that early day.

One day Murlock was found in his cabin dead. It was not a time and
place for coroners and newspapers, and I suppose it was agreed that he
had died from natural causes or I should have been told, and should
remember. I know only that with what was probably a sense of the fitness
of things the body was buried near the cabin, alongside the grave of his
wife, who had preceded him by so many years that local tradition had
retained hardly a hint of her existence. That closes the final chapter of
this true story – excepting, indeed, the circumstance that many years
afterwards, in company with an equally intrepid spirit, I penetrated to
the place and ventured near enough to the ruined cabin to throw a stone
against it, and ran away to avoid the ghost which every well-informed
boy thereabout knew haunted the spot. But there is an earlier chapter –
that supplied by my grandfather.

When Murlock built his cabin and began laying sturdily about with
his axe to hew out a farm – the rifle, meanwhile, his means of support –
he was young, strong and full of hope. In that eastern country whence
he came he had married, as was the fashion, a young woman in all ways
worthy of his honest devotion, who shared the dangers and privations
of his lot with a willing spirit and light heart. There is no known record
of her name; of her charms of mind and person tradition is silent and the
doubter is at liberty to entertain his doubt; but God forbid that I should
share it! Of their affection and happiness there is abundant assurance in
every added day of the man's widowed life; for what but the magnetism
of a blessed memory could have chained that venturesome spirit to a lot
like that?

One day Murlock returned from gunning in a distant part of the forest
to find his wife prostrate with fever, and delirious. There was no physician
within miles, no neighbour; nor was she in a condition to be left, to
summon help. So he set about the task of nursing her back to health,
but at the end of the third day she fell into unconsciousness and so passed
away, apparently, with never a gleam of returning reason.

From what we know of a nature like his we may venture to sketch in
some of the details of the outline picture drawn by my grandfather.
When convinced that she was dead, Murlock had sense enough to
remember that the dead must be prepared for burial. In performance

of this sacred duty he blundered now and again, did certain things incorrectly, and others which he did correctly were done over and over. His occasional failures to accomplish some simple and ordinary act filled him with astonishment, like that of a drunken man who wonders at the suspension of familiar natural laws. He was surprised, too, that he did not weep – surprised and a little ashamed; surely it is unkind not to weep for the dead. 'Tomorrow,' he said aloud, 'I shall have to make the coffin and dig the grave; and then I shall miss her, when she is no longer in sight; but now – she is dead, of course, but it is all right – it *must* be all right, somehow. Things cannot be so bad as they seem.'

He stood over the body in the fading light, adjusting the hair and putting the finishing touches to the simple toilet, doing all mechanically, with soulless care. And still through his consciousness ran an undersense of conviction that all was right – that he should have her again as before, and everything explained. He had had no experience in grief; his capacity had not been enlarged by use. His heart could not contain it all, nor his imagination rightly conceive it. He did not know he was so hard struck; *that* knowledge would come later, and never go. Grief is an artist of powers as various as the instruments upon which he plays his dirges for the dead, evoking from some the sharpest, shrillest notes, from others the low, grave chords that throb recurrent like the slow beating of a distant drum. Some natures it startles; some it stupefies. To one it comes like the stroke of an arrow, stinging all the sensibilities to a keener life; to another as the blow of a bludgeon which, in crushing, benumbs. We may conceive Murlock to have been that way affected, for (and here we are upon surer ground than that of conjecture) no sooner had he finished his pious work than, sinking into a chair by the side of the table upon which the body lay, and noting how white the profile showed in the deepening gloom, he laid his arms upon the table's edge, and dropped his face into them, tearless yet and unutterably weary. At that moment came in through the open window a long, wailing sound like the cry of a lost child in the far deeps of the darkening wood! But the man did not move. Again, and nearer than before, sounded that unearthly cry upon his failing sense. Perhaps it was a wild beast; perhaps it was a dream. For Murlock was asleep.

Some hours later, as it afterwards appeared, this unfaithful watcher awoke, and lifting his head from his arms intently listened – he knew not why. There in the black darkness by the side of the dead, recalling all without a shock, he strained his eyes to see – he knew not what. His senses were all alert, his breath was suspended, his blood had stilled its tides as if to assist the silence. Who – what had waked him, and where was it?

Suddenly the table shook beneath his arms, and at the same moment he heard, or fancied that he heard, a light, soft step – another – sounds as of bare feet upon the floor!

He was terrified beyond the power to cry out or move. Perforce he waited – waited there in the darkness through seeming centuries of such dread as one may know, yet live to tell. He tried vainly to speak the dead woman's name, vainly to stretch forth his hand across the table to learn if she were there. His throat was powerless, his arms and hands were like lead. Then occurred something most frightful. Some heavy body seemed hurled against the table with an impetus that pushed it against his breast so sharply as nearly to overthrow him, and at the same instant he heard and felt the fall of something upon the floor with so violent a thump that the whole house was shaken by the impact. A scuffling ensued, and a confusion of sounds impossible to describe. Murlock had risen to his feet. Fear had by excess forfeited control of his faculties. He flung his hands upon the table. Nothing was there!

There is a point at which terror may turn to madness; and madness incites to action. With no definite intent, from no motive but the wayward impulse of a madman, Murlock sprang to the wall, with a little groping seized his loaded rifle, and without aim discharged it. By the flash which lit up the room with a vivid illumination, he saw an enormous panther dragging the dead woman towards the window, its teeth fixed in her throat! Then there were darkness blacker than before, and silence; and when he returned to consciousness the sun was high and the wood vocal with songs of birds.

The body lay near the window, where the beast had left it when frightened away by the flash and report of the rifle. The clothing was deranged, the long hair in disorder, the limbs lay anyhow. From the throat, dreadfully lacerated, had issued a pool of blood not yet entirely coagulated. The ribbon with which he had bound the wrists was broken; the hands were tightly clenched. Between the teeth was a fragment of the animal's ear.

# The Mannikin

## *Robert Bloch*

Mind you, I cannot swear that my story is true. It may have been a dream; or worse, a symptom of some severe mental disorder. But I believe it is true. After all, how are we to know what things there are on earth? Strange monstrosities still exist, and foul, incredible perversions. Every year, each new geographical or scientific discovery, brings to light some new bit of ghastly evidence that the world is not altogether the same place we fondly imagine it to be. Sometimes peculiar incidents occur which hint of utter madness.

How can we be sure that our smug conceptions of reality actually exist? To one man in a million dreadful knowledge is revealed, and the rest of us remain mercifully ignorant. There have been travellers who never came back, and research workers who disappeared. Some of those who did return were deemed mad because of what they told, and others sensibly concealed the wisdom that had so horribly been revealed. Blind as we are, we know a little of what lurks beneath our normal life. There have been tales of sea-serpents and creatures of the deep; legends of dwarfs and giants; records of queer medical horrors and unnatural births. Stunted nightmares of men's personalities have blossomed into being under the awful stimulus of war, or pestilence, or famine. There have been cannibals, necrophiles, and ghouls; loathsome rites of worship and sacrifice; maniacal murders, and blasphemous crimes. When I think, then, of what *I* saw and heard, and compare it with certain other grotesque and unbelievable authenticities, I begin to fear for my reason.

But if there is any *sane* explanation to this matter, I wish to God I may be told before it is too late. Doctor Pierce tells me that I must be calm; he advised me to write this account in order to allay my apprehension. But I am not calm, and I never can be calm until I know the truth, once and for all; until I am wholly convinced that my fears are not founded on a hideous reality.

I was already a nervous man when I went to Bridgetown for a rest. It had been a hard grind that year at school, and I was very glad to get away from the tedious classroom routine. The success of my lecture courses assured my position on the faculty for the year to come, and

consequently I dismissed all academic speculation from my mind when
I decided to take a vacation. I chose to go to Bridgetown because of the
excellent facilities the lake afforded for trout-fishing. The resort I chose
from the voluminous array of hotel literature was a quiet, peaceful place,
according to the simple prospectus. It did not offer a golf-course, a bridle-
path, or an indoor swimming-pool. There was no mention made of a
grand ballroom, an eighteen-piece orchestra, no formal dinner. Best of
all, the advertisement in no way extolled the scenic grandeur of the lake
and woods. It did not polysyllabically proclaim that Lake Kane was
'Nature's eternal paradise, where cerulean skies and verdant wilderness
beckon the happy visitor to taste the joys of youth.' For that reason I
wired in a reservation, packed my bag, assembled my pipes, and left.

I was more than satisfied with the place when I arrived. Bridgetown
is a small, rustic village; a quaint survival of older and simpler days.
Situated on Lake Kane itself, it is surrounded by rambling woods, and
sloping, sun-splashed meadows where the farm-folk toil in serene content.
The blight of modern civilization has but dimly fallen upon these people
and their quiet ways. Automobiles, tractors, and the like are few. There
are several telephones, and five miles away the State Highway affords
easy access to the city. That is all. The homes are old, the streets cobbled.
Artists, suburban dilettantes and professional aesthetes have not yet
invaded the pastoral scene. The quota of summer guests is small and
select. A few hunters and fishers come, but none of the ordinary pleasure-
hunting crowd. The families thereabout do not cater to such tastes;
ignorant and unsophisticated as they are, they can recognize vulgarity.

So my surroundings were ideal. The place I stayed at was a three-
storey hostelry on the lake itself – the Kane House, run by Absolom
Gates. He was a character of the old school; a grizzled, elderly veteran
whose father had been in the fishery business back in the sixties. He,
himself, was a devotee of things piscatorial; but only from the Waltonian
view. His resort was a fisherman's Mecca. The rooms were large and
airy; the food plentiful and excellently prepared by Gates' widowed
sister. After my first inspection, I prepared to enjoy a remarkably
pleasant stay.

Then, upon my first visit to the village, I bumped into Simon Maglore
on the street.

I first met Simon Maglore during my second term as an instructor
back at college. Even then, he had impressed me greatly. This was not
due to his physical characteristics alone, though they were unusual
enough. He was tall and thin, with massive, stooping shoulders, and a
crooked back. He was not a hunchback in the usual sense of the word,
but was afflicted with a peculiar tumorous growth beneath his left
shoulder-blade. This growth he took some pains to conceal, but its

prominence made such attempts unsuccessful. Outside of this unfortunate deformity, however, Maglore had been a very pleasant-looking fellow. Black-haired, grey-eyed, fair of skin, he seemed a fine specimen of intelligent manhood. And it was this intelligence that had so impressed me. His class-work was strikingly brilliant, and at times his theses attained heights of sheer genius. Despite the peculiarly morbid trend of his work in poetry and essays, it was impossible to ignore the power and imagination that could produce such wild imagery and eldritch colour. One of his poems – *The Witch Is Hung* – won for him the Edsworth Memorial Prize for that year, and several of his major themes were republished in certain private anthologies.

From the first, I had taken a great interest in the young man and his unusual talent. He had not responded to my advances at first; I gathered that he was a solitary soul. Whether this was due to his physical peculiarity or his mental trend, I cannot say. He had lived alone in town, and was known to have ample means. He did not mingle with the other students, though they would have welcomed him for his ready wit, his charming disposition, and his vast knowledge of literature and art. Gradually, however, I managed to overcome his natural reticence, and won his friendship. He invited me to his rooms, and we talked.

I had then learned of his earnest belief in the occult and esoteric. He had told me of his ancestors in Italy, and their interest in sorcery. One of them had been an agent of the Medici. They had migrated to America in the early days, because of certain charges made against them by the Holy Inquisition. He also spoke of his own studies in the realms of the unknown. His rooms were filled with strange drawings he had made from dreams, and still stranger images done in clay. The shelves of his bookcases held many odd and ancient books. I noted Ranfts' *De Masticatione Mortuorum in Tumulis* (1734); the almost priceless *Cabala of Saboth* (Greek translation, circa 1686); Mycroft's *Commentaries on Witchcraft*; and Ludvig Prinn's infamous *Mysteries of the Worm*.

I made several visits to the apartments before Maglore left school so suddenly in the fall of '33. The death of his parents called him to the East, and he left without saying farewell. But in the interim I had learned to respect him a good deal, and had taken a keen interest in his future plans, which included a book on the history of witch cult survivals in America, and a novel dealing with the psychological effects of superstition on the mind. He had never written to me, and I heard no more about him until this chance meeting on the village street.

He recognized me. I doubt if I should have been able to identify him. He had changed. As we shook hands I noted his unkempt appearance and careless attire. He looked older. His face was thinner, and much paler. There were shadows around his eyes – and in them. His hands trembled; his face forced a lifeless smile. His voice was deeper when he spoke, but he inquired after my health in the same charming fashion he had always affected. Quickly I explained my presence, and began to question him.

He informed me that he lived here in town; he had lived here ever since the death of his parents. He was working very hard just now on his books, but he felt that the result of his labours more than justified any physical inconveniences he might suffer. He apologized for his untidy apparel and his tired manner. He wanted to have a long talk with me sometime soon, but he would be very busy for the next few days. Possibly next week he would look me up at the hotel – just now he must get some paper at the village store and go back to his home. With an abrupt farewell, he turned his back on me and departed.

As he did so I received another start. The hump on his back had grown. It was now virtually twice the size it had been when I first met him, and it was no longer possible to hide it in the least. Undoubtedly the hard work had taken severe toll of Maglore's energies. I thought of a sarcoma, and shuddered.

Walking back to the hotel, I did some thinking. Simon's haggardness appalled me. It was not healthful for him to work so hard, and his choice of subject was not any too wholesome. The constant isolation and the nervous strain were combining to undermine his constitution in an alarming way, and I determined to appoint myself a mentor over his course. I resolved to visit him at the earliest opportunity, without waiting for a formal invitation. Something must be done.

Upon my arrival at the hotel I got another idea. I would ask Gates what he knew about Simon and his work. Perhaps there was some interesting sidelight on his activity which might account for his curious transformation. I therefore sought out the worthy gentleman and broached the subject to him.

What I learned from him startled me. It appears that the villagers did not like Master Simon, or his family. The old folks had been wealthy enough, but their name had a dubious repute cast upon it ever since the early days. Witches and warlocks, one and all, made up the family line. Their dark deeds had been carefully hidden from the first, but the folk around them could tell. It appears that nearly all the Maglores had possessed certain physical malformations that had made them conspicuous. Some had been born with veils; others with club-feet. One or two were dwarfed, and all had at some time or another been accused of possessing the fabled 'evil eye'. Several of them had been nyctalops – they could see in the dark. Simon was not the first crookback in the family, by any means. His grandfather had it, and *his* grandsire before him.

There was much talk of inbreeding and clan-segregation, too. That, in the opinion of Gates and his fellows, clearly pointed to one thing – wizardry. Nor was this their only evidence. Did not the Maglores shun the village and shut themselves away in the old house on the hill? None of them attended church either. Were they not known to take long walks after dark, on nights when all decent, self-respecting people were safe in bed?

There were probably good reasons why they were unfriendly. Perhaps they had things they wished to hide in their old house, and maybe they were afraid of letting any talk get around. Folk had it that the place was full of wicked and heathenish books, and there was an old story that the whole family were fugitives from some foreign place or other because of what they had done. After all, who could say? They looked suspicious; they acted queerly; maybe they were. Of course, nobody could rightly tell. The mass hysteria of witch-burning and the herd-mania of satanic possession had not penetrated to this part of the country. There was no talk of altars in the woods, and the spectral forest presences of Indian myth. No disappearances – bovine or human – could be laid at the doors of the Maglore family. Legally, their record was clear. But folk feared them. And this new one – Simon – was the worst.

He never had acted right. His mother died at his birth. Had to get a doctor from out of the city – no local man would handle such a case. The boy had nearly died, too. For several years nobody had seen him. His father and his uncle had spent all their time taking care of him. When he was seven, the lad had been sent away to a private school. He came back once, when he was about twelve. That was when his uncle died. He went mad, or something of the sort. At any rate, he had an attack which resulted in a cerebral haemorrhage, as the doctor called it.

Simon then was a nice-looking lad – except for the hump, of course. But it did not seem to bother him at the time – indeed, it was quite small. He had stayed several weeks and then gone off to school again. He had not reappeared until his father's death, two years ago. The old man died all alone in that great house, and the body was not discovered until several weeks later. A passing pedlar had called; walked into the open parlour, and found old Jeffrey Maglore dead in his great chair. His eyes were open, and filled with a look of frightful dread. Before him was a great iron book, filled with queer, undecipherable characters.

A hurriedly summoned physician pronounced it death due to heart-failure. But the pedlar, after staring into those fear-filled eyes, and glancing at the odd, disturbing figures in the book, was not so sure. He had no opportunity to look around any further, however, for that night the son arrived.

People looked at him very queerly when he came, for no notice had yet been sent to him of his father's death. They were very still indeed when he exhibited a two-weeks' old letter in the old man's handwriting which announced a premonition of imminent death, and advised the young man to come home. The carefully guarded phrases of this letter seemed to hold a secret meaning; for the youth never even bothered to ask the circumstances of his father's death. The funeral was private; the customary interment being held in the cellar vaults beneath the house.

The gruesome and peculiar events of Simon Maglore's homecoming immediately put the country-folk on their guard. Nor did anything occur to alter their original opinion of the boy. He stayed on all alone in the silent house. He had no servants, and made no friends. His infrequent trips to the village were made only for the purpose of obtaining supplies. He took the purchases back himself, in his car. He bought a good deal of meat and fish. Once in a while he stopped in at the drug-store, where he purchased sedatives. He never appeared talkative, and replied to questions in monosyllables. Still, he was obviously well educated. It was generally rumoured that he was writing a book. Gradually his visits became more and more infrequent.

People now began to comment on his changed appearance. Slowly but surely he was altering, in an unpleasant way. First of all, it was noticed that his deformity was increasing. He was forced to wear a voluminous overcoat to hide its bulk. He walked with a slight stoop, as though its weight troubled him. Still, he never went to a doctor, and none of the townsfolk had the courage to comment or question him on his condition. He was ageing, too. He began to resemble his uncle Richard, and his eyes had taken on that lambent cast which hinted of a nyctaloptic power. All this excited its share of comment among people to whom the Maglore family had been a matter of interesting conjecture for generations.

Later this speculation had been based on more tangible developments. For recently Simon had made an appearance at various isolated farm-houses throughout the region, on a furtive errand.

He questioned the old folks, mostly. He was writing a book, he told them, on folk-lore. He wanted to ask them about the old legends of the neighbourhood. Had any of them ever heard stories concerning local cults, or rumours about rites in the woods? Were there any haunted houses, or shunned places in the forest? Had they ever heard the name 'Nyarlathotep', or references to 'Shub-Niggurath' and 'the Black Messenger'? Could they recall anything of the old Pasquantog Indian myths about 'the beast-men', or remember stories of black covens that sacrificed cattle on the hills? These and similar questions put the naturally suspicious farmers on their guard. If they had any such knowledge, it was decidedly unwholesome in its nature, and they did not care to reveal it to this self-avowed outsider. Some of them knew of such things from old tales brought them from the upper coast, and others had heard whispered nightmares from recluses in the eastern hills. There were a lot of things about these matters which they frankly did not know, and what they suspected was not for outside ears to hear. Everywhere he went, Maglore met with evasions or frank rebuffs, and he left behind a distinctly bad impression.

The story of these visits spread. They became the topic for an elaborate discussion. One oldster in particular – a farmer named Thatcherton, who lived alone in a secluded stretch to the west of the lake, off the main highway – had a singularly arresting story to tell. Maglore had appeared one night around eight o'clock, and knocked on the door. He persuaded his host to admit him to the parlour, and then tried to cajole him into revealing certain information regarding the presence of an abandoned cemetery that was reputed to exist somewhere in the vicinity.

The farmer said that his guest was in an almost hysterical state, that he rambled on and on in a most melodramatic fashion, and made frequent allusion to a lot of mythological gibberish about 'secrets of the grave', 'the thirteenth covenant', 'the Feast of Ulder', and the 'Doel chants'. There was also talk of 'the ritual of Father Yig', and certain names were brought up in connection with queer forest ceremonies said to occur near this graveyard. Maglore asked if cattle ever disappeared, and if his host ever heard 'voices in the forest that made proposals'.

These things the man absolutely denied, and he refused to allow his visitor to come back and inspect the premises by day. At this the unexpected guest became very angry, and was on the point of making a heated rejoinder, when something strange occurred. Maglore suddenly turned very pale, and asked to be excused. He seemed to have a severe attack of internal cramps; for he doubled up and staggered to the door. As he did so, Thatcherton received the shocking impression that the hump on his back was *moving*! It seemed to writhe and slither on Maglore's shoulders, as though he had an animal concealed beneath his coat! At this juncture Maglore turned around sharply, and backed towards the exit, as if trying to conceal this unusual phenomenon. He went out hastily, without another word, and raced down the drive to the car. He ran like an ape, vaulted madly into the driver's seat, and sent the wheels spinning as he roared out of the yard. He disappeared into the night, leaving behind him a sadly puzzled man, who lost no time in spreading the tale of his fantastic visitor among his friends.

Since then such incidents had abruptly ceased, and until this afternoon Maglore had not reappeared in the village. But people were still talking, and he was not welcome. It would be well to avoid the man, whatever he was.

Such was the substance of my friend Gates' story. When he concluded, I retired to my room without comment, to meditate upon the tale.

I was not inclined to share the local superstitions. Long experience in such matters made me automatically discredit the bulk of its detail. I knew enough of rural psychology to realize that anything out of the ordinary is looked upon with suspicion. Suppose the Maglore family were reclusive: what then? Any group of foreign extraction would naturally be. Granted that they were racially deformed – that did not make them witches. Popular fancy has persecuted many people for sorcery whose only crime lay in some physical defect. Even inbreeding was naturally to be expected when social ostracism was inflicted. But what is there of magic in that? It's common enough in such rural back-waters, heaven knows, and not only among foreigners, either. Queer books? Likely. Nyctalops? Common enough among all peoples. Insanity? Perhaps – lonely minds often degenerate. Simon was brilliant, however. Unfortunately, his trend towards the mystical and the unknown was leading him astray. It had been poor judgement that led him to seek information for his book from the illiterate country people. Naturally, they were intolerant and distrustful. And his poor physical condition assumed exaggerated importance in the eyes of these credulous folk.

Still, there was probably enough truth in these distorted accounts to make it imperative that I talk to Maglore at once. He must get out of this unhealthful atmosphere, and see a reputable physician. His genius should not be wasted or destroyed through such an environmental obstacle. It would wreck him, mentally and physically. I decided to visit him on the morrow.

After this resolution, I went downstairs to supper, took a short stroll along the shores of the moonlit lake, and retired for the night.

The following afternoon, I carried out my intention. The Maglore mansion stood on a bluff about a half-mile out of Bridgetown, and frowned dismally down upon the lake. It was not a cheerful place; it was too old, and too neglected. I conjured up a mental image of what those gaping windows must look like on a moonless night, and shuddered. Those empty openings reminded me of a blind bat. The two gables resembled its hooded head, and the broad, peaked side-chambers might serve as wings. When I realized the trend of my thought I felt surprised and disturbed. As I walked up the long, tree-shadowed walk I endeav-oured to gain a firm command over my imagination. I was here on a definite errand.

I was almost composed when I rang the bell. Its ghostly tinkle echoed down the serpentine corridors within. Faint, shuffling footsteps sounded, and then, with a grating clang, the door opened. There, limned against the doorway, stood Simon Maglore.

Maglore crouched there in the grey twilight, and the blurred outline of his body was mercifully obscured in wavering shadows. There was something sinister in the repellent angle at which he stooped, and I did not care to peer too closely at his humped back or slackly dangling arms.

Only his face was wholly visible. It was a waxen mask of death, set in an empty stare in which I read no recognition.

His eyes alone were alive. Their lambent glare welled forth in the darkness with feline fixity. I gazed into them, seeking to master the inexplicable repulsion rising within me.

'Simon,' I said. 'I've come to –'

His lips curled back. Was it a trick of light, or were those lips white worms that writhed across his face? Was it an illusion, or was his mouth a black cavern from which his words crawled forth?

I did not know. There was but one certainty; the voice that rustled faintly in my ears was not the voice of the Simon Maglore I knew. It was small, shrill, and filled with hidden mockery.

'Go away. I cannot see you today,' it whispered.

'But I wanted to help you. I–'

'Go away, you fool – go away!'

The door slammed in my astounded face, and I found myself alone.

But I was not alone on the walk back to town. My thoughts were haunted by the presence of another – that crouching, alien presence that had once been my friend, Simon Maglore.

## 2

I was still dazed when I arrived back in the village. But after I had reached my room in the hotel, I began to reason with myself. That romantic imagination of mine had played me a sorry trick. Poor Maglore was ill – probably a victim of some severe nervous disorder. I recalled the report of his buying sedatives at the local pharmacy. In my foolish emotionalism I had sadly misconstrued his unfortunate sickness. What a child I had been! I must go back tomorrow, and apologize. After that, Maglore must be persuaded to go away and get himself back into proper shape once more. He *had* looked pretty bad, and his temper was getting the best of him, too. How the man had changed!

That night I slept but little. Early the following morning I again set out. This time I carefully avoided the disquieting mental images that the old house suggested to my susceptible mind. I was all business when I rang the bell.

It was a different Maglore who met me. He, too, had changed for the better. He looked ill, and old, but there was a normal light in his eyes and a saner intonation in his voice as he courteously bade me enter, and apologized for his delirious spasm of the day before. He was subject to frequent attacks, he told me, and planned to get away very shortly and take a long rest. He was eager to complete his book – there was only a little to do, now – and go back to his work at college. From this statement he abruptly switched the conversation to a series of reminiscent interludes. He recalled our mutual association on the campus as we sat in the parlour, and seemed eager to hear about the affairs at school. For nearly an hour he virtually monopolized the conversation and steered it in such a manner as to preclude any direct inquiries or questions of a personal nature on my part.

Nevertheless, it was easy to me to see that he was far from well. He sounded as though he were labouring under an intense strain; his words seemed forced, his statements stilted. Once again I noted how pale he was; how bloodless. His malformed back seemed immense; his body correspondingly shrunken. I recalled my fears of a cancerous tumour, and wondered. Meanwhile he rambled on, obviously ill at ease. The parlour seemed almost bare; the book-cases were unlined, and the empty spaces filled with dust. No papers or manuscripts were visible on the table. A spider had spun its web upon the ceiling.

During a pause in his conversation, I asked him about his work. He answered vaguely that it was very involved, and was taking up most of his time. He had made some very interesting discoveries, however, which would amply repay him for his pains. It would excite him too much in his present condition if he went into detail about what he was doing, but he could tell me that his findings in the field of witchcraft alone would add new chapters to anthropological and metaphysical history. He was particularly interested in the old lore about 'familiars' – the tiny creatures who were said to be emissaries of the devil, and were supposed to attend the witch or wizard in the form of a small animal – rat, cat, mouse, or ousel. Sometimes they were represented as existing on the body of the warlock himself, or subsisting upon it for their nourishment. The idea of a 'devil's teat' on the witches' bodies from which their familiar drew sustenance in blood was fully illuminated by Maglore's findings. His book had a medical aspect, too; it really endeavoured to put such statements on a scientific basis. The effects of glandular disorders in cases of so-called 'demonic possession' were also treated.

At this point Maglore abruptly concluded. He felt very tired, he said, and must get some rest. But he hoped to be finished with his work very shortly, and then he wanted to get away for a long rest. It was not wholesome for him to live alone in this old house, and at times he was troubled with disturbing fancies and queer lapses of memory. He had no alternative, however, at present, because the nature of his investigations demanded both privacy and solitude. At times his experiments impinged on certain ways and courses best left undisturbed, and he was not sure just how much longer he would be able to stand the strain. It was in his blood, though – I probably was aware that he came from a necromantic line. But enough of such things. He requested that I go at once. I would hear from him again early next week.

As I rose to my feet I again noticed how weak and agitated Simon appeared. He walked with an exaggerated stoop, now, and the pressure on his swollen back must be enormous. He conducted me down the long hall to the door, and as he led the way I noted the trembling of his body, as it limned itself against the flaming dusk that licked against the window-panes ahead. His shoulders heaved with a slow, steady undulation, as if the hump on his back was actually pulsing with life. I recalled the tale of Thatcherton, the old farmer, who claimed that he actually saw such a movement. For a moment I was assailed by a powerful nausea; then I realized that the flickering light was creating a commonplace optical illusion.

When we reached the door, Maglore endeavoured to dismiss me very hastily. He did not even extend his hand for a parting clasp, but merely mumbled a curt 'good evening', in a strained, hesitant voice. I gazed at him for a moment in silence, mentally noting how wan and emaciated his once-handsome countenance appeared, even in the sunset's ruby light. Then, as I watched, a shadow crawled across his face. It seemed to purple and darken in a sudden eerie metamorphosis. The adumbration deepened, and I read stark panic in his eyes. Even as I forced myself to respond to his farewell, horror crept into his face. His body fell into that odd, shambling posture I had noted once before, and his lips leered in a ghastly grin. For a moment I actually thought the man was going to attack me. Instead he laughed – a shrill, tittering chuckle that pealed blackly in my brain. I opened my mouth to speak, but he scrambled back into the darkness of the hall and shut the door.

Astonishment gripped me, not unmingled with fear. Was Maglore ill, or was he actually demented? Such grotesqueries did not seem possible in a normal man.

I hastened on, stumbling through the glowing sunset. My bewildered mind was deep in ponderment, and the distant croaking of ravens blended in evil litany with my thoughts.

## 3

The next morning, after a night of troubled deliberation, I made my decision. Work or no work, Maglore must go away, and at once. He was on the verge of serious mental and physical collapse. Knowing how useless it would be for me to go back and argue with him, I decided that stronger methods must be employed to make him see the light.

That afternoon, therefore, I sought out Doctor Carstairs, the local practitioner, and told him all I knew. I particularly emphasized the distressing occurrence of the evening before, and frankly told him what I already suspected. After a lengthy discussion, Carstairs agreed to accompany me to the Maglore house at once, and there take what steps were necessary in arranging for his removal. In response to my request the doctor took along the materials necessary for a complete physical examination. Once I could persuade Simon to submit to a medical diagnosis, I felt sure he would see that the results made it necessary for him to place himself under treatment at once.

The sun was sinking when we climbed into the front seat of Doctor Carstairs' battered Ford and drove out of Bridgetown along the south road where the ravens croaked. We drove slowly, and in silence. Thus it was that we were able to hear clearly that single high-pitched shriek from the old house on the hill. I gripped the doctor's arm without a word, and a second later we were whizzing up the drive and into the frowning gateway. 'Hurry,' I muttered as I vaulted from the running-board and dashed up the steps to the forbidding door.

We battered upon the boards with futile fists, then dashed around to the left-wing window. The sunset faded into tense, waiting darkness as we crawled hastily through the openings and dropped to the floor within. Doctor Carstairs produced a pocket flashlight, and we rose to our feet. My heart hammered in my breast, but no other sound broke the tomb-like silence as we threw open the door and advanced down the darkened hall to the study. All about us I sensed a gloating Presence; a lurking demon who watched our progress with eyes of gleeful mirth, and whose sable soul shook with hell-born laughter as we opened the door of the study and stumbled across that which lay within.

We both screamed then. Simon Maglore lay at our feet, his twisted head and straining shoulders resting in a little lake of fresh, warm blood. He was on his face, and his clothes had been torn off above his waist, so that his entire back was visible. When we saw what rested there we became quite crazed, and then began to do what must be done, averting our gaze whenever possible from that utterly monstrous thing on the floor.

Do not ask me to describe it to you in detail. I can't. There are some times when the senses are mercifully numbed, because complete acuteness would be fatal. I do not know certain things about that abomination even now, and I dare not let myself recall them. I shall not tell you, either, of the books we found in that room, or of the terrible document on the table that was Simon Maglore's unfinished masterpiece.

We burned them all in the fire, before calling the city for a coroner; and if the doctor had had his way, we should have destroyed the *thing*, too. As it was, when the coroner did arrive for his examination, the three of us swore an oath of silence concerning the exact way in which Simon Maglore met his death. Then we left, but not before I had burned the other document – the letter, addressed to me, which Maglore was writing when he died.

And so, you see, nobody ever knew. I later found that the property was left to me, and the house is being razed even as I pen these lines. But I must speak, if only to relieve my own torment.

I dare not quote that letter in its entirety; I can but record a part of that stupendous blasphemy:

'. . . and that, of course, is why I began to study witchcraft. *It* was forcing me to. God, if I can only make you feel the horror if it! To be born that way – with that thing, that mannikin, that *monster*! At first it was small; the doctors all said it was an undeveloped twin. But it was alive! It had a face, and two hands, but its legs ran off into the lumpy flesh that connected it to my body. . . .

'For three years they had it under secret study. It lay face downward on my back, and its hands were clasped around my shoulders. The men said that it had its own tiny set of lungs, but no stomach organs or digestive system. It apparently drew nourishment through the fleshy tube that bound it to my body. Yet it *grew*! Soon its eyes were open, and it began to develop tiny teeth. Once it nipped one of the doctors on the hand . . . So they decided to send me home. It was obvious that it could not be removed. I swore to keep the whole affair a secret, and not even my father knew, until near the end. I wore the straps, and it never grew much until I came back . . . Then, that hellish change!

'It talked to me, I tell you, it talked to me! . . . that little, wrinkled face, like a monkey's . . . the way it rolled those tiny, reddish eyes . . . that squeaking little voice calling "more blood, Simon – I want more" . . . and then it grew; I had to feed it twice a day, and cut the nails on its little black hands . . .

'But I never knew *that*; I never realized how it was taking control! I would have killed myself first; I swear it! Last year it began to get hold of me for hours and give me those fits. It directed me to write the book, and sometimes it sent me out at night on queer errands . . . More and more blood it took, and I was getting weaker and weaker. When I was myself I tried to combat it. I looked up that material on the familiar legend, and cast around for some means of overcoming its mastery. But in vain. And all the while it was growing, growing; it got stronger, and bolder, and wiser. It talked to me now, and sometimes it taunted me. I knew that it wanted me to listen, and obey it all the time. The promises

it made with that horrible little mouth! I should call upon the Black One
and join a coven. Then we would have power to rule, and admit new
evil to the earth.

'I didn't want to obey – you know that. But I was going mad, and
losing all that blood . . . it took control nearly all the time now, and it
got so that I was afraid to go into town any more, because that devilish
thing knew I was trying to escape, and it would move on my back and
frighten folk . . . I wrote all the time I had those spells when it ruled my
brain . . . then you came.

'I know you want me to go away, but it won't let me. It's too cunning
for that. Even as I try to write this, I can feel it boring its commands into
my brain to stop. But I will not stop. I will tell you, while I still have a
chance; before it overcomes me for ever and works its black will with my
poor body and masters my helpless soul. I want you to know where my
book is, so that you can destroy it, should anything ever happen. I want
to tell you how to dispose of those awful old volumes in the library. And
above all, I want you to kill me, if ever you see that the mannikin has
gained complete control. God knows what it intends to do when it has
me for certain! . . . How hard it is for me to fight, while all the while it is
commanding me to put down my pen and tear this up! But I will fight –
I must, until I can tell you what the creature told me – what it plans to
let loose on the world when it has me utterly enslaved . . . I will tell . . . I
can't think . . . I *will* write it, damn you! Stop! . . . No! Don't do that! Get
your hands –'

That's all. Maglore stopped there because he died; because the Thing
did not want its secrets revealed. It is dreadful to think about that
nightmare-nurtured horror, but that thought is not the worst. What
troubles me is what I saw when we opened the door – the sight that
explained how Maglore died.

There was Maglore, on the floor, in all that blood. He was naked to
the waist, as I have said; and he lay face downward. But on his back was
the Thing, just as he had described it. And it was that little monster,
afraid its secrets would be revealed, that had climbed a trifle higher on
Simon Maglore's back, wound its tiny black paws around his unprotected
neck, *and bitten him to death*!

# They Bite

*Anthony Boucher*

There was no path, only the almost vertical ascent. Crumpled rock for a few yards, with the roots of sage finding their scanty life in the dry soil. Then jagged outcroppings of crude crags, sometimes with accidental footholds, sometimes with overhanging and untrustworthy branches of greasewood, sometimes with no aid to climbing but the leverage of your muscles and the ingenuity of your balance.

The sage was as drably green as the rock was drably brown. The only colour was the occasional rosy spikes of a barrel cactus.

Hugh Tallant swung himself up onto the last pinnacle. It had a deliberate, shaped look about it – a petrified fortress of Lilliputians, a Gibraltar of pygmies. Tallant perched on its battlements and unslung his field-glasses.

The desert valley spread below him. The tiny cluster of buildings that was Oasis, the exiguous cluster of palms that gave name to the town and shelter of his own tent and to the shack he was building, the dead-ended highway leading straightforwardly to nothing, the oiled roads diagramming the vacant blocks of an optimistic subdivision.

Tallant saw none of these. His glasses were fixed beyond the oasis and the town of Oasis on the dry lake. The gliders were clear and vivid to him, and the uniformed men busy with them were as sharply and minutely visible as a nest of ants under glass. The training school was more than usually active. One glider in particular, strange to Tallant, seemed the focus of attention. Men would come and examine it and glance back at the older models in comparison.

Only the corner of Tallant's left eye was not preoccupied with the new glider. In that corner something moved, something little and thin and brown as the earth. Too large for a rabbit, much too small for a man. It darted across that corner of vision, and Tallant found gliders oddly hard to concentrate on.

He set down the bi-focals and deliberately looked about him. His pinnacle surveyed the narrow, flat area of the crest. Nothing stirred. Nothing stood out against the sage and rock but one barrel of rosy spikes.

He took up the glasses again and resumed his observations. When he was done, he methodically entered the results in the little black notebook.

His hand was still white. The desert is cold and often sunless in winter. But it was a firm hand, and as well trained as his eyes, fully capable of recording faithfully the designs and dimensions which they had registered so accurately.

Once his hand slipped, and he had to erase and redraw, leaving a smudge that displeased him. The lean, brown thing had slipped across the edge of his vision again. Going towards the east edge, he would swear, where that set of rocks jutted like the spines on the back of a stegosaur.

Only when his notes were completed did he yield to curiosity, and even then with cynical self-reproach. He was physically tired, for him an unusual state, from this daily climbing and from clearing the ground for his shack-to-be. The eye muscles play odd nervous tricks. There could be nothing behind the stegosaur's armour.

There was nothing. Nothing alive and moving. Only the torn and half-plucked carcass of a bird, which looked as though it had been gnawed by some small animal.

It was halfway down the hill – hill in Western terminology, though anywhere east of the Rockies it would have been considered a sizeable mountain – that Tallant again had a glimpse of a moving figure.

But this was no trick of a nervous eye. It was not little nor thin nor brown. It was tall and broad and wore a loud red-and-black lumberjacket. It bellowed, 'Tallant!' in a cheerful and lusty voice.

Tallant drew near the man and said, 'Hello.' He paused and added, 'Your advantage, I think.'

The man grinned broadly. 'Don't know me? Well, I dare say ten years is a long time, and the California desert ain't exactly the Chinese rice fields. How's stuff? Still loaded down with Secrets for Sale?'

Tallant tried desperately not to react to that shot, but he stiffened a little. 'Sorry. The prospector get-up had me fooled. Good to see you again, Morgan.'

The man's eyes narrowed. 'Just having my little joke,' he smiled. 'Of course you wouldn't have no serious reason for mountain climbing around a glider school, now, would you? And you'd kind of need field-glasses to keep an eye on the pretty birdies.'

'I'm out here for my health.' Tallant's voice sounded unnatural even to himself.

'Sure, sure. You were always in it for your health. And come to think of it, my own health ain't been none too good lately. I've got me a little cabin way to hell-and-gone around here, and I do me a little prospecting now and then. And somehow it just strikes me, Tallant, like maybe I hit a pretty good lode today.'

'Nonsense, old man. You can see –'

'I'd sure hate to tell any of them Army men out at the field some of the stories I know about China and the kind of men I used to know out there. Wouldn't cotton to them stories a bit, the Army wouldn't. But if I was to have a drink too many and get talkative-like –'

'Tell you what,' Tallant suggested brusquely. 'It's getting near sunset now, and my tent's chilly for evening visits. But drop around in the morning and we'll talk over old times. Is rum still your tipple?'

'Sure is. Kind of expensive now, you understand –'

'I'll lay some in. You can find the place easily – over by the oasis. And we . . . we might be able to talk about your prospecting, too.'

Tallant's thin lips were set firm as he walked away.

The bartender opened a bottle of beer and plunked it on the damp-circled counter. 'That'll be twenty cents,' he said, then added as an afterthought, 'want a glass? Sometimes tourists do.'

Tallant looked at the others sitting at the counter – the red-eyed and unshaven old man, the flight-sergeant unhappily drinking a Coke – it was after Army hours for beer – the young man with the long, dirty trench-coat and the pipe and the new-looking brown beard – and saw no glasses. 'I guess I won't be a tourist,' he decided.

This was the first time Tallant had had a chance to visit the Desert Sport Spot. It was as well to be seen around in a community. Otherwise people begin to wonder and say, 'Who is that man out by the oasis? Why don't you ever see him any place?'

The Sport Spot was quiet that night. The four of them at the counter, two Army boys shooting pool, and a half-dozen of the local men gathered about a round poker table, soberly and wordlessly cleaning a construction worker whose mind seemed more on his beer than on his cards.

'You just passing through?' the bartender asked sociably.

Tallant shook his head. 'I'm moving in. When the Army turned me down for my lungs, I decided I better do something about it. Heard so much about your climate here I thought I might as well try it.'

'Sure thing,' the bartender nodded. 'You take up until they started this glider school, just about every other guy you meet in the desert is here for his health. Me, I had sinus, and look at me now. It's the air.'

Tallant breathed the atmosphere of smoke and beer suds, but did not smile. 'I'm looking forward to miracles.'

'You'll get 'em. Whereabouts you staying?'

'Over that way a bit. The agent called it "the old Carker place".'

Tallant felt the curious listening silence and frowned. The bartender had started to speak and then thought better of it. The young man with the beard looked at him oddly. The old man fixed him with red and watery eyes that had a faded glint of pity in them. For a moment, Tallant felt a chill that had nothing to do with the night air of the desert.

The old man drank his beer in quick gulps and frowned as though trying to formulate a sentence. At last he wiped beer from his bristly lips and said, 'You wasn't aiming to stay in the adobe, was you?'

'No. It's pretty much gone to pieces. Easier to rig me up a little shack than try to make the adobe liveable. Meanwhile, I've got a tent.'

'That's all right, then, mebbe. But mind you don't go poking around that there adobe.'

'I don't think I'm apt to. But why not? Want another beer?'

The old man shook his head reluctantly and slid from his stool to the ground. 'No thanks. I don't rightly know as I – '

'Yes?'

'Nothing. Thanks all the same.' He turned and shuffled to the door.

Tallant smiled. 'But why should I stay clear of the adobe?' he called after him.

The old man mumbled.

'What?'

'They bite,' said the old man, and went out shivering into the night.

The bartender was back at his post. 'I'm glad he didn't take that beer you offered him,' he said. 'Along about this time in the evening I have to stop serving him. For once he had the sense to quit.'

Tallant pushed his own empty bottle forward. 'I hope I didn't frighten him away.'

'Frighten? Well, mister, I think maybe that's just what you did do. He didn't want beer that sort of came, like you might say, from the old Carker place. Some of the old-timers here, they're funny that way.'

Tallant grinned. 'Is it haunted?'

'Not what you'd call haunted, no. No ghosts there that I ever heard of.' He wiped the counter with a cloth and seemed to wipe the subject away with it.

The flight-sergeant pushed his Coke bottle away, hunted in his pocket for nickels, and went over to the pinball machine. The young man with the beard slid on to his vacant stool. 'Hope old Jake didn't worry you,' he said.

Tallant laughed. 'I suppose every town has its deserted homestead with a grisly tradition. But this sounds a little different. No ghosts, and they bite. Do you know anything about it?'

'A little,' the young man said seriously. 'A little. Just enough to – '

Tallant was curious. 'Have one on me and tell me about it.'

The flight-sergeant swore bitterly at the machine.

Beer gurgled through the beard. 'You see,' the young man began, 'the desert's so big you can't be alone in it. Ever notice that? It's all empty and there's nothing in sight, but there's always something moving over there where you can't quite see it. It's something very dry and thin and brown, only when you look around it isn't there. Ever see it?'

'Optical fatigue –' Tallant began

'Sure. I know. Every man to his own legend. There isn't a tribe of Indians hasn't got some way of accounting for it. You've heard of the Watchers? And the twentieth-century White man comes along, and it's optical fatigue. Only in the nineteenth century things weren't quite the same, and there were the Carkers.'

'You've got a special localized legend?'

'Call it that. You glimpse things out of the corner of your mind, same like you glimpse lean, dry things out of the corner of your eye. You encase 'em in solid circumstance and they're not so bad. That is known as the Growth of Legend. The Folk Mind in Action. You take the Carkers and the things you don't quite see and you put 'em together. And they bite.'

Tallant wondered how long that beard had been absorbing beer. 'And what were the Carkers?' he prompted politely.

'Ever hear of Sawney Bean? Scotland – reign of James First, or maybe the Sixth, though I think Roughead's wrong on that for once. Or let's be more modern – ever hear of the Benders? Kansas in the 1870s? No? Ever hear of Procrustes? Or Polyphemus? Or Fee-fi-fo-fum?

'There are ogres, you know. They're no legend. They're fact, they are. The inn where nine guests left for every ten that arrived, the mountain cabin that sheltered travellers from the snow, sheltered them all winter till the melting spring uncovered their bones, the lonely stretches or road that so many passengers travelled halfway – you'll find 'em everywhere. All over Europe and pretty much in this country too before communications became what they are. Profitable business. And it wasn't just the profit. The Benders made money, sure; but that wasn't why they killed all their victims as carefully as a kosher butcher. Sawney Bean got so he didn't give a damn about the profit; he just needed to lay in more meat for the winter.

'And think of the chances you'd have at an oasis.'

'So these Carkers of yours were, as you call them, ogres?'

'Carkers, ogres – maybe they were Benders. The Benders were never seen alive, you know, after the townspeople found those curiously butchered bones. There's a rumour they got this far west. And the time checks pretty well. There wasn't any town here in the eighties. Just a

couple of Indian families, last of a dying tribe living on at the oasis. They
vanished after the Carkers moved in. That's not so surprising. The White
race is a sort of super-ogre, anyway. Nobody worried about them. But
they used to worry about why so many travellers never got across this
stretch of desert. The travellers used to stop over at the Carkers', you
see, and somehow they often never got any further. Their wagons'd be
found maybe fifteen miles beyond in the desert.   Sometimes they
found the bones, too, parched and white. Gnawed-looking, they said
sometimes.'

'And nobody ever did anything about these Carkers?'

'Oh, sure. We didn't have King James Sixth – only I still think it was
First – to ride up on a great white horse for a gesture, but twice Army
detachments came here and wiped them all out.'

'Twice? One wiping-out would do for most families.' Tallant smiled.

'Uh-uh. That was no slip. They wiped out the Carkers twice because,
you see, once didn't do any good. They wiped 'em out and still travellers
vanished and still there were gnawed bones. So they wiped 'em out
again. After that they gave up, and people detoured the oasis. It made
a longer, harder trip, but after all – '

Tallant laughed. 'You mean to say these Carkers were immortal?'

'I don't know about immortal. They somehow just didn't die very
easy.  Maybe, if they were the Benders – and I sort of like to think they
were – they learned a little more about what they were doing out here
on the desert.  Maybe they put together what the Indians knew and
what they knew, and it worked. Maybe whatever they made their
sacrifices to understood them better out here than in Kansas.'

'And what's become of them – aside from seeing them out of the corner
of the eye?'

'There's forty years between the last of the Carker history and this
new settlement at the oasis.  And people won't talk much about what
they learned here in the first year or so. Only that they stay away from
that old Carker adobe. They tell some stories – The priest says he was
sitting in the confessional one hot Saturday afternoon and thought he
heard a penitent come in. He waited a long time and finally lifted the
gauze to see was anybody there. Something was there, and it bit. He's
got three fingers on his right hand now, which looks funny as hell when
he gives a benediction.'

Tallant pushed their two bottles towards the bartender. 'That yarn,
my young friend, has earned another beer. How about it, bartender? Is
he always cheerful like this, or is this just something he's improvised for
my benefit?'

The bartender set out the fresh bottles with great solemnity. 'Me, I wouldn't've told you all that myself, but then, he's a stranger too and maybe don't feel the same way we do here. For him it's just a story.'

'It's more comfortable that way,' said the young man with the beard, and he took a firm hold on his beer bottle.

'But as long as you've heard that much,' said the bartender, 'you might as well – It was last winter, when we had that cold spell. You heard funny stories that winter. Wolves coming into prospectors' cabins just to warm up. Well, business wasn't so good. We don't have a licence for hard liquor, and the boys don't drink much beer when it's that cold. But they used to come in anyway because we've got that big oil burner.

'So one night there's a bunch of 'em in here – old Jake was here, that you was talking to, and his dog Jigger – and I think I hear somebody else come in. The door creaks a little. But I don't see nobody, and the poker game's going, and we're talking just like we're talking now, and all of a sudden I hear a kind of a noise like crack! over there in that corner behind the jukebox near the burner.

'I go over to see what goes and it gets away before I can see it very good. But it was little and thin and it didn't have no clothes on. It must've been damned cold that winter.'

'And what was the cracking noise?' Tallant asked dutifully.

'That? That was a bone. It must've strangled Jigger without any noise. He was a little dog. It ate most of the flesh, and if it hadn't cracked the bone for the marrow it could've finished. You can still see the spots over there. The blood never did come out.'

There had been silence all through the story. Now suddenly all hell broke loose. The flight-sergeant let out a splendid yell and began pointing excitedly at the pinball machine and yelling for his pay off. The construction worker dramatically deserted the poker game, knocking his chair over in the process, and announced lugubriously that these guys here had their own rules, see?

Any atmosphere of Carker-inspired horror was dissipated. Tallant whistled as he walked over to put a nickel in the jukebox. He glanced casually at the floor. Yes, there was a stain, for what that was worth.

He smiled cheerfully and felt rather grateful to the Carkers. They were going to solve his blackmail problem very neatly.

Tallant dreamed of power that night. It was a common dream with him. He was a ruler of the new American Corporate State that would follow the war; and he said to this man, 'Come!' and he came, and to that man, 'Go!' and he went, and to his servants, 'Do this!' and they did it.

Then the young man with the beard was standing before him, and the dirty trench-coat was like the robes of an ancient prophet. And the young man said, 'You see yourself riding high, don't you? Riding the crest of the wave – the Wave of the Future, you call it. But there's a deep, dark undertow that you don't see, and that's a part of the Past. And the Present and even your Future. There is evil in mankind that is blacker even than your evil, and infinitely more ancient.'

And there was something in the shadows behind the young man, something little and lean and brown.

Tallant's dream did not disturb him the following morning. Nor did the thought of the approaching interview with Morgan. He fried his bacon and eggs and devoured them cheerfully. The wind had died down for a change, and the sun was warm enough so that he could strip to the waist while he cleared land for his shack. His machete glinted brilliantly as it swung through the air and struck at the roots of the brush.

When Morgan arrived his full face was red and sweating.

'It's cool over there in the shade of the adobe,' Tallant suggested. 'We'll be comfortable.' And in the comfortable shade of the adobe he swung the machete once and clove Morgan's full, red, sweating face in two.

It was so simple. It took less effort than uprooting a clump of sage. And it was so safe. Morgan lived in a cabin way to hell-and-gone and was often away on prospecting trips. No one would notice his absence for months, if then. No one had any reason to connect him with Tallant. And no one in Oasis would hunt for him in the Carker-haunted adobe.

The body was heavy, and the blood dripped warm on Tallant's bare skin. With relief he dumped what had been Morgan on the floor of the adobe. There were no boards, no flooring. Just the earth. Hard, but not too hard to dig a grave in. And no one was likely to come poking around in this taboo territory to notice the grave. Let a year or so go by, and the grave and the bones it contained would be attributed to the Carkers.

The corner of Tallant's eye bothered him again. Deliberately he looked about the interior of the adobe.

The little furniture was crude and heavy, with no attempt to smooth down the strokes of the axe. It was held together with wooden pegs or half-rotted thongs. There were age-old cinders in the fireplace, and the dusty shards of a cooking jar among them.

And there was a deeply hollowed stone, covered with stains that might have been rust, if stone rusted. Behind it was a tiny figure, clumsily fashioned of clay and sticks. It was something like a man and something like a lizard, and something like the things that flit across the corner of the eye.

Curious now, Talland peered about further. He penetrated to the corner that the one unglassed window lighted but dimly. And there he let out a little choking gasp. For a moment he was rigid with horror. Then he smiled and all but laughed aloud.

This explained everything. Some curious individual had seen this, and from his accounts had burgeoned the whole legend. The Carkers had indeed learned something from the Indians, but that secret was the art of embalming.

It was a perfect mummy. Either the Indian art had shrunk bodies, or this was that of a ten-year-old boy. There was no flesh. Only skin and bone and taut, dry stretches of tendon between. The eyelids were closed; the sockets looked hollow under them. The nose was sunken and almost lost. The scant lips were tightly curled back from the long and very white teeth, which stood forth all the more brilliantly against the deep-brown skin.

It was a curious little trove, this mummy. Tallant was already calculating the chances for raising a decent sum of money from an interested anthropologist – murder can produce such delightfully profitable chance by-products – when he noticed the infinitesimal rise and fall of the chest.

The Carker was not dead. It was sleeping.

Tallant did not dare to stop beyond the instant. This was no time to pause to consider if such things were possible in a well-ordered world. It was no time to reflect on the disposal of the body of Morgan. It was a time to snatch up your machete and get out of there.

But in the doorway he halted. There, coming across the desert, heading for the adobe, clearly seen this time, was another – a female.

He made an involuntary gesture of indecision. The blade of the machete clanged ringingly against the adobe wall. He heard the dry shuffling of a roused sleeper behind him.

He turned fully now, the machete raised. Dispose of this nearer one first, then face the female. There was no room even for terror in his thoughts, only for action.

The lean brown shape darted at him avidly. He moved lightly away and stood poised for its second charge. It shot forward again. He took one step back, machete arm raised, and fell headlong over the corpse of Morgan. Before he could rise, the thin thing was upon him. Its sharp teeth had met through the palm of his left hand.

The machete moved swiftly. The thin dry body fell headless to the floor. There was no blood.

The grip of the teeth did not relax. Pain coursed up Tallant's left arm – a sharper, more bitter pain than you would expect from the bite. Almost as though venom –

He dropped the machete, and his strong white hand plucked and twisted at the dry brown lips. The teeth stayed clenched, unrelaxing.

He sat bracing his back against the wall and gripped the head between his knees. He pulled. His flesh ripped, and blood formed dusty clots on the dirt floor. But the bite was firm.

His world had become reduced now to that hand and that head. Nothing outside mattered. He must free himself. He raised his aching arm to his face, and with his own teeth he tore at that unrelenting grip. The dry flesh crumbled away in desert dust, but the teeth were locked fast. He tore his lip against their white keenness, and tasted in his mouth the sweetness of blood and something else.

He staggered to his feet again. He knew what he must do. Later he could use cautery, a tourniquet, see a doctor with a story about a Gila monster – their heads grip too, don't they? – but he knew what he must do now.

He raised the machete and struck again.

His white hand lay on the brown floor, gripped by the white teeth in the brown face. He propped himself against the adobe wall, momentarily unable to move. His open wrist hung over the deeply hollowed stone. His blood and his strength and his life poured out before the little figure of sticks and clay.

The female stood in the doorway now, the sun bright on her thin brownness. She did not move. He knew that she was waiting for the hollow stone to fill.

# The Demon Lover

*Elizabeth Bowen*

Towards the end of her day in London Mrs Drover went round to her shut-up house to look for several things she wanted to take away. Some belonged to herself, some to her family, who were by now used to their country life. It was late August; it had been a steamy, showery day: at the moment the trees down the pavement glittered in an escape of humid yellow afternoon sun. Against the next batch of clouds, already piling up ink-dark, broken chimneys and parapets stood out. In her once familiar street, as in any unused channel, an unfamiliar queerness had silted up; a cat wove itself in and out of railings, but no human eye watched Mrs Drover's return. Shifting some parcels under her arm, she slowly forced round her latchkey in an unwilling lock, then gave the door, which had warped, a push with her knee. Dead air came out to meet her as she went in.

The staircase window having been boarded up, no light came down into the hall. But one door, she could just see, stood ajar, so she went quickly through into the room and unshuttered the big window in there. Now the prosaic woman, looking about her, was more perplexed than she knew by everything that she saw, by traces of her long former habit of life – the yellow smoke-stain up the white marble mantelpiece, the ring left by a vase on the top of the escritoire; the bruise in the wallpaper where, on the door being thrown open widely, the china handle had always hit the wall. The piano, having gone away to be stored, had left what looked like claw-marks on its part of the parquet. Though not much dust had seeped in, each object wore a film of another kind; and, the only ventilation being the chimney, the whole drawing-room smelled of the cold hearth. Mrs Drover put down her parcels on the escritoire and left the room to proceed upstairs; the things she wanted were in a bedroom chest.

She had been anxious to see how the house was – the part-time caretaker she shared with some neighbours was away this week on his holiday, known to be not yet back. At the best of times he did not look in often, and she was never sure that she trusted him. There were some cracks in the structure, left by the last bombing, on which she was anxious to keep an eye. Not that one could do anything –

A shaft of refracted daylight now lay across the hall. She stopped dead and stared at the hall table – on this lay a letter addressed to her.

She thought first – then the caretaker *must* be back. All the same, who, seeing the house shuttered, would have dropped a letter in at the box? It was not a circular, it was not a bill. And the post office redirected, to the address in the country, everything for her that came through the post. The caretaker (even if he *were* back) did not know she was due in London today – her call here had been planned to be a surprise – so his negligence in the manner of this letter, leaving it to wait in the dusk and the dust, annoyed her. Annoyed, she picked up the letter, which bore no stamp. But it cannot be important, or they would know ... She took the letter rapidly upstairs with her, without a stop to look at the writing till she reached what had been her bedroom, where she let in light. The room looked over the garden and other gardens: the sun had gone in; as the clouds sharpened and lowered, the trees and rank lawns seemed already to smoke with dark. Her reluctance to look again at the letter came from the fact that she felt intruded upon – and by someone contemptuous of her ways. However, in the tenseness preceding the fall of rain she read it: it was a few lines.

DEAR KATHLEEN,

You will not have forgotten that today is our anniversary, and the day we said. The years have gone by at once slowly and fast. In view of the fact that nothing has changed, I shall rely upon you to keep your promise. I was sorry to see you leave London, but was satisfied that you would be back in time. You may expect me, therefore, at the hour arranged.

Until then ...

K.

Mrs Drover looked for the date: it was today's. She dropped the letter on to the bed-springs, then picked it up to see the writing again – her lips, beneath the remains of lipstick, beginning to go white. She felt so much the change in her own face that she went to the mirror, polished a clear patch in it and looked at once urgently and stealthily in. She was confronted by a woman of forty-four, with eyes starting out under a hat-brim that had been rather carelessly pulled down. She had not put on any more powder since she left the shop where she ate her solitary tea. The pearls her husband had given her on their marriage hung loose round her now rather thinner throat, slipping into the V of the pink wool jumper her sister knitted last autumn as they sat round the fire. Mrs Drover's most normal expression was one of controlled worry, but of assent. Since the birth of the third of her little boys, attended by a quite serious illness, she had had an intermittent muscular flicker to the left of her mouth, but in spite of this she could always sustain a manner that was at once energetic and calm.

Turning from her own face as precipitately as she had gone to meet it, she went to the chest where the things were, unlocked it, threw up the lid and knelt to search. But as rain began to come crashing down she could not keep from looking over her shoulder at the stripped bed on which the letter lay. Behind the blanket of rain the clock of the church that still stood struck six – with rapidly heightening apprehension she counted each of the slow strokes. 'The hour arranged ... My God,' she said, '*what* hour? How should I ...? After twenty-five years ...'

The young girl talking to the soldier in the garden had not ever completely seen his face. It was dark; they were saying goodbye under a tree. Now and then – for it felt, from not seeing him at this intense moment, as though she had never seen him at all – she verified his presence for these few moments longer by putting out a hand, which he each time pressed, without very much kindness, and painfully, on to one of the breast buttons of his uniform. That cut of the button on the palm of her hand was, principally, what she was to carry away. This was so near the end of a leave from France that she could only wish him already gone. It was August 1916. Being not kissed, being drawn away from and looked at intimidated Kathleen till she imagined spectral glitters in the place of his eyes. Turning away and looking back up the lawn she saw, through branches of trees, the drawing-room window alight: she caught a breath for the moment when she could go running back there into the safe arms of her mother and sister, and cry: 'What shall I do, what shall I do? He has gone.'

Hearing her catch her breath, her fiancé said, without feeling, 'Cold?'

'You're going away such a long way.'

'Not so far as you think.'

'I don't understand?'

'You don't have to,' he said. 'You will. You know what we said.'

'But that was – suppose you – I mean, suppose.'

'I shall be with you,' he said, 'sooner or later. You won't forget that. You need do nothing but wait.'

Only a little more than a minute later she was free to run up the silent lawn. Looking in through the window at her mother and sister, who did not for the moment perceive her, she already felt that unnatural promise drive down between her and the rest of all human kind. No other way of having given herself could have made her feel so apart, lost and foresworn. She could not have plighted a more sinister troth.

Kathleen behaved well when, some months later, her fiancé was reported missing, presumed killed. Her family not only supported her but were able to praise her courage without stint because they could not regret, as a husband for her, the man they knew almost nothing about. They hoped she would, in a year or two, console herself – and had it been only a question of consolation things must have gone much straighter ahead. But her trouble, behind just a little grief, was a complete dislocation from everything. She did not reject other lovers, for these failed to appear: for years she failed to attract men – and with the approach of her thirties she became natural enough to share her family's anxiousness on this score. She began to put herself out, to wonder; and at thirty-two she was very greatly relieved to find herself being courted by William Drover. She married him, and the two of them settled down in this quiet, arboreal part of Kensington: in this house the years piled up, her children were born and they all lived till they were driven out by the bombs of the next war. Her movements as Mrs Drover were circumscribed, and she dismissed any idea that they were still watched.

As things were – dead or living the letter-writer sent her only a threat. Unable, for some minutes, to go on kneeling with her back exposed to the empty room, Mrs Drover rose from the chest to sit on an upright chair whose back was firmly against the wall. The desuetude of her former bedroom, her married London home's whole air of being a cracked cup from which memory, with its reassuring power, had either evaporated or leaked away, made a crisis – and at just this crisis the letter-writer had, knowledgeably, struck. The hollowness of the house this evening cancelled years on years of voices, habits and steps. Through the shut windows she only heard rain fall on the roofs around. To rally herself, she said she was in a mood – and, for two or three seconds shutting her eyes, told herself that she had imagined the letter. But she opened them – there it lay on the bed.

On the supernatural side of the letter's entrance she was not permitting her mind to dwell. Who, in London, knew she meant to call at the house today? Evidently, however, this has been known. The caretaker, *had* he come back, had had no cause to expect her: he would have taken the letter in his pocket, to forward it, at his own time, through the post. There was no other sign that the caretaker had been in – but, if not? Letters dropped in at doors of deserted houses do not fly or walk to tables in halls. They do not sit on the dust of empty tables with the air of certainty that they will be found. There is needed some human hand – but nobody but the caretaker had a key. Under circumstances she did not care to consider, a house can be entered without a key. It was possible that she was not alone now. She might be being waited for, downstairs.

Waited for – until when? Until 'the hour arranged'. At least that was not six o'clock: six has struck.

She rose from the chair and went over and locked the door.

The thing was, to get out. To fly? No, not that: she had to catch her train. As a woman whose utter dependability was the keystone of her family life she was not willing to return to the country, to her husband, her little boys and her sister, without the objects she had come up to fetch. Resuming work at the chest she set about making up a number of parcels in a rapid, fumbling-decisive way. These, with her shopping parcels, would be too much to carry; these meant a taxi – at the thought of the taxi her heart went up and her normal breathing resumed. I will ring up the taxi now; the taxi cannot come too soon: I shall hear the taxi out there running its engine, till I walk calmly down to it through the hall. I'll ring up – But no: the telephone is cut off . . . She tugged at a knot she had tied wrong.

The idea of flight . . . He was never kind to me, not really. I don't remember him kind at all. Mother said he never considered me. He was set on me, that was what it was – not love. Not love, not meaning a person well. What did he do, to make me promise like that? I can't remember – But she found that she could.

She remembered with such dreadful acuteness that the twenty-five years since then dissolved like smoke and she instinctively looked for the weal left by the button on the palm of her hand. She remembered not only all that he said and did but the complete suspension of *her* existence during that August week. I was not myself – they all told me so at the time. She remembered – but with one white burning blank as where acid has dropped on a photograph: *under no conditions* could she remember his face.

So, wherever he may be waiting, I shall not know him. You have no time to run from a face you do not expect.

The thing was to get to the taxi before any clock struck what could be the hour. She would slip down the street and round the side of the square to where the square gave on the main road. She would return in the taxi, safe, to her own door, and bring the solid driver into the house with her to pick up the parcels from room to room. The idea of the taxi driver made her decisive, bold: she unlocked her door, went to the top of the staircase and listened down.

She heard nothing – but while she was hearing nothing the *passé* air of the staircase was disturbed by a draught that travelled up to her face. It emanated from the basement: down there a door or window was being opened by someone who chose this moment to leave the house.

The rain had stopped; the pavements steamily shone as Mrs Drover let herself out by inches from her own front door into the empty street.

The unoccupied houses opposite continued to meet her look with their damaged stare. Making towards the thoroughfare and the taxi, she tried not to keep looking behind. Indeed, the silence was so intense – one of those creeks of London silence exaggerated this summer by the damage of war – that no tread could have gained on hers unheard. Where her street debouched on the square where people went on living, she grew conscious of, and checked, her unnatural pace. Across the open end of the square two buses impassively passed each other: women, a perambulator, cyclists, a man wheeling a barrow signalized, once again, the ordinary flow of life. At the square's most populous corner should be – and was – the short taxi rank. This evening, only one taxi – but this, although it presented its blank rump, appeared already to be alertly waiting for her. Indeed, without looking round the driver started his engine as she panted up from behind and put her hand on the door. As she did so, the clock struck seven. The taxi faced the main road: to make the trip back to her house it would have to turn – she had settled back on the seat and the taxi *had* turned before she, surprised by its knowing movement, recollected that she had not 'said where'. She leaned forward to scratch at the glass panel that divided the driver's head from her own.

The drive braked to what was almost a stop, turned round and slid the glass panel back: the jolt of this flung Mrs Drover forward till her face was almost into the glass. Through the aperture driver and passenger, not six inches between them, remained for an eternity eye to eye. Mrs Drover's mouth hung open for some seconds before she could issue her first scream. After that she continued to scream freely and to beat with her gloved hands on the glass all round as the taxi, accelerating without mercy, made off with her into the hinterland of deserted streets.

# The Crown Derby Plate

*Marjorie Bowen*

Martha Pym said that she had never seen a ghost and that she would very much like to do so, 'particularly at Christmas, for you can laugh as you like, that is the correct time to see a ghost.'

'I don't suppose you ever will,' replied her cousin Mabel comfortably, while her cousin Clara shuddered and said that she hoped they would change the subject for she disliked even to think of such things.

The three elderly, cheerful women sat round a big fire, cosy and content after a day of pleasant activities; Martha was the guest of the other two, who owned the handsome, convenient country house; she always came to spend her Christmas with the Wyntons and found the leisurely country life delightful after the bustling round of London, for Martha managed an antique shop of the better sort and worked extremely hard. She was, however, still full of zest for work or pleasure, though sixty years old, and looked backwards and forwards to a succession of delightful days.

The other two, Mabel and Clara, led quieter but none the less agreeable lives; they had more money and fewer interests, but nevertheless enjoyed themselves very well.

'Talking of ghosts,' said Mabel, 'I wonder how that old woman at "Hartleys" is getting on, for "Hartleys", you know, is supposed to be haunted.'

'Yes, I know,' smiled Miss Pym, 'but all the years that we have known of the place we have never heard anything definite, have we?'

'No,' put in Clara; 'but there *is* that persistent rumour that the house is uncanny, and for myself, *nothing* would induce me to live there!'

'It is certainly very lonely and dreary down there on the marshes,' conceded Mabel. 'But as for the ghost – you never hear *what* it is supposed to be even.'

'Who has taken it?' asked Miss Pym, remembering 'Hartleys' as very desolate indeed, and long shut up.

'A Miss Lefain, an eccentric old creature – I think you met her here once, two years ago –'

'I believe that I did, but I don't recall her at all.'

'We have not seen her since, "Hartleys" is so un-get-at-able and she didn't seem to want visitors. She collects china, Martha, so really you ought to go and see her and talk "shop".'

With the word 'china' some curious associations came into the mind of Martha Pym; she was silent while she strove to put them together, and after a second or two they all fitted together into a very clear picture.

She remembered that thirty years ago – yes, it must be thirty years ago, when, as a young woman, she had put all her capital into the antique business, and had been staying with her cousins (her aunt had then been alive), that she had driven across the marsh to 'Hartleys', where there was an auction sale; all the details of this she had completely forgotten, but she could recall quite clearly purchasing a set of gorgeous china which was still one of her proud delights, a perfect set of Crown Derby save that one plate was missing.

'How odd,' she remarked, 'that this Miss Lefain should collect china too, for it was at "Hartleys" that I purchased my dear old Derby service – I've never been able to match that plate –'

'A plate was missing? I seem to remember,' said Clara. 'Didn't they say that it must be in the house somewhere and that it should be looked for?'

'I believe they did, but of course I never heard any more and that missing plate has annoyed me ever since. Who had "Hartleys"?'

'An old connoisseur, Sir James Sewell; I believe he was some relation to this Miss Lefain, but I don't know –'

'I wonder if she has found the plate,' mused Miss Pym. 'I expect she has turned out and ransacked the whole place –'

'Why not trot over and ask?' suggested Mabel. 'It's not much use to her, if she has found it, one odd plate.'

'Don't be silly,' said Clara. 'Fancy going over the marshes, this weather, to ask about a plate missed all those years ago. I'm sure Martha wouldn't think of it –'

But Martha did think of it; she was rather fascinated by the idea; how queer and pleasant it would be if, after all these years, nearly a lifetime, she should find the Crown Derby plate, the loss of which had always irked her! And this hope did not seem so altogether fantastical, it was quite likely that old Miss Lefain, poking about in the ancient house, had found the missing piece.

And, of course, if she had, being a fellow-collector, she would be quite willing to part with it to complete the set.

Her cousin endeavoured to dissuade her; Miss Lefain, she declared, was a recluse, an odd creature who might greatly resent such a visit and such a request.

'Well, if she does I can but come away again,' smiled Miss Pym. 'I suppose she can't bite my head off, and I rather like meeting these curious types – we've got a love for old china in common, anyhow.'

'It seems so silly to think of it – after all these years – a plate!'

'A Crown Derby plate,' corrected Miss Pym. 'It is certainly strange that I didn't think of it before, but now that I have got it into my head I can't get it out. Besides,' she added hopefully, 'I might see the ghost.'

So full, however, were the days with pleasant local engagements that Miss Pym had no immediate chance of putting her scheme into practice; but she did not relinquish it, and she asked several different people what they knew about 'Hartleys' and Miss Lefain.

And no one knew anything save that the house was supposed to be haunted and the owner 'cracky'.

'Is there a story?' asked Miss Pym, who associated ghosts with neat tales into which they fitted as exactly as nuts into shells.

But she was always told: 'Oh, no, there isn't a story, no one knows anything about the place, don't know how the idea got about; old Sewell was half-crazy, I believe, he was buried in the garden and that gives a house a nasty name –'

'Very unpleasant,' said Martha Pym, undisturbed.

This ghost seemed too elusive for her to track down; she would have to be content if she could recover the Crown Derby plate; for that at least she was determined to make a try and also to satisfy that faint tingling of curiosity roused in her by this talk about 'Hartleys' and the remembrance of that day, so long ago, when she had gone to the auction sale at the lonely old house.

So the first free afternoon, while Mabel and Clara were comfortably taking their afternoon repose, Martha Pym, who was of a more lively habit, got out her little governess cart and dashed away across the Essex flats.

She had taken minute directions with her, but she had soon lost her way.

Under the wintry sky, which looked as grey and hard as metal, the marshes stretched bleakly to the horizon, the olive-brown broken reeds were harsh as scars on the saffron-tinted bogs, where the sluggish waters that rose so high in winter were filmed over with the first stillness of a frost; the air was cold but not keen, everything was damp; faintest of mists blurred the black outlines of trees that rose stark from the ridges above the stagnant dykes; the flooded fields were haunted by black birds and white birds, gulls and crows, whining above the long ditch grass and wintry wastes.

Miss Pym stopped the little horse and surveyed this spectral scene, which had a certain relish about it to one sure to return to a homely village, a cheerful house and good company.

A withered and bleached old man, in colour like the dun landscape, came along the road between the sparse alders.

Miss Pym, buttoning up her coat, asked the way to 'Hartleys' as he passed her; he told her, straight on, and she proceeded, straight indeed across the road that went with undeviating length across the marshes.

'Of course,' thought Miss Pym, 'if you live in a place like this, you are bound to invent ghosts.'

The house sprang up suddenly on a knoll ringed with rotting trees, encompassed by an old brick wall that the perpetual damp had overrun with lichen, blue, green, white colours of decay.

'Hartleys', no doubt, there was no other residence of human being in sight in all the wide expanse; besides, she could remember it, surely, after all this time, the sharp rising out of the marsh, the colony of tall trees, but then fields and trees had been green and bright – there had been no water on the flats, it had been summer-time.

'She certainly,' thought Miss Pym, 'must be crazy to live here. And I rather doubt if I shall get my plate.'

She fastened up the good little horse by the garden gate which stood negligently ajar and entered; the garden itself was so neglected that it was quite surprising to see a trim appearance in the house, curtains at the window and a polish on the brass door knocker, which must have been recently rubbed there, considering the taint in the sea damp which rusted and rotted everything.

It was a square-built, substantial house with 'nothing wrong with it but the situation', Miss Pym decided, though it was not very attractive, being built of that drab plastered stone so popular a hundred years ago, with flat windows and door, while one side was gloomily shaded by a large evergreen tree of the cypress variety which gave a blackish tinge to that portion of the garden.

There was no pretence at flower-beds nor any manner of cultivation in this garden where a few rank weeds and straggling bushes matted together above the dead grass; on the enclosing wall which appeared to have been built high as protection against the ceaseless winds that swung along the flats were the remains of fruit trees; their crucified branches, rotting under the great nails that held them up, looked like the skeletons of those who had died in torment.

Miss Pym took in these noxious details as she knocked firmly at the door; they did not depress her; she merely felt extremely sorry for anyone who could live in such a place.

She noticed, at the far end of the garden, in the corner of the wall, a headstone showing above the sodden colourless grass, and remembered what she had been told about the old antiquary being buried there, in the grounds of 'Hartleys'.

As the knock had no effect she stepped back and looked at the house; it was certainly inhabited – with those neat windows, white curtains and drab blinds all pulled to precisely the same level.

And when she brought her glance back to the door she saw that it had been opened and that someone, considerably obscured by the darkness of the passage, was looking at her intently.

'Good afternoon,' said Miss Pym cheerfully. 'I just thought that I would call to see Miss Lefain – it is Miss Lefain, isn't it?'

'It's my house,' was the querulous reply.

Martha Pym had hardly expected to find any servants here, though the old lady must, she thought, work pretty hard to keep the house so clean and tidy as it appeared to be.

'Of course,' she replied. 'May I come in? I'm Martha Pym, staying with the Wyntons, I met you there –'

'Do come in,' was the faint reply. 'I get so few people to visit me, I'm really very lonely.'

'I don't wonder,' thought Miss Pym; but she had resolved to take no notice of any eccentricity on the part of her hostess, and so she entered the house with her usual agreeable candour and courtesy.

The passage was badly lit, but she was able to get a fair idea of Miss Lefain; her first impression was that this poor creature was most dreadfully old, older than any human being had the right to be, why, she felt young in comparison – so faded, feeble, and pallid was Miss Lefain.

She was also monstrously fat; her gross, flaccid figure was shapeless and she wore a badly cut, full dress of no colour at all, but stained with earth and damp where Miss Pym supposed she had been doing futile gardening; this gown was doubtless designed to disguise her stoutness, but had been so carelessly pulled about that it only added to it, being rucked and rolled 'all over the place' as Miss Pym put it to herself.

Another ridiculous touch about the appearance of the poor old lady was her short hair; decrepit as she was, and lonely as she lived she had actually had her scanty relics of white hair cropped round her shaking head.

'Dear me, dear me,' she said in her thin treble voice. 'How very kind of you to come. I suppose you prefer the parlour? I generally sit in the garden.'

'The garden? But not in this weather?'

'I get used to the weather. You've no idea how used one gets to the weather.'

'I suppose so,' conceded Miss Pym doubtfully. 'You don't live here quite alone, do you?'

'Quite alone, lately. I had a little company, but she was taken away,

I'm sure I don't know where. I haven't been able to find a trace of her anywhere,' replied the old lady peevishly.

'Some wretched companion that couldn't stick it, I suppose,' thought Miss Pym. 'Well, I don't wonder – but someone ought to be here to look after her.'

They went into the parlour, which, the visitor was dismayed to see, was without a fire but otherwise well kept.

And where, on dozens of shelves was a choice array of china at which Martha Pym's eyes glistened.

'Aha!' cried Miss Lefain. 'I see you've noticed my treasures! Don't you envy me? Don't you wish that you had some of those pieces?'

Martha Pym certainly did and she looked eagerly and greedily round the walls, tables, and cabinets while the old woman followed her with little thin squeals of pleasure.

It was a beautiful little collection, most choicely and elegantly arranged, and Martha thought it marvellous that this feeble ancient creature should be able to keep it in such precise order as well as doing her own housework.

'Do you really do everything yourself here and live quite alone?' she asked, and she shivered even in her thick coat and wished that Miss Lefain's energy had risen to a fire, but then probably she lived in the kitchen, as these lonely eccentrics often did.

'There was someone,' answered Miss Lefain cunningly, 'but I had to send her away. I told you she's gone, I can't find her, and I am so glad. Of course,' she added wistfully, 'it leaves me very lonely, but then I couldn't stand her impertinence any longer. She used to say that it was *her* house and her collection of china! Would you believe it? She used to try to chase me away from looking at my own things?'

'How very disagreeable,' said Miss Pym, wondering which of the two women had been crazy. 'But hadn't you better get someone else.'

'Oh, no,' was the jealous answer. 'I would rather be alone with my things, I daren't leave the house for fear someone takes them away – there was a dreadful time once when an auction sale was held here –'

'Were you here then?' asked Miss Pym; but indeed she looked old enough to have been anywhere.

'Yes, of course,' Miss Lefain replied rather peevishly and Miss Pym decided that she must be a relation of old Sir James Sewell. Clara and Mabel had been very foggy about it all. 'I was very busy hiding all the china – but one set they got – a Crown Derby tea service –'

'With one plate missing!' cried Martha Pym. 'I bought it, and do you know, I was wondering if you'd found it –'

'I hid it,' piped Miss Lefain.

'Oh, you did, did you? Well, that's rather funny behaviour. Why did you hide the stuff away instead of buying it?'

'How could I buy what was mine?'

'Old Sir James left it to you, then?' asked Martha Pym, feeling very muddled.

'*She* bought a lot more,' squeaked Miss Lefain, but Martha Pym tried to keep her to the point.

'If you've got the plate,' she insisted, 'you might let me have it – I'll pay quite handsomely, it would be so pleasant to have it after all these years.'

'Money is no use to me,' said Miss Lefain mournfully. 'Not a bit of use. I can't leave the house or the garden.'

'Well, you have to live, I suppose,' replied Martha Pym cheerfully. 'And, do you know, I'm afraid you are getting rather morbid and dull, living here all alone – you really ought to have a fire – why, it's just on Christmas and very damp.'

'I haven't felt the cold for a long time,' replied the other; she seated herself with a sigh on one of the horsehair chairs and Miss Pym noticed with a start that her feet were covered only by a pair of white stockings; 'one of those nasty health fiends', thought Miss Pym, 'but she doesn't look too well for all that.'

'So you don't think that you could let me have the plate?' she asked briskly, walking up and down, for the dark, neat, clean parlour was very cold indeed, and she thought that she couldn't stand this much longer; as there seemed no sign of tea or anything pleasant and comfortable she had really better go.

'I might let you have it,' sighed Miss Lefain, 'since you've been so kind as to pay me a visit. After all, one plate isn't much use, is it?'

'Of course not, I wonder you troubled to hide it –'

'I couldn't *bear*,' wailed the other, 'to see the things going out of the house!'

Martha Pym couldn't stop to go into all this; it was quite clear that the old lady was very eccentric indeed and that nothing very much could be done with her; no wonder that she had 'dropped out' of everything and that no one ever saw her or knew anything about her, though Miss Pym felt that some effort ought really to be made to save her from herself.

'Wouldn't you like a run in my little governess cart?' she suggested. 'We might go to tea with the Wyntons on the way back, they'd be delighted to see you, and I really think that you do want taking out of yourself.'

'I was taken out of myself some time ago,' replied Miss Lefain. 'I really was, and I couldn't leave my things – though,' she added with pathetic gratitude, 'it is very, very kind of you –'

'Your things would be quite safe, I'm sure,' said Martha Pym, humouring her. 'Who ever would come up here, this hour of a winter's day?'

'They do, oh, they do! And *she* might come back, prying and nosing and saying that it was all hers, all my beautiful china, hers!'

Miss Lefain squealed in her agitation and rising up, ran round the wall fingering with flaccid yellow hands the brilliant glossy pieces on the shelves.

'Well, then, I'm afraid that I must go, they'll be expecting me, and it's quite a long ride; perhaps some other time you'll come and see us?'

'Oh, must you go?' quavered Miss Lefain dolefully. 'I do like a little company now and then and I trusted you from the first – the others, when they do come, are always after my things and I have to frighten them away!'

'Frighten them away!' replied Martha Pym. 'However do you do that?'

'It doesn't seem difficult, people are so easily frightened, aren't they?'

Miss Pym suddenly remembered that 'Hartleys' had the reputation of being haunted – perhaps the queer old thing played on that; the lonely house with the grave in the garden was dreary enough around which to create a legend.

'I suppose you've never seen a ghost?' she asked pleasantly. 'I'd rather like to see one, you know –'

'There is no one here but myself,' said Miss Lefain.

'So you've never seen anything? I thought it must be all nonsense. Still, I do think it rather melancholy for you to live here all alone –'

Miss Lefain sighed:

'Yes, it's very lonely. Do stay and talk to me a little longer.' Her whistling voice dropped cunningly. 'And I'll give you the Crown Derby plate!'

'Are you sure you've really got it?' Miss Pym asked.

'I'll show you.'

Fat and waddling as she was, she seemed to move very lightly as she slipped in front of Miss Pym and conducted her from the room, going slowly up the stairs – such a gross odd figure in that clumsy dress with the fringe of white hair hanging on to her shoulders.

The upstairs of the house was as neat as the parlour, everything well in its place; but there was no sign of occupancy; the beds were covered with dust sheets, there were no lamps or fires set ready. 'I suppose,' said Miss Pym to herself, 'she doesn't care to show me where she really lives.'

But as they passed from one room to another, she could not help saying:

'Where *do* you live, Miss Lefain?'

'Mostly in the garden,' said the other.

Miss Pym thought of those horrible health huts that some people indulged in.

'Well, sooner you than I,' she replied cheerfully.

In the most distant room of all, a dark, tiny closet, Miss Lefain opened a deep cupboard and brought out a Crown Derby plate which her guest received with a spasm of joy, for it was actually that missing from her cherished set.

'It's very good of you,' she said in delight. 'Won't you take something for it, or let me do something for you?'

'You might come and see me again,' replied Miss Lefain wistfully.

'Oh, yes, of course I should like to come and see you again.'

But now that she had got what she had really come for, the plate, Martha Pym wanted to be gone; it was really very dismal and depressing in the house and she began to notice a fearful smell – the place had been shut up too long, there was something damp rotting somewhere, in this horrid little dark closet no doubt.

'I really must be going,' she said hurriedly.

Miss Lefain turned as if to cling to her, but Martha Pym moved quickly away.

'Dear me,' wailed the old lady. 'Why are you in such haste?'

'There's – a smell,' murmured Miss Pym rather faintly.

She found herself hastening down the stairs, with Miss Lefain complaining behind her.

'How peculiar people are – *she* used to talk of a smell –'

'Well, you must notice it yourself.'

Miss Pym was in the hall; the old woman had not followed her, but stood in the semi-darkness at the head of the stairs, a pale shapeless figure.

Martha Pym hated to be rude and ungrateful but she could not stay another moment; she hurried away and was in her cart in a moment – really – that smell –

'Goodbye!' she called out with false cheerfulness, 'and thank you *so* much!'

There was no answer from the house.

Miss Pym drove on; she was rather upset and took another way than that by which she had come, a way that led past a little house raised above the marsh; she was glad to think that the poor old creature at 'Hartleys' had such near neighbours, and she reined up the horse, dubious as to whether she should call someone and tell them that poor old Miss Lefain really wanted a little looking after, alone in a house like that, and plainly not quite right in her head.

A young woman, attracted by the sound of the governess cart, came to the door of the house and seeing Miss Pym called out, asking if she wanted the keys of the house?

'What house?' asked Miss Pym.

'"Hartleys", mum, they don't put a board out, as no one is likely to pass, but it's to be sold. Miss Lefain wants to sell or let it –'

'I've just been up to see her –'

'Oh, no, mum – she's been away a year, abroad somewhere, couldn't stand the place, it's been empty since then, I just run in every day and keep things tidy –'

Loquacious and curious the young woman had come to the fence; Miss Pym had stopped her horse.

'Miss Lefain is there now,' she said. 'She must have just come back –'

'She wasn't there this morning, mum, 'tisn't likely she'd come, either – fair scared she was, mum, fair chased away, didn't dare move her china. Can't say I've noticed anything myself, but I never stay long – and there's a smell –'

'Yes,' murmured Martha Pym faintly, 'there's a smell. What – what – chased her away?'

The young woman, even in that lonely place, lowered her voice.

'Well, as you aren't thinking of taking the place, she got an idea in her head that old Sir James – well, he couldn't bear to leave "Hartleys", mum, he's buried in the garden, and she thought he was after her, chasing round them bits of china –'

'Oh!' cried Miss Pym.

'Some of it used to be his, she found a lot stuffed away, he said they were to be left in "Hartleys", but Miss Lefain would have the things sold, I believe – that's years ago –'

'Yes, yes,' said Miss Pym with a sick look. 'You don't know what he was like, do you?'

'No, mum – but I've heard tell he was very stout and very old – I wonder who it was you saw up at "Hartleys"?'

Miss Pym took a Crown Derby plate from her bag.

'You might take that back when you go,' she whispered. 'I shan't want it, after all –'

Before the astonished young woman could answer Miss Pym had darted off across the marsh; that short hair, that earth-stained robe, the white socks, 'I generally live in the garden –'

Miss Pym drove away, at breakneck speed, frantically resolving to mention to no one that she had paid a visit to 'Hartleys', nor lightly again to bring up the subject of ghosts.

She shook and shuddered in the damp, trying to get out of her clothes and her nostrils – that indescribable smell.

# The Kite

## *Christianna Brand*

Buzzards you might see aplenty; but the kite, the majestic kite – he was rare, and being rare, was precious. Perhaps a dozen pairs were left in the whole of Great Britain; and Miss Bellingham actually had a pair nesting on her land.

If a pair of kites nested on your land and reared their young, you were awarded a bounty; and Miss Bellingham duly received her bounty. Not that she needed an odd five pounds – she was well enough off, and if she chose to live in a cottage in the deep heart of Wales, if she had made it as comfortable as a rather stout elderly lady could require and lived there solely because she preferred to, that was her personal business.

No, it was not the money; it was the pride – the pride and the feeling that from now on these kites belonged to *her*. She took to keeping an account of their movements, sending off innumerable postcards to the official guardians of kites, full of information, and confirmation or denial of information, already perfectly well known to them. The guardians threw the postcards away; all they required of Miss Bellingham was that she should protect the nest.

And she did protect it. Not a soul was allowed near the cottage or in the surrounding woods; in sunshine and in rain she patrolled her few acres and drove away all who might disturb the great one and his queen. Not that there were many visitors – the cottage was too remotely situated to be troubled by more than an occasional motoring tourist, probing into the lonely, lovely valleys for more scenic delights; but the kindly farmers would every now and again jog over in their Land-rovers, up Miss Bellingham's rutty lane, 'just to see if the old lady's all right' – and by no means appreciated being turned back with brusque assurances that she lacked for nothing and would have to say goodbye now, as she was very busy.

For of course she said nothing of the nesting kites; above all, one must keep them secret against the curious, the predatory, the undisciplined ignorant; and from the irreverent.

The years passed; the kites moved elsewhere to nest; but his lordship still visited Miss Bellingham's land – sailing over, high, serene, majestical, whenever the whim seized him, and always to Miss Bellingham's delight. *Kite visited today, twelve noon,* she would write on a postcard to the kite guardians, perhaps once a week; in a life almost totally devoid of other incident, this was always a red-letter day.

Others must watch for the long forked tail, for the glint of russet, for the crook of the wingtips, to distinguish the kite from the blunt-rumped buzzard; but not Miss Bellingham. She knew him for himself – for his lazy sweep of the air he owned, for the swift controlled swoop, for the calm, unhurried return, slowly upward-circling into the blue remoteness of his kingdom. The buzzard might be hustled and harried by raven flocks; the lord of the air sailed on through the scruffy ranks, unruffled, and the foe fell back. . .

The seasons came and went, and spring came; and in April – surprisingly in those parts, where even in the heart of winter a bitter cold is unusual – came the snow. At the first sign of it, while the country was still an exquisite pearly green not yet blotted out by white, came the farmers, bucketing and sliding up and down the steep hills with chains on their wheels.

'Better get out, Miss Bellingham, while you can. You know what it's like here when the snow drifts – this road will be impassable, it always it. And who knows how long it will last? Better get out.'

But Miss Bellingham had no intention of getting out. Every winter her relatives came and forced her away, took her to homes where, long used to her solitudes, she felt cramped, harassed, ill at ease. But they would not discover, until it was too late to reach her, the news of snow in these faraway valleys; she would escape them this time.

On the other hand, she could not have the farmers struggling over – she had no telephone – fighting their way through to her, just because she chose to be obstinate and remain. 'It's all arranged for,' she lied. 'My nephew will be coming for me later today. You know, they never leave me here in hard weather. Yes, he's coming for me today.'

They went away, reassured, and passed the word round the tiny community. No need to worry about Miss Bellingham – her family was taking her to safety till the snow was gone. Miss Bellingham sighed happily and settled down to her self-created besiegement.

The small birds were grateful for her presence, poor little things – the sparrow, the robin, the tiny Jenny Wren, and of course the sly jackdaw with his monastic gray cowl. And seeing them all feeding there as the bitter weather went on, the buzzards swooped down also, to see what was going on. And then one day – one day, royalty itself: her kite.

Who said that wild creatures couldn't be taught by man? The buzzards, consistently driven off by her flapping arms and screeching voice, soon learned to come no more. The kite, on the other hand, enticed with lumps of meat from the deep-freeze, soon knew he was welcome. At first she must go far afield to tempt him down, slipping and stumbling over the frozen paths, over the fields when the paths became indistinguishable from the rest of the land, to place the offerings only as near as his wary aloofness would permit.

But soon, because her legs were growing weak under the unaccustomed exercise, she must place the lumps of meat closer; and still he came, and came nearer, starved into daring, until one day he took meat from the wooden table set up just outside her door, where in summertime she would sit and take her own meals – took meat from the very table where Miss Bellingham herself would eat. From within her small deep-set cottage window she watched him and could have cried for joy. She had taken the King's Bounty; now she would earn it and place him forever in her debt.

She could send no postcards; the postwoman came no more, crawling like a bug in her little green car up the twisty lane; but Miss Bellingham started a diary in an old exercise book: *Today, April 6th, kite approached within two yards of house. Quite true that rim of eye is pronounced yellow. Eye very bright and proud.*

The days passed; the snow no longer fell but still lay deep, windswept into drifts along the lane, leveling the fields into flat white sheets, damming up, icing over, the sluggish stream. No thaw came. The resources of the deep-freeze began to get low, and Miss Bellingham cut down the kite's ration and her own.

He came regularly now to the table; he had seen her watching from the window, and after the first shock and swift evading flight, took no further heed of her. For more and more it was becoming an effort for her to get out to the table; the snow, iced over by the back-and-forth passing of her feet on her errands of mercy, had grown skiddy and treacherous. Once or twice she slipped and fell, and the effort of raising herself again to her feet made her heart thump and her mind grow grey and blurred.

One day, standing at the table with the meat in her hand, she felt suddenly strangely ill and was obliged to sit down abruptly in the old wooden armchair and let the world swim round her in a swirling of darkness and light. And her hand dropped the meat without volition, and somehow – somehow it came to her that time had passed without her knowing anything of it. The kite was wheeling close above her head; he had not been there before. 'I have had a little faint,' she said to herself. But she knew it was more than that.

The kite hardly waited for her slow, stumbling return inside the cottage before he swooped down upon the meat. *Kite came within five feet,* she wrote in the diary. *True that bill is strongly hooked.*

The next day she waited, very, very quiet, only halfway to the table –

and again down he came; and that afternoon she stayed even nearer the table; and still he came. It was very cold waiting there – but worth it, worth it! One day, she thought, if the freeze lasts long enough, if I am patient enough – he will take the meat from my hand.

She ate very little now. The other birds had finished her store of frozen fruit and vegetables and nowadays sought elsewhere or sought no more, poor little things, clamped frozen to the frozen twigs. And the bread was all gone, and even such meat as she allowed herself, she begrudged for the kite's sake. And there came another of the little fainting spells, and this time a numbness of her left arm and leg; and Miss Bellingham recognized, in a mind growing increasingly woolly and vague, that she could not go on much longer. And if she were to die – who, then, was going to feed the kite?

She feared that she would have the strength for very few more journeys out to the table. Fortunately she had, while she still could, removed what was left of the meat from the depths of the refrigerator: the weather was sufficiently cold to keep it wholesome, and the kite could not have eaten it frozen solid. She looked at the meat despairingly – so little left that she must eke it out day by day; if she were to place it all out on the table in one last great effort, would he not take it all at once and then have none left for the rest of the time until the thaw came? Might not – worse and worse – the buzzards return, and seeing the meat there, unguarded, swoop down and help themselves?

*I would have liked before I die*, she confided to the diary, painfully scrawling with her stub of pencil, *to have had him take the meat from my hand, just once.*

And that day – that very day – he did. Limping and struggling, dragging herself by slow painful inches, she had got out to the table and there collapsed again into the chair and for a long time lay sprawled there, the meat still held in her outstretched hand. So long, indeed, that the kite grew weary of circling, unobserved, above the old grey tumbled head, and came down closer, closer – closer; and since the enemy made no move, swooped at last and with a wild snatch tore the food from her lax fingers and with two great thrashing flaps of dappled brown wings, soared up again into the whiteness of the sky.

The violence of his up-winging awakened and startled her. She felt very ill, and the halting journey back inside the house took longer than it ever had before. But that night she scrawled triumphantly in her diary: *Not true that kite will not feed from the human hand.*

The next day she retained her consciousness but lay as she had before, across the table; only this time she watched him. The cold was bitter, but wrapped in her old winter coat, she seemed, strangely, hardly to suffer from it, sitting there hour after hour waiting for his coming, the meat held out temptingly; waiting, when the meat was gone, to gather her strength to make the slow creeping journey indoors again.

That night she did not undress, just lay down beside the warm electric radiator and slept her oddly untroubled sleep, building up courage for the next day's effort. But again that evening she had been able to record faithfully in the diary: *Kite alighted on table, took food from hand, ate it close by. Beak very fierce and strong. True that crown of head is almost white.*

But still the freeze held; and now there was meat for only one more day.

She sat for a long time that morning, pressing against the warm radiator, thinking. No more food for the kite, and if the cold lasted much longer – already it must be unprecedented for this time of year – what would become of him? What would become of him, her love, her lord, her king of the air?

No man in all her life had claimed ascendancy over the heart of Miss Bellingham; mind and body, she had remained all too free of the dominance of the male over feminine frailty; in her youth much longed for, in age deeply regretted – the sweet, the easeful submission to a strength superior to her own. Now into her blurred mind, shot through with fantasies of that long-ago starved youth, had come some hazy recognition that here he was at last – her overlord, to be submitted to, sacrificed to, body and soul. . .

*Alive I have served him,* she wrote, the letters straggling crazily across the page of her diary; *why shouldn't I, dead, serve him still? In life I have suffered in serving him. I shan't suffer when I am dead.*

And she struggled out of the old coat, and thinly clad, carrying only the diary and stub of pencil, with the last of the meat, she made the painful journey, crawling now on hands and knees, out to the table; and hoisted herself up somehow, and once again, exhausted by the effort, fell back unconscious in the wooden armchair.

And this time when she awoke to sensibility, sensibility was indeed almost all that remained to her. In the right hand a little strength, in the left less, not enough any longer to move the dead weight of even her hand. Willing or not, now there was no more possibility of changing her mind. The die was cast: at this sacrificial altar, the victim had tethered herself without hope of escape. Painfully she wrote in the diary: *Do not be distressed. It is what I have chosen to do.*

The whirr of his wings was like thunder as he swooped. Proud as a king, an emperor, proud as a god – scornful of danger now, he strutted, with a click of curved talons, the bleached silver of the birchwood boards. Fierce was the yellow-rimmed brilliance of his pale eye, sizing her up.

Feebly she added a note in the diary: *He is only waiting till I am* – The writing tailed off.

And she wrote once more – how much later, how many hours or even days later, who could tell? They found the words, almost indecipherable, straggling across the bloodstained page.

*Not true.*

Not true that the bird of prey waits to feed until the victim is dead.

# Blind Man's Hood

*John Dickson Carr*

Although one snowflake had already sifted past the lights, the great doors of the house stood open. It seemed less a snowflake than a shadow; for a bitter wind whipped after it, and the doors creaked. Inside, Rodney and Muriel Hunter could see a dingy, narrow hall paved in dull red tiles, with a Jacobean staircase at the rear. (At that time, of course, there was no dead woman lying inside.)

To find such a place in the loneliest part of the Weald of Kent – a seventeenth-century country house whose floors had grown humped and its beams scrubbed by the years – was what they had expected. Even to find electricity was not surprising. But Rodney Hunter thought he had seldom seen so many lights in one house, and Muriel had been equally startled by the display. 'Clearlawns' lived up to its name. It stood in the midst of a slope of flat grass, now wiry white with frost, and there was no tree or shrub within twenty yards of it. Those lights contrasted with a certain inhospitable and damp air about the house, as though the owner were compelled to keep them burning all the time.

'But why is the front door *open*?' insisted Muriel.

In the drive-way, the engine of their car coughed and died. The house was now a secret blackness of gables, emitting light at every chink, and silhouetting the stalks of the wisteria vines which climbed it. On either side of the front door were little-paned windows whose curtains had not been drawn. Towards their left they could see into a low dining-room, with table and sideboard set for a cold supper; towards their right was a darkish library moving with the reflections of a bright fire.

The sight of the fire warmed Rodney Hunter, but it made him feel guilty. They were very late. At five o'clock, without fail, he had promised Jack Bannister, they would be at 'Clearlawns' to inaugurate the Christmas party.

Engine-trouble in leaving London was one thing; idling at a country pub along the way, drinking hot ale and listening to the wireless sing carols until a sort of Dickensian jollity stole into you, was something else. But both he and Muriel were young; they were very fond of each other and of things in general; and they had worked themselves into a glow of Christmas, which – as they stood before the creaking doors of 'Clearlawns' – grew oddly cool.

There was no real reason, Rodney thought, to feel disquiet. He hoisted their luggage, including a big box of presents for Jack and Molly's children, out of the rear of the car. That his footsteps should sound loud on the gravel was only natural. He put his head into the doorway and whistled. Then he began to bang the knocker. Its sound seemed to seek out every corner of the house and then come back like a questing dog; but there was no response.

'I'll tell you something else,' he said. 'There's nobody in the house.'

Muriel ran up the three steps to stand beside him. She had drawn her fur coat close around her, and her face was bright with cold.

'But that's impossible!' she said. 'I mean, even if they're out, the servants –! Molly told me she keeps a cook and two maids. Are you sure we've got the right place?'

'Yes. The name's on the gate, and there's no other house within a mile.'

With the same impulse they craned their necks to look through the windows of the dining-room on the left. Cold fowl on the sideboard, a great bowl of chestnuts; and, now they could see it, another good fire, before which stood a chair with a piece of knitting put aside on it. Rodney tried the knocker again, vigorously, but the sound was all wrong. It was as though they were even more lonely in that core of light, with the east wind rushing across the Weald, and the door creaking again.

'I suppose we'd better go in,' said Rodney. He added, with a lack of Christmas spirit: 'Here, this is a devil of a trick! What do you think has happened? I'll swear that fire has been made up in the last fifteen minutes.'

He stepped into the hall and set down the bags. As he was turning to close the door, Muriel put her hand on his arm.

'I say, Rod. Do you think you'd better close it?'

'Why not?'

'I – I don't know.'

'The place is getting chilly enough as it is,' he pointed out, unwilling to admit that the same thought had occurred to him. He closed both doors and shot their bar into place; and, at the same moment, a girl came out of the door to the library on the right.

She was such a pleasant-faced girl that they both felt a sense of relief. Why she had not answered the knocking had ceased to be a question, she filled a void. She was pretty, not more than twenty-one or two, and had an air of primness which made Rodney Hunter vaguely associate her with a governess or a secretary, though Jack Bannister had never mentioned any such person. She was plump, but with a curiously narrow waist; and she wore brown. Her brown hair was neatly parted, and her brown eyes – long eyes, which might have given a hint of secrecy or curious smiles if they had not been so placid – looked concerned. In one hand she carried what looked like a small white bag of linen or cotton. And she spoke with a dignity which did not match her years.

'I am most terribly sorry,' she told them. 'I *thought* I heard someone, but I was so busy that I could not be sure. Will you forgive me?'

She smiled. Hunter's private view was that his knocking had been loud enough to wake the dead; but he murmured conventional things. As though conscious of some faint incongruity about the white bag in her hand, she held it up.

'For Blind Man's Bluff,' she explained. 'They do cheat so, I'm afraid, and not only the children. If one uses an ordinary handkerchief tied round the eyes, they always manage to get a corner loose. But if you take this, and you put it fully over a person's head, and you tie it round the neck' – a sudden gruesome image occurred to Rodney Hunter – 'then it works so much better, don't you think?' Her eyes seemed to turn inward, and to grow absent. 'But I must not keep you talking here. You are –?'

'My name is Hunter. This is my wife. I'm afraid we've arrived late, but I understood Mr Bannister was expecting –'

'He did not tell you?' asked the girl in brown.

'Tell me what?'

'Everyone here, including the servants, is always out of the house at this hour on this particular date. It is the custom; I believe it has been the custom for more than sixty years. There is some sort of special church service.'

Rodney Hunter's imagination had been devising all sorts of fantastic explanations: the first of them being that this demure lady had murdered the members of the household, and was engaged in disposing of the bodies. What put this nonsensical notion into his head he could not tell, unless it was his own profession of detective-story writing. But he felt relieved to hear a commonplace explanation. Then the woman spoke again.

'Of course, it's a pretext really. The rector, that dear man, invented it all those years ago to save embarrassment. What happened here had nothing to do with the murder, since the dates were so different; and I suppose most people have forgotten now why the tenants *do* prefer to stay away during seven and eight o'clock on Christmas Eve. I doubt if Mrs Bannister even knows the real reason, though I should imagine Mr Bannister must know it. But what happens here cannot be very pleasant, and it wouldn't do to have the children see it – would it?'

Muriel spoke with such sudden directness that her husband knew she was afraid. 'Who are you?' Muriel said. 'And what on earth are you talking about?'

'I am quite sane, really,' their hostess assured them, with a smile that was half-cheery and half-coy. 'I dare say it must be all very confusing to you, poor dear. But I am forgetting my duties. Please come in and sit down before the fire, and let me offer you something to drink.'

She took them into the library on the right, going ahead with a walk that was like a bounce, and looking over her shoulder out of those long eyes. The library was a long, low room with beams. The windows towards the road were uncurtained; but those in the side-wall, where a faded red-brick fireplace stood, were bay windows with draperies closed across them. As their hostess put them before the fire, Hunter could have sworn he saw one of the draperies move.

'You need not worry about it,' she assured him, following his glance towards the bay. 'Even if you looked in there, you might not see anything now. I believe some gentleman did try it once, a long time ago. He stayed in the house for a wager. But when he pulled the curtain back, he did not see anything in the bay – at least, anything quite. He felt some hair, and it moved. That is why they have so many lights nowadays.'

Muriel had sat down on a sofa, and was lighting a cigarette: to the rather prim disapproval of their hostess, Hunter thought.

'May we have a hot drink?' Muriel asked crisply. 'And then, if you don't mind, we might walk over and meet the Bannisters coming from church.'

'Oh, please don't do that!' cried the other. She had been standing by the fireplace, her hands folded and turned outwards. Now she ran across to sit down beside Muriel; and the swiftness of her movement, no less than the touch of her hand on Muriel's arm, made the latter draw back.

Hunter was now completely convinced that their hostess was out of her head. Why she held such fascination for him, though, he could not understand. In her eagerness to keep them there, the girl had come upon a new idea. On a table behind the sofa, book-ends held a row of modern novels. Conspicuously displayed – probably due to Molly Bannister's tact – were two of Rodney Hunter's detective stories. The girl put a finger on them.

'May I ask if you wrote these?'

He admitted it.

'Then,' she said with sudden composure, 'it would probably interest you to hear about the murder. It was a most perplexing business, you know; the police could make nothing of it, and no one ever has been able to solve it.' An arresting eye fixed on his. 'It happened out in the hall there. A poor woman was killed where there was no one to kill her, and no one could have done it. But she was murdered.'

Hunter started to get up from his chair; then he changed his mind, and sat down again. 'Go on,' he said.

'You must forgive me if I am a little uncertain about dates,' she urged. 'I think it was in the early eighteen-seventies, and I am sure it was in early February – because of the snow. It was a bad winter then; the farmers' livestock all died. My people have been bred up in the district for years, and I know that. The house here was much as it is now, except that there was none of this lighting (only paraffin lamps, poor girl!); and you were obliged to pump up what water you wanted; and people read the newspaper quite through, and discussed it for days.

'The people were a little different to look at, too. I am sure I do not understand why we think beards are so strange nowadays; they seem to think that men who had beards never had any emotions. But even young men wore them then, and looked handsome enough. There was a newly married couple living in this house at the time: at least, they had been married only the summer before. They were named Edward and Jane Waycross, and it was considered a good match everywhere.

'Edward Waycross did not have a beard, but he had bushy side-whiskers which he kept curled. He was not a handsome man, either, being somewhat dry and hard-favoured; but he was a religious man, and a good man, and an excellent man of business, they say: a manufacturer of agricultural implements at Hawkhurst. He had determined that Jane Anders (as she was) would make him a good wife, and I dare say she did. The girl had several suitors. Although Mr Waycross was the best match, I know it surprised people a little when she accepted him, because she was thought to have been fond of another man – a more striking man, whom many of the young girls were after. This was Jeremy Wilkes: who came of a very good family, but was considered wicked. He was no younger than Mr Waycross, but he had a great black beard, and wore white waistcoats with gold chains, and drove a gig. Of course, there had been gossip, but that was because Jane Anders was considered pretty.'

Their hostess had been sitting back against the sofa, quietly folding the little white bag with one hand, and speaking in a prim voice. Now she did something which turned her hearers cold.

You have probably seen the same thing done many times. She had been touching her cheek lightly with the fingers of the other hand. In doing so, she touched the flesh at the corner under her lower eyelid, and identally drew down the corner of that eyelid – which should have exposed the red part of the inner lid at the corner of the eye. It was not red. It was of a sickly pale colour.

'In the course of his business dealing,' she went on, 'Mr Waycross had often to go to London, and usually he was obliged to remain overnight.

But Jane Waycross was not afraid to remain alone in the house. She had a good servant, a staunch old woman, and a good dog. Even so, Mr Waycross commended her for her courage.'

The girl smiled. 'On the night I wish to tell you of, in February, Mr Waycross was absent. Unfortunately, too, the old servant was absent; she had been called away as a midwife to attend her cousin, and Jane Waycross had allowed her to go. This was known in the village, since all such affairs are well known, and some uneasiness was felt – this house being isolated, as you know. But she was not afraid.

'It was a very cold night, with a heavy fall of snow which had stopped about nine o'clock. You must know, beyond doubt, that poor Jane Waycross was alive after it had stopped snowing. It must have been nearly half-past nine when a Mr Moody – a very good and sober man who lived in Hawkhurst – was driving home along the road past this house. As you know, it stands in the middle of a great bare stretch of lawn; and you can see the house clearly from the road. Mr Moody saw poor Jane at the window of one of the upstairs bedrooms, with a candle in her hand, closing the shutters. But he was not the only witness who saw her alive.

'On that same evening, Mr Wilkes (the handsome gentleman I spoke to you of a moment ago) had been at a tavern in the village of Five Ashes with Dr Sutton, the local doctor, and a racing gentleman named Pawley. At about half-past eleven they started to drive home in Mr Wilkes's gig to Cross-in-Hand. I am afraid they had been drinking, but they were all in their sober senses. The landlord of the tavern remembered the time because he had stood in the doorway to watch the gig, which had fine yellow wheels, go spanking away as though there were no snow; and Mr Wilkes in one of the new round hats with a curly brim.

'There was a bright moon. "And no danger," Dr Sutton always said afterwards; "shadows of trees and fences as clear as though a silhouette-cutter had made 'em for sixpence." But when they were passing this house Mr Wilkes pulled up sharp. There was a bright light in the window of one of the downstairs rooms – this room, in fact. They sat out there looking round the hood of the gig, and wondering.

'Mr Wilkes spoke: "I don't like this," he said. "You know, gentlemen, that Waycross is still in London; and the lady in question is in the habit of retiring early. I am going up there to find out if anything is wrong."

'With that he jumped out of the gig, his black beard jutting out and his breath smoking. He said: "And if it is a burglar, then, by Something, gentlemen" – I will not repeat the word he used – "by Something, gentlemen, I'll settle him." He walked through the gate and up to the house – they could follow every step he made – and looked into the windows of this room here. Presently he returned looking relieved (they could see him by the light of the gig lamps), but wiping the moisture off his forehead.

'"It is all right," he said to them; "Waycross has come home. But, by Something, gentlemen, he is growing thinner these days, or it is shadows."

'Then he told them what he had seen. If you look through the front windows – there – you can look sideways and see out through the doorway into the main hall. He said he had seen Mrs Waycross standing in the hall with her back to the staircase, wearing a blue dressing-wrap over her nightgown, and her hair down round her shoulders. Standing in front of her, with his back to Mr Wilkes, was a tallish, thin man like Mr Waycross, with a long greatcoat and a tall hat like Mr Waycross's. *She* was carrying either a candle or a lamp; and he remembered how the tall hat seemed to wag back and forth, as though the man were talking to her or putting out his hands towards her. For he said he could not see the woman's face.

'Of course, it was not Mr Waycross; but how were they to know that?

'At about seven o'clock next morning, Mrs Randall, the old servant, returned. (A fine boy had been born to her cousin the night before.) Mrs Randall came home through the white dawn and the white snow, and found the house all locked up. She could get no answer to her knocking. Being a woman of great resolution, she eventually broke a window and got in. But, when she saw what was in the front hall, she went out screaming for help.

'Poor Jane was past help. I know I should not speak of these things; but I must. She was lying on her face in the hall. From the waist down her body was much charred and – unclothed, you know, because fire had burnt away most of the nightgown and the dressing-wrap. The tiles of the hall were soaked with blood and paraffin oil having come from a broken lamp with a thick blue-silk shade which was lying a little distance away. Near it was a china candlestick with a candle. This fire had also charred a part of the panelling of the wall, and a part of the staircase. Fortunately, the floor is of brick tiles, and there had not been much paraffin left in the lamp, or the house would have been set afire.

'But she had not died from burns alone. Her throat had been cut with a deep slash from some very sharp blade. But she had been alive for a while to feel both things, for she had crawled forward on her hands while she was burning. It was a cruel death, a horrible death for a soft person like that.'

There was a pause. The expression on the face of the narrator, the plump girl in the brown dress, altered slightly. So did the expression of her eyes. She was sitting beside Muriel; and moved a little closer.

'Of course, the police came. I do not understand such things, I am afraid, but they found that the house had not been robbed. They also noticed the odd thing I have mentioned, that there was both a lamp *and* a candle in a candlestick near her. The lamp came from Mr and Mrs Waycross's bedroom upstairs, and so did the candlestick: there were no other lamps or candles downstairs except the lamps waiting to be filled next morning in the back kitchen. But the police thought she would not have come downstairs carrying both the lamp *and* the candle as well.

'She must have brought the lamp, because that was broken. When the murderer took hold of her, they thought, she had dropped the lamp, and it went out; the paraffin spilled, but did not catch fire. Then this man in the tall hat, to finish his work after he had cut her throat, went upstairs, and got a candle, and set fire to the spilled oil. I am stupid at these things; but even I should have guessed that this must mean someone familiar with the house. Also, if she came downstairs, it must have been to let someone in at the front door; and that could not have been a burglar.

'You may be sure all the gossips were like police from the start, even when the police hemm'd and haw'd, because they knew Mrs Waycross must have opened the door to a man who was not her husband. And immediately they found an indication of this, in the mess that the fire and blood had made in the hall. Some distance away from poor Jane's body there was a medicine-bottle, such as chemists use. I think it had been broken in two pieces; and on one intact piece they found sticking some fragments of a letter that had not been quite burned. It was in a man's handwriting, not her husband's, and they made out enough of it to understand. It was full of – expressions of love, you know, and it made an appointment to meet her there on that night.'

Rodney Hunter, as the girl paused, felt impelled to ask a question.

'Did they know whose handwriting it was?'

'It was Jeremy Wilkes's,' replied the other simply. 'Though they never proved that, never more than slightly suspected it, and the circumstances did not bear it out. In fact, a knife stained with blood was actually found in Mr Wilkes's possession. But the police never brought it to anything, poor souls. For, you see, not Mr Wilkes – or anyone else in the world – could possibly have done the murder.'

'I don't understand that,' said Hunter, rather sharply.

'Forgive me if I am stupid about telling things,' urged their hostess in a tone of apology. She seemed to be listening to the chimney growl under a cold sky, and listening with hard, placid eyes. 'But even the village gossips could tell that. When Mrs Randall came here to the house on that morning, both the front and the back doors were locked and securely bolted on the inside. All the windows were locked on the inside. If you will look at the fastenings in this dear place, you will know what that means.

'But, bless you, that was the least of it! I told you about the snow. The snowfall had stopped at nine o'clock in the evening, hours and hours before Mrs Waycross was murdered. When the police came, there were only two separate sets of footprints in the great unmarked half-acre of snow round the house. One set belonged to Mr Wilkes, who had come up and looked in through the window the night before. The other belonged to Mrs Randall. The police could follow and explain both sets of tracks; but there were no other tracks at all, and no one was hiding in the house.

'Of course, it was absurd to suspect Mr Wilkes. It was not only that he told a perfectly straight story about the man in the tall hat; but both Dr Sutton and Mr Pawley, who drove back with him from Five Ashes, were there to swear he could not have done it. You understand, he came no closer to the house than the windows of this room. They could watch every step he made in the moonlight, and they did. Afterwards he drove home with Dr Sutton, and slept there; or, I should say, they continued their terrible drinking until daylight. It is true that they found in his possession a knife with blood on it, but he explained that he had used the knife to gut a rabbit.

'It was the same with poor Mrs Randall, who had been up all night about her midwife's duties, though naturally it was even more absurd to think of *her*. But there were no other footprints at all, either coming to or going from the house, in all that stretch of snow; and all the ways in or out were locked on the inside.'

It was Muriel who spoke then, in a voice that tried to be crisp, but wavered in spite of her. 'Are you telling us that all this is true?' she demanded.

'I am teasing you a little, my dear,' said the other. 'But, really and truly, it all did happen. Perhaps I will show you in a moment.'

'I suppose it was really the husband who did it?' asked Muriel in a bored tone.

'Poor Mr Waycross!' said their hostess tenderly. 'He spent that night in a temperance hotel near Charing Cross Station, as he always did, and, of course, he never left it. When he learned about his wife's duplicity' – again Hunter thought she was going to pull down a corner of her eyelid – 'it nearly drove him out of his mind, poor fellow. I think he gave up agricultural machinery and took to preaching, but I am not sure. I know he left the district soon afterwards, and before he left he insisted on burning the mattress of their bed. It was a dreadful scandal.'

'But in that case,' insisted Hunter, 'who did kill her? And, if there were no footprints and all the doors were locked, how did the murderer come or go? Finally, if all this happened in February, what does it have to do with people being out of the house on Christmas Eve?'

'Ah, that is the real story. That is what I meant to tell you.'

She grew very subdued.

'It must have been very interesting to watch the people alter and grow older, or find queer paths, in the years afterwards. For, of course, nothing did happen as yet. The police presently gave it all up; for decency's sake it was allowed to rest. There was a new pump built in the market square; and the news of the Prince of Wales's going to India in '75 to talk about; and presently a new family came to live at 'Clearlawns,' and began to raise their children. The trees and the rains in summer were just the same, you know. It must have been seven or eight years before anything happened, for Jane Waycross was very patient.

'Several of the people had died in the meantime. Mrs Randall had, in a fit of quinsy; and so had Dr Sutton, but that was a great mercy, because he fell by the way when he was going out to perform an amputation with too much of the drink in him. But Mr Pawley had prospered – and, above all, so had Mr Wilkes. He had become an even finer figure of a man, they tell me, as he drew near middle age. When he married he gave up all his loose habits. Yes, he married; it was the Tinsley heiress, Miss Linshaw, whom he had been courting at the time of the murder; and I have heard that poor Jane Waycross, even after *she* was married to Mr Waycross, used to bite her pillow at night because she was so horribly jealous of Miss Linshaw.

'Mr Wilkes had always been tall, and now he was finely stout. He always wore frock-coats. Though he had lost most of his hair, his beard was full and curly; he had twinkling black eyes, and twinkling ruddy cheeks, and a bluff voice. All the children ran to him. They say he broke as many feminine hearts as before. At any wholesome entertainment he was always the first to lead the cotillion or applaud the fiddler, and I do not know what hostesses would have done without him.

'On Christmas Eve, then – remember, I am not sure of the date – the Fentons gave a Christmas party. The Fentons were the very nice family who had taken this house afterwards, you know. There was to be no dancing, but all the old games. Naturally, Mr Wilkes was the first of all to be invited, and the first to accept; for everything was all smoothed away by time, like the wrinkles in last year's counterpane; and what past *is* past, or so they say. They had decorated the house with holly and mistletoe, and guests began to arrive as early as two in the afternoon.

'I had all this from Mrs Fenton's aunt (one of the Warwickshire Abbotts), who was actually staying here at the time. In spite of such a festal season, the preparations had not been going at all well that day, though such preparations usually did. Miss Abbott complained that there was a nasty earthy smell in the house. It was a dark and raw day, and the chimneys did not seem to draw as well as they should. What is more, Mrs Fenton cut her finger when she was carving the cold fowl, because she said one of the children had been hiding behind the window-curtains in here, and peeping out at her; she was very angry. But Mr Fenton, who was going about the house in his carpet slippers before the arrival of the guests, called her "Mother" and said that it was Christmas.

'It is certainly true that they forgot all about this when the fun of the games began. Such squealings you never heard! – or so I am told. Foremost of all at Bobbing for Apples or Nuts in May was Mr Jeremy Wilkes. He stood, gravely paternal, in the midst of everything, with his ugly wife beside him, and stroked his beard. He saluted each of the ladies on the cheek under the mistletoe; there was also some scampering to salute him; and, though he *did* remain for longer than was necessary behind the window-curtains with the younger Miss Twigelow, his wife only smiled. There was only one unpleasant incident, soon forgotten. Towards dusk a great gusty wind began to come up, with the chimneys smoking worse than usual. It being nearly dark, Mr Fenton said it was time to fetch in the Snapdragon Bowl, and watch it flame. You know the game? It is a great bowl of lighted spirit, and you must thrust in your hand and pluck out a raisin from the bottom without scorching your fingers. Mr Fenton carried it in on a tray in the half-darkness; it was flickering with that bluish flame you have seen on Christmas puddings. Miss Abbott said that once, in carrying it, he started and turned round. She said that for a second she thought there was a face looking over his shoulder, and it wasn't a nice face.

'Later in the evening, when the children were sleepy and there was tissue-paper scattered all over the house, the grown-ups began their games in earnest. Someone suggested Blind Man's Bluff. They were mostly using the hall and this room here, as having more space than the dining-room. Various members of the party were blindfolded with the men's handkerchiefs; but there was a dreadful amount of cheating. Mr Fenton grew quite annoyed about it, because the ladies almost always caught Mr Wilkes when they could; Mr Wilkes was laughing and perspiring heartily, and his great cravat with the silver pin had almost come loose.

'To make it certain nobody could cheat, Mr Fenton got a little white linen bag – like this one. It was the pillow-cover off the baby's cot, really; and he said nobody could look through that if it were tied over the head.

'I should explain that they had been having some trouble with the lamp in this room. Mr Fenton said: "Confound it, mother, what is wrong with that lamp? Turn up the wick, will you?" It was really quite a good lamp from Spence and Minstead's, and should not have burned so dull as it did. In the confusion, while Mrs Fenton was trying to make the light better, and he was looking over his shoulder at her, Mr Fenton had been rather absently fastening the bag on the head of the last person caught. He has said since that he did not notice who it was. No one else noticed, either, the light being so dim and there being such a large number of people. It seemed to be a girl in a broad bluish kind of dress, standing over near the door.

'Perhaps you know how people act when they have just been blind-folded in this game. First they usually stand very still, as though they were smelling or sensing in which direction to go. Sometimes they make a sudden jump, or sometimes they begin to shuffle gently forward. Everyone noticed what an air of *purpose* there seemed to be about this person whose face was covered; she went forward very slowly, and seemed to crouch down a bit.

'It began to move towards Mr Wilkes in very short but quick little jerks, the white bag bobbing on its face. At this time Mr Wilkes was sitting at the end of the table, laughing, with his face pink above the beard, and a glass of our Kentish cider in his hand. I want you to imagine this room as being very dim, and much more cluttered, what with all the tassels they had on the furniture then; and the high-piled hair of the ladies, too. The hooded person got to the edge of the table. It began to edge along towards Mr Wilkes's chair; and then it jumped!

'Mr Wilkes got up and skipped (yes, skipped) out of its way, laughing. It waited quietly, after which it went, in the same slow way, towards him again. It nearly got him again, by the edge of the potted plant. All this time it did not say anything, you understand, although everyone was applauding it and crying encouraging advice. It kept its head down. Miss Abbott says she began to notice an unpleasant faint smell of burnt cloth or something worse, which turned her half-ill. By the time the hooded person came stooping clear across the room, as certainly as though it could see him, Mr Wilkes was not laughing any longer.

'In the corner by one bookcase, he said out loud: "I'm tired of this silly, rotten game; go away, do you hear?" Nobody there had ever heard him speak like that, in such a loud, wild way, but they laughed and thought it must be the Kentish cider. "Go away!" cried Mr Wilkes again, and began to strike at it with his fist. All this time, Miss Abbott says, she had observed his face gradually changing. He dodged again, very pleasant and nimble for such a big man, but with the perspiration running down his face. Back across the room he went again, with it following him; and he cried out something that most naturally shocked them all inexpressibly.

'He screamed out: "For God's sake, Fenton, take it off me!"

'And for the last time the thing jumped.

'They were over near the curtains of that bay window, which were drawn as they are now. Miss Twigelow, who was nearest, says that Mr Wilkes could not have seen anything, because the white bag was still drawn over the woman's head. The only thing she noticed was that at the lower part of the bag, where the face must have been, there was a curious kind of discoloration, a stain of some sort which had not been there before: something seemed to be seeping through. Mr Wilkes fell back between the curtains, with the hooded person after him, and screamed again. There was a kind of thrashing noise in or behind the curtains; then they fell straight again, and everything grew quiet.

'Now, our Kentish cider is very strong, and for a moment Mr Fenton did not know what to think. He tried to laugh at it, but the laugh did not sound well. Then he went over to the curtains, calling out gruffly to them to come out of there and not play the fool. But, after he had looked inside the curtains, he turned round very sharply and asked the rector to get the ladies out of the room. This was done, but Miss Abbott often said that she had one quick peep inside. Though the bay windows were locked on the inside, Mr Wilkes was now alone on the window seat. She could see his beard sticking up, and the blood. He was dead, of course. But, since he had murdered Jane Waycross, I sincerely think that he deserved to die.'

For several seconds the two listeners did not move. She had all too successfully conjured up this room in the late 'seventies, whose stuffiness still seemed to pervade it now.

'But look here!' protested Hunter, when he could fight down an inclination to get out of the room quickly. 'You say he killed her after all? And yet you told us he had an absolute alibi. You said he never went closer to the house than the windows ...'

'No more he did, my dear,' said the other.

'He was courting the Linshaw heiress at the time,' she resumed; 'and Miss Linshaw was a very proper young lady who would have been horrified if she had heard about him and Jane Waycross. She would have broken off the match, naturally. But poor Jane Waycross meant her to hear. She was much in love with Mr Wilkes, and she was going to tell the whole matter publicly: Mr Wilkes had been trying to persuade her not to do so.'

'But –'

'Oh, don't you see what happened?' cried the other in a pettish tone. 'It is so dreadfully simple. I am not clever at these things, but I should have seen it in a moment: even if I did not already know. I told you everything so that you should be able to guess.

'When Mr Wilkes and Dr Sutton and Mr Pawley drove past here in the gig that night, they saw a bright light burning in the windows of this room. I told you that. But the police never wondered, as anyone should, what caused that light. Jane Waycross never came into this room, as you know; she was out in the hall, carrying either a lamp or a candle. But that lamp in the thick blue-silk shade, held out there in the hall, would not have caused a bright light to shine through this room and illuminate it. Neither would a tiny candle; it is absurd. And I told you there were no other lamps in the house except some empty ones waiting to be filled in the back kitchen. There is only one thing they could have seen. They saw the great blaze of the paraffin oil round Jane Waycross's body.

'Didn't I tell you it was dreadfully simple? Poor Jane was upstairs waiting for her lover. From the upstairs window she saw Mr Wilkes's gig, with the fine yellow wheels, drive along the road in the moonlight, and she did not know there were other men in it; she thought he was alone. She came downstairs –

'It is an awful thing that the police did not think more about that broken medicine-bottle lying in the hall, the large bottle that was broken in just two pieces. She must have had a use for it; and, of course, she had. You knew that the oil in the lamp was almost exhausted, although there was a great blaze round the body. When poor Jane came downstairs, she was carrying the unlighted lamp in one hand; in the other hand she was carrying a lighted candle, and an old medicine-bottle containing paraffin oil. When she got downstairs, she meant to fill the lamp from the medicine-bottle, and then light it with the candle.

'But she was too eager to get downstairs, I am afraid. When she was more than half-way down, hurrying, that long nightgown tripped her. She pitched forward down the stairs on her face. The medicine-bottle broke on the tiles under her, and poured a lake of paraffin round her body. Of course, the lighted candle set the paraffin blazing when it fell; but that was not all. One intact side of that broken bottle, long and sharp and cleaner than any blade, cut into her throat when she fell on the smashed bottle. She was not quite stunned by the fall. When she felt herself burning, and the blood almost as hot, she tried to save herself. She tried to crawl forward on her hands, forward into the hall, away from the blood and oil and fire.

'That was what Mr Wilkes really saw when he looked in the window.

'You see, he had been unable to get rid of the two fuddled friends, who insisted on clinging to him and drinking with him. He had been obliged to drive them home. If he could not go to 'Clearlawns' now, he wondered how at least he could leave a message; and the light in the window gave him an excuse.

'He saw pretty Jane propped up on her hands in the hall, looking out at him beseechingly while the blue flame ran up and turned yellow. You might have thought he would have pitied, for she loved him very much. Her wound was not really a deep wound. If he had broken into the house at that moment, he might have saved her life. But he preferred to let her die: because now she would make no public scandal and spoil his chances with the rich Miss Linshaw. That was why he returned to his friends and told a lie about a murderer in a tall hat. It is why, in heaven's truth, he murdered her himself. But when he returned to his friends, I do not wonder that they saw him mopping his forehead. You know now how Jane Waycross came back for him, presently.'

There was another heavy silence.

The girl got to her feet, with a sort of bouncing motion which was as suggestive as it was vaguely familiar. It was as though she were about to run. She stood there, a trifle crouched, in her prim brown dress, so oddly narrow at the waist after an old-fashioned pattern; and in the play of light on her face Rodney Hunter fancied that its prettiness was only a shell.

'The same thing happened afterwards, on some Christmas Eves,' she explained. 'They played Blind Man's Bluff over again. That is why people who live here do not care to risk it nowadays. It happens at a quarter-past seven –'

Hunter stared at the curtains. 'But it was a quarter-past seven when we got here!' he said. 'It must now be –'

'Oh, yes,' said the girl, and her eyes brimmed over. 'You see, I told you you had nothing to fear; it was all over then. But that is not why I thank you. I begged you to stay, and you did. You have listened to me, as no one else would. And now I have told it at last, and now I think both of us can sleep.'

Not a fold stirred or altered in the dark curtains that closed the window bay; yet, as though a blurred lens had come into focus, they now seemed innocent and devoid of harm. You could have put a Christmas-tree there. Rodney Hunter, with Muriel following his gaze, walked across and threw back the curtains. He saw a quiet window-seat covered with chintz, and the rising moon beyond the window. When he turned round, the girl in the old-fashioned dress was not there. But the front doors were open again, for he could feel a current of air blowing through the house.

With his arm round Muriel, who was white-faced, he went out into the hall. They did not look long at the scorched and beaded stains at the foot of the panelling, for even the scars of fire seemed gentle now. Instead, they stood in the doorway looking out, while the house threw its great blaze of light across the frosty Weald. It was a welcoming light. Over the rise of a hill, black dots trudging in the frost showed that

Jack Bannister's party was returning; and they could hear the sound of voices carrying far. They heard one of the party carelessly singing a Christmas carol for glory and joy, and the laughter of children coming home.

# The Door

## R. Chetwynd-Hayes

'Why a door?' Rosemary asked. 'I mean to say, the house has a full complement of perfectly satisfactory doors.'

William continued to run his hands over his latest acquisition, his eyes alight with that glow of pure pleasure that is peculiar to the ardent collector.

'I liked it,' he explained, 'besides it is very old. Three hundred years, if a day.'

'But it doesn't match the paintwork or anything,' Rosemary protested, 'and it's so heavy.'

She was right of course. The door was massive; made of solid walnut, fully four feet wide and seven feet high, the panels embossed with an intricate pattern that seemed to grow more complicated the longer it was examined. It had a great tarnished brass knob on the left side, and four butt hinges on the right.

'What are you going to do with it?' Rosemary asked after a while. 'Hang it on the wall?'

'Don't be so silly.' William tapped the panels with his knuckles. 'I'm going to put it to its proper use. You know that cupboard in my study? Well, it's dead centre in the wall opposite my desk; I'll get the builders to take away the old door, enlarge the aperture, and hang this one in its place.'

'A great thing like that as a cupboard door!' Rosemary gasped.

'Then,' William went on, 'I'll hang a large sixteenth-century print on either side, a couple of crossed swords over the top, and the result should be pretty impressive.'

'Like a museum,' Rosemary observed.

'It will inspire me,' William nodded slowly, and Rosemary, with a woman's inconsistency, thought he looked very sweet. 'It must be French polished of course, and the lock burnished and then lacquered.'

'Where did you find it?' Rosemary asked.

'At Murray's. You know, the demolition people. Old Murray said it came from a sixteenth-century manor house he knocked down last year. I can't wait to see the door in position, can you?'

'No,' Rosemary said doubtfully. 'No, I can hardly wait.'

The builders made an awful mess, as she knew they would, but when the job was finished, and of course the study had to be completely redecorated, the effect was certainly very impressive. The entire wall was covered with red wallpaper, and in the exact centre was the door, now resplendent with polish, the brass knob and hinges gleaming like gold, giving the impression that behind must lie a gracious drawing-room instead of an eighteen inches deep stationery cupboard. On either side hung a Rembrandt print, each one housed in a magnificent gilt frame, and over the door were two crossed sabres with shining brass hilts. William sat behind his desk, his face wearing the look of a man well satisfied with the world and all it contained.

'Wonderful,' he breathed, 'absolutely marvellous.'

'Well, as long as you're satisfied.' Rosemary frowned, and puckered her lips into an expression of faint distaste. 'Frankly I'm not certain I like it.'

'What!' William scowled his displeasure. He liked people to share his enthusiasm. 'What's wrong with it?'

'It looks very nice and original,' Rosemary admitted, 'but some-how . . .' she paused . . . 'it's rather creepy.'

'What utter rot.'

'Yes, I suppose it must sound that way, but I can't help wondering what lies behind.'

'What lies . . . !' William stared at his wife with growing amazement. 'You know what lies behind, an ordinary stationery cupboard.'

'Yes, I know, and you don't have to shout at me. I keep telling myself it is only a door and behind is a shallow cupboard lined with shelves, but I can't really believe it. I mean, cupboards don't have grand doors like that, they have cheap ply-panelled ones covered with layers and layers of old paint, and they're sort of humble. If they could talk, they'd say: "I'm a cupboard door, and I don't pretend to be anything else." But that thing . . .' She jerked her head in the direction of the large door. 'That wouldn't say anything. Just stare at you and wait to be opened by a butler.'

'What an imagination,' William pointed to his typewriter. 'You ought to be doing my job. But you're right. I never thought about it. A door must take on the character of the room it guards, in the same way a face assumes the character of the brain behind it. Now . . .' He got up, walked round the desk, and moved over to the great gleaming door. 'What kind of room do you suppose this once guarded?'

'A big one,' Rosemary said with conviction. 'Yes, I'd say a big room.'

'A reasonable deduction.' William nodded. 'Large door, large room. What else?'

'I think it must have been a beautiful room. Sinister maybe, cold, but beautiful. A big expanse of carpet, a great fireplace, high blue walls, a big window with an olde worlde garden beyond . . . blue velvet chairs. I think it would have been a room like that.'

'Could well be.' William nodded again. 'A large drawing-room that hardly changed with the years. There again, it might have been a picture gallery – anything. Tell you what, I'll ring up Murray and find out what he can tell me.'

'A big room,' Rosemary murmured, more to herself than to her husband. 'I'm certain it was a large drawing-room. Certain.'

'Good morning, Mr Seaton. What can I do for you?'

'About that door I bought.' William pressed the telephone receiver closer to his ear. 'I wondered if you could tell me something about the house from which it came.'

'The house?' Murray sounded a little impatient. 'Clavering Grange, you mean. An old place down in Kent. The last owner, Sir James Sinclair, died recently, and the chap who inherited – Hackett was his name – had no use for it, falling to pieces it was, so he sold the lot to a building contractor. We had the job of clearing the site. Why do you ask?'

'Oh, my wife and I wondered what sort of room went with such a fine door. I suppose you wouldn't know?'

Murray chuckled. 'Matter of fact I do. It came from the blue drawing-room. A great barn of a place with a ruddy great fireplace. Very grand in its day I'm sure, but was a bit of a mess when we came to drive our bulldozer through it. You know, damp, the paper peeling from the walls. Can't tell you much else.'

'Well, thanks anyway. My wife was right. She thought it was a large drawing-room, and, strangely enough, she guessed it was blue.'

'You don't say? What do you know about that? Must be psychic or something.'

'Probably something,' William laughed. 'Well, thanks again. 'Bye.'

'So.' William spoke aloud. 'We have established a blue drawing-room should be behind you, but there isn't, is there? Only a horrible little cupboard, so you had better get used to your reduced circumstances, and be mighty grateful you didn't finish up as firewood.'

The door ignored him.

William often worked late into the night, finding the peace and quiet of the small hours conducive to creative thinking. Usually there was a feeling of serene contentment when he settled down in his old chair, heard the muted roar of a passing car, and let his brain churn out a steady flow of dialogue. But once the door was installed he found his attention was apt to wander to it, or rather to what had once lain behind it. The blue room. Grand old country houses seemed to go in for that kind of thing. Blue rooms, red rooms, yellow rooms. Presumably if one had a lot of rooms, it was as good a way as any to identify one from the other. Also, decorating must be greatly simplified. Blue walls, blue hangings, carpet, upholstery – William chuckled to himself – there was really no limit. Why not have blue flowers just outside the great window, or perhaps a little blue creeper that completely surrounded the window and in fact gently tapped the glass panes on a windy night. He must get old Jem to cut it back.

William sat upright, dropped his pen, and frowned. Who the blazes was old Jem? It was all very well having a powerful, cultivated imagination, but he must keep it under control. But still... He stared at the door thoughtfully; there was a certain rather eerie satisfaction in creating an imaginary world for the door to guard. William lay back in his chair and half closed his eyes. First of all the room; it must be reconstructed properly. You open the door, walk onto a thick, extremely beautiful, blue carpet, clearly made to measure, for it stretches from wainscoting to wainscoting, and in front of that great fireplace with its roaring log-fire is a dark blue rug. So much for the floor, now the furniture. Situated some six feet back from the fireplace is a settee, at least so William supposed it to be, for it had a high back, a round arm on each side, would seat possibly four people at one time, and was covered with blue brocade. Six matching chairs were placed around the room, and William sank down onto one. It was very comfortable. He examined the walls. Blue of course, but the covering appeared to be some kind of material, embossed with dark blue flowers, and there were several pictures in blue velvet-edged frames. Indeed this is a blue room. Or it was. Funny this obsession for blue. What kind of man had he been ... or was? There was a portrait of him over the mantelpiece, painted when he was a young man; his face still clean, not yet scarred by lines of debauchery and evil, but the eyes... By God and all his saints, the eyes...

William got up and walked towards the fireplace; he could feel the heat of the fire; a log settled and sent a shower of sparks rocketing up the chimney. An oval face with the dark beauty of a fallen angel, long, black hair that curled down to his shoulders, lace collar, blue velvet doublet, the epitome of a Restoration gentleman. The dark, terrible eyes watched him, and William pulled his gaze away, then walked to the window. The garden was a place of beauty, close-clipped lawns, islands of flowers, trees beyond, further still, blue-crested hills.

He turned and went over to the great desk; a quill-pen grew out of an ink-horn, a blue velvet-covered book lay upon the desk and his hand went down to open it, when . . .

Footsteps outside, just beyond the windows, slow, halting steps, punctuated by an occasional dragging sound, like a lame old man who is trying to overcome his handicap; drawing nearer, and the room was becoming colder. William shivered, then, overcome by an unreasoning fear, darted towards the door. He opened it, went out, closed it carefully behind him, then went over and sat down behind his desk.

He opened his eyes.

Five minutes passed. William got up, moved very slowly towards the door, turned the brass knob, then pulled. A cupboard, eighteen inches deep, filled with shelves on which nestled stacks of typing paper, carbons, ribbons, the familiar materials of his trade. He shut the door, then opened it again, finally closed it with a bang before returning to his desk.

He sat there for some time, then suddenly was seized by a fit of shivering that made his body shake like a dead leaf beaten by the wind. Gradually the spasm passed, leaving him weak, drenched with perspiration, but strangely at peace, like a man who has recently recovered from a brief, but serious illness. A dream, an illusion, or perhaps a rebellion on the part of an overworked imagination. What did it matter? It had been an experience, an exercise of the mind, and no writer worthy of his ink should be afraid of a journey into the unknown.

He watched the door for the rest of the night, and the door stared right back at him. Once he thought the handle began to turn, and he waited with breathless expectancy, but it must have been an illusion caused by his overstrained eyes, for the door remained closed.

The door became an obsession. His work was neglected, a bewildered agent telephoned at regular intervals, muttering dark threats about deadlines, broken contracts, and William tried to flog his brain back to its former production line, but to no avail. The door was always there, and with it the memory of a room; a study in blue, an ante-room to another age. 'Next time,' he told himself, 'I will go out through the great window, and walk across the garden and rediscover yesterday.'

He sat by the hour with closed eyes trying to recreate the dream, willing himself back into that armchair, gazing up at the portrait over the mantelpiece, but the twentieth century remained obstinately present, and several times he fell asleep. Rosemary was becoming worried.

'What's the matter? Are you ill?'

'No.' He barked the denial, his irritation growing each time the gentle inquiry was made. 'Leave me alone. How am I to work?'

'But you're not working,' she persisted, 'neither are you eating. William, this must stop.'

'What?'

'You and that damned door.' She glared at the door. 'I do not pretend to understand, but ever since that lump of old wood came into this house, you haven't been the same man. It scares me. William, have it taken out. Let's burn it in the boiler.'

He laughed harshly, and experienced a pang of fear at her suggestion, and saw the startled expression on Rosemary's face.

'Don't worry so much. The truth is I've run dry. Writers do occasionally. It's happened before and the old brain has always started ticking over once it was good and ready. But it makes me a bit irritable.'

'That's all right.' She brightened up at once. 'I don't mind you being a bit testy, but you're getting so thin. Are you sure that nothing else is bothering you?'

For a mad moment he toyed with the idea of telling her about the room, the dream, then instantly discarded it. She would not understand or believe, so he kissed her gently and said, 'Absolutely nothing.'

'Then pack it in for a bit,' she pleaded, 'and let me cook you a decent meal. One you will eat.'

It was suddenly very important she be pacified, her mind be put at rest.

'All right. I'll give you a hand.'

He helped her in the kitchen, was surprised to hear himself making small talk, while all the time his mind, his very soul hungered for the blue room and the fear that lurked in the garden. For that was the truth, and the realization burst upon him like a blast of light. The terror inspired by approaching footsteps, the heart-stopping, exciting horror of wondering what would come in through the great French windows, the craving for a new experience, even if fulfilment meant madness or worse.

They ate in the kitchen, two young, beautiful people, as modern as Carnaby Street. He tall, lean, dark, she petite, blonde, blue-eyed. His dark, clever eyes watched her, and he smiled often.

That night they retired to bed early, and long after Rosemary had fallen asleep he lay thinking about the room behind the door.

'It does not exist,' he told himself. 'Maybe it did long ago, but not now. A bulldozer flattened the house, and only the blue-room door remains. A flat piece of polished wood.'

There was comfort in that thought, and presently sleep closed his eyes with soft fingers, and for a while he was at rest.

The room had not altered, the log-fire still spluttered, the chairs were in the same position as on his last visit, and the blue journal lay upon the desk. William found he was dressed in his pyjamas and his feet were bare.

'I must have sleep-walked,' he whispered, 'but now I am wide awake. This is not a dream.'

He walked over to the door, opened it and stared into the gloom; a few yards away the outline of his desk shimmered softly, the door of his study was open, beyond was darkness. William closed the door, crossed the blue carpet and flattened his nose against the French windows. Back in his own world it was night, out in the garden it was sunset; long shadows lay across the smooth lawn, the trees were giant sentinels rearing up against the evening sky, and although it all looked beautiful and peaceful, there was something eerie about the scene. Suddenly William knew why. Nothing moved. There were no birds, the leaves did not stir, the flowers stood upright; it was as though he were looking at a three-dimensional picture.

He shivered, then turned and walked over to the desk. The blue journal lay waiting, and he fingered the soft velvet cover before sitting down, then with a strange reluctance opened the book: crisp parchment, about fifty pages he estimated, bound together. The first one was blank, serving as a fly-leaf. He turned it slowly, then read the clear, beautiful copperplate inscription.

## AN EXPERIMENT IN DARKNESS
### BY
#### SIR MICHAEL SINCLAIR, BART.

of the county of Kent, Lord of the Manor of Clavering, written in this the twenty-second year of the reign of his gracious majesty, King Charles the Second.

It took a great effort of will to turn the title page, for the room seemed suddenly to have become very cold, and the dying sun sent its last shafts of light through the window, making the shadows scurry like so many disturbed mice. But he had to read on; the page went over with a disturbingly loud crackling sound.

### PART I
#### INSTRUCTIONS AS TO THE ENTRAPMENT OF THE UNBORN

Having kept myself aloof from the troubles of the preceding reign, I have devoted these many years to the pursuit of that knowledge which fools call evil, and from which, even those men that are dubbed wise, cover their faces, even as the night hides from the rising sun.

To say that the knowledge I have confined to these pages is the unadulterated fruit of my own labours would not be true, for I have been helped by the old masters, such as Astaste and his *Book of Forbidden Knowledge*, Conrad von Leininstein with his invaluable *Transformation of Living Matter Through Quickening Time*, and many others. But I have gone beyond them, have made myself as a seething-pot, created an essence of bubbling truth such as no man has yet conceived.

Men avert their eyes rather than meet my glance, for I wear my knowledge about me like a cloak; they whisper about me in corners, and there is much talk of witchcraft, and were I not who I am, I might fear the stake.

I prepared me the room after many years and the expense of much blood, and the damnation of my soul should the Black One whose name must never be uttered ever assume power over me. I brought me slaves from the Africas; young persons whose disappearance would never be commented upon, although their screams have doubtless been heard, but such is the reputation of this house, the fools merely cross themselves and take to their heels. It was necessary to kill their body with a painful slowness, and draw off their soul or life essence while the blue room and all pertaining to it was imprinted upon their dying gaze. Thus did I make a *karma* or ghost room, kept alive by the life essence of those who had been sacrificed to it. But even as the body needs food, the earth needs fertilizing, so the room, from time to time, must be fed. Many of the Africans have a poor lasting quality, the power fades and my soul trembles lest *He* be able to enter. Therefore, I prepared me the door, seeping it in blood that was still warm, and making it into a trap that will function for a brief spell in the time that has yet to come. I pray that this be not destroyed in the centuries yet unborn, for without it will I be unable to acquire that which is needful, and be lost for all eternity.

The unborn must come in when the time is ripe, and should he be of the right mixture, then shall he give of his body and soul that I and the room may continue to be; or I will go forth beyond the door and find me a woman of his kind, which would be better, for a woman have a more lasting quality . . .

William slammed the book closed and looked about him with sudden fear. A sound had disturbed him and for a moment he could not be sure what it had been. Then it came again – a slow, halting footstep, just beyond the French windows. William seemed to be frozen to his chair; he wanted to get up and run back to the safety of his own world; at the same time, there was an irritating curiosity to know who – what, would shortly come in through the window.

Suddenly the overhead chandelier lit up; every one of its candles took on a yellow spear-shaped light, and beyond the window it was night, a black impregnable wall of darkness. But the slow, faltering footsteps continued to draw nearer, and it seemed as though the room shivered with fear at the approach of its dread master, for the coldness grew more intense, and William whimpered like a terrified puppy.

The French windows opened, and slowly a black figure emerged from the darkness and limped into the room. The scarlet doublet was rotten with age, the blue velvet hat had long since lost its plume, the knee-breeches were threadbare, the black boots cracked and down at heel, and He – It – had no face. Just an oval-shaped expanse of dead-white skin surrounded by a mass of bedraggled white hair.

William screamed once, a long-drawn-out shriek, then he was on his feet and racing for the door. He pulled it open, crossed the dark study in a fear-mad rush, barked his shins on a chair, then tore out into the hall, and up the stairs, finally to collapse on the landing, where he lay panting and trembling like a hunted animal.

Slowly he recovered, fought back the terror, mastered his shaking limbs, and marshalled his thoughts. He crawled forward and peered down through the banisters to the dark hall below. He could see the pale oblong that marked his study doorway. The huge door was still open. Then another more terrible thought exploded and sent slivers of fear across his brain. *The door was open.* What had he read in the blue-covered book?

'Therefore I prepared me the door . . . making it into a trap that will function for a brief spell . . . or I will go forth beyond the door and find me a woman of his kind, which would be better, for a woman have a more lasting quality.'

Rosemary! If Sir Michael was beyond the door, then he might be but a few feet away, hidden by the darkness, peering down at William with that face that was not a face, perhaps even moving silently towards the bedroom where Rosemary lay asleep.

William got to his feet, stretched out a hand and groped wildly for the light switch. He found it, pressed, and the sudden light blasted the darkness, shattered it into splinters, sent the shadows racing for protecting corners, forced imagination to face reality. The landing was empty; the familiar cold linoleum, the white painted doors, the brown banisters, the stairs. . . William peered down into the hall. The landing light did not extend to more than half way down the stairs; the hall was still in total darkness. It took great courage to descend the stairs, and a great effort of will to press the hall switch. Light, like truth, is all-revealing; the hall table was in its proper place, the carpet he and Rosemary had chosen with such care covered the floor, two prints still hung on the green-papered walls, and all doors were closed, save the one leading to his study; and standing in the opening was something extra – a bedraggled, nightmare figure with no face. Almost no face, for since William had seen it last, it had acquired a mouth. Two thin lines that opened.

'Thank you.' The voice came as a harsh, vibrant whisper. 'Thank you very much.'

For the first time in his life, William fainted.

Rosemary was crying. Sitting by his bed sobbing, but when she saw his eyes were open, a smile lit up her face, the sun peeping through the rainclouds.

'Oh, William, you're awake. Thank goodness. When I found you down on the hall floor, I thought... Do you feel better now? The doctor said you have a slight concussion. Hit your head when you fell.'

He felt very weak, and his head hurt, a dull ache. There was also a nagging fear at the back of his mind, trying to remind him of something he wanted to forget.

'I feel fine,' he said. 'Great, simply great. What happened?'

'I don't know.' Rosemary was wiping her eyes. 'I guess you must have walked in your sleep, and fallen downstairs. I didn't find you until this morning, and you lay so still...'

She began to cry again and he wanted to comfort her, but the nagging fear was coming out into the open, making him remember, causing him to shiver.

'You must leave this house.' He tried to sit upright. 'He is looking for someone – a woman who has ...' he giggled inanely, '... who has a lasting quality.'

'Oh, no.' Rosemary had both hands clutched to her mouth, staring at him with fear-filled eyes. 'Your poor head.'

'I'm not mad.' William clutched her arm. 'Please believe me. He – It, I don't know, but there is a room behind the door, and He made it – kept it alive and himself by the life essence – soul's-blood, of living people. I know the door is a trap, is only active for a little while at certain periods, and *now* happens to be one of them. I don't know why sometimes I can go through, and at others I cannot, but it is so. But the point is, He – Sir Michael – has come through. He is on this side of the door. He wants a woman he can take back – make part of the room – take to pieces, tear soul from body. But you won't die – you won't be so lucky.'

Rosemary ran from the room, raced down the stairs, and he heard the telephone receiver being removed; she was telephoning the doctor, convinced beyond all doubt he was mad.

Perhaps he was, or at the very best a victim of a walking hallucination. He was suddenly very confused. He had lived off his imagination for years – it could have rebelled, manufactured a sleep-walking nightmare.

After all, his first 'visit' had begun by him mentally building up the room item by item.

He pretended to be asleep when Rosemary returned.

The doctor said: 'Run down,' remarked sagely on the effects of overwork, strain, advised rest, wrote out a prescription, and then departed. William felt almost happy after his visit, quite willing to accept the certainty that his experience had been nothing more than a vivid and unpleasant dream. He would rest, stay in bed, then in a few days he and Rosemary would go away for a long holiday, and during their absence a builder could remove the door. That was the sensible solution.

'Sorry if I scared you,' he told Rosemary, 'but I had such a horrible nightmare – a sort of two-part dream, and it seemed so real. We'll go away when I feel fit.'

She was delighted, chatted happily about where they should go, spent as much time as possible by his bedside, and left all the doors open when she went downstairs, so she could hear should he call out. The day passed, and as the shadows of night darkened the windows, a faint chill of returning fear began to haunt his mind. Rosemary turned on the lights, drew the curtains, smiled at him, but there was an expression of unease in her eyes, and it was then he knew his hard-won peace of mind was merely self-deception.

'Anything wrong?' He tried to make the question sound casual.

'No.' She straightened the counterpane. 'No, nothing.'

'Tell me,' he whispered, fearful lest the very walls were listening. 'Please, tell me.'

She averted her head.

'It's nothing, only silliness on my part. But – that door – it won't remain shut. Every time I close it, the handle turns, and it opens.'

'Then I was right, it was not a dream.'

'Nonsense.' She was pushing him back onto the pillows. 'The door is shrinking, the warm air is making it contract, that must be the answer. It must be.'

'Did ... did you see anything beyond the door?'

'Only the cupboard shelves, but ...'

She paused, and he did not want her to go on, tried to blot out her voice, but the words came to him, like echoes from yesteryear.

'I keep thinking there is someone else in the house.'

He shook his head: 'No ... no ...'

'I know it's pure imagination, but ... I thought I saw a face looking down at me over the banisters.'

'Rosemary.' He took her hand. 'Don't say anything more, just do as I say. Go downstairs, get the car out of the garage and wait for me. I'll pack a bag and will be with you in a few minutes.'

'But . . .' Her eyes were wide open, glazed with fear, and she made a faint protest when he clambered out of bed.

'Please do as I say. Now.'

She ran from the room, and William was reaching for his clothes when he had a glimpse of a figure gliding across the open doorway. For a moment he stood petrified, then he shouted once: 'Rosemary!'

'What's the matter?' Her voice, hoarse with fear, came up from the hall. 'What . . .'

Her scream seared his brain like a hot knife and he raced for the landing, ran down the stairs, then stood in the hall, calling out her name, trying to master his fear, the weakness in his legs.

'William . . . !'

The scream came from his study, and for a moment he surrendered to the paralysing terror, stood trembling like a statue on the brink of unnatural life, then with a great effort of will he moved forward, staggered rather than ran through the doorway and took in the scene with one all-embracing glance.

He – It – Sir Michael, was complete, rejuvenated by the life force of the girl who lay limp in his arms. The face was now lit by a pair of dark, terrible eyes, the nose was arched, cruel, the lips parted in a triumphant smile, the long hair only slightly flecked with grey, but his clothes were still ragged, old, besmirched with grave mire.

The door was open but the room beyond was slightly out of focus; the walls had a shimmering quality, the chandelier candles were spluttering, making light dance with shadow; a chair suddenly lost one leg and fell over onto the floor.

Sir Michael watched William, eyes glistening with sardonic amusement, and made no attempt to intervene as the young man edged round the walls towards the door. When William stood in the open doorway, with the blue room behind him, the thin lips parted again, and the harsh voice spoke.

'I must thank you again. The woman may have a more lasting quality, but two bodies and souls were always better than one.'

He moved forward, and Rosemary, now mercifully unconscious, lay in his arms, her head flung back so that her long hair brushed the desk top as they passed.

'The door,' William's brain screamed. 'Destroy the door!'

He would have given twenty years of his life for an axe. Then he remembered the crossed sabres hanging just above the door frame. He reached up and gripped the brass hilts, jerked, and they came away, then he spun round to face the approaching figure.

Sir Michael chuckled as he slowly shook his head.

'Never. You will only harm the lady.'

William swung the sabre in his right hand sideways and struck the door with a resounding crash. Instantly Sir Michael flinched, falling back a few paces as though the blade had been aimed at him.

'No-o-o.' The protest was a cry of pain; William struck again, and red fluid began to seep out of the door panel, and something crashed in the room behind. Then, in a fear-inspired frenzy, William slashed wildly at the door, and was dimly aware that Sir Michael had dropped Rosemary and was feeling around the study, jerking as each blow fell, emitting harsh animal-like cries, his eyes black pools of pain-racked hate.

The door shivered, then split; one half, now splintered, soggy, crashed to the floor; William swung his right-hand sabre and struck at the hinges, the door frame, and did not cease until the brickwork lay bare.

Sir Michael disintegrated. The face dissolved into an oval, featureless mask, the hair turned white, then seemed to melt into a white powder; the entire body collapsed and became an untidy heap of rags and white bones. In a few minutes these too faded away and William was left staring at a dirty patch of carpet.

He had one last fleeting glimpse of the blue room. The walls and ceiling appeared to fall in, turn into a mass of swirling blue-mist; he saw a great jumble of faces: Negroes with frizzy hair and large, black eyes, young fair-haired girls, children, even animals. Then the shelves of his stationery cupboard came into being, typing paper, ribbons, carbon paper, all merged into their proper place, and William turned his attention to Rosemary, who was stirring uneasily.

He gathered her up into his arms.

The splintered remains of the door lay all around, crumbling, rotten with age.

# The Strange Case of
# Sir Arthur Carmichael

*Agatha Christie*

(Taken from the notes of the late Dr Edward Carstairs, MD, the eminent psychologist.)

I am perfectly aware that there are two distinct ways of looking at the strange and tragic events which I have set down here. My own opinion has never wavered. I have been persuaded to write the story out in full, and indeed I believe it to be due to science that such strange and inexplicable facts should not be buried in oblivion.

It was a wire from my friend, Dr Settle, that first introduced me to the matter. Beyond mentioning the name Carmichael, the wire was not explicit, but in obedience to it I took the 12.20 train from Paddington to Wolden, in Hertfordshire.

The name of Carmichael was not unfamiliar to me. I had been slightly acquainted with the late Sir William Carmichael of Wolden, though I had seen nothing of him for the last eleven years. He had, I knew, one son, the present baronet, who must now be a young man of about twenty-three. I remembered vaguely having heard some rumours about Sir William's second marriage, but could recall nothing definite unless it were a vague impression detrimental to the second Lady Carmichael.

Settle met me at the station.

'Good of you to come,' he said as he wrung my hand.

'Not at all. I understand this is something in my line?'

'Very much so.'

'A mental case, then?' I hazarded. 'Possessing some unusual features?'

We had collected my luggage by this time and were seated in a dogcart driving away from the station in the direction of Wolden, which lay about three miles away. Settle did not answer for a minute or two. Then he burst out suddenly.

'The whole thing's incomprehensible! Here is a young man, twenty-three years of age, thoroughly normal in every respect. A pleasant amiable boy, with no more than his fair share of conceit, not brilliant intellectually perhaps, but an excellent type of the ordinary upperclass young Englishman. Goes to bed in his usual health one evening, and is found the next morning wandering about the village in a semi-idiotic condition incapable of recognizing his nearest and dearest.'

'Ah!' I said, stimulated. This case promised to be interesting. 'Complete loss of memory? And this occurred – ?'

'Yesterday morning. The 9th of August.'

'And there has been nothing – no shock that you know of – to account for this state?'

'Nothing.'

I had a sudden suspicion.

'Are you keeping anything back?'

'N – no.'

His hesitation confirmed my suspicion.

'I must know everything.'

'It's nothing to do with Arthur. It's to do with – with the house.'

'With the house,' I repeated, astonished.

'You've had a great deal to do with that sort of thing, haven't you, Carstairs? You've "tested" so-called haunted houses. What's your opinion of the whole thing?'

'In nine cases of ten, fraud,' I replied. 'But the tenth – well, I have come across phenomena that is absolutely unexplainable from the ordinary materialistic standpoint. I am a believer in the occult.'

Settle nodded. We were just turning in at the Park gates. He pointed with his whip at a low-lying white mansion on the side of a hill.

'That's the house,' he said. 'And – there's *something* in that house, something uncanny – horrible. We all feel it... And I'm not a super-stitious man...'

'What form does it take?' I asked.

He looked straight in front of him. 'I'd rather you knew nothing. You see, if you – coming here unbiased – knowing nothing about it – see it too – well –'

'Yes,' I said, 'it's better so. But I should be glad if you will tell me a little more about the family.'

'Sir William,' said Settle, 'was twice married. Arthur is the child of his first wife. Nine years ago he married again, and the present Lady Carmichael is something of a mystery. She is only half English, and, I suspect, has Asiatic blood in her veins.'

He paused.

'Settle,' I said, 'you don't like Lady Carmichael.'

He admitted it frankly. 'No, I don't. There has always seemed to me to be something sinister about her. Well, to continue, by his second wife Sir William had another child, also a boy, who is now eight years old. Sir William died three years ago, and Arthur came into the title and place. His stepmother and half brother continued to live with him at

Wolden. The estate, I must tell you, is very much impoverished. Nearly the whole of Sir Arthur's income goes to keeping it up. A few hundreds a year was all Sir William could leave his wife, but fortunately Arthur has always got on splendidly with his stepmother, and has been only too delighted to have her live with him. Now – '

'Yes?'

'Two months ago Arthur became engaged to a charming girl, a Miss Phyllis Patterson.' He added, lowering his voice with a touch of emotion: 'They were to have been married next month. She is staying here now. You can imagine her distress – '

I bowed my head silently.

We were driving up close to the house now. On our right the green lawn sloped gently away. And suddenly I saw a most charming picture. A young girl was coming slowly across the lawn to the house. She wore no hat, and the sunlight enhanced the gleam of her glorious golden hair. She carried a great basket of roses, and a beautiful grey Persian cat twined itself lovingly round her feet as she walked.

I looked at Settle interrogatively.

'That is Miss Patterson,' he said.

'Poor girl,' I said, 'poor girl. What a picture she makes with the roses and her grey cat.'

I heard a faint sound and looked quickly round at my friend. The reins had slipped out of his fingers, and his face was quite white.

'What's the matter?' I exclaimed.

He recovered himself with an effort.

In a few moments more we had arrived, and I was following him into the green drawing-room, where tea was laid out.

A middle-aged but still beautiful woman rose as we entered and came forward with an outstretched hand.

'This is my friend, Dr Carstairs, Lady Carmichael.'

I cannot explain the instinctive wave of repulsion that swept over me as I took the proffered hand of this charming and stately woman who moved with the dark and languorous grace that recalled Settle's surmise of Oriental blood.

'It is very good of you to come, Dr Carstairs,' she said in a low musical voice, 'and to try and help us in our great trouble.'

I made some trivial reply and she handed me my tea.

In a few minutes the girl I had seen on the lawn outside entered the room. The cat was no longer with her, but she still carried the basket of roses in her hand. Settle introduced me and she came forward impulsively.

'Oh! Dr Carstairs, Dr Settle has told us so much about you. I have a feeling that you will be able to do something for poor Arthur.'

Miss Patterson was certainly a very lovely girl, though her cheeks were pale, and her frank eyes were outlined with dark circles.

'My dear young lady,' I said reassuringly, 'indeed you must not despair. These cases of lost memory, or secondary personality, are often of very short duration. At any minute the patient may return to his full powers.'

She shook her head. 'I can't believe in this being a second personality,' she said. '*This* isn't Arthur at all. It is *no* personality of his. It isn't *him*. I –'

'Phyllis, dear,' said Lady Carmichael's soft voice, 'here is your tea.'

And something in the expression of her eyes as they rested on the girl told me that Lady Carmichael had little love for her prospective daughter-in-law.

Miss Patterson declined the tea, and I said, to ease the conversation: 'Isn't the pussy cat going to have a saucer of milk?'

She looked at me rather strangely.

'The – pussy cat?'

'Yes, your companion of a few moments ago in the garden –'

I was interrupted by a crash. Lady Carmichael had upset the tea kettle, and the hot water was pouring all over the floor. I remedied the matter, and Phyllis Patterson looked questioningly at Settle. He rose.

'Would you like to see your patient now, Carstairs?'

I followed him at once. Miss Patterson came with us. We went upstairs and Settle took a key from his pocket.

'He sometimes has a fit of wandering,' he explained. 'So I usually lock the door when I'm away from the house.'

He turned the key in the lock and we went in.

A young man was sitting on the window seat where the last rays of the westerly sun struck broad and yellow. He sat curiously still, rather hunched together, with every muscle relaxed. I thought at first that he was quite unaware of our presence until I suddenly saw that, under immovable lids, he was watching us closely. His eyes dropped as they met mine, and he blinked. But he did not move.

'Come, Arthur,' said Settle cheerfully. 'Miss Patterson and a friend of mine have come to see you.'

But the young fellow on the window seat only blinked. Yet a moment or two later I saw him watching us again – furtively and secretly.

'Want your tea?' asked Settle, still loudly and cheerfully, as though talking to a child.

He set on the table a cup full of milk. I lifted my eyebrows in surprise, and Settle smiled.

'Funny thing,' he said, 'the only drink he'll touch is milk.'

In a moment or two, without undue haste, Sir Arthur uncoiled himself, limb by limb, from his huddled position, and walked slowly over to the table. I recognized suddenly that his movements were absolutely silent, his feet made no sound as they trod. Just as he reached the table he gave a tremendous stretch, poised on one leg forward, the other stretching out behind him. He prolonged this exercise to its utmost extent, and then yawned. Never have I seen such a yawn! It seemed to swallow up his entire face.

He now turned his attention to the milk, bending down to the table until his lips touched the fluid.

Settle answered my inquiring look.

'Won't make use of his hands at all. Seems to have returned to a primitive state. Odd, isn't it?'

I felt Phyllis Patterson shrink against me a little, and I laid my hand soothingly on her arm.

The milk was finished at last, and Arthur Carmichael stretched himself once more, and then with the same quiet noiseless footsteps he regained the window seat, where he sat, huddled up as before, blinking at us.

Miss Patterson drew us out into the corridor. She was trembling all over.

'Oh! Dr Carstairs,' she cried. 'It *isn't* him – that thing in there isn't Arthur! I should feel – I should know – '

I shook my head sadly.

'The brain can play strange tricks, Miss Patterson.'

I confess that I was puzzled by the case. It presented unusual features. Though I had never seen young Carmichael before there was something about his peculiar manner of walking, and the way he blinked, that reminded me of someone or something that I could not quite place.

Our dinner that night was a quiet affair, the burden of conversation being sustained by Lady Carmichael and myself. When the ladies had withdrawn Settle asked me my impression of my hostess.

'I must confess,' I said, 'that for no cause or reason I dislike her intensely. You were quite right, she has Eastern blood, and, I should say, possesses marked occult powers. She is a woman of extraordinary magnetic force.'

Settle seemed on the point of saying something, but checked himself and merely remarked after a minute or two: 'She is absolutely devoted to her little son.'

We sat in the green drawing-room again after dinner. We had just finished coffee and were conversing rather stiffly on the topics of the day when the cat began to miaw piteously for admission outside the door. No one took any notice, and, as I am fond of animals, after a moment or two I rose.

'May I let the poor thing in?' I asked Lady Carmichael.

Her face seemed very white, I thought, but she made a faint gesture of the head which I took as assent and, going to the door, I opened it. But the corridor outside was quite empty.

'Strange,' I said, 'I could have sworn I heard a cat.'

As I came back to my chair I noticed they were all watching me intently. It somehow made me feel a little uncomfortable.

We retired to bed early. Settle accompanied me to my room.

'Got everything you want?' he asked, looking round.

'Yes, thanks.'

He still lingered rather awkwardly as though there was something he wanted to say but could not quite get out.

'By the way,' I remarked, 'you said there was something uncanny about this house? As yet it seems most normal.'

'You call it a cheerful house?'

'Hardly that, under the circumstances. It is obviously under the shadow of a great sorrow. But as regards any abnormal influence, I should give it a clean bill of health.'

'Goodnight,' said Settle abruptly. 'And pleasant dreams.'

Dream I certainly did. Miss Patterson's grey cat seemed to have impressed itself upon my brain. All night long, it seemed to me, I dreamt of the wretched animal.

Awaking with a start, I suddenly realized what had brought the cat so forcibly into my thoughts. The creature was miawing persistently outside my door. Impossible to sleep with that racket going on. I lit my candle and went to the door. But the passage outside my room was empty, though the miawing still continued. A new idea struck me. The unfortunate animal was shut up somewhere, unable to get out. To the left was the end of the passage, where Lady Carmichael's room was situated. I turned therefore to the right and had taken but a few paces when the noise broke out again from behind me. I turned sharply and the sound came again, this time distinctly on the *right* of me.

Something, probably a draught in the corridor, made me shiver, and I went sharply back to my room. Everything was silent now, and I was soon asleep once more – to wake to another glorious summer's day.

As I was dressing I saw from my window the disturber of my night's rest. The grey cat was creeping slowly and stealthily across the lawn. I judged its object of attack to be a small flock of birds who were busy chirruping and preening themselves not far away.

And then a very curious thing happened. The cat came straight on and passed through the midst of the birds, its fur almost brushing against them – and the birds did not fly away. I could not understand it – the thing seemed incomprehensible.

So vividly did it impress me that I could not refrain from mentioning it at breakfast.

'Do you know?' I said to Lady Carmichael, 'that you have a very unusual cat?'

I heard the quick rattle of a cup on a saucer, and I saw Phyllis Patterson, her lips parted and her breath coming quickly, gazing earnestly at me.

There was a moment's silence, and then Lady Carmichael said in a distinctly disagreeable manner: 'I think you must have made a mistake. There is no cat here. I have never had a cat.'

It was evident that I had managed to put my foot in it badly, so I hastily changed the subject.

But the matter puzzled me. Why had Lady Carmichael declared there was no cat in the house? Was it perhaps Miss Patterson's, and its presence concealed from the mistress of the house? Lady Carmichael might have one of those strange antipathies to cats which are so often met with nowadays. It hardly seemed a plausible explanation, but I was forced to rest content with it for the moment.

Our patient was still in the same condition. This time I made a thorough examination and was able to study him more closely than the night before. At my suggestion it was arranged that he should spend as much time with the family as possible. I hoped not only to have a better opportunity of observing him when he was off his guard, but that the ordinary everyday routine might awaken some gleam of intelligence. His demeanour, however, remained unchanged. He was quiet and docile, seemed vacant, but was, in point of fact, intensely and rather slyly watchful. One thing certainly came as a surprise to me, the intense affection he displayed towards his stepmother. Miss Patterson he ignored completely, but he always managed to sit as near Lady Carmichael as possible, and once I saw him rub his head against her shoulder in a dumb expression of love.

I was worried about the case. I could not but feel that there was some clue to the whole matter which had so far escaped me.

'This is a very strange case,' I said to Settle.

'Yes,' said he, 'it's very – suggestive.'

He looked at me – rather furtively, I thought.

'Tell me,' he said. 'He doesn't – remind you of anything?'

The words struck me disagreeably, reminding me of my impression of the day before.

'Remind me of what?' I asked.

He shook his head.

'Perhaps it's my fancy,' he muttered. 'Just my fancy.'

And he would say no more on the matter.

Altogether there was mystery shrouding the affair. I was still obsessed with that baffling feeling of having missed the clue that should elucidate it to me. And concerning a lesser matter there was also mystery. I mean that trifling affair of the grey cat. For some reason or other the thing was getting on my nerves. I dreamed of cats – I continually fancied I heard them. Now and then in the distance I caught a glimpse of the beautiful animal. And the fact that there was some mystery connected with it fretted me unbearably. On a sudden impulse I applied one afternoon to the footman for information.

'Can you tell me anything,' I said, 'about the cat I see?'

'The cat, sir?' He appeared politely surprised.

'Wasn't there – isn't there – a cat?'

'Her ladyship *had* a cat, sir. A great pet. Had to be put away though. A great pity, as it was a beautiful animal.'

'A grey cat?' I asked slowly.

'Yes, sir. A Persian.'

'And you say it was destroyed?'

'Yes, sir.'

'You're quite sure it was destroyed?'

'Oh! quite sure, sir. Her ladyship wouldn't have him sent to the vet – but did it herself. A little less than a week ago now. He's buried out there under the copper beech, sir.' And he went out of the room, leaving me to my meditations.

Why had Lady Carmichael affirmed so positively that she had never had a cat?

I felt an intuition that this trifling affair of the cat was in some way significant. I found Settle and took him aside.

'Settle,' I said. 'I want to ask you a question. Have you, or have you not, both seen and heard a cat in this house?'

He did not seem surprised at the question. Rather did he seem to have been expecting it.

'I've heard it,' he said. 'I've not seen it.'

'But that first day,' I cried. 'On the lawn with Miss Patterson!'

He looked at me very steadily.

'I saw Miss Patterson walking across the lawn. Nothing else.'

I began to understand. 'Then,' I said, 'the cat – ?'

He nodded.

'I wanted to see if you – unprejudiced – would hear what we all hear. . . ?'

'You all hear it then?'

He nodded again.

'It's strange,' I murmured thoughtfully. 'I never heard of a cat haunting a place before.'

I told him what I had learnt from the footman, and he expressed surprise.

'That's news to me. I didn't know that.'

'But what does it mean?' I asked helplessly.

He shook his head. 'Heaven only knows! But I'll tell you, Carstairs – I'm afraid. The – thing's voice sounds – menacing.'

'Menacing?' I said sharply. 'To whom?'

He spread out his hands. 'I can't say.'

It was not till that evening after dinner that I realized the meaning of his words. We were sitting in the green drawing-room, as on the night of my arrival, when it came – the loud insistent miawing of a cat outside the door. But this time it was unmistakably angry in its tone – a fierce cat yowl, long-drawn and menacing. And then as it ceased the brass hook outside the door was rattled violently as by a cat's paw.

Settle started up.

'I swear that's real,' he cried.

He rushed to the door and flung it open.

There was nothing there.

He came back mopping his brow. Phyllis was pale and trembling, Lady Carmichael deathly white. Only Arthur, squatting contentedly like a child, his head against his stepmother's knee, was calm and undisturbed.

Miss Patterson laid her hand on my arm and we went upstairs.

'Oh! Dr Carstairs,' she cried. 'What is it? What does it all mean?'

'We don't know yet, my dear young lady,' I said. 'But I mean to find out. But you mustn't be afraid. I am convinced there is no danger to you personally.'

She looked at me doubtfully. 'You think that?'

'I am sure of it,' I answered firmly. I remembered the loving way the grey cat had twined itself round her feet, and I had no misgivings. The menace was not for her.

I was some time dropping off to sleep, but at length I fell into an uneasy slumber from which I awoke with a sense of shock. I heard a scratching sputtering noise as of something being violently ripped or torn. I sprang out of bed and rushed out into the passage. At the same moment Settle burst out of his room opposite. The sound came from our left.

'You hear it, Carstairs?' he cried. 'You hear it?'

We came swiftly up to Lady Carmichael's door. Nothing had passed us, but the noise had ceased. Our candles glittered blankly on the shiny panels of Lady Carmichael's door. We stared at one another.

'You know what it was?' he half whispered.

I nodded. 'A cat's claws ripping and tearing something.' I shivered a little. Suddenly I gave an exclamation and lowered the candle I held.

'Look here, Settle.'

'Here' was a chair that rested against the wall – and the seat of it was ripped and torn in long strips...

We examined it closely. He looked at me and I nodded.

'Cat's claws,' he said, drawing in his breath sharply. 'Unmistakable.' His eyes went from the chair to the closed door. 'That's the person who is menaced. Lady Carmichael!'

I slept no more that night. Things had come to a pass where something must be done. As far as I knew there was only one person who had the key to the situation. I suspected Lady Carmichael of knowing more than she chose to tell.

She was deathly pale when she came down the next morning, and only toyed with the food on her plate. I was sure that only an iron determination kept her from breaking down. After breakfast I requested a few words with her. I went straight to the point.

'Lady Carmichael,' I said. 'I have reason to believe that you are in very grave danger.'

'Indeed?' She braved it out with wonderful unconcern.

'There is in this house,' I continued, 'a Thing – a Presence – that is obviously hostile to you.'

'What nonsense,' she murmured scornfully. 'As if I believed in any rubbish of that kind.'

'The chair outside your door,' I remarked dryly, 'was ripped to ribbons last night.'

'Indeed?' With raised eyebrows she pretended surprise, but I saw that I had told her nothing she did not know. 'Some stupid practical joke, I suppose.'

'It was not that,' I replied with some feeling. 'And I want you to tell me – for your own sake – ' I paused.

'Tell you what?' she queried.

'Anything that can throw light on the matter,' I said gravely.

She laughed.

'I know nothing,' she said. 'Absolutely nothing.'

And no warnings of danger could induce her to relax the statement. Yet I was convinced that she *did* know a great deal more than any of us, and held some clue to the affair of which we were absolutely ignorant. But I saw that it was quite impossible to make her speak.

I determined, however, to take every precaution that I could, convinced as I was that she was menaced by a very real and immediate danger. Before she went to her room the following night Settle and I made a thorough examination of it. We had agreed that we would take it in turns to watch in the passage.

I took the first watch, which passed without incident, and at three o'clock Settle relieved me. I was tired after my sleepless night the day before, and dropped off at once. And I had a very curious dream.

I dreamed that the grey cat was sitting at the foot of my bed and that its eyes were fixed on mine with a curious pleading. Then, with the ease of dreams, I knew that the creature wanted me to follow it. I did so, and it led me down the great staircase and right to the opposite wing of the house to a room which was obviously the library. It paused there at one side of the room and raised its front paws till they rested on one of the lower shelves of books, while it gazed at me once more with that same moving look of appeal.

Then – cat and library faded, and I awoke to find that morning had come.

Settle's watch had passed without incident, but he was keenly interested to hear of my dream. At my request he took me to the library, which coincided in every particular with my vision of it. I could even point out the exact spot where the animal had given me that last sad look.

We both stood there in silent perplexity. Suddenly an idea occurred to me, and I stopped to read the title of the book in that exact place. I noticed that there was a gap in the line.

'Some book has been taken out of here,' I said to Settle.

He stooped also to the shelf.

'Hallo,' he said. 'There's a nail at the back here that has torn off a fragment of the missing volume.'

He detached the little scrap of paper with care. It was not more than an inch square – but on it were printed two significant words: 'The cat. . .'

'This thing gives me the creeps,' said Settle. 'It's simply horribly uncanny.'

'I'd give anything to know,' I said, 'what book it is that is missing from here. Do you think there is any way of finding out?'

'May be a catalogue somewhere. Perhaps Lady Carmichael –'

I shook my head.

'Lady Carmichael will tell you nothing.'

'You think so?'

'I am sure of it. While we are guessing and feeling about in the dark Lady Carmichael *knows*. And for reasons of her own she will say nothing. She prefers to run a most horrible risk sooner than break silence.'

The day passed with an uneventfulness that reminded me of the calm before a storm. And I had a strange feeling that the problem was near solution. I was groping about in the dark, but soon I should see. The facts were all there, ready, waiting for the little flash of illumination that should weld them together and show out their significance.

And come it did! In the strangest way!

It was when we were all sitting together in the green drawing-room as usual after dinner. We had been very silent. So noiseless indeed was the room that a little mouse ran across the floor – and in an instant the thing happened.

With one long spring Arthur Carmichael leapt from his chair. His quivering body was swift as an arrow on the mouse's track. It had disappeared behind the wainscoting, and there he crouched – watchful – his body still trembling with eagerness.

It was horrible! I have never known such a paralysing moment. I was no longer puzzled as to that something that Arthur Carmichael reminded me of with his stealthy feet and watching eyes. And in a flash an explanation, wild, incredible, unbelievable, swept into my mind. I rejected it as impossible – unthinkable! But I could not dismiss it from my thoughts.

I hardly remember what happened next. The whole thing seemed blurred and unreal. I know that somehow we got upstairs and said our goodnights briefly, almost with a dread of meeting each other's eyes, lest we should see there some confirmation of our own fears.

Settle established himself outside Lady Carmichael's door to take the first watch, arranging to call me at three a.m. I had no special fears for Lady Carmichael; I was too taken up with my fantastic impossible theory. I told myself it was impossible – but my mind returned to it, fascinated.

And then suddenly the stillness of the night was disturbed. Settle's voice rose in a shout, calling me. I rushed out into the corridor.

He was hammering and pounding with all his might on Lady Carmichael's door.

'Devil take the woman!' he cried. 'She's locked it!'

'But –'

'*It's* in there, man! In with her! Can't you hear it?'

From behind the locked door a long-drawn cat yowl sounded fiercely. And then following it a horrible scream – and another. . . I recognized Lady Carmichael's voice.

'The door!' I yelled. 'We must break it in. In another minute we shall be too late.'

We set our shoulders against it, and heaved with all our might. It gave with a crash – and we almost fell into the room.

Lady Carmichael lay on the bed bathed in blood. I have seldom seen a more horrible sight. Her heart was still beating, but her injuries were terrible, for the skin of the throat was all ripped and torn... Shuddering, I whispered: 'The Claws...' A thrill of superstitious horror ran over me.

I dressed and bandaged the wounds carefully and suggested to Settle that the exact nature of the injuries had better be kept secret, especially from Miss Patterson. I wrote out a telegram for a hospital nurse, to be despatched as soon as the telegraph office was open.

The dawn was now stealing in at the window. I looked out on the lawn below.

'Get dressed and come out,' I said abruptly to Settle. 'Lady Carmichael will be all right now.'

He was soon ready, and we went out into the garden together.

'What are you going to do?'

'Dig up the cat's body,' I said briefly. 'I must be sure –'

I found a spade in a toolshed and we set to work beneath the large copper beech tree. At last our digging was rewarded. It was not a pleasant job. The animal had been dead a week. But I saw what I wanted to see.

'That's the cat,' I said. 'The identical cat I saw the first day I came here.'

Settle sniffed. An odour of bitter almonds was still perceptible.

'Prussic acid,' he said.

I nodded.

'What are you thinking?' he asked curiously.

'What you think too!'

My surmise was no new one to him – it had passed through his brain also, I could see.

'It's impossible,' he murmured. 'Impossible! It's against all science – all nature...' His voice tailed off in a shudder. 'That mouse last night,' he said. 'But – oh! it couldn't be!'

'Lady Carmichael,' I said, 'is a very strange woman. She has occult powers – hypnotic powers. Her forebears came from the East. Can we know what use she might have made of these powers over a weak lovable nature such as Arthur Carmichael's? And remember, Settle, if Arthur Carmichael remains a hopeless imbecile, devoted to her, the whole property is practically hers and her son's – whom you have told me she adores. And Arthur was going to be married!'

'But what are we going to do, Carstairs?'

'There's nothing to be done,' I said. 'We'll do our best though to stand between Lady Carmichael and vengeance.'

Lady Carmichael improved slowly. Her injuries healed themselves as well as could be expected – the scars of that terrible assault she would probably bear to the end of her life.

I had never felt more helpless. The power that defeated us was still at large, undefeated, and though quiescent for the minute we could hardly regard it as doing otherwise than biding its time. I was determined upon one thing. As soon as Lady Carmichael was well enough to be moved she must be taken away from Wolden. There was just a chance that the terrible manifestation might be unable to follow her. So the days went on.

I had fixed September 18th as the date of Lady Carmichael's removal. It was on the morning of the 14th when the unexpected crisis arose.

I was in the library discussing details of Lady Carmichael's case with Settle when an agitated housemaid rushed into the room.

'Oh! sir,' she cried. 'Be quick! Mr Arthur – he's fallen into the pond. He stepped on the punt and it pushed off with him, and he overbalanced and fell in! I saw it from the window.'

I waited for no more, but ran straight out of the room followed by Settle. Phyllis was just outside and had heard the maid's story. She ran with us.

'But you needn't be afraid,' she cried. 'Arthur is a magnificent swimmer.'

I felt forebodings, however, and redoubled my pace. The surface of the pond was unruffled. The empty punt floated lazily about – but of Arthur there was no sign.

Settle pulled off his coat and his boots. 'I'm going in,' he said. 'You take the boathook and fish about from the other punt. It's not very deep.'

Very long the time seemed as we searched vainly. Minute followed minute. And then, just as we were despairing, we found him, and bore the apparently lifeless body of Arthur Carmichael to shore.

As long as I live I shall never forget the hopeless agony of Phyllis's face.

'Not – not –' her lips refused to frame the dreadful word.

'No, no, my dear,' I cried. 'We'll bring him round, never fear.'

But inwardly I had little hope. He had been under water for half an hour. I sent off Settle to the house for hot blankets and other necessaries, and began myself to apply artificial respiration.

We worked vigorously with him for over an hour but there was no sign of life. I motioned to Settle to take my place again, and I approached Phyllis.

'I'm afraid,' I said gently, 'that it is no good. Arthur is beyond our help.'

She stayed quite still for a moment and then suddenly flung herself down on the lifeless body.

'Arthur!' she cried desperately. 'Arthur! Come back to me! Arthur – come back – come back!'

Her voice echoed away into silence. Suddenly I touched Settle's arm. 'Look!' I said.

A faint tinge of colour crept into the drowned man's face. I felt his heart.

'Go on with the respiration,' I cried. 'He's coming round!'

The moments seemed to fly now. In a marvellously short time his eyes opened.

Then suddenly I realized the difference. *These were intelligent eyes, human eyes...*

They rested on Phyllis.

'Hallo! Phil,' he said weakly. 'Is it you? I thought you weren't coming until tomorrow.'

She could not yet trust herself to speak but she smiled at him. He looked round with increasing bewilderment.

'But, I say, where am I? And – how rotten I feel! What's the matter with me? Hallo, Dr Settle!'

'You've been nearly drowned – that's what's the matter,' returned Settle grimly.

Sir Arthur made a grimace.

'I've always heard it was beastly coming back afterwards! But how did it happen? Was I walking in my sleep?'

Settle shook his head.

'We must get him to the house,' I said, stepping forward.

He stared at me, and Phyllis introduced me. 'Dr Carstairs, who is staying here.'

We supported him between us and started for the house. He looked up suddenly as though struck by an idea.

'I say, doctor, this won't knock me up for the 12th, will it?'

'The 12th?' I said slowly, 'you mean the 12th of August?'

'Yes – next Friday.'

'Today is the 14th of September,' said Settle abruptly.

His bewilderment was evident.

'But – but I thought it was the 8th of August? I must have been ill then?'

Phyllis interposed rather quickly in her gentle voice.

'Yes,' she said, 'you've been very ill.'

He frowned. 'I can't understand it. I was perfectly all right when I went to bed last night – at least of course it wasn't really last night. I had dreams though, I remember, dreams...' His brow furrowed itself still more as he strove to remember. 'Something – what was it? – something dreadful – someone had done it to me – and I was angry – desperate... And then I dreamed I was a cat – yes, a cat! Funny, wasn't it? But it wasn't a funny dream. It was more – horrible! But I can't remember. It all goes when I think.'

I laid my hand on his shoulder. 'Don't try to think, Sir Arthur,' I said gravely. 'Be content – to forget.'

He looked at me in a puzzled way and nodded. I heard Phyllis draw a breath of relief. We had reached the house.

'By the way,' said Sir Arthur suddenly, 'where's the mater?'

'She has been – ill,' said Phyllis after a momentary pause.

'Oh! poor old mater!' His voice rang with genuine concern. 'Where is she? In her room?'

'Yes,' I said, 'but you had better not disturb –'

The words froze on my lips. The door of the drawing-room opened and Lady Carmichael, wrapped in a dressing-gown, came out into the hall.

Her eyes were fixed on Arthur, and if ever I have seen a look of absolute guilt-stricken terror I saw it then. Her face was hardly human in its frenzied terror. Her hand went to her throat.

Arthur advanced towards her with boyish affection.

'Hello, mater! So you've been knocked up too? I say, I'm awfully sorry.'

She shrank back before him, her eyes dilating. Then suddenly, with the shriek of a doomed soul, she fell backwards through the open door.

I rushed and bent over her, then beckoned to Settle.

'Hush,' I said. 'Take him upstairs quietly and then come down again. Lady Carmichael is dead.'

He returned in a few minutes.

'What was it?' he asked. 'What caused it?'

'Shock,' I said grimly. 'The shock of seeing Arthur Carmichael, the *real* Arthur Carmichael, restored to life! Or you may call it, as I prefer to, the judgement of God!'

'You mean –' he hesitated.

I looked at him in the eyes so that he understood.

'A life for life,' I said significantly.

'But –'

'Oh! I know that a strange and unforeseen accident permitted the spirit of Arthur Carmichael to return to his body. But, nevertheless, Arthur Carmichael was murdered.'

He looked at me half fearfully. 'With prussic acid?' he asked in a low tone.

'Yes,' I answered. 'With prussic acid.'

Settle and I have never spoken of our belief. It is not one likely to be credited. According to the orthodox point of view Arthur Carmichael merely suffered from loss of memory, Lady Carmichael lacerated her own throat in a temporary fit of mania, and the apparition of the Grey Cat was mere imagination.

But there are two facts that to my mind are unmistakable. One is the ripped chair in the corridor. The other is even more significant. A catalogue of the library was found, and after exhaustive search it was proved that the missing volume was an ancient and curious work on the possibilities of the metamorphosis of human beings into animals!

One thing more. I am thankful to say that Arthur knows nothing. Phyllis has locked the secret of those weeks in her own heart, and she will never, I am sure, reveal them to the husband she loves so dearly, and who came back across the barrier of the grave at the call of her voice.

# Blackberries

## *Roger Clarke*

Edward arranged the soldiers rank and file in scattered lines on the grass. All advanced (acting under orders) while he provided many blood-curdling and realistic battle cries and death screams. They moved relentlessly in the push for the monastery: without air-cover or tank support, bravely and with speed. Edward began to find their range with his spring Howitzer. A devastating volley of matchsticks began falling on their heads to destroy them utterly and kill morale, boom. He knew it was probably against the Geneva Convention to use such weapons against troops, but he had no scruples; some things just had to be done, and this was war. Anyhow, at least he wasn't using his water-pistol.

Edward was sitting on the big lawn behind the house. Trucks, lorries, special vehicles, tanks and plastic soldiers were all spread out before him like a picnic. It was a hot afternoon for late summer with the sun still trying its hardest. The heat was ponderous, and the haze gathered its thoughts in the distance.

Edward fired off more matchsticks, and then the missiles, which he picked up and reloaded. It was so easy to kill them off. However, it was not long before he tired of such delicate and exacting methods of slaughter, and reached over to take his red-pocked cricket bat, jumping up, tucking the spatulate end into the side and aiming carelessly. A deathly rattle from his throat breech – ack-ack-ack – and that was enough; he sneered at the slain with godlike triumph, amused to see them fall into the grass. Running up to the troops like a footballer, he gave an almighty kick, which sent them everywhere and into the flower beds. 'No prisoners!' he shouted. 'Fix bayonets!'

He looked around to check his position and was suddenly aware that a branch moved in the azaleas to his right. A sniper! Must have got a bead on his cigarette – had to hit the dirt. He rolled over several times and took aim. Momentarily, the sun caught in his eye and he was dazzled white; he blinked several times and his vision began to trickle back in a tone of sepia. There was movement all right, but it was nothing in the bushes as he had supposed. A figure was emerging from beside the crisp-cut yew hedge to his left. It was Charlie.

Fancy him creeping up like that, cunning and quiet, like a spy. Some friend, to crawl along out of sight.

'What are you doing, trying to sneak up and frighten me?' Edward demanded, rapidly getting to his feet in case Charlie should take a run at him when he was vulnerable.

'Worried about being frightened?'

'That's how you get shot.'

Charlie, hands bulging in his trouser pockets, began a slow, ambiguous saunter over the short distance to where Edward stood ready for him. But he neither said nor did a thing. Dispassionately, but like a connoisseur, he eyed the carnage of the battle spread about. He nosed at a truck with his foot. Edward looked baffled; he did not seem to want a fight.

'How odd,' said Charlie in theatrical manner as he stooped to retrieve a soldier without a head, holding it up with two fingers, like something dainty. 'You think I was spying, do you not?' he went on seriously. 'Well, I'll tell you, I wasn't, so that is it.' His voice was very smooth and sure. 'But I have heard that another's eyes are even now upon you.'

Edward looked instinctively towards the cake-white Palladian house at the end of the lawn, but could discern no face at any window, only squares of blank glass with oblique white reflections in each one.

'She's washing leeks and looking out,' said Charlie. 'The basin is all full of grit and slugs.'

'You're a slug.' Edward snatched the headless soldier from Charlie's hand.

'Leek and potato soup. That's the first course.'

'What course, Slug?'

'For your dinner, dumbo. Or should I say John's dinner, since it *is* for him when he comes tomorrow.'

'No, it isn't John's dinner.'

'Jolly for you, Ed, having a new dad. Is it Christmas, I ask?'

Edward did not think it was on to tease people about their parents – that was what they always felt at school. Charlie ought to know better.

'It doesn't matter,' retorted Edward airily. 'It isn't as if my mother can marry someone else, is it? She is allowed friends. She can't marry John, so that's all right.'

'' Course she can. Your father is dead.'

'But she is still married to him.'

'Look – he's dead. He's in a coffin. He's filed underground in the great filing cabinet of the world. He's gone – I mean, permanently gone, right? She can marry anyone she likes.'

'No.'

'She can go to an airport and say: "Right, I'll have him!"''

Edward threw a very hard punch, but it missed. He would have thrown another, but Charlie was beginning to walk away. Let him go.

'What is the worry?' said Charlie from near the yew hedge. 'You can get used to him. You can get used to anything in time, even torture.'

'No,' said Edward desperately. 'No, I won't get used to him. He's not my father. I won't get . . .'

'Make your mother happy for a change. How nice. Stop her hating you just once.'

'She doesn't hate me.'

'She does, old man. You are getting in the way of her remarriage. Be sensible. Compromise. He'll give you presents.'

'You'd better go,' said Edward stiffly. And, indeed, Charlie seemed entirely to vanish, to dissolve into an expanse of colour.

'Ed-ward?' The sound was unmistakable. Two long-drawn-out syllables coming across the daisied lawn. 'Ed-ward?' He lay flat on the ground and tried to turn green, to merge in. She would want him to do something for her. 'Are you doing anything?' she would say, knowing full well that he was. 'Lay the table.' 'Dig the potatoes.'

'I can see-ee you, Ed-ward.'

Edward peered through the figures with which he covered his face, and realized she probably could. He got up, grudgingly. Bits of grass stuck to his clothes.

'Hurry up and come here a minute.'

The soldiers he left in rotting heaps; the lorries he abandoned to belch their tarry smoke and explode. He went round to the front. He preferred the front of the house because it had a huge, white staircase which reminded him of history and carriages. If he went through the grand door, perhaps the footman missing for so long would suddenly appear and bow for his gloves.

All the doors of all the rooms were open, and so were the windows, to let in what little air there was. Sunlight wallowed in the woodpolished, ormolu-clocked atmosphere of the ancient lime-green walls. To get to the kitchen meant a trip through the servants' quarters, which were very dim, quite cool and with a sadness somehow accentuated by the plain, glassy tiles.

Even before he got there, Edward could hear his mother splashing water about as she washed the vegetables to get the garden out of them. She sliced off the tousled roots. As Edward entered the room, she did not turn round.

'Are you doing anything?' she said.

'Only playing,' Edward replied.

'With whom? By yourself?'

'No, with Charlie.'

'Charles who?'

'Charlie Charlie. I don't know his other name.'

She turned to examine him, coolly, in a superior way. She picked at the ends of her rubber gloves and they made a wet, snapping noise. The way she looked, Edward might have been a side of bacon.

'You mean you didn't ask?' she said, in her what-an-imbecile-for-a-son voice. 'How could you be playing with a boy and you don't even know his name? You are truly absurd. You are just saying this to make me angry because you know it does. Of course you have his name.'

'I do not.'

She put her hand to her head as if she had a headache and heaved a huge sigh of weary exasperation.

'Now what Charleses are there nearby? Charles Stock, Charles Randolph . . .' She was talking to herself now. Perhaps he should tell her *all* about Charlie. She would have a fit. He smiled cleverly in the knowledge of his power over her.

She turned to him again. 'Where is his address?'

'Nowhere,' said Edward.

'Never-Never Land. I might have guessed it, too. Yet another ghostly companion, another Peter Pan.'

'Charlie.'

'Why do you persistently lie to me, Edward?'

'I don't lie.'

'Is it better to have a liar or a lunatic as a son, I wonder.'

'Charlie is real and I like him.'

She splashed the water in increasing agitation, and some went on the floor. 'It doesn't really matter. Choose who you like to be your friends. Make up all the ones you want! You won't get them any other way. When I remember how you treated those children I invited over – it is just too much – and what their mothers must have thought of me . . .'

Edward's mother had invited a batch of about twelve, with only their age in common, to a Sunday tea in the vague hope that they would play together. Edward suggested Cowboys and Indians, which was generally approved, and they managed to tie the girls to trees quite far from the house so they could not shout help. The boys had left them there, mewing and boo-hooing and yelling for help, although he had explained it was no good doing so. The boys, strutting with their success, agreed on Pirates next. He got them all into the boat on the lake and gave it a great push-off, with the oars. Charlie appeared and they had a long laugh.

'I suppose,' his mother was saying, 'you are too silly and immature to get on sensibly with other people. Not that it makes it any easier for me, but I do not suppose you think about that . . .'

Edward stared at the plates on the dresser. They had a blue geometry that circled round and round like a bicycle wheel.

'Perhaps no one else is good enough for you, is that it?'

Now she was getting brisk and tight-lipped, in one of her starchy moods when anything he said would be wrong. He wanted to leave, but he knew she would love him to do that. He would never hear the end of it. Another 'Tales of My Dreadful Child' to astonish and enthral one's drinks-party guests. Other parents might nod in deep sympathy.

'How was he going to get out of this? Perhaps he should try to tell the truth – that's what she always said he ought to do – make her understand everything. He spoke with hesitation.

'I – I just don't like . . . everyone.'

The lecturing tone switched in immediately.

'We all,' she said, in a sage way, 'must be prepared to make sacrifices, Edward. If we do not enjoy the social life, we must at least be civil and polite to others. It is simply a question of being considerate! It isn't much to ask. You, on the other hand, cannot even bother yourself with common courtesy.'

'No,' said Edward. She was so stupid, it was funny.

'You dislike John and you make no effort to hide it.' She was really getting steamed up now.

'No,' said Edward, with an infuriating grin.

'You are so abominably rude to everyone, it is an embarrassment to be your mother! There is no excuse for it but childish tantrums. John has offered to come and watch your football and take you out to tea from school . . .'

Shortcake in an empty resort café overlooking a dismal Channel seaswell.

'. . . He's tried very hard to be friendly to you. He has even tried to be a father to you.'

Edward had been standing all the time, as if in the dock, but now he moved over to the table, took out a chair, sat down, and stared sullenly down at his shoes. 'There is,' he said quietly, 'no need for him to do that.'

His mother laughed, misunderstanding. 'School meals can't be that bad, then.'

'School is all right.'

'Perhaps,' she said in her clever voice, 'you should stay there through the holidays, since you like it so much.'

'But no one else would be there. It would be empty. That would be no fun.'

'Oh, thank you, your worship. So home isn't so bad, after all.' His mother, to Edward's great surprise, seemed genuinely pleased. Her tone softened.

'I am making dinner for tomorrow night, when John comes,' she said. 'It will be only us three.'

Edward decided to anticipate her. 'What do you want me to do?'

'Would you go to Barley Lane and pick me a basketful of blackberries? I shall make ice-cream and freeze it overnight. You'll like that.'

'But that is miles. It will take me hours. Blackberries are stupid to have for pudding.'

'It is certainly not stupid, Edward. John told me he liked them. So we shall have them, whether you want to or not. You can have bread and cheese.'

Blackberries – stupid, sour, pippy things. That was her funeral, if she wanted them. He didn't want them. John, John, John.

'The best blackberries,' said Edward informatively, 'are at Dodpits. I've seen them.'

'No, darling. I am told the Barley Lane crop are especially fine this year. Will you go there, please, like a good boy?'

'They are better at Dodpits,' he repeated firmly.

She left the sink and came nearer, to concentrate on him. She still had a knife in her hand. She looked very angry.

'I have told you before that Dodpits is unsafe and out of bounds. Of course you have been there – you never take any notice of what I tell you. It would have served you right if you had fallen and broken something. Now you will go to Barley Lane, and that is final.'

'If you want nice blackberries,' he retorted indignantly, 'then you should let me go to Dodpits. But since I am not eating them, it doesn't bother me if they are horrible.'

'You cannot resist the temptation to make life more difficult for me, can you? You have eaten them before now.'

'Yes, and now I have changed my mind. I am allowed to change my mind. From now on I hate them and they make me sick.'

'You will eat what you are given, and be grateful.'

Just think of all the people who are starving . . . The words remained unsaid. The two were glaring at each other, each trying to superimpose their will upon the other in a terrible, mute battle.

'I don't suppose,' his mother hissed, 'that this urge to go to Dodpits has anything to do with the dead crows on the fence outside Barley Lane?'

Edward's heart sank. She knew. He must have told her once . . .

She laughed victoriously when she saw the change in his face. 'You poor darling,' she cried. 'So frightened of such silly dead things, frightened like a girl. I ought to tie your hair in ribbons.'

Edward felt such utter anger, he wanted to hit her, he wanted to tell her exactly what he thought of her in the way she always told him what she thought of him.

'I am going to Dodpits, Mother.' His voice was winter cold. He about-turned and began to march away towards the garden. Through his daze, he was aware that his mother was running after him, waving and shaking her hands, shouting at him. For a moment he thought she would attack him.

'Then beware of the dead man who lives at Dodpits,' she was yelling insanely. 'He feels like a slug and moves like a worm. His eyes have fallen out, but he can still smell you a mile off. He crawls along the ground out of his hole in the earth lined with ... with tombstones and sheep guts. And he will slither up behind you when you aren't looking, and suddenly you will feel his dead grey fingers crunching your leg bones, and then he will drag you away to ...'

She had stopped at the back door and her voice was fading away as Edward crossed the garden.

Barley Lane was about half a mile away, across a road and some fields. Dodpits was just past it, farther on.

Edward walked through a particularly large meadow, full of yellow flowers and smelling sweet as tea. He was aware of a great summery heat bubbling all about him. He could not think much; his mind hardly seemed to be working. The sky above was so wide, the clouds pulled out in a thin gauze up very high.

After that hedge ended there, in a little distance, it would curve inwards and be replaced by a wire fence. The entrance of Barley Lane was kept by an odd metal turnstile to keep animals out.

The crows, when he smelt them, when he saw them, made no difference. Five reeking little bundles of black feathers sticking to exposed bone were gibbeted from the fence beside the entrance to Barley Lane. The weight of their bodies had stretched their necks into a long strand of grey steel cable, which pressure had made their beaks open in a permanent stinking caw of defiance.

Edward felt a little light-headed and sick at their presence, but they no longer seemed to worry him. Certainly, they were not the reason he walked without hesitation straight past Barley Lane.

Dodpits had been a quarry for limestone since the Industrial Revolution and had been abandoned for fifty years. It was supposed to be dangerous, full of potholes and crumbling rock, and there were notices everywhere saying 'Danger! Keep Out'. There was a path down to its dark hollow, and that was where the blackberries grew. Its entrance was gated and chained up. When you got over the gate, you had to be careful of the barbed wire twisted around the top bar as a vicious afterthought. Everything clattered, and the chains jangled as Edward traversed the barricade.

The Dodpits path was a steady slope down. It wound round and round in a series of concentric circles until it reached the quarry itself. Everything there was unkempt and unused; the path was almost overgrown. The blackberry bushes had nearly closed the gap between them, and knee-length grass marked what had once been a busy thoroughfare.

There was a curious claustrophobic atmosphere in the path, a kind of muffled dreaminess brought on by the sun, the lazy Chalkland Blue butterflies, and mostly by the huge walls of vigorously growing bramble that towered about seven feet on either side.

It was really too early for blackberries, but he could find them if he tried hard enough. The plants were at several stages at once: there were still many flowers – but some were faded or wilted, their loosened petals fluttering down upon him and sticking to his hair and clothes. Many blackberries were green and skinny, or reddish purple, wizened and bristled like old men. A few were just right. Some were gouty, overweight portwiners who burst in your hand and stained them mauve.

On the way out of the kitchen, he had grabbed a cardboard basket with a tin handle of the type commonly used for fruit picking, and now he began to fill it with a slow but steady supply. They made a pleasing noise as they hit the base of the basket. Tap, tap. After a while the bottom was filled up with fruit, and it did not make the same sound.

When he had picked a fair number, he stopped for a moment to look around. For a blissful while he had been totally absorbed in his task, without a care. He had barely noticed his steady progress along the path, and by now he was quite deeply into Dodpits. The brambles were just as high, but it was now somewhat darker, because of the descent towards the quarry. The plants were just as argumentative, scratching at his hand and refusing to let go of a blackberry.

Edward stooped to lift up the canopy of leaves near the ground, where there were often the most to be discovered. As he looked up again, to his great surprise he saw someone standing not very far away from him, almost obscured by the next bend.

Edward did not recognize him. He was quite tall, dressed in a long and tattered coat, with a broad-rimmed black velvet hat. Edward felt a bit annoyed that someone else was there, destroying the welcome solitude. It was strange the way he just stood there, not moving, staring at a sandy bank full of rabbit holes.

What was so interesting about rabbits? He must be a professor of rabbitology. Maybe he was doing rabbits for TV, like David

Attenborough. Of course, they were great friends, shared notes. Maybe he could get him David Attenborough's autograph. Maybe he was the dead man.

He didn't know it was the dead man; he couldn't know for sure. Why did he have to go and think that? Could be anyone at all. He could clear it up by going up to him and seeing who he was. He could do that. What if it *was* the dead man, what then? There would be no chance of escape. He would be in his hands.

Of course, he *could* just turn around and slip back out of the lane, without any fuss. No need to go up to the strange tall man with the hat. Quietly work his way back up the path. He had enough blackberries to pass off. He could say he could not find any more. Hopefully, his mother would taste the Dodpits in them.

But as he was preparing to leave, something very disturbing happened. He glimpsed something very small and pink in one of the rabbit holes. The man must be looking at it. As he looked, Edward saw it was a rabbit, bald and bloated through the ravage of myxomatosis.

Edward saw then that the man wore no socks. He wore no shoes. His feet were an ugly whiteness against the ground.

Now the man cocked his head, as if to listen. He tested the air, smelling it like a fox.

He knew Edward was there behind him. He was the dead man.

Edward almost dropped the basket in fright as he began to run back the way he had come; he did not know how far it was. All he knew was that he had to run and get out of there as quickly as he could.

His clothes kept catching upon thorns; the leaves of the bushes rustled and rustled more than they needed to as he ran past, as if they were trying to give him away. And the grass swished at his feet and slowed him down. All this noise and commotion would give him away; the dead man must have heard by now and would be after him in a flash.

Because the path was a spiral there was always a corner which you never came round, there was always somewhere out of sight, something you could not see. Round and round went Edward. He was becoming dizzy as well as out of breath, and was beginning to get a great, moaning stitch in his side. It was farther than he thought, the entrance; he would have to slow down soon whether he liked it or not; he was becoming exhausted. He looked over his shoulder and could see nothing in pursuit. He began to trot, then to walk. Then he stopped altogether, panting.

But the noise of his flight did not stop when he did. It continued in a swishing, boiling rush that grew louder and louder as whatever it was, moving at speed through the undergrowth, came towards him.

Edward began a tired, terrified run once more. This all had been a trap; he felt he was in a lobsterpot, a labyrinth, a working nightmare of a hot summer day with the cliffs of bramble rising dense and high all around him, so high, high, he felt they would topple inwards and the weight crush him. And although he was running still, on and on, he was unwilling to go too fast because any moment could reveal the dead man waiting before him with arms opened wide to snap shut, and every flagging footstep might have the dead man clutching at his heels. He pushed himself on and on and on in a terrible monotony, and still he came no nearer an escape. The path seemed a complete circle. Was it his imagination, or was there no longer a slope to climb?

He stopped for a second without realizing what he was doing, and after he had done so there was a powerful feeling that whatever had been pursuing him was no longer there.

Edward began to walk a little. He looked forlornly into the basket, which was almost empty. The blackberries had fallen out while he was running.

Just up ahead there seemed to be a widening of the path into an area of close-cropped grass, overshadowed by an oak. He would sit down there awhile. He could see things coming more easily, if they came.

Very cautiously, he approached the spot, looking around and listening for the least whisper of the dead man. It was a relief to find a place not cramped and crowded in by vast bramble bushes. There was a bit of space here, a bit of air. He sat beneath the tree and, as he did so, he realized why the grass was as short as it was: rabbits. It could easily have been a rabbit in the undergrowth. He still had no evidence there was any dead man.

Yet it was just the sort of thing likely to happen: if he was to gain a false sense of security, dismiss it all like a logical adult the dead man really *would* creep up and grab him ... that was exactly what would happen. He was not going to be fooled. He knew now it was the dead man, and he knew he had to keep vigilant.

He was not entirely sure he recognized this place, though that was stupid; he would have had to have gone past it before. And there were no paths leading off elsewhere, as far as he knew. Yet he must somehow have strayed onto a path he never realized was there. He had no idea where he was. He was completely lost.

He could climb the tree, of course, and see from there where he was.

He stumbled to his feet and searched eagerly for a foothold, looking up into the twisted branches of the oak.

It was a bat.

He was sure it was a bat; and when he knew that it was not, it was too late. Something that had been squatting on the branches above his head now fell heavily upon him.

The skin was the colour of stale, coagulated cream. Its eyes were without eyes, like the crows hung up. Its arms were thin as bones and covered in a glutinous slime.

The coat had given the illusion of wings.

Emaciated fingers were in hands that squeezed round his throat. There was an overpowering smell of puppies left in rain barrels. The flesh smeared and spread like fishpaste on his face.

He struggled for a while, until his eyes began to glaze and bulge. He wheezed, coughed, tried to speak.

'You're not real!' he gargled thickly. 'My mother made you up to frighten me . . .'

And his darkening tongue began to poke rudely from between his teeth, purple as a very ripe blackberry.

# The Moon Web

## *Adrian Cole*

Tobias the gardener bent down outside the high window of the kitchens and attended to the small shrubs that were growing there. It was a bright day, with hardly a puff of wind, and the voices that came to the ears of Tobias from the small window carried clearly, so that he could hear every word. He was not one for gossip and, as a rule, kept well clear of the kitchen staff, who seemed to revel in it. However, for once the introspective gardener was intrigued by what he heard.

'Bound to be some changes here,' came the first female voice.

'How's that, then?' said the other.

'Amelia's not a child any more. She was no more than a skinny, ill-mannered brat when she went off to that Swiss finishing school. See her now that she's back, though! Quite the young woman. Beautiful, too. Got a mind of her own.'

'Yes, her father was too fond of her. Spoiled her something rotten. You think she's outgrown all her old ways?'

'Maybe. Those fêtes and gymkhanas that her father used to hold – I think we'll see them again before long.'

'Her brother won't like that. Since they've managed the estate, things have been very quiet. They won't appreciate any reckless squandering of the family money.'

'Yes, but Amelia shares the inheritance. You forget – she's come of age now. You mark my words, she'll want to change things.'

'In a way I hope she does. I liked the old times. Plenty of life. It's been very dull here since Nathan Darlington died.'

Tobias shuddered as he finished his work, moving away quietly. So the beautiful young woman he had seen the other day was Amelia, sister of the two Darlington brothers. Tobias, who was not an attractive man, and one who kept well to himself, had felt some alien emotion stir in his breast as he had seen the girl, though he had quickly smothered it. Now he prayed that there would not be changes, for he was well content with the subdued life of the manor.

Over the course of the next few months, however, it quickly became apparent that Amelia certainly did intend to alter things at the big house. In fact, she began to bend her brothers to her will, and the ways of their father were revived. There were parties and social functions. People thronged to the manor, not least of all to meet the delightful beauty who seemed to be running things. Eliot and Daniel, both solicitors of repute, allowed their sister to have her head, though with some trepidation, for she did indeed have a share of the Darlington fortune.

Tobias led a sheltered life at the best of times, but now he found it less easy to remain insular. His feelings for Amelia were confused – she praised his work (the gardens and lawns were always immaculate) but she caused him more toil by having so many outsiders visit the estate. Still, Tobias found himself irresistibly drawn to her; her natural beauty and freshness stirred him in a way that he had never experienced before. Naturally, he tried to smother his feelings, being a humble gardener, and he contented himself by drinking steadily in one of his local haunts in the village. Meanwhile, there were a good many young men of substance who courted Amelia, but she mocked and teased them all coquettishly, attaching herself to none.

It was during a spell of remarkably good weather, when the sun blazed down in an almost Mediterranean fashion, that Tobias came close to stumbling over Amelia as she lay in a secluded part of the extensive gardens, sleek with sun tan oil, all but naked in the tiny, provocative bikini that clung to her slender, golden figure. She was alone, stretched out on a blanket, like a magnificent nymph of the woods. Tobias sucked in his breath and drew back into the shadows of the surrounding trees, but Amelia's head jerked up, her sharp ears catching the sound of rustling leaves.

'Is there somebody there?' she challenged, but she was smiling as she sat up, stretching like a cat, her body glistening. Tobias felt his heart lurch, but he remained motionless. 'Who is there? Tobias? Is it you? You'd better not be playing games with me! Come out at once!'

Reluctantly, Tobias shuffled out of the undergrowth and crossed the lawn to her. She made no attempt to get up, settling back on her elbows as she studied him.

'So it was you.' She appeared to be enjoying his discomfort.

'Your pardon, miss. I was working. I had no mind to disturb you.'

'What were you hoping to see?' she said, her eyes teasing him. She sat up and her breasts quivered. Tobias dragged his gaze from them.

'Nothing, miss. I didn't know you were here.'

'Yes, well I thought this would be a good spot to get away from everyone.'

'No one comes here, miss,' affirmed Tobias. 'If I'd known, I'd have kept *my* distance, too.' He looked about him anxiously.

She laughed softly, arching her neck back sensuously. She glowed with enticement. After a moment's thought she regarded him oddly. 'You're a lover of nature, Tobias. Tell me, am I beautiful? Do you like me? You are used to caressing the flowers, gently tending the plants – am I desirable?'

He swallowed hard. If the Darlington men caught him here, they would punish him for his impudence. 'I . . .'

'Oh, come, Tobias,' she taunted, leaning forward. 'Surely you have desires?' She ran a hand through her hair. 'You must have.'

'I . . . must get on with my work, miss,' he said abruptly, turning and hurrying off before she could tease him more. Her tinkling laughter followed him into the bushes. It was a sound that stayed with him throughout the sweltering day, and that night, tossing on his lonely bed in his outhouse, it trickled into his dreams.

After that, whenever he saw Amelia, or when they met in the gardens, he could never look into her eyes. She had at once sensed his embarrassment, having also sensed his emotional turbulence, his desire. For his part, Tobias felt a continuation, a heightening of his – what was it, lust? He knew at least that he wanted her, though he knew also that his station in life, his unattractiveness, made that thought ridiculous. Yet in spite of this she continued to tease him, to pout at him, as though leading him on. But he knew she toyed with him. He had seen her making fools of all those so-called suitors who flocked here to pay court. He would not allow her to ridicule him.

Whenever he felt that he had come to terms with his welling desires, it seemed that Amelia knew of it, for she would mock him deliberately and flaunt herself unashamedly until he could not bear it. He could never realize his needs, so he must find a method of punishing her heartlessness. There seemed no good reason for her behaviour; it must be sheer spite. Certainly he could not accept that she felt anything for him.

Eventually, when he could bear it no longer, he decided he would ravish her. How it could be done he had no idea, for her brothers would kill him if they found out he had as much as touched her. But he must do it! Patiently he brooded, determined now to find some way of dishonouring the temptress.

It was during this period that the first hints that something was amiss in the Darlington household began to vibrate along the servants' grapevine. Tobias had little to do with the rest of the staff (an arrangement which suited them) but he heard the rumours. Apparently, Amelia's behaviour had upset her brothers, though what exactly she had done no one knew or was saying. Tobias blessed his fortune, thinking that perhaps he would be able to use Amelia's indiscretions against her somehow. Discreetly, he listened for more shreds of gossip.

A few days after the first murmurs of unrest, Tobias found himself in the unlooked-for company of a local man by the name of Jarks. This loud fellow, reputed to be a gossip, and a man with a nose for embarrassing tidbits of information, had sidled up to where Tobias was already slumped in one of his regular bars. Jarks put his pint glass down on the bare table in front of Tobias and smacked his lips as he contemplated it. He knuckled his big red nose and looked away, as if Tobias were no more than a piece of furniture. But the gardener knew he had seated himself so close for distinct reasons. Tobias sipped his own beer, saying nothing.

'Don't mind me,' said Jarks, still looking everywhere but at Tobias.

'Tobias sipped and ignored the man. He loathed him and his prying nature, his false friendliness.

'How's this weather suiting your plants, then? Could do with a drop of rain, I expect.'

Tobias put down his glass and spat on to the faded linoleum. 'What do you want?' he said quietly.

Jarks looked taken aback. He gulped noisily, piggishly at his beer. 'No need to be stand-offish. Just passing the time of day.'

'What do you want?' repeated Tobias testily.

'Well, since you've no mind to be sociable, I'll tell you straight,' said Jarks uncomfortably. His deep-set eyes were darting hither and thither, though there were only a few men in the bar, and they were deeply embroiled in discussions of their own, oblivious to the world. 'It's the manor house,' Jarks went on hesitantly.

Tobias waited.

'Word gets out, you know,' went on Jarks, as though prodding Tobias into admitting something relevant. But the latter remained stone-faced and silent.

'Me and the boys – we've heard things.'

'Have you?' said Tobias, without a hint of interest. But internally he was excited. Jarks sought information, but Tobias felt that he would, ironically, be supplying it.

'We've heard one or two stories about the Darlingtons. Things up there have been a bit queer of late.'

Tobias remained impassive.

'Just wondered if you knew anything . . .'

'I'm just the gardener. I keep to myself.'

'I know that, Tobias. But you must have noticed something going on. I've seen Jim Fallows, the chauffeur. Had a few drinks with him the other night. Me and some of the boys. He told us about queer goings-on.'

Tobias frowned. 'Like what?'

Jarks glanced suspiciously towards the bar. His voice dropped. 'Miss Amelia. Been getting up to some funny tricks.'

Tobias felt his own eyes narrow, but controlled himself. 'Oh?'

'Strange things . . . at night.' Jarks nodded, as though this revelation had to strike the chord of response in Tobias that would reveal all. Tobias stubbornly remained unresponsive.

'And these here spiders – '

Tobias at last looked interested. 'Eh? What's that you say?'

Jarks was taken aback. 'Don't you know about it?'

'Spiders? What about spiders?' Tobias had never shared the secret with anyone, but he had an odd affection for the little arachnids, which were good friends to the gardener.

'Her. Miss Amelia. You saying you ain't heard?'

Tobias shook his head, puzzled.

'Jim Fallows told us. He was a bit drunk. Forgot himself.'

'He knows more than I do.'

'He said the maid ran out shaking,' said Jarks. 'She went in to clean out Miss Amelia's room, and there were dozens of them. Spiders. Crawling all over the bedclothes. Little black spiders.'

Tobias shuddered visibly, downing half his drink in one. The image was disturbing. 'First I've heard of it.'

'Ah, there's more, though, Tobias. Word's got round. Seems like Miss Amelia is fond of the little horrors. Encourages them.'

Tobias scowled. 'What do you mean?'

'The maid says she keeps them. Like pets. Got glass cases hidden away with hundreds of them. Different types and all. Ain't you heard nothing? Ain't you see anything peculiar?'

'No! Crazy talk.'

Jarks snorted. 'What about at night? Heard anything?'

'I sleep sound. What would I hear?'

'Fallows heard a row. Eliot Darlington was giving Miss Amelia a good telling-off. She'd been out in the gardens. Fallows couldn't hear much, but it was something about the spiders.'

'Not my business to know.'

'Something funny going on, though, eh? What's she up to? You sure you don't know anything?'

Tobias abruptly stood up, ignoring his beer. His skin crawled. Damn Jarks's tongue! Jarks thought Tobias was about to speak, but Tobias scowled and walked away. Evidently the brief conversation was at an end.

In his room that night, Tobias watched the tapering candle burn right down. Something very unusual must indeed be going on, particularly if the other retainers were going into the village and blabbering about it, for they would rarely discuss the affairs of the Darlingtons save among themselves; an unofficial servants' code. Somehow, Tobias had to get at the roots of the mystery, for there would lie the key to the furtherance of his own special plans.

He knew that it would be impossible to sleep tonight. His mind was in a complete turmoil, and Jarks's comments about the spiders had made him even more curious about Amelia. He lifted a skinny hand to scratch at his face, and a suggestive shadow was projected by the candle on to the cracked wall. Tobias grinned a rare grin at his spider fantasies. But the closed room made him restless. He got up hastily. With a grunt, he pushed open the door and stood looking out at the night, inhaling the scent of fir and honeysuckle.

The moon was almost full; it sailed majestically through a few wisps of cloud, dabbing the trees and the lawns with a touch of whiteness. Tobias delighted in the scent of the country. It calmed him. He would walk a little, and when he returned he would sleep.

Across the lawns he went, a slight dew gleaming like spilled jewels before him. There was no wind – indeed, hardly a puff of air. Just the absolute stillness. The trees were limned beyond, statuesque and petrified, waiting. Tobias walked to their edge, thinking about Amelia and her strange bed-fellows. But there must be an explanation for what the maid had seen. Could Amelia be strangely obsessed with the spiders? Tobias appreciated them more than most, but to actively encourage countless numbers of them . . .

Lilting across the treetops like the song of an invisible nightingale, there came an odd trill of sound. Tobias stiffened. He knew the sounds of the country, but this was unfamiliar. His head inclined as he listened. It came again – hard to define, but clear, like the peal of a tiny bell, elfin, a note out of place in the woodland symphony. The moon watched him, as though his next movement would fascinate it.

He slipped into the tunnel of trees, trying to locate the faint sounds. It grew very dark, and the branches above contrived to blot out the curious moonlight. Tobias hesitated. The branches were still, but they hung like frozen claws, spiderish. He shuddered, about to draw back. As he did so, he saw the flicker of something ahead. Will-o'-the-wisp or firefly? He took a few more steps. No, it was motionless, fixed, like a candle.

Quietly he went towards it, his years of experience enabling him to keep as silent as a hunting animal. Through the trees he padded. Before him was a dip and a glade. He knew the place. It was a favourite picnic spot for the Darlingtons on the occasions when they decided to spend the day *en famille*, enjoying the freedom of their estates. Trees ringed it secretively, blotting out the eyes and cares of the world.

There in the little haven of solitude, the source of the light gleamed. It was a small lamp. Tobias sucked his breath through his teeth and bent low to retain his inconspicuousness. There was someone here – a lone figure, arms raised as though in a silent invocation to the moon. *Amelia!* Her form was unmistakable to the one who had clandestinely studied it for so long. But why was she here? Had something within her mind turned, leaving her not quite sane? Was this what had so disturbed her brothers?

Her voice emitted a single note, pure and sweet. Tobias, heart thudding, felt his emotions welling like a spring. Amelia's head turned, quick as a bird's, and she looked directly towards him, as though he were a beacon of evil thoughts. Flushed, he spun round and blundered off, running as fast as he could, careless now of sound. He ran all the way back to his room, closing the door and slipping the bolt. He got into bed and kept very still, waiting. But nothing came to disturb him.

The early morning found Tobias spraying a rose bed some distance from the manor house. It was a warm day already, and the sky had rid itself of the last wispy tatters of cirrus. It would be too hot to work later on, so Tobias had risen early. He wasted little time puzzling over the unusual events of the night, which in retrospect were no longer unsettling. Amelia's remarkable behaviour was something he could not begin to explain, so he did not try. Instead, he tried to think of how he could turn it to his own advantage. Would her nocturnal strayings into the picnic dell be regular? Was this the sort of secretive activity that had so upset the rhythm of the household? Tobias tended his roses. His fears had been melted by the bright daylight, no more remembered than a passing dream.

As he bent to inspect a pink-hued bloom, he sensed movement behind him. Straightening, he turned. Amelia faced him, alone, an almost coy smile on her unblemished face.

'Good day, Tobias,' she said sweetly. He shivered apprehensively, feeling like some insect enmeshed in the sticky cobwebs she had woven. The image upset him even more, and he stepped back, almost tripping over the spray tube.

'Are you frightened of me?' She laughed softly, and he recalled her pure voice in the night. He was not sure how to react, but he shook his head.

'Not going to run away from me again?' The words hung delicately on the air, rich in suggestion.

Again. She had seen and recognized him, then. He shrugged, watching her as though she were stalking him. Her eyes were alive, but bore no trace of malice.

'Don't know what you mean, miss.'

She stepped lightly closer. 'Yes you do, Tobias.' Her slim fingers reached out and caressed the petals of a rose. It seemed somehow sinister, that caress.

Tobias nodded, his mouth slack.

'Have you told anybody?' she hissed, her eyes suddenly cold.

He shook his head.

'You're sure?' She stepped even closer; he was fascinated.

'No one, miss. No one will know.'

'That's good, Tobias. Very good. Do you know what I was doing?' She moved away, walking slowly along the edge of the rose bed. Tobias felt himself held in her uncanny spell, and again the idea of a thin thread tugging him to her suggested itself. Like a faithful dog, he followed a few paces behind.

'No, miss.'

She turned and faced him, her eyes alight. Mocking? Was she? He felt a stab of anger. If she was to begin that again, he would lose control – the spell would snap. He could feel his libido stirring.

'Communing, Tobias. I was communing.'

'I . . . don't understand, miss.'

'You will.' She turned lithely away again, leaving an enigmatic void. Tobias stood rooted.

'Does it interest you, Tobias? You're a lover of nature and the wild things. Your spirit drifts with the breeze, the stream, and your heart beats in tune with the things that grow. You hear the tread of the tiny creatures and smell the plants, sense their whispers. You understand, don't you? You are alive. All the others – they know nothing. Their senses are paralysed. They are blind.

'Shall I tell you something? They sent me away, abroad. To learn. Well, I did. I learned things there that I had never been aware of. In Switzerland, amongst those giddy heights, I tasted the truth. I learned to listen to the earth breathe. I learned to love all the livimg things, no matter how small. Am I mad, Tobias? Do you think I'm talking nonsense?'

He cleared his throat. 'No, miss. Folks just don't realize. You're right in what you say. I . . . heard you singing. It was . . . very beautiful.'

She seemed to be pleased by that. He prayed that she was not mocking him. He had wanted to ravish her, to hurt her, but now he felt only warmth, closeness. She had touched at the strings that moved him – she *knew* the realities of what surrounded them all. There was no madness in that.

'I was communing when you found me last night,' she said. 'You startled me, otherwise I would have asked you to . . . join me.'

He was slightly bemused. *Join* her? Why should a goddess favour one so low?

'Didn't mean to pry. I saw the light . . . thought it was poachers.'

'That's all right. At least you know why I love the woods at night. The peace of the night is unspoiled. To be one with that peace is everything.'

'Yes.'

'Your flowers,' she said, again touching the soft petals lightly, and this time there was nothing sinister in the motion. 'They are beautiful. They reflect what is in you, Tobias.'

She had never spoken to him this way before. Gone were the teasing jibes and the veiled insults. It was almost intimate. His breathing quickened.

'Tonight,' she said, 'I will be there again. Will you come?'

Was she insane to ask him? Was there some grim joke attached to this? 'I . . .'

'No one will know. My brothers will be out of the county on business. Come to the dell tonight. It will be our secret.'

He stood for a long moment, like a machine that had been immobilized. She smiled, and then was gone, sudden as a breeze. Behind her she left a cocoon of magic, and within it Tobias felt his pulse juddering.

The day floated by. When it was dark and the full moon soared high in a spangled sky, with silence settled on the grounds and woods of the estate, Tobias sat again in his room, watching the sputtering candle sleeplessly. Should he go? Certainly he longed to venture out into the shadows of the woods to the dell, but it was all madness. What could Amelia possibly have in mind? A tryst? That was unthinkable – she was so beautiful. She could choose any man she pleased. Yet she had told him that only he understood the nature of the wilds. It would be their secret.

He turned to stare at his bed, resolved not to go out. A lifetime of loneliness could not be reversed. She would shame him. He shied from the demands of communicating with her. As he turned, something gently brushed his face, a silk kiss. He flicked at something and examined it in the poor light. It was a money spider. He let it drop gently on its thread to the floor. Overhead, dangling from the beams of the low ceiling, were a handful of the tiny creatures. They reminded him of her and her affinity for everything natural. Would she really be there again? His decision to remain here crumbled, and minutes later he was running across the lawns, heading for the trees.

Just as he had heard the strange notes of her voice last night and seen the light, he again sensed them now, a magical part of the woods. He went slowly, silently, but with less apprehension. At the lip of the natural, scooped-out dell, he stopped, looking down at the lamp that cast its glow of pale light round the glade.

She was there, wrapped in a flowing silk robe, her hair loose, her arms bare and white as milk. The magnetism that she exerted upon him was at its most powerful. Like a tide tugged by the moon, he stepped forward, his heartbeat expanding like thunder throughout his whole body. She had readied herself for him. He must possess her, his pounding blood told him, *he must!*

'Come, Tobias,' he heard her softly call, and his blood roared. Beyond her, through a break in the trees, he could see the moon, huge and full, like some bloated and luminescent puff-ball, a great, blazing eye. Mechanically, he came to stand very close, the halo of light embracing him. There was an earthy smell to the glade. The whole place seemed to listen, as though the ground were alive, attuned to each step, each breath. Every leaf, every vein in it, pulsed as though a faint but virile rhythm was in motion. Her enchantment had evoked from the night its stream of life.

'Do you feel it, Tobias?' she whispered, her voice as soft as the stirring leaves.

Entranced, intoxicated, he nodded. His body throbbed. He wanted to reach out and touch that white skin. Before he came close to her, she let fall her robe, and he drew in his breath, seeing the moon-washed contours of her divine body. His head swam with the giddy beauty of it. His palms were hot with sweat. It had become an ache, his longing unbearable.

She began to sway and sing, high notes spilling out. The forest listened, its every atom intent on the melody of that emotive, stirring sound. Her arms came up, her breasts full, her waist curving in, its arc precise, perfect. For a long time Tobias watched her, trembling, saw her swaying.

Something snapped. He lurched forward, drunk with lust. As though she had been anticipating his movement, she swept aside like a shadow. Tobias closed in on air, stumbling, falling, sprawling. The rich earth welcomed him as he toppled, smearing him. He looked up, stunned, and on Amelia's face was a malevolent gleam of triumph. She began to sing and weave about him, arms held out at strange, unnatural angles.

Tobias watched her, a bird watching a snake. He could not move. She had become the spider of the web, spinning her evil about him to hold him down. He tried to rise, but could only grovel. Then, from out of the earth and from the grass, they came. They tickled across his hands – ten, a score, a hundred. They seemed to scuttle from every leaf and every blade of grass in that silent place, moving rhythms in sympathy with the voice of the girl.

Spiders. An army of them had materialized, popping out from an unseen dimension of the dark. Amelia continued to weave her diabolical dance, as though it was by her command that these crawling legions poured forth towards the bemused Tobias. His arms were covered. He beat at them, eyes beginning to widen in fear. It was as though the entire glade had come to life. *Communing*. Millions of the little black shapes marched like ants to the focal point that Tobias had become.

He screamed. The awful stridency pierced the night, but the trees muffled it as though they were a party to the terrible events. At last Tobias got to his feet. The spiders still came on, a ghastly, endless parade, yet they avoided their mistress, who continued to sing. Her voice was like some supernormal force, the tide that carried these myriad creatures to their feast, her notes a web that united them.

Shrieking, Tobias ran from the grove, away from the place where he had entered the woods. He ran towards the moon itself, which glowered down without pity. As he rushed at it, a new element was added to his terror. Amelia had unleashed some further power that dipped deep into the bounds of insanity.

For as Tobias looked to that great moon filling his horizon, he saw gigantic fronds of web, swaying down, as if earth and moon were moored together by the dangling, silken cords. They swayed, beckoning. He had forgotten the moving carpet of creatures on which he trod as he blundered on. He burst out of the woods, refusing to believe what he saw. Across a wide field he ran, throat raw, breath rasping, away from the nightmare grove and the weaving arms of the temptress.

He ran up the grassy slope of a low hill, heedless of direction, eyes half closed in exertion. Then the last of the night's horrors confronted him. It was a vision of pure madness, a huge, monstrous travesty of everything sane and coherent. Melody had become discord, reality disjointedness. Tobias screamed again, his eyes bulging, as that appalling sight mocked his reason.

From down those gigantic, impossible cobwebs of the moon lurched a titanic shape, its legs spread far across the hill as it came for him. It was a spider, rearing up hundreds of feet, its mandibles waiting, greedily, to snap him up.

George Pethick was walking steadily up the incline in the sunlight, a weather eye on the stragglers of his flock as the sheep bleated, looking for the best grazing. George's two sheepdogs were running alongside the flanks of the flock, content to leave the sheep alone until George gave them a particular order. The farmer wiped sweat from his neck with a grubby scarf. Going to be another hot one today. Must have some rain soon.

One of the dogs began to bark loudly. It had moved uphill, away from the sheep, and was worrying at something in the grass.

'Calm down, boy!' George called, climbing to investigate. 'What you found, eh? – God almighty!'

He had reached the place and stood back in shock, for it was a body. Tobias was sprawled on his back, his face a mask of horror as he stared skywards. He was dead.

George turned away, aghast.

'All right, boy, leave it be!'

He moved off downhill towards home with a last glance back at Tobias. The sun blazed down, casting a huge shadow, the edge of it touching the corpse. The dead eyes gazed up, apparently still fixed on the arms of the humming pylon.

# The Horror of Abbot's Grange

*Frederick Cowles*

## I

It was Joan who fell in love with Abbot's Grange. I must confess that, from the first, I thought the place had a brooding and sinister air about it.

For three months we had been house-hunting, and then a chance visit to Ritton had led to the discovery of the Grange. As far as country houses go, it was perfect. It had been erected in the fifteenth century by the Cistercian monks of Ritton Abbey, and a tiny detached chapel was a relic of the monastic days. Yet, in spite of the fact that Joan was mad about it, I did not like the place.

The next day we sought out the estate agent, and he willingly agreed to conduct us over the house. It turned out to be the property of Lord Salton, and it was his desire to let the place furnished. That suited us as, being birds of passage, we had no furniture of our own.

It was not a large house, but the rooms were spacious. The entrance hall was really quite palatial and hung with paintings of the dead and gone Saltons. I examined the portraits whilst the agent was revealing the charms of the Grange to Joan.

They were not a very imposing lot, those Saltons of the past. One was a bishop, looking very uncomfortable in his robes; another a general, mounted on a weird-looking charger. Not one of them really interested me until I came upon a dingy painting hung in a dark corner near the stairs.

It represented a tall, sallow-featured man, dressed in sombre garments of early sixteenth-century style. His face was thin and brooding and strangely pale, but the lips were intensely red and were drawn back to show white, fang-like teeth. The whole expression was one of diabolical cruelty, and I shuddered involuntarily as I looked at it.

An inscription in the right-hand corner of the painting caught my eye. The writing was rather faded, but I was just able to make out the words: 'William Salton, pxt. 1572', and below, in rather brighter colours, was a small cross and the sentence: 'Seeking whom he may devour. God frustrate him always.'

Joan and the agent returned just then, and I called their attention to the portrait. It may have been my imagination, but I thought a shade of fear passed over the man's face. I asked him who the sinister gentleman was, and, with some slight show of reluctance, he answered: 'That is a picture of the first Lord Salton. He is said to have been a monk at Ritton Abbey, but they turned him out. At the dissolution he revenged himself upon the community by giving evidence against them. Many of the monks were executed, and as a reward William Salton was made Lord Salton, and this house was given to him.'

'How exciting,' exclaimed Joan. 'He looks just the sort of person to do a thing like that. We really must have this house, Michael. It is just what we have been looking for.'

When Joan makes up her mind there is no gainsaying her. Within an hour I had paid a deposit, signed the lease, and received the keys of Abbot's Grange.

As he handed the keys over to me the agent pointed out an exceptionally large one, and said: 'This, sir, is the key of the chapel. It has been closed for nearly three hundred years, and Lord Salton particularly requested that you will not enter the place. If you should feel you want to visit it go in the daytime, and be sure to lock the door when you leave. *On no account allow the door to be unlocked between dusk and daybreak.*'

'But,' I exclaimed, 'that is a curious condition. What is the reason for it?'

The agent's face was blank as he answered: 'I do not know, sir. Those are Lord Salton's instructions to me.' With that I had to be content, although I felt that the man could have told more if he had cared to.

Three weeks later, with a staff engaged by Joan and my sister, we took up residence at Abbot's Grange.

2

Of course Joan had to have a house-warming party. By making up extra beds on sofas and floors we managed to invite about twenty people down. Then there were a few local residents, such as the vicar and the doctor, who were asked to dinner.

Before the meal I was standing in front of the fire in the hall. The others were all dressing, and there was only a dim light burning on the staircase. I was thinking how impressive the place looked when, quite suddenly, somebody switched on all the lights. It was the butler taking some glasses to the dining-room.

'Good Lord, man,' I shouted, 'why on earth did you switch all those lights on like that?'

He looked rather confused, and then he blurted out: 'I always do it, sir. None of us will come into the hall after dark unless the lights are full on.'

'What on earth is there to be frightened of here?' I stormed. 'You must be like a lot of children afraid of the dark.'

The man's voice was apologetic as he replied: 'It isn't that, sir. It's that painting under the stairs. His eyes seem to follow you about.'

I glanced over at the portrait of the first Lord Salton, and, whether it was a trick of the artist or a trick of the light, the eyes certainly did seem to glare out of the canvas. They almost seemed to be illuminated by an uncanny glow.

The butler stood expecting a further reprimand when the vicar was announced. The clergyman turned out to be quite an affable little man, the usual type of country parson, but endowed with more brains than most. We discussed the weather, the political situation, and a few other minor things. Then I asked him if he knew anything about the first Lord Salton.

'Quite enough to make me detest him,' he replied. 'He was a hateful type. A man who became a Cistercian monk, and then gave information against the abbot and brethren.'

'Wasn't he turned out of the Abbey long before the suppression?' I inquired.

'Yes. He was accused of practising black magic and they expelled him from the Order. I think the details are given in a manuscript that used to be in the library. If you like we will look and see if it is still there.'

I readily agreed, and we were just moving off when the gong went and the guests began to come down for dinner. So we had to postpone our visit to the library.

The meal was quite a jolly function. As usual, Joan had managed to assemble quite a distinguished and interesting company. There was Vincent Dunn, the actor; Rita Young, the film star; Edmund Morton, the novelist; Malcolm Dale, the explorer; and a host of other celebrities of one sort or another. And they were all quite human, which says a lot for Joan's taste. It was Morton who asked about the chapel, and I had to tell them all about the conditions relating to it.

'And have you been inside yet?' asked Dale.

'Not I,' I replied. 'I put the key in the Chinese vase in the hall and there it stays until my lease is up.'

They all seemed to think it very jolly to have a private chapel, and the possibility of it being haunted was freely discussed. Then the talk drifted round to plays and films, and the chapel was forgotten – at least I thought it was.

There was dancing in the hall afterwards, and as soon as we could reasonably do so, the vicar and I slipped off to the library.

He found the book without any trouble. It was a musty, calf-bound volume filled with crabbed handwriting. It seemed to be a catalogue of the pictures in the hall, with some biographical notes, and the first person mentioned was William Salton. The following is the extract relating to him:

William Salton born 1501. Entered the Abbey of Our Lady of Ritton 1522. Accused of practising witchcraft, sorcery and black magic, and expelled from the monastery in 1530. In 1539 gave evidence before the commissioners against the abbot and community, which resulted in the abbot and six of the brethren being condemned to death. Evidence afterwards proved to be false, but Salton was made Lord Salton and received the Abbey Grange. Lived the life of a recluse, and commonly believed to have been a wizard and a vampire. Died in 1597, and buried in the private chapel of Abbot's Grange. No priest would perform the burial-rites, and he was interred without prayer or ceremony.

Then, in another hand, followed a later entry:

On the 16th day of May 1640 the tomb of William Lord Salton was sealed by me, John Rogers, clerk in holy orders. Let none loose the chapel door between sunset and sunrise lest, perchance, he come abroad again seeking whom he may devour. God frustrate him always.

'What does that mean?' I asked.

'Well,' answered the parson, 'I should say that the first Lord Salton could not rest in his grave, and John Rogers was called in to lay his unquiet spirit.'

An argument on ghosts seemed to be impending when Malcolm Dale burst into the room. I have never seen a man looking so utterly terrified. He sank into a chair, asked for a drink, and gulped down the brandy I handed to him. It was some time before he could speak coherently, but, at last, he managed to blurt out his story.

It appeared that the mention of the chapel had fired his curiosity, and that, when the dancing was well on the go, he had taken the key from the vase and had gone out to investigate. He took an electric flash-light with him, but had some difficulty in unlocking the door. The keyhole, he declared, was filled with rubbish, and he had to scrape it clean with his pocket-knife. At last he got the key in, and then it wouldn't turn. So he went over to the garage and got a spanner. With this he managed to twist the key in the lock. The rest of the story shall be told in his own words.

'When I got into the place I noticed at once how intensely cold it was, even colder than most old churches. My light was just enough for me to see that there were no seats in the building, and precious little else. I had almost decided to go out again when I noticed a sort of table tomb near the east end, and so went up to examine it. Suddenly, without any warning, it seemed to crack, and out of it sprang the figure of a man with a deadly white face and long, sharp teeth. He glared at me for a moment, and I saw the beam of my light reflect redly in his eyes. Then I turned tail and fled, but, all the way back, I felt that he was after me.'

His voice rose to a scream as he came to the end of his tale, and I could see that he was all in.

'Then you left the chapel door open?' asked the vicar.

Dale nodded dumbly as if he dared not trust himself to speak.

'God frustrate him,' the parson murmured, and then, springing to his feet, he said to me: 'Come. There is not a moment to be lost. We must go over and lock the door.'

I seized the torch, which Dale still held, and within a few minutes we had reached the chapel. It looked quiet and desolate enough, but the vicar insisted on entering and seeing the tomb. It was quite an ordinary table tomb of white marble, but the top of it was cracked right across, and it was easy to see that *the crack was newly made*.

The parson crossed himself, and together we left the building, swung the ponderous door shut and locked it. We did not speak as we returned to the house.

## 3

We got Dale to bed without letting any other members of the party suspect that anything was wrong. He was in a blue funk, and I was nearly as bad. When the vicar suggested that I should give him a shakedown in my room and let him stay the night I almost embraced him.

Well, dancing went on until about half-past one, and by two o'clock everybody had gone to bed. The vicar (whose name, by the way, was Parker) went round the house with me, and we saw that all windows and doors were secured. Wolf, the Alsatian, we brought into the hall, and left him comfortably settled in front of the fire. Then we went upstairs, and, in spite of the excitement, I, for one, was soon asleep.

It must have been about three o'clock when I was suddenly awakened by the howling of the dog. Parker was already astir. 'Did you hear that?' he whispered.

Again it came – not an ordinary howl, but a howl of sheer terror. It was a sound that seemed to freeze the blood in my veins, and made my hair literally stand on end. Then came a shriek of horrible laughter that was even more nerve-racking.

'Come along,' said Parker, 'we must see what is wrong,' and he made for the door.

I slipped into a dressing-gown and followed him, although, I must confess, I would have preferred to have stayed in my room with the door locked.

The landing was dark, except for the pale light of the moon filtering through the leaded windows, and the electric-light switch was at the head of the stairs. Before we could reach it Parker suddenly gripped my arm and whispered: 'Look! Just beyond that suit of armour.' I looked to the spot he indicated. At first only a shadow was visible, and then, gradually appearing out of the darkness, I made out a white, grinning face – the features of the first Lord Salton. Even as I looked, the figure moved and glided away down the staircase.

I was badly shaken, but Parker, who seemed to possess nerves of steel, bounded over to the switch and flooded the staircase with light. There was nothing to be seen, but, in a wave, a deadly, sickening smell came up the stairs to us. It was the fetid odour of corruption, a nauseating, vile stink that made me feel ill.

Parker led the way down the staircase, and at once turned all the lights on in the hall. I noticed that his lips were moving in prayer, and beads of perspiration stood on his brow. The place was empty and it was some minutes before we saw the dog. Poor Wolf was lying near the door, and he was quite dead. Somehow the body seemed shrunken, although, when we examined it, the only marks we could find were two tiny wounds in the throat.

'Doesn't he look to you as if he has shrunk?' I asked Parker.

'Yes,' he replied. 'Every drop of blood has been drained from his body.'

At that moment a voice came from the top of the stairs. 'Is anything wrong, sir?' It was the butler, and he was shaking with fright.

'Come down, man,' I called, and then turned back to the dog.

'We are up against a –' began Parker, and then he was interrupted by a terrified scream. We jumped up at once and there was the butler, gibbering like a maniac, at the foot of the stairs.

'Be quiet,' hissed Parker, crossing the hall.

'Look! Look!' wailed the man. His quivering finger pointed towards the picture of the first Lord Salton, but there was no picture in the frame. The canvas was blank.

4

It is difficult to write of those three hours before daybreak. We sat together in the library, and prayed for the dawn. It found us wild-eyed, and white-faced.

When it was quite light, Parker said: 'I must see that picture again.'

We followed him out into the hall, and there was the portrait of William Lord Salton leering at us from its frame. It was only a painting (we touched it to see), but the eyes glowed with a hellish fire, and the cruel lips seemed twisted in a triumphant smile.

Back in the library we sat down to discuss our plan of action. The butler, his name was Clarke, took things quite well, and Parker included him in the discussion.

'It all seems too terrible to be true,' I said. 'What can we do?'

'Well,' replied Parker, 'I am going to make a suggestion. I have a friend, a Benedictine monk at Fairly Abbey. He happens to be an expert on occult matters, and has often been brought up against queer things. I wonder if you would allow me to invite him over?'

Naturally I agreed at once, and Parker telephoned to the Abbey, which was only about five miles from Ritton. He gave no particulars over the line, but I heard him assuring the priest that it was 'something of vital and terrible importance'.

'Good,' he said, as he laid the receiver down. 'Father Vincent will be over about ten o'clock.'

After that we went upstairs to dress and freshen ourselves up. Clarke saw to the removal of the body of the dog before any of the guests came down, and breakfast was almost a jolly meal. Most of the visitors left soon after nine, but Dale and Morton were staying on until the weekend.

Punctually at ten o'clock Father Vincent was announced and joined the vicar and myself in the library. He was a quiet little man, with twinkling brown eyes shining behind thick spectacles. Anyone less like a ghost-hunter it would be difficult to imagine.

Parker told him all that had happened since Dale had unlocked the chapel, and Clarke was called in to confirm the part about the portrait. The monk asked a few questions, and then he said: 'I may as well tell you that you are up against a most hellish thing – a man who should have died over three hundred years ago, and yet, by devilish arts, has kept his evil mind alive within the tomb.'

He went on to suggest that Joan, Dale, and Morton be taken into our confidence, and asked to help if necessary. I was a little doubtful about frightening Joan, but Father Vincent soon convinced me that it would be unwise to leave her in ignorance. So we asked the three of them to come down to the library.

Dale, with his experience of the previous night fresh in his mind, was easily convinced; Morton and Joan were frankly incredulous but, I could see, our seriousness impressed them.

It was finally decided that the Benedictine should return to his abbey for some things he required, and then stay the night with us.

'If it is what I suspect I shall have to ask you to get in touch with Lord Salton,' he said. 'But we can leave that until tomorrow.'

'A wonderful man,' remarked Parker, when the monk had gone. 'These Roman priests are the only chaps who understand anything about occult phenomena. I take off my hat to them when it comes to a real tussle with the devil.'

Lunch was a quiet meal, and, afterwards, Morton and Joan played tennis, and Dale, Parker, and I went over to the chapel. The key turned quite easily in the lock, and the interior did not look at all sinister in the bright light of the afternoon sun.

It was quite an interesting little building, dating, I should say, mostly from the middle fifteenth century. Some fragments of good stained glass remained in the windows, there was a stone altar, a few benches, and the marble table tomb.

Whilst we were looking round Father Vincent joined us.

'I have just arrived,' he exclaimed, 'and they told me you were here, so I thought I would stroll down and look over the place.'

We showed him the crack in the tomb, and he agreed that it was certainly new. He also pointed out a number of dark stains on the flat top of the monument, and it was not long before he discovered similar stains on the stone slab of the altar.

'What do you make of them?' asked Parker.

'They look to me like bloodstains,' answered the priest. 'It is a horrible thought but, if they are, something has been killed on this altar. You notice how the stain runs down the side, just as if the blood of a victim has dropped from the slab to the floor.'

Clarke met us, as we were returning to the house, with the news that one of the parlour-maids had been found in the hall in a dead faint. On recovering she had declared that she was going upstairs when a man dressed in black, with a deathly white face, had pounced out at her.

We interviewed the girl and she not only stuck to her story, but also avowed that she could still feel the grip of his cold fingers on her wrist.

At dinner we were a very dull company in spite of the little priest's efforts to keep us amused. Afterwards we all went along to the library, and Joan, Parker, Morton, and Dale made up a four for bridge, whilst Father Vincent and I settled down to talk and smoke. I never knew that a monk could be such good company. He seemed to have travelled all over the world, and had a fund of excellent stories about all manner of places and all sorts of people.

The time passed pleasantly enough until about eleven o'clock when Clarke came in with the whisky. I remember that he was just squirting the soda into Parker's drink when, eerie and shrill, a burst of wicked laughter echoed through the house.

For a moment or so none moved, then the priest sprang to his feet and rushed out into the hall. We were not slow to follow him. Instinctively our first glance was towards the portrait of William Salton. Only a blank canvas filled the frame: the figure had gone.

# 5

I don't think the servants will come to any harm,' said the priest later on. 'He will hardly go into the new wing of the house.'

We had sent Joan off to bed, and Father Vincent had carefully fastened a crucifix to the door of her room, and sprinkled the threshold with holy water. The rest of us, including Clarke the butler, had agreed to keep watch in the hall.

The monk had made us sit in a semi-circle round the fire. All around he had sprinkled his holy water, and on the mantelpiece he had lighted two blessed candles. He himself took up a position near the fireplace.

'It is as well for you to know what you are up against,' he went on. 'This William Salton, however melodramatic it may sound, undoubtedly sold his soul to the devil. Unholy sacrifices were offered by him in the chapel, and, after death, there was no rest for him in the grave. He became what we call a vampire. Evidently the portrait is connected with him in some very intimate way, and he can, by some fell means, animate the painted figure for his own ends.

'Around you I have sprinkled holy water, blessed with the rites of Holy Church, and I want no one to pass beyond that circle until the portrait is back in its frame.'

'You think it will return, then?' asked Morton.

'It must return,' was the reply. 'You,' the monk went on, turning to me, 'must watch the frame very carefully and let us know if you see anything out of the ordinary. I want Mr Parker to keep an eye on the staircase, Mr Dale to watch the door, and Mr Morton to keep the passage to the kitchens under observation.'

We sat there smoking in silence. The priest had his Breviary and was reading his Office, and Parker idly turned the pages of a magazine. Then, without any warning, the place seemed to go very cold, and again came that rotten odour of decay.

Father Vincent motioned us to remain still, and I could see that his lips were moving rapidly in prayer. Suddenly the candle-flames flickered, and changed to a peculiar shade of blue.

It was getting too much for us. Our nerves were all keyed up to breaking-pitch, and I was not surprised to hear Dale move his chair, and notice him throw his head back in a queer way he had. What followed is too horrible to think about. There came a sickening sucking sound, poor Dale screamed, and I had a vague vision of two fang-like teeth at his throat.

It was all over in a moment. We jumped up, and, as we did so, there came that peal of wicked laughter again. We looked towards the picture: the figure was there once more.

Dale was unconscious, and the others carried him up to his room whilst I telephoned the doctor.

'Better not say too much to the medico,' said Parker. 'He wouldn't understand.'

'I wonder exactly what did happen,' remarked Morton.

'I think poor Dale pushed his chair back and got his head beyond the circle of holy water,' answered Father Vincent.

We waited up in Dale's room for the doctor to come, and, as soon as we heard the sound of his car in the drive, Clarke went to let him in. He was a fussy little man, and cleared us all out of the room whilst he made his examination.

He was soon out again. His brow was crinkled in a puzzled frown, and he inquired at once how it had happened.

'We were sitting in the hall,' I replied, 'and he suddenly went off – just a gasp, and then he was unconscious.'

'Just so! Just so!' he went on. 'Weak heart. Seems to me that the trouble is long-standing. Has he been in the tropics at all?'

'He is an explorer,' I answered, 'and has been in all parts of the world. In fact, he has only just come back from the East.'

'That accounts for it. So many of these people get heart trouble and never bother about it. One thing puzzles me, and that is two tiny, festering punctures in the throat. Looks as if he may have scraped a couple of pimples whilst shaving.'

We made no comment, but I saw Parker start forward as if to say something and then thought better of it.

'Don't worry about him. He will be all right as soon as he recovers consciousness,' the doctor assured us.

· But he was wrong. Poor Dale never recovered consciousness, and by eight o'clock he was dead.

6

Father Vincent put a telephone call through to Lord Salton, and was fortunate enough to find him at home. He promised to leave London at once, and, true to his word, he was at Abbot's Grange soon after lunch. He turned out to be quite a young man, and greeted both Parker and Father Vincent as old friends.

We gathered in the library, and Father Vincent gave him the facts of the case. I could see that the boy was very much upset, particularly when we had to tell him of the death of Dale.

'I will most willingly tell you all I know,' he said. 'William Salton has always been the skeleton in our cupboard. Each heir to the title, at his coming of age, is told the story of the first Lord, and warned never to leave the chapel door open between dusk and sunrise. I have never taken the matter very seriously, and, I am afraid, I ought not to have left the key with the agent.

'As you already know, my ancestor was once a Cistercian monk, but he was turned out of the monastery for practising witchcraft and the black art. Really he was a greater villain than even the monks suspected.

'At the dissolution he gave evidence against the abbot and brethren of Ritton, and, for his services, was made Lord Salton, and given this house.

'Under his rule Abbot's Grange became a temple of Satan. He is said to have celebrated the Black Mass in the chapel, and to have sacrificed living children on the altar. The picture in the hall is a self-portrait, and tradition says that the canvas is really the skin of one of his victims coated over with human blood.

'Even after his death he terrorized the district. For over half a century there were tales of children stolen from their cradles in the dead of night by a man with a strangely white face. Then, in 1640, the Lord Salton of the time went into the chapel and found the altar dripping with fresh blood. He called in a parson named John Rogers, who carried out some religious ceremony there, and, since then, the chapel has not been opened after sunset until this week.'

With a word of apology he got up and went over to one of the oak bookcases. Sliding a concealed panel at the end, he took out, from the cavity behind, two small vellum-bound books. Laying these on the table, he went on:

'These books are diaries kept by William Salton. I have never read them through, but I know of two passages which may interest you.' He opened one of the books and read from it.

'At last I have completed the portrait in the manner laid down by the master Setharius. Now, even if my body decays, I have that which will give me the semblance of life.

'The other note,' he continued, 'was made in the second volume by John Rogers. Ah! Here it is.

'Terrible is the power of the evil one. He that is dead yet wanders abroad seeking whom he may devour. I have watched and prayed, and it seems that he may only be free of the grave for three days at a time. Then for three days he must rest within the tomb. I have sealed him there, but should he ever break free again let it be remembered that on the third day he will return to the grave.'

'That will be tomorrow,' interpolated Father Vincent. 'God grant that nothing happens tonight.'

'You must see that it doesn't,' answered Salton.

'If I am able to keep him within the picture for tonight have I your permission to do whatever I think fit in the morning?' asked the priest.

'You can do whatever you like,' was the reply. 'I am only too anxious that such a heritage of evil shall not be handed on to my successors.'

Salton asked if I could put him up for the night, and we were all very glad to have him to stay. With Dale dead upstairs and the horror of the unknown hanging over us, we were not a very lively party.

The priest made his preparations early in the evening. A semi-circle of salt was made round the picture, this was sprinkled with holy water, and, in the centre, he placed a crucifix.

Just before midnight we began our watch. We hadn't long to wait. About twenty minutes past the hour the figure in the frame began to move. It jumped to life with curious, jerky, mechanical movements. Then it tried to step down, but was evidently prevented by the arrangements the monk had made.

A look of diabolical hate passed over its features, and then it laughed. As the laughter died it began to intone a kind of weird chant. I could not understand the words, but I knew it for some incantation to the devil.

Suddenly Morton screamed, and pointed to the stairs. We all looked up, and there, moving slowly down, was the figure of Malcolm Dale, the man whose dead body lay upstairs.

Morton screamed again, and then fainted. I saw the monk step forward with crucifix in one hand and Breviary in the other. In a clear voice he began to read the office of exorcism, and all the time that terrible incantation went on. Louder and louder rose the infernal chant, and clearer rang the voice of the priest. It seemed that the forces of good were waging a battle with the powers of evil. The perspiration ran in great drops down the monk's face, and I found myself praying the words of the 'Our Father' – the only prayer I knew.

Gradually the hellish chant got quieter, whilst Father Vincent's voice grew stronger in volume. Then a strange thing happened. A beautiful smile came over the face of the thing that looked like Malcolm Dale, and, still smiling, it slowly faded away.

From the picture came a most unearthly shriek and, for a few moments, the figure in the frame seemed to writhe in agony. Then it became still. It was only a painting once again.

'We have won the first round of the fight, my friends,' said the little priest.

## 7

It was three o'clock in the afternoon of the following day.

'If John Rogers' calculations are correct,' said Father Vincent, 'the monster should be back in his grave by now.'

Armed with crowbars we were making our way to the chapel. The priest carried a small Spanish dagger with a cross handle.

Salton unlocked the door and we went inside. The place was rather gloomy, for it was a dull day, but nothing seemed to have been disturbed.

'Now we come to the worst part of this horrible business,' said the priest.

Taking a crowbar from Morton he went up to the tomb, and inserted the implement under the slab. I put mine under the other side, and together we levered until the top swung up. It was an easy matter to lift it off. Inside was a brass-bound coffin, and all over it were dark-brown stains.

We lifted the coffin out of the tomb, and laid it before the altar.

'If any of you feel at all nervous you may go outside,' said Father Vincent. Morton took him at his word, but Salton, Parker, and I stayed on.

It did not take long to remove the lid, and inside was no crumbling skeleton, but the body of William, Lord Salton, looking just as he must have looked in life. His eyes gleamed at us with a malevolent stare; his lips were unnaturally red; and his white, fang-like teeth protruded over his bottom lip.

'Stand back!' cried the monk.

He raised his dagger aloft, and then, praying in Latin, brought it down into the creature's heart. The red mouth opened in a piercing shriek, the body writhed as if in agony, and then it slowly crumbled to dust before our eyes.

We sealed the coffin and placed it back in the tomb. The slab was returned to its position, and Salton promised to see that it was cemented down.

One more task remained. We took down the portrait of William Salton, carried it into the grounds, soaked it in petrol, and set fire to it. As the flames licked that white face it seemed to leer at us again, and I fancied the lips parted in a snarl.

Salton was very good about the lease for, naturally neither Joan nor I felt that we could remain on at Abbot's Grange after what had happened. I took her away to the south of France, where the sunshine and gaiety helped her to forget the nightmare of that tragic week.

But I saw Malcolm Dale die, the picture come to life, Dale's ghost walk at the bidding of the monster, and the corpse of William Salton living after over three hundred years in the tomb. It will be many years before I can forget the horror of Abbot's Grange.

# The Screaming Skull

## *F. Marion Crawford*

I have often heard it scream. No, I am not nervous, I am not imaginative, and I never believed in ghosts, unless that thing is one. Whatever it is, it hates me almost as much as it hated Luke Pratt, and it screams at me.

If I were you, I would never tell ugly stories about ingenious ways of killing people, for you never can tell but that some one at the table may be tired of his or her nearest and dearest. I have always blamed myself for Mrs Pratt's death, and I suppose I was responsible for it in a way, though heaven knows I never wished her anything but long life and happiness. If I had not told that story she might be alive yet. That is why the thing screams at me, I fancy.

She was a good little woman, with a sweet temper, all things considered, and a nice gentle voice; but I remember hearing her shriek once when she thought her little boy was killed by a pistol that went off, though everyone was sure that it was not loaded. It was the same scream; exactly the same, with a sort of rising quaver at the end; do you know what I mean? Unmistakable.

The truth is, I had not realized that the doctor and his wife were not on good terms. They used to bicker a bit now and then when I was here, and I often noticed that little Mrs Pratt got very red and bit her lip hard to keep her temper, while Luke grew pale and said the most offensive things. He was that sort when he was in the nursery, I remember, and afterwards at school. He was my cousin, you know; that is how I came by this house; after he died, and his boy Charley was killed in South Africa, there were no relations left. Yes, it's a pretty little property, just the sort of thing for an old sailor like me who has taken to gardening.

One always remembers one's mistakes much more vividly than one's cleverest things, doesn't one? I've often noticed it. I was dining with the Pratts one night, when I told them the story that afterwards made so much difference. It was a wet night in November, and the sea was moaning. Hush! – if you don't speak you will hear it now...

Do you hear the tide? Gloomy sound, isn't it? Sometimes, about this time of year – hallo! – there it is! Don't be frightened, man – it won't eat you – it's only a noise, after all! But I'm glad you've heard it, because there are always people who think it's the wind, or my imagination, or something. You won't hear it again tonight, I fancy, for it doesn't often come more than once. Yes – that's right. Put another stick on the fire, and a little more stuff into that weak mixture you're so fond of. Do you remember old Blauklot the carpenter, on that German ship that picked us up when the *Clontarf* went to the bottom? We were hove to in a howling gale one night, as snug as you please, with no land within five hundred miles, and the ship coming up and falling off as regularly as clockwork – 'Biddy te boor beebles ashore tis night, poys!' old Blauklot sang out, as he went off to his quarters with the sail-maker. I often think of that, now that I'm ashore for good and all.

Yes, it was on a night like this, when I was at home for a spell, waiting to take the *Olympia* out on her first trip – it was on the next voyage that she broke the record, you remember – but that dates it. Ninety-two was the year, early in November.

The weather was dirty, Pratt was out of temper, and the dinner was bad, very bad indeed, which didn't improve matters, and cold, which made it worse. The poor little lady was very unhappy about it, and insisted on making a Welsh rarebit on the table to counteract the raw turnips and the half-boiled mutton. Pratt must have had a hard day. Perhaps he had lost a patient. At all events, he was in a nasty temper.

'My wife is trying to poison me, you see!' he said. 'She'll succeed some day.' I saw that she was hurt, and I made believe to laugh, and said that Mrs Pratt was much too clever to get rid of her husband in such a simple way; and then I began to tell them about Japanese tricks with spun glass and chopped horsehair and the like.

Pratt was a doctor, and knew a lot more than I did about such things, but that only put me on my mettle, and I told a story about a woman in Ireland who did for three husbands before anyone suspected foul play.

Did you never hear that tale? The fourth husband managed to keep awake and caught her, and she was hanged. How did she do it? She drugged them, and poured melted lead into their ears through a little horn funnel when they were asleep... No – that's the wind whistling. It's backing up to the southward again. I can tell by the sound. Besides, the other thing doesn't often come more than once in an evening even at this time of year – when it happened. Yes, it was in November. Poor Mrs Pratt died suddenly in her bed not long after I dined here. I can fix the date, because I got the news in New York by the steamer that followed the *Olympia* when I took her out on her first trip. You had the *Leofric* the same year? Yes, I remember. What a pair of old buffers we are coming to be, you and I. Nearly fifty years since we were apprentices together on the *Clontarf*. Shall you ever forget old Blauklot? 'Biddy te boor beebles ashore, poys!' Ha, ha! Take a little more, with all that water. It's the old Hulstkamp I found in the cellar when this house came to me, the same I brought Luke from Amsterdam five-and-twenty years ago. He had never touched a drop of it. Perhaps he's sorry now, poor fellow.

Where did I leave off? I told you that Mrs Pratt died suddenly – yes. Luke must have been lonely here after she was dead, I should think; I came to see him now and then, and he looked worn and nervous, and told me that his practice was growing too heavy for him, though he wouldn't take an assistant on any account. Years went on, and his son was killed in South Africa, and after that he began to be queer. There was something about him not like other people. I believe he kept his senses in his profession to the end; there was no complaint of his having made mad mistakes in cases, or anything of that sort, but he had a look about him –

Luke was a red-headed man with a pale face when he was young, and he was never stout; in middle age he turned a sandy grey, and after his son died he grew thinner and thinner, till his head looked like a skull with parchment stretched over it very tight, and his eyes had a sort of glare in them that was very disagreeable to look at.

He had an old dog that poor Mrs Pratt had been fond of, and that used to follow her everywhere. He was a bulldog, and the sweetest tempered beast you ever saw, though he had a way of hitching his upper lip behind one of his fangs that frightened strangers a good deal. Sometimes, of an evening, Pratt and Bumble – that was the dog's name – used to sit and look at each other a long time, thinking about old times, I suppose, when Luke's wife used to sit in that chair you've got. That was always her place, and this was the doctor's, where I'm sitting. Bumble used to climb up by the footstool – he was old and fat by that time, and could not jump much, and his teeth were getting shaky. He would look steadily at Luke, and Luke looked steadily at the dog, his face growing more and more like a skull with two little coals for eyes; and after about five minutes or so, though it may have been less, old Bumble would suddenly begin to shake all over, and all on a sudden he would set up an awful howl, as if he had been shot, and tumble out of the easy-chair and trot away, and hide himself under the sideboard, and lie there making odd noises.

Considering Pratt's looks in those last months, the thing is not surprising, you know. I'm not nervous or imaginative, but I can quite believe he might have sent a sensitive woman into hysterics – his head looked so much like a skull in parchment.

At last I came down one day before Christmas, when my ship was in dock and I had three weeks off. Bumble was not about, and I said casually that I supposed the old dog was dead.

'Yes,' Pratt answered, and I thought there was something odd in his tone even before he went on after a little pause. 'I killed him,' he said presently. 'I could stand it no longer.'

I asked what it was that Luke could not stand, though I guessed well enough.

'He had a way of sitting in her chair and glaring at me, and then howling,' Luke shivered a little. 'He didn't suffer at all, poor old Bumble,' he went on in a hurry, as if he thought I might imagine he had been cruel. 'I put dionine into his drink to make him sleep soundly, and then I chloroformed him gradually, so that he could not have felt suffocated even if he was dreaming. It's been quieter since then.'

I wondered what he meant, for the words slipped out as if he could not help saying them. I've understood since. He meant that he did not hear that noise so often after the dog was out of the way. Perhaps he thought at first that it was old Bumble in the yard howling at the moon, though it's not that kind of noise, is it? Besides, I know what it is, if Luke didn't. It's only a noise after all, and a noise never hurt anybody yet. But he was much more imaginative than I am. No doubt there really is something about this place that I don't understand; but when I don't understand a thing, I call it a phenomenon, and I don't take it for granted that it's going to kill me, as he did. I don't understand everything, by long odds, nor do you, nor does any man who has been to sea. We used to talk of tidal waves, for instance, and we could not account for them; now we account for them by calling them submarine earthquakes, and we branch off into fifty theories, any one of which might make earthquakes quite comprehensible if we only knew what they were. I fell in with one of them once, and the inkstand flew straight up from the table against the ceiling of my cabin. The same thing happened to Captain Lecky – I dare say you've read about it in his 'Wrinkles'. Very good. If that sort of thing took place ashore, in this room for instance, a nervous person would talk about spirits and levitation and fifty things that mean nothing, instead of just quietly setting it down as a 'phenomenon' that has not been explained yet. My view of that voice, you see.

Besides, what is there to prove that Luke killed his wife? I would not even suggest such a thing to anyone but you. After all, there was nothing but the coincidence that poor little Mrs Pratt died suddenly in her bed a few days after I told that story at dinner. She was not the only woman who ever died like that. Luke got the doctor over from the next parish, and they agreed that she had died of something the matter with her heart. Why not? It's common enough.

Of course, there was the ladle. I never told anybody about that, and it made me start when I found it in the cupboard in the bedroom. It was new, too – a little tinned iron ladle that had not been in the fire more than once or twice, and there was some lead in it that had been melted, and stuck to the bottom of the bowl, all grey, with hardened dross on it. But that proves nothing. A country doctor is generally a handy man, who does everything for himself, and Luke may have had a dozen reasons for melting a little lead in a ladle. He was fond of sea-fishing, for instance, and he may have cast a sinker for a night-line; perhaps it was a weight for the hall clock, or something like that. All the same, when I found it I had a rather queer sensation, because it looked so much like the thing I had described when I told them the story. Do you understand? It affected me unpleasantly, and I threw it away; it's at the bottom of the sea a mile from the Spit, and it will be jolly well rusted beyond recognizing if it's ever washed up by the tide.

You see, Luke must have bought it in the village, years ago, for the man sells just such ladles still. I suppose they are used in cooking. In any case, there was no reason why an inquisitive housemaid should find such a thing lying about, with lead in it, and wonder what it was, and perhaps talk to the maid who heard me tell the story at dinner – for that girl married the plumber's son in the village, and may remember the whole thing.

You understand me, don't you? Now that Luke Pratt is dead and gone, and lies buried beside his wife, with an honest man's tombstone at his head, I should not care to stir up anything that could hurt his memory. They are both dead, and their son, too. There was trouble enough about Luke's death, as it was.

How? He was found dead on the beach one morning, and there was a coroner's inquest. There were marks on his throat, but he had not been robbed. The verdict was that he had come to his end 'By the hands or teeth of some person or animal unknown,' for half the jury thought it might have been a big dog that had thrown him down and gripped his windpipe, though the skin of his throat was not broken. No one knew at what time he had gone out, nor where he had been. He was found lying on his back above high-water mark, and an old cardboard bandbox that had belonged to his wife lay under his hand, open. The lid had fallen off. He seemed to have been carrying home a skull in the box – doctors are fond of collecting such things. It had rolled out and lay near his head, and it was a remarkably fine skull, rather small, beautifully shaped and very white, with perfect teeth. That is to say, the upper jaw was perfect, but there was no lower one at all, when I first saw it.

Yes, I found it here when I came. You see, it was very white and polished, like a thing meant to be kept under a glass case, and the people did not know where it came from, nor what to do with it; so they put it back into the bandbox and set it on the shelf of the cupboard in the best bedroom, and of course they showed it to me when I took possession. I was taken down to the beach, too, to be shown the place where Luke was found, and the old fisherman explained just how he was lying, and the skull beside him. The only point he could not explain was why the skull had rolled up the sloping sand towards Luke's head instead of rolling downhill to his feet. It did not seem odd to me at the time, but I have often thought of it since, for the place is rather steep. I'll take you there tomorrow if you like – I made a sort of cairn of stones there afterwards.

When he fell down, or was thrown down – whichever happened – the bandbox struck the sand, and the lid came off, and the thing came out and ought to have rolled down. But it didn't. It was close to his head, almost touching it, and turned with the face towards it. I say it didn't strike me as odd when the man told me; but I could not help thinking about it afterwards, again and again, till I saw a picture of it all when I closed my eyes; and then I began to ask myself why the plaguey thing had rolled up instead of down, and why it had stopped near Luke's head instead of anywhere else, a yard away, for instance.

You naturally want to know what conclusion I reached, don't you? None that at all explained the rolling, at all events. But I got something else into my head, after a time, that made me feel downright uncomfortable.

Oh, I don't mean as to anything supernatural! There may be ghosts, or there may not be. If there are, I'm not inclined to believe that they can hurt living people except by frightening them, and, for my part, I would rather face any shape of ghost than a fog in the Channel when it's crowded. No. What bothered me was just a foolish idea, that's all, and I cannot tell how it began, nor what made it grow till it turned into a certainty.

I was thinking about Luke and his poor wife one evening over my pipe and a dull book, when it occurred to me that the skull might possibly be hers, and I have never got rid of the thought since. You'll tell me there's no sense in it, no doubt, that Mrs Pratt was buried like a Christian and is lying in the churchyard where they put her, and that it's perfectly monstrous to suppose her husband kept her skull in her old bandbox in his bedroom. All the same, in the face of reason, and common sense, and probability, I'm convinced that he did. Doctors do all sorts of queer things that would make men like you and me feel creepy, and those are just the things that don't seem probable, nor logical, nor sensible to us.

Then, don't you see? – if it really was her skull, poor woman, the only way of accounting for his having it is that he really killed her, and did it in that way, as the woman killed her husbands in the story, and that he was afraid there might be an examination some day which would betray him. You see, I told that too, and I believe it had really happened some fifty or sixty years ago. They dug up the three skulls, you know, and there was a small lump of lead rattling about in each one. That was what hanged the woman. Luke remembered that, I'm sure. I don't want to know what he did when he thought of it; my taste never ran in the direction of horrors, and I don't fancy you care for them either, do you? No. If you did, you might supply what is wanting to the story.

It must have been rather grim, eh? I wish I did not see the whole thing so distinctly, just as everything must have happened. He took it the night before she was buried, I'm sure, after the coffin had been shut, and when the servant girl was asleep. I would bet anything, that when he'd got it, he put something under the sheet in its place, to fill up and look like it. What do you suppose he put there, under the sheet?

I don't wonder you take me up on what I'm saying! First I tell you that I don't want to know what happened, and that I hate to think about horrors, and then I describe the whole thing to you as if I had seen it. I'm quite sure that it was her work-bag that he put there. I remember the bag very well, for she always used it of an evening; it was made of brown plush, and when it was stuffed full it was about the size of – you understand. Yes, there I am, at it again! You may laugh at me, but you don't live here alone, where it was done, and you didn't tell Luke the story about the melted lead. I'm not nervous, I tell you, but sometimes I begin to feel that I understand why some people are. I dwell on all this when I'm alone, and I dream of it, and when that thing screams – well, frankly, I don't like the noise any more than you do, though I should be used to it by this time.

I ought not to be nervous. I've sailed in a haunted ship. There was a Man in the Top, and two-thirds of the crew died of the West Coast fever inside of ten days after we anchored; but I was all right, then and afterwards. I have seen some ugly sights, too, just as you have, and all the rest of us. But nothing ever stuck in my head in the way this does.

You see, I've tried to get rid of the thing, but it doesn't like that. It wants to be there in its place, in Mrs Pratt's bandbox in the cupboard in the best bedroom. It's not happy anywhere else. How do I know that? Because I've tried it. You don't suppose that I've not tried, do you? As long as it's there it only screams now and then, generally at this time of year, but if I put it out of the house it goes on all night, and no servant will stay here twenty-four hours. As it is, I've often been left alone and have been obliged to shift for myself for a fortnight at a time. No one from the village would ever pass a night under the roof now, and as for selling the place, or even letting it, that's out of the question. The old women say that if I stay here I shall come to a bad end myself before long.

I'm not afraid of that. You smile at the mere idea that anyone could take such nonsense seriously. Quite right. It's utterly blatant nonsense, I agree with you. Didn't I tell you that it's only a noise after all when you started and looked round as if you expected to see a ghost standing behind your chair?

I may be all wrong about the skull, and I like to think that I am – when I can. It may be just a fine specimen which Luke got somewhere long ago, and what rattles about inside when you shake it may be nothing but a pebble, or a bit of hard clay, or anything. Skulls that have lain long in the ground generally have something inside them that rattles, don't they? No, I've never tried to get it out, whatever it is; I'm afraid it might be lead, don't you see? And if it is, I don't want to know the fact, for I'd much rather not be sure. If it really is lead, I killed her quite as much as if I had done the deed myself. Anybody must see that, I should think. As long as I don't know for certain, I have the consolation of saying that it's all utterly ridiculous nonsense, that Mrs Pratt died a natural death and that the beautiful skull belonged to Luke when he was a student in London. But if I were quite sure, I believe I should have to leave the house; indeed I do, most certainly. As it is, I had to give up trying to sleep in the best bedroom where the cupboard is.

You ask me why I don't throw it into the pond – yes, but please don't call it a 'confounded bugbear' – it doesn't like being called names.

There! Lord, what a shriek! I told you so! You're quite pale, man. Fill up your pipe and draw your chair nearer to the fire, and take some more drink. Old Hollands never hurt anybody yet. I've seen a Dutchman in Java drink half a jug of Hulstkamp in a morning without turning a hair. I don't take much rum myself, because it doesn't agree with my rheumatism, but you are not rheumatic and it won't damage you. Besides, it's a very damp night outside. The wind is howling again, and it will soon be in the south-west; do you hear how the windows rattle? The tide must have turned too, by the moaning.

We should not have heard the thing again if you had not said that. I'm pretty sure we should not. Oh yes, if you choose to describe it as a coincidence, you are quite welcome, but I would rather that you should not call the thing names again, if you don't mind. It may be that the poor little woman hears, and perhaps it hurts her, don't you know? Ghosts? No! You don't call anything a ghost that you can take in your hands and look at in broad daylight, and that rattles when you shake it. Do you, now? But it's something that hears and understands; there's no doubt about that.

I tried sleeping in the best bedroom when I first came to the house, just because it was the best and most comfortable, but I had to give it up. It was their room, and there's the big bed she died in, and the cupboard is in the thickness of the wall, near the head, on the left. That's where it likes to be kept, in its bandbox. I only used the room for a fortnight after I came, and then I turned out and took the little room downstairs, next to the surgery, where Luke used to sleep when he expected to be called to a patient during the night.

I was always a good sleeper ashore; eight hours is my dose, eleven to seven when I'm alone, twelve to eight when I have a friend with me. But I could not sleep after three o'clock in the morning in that room – a quarter past, to be accurate – as a matter of fact, I timed it with my old pocket chronometer, which still keeps good time, and it was always at exactly seventeen minutes past three. I wonder whether that was the hour when she died?

It was not what you have heard. If it had been that, I could not have stood it two nights. It was just a start and a moan and hard breathing for a few seconds in the cupboard, and it could never have waked me under ordinary circumstances, I'm sure. I suppose you are like me in that, and we are just like other people who have been to sea. No natural sounds disturb us at all, not all the racket of a square-rigger hove to in a heavy gale, or rolling on her beam ends before the wind. But if a lead pencil gets adrift and rattles in the drawer of your cabin table you are awake in a moment. Just so – you always understand. Very well, the noise in the cupboard was no louder than that, but it waked me instantly.

I said it was like a 'start'. I know what I mean, but it's hard to explain without seeming to talk nonsense. Of course you cannot exactly 'hear' a person 'start'; at the most, you might hear the quick drawing of the breath between the parted lips and closed teeth, and the almost imperceptible sound of clothing that moved suddenly though very slightly. It was like that.

You know how one feels what a sailing vessel is going to do, two or three seconds before she does it, when one has the wheel. Riders say the same of a horse, but that's less strange, because the horse is a live animal with feelings of its own, and only poets and landsmen talk about a ship being alive, and all that. But I have always felt somehow that besides being a steaming machine or a sailing machine for carrying weights, a vessel at sea is a sensitive instrument, and a means of communication between nature and man, and most particularly the man at the wheel, if she is steered by hand. She takes her impressions directly from wind and sea, tide and stream, and transmits them to the man's hand, just as the wireless telegraphy picks up the interrupted currents aloft and turns them out below in the form of a message.

You see what I am driving at; I felt that something started in the cupboard, and I felt it so vividly that I heard it, though there may have been nothing to hear, and the sound inside my head waked me suddenly.

But I really heard the other noise. It was as if it were muffled inside a box, as far away as if it came through a long-distance telephone; and yet I knew that it was inside the cupboard near the head of my bed. My hair did not bristle and my blood did not run cold that time. I simply resented being waked up by something that had no business to make a noise, any more than a pencil should rattle in the drawer of my cabin table on board ship. For I did not understand; I just supposed that the cupboard had some communication with the outside air, and that the wind had got in and was moaning through it with a sort of very faint screech. I struck a light and looked at my watch, and it was seventeen minutes past three. Then I turned over and went to sleep on my right ear. That's my good one; I'm pretty deaf with the other, for I struck the water with it when I was a lad in diving from the fore-topsail yard. Silly thing to do, it was, but the result is very convenient when I want to go to sleep when there's a noise.

That was the first night, and the same thing happened again and several times afterwards, but not regularly, though it was always at the same time, to a second; perhaps I was sometimes sleeping on my good ear, and sometimes not. I overhauled the cupboard and there was no way by which the wind could get in, or anything else, for the door makes a good fit, having been meant to keep out moths, I suppose; Mrs Pratt must have kept her winter things in it, for it still smells of camphor and turpentine.

After about a fortnight I had had enough of the noises. So far I had said to myself that it would be silly to yield to it and take the skull out of the room. Things always look differently by daylight, don't they? But the voice grew louder – I suppose one may call it a voice – and it got inside my deaf ear, too, one night. I realized that when I was wide awake, for my good ear was jammed down on the pillow, and I ought not to have heard a foghorn in that position. But I heard that, and it made me lose my temper, unless it scared me, for sometimes the two are not far apart. I struck a light and got up, and I opened the cupboard, grabbed the bandbox and threw it out of the window, as far as I could.

Then my hair stood on end. The thing screamed in the air, like a shell from a twelve-inch gun. It fell on the other side of the road. The night was very dark, and I could not see it fall, but I know it fell beyond the road. The window is just over the front door, it's fifteen yards to the fence, more or less, and the road is ten yards wide. There's a thick-set hedge beyond, along the glebe that belongs to the vicarage.

I did not sleep much more than night. It was not more than half an hour after I had thrown the bandbox out when I heard a shriek outside – like what we've had tonight, but worse, more despairing, I should call it; and it may have been my imagination, but I could have sworn that the screams came nearer and nearer each time. I lit a pipe, and walked up and down for a bit, and then took a book and sat up reading, but I'll be hanged if I can remember what I read nor even what the book was, for every now and then a shriek came up that would have made a dead man turn in his coffin.

A little before dawn someone knocked at the front door. There was no mistaking that for anything else, and I opened my window and looked down, for I guessed that someone wanted the doctor, supposing that the new man had taken Luke's house. It was rather a relief to hear a human knock after that awful noise.

You cannot see the door from above, owing to the little porch. The knocking came again, and I called out, asking who was there, but nobody answered, though the knock was repeated. I sang out again, and said that the doctor did not live here any longer. There was no answer, but it occurred to me that it might be some old countryman who was stone deaf. So I took my candle and went down to open the door. Upon my word, I was not thinking of the thing yet, and I had almost forgotten the other noises. I went down convinced that I should find somebody outside, on the doorstep, with a message. I set the candle on the hall table, so that the wind should not blow it out when I opened. While I was drawing the old-fashioned bolt I heard the knocking again. It was not loud, and it had a queer, hollow sound, now that I was close to it, I remember, but I certainly thought it was made by some person who wanted to get in.

It wasn't. There was nobody there, but as I opened the door inward, standing a little on one side, so as to see out at once, something rolled across the threshold and stopped against my foot.

I drew back as I felt it, for I knew what it was before I looked down. I cannot tell you how I knew, and it seemed unreasonable, for I am still quite sure that I had thrown it across the road. It's a French window, that opens wide, and I got a good swing when I flung it out. Besides, when I went out early in the morning, I found the bandbox beyond the thick hedge.

You may think it opened when I threw it, and that the skull dropped out; but that's impossible, for nobody could throw an empty cardboard box so far. It's out of the question; you might as well try to fling a ball of paper twenty-five yards, or a blown bird's egg.

To go back, I shut and bolted the hall door, picked the thing up carefully, and put it on the table beside the candle. I did that mechanically, as one instinctively does the right thing in danger without thinking at all – unless one does the opposite. It may seem odd, but I believe my first thought had been that somebody might come and find me there on the threshold while it was resting against my foot, lying a little on its side, and turning one hollow eye up at my face, as if it meant to accuse me. And the light and shadow from the candle played in the hollows of the eyes as it stood on the table, so that they seemed to open and shut at me. Then the candle went out quite unexpectedly, though the door was fastened and there was not the least draught; and I used up at least half a dozen matches before it would burn again.

I sat down rather suddenly, without quite knowing why. Probably I had been badly frightened, and perhaps you will admit there was no great shame in being scared. The thing had come home, and it wanted to go upstairs, back to its cupboard. I sat still and stared at it for a bit, till I began to feel very cold; then I took it and carried it up and set it in its place, and I remember that I spoke to it, and promised that it should have its bandbox again in the morning.

You want to know whether I stayed in the room till daybreak? Yes, but I kept a light burning, and sat up smoking and reading, most likely out of fright; plain, undeniable fear, and you need not call it cowardice either, for that's not the same thing. I could not have stayed alone with that thing in the cupboard; I should have been scared to death, though I'm not more timid than other people. Confound it all, man, it had crossed the road alone, and had got up the doorstep and had knocked to be let in.

When the dawn came, I put on my boots and went out to find the bandbox. I had to go a good way round, by the gate near the high road, and I found the box open and hanging on the other side of the hedge. It had caught on the twigs by the string, and the lid had fallen off and was lying on the ground below it. That shows that it did not open till it was well over; and if it had not opened as soon as it left my hand, what was inside it must have gone beyond the road too.

That's all. I took the box upstairs to the cupboard, and put the skull back and locked it up. When the girl brought me my breakfast she said she was sorry, but that she must go, and she did not care if she lost her month's wages. I looked at her, and her face was a sort of greenish, yellowish white. I pretended to be surprised, and asked what was the matter; but that was of no use, for she just turned on me and wanted to know whether I meant to stay in a haunted house, and how long I expected to live if I did, for though she noticed I was sometimes a little hard of hearing, she did not believe that even I could sleep through those screams again – and if I could, why had I been moving about the house and opening and shutting the front door, between three and four in the morning? There was no answering that, since she had heard me, so off she went, and I was left to myself. I went down to the village during the morning and found a woman who was willing to come and do the little work there is and cook my dinner, on condition that she might go home every night. As for me, I moved downstairs that day, and I have never tried to sleep in the best bedroom since. After a little while I got a brace of middle-aged Scotch servants from London, and things were quiet enough for a long time. I began by telling them that the house was in a very exposed position, and that the wind whistled round it a good deal in the autumn and winter, which had given it a bad name in the village, the Cornish people being inclined to superstition and telling ghost stories. The two hard-faced, sandy-haired sisters almost smiled, and they answered with great contempt that they had no great opinion of any Southern bogey whatever, having been in service in two English haunted houses, where they had never seen so much as the Boy in Grey, whom they reckoned no very particular rarity in Forfarshire.

They stayed with me several months, and while they were in the house we had peace and quiet. One of them is here again now, but she went away with her sister within the year. This one – she was the cook – married the sexton, who works in my garden. That's the way of it. It's a small village and he has not much to do, and he knows enough about flowers to help me nicely, besides doing most of the hard work; for though I'm fond of exercise, I'm getting a little stiff in the hinges. He's a sober, silent sort of fellow, who minds his own business, and he was a widower when I came here – Trehearn is his name, James Trehearn. The Scottish sisters would not admit that there was anything wrong about the house, but when November came they gave me warning that they were going, on the ground that the chapel was such a long walk from here, being in the next parish, and that they could not possibly go to our church. But the younger one came back in the spring, and as soon as the banns could be published she was married to James Trehearn by the vicar, and she seems to have had no scruples about hearing him preach since then. I'm quite satisfied, if she is! The couple live in a small cottage that looks over the churchyard.

I suppose you are wondering what all this has to do with what I was talking about. I'm alone so much that when an old friend comes to see me, I sometimes go on talking just for the sake of hearing my own voice. But in this case there is really a connection of ideas. It was James Trehearn who buried poor Mrs Pratt, and her husband after her in the same grave, and it's not far from the back of his cottage. That's the connection in my mind, you see. It's plain enough. He knows something; I'm quite sure that he does, though he's such a reticent beggar.

Yes, I'm alone in the house at night now, for Mrs Trehearn does everything herself, and when I have a friend the sexton's niece comes in to wait on the table. He takes his wife home every evening in winter, but in summer, when there's light, she goes by herself. She's not a nervous woman, but she's less sure than she used to be that there are no bogies in England worth a Scotch-woman's notice. Isn't it amusing, the idea that Scotland has a monopoly of the supernatural? Odd sort of national pride, I call that, don't you?

That's a good fire, isn't it? When driftwood gets started at last there's nothing like it, I think. Yes, we get lots of it, for I'm sorry to say there are still a great many wrecks about here. It's a lonely coast, and you may have all the wood you want for the trouble of bringing it in. Trehearn and I borrow a cart now and then, and load it between here and the Spit. I hate a coal fire when I can get wood of any sort. A log is company, even if it's only a piece of a deck beam or timber sawn off, and the salt in it makes pretty sparks. See how they fly, like Japanese hand-fireworks! Upon my word, with an old friend and a good fire and a pipe, one forgets all about that thing upstairs, especially now that the wind has moderated. It's only a lull, though, and it will blow a gale before morning.

You think you would like to see the skull? I've no objection. There's no reason why you shouldn't have a look at it, and you never saw a more perfect one in your life, except that there are two front teeth missing in the lower jaw.

Oh yes – I had not told you about the jaw yet. Trehearn found it in the garden last spring when he was digging a pit for a new asparagus bed. You know we make asparagus beds six or eight feet deep here. Yes, yes – I had forgotten to tell you that. He was digging straight down, just as he digs a grave; if you want a good asparagus bed made, I advise you to get a sexton to make it for you. Those fellows have a wonderful knack at that sort of digging.

Trehearn had got down about three feet when he cut into a mass of white lime in the side of the trench. He had noticed that the earth was a little looser there, though he says it had not been disturbed for a number of years. I suppose he thought that even old lime might not be good for asparagus, so he broke it out and threw it up. It was pretty hard, he says, in biggish lumps, and out of sheer force of habit he cracked the lumps with his spade as they lay outside the pit beside him; the jaw bone of the skull dropped out of one of the pieces. He thinks he must have knocked out the two front teeth in breaking up the lime, but he did not see them anywhere. He's a very experienced man in such things, as you may imagine, and he said at once that the jaw had probably belonged to a young woman, and that the teeth had been complete when she died. He brought it to me, and asked me if I wanted to keep it; if I did not, he said he would drop it into the next grave he made in the churchyard, as he supposed it was a Christian jaw, and ought to have decent burial, wherever the rest of the body might be. I told him that doctors often put bones into quicklime to whiten them nicely, and that

I supposed Dr Pratt had once had a little lime pit in the garden for that purpose, and had forgotten the jaw. Trehearn looked at me quietly.

'Maybe it fitted that skull that used to be in the cupboard upstairs, sir,' he said. 'Maybe Dr Pratt had put the skull into the lime to clean it, or something, and when he took it out he left the lower jaw behind. There's some human hair sticking in the lime, sir.'

I saw there was, and that was what Trehearn said. If he did not suspect something, why in the world should he have suggested that the jaw might fit the skull? Besides, it did. That's proof that he knows more than he cares to tell. Do you suppose he looked before she was buried? Or perhaps – when he buried Luke in the same grave –

Well, well, it's of no use to go over that, is it? I said I would keep the jaw with the skull, and I took it upstairs and fitted it into its place. There's not the slightest doubt about the two belonging together, and together they are.

Trehearn knows several things. We were talking about plastering the kitchen a while ago, and he happened to remember that it had not been done since the very week when Mrs Pratt died. He did not say that the mason must have left some lime on the place, but he thought it, and that it was the very same lime he had found in the asparagus pit. He knows a lot. Trehearn is one of your silent beggars who can put two and two together. That grave is very near the back of his cottage, too, and he's one of the quickest men with a spade I ever saw. If he wanted to know the truth, he could, and no one else would ever be the wiser unless he chose to tell. In a quiet village like ours, people don't go and spend the night in the churchyard to see whether the sexton potters about by himself between ten o'clock and daylight.

What is awful to think of, is Luke's deliberation, if he did it; his cool certainty that no one would find him out; above all, his nerve, for that must have been extraordinary. I sometimes think it's bad enough to live in the place where it was done, if it really was done. I always put in the condition, you see, for the sake of his memory, and a little bit for my own sake, too.

I'll go upstairs and fetch the box in a minute. Let me light my pipe; there's no hurry! We had supper early, and it's only half-past nine o'clock. I never let a friend go to bed before twelve, or with less than three glasses – you may have as many more as you like, but you shan't have less, for the sake of old times.

It's breezing up again, do you hear? That was only a lull just now, and we are going to have a bad night.

A thing happened that made me start a little when I found that the jaw fitted exactly. I'm not very easily startled in that way myself, but I have seen people make a quick movement, drawing their breath sharply, when they had thought they were alone and suddenly turned and saw someone very near them. Nobody can call that fear. You wouldn't, would you? No. Well, just when I had set the jaw in its place under the skull, the teeth closed sharply on my finger. It felt exactly as if it were biting me hard, and I confess that I jumped before I realized that I had been pressing the jaw and the skull together with my other hand. I assure you I was not at all nervous. It was broad daylight, too, and a fine day, and the sun was streaming into the best bedroom. It would have been absurd to be nervous, and it was only a quick mistaken impression, but it really made me feel queer. Somehow it made me think of the funny verdict of the coroner's jury on Luke's death, 'by the hand or teeth of some person or animal unknown'. Ever since that I've wished I had seen those marks on his throat, though the lower jaw was missing then.

I have often seen a man do insane things with his hands that he does not realize at all. I once saw a man hanging on by an old awning stop with one hand, leaning backward, outboard, with all his weight on it, and he was just cutting the stop with the knife in his other hand when I got my arms round him. We were in mid-ocean, going twenty knots. He had not the smallest idea what he was doing; neither had I when I managed to pinch my finger between the teeth of that thing. I can feel it now. It was exactly as if it were alive and were trying to bite me. It would if it could, for I know it hates me, poor thing! Do you suppose that what rattles about inside is really a bit of lead? Well, I'll get the box down presently, and if whatever it is happens to drop out into your hands, that's your affair. If it's only a clod of earth or a pebble, the whole matter would be off my mind, and I don't believe I should ever think of the skull again; but somehow I cannot bring myself to shake out the bit of hard stuff myself. The mere idea that it may be lead makes me confoundedly uncomfortable, yet I've got the conviction that I shall know before long. I shall certainly know. I'm sure Trehearn knows, but he's such a silent beggar.

I'll go upstairs now and get it. What? You had better go with me? Ha, ha! do you think I'm afraid of a bandbox and a noise? Nonsense!

Bother the candle, it won't light! As if the ridiculous thing understood what it's wanted for! Look at that – the third match. They light fast enough for my pipe. There, do you see? It's a fresh box, just out of the tin safe where I keep the supply on account of the dampness. Oh, you think the wick of the candle may be damp, do you? All right, I'll light the beastly thing in the fire. That won't go out, at all events. Yes, it sputters a bit, but it will keep lighted now. It burns just like any other candle, doesn't it? The fact is, candles are not very good about here. I don't know where they come from, but they have a way of burning low occasionally, with a greenish flame that spits tiny sparks, and I'm often annoyed by their going out of themselves. It cannot be helped, for it will be long before we have electricity in our village. It really is rather a poor light, isn't it?

You think I had better leave you the candle and take the lamp, do you? I don't like to carry lamps about, that's the truth. I never dropped one in my life, but I have always thought I might, and it's so confoundedly dangerous if you do. Besides, I am pretty well used to these rotten candles by this time.

You may as well finish that glass while I'm getting it, for I don't mean to let you off with less than three before you go to bed. You won't have to go upstairs, either, for I've put you in the old study next to the surgery – that's where I live myself. The fact is, I never ask a friend to sleep upstairs now. The last man who did was Crackenthorpe, and he said he was kept awake all night. You remember old Crack, don't you? He stuck to the Service, and they've just made him an admiral. Yes, I'm off now – unless the candle goes out. I couldn't help asking if you remembered Crackenthorpe. If anyone had told us that the skinny little idiot he used to be was to turn out the most successful of the lot of us, we should have laughed at the idea, shouldn't we? You and I did not do badly, it's true – but I'm really going now. I don't mean to let you think that I've been putting it off by talking! As if there were anything to be afraid of! If I were scared, I should tell you so quite frankly, and get you to go upstairs with me.

Here's the box. I brought it down very carefully, so as not to disturb it, poor thing. You see, if it were shaken, the jaw might get separated from it again, and I'm sure it wouldn't like that. Yes, the candle went out as I was coming downstairs, but that was the draught from the leaky window on the landing. Did you hear anything? Yes, there was another scream. Am I pale, do you say? That's nothing. My heart is a little queer sometimes, and I went upstairs too fast. In fact, that's one reason why I really prefer to live altogether on the ground floor.

Wherever the shriek came from, it was not from the skull, for I had the box in my hand when I heard the noise, and here it is now; so we have proved definitely that the screams are produced by something else. I've no doubt I shall find out some day what makes them. Some crevice in the wall, of course, or a crack in a chimney, or a chink in the frame of a window. That's the way all ghost stories end in real life. Do you know, I'm jolly glad I thought of going up and bringing it down for you to see, for that last shriek settles the question. To think that I should have been so weak as to fancy that the poor skull could really cry out like a living thing!

Now I'll open the box, and we'll take it out and look at it under the bright light. It's rather awful to think that the poor lady used to sit there, in your chair, evening after evening, in just the same light, isn't it? But then – I've made up my mind that it's all rubbish from beginning to end, and that it's just an old skull that Luke had when he was a student; and perhaps he put it into the lime merely to whiten it, and could not find the jaw.

I made a seal on the string, you see, after I had put the jaw in its place, and I wrote on the cover. There's the old white label on it still, from the milliner's, addressed to Mrs Pratt when the hat was sent to her, and as there was room I wrote on the edge: 'A skull, once the property of the late Luke Pratt, MD.' I don't quite know why I wrote that, unless it was with the idea of explaining how the thing happened to be in my possession. I cannot help wondering sometimes what sort of hat it was that came in the bandbox. What colour was it, do you think? Was it a gay spring hat with a bobbing feather and pretty ribands? Strange that the very same box should hold the head that wore the finery – perhaps. No – we made up our minds that it just came from the hospital in London where Luke did his time. It's far better to look at it in that light, isn't it? There's no more connection between that skull and poor Mrs Pratt than there was between my story about the lead and –

Good Lord! Take the lamp – don't let it go out, if you can help it – I'll have the window fastened again in a second – I say, what a gale! There, it's out! I told you so! Never mind, there's the firelight – I've got the window shut – the bolt was only half down. Was the box blown off the table? Where the deuce is it? There! That won't open again, for I've put up the bar. Good dodge, an old-fashioned bar – there's nothing like it. Now, you find the bandbox while I light the lamp. Confound those wretched matches! Yes, a pipe spill is better – it must light in the fire – I hadn't thought of it – thank you – there we are again. Now, where's the box? Yes, put it back on the table, and we'll open it.

That's the first time I have ever known the wind to burst that window open; but it was partly carelessness on my part when I last shut it. Yes, of course I heard the scream. It seemed to go all round the house before it broke in at the window. That proves that it's always been the wind and nothing else, doesn't it? When it was not the wind, it was my imagination. I've always been a very imaginative man: I must have been, though I did not know it. As we grow older we understand ourselves better, don't you know?

I'll have a drop of the Hulstkamp neat, by way of an exception, since you are filling up your glass. That damp gust chilled me, and with my rheumatic tendency I'm very much afraid of a chill, for the cold sometimes seems to stick in my joints all winter when it once gets in.

By George, that's good stuff! I'll just light a fresh pipe, now that

everything is snug again, and then we'll open the box. I'm so glad we
heard that last scream together, with the skull here on the table between
us, for a thing cannot possibly be in two places at the same time, and the
noise most certainly came from outside, as any noise the wind makes
must. You thought you heard it scream through the room after the
window was burst open? Oh yes, so did I, but that was natural enough
when everything was open. Of course we heard the wind. What could
one expect?

Look here, please. I want you to see that the seal is intact before we
open the box together. Will you take my glasses? No, you have your
own. All right. The seal is sound, you see, and you can read the words
of the motto easily. 'Sweet and low' – that's it – because the poem goes
on 'Wind of the Western Sea', and says, 'blow him again to me', and all
that. Here is the seal on my watch chain, where it's hung for more than
forty years. My poor little wife gave it to me when I was courting, and
I never had any other. It was just like her to think of those words – she
was always fond of Tennyson.

It's no use to cut the string, for it's fastened to the box, so I'll just break
the wax and untie the knot, and afterwards we'll seal it up again. You
see, I like to feel that the thing is safe in its place, and that nobody can
take it out. Not that I should suspect Trehearn of meddling with it, but
I always feel that he knows a lot more than he tells.

You see, I've managed it without breaking the string, though when I
fastened it I never expected to open the bandbox again. The lid comes
off easily enough. There! Now look!

What! Nothing in it! Empty! It's gone, man, the skull is gone!

No, there's nothing the matter with me. I'm only trying to collect my
thoughts. It's so strange. I'm positively certain that it was inside when
I put on the seal last spring. I can't have imagined that: it's utterly
impossible. If I ever took a stiff glass with a friend now and then, I would
admit that I might have made some idiotic mistake when I had taken
too much. But I don't, and I never did. A pint of ale at supper and half
a go of rum at bedtime was the most I ever took in my good days. I
believe it's always we sober fellows who get rheumatism and gout! Yet
there was my seal, and there is the empty bandbox. That's plain enough.

I say, I don't half like this. It's not right. There's something wrong
about it, in my opinion. You needn't talk to me about supernatural
manifestations, for I don't believe in them, not a little bit! Somebody
must have tampered with the seal and stolen the skull. Sometimes, when
I go out to work in the garden in summer, I leave my watch and chain
on the table. Trehearn must have taken the seal then, and used it, for he
would be quite sure that I should not come in for at least an hour.

If it was not Trehearn – oh, don't talk to me about the possibility that the thing has got out by itself! If it has, it must be somewhere about the house, in some out-of-the-way corner, waiting. We may come upon it anywhere, waiting for us, don't you know? – just waiting in the dark. Then it will scream at me; it will shriek at me in the dark, for it hates me, I tell you!

The bandbox is quite empty. We are not dreaming, either of us. There, I turn it upside down.

What's that? Something fell out as I turned it over. It's on the floor, it's near your feet. I know it is, and we must find it. Help me to find it, man. Have you got it? For God's sake, give it to me, quickly!

Lead! I knew it when I heard it fall. I knew it couldn't be anything else by the little thud it made on the hearthrug. So it was lead after all and Luke did it.

I feel a little bit shaken up – not exactly nervous, you know, but badly shaken up, that's the fact. Anybody would, I should think. After all, you cannot say that it's fear of the thing, for I went up and brought it down – at least, I believed I was bringing it down, and that's the same thing, and by George, rather than give in to such silly nonsense, I'll take the box upstairs again and put it back in its place. It's not that. It's the certainty that the poor little woman came to her end in that way, by my fault, because I told the story. That's what is so dreadful. Somehow, I had always hoped that I should never be quite sure of it, but there is no doubting it now. Look at that!

Look at it! That little lump of lead with no particular shape. Think of what it did, man! Doesn't it make you shiver? He gave her something to make her sleep, of course, but there must have been one moment of awful agony. Think of having boiling lead poured into your brain. Think of it. She was dead before she could scream, but only think of – oh! there it is again – it's just outside – I know it's just outside – I can't keep it out of my head! – oh! – oh!

You thought I had fainted? No, I wish I had, for it would have stopped sooner. It's all very well to say that it's only a noise, and that a noise never hurt anybody – you're as white as a shroud yourself. There's only one thing to be done, if we hope to close an eye tonight. We must find it and put it back into its bandbox and shut it up in the cupboard, where it likes to be. I don't know how it got out, but it wants to get in again. That's why it screams so awfully tonight – it was never so bad as this – never since I first –

Bury it? Yes, if we can find it, we'll bury it, if it takes us all night. We'll bury it six feet deep and ram down the earth over it, so that it shall never get out again, and if it screams, we shall hardly hear it so deep down. Quick, we'll get the lantern and look for it. It cannot be far away; I'm sure it's just outside – it was coming in when I shut the window, I know it.

Yes, you're quite right. I'm losing my senses, and I must get hold of myself. Don't speak to me for a minute or two; I'll sit quite still and keep my eyes shut and repeat something I know. That's the best way.

'Add together the altitude, the latitude, and the polar distance, divide by two and subtract the altitude from the half-sum; then add the logarithm of the secant of the latitude, the cosecant of the polar distance, the cosine of the half-sum and the sine of the half-sum minus the altitude' – there! Don't say that I'm out of my senses, for my memory is all right, isn't it?

Of course, you may say that it's mechanical, and that we never forget the things we learned when we were boys and have used almost every day for a lifetime. But that's the very point. When a man is going crazy, it's the mechanical part of his mind that gets out of order and won't work right; he remembers things that never happened, or he sees things that aren't real, or he hears noises when there is perfect silence. That's not what is the matter with either of us, is it?

Come, we'll get the lantern and go round the house. It's not raining – only blowing like old boots, as we used to say. The lantern is in the cupboard under the stairs in the hall, and I always keep it trimmed in case of a wreck.

No use to look for the thing? I don't see how you can say that. It was nonsense to talk of burying it, of course, for it doesn't want to be buried; it wants to go back into its bandbox and be taken upstairs, poor thing! Trehearn took it out, I know, and made the seal over again. Perhaps he took it to the churchyard, and he may have meant well. I dare say he thought that it would not scream any more if it were quietly laid in consecrated ground, near where it belongs. But it has come home. Yes, that's it. He's not half a bad fellow, Trehearn, and rather religiously inclined, I think. Does not that sound natural, and reasonable, and well meant? He supposed it screamed because it was not decently buried – with the rest. But he was wrong. How should he know that it screams at me because it hates me, and because it's my fault that there was that little lump of lead in it?

No use to look for it, anyhow? Nonsense! I tell you it wants to be found – Hark! what's that knocking? Do you hear it? Knock – knock – knock – three times, then a pause, and then again. It has a hollow sound, hasn't it?

It has come home. I've heard that knock before. It wants to come in and be taken upstairs in its box. It's at the front door.

Will you come with me? We'll take it in. Yes, I own that I don't like to go alone and open the door. The thing will roll in and stop against my foot, just as it did before, and the light will go out. I'm a good deal shaken by finding that bit of lead, and, besides, my heart isn't quite right – too much strong tobacco, perhaps. Besides, I'm quite willing to own that I'm a bit nervous tonight, if I never was before in my life.

That's right, come along! I'll take the box with me, so as not to come back. Do you hear the knocking? It's not like any other knocking I ever heard. If you will hold this door open, I can find the lantern under the stairs by the light from this room without bringing the lamp into the hall – it would only go out.

The thing knows we are coming – hark! It's impatient to get in. Don't shut the door till the lantern is ready, whatever you do. There will be the usual trouble with the matches, I suppose – no, the first one, by Jove! I tell you it wants to get in, so there's no trouble. All right with that door now; shut it, please. Now come and hold the lantern, for it's blowing so hard outside that I shall have to use both hands. That's it, hold the light low. Do you hear the knocking still? Here goes – I'll open just enough with my foot against the bottom of the door – now!

Catch it! it's only the wind that blows it across the floor, that's all – there's half a hurricane outside, I tell you! Have you got it? The bandbox is on the table. One minute, and I'll have the bar up. There!

Why did you throw it into the box so roughly? It doesn't like that, you know.

What do you say? Bitten your hand? Nonsense, man! You did just what I did. You pressed the jaws together with your other hand and pinched yourself. Let me see. You don't mean to say you have drawn blood? You must have squeezed hard by Jove, for the skin is certainly torn. I'll give you some carbolic solution for it before we go to bed, for they say a scratch from a skull's tooth may go bad and give trouble.

Come inside again and let me see it by the lamp. I'll bring the bandbox – never mind the lantern, it may just as well burn in the hall, for I shall need it presently when I go up the stairs. Yes, shut the door if you will; it makes it more cheerful and bright. Is your finger still bleeding? I'll get you the carbolic in an instant; just let me see the thing.

Ugh! There's a drop of blood on the upper jaw. It's on the eyetooth. Ghastly, isn't it? When I saw it running along the floor of the hall, the strength almost went out of my hands, and I felt my knees bending; then I understood that it was the gale, driving it over the smooth boards. You don't blame me? No, I should think not! We were boys together, and we've seen a thing or two, and we may just as well own to each other that we were both in a beastly funk when it slid across the floor at you. No wonder you pinched your finger picking it up, after that, if I did the same thing out of sheer nervousness, in broad daylight, with the sun streaming in on me.

Strange that the jaw should stick to it so closely, isn't it? I suppose it's the dampness, for it shuts like a vice – I have wiped off the drop of blood, for it was not nice to look at. I'm not going to try to open the jaws, don't be afraid! I shall not play any tricks with the poor thing, but I'll just seal the box again, and we'll take it upstairs and put it away where it wants to be. The wax is on the writing-table by the window. Thank you. It will be long before I leave my seal lying about again, for Trehearn to use, I can tell you. Explain? I don't explain natural phenomena, but if you choose to think that Trehearn had hidden it somewhere in the bushes, and that the gale blew it to the house against the door, and made it knock, as if it wanted to be let in, you're not thinking the impossible, and I'm quite ready to agree with you.

Do you see that? You can swear that you've actually seen me seal it this time, in case anything of the kind should occur again. The wax fastens the strings to the lid, which cannot possibly be lifted, even enough to get in one finger. You're quite satisfied, aren't you? Yes. Besides, I shall lock the cupboard and keep the key in my pocket hereafter.

Now we can take the lantern and go upstairs. Do you know? I'm very much inclined to agree with your theory that the wind blew it against the house. I'll go ahead, for I know the stairs; just hold the lantern near my feet as we go up. How the wind howls and whistles! Did you feel the sand on the floor under your shoes as we crossed the hall?

Yes – this is the door of the best bedroom. Hold up the lantern, please. This side, by the head of the bed. I left the cupboard open when I got the box. Isn't it queer how the faint odour of women's dresses will hang about an old closet for years? This is the shelf. You've seen me set the box there, and now you see me turn the key and put it into my pocket. So that's done!

Goodnight. Are you sure you're quite comfortable? It's not much of a room, but I dare say you would as soon sleep here as upstairs tonight. If you want anything, sing out; there's only a lath and plaster partition between us. There's not so much wind on this side by half. There's the Hollands on the table, if you'll have one more nightcap. No? Well, do as you please. Goodnight again, and don't dream about that thing, if you can.

The following paragraph appeared in the *Penraddon News*, 23rd November 1906:

### MYSTERIOUS DEATH OF A RETIRED SEA CAPTAIN

The village of Tredcombe is much disturbed by the strange death of Captain Charles Braddock, and all sorts of impossible stories are circulating with regard to the circumstances, which certainly seem difficult of explanation. The retired captain, who had successfully commanded in his time the largest and fastest liners belonging to one of the principal transatlantic steamship companies, was found dead in his bed on Tuesday morning in his own cottage, a quarter of a mile from the village. An examination was made at once by the local practitioner, which revealed the horrible fact that the deceased had been bitten in the throat by a human assailant, with such amazing force as to crush the windpipe and cause death. The marks of the teeth of both jaws were so plainly visible on the skin that they could be counted, but the perpetrator of the deed had evidently lost the two lower middle incisors. It is hoped that this peculiarity may help to identify the murderer, who can only be a dangerous escaped maniac. The deceased, though over sixty-five years of age, is said to have been a hale man of considerable physical strength, and it is remarkable that no signs of any struggle were visible in the room, nor could it be ascertained how the murderer had entered the house. Warning has been sent to all the insane asylums in the United Kingdom, but as yet no information has been received regarding the escape of any dangerous patient.

The coroner's jury returned the somewhat singular verdict that Captain Braddock came to his death 'by the hands or teeth of some person unknown'. The local surgeon is said to have expressed privately the opinion that the maniac is a woman, a view he deduces from the small size of the jaws, as shown by the marks of the teeth. The whole affair is shrouded in mystery. Captain Braddock was a widower, and lived alone. He leaves no children.

(AUTHOR'S NOTE. – Students of ghost lore and haunted houses will find the foundation of the foregoing story in the legends about a skull which is still preserved in the farmhouse called Bettiscombe Manor, situated, I believe, on the Dorsetshire coast.)

# Pig

*Roald Dahl*

## I

Once upon a time, in the City of New York, a beautiful baby boy was born into this world, and the joyful parents named him Lexington.

No sooner had the mother returned home from the hospital carrying Lexington in her arms than she said to her husband, 'Darling, now you must take me out to a most marvellous restaurant for dinner so that we can celebrate the arrival of our son and heir.'

Her husband embraced her tenderly and told her that any woman who could produce such a beautiful child as Lexington deserved to go absolutely anywhere she wanted. But was she strong enough yet, he inquired, to start running around the city late at night?

'No,' she said, she wasn't. But what the hell.

So that evening they both dressed themselves up in fancy clothes, and leaving little Lexington in care of a trained infant's nurse who was costing them twenty dollars a day and was Scottish into the bargain, they went out to the finest and most expensive restaurant in town. There they each ate a giant lobster and drank a bottle of champagne between them, and after that, they went on to a nightclub, where they drank another bottle of champagne and then sat holding hands for several hours while they recalled and discussed and admired each individual physical feature of their lovely newborn son.

They arrived back at their house on the East Side of Manhattan at around two o'clock in the morning and the husband paid off the taxi driver and then began feeling in his pockets for the key to the front door. After a while, he announced that he must have left it in the pocket of his other suit, and he suggested they ring the bell and get the nurse to come down and let them in. An infant's nurse at twenty dollars a day must expect to be hauled out of bed occasionally in the night, the husband said.

So he rang the bell. They waited. Nothing happened. He rang it again, long and loud. They waited another minute. Then they both stepped back on to the street and shouted the nurse's name (McPottle) up at the nursery windows on the third floor, but there was still no response. The house was dark and silent. The wife began to grow apprehensive. Her baby was imprisoned in this place, she told herself. Alone with McPottle. And who was McPottle? They had known her for two days, that was all, and she had a thin mouth, a small disapproving eye, and a starchy bosom, and quite clearly she was in the habit of sleeping too soundly for safety. If she couldn't hear the front-door bell, then how on earth did she expect to hear a baby crying? Why, this very second the poor thing might be swallowing its tongue or suffocating on its pillow.

'He doesn't use a pillow,' the husband said. 'You are not to worry. But I'll get you in if that's what you want.' He was feeling rather superb after all the champagne, and now he bent down and undid the laces of one of his black patent-leather shoes, and took it off. Then, holding it by the toe, he flung it hard and straight through the dining-room window on the ground floor.

'There you are,' he said, grinning. 'We'll deduct it from McPottle's wages.'

He stepped forward and very carefully put a hand through the hole in the glass and released the catch. Then he raised the window.

'I shall lift you in first, little mother,' he said, and he took his wife around the waist and lifted her off the ground. This brought her big red mouth up level with his own, and very close, so he started kissing her. He knew from experience that women like very much to be kissed in this position, with their bodies held tight and their legs dangling in the air, so he went on doing it for quite a long time, and she wiggled her feet, and made loud gulping noises down in her throat. Finally, the husband turned her round and began easing her gently through the open window into the dining-room. At this point, a police patrol car came nosing silently along the street towards them. It stopped about thirty yards away, and three cops of Irish extraction leaped out of the car and started running in the direction of the husband and wife, brandishing revolvers.

'Stick 'em up!' the cops shouted. 'Stick 'em up!' But it was impossible for the husband to obey this order without letting go of his wife, and had he done this she would either have fallen to the ground or would have been left dangling half in and half out of the house, which is a terribly uncomfortable position for a woman; so he continued gallantly to push her upward and inward through the window. The cops, all of whom had received medals before for killing robbers, opened fire immediately, and although they were still running, and although the wife in particular was presenting them with a very small target indeed, they succeeded in scoring several direct hits on each body – sufficient anyway to prove fatal in both cases.

Thus, when he was no more than twelve days old, little Lexington became an orphan.

2

The news of this killing, for which the three policemen subsequently received citations, was eagerly conveyed to all relatives of the deceased couple by newspaper reporters, and the next morning the closest of these relatives, as well as a couple of undertakers, three lawyers, and a priest, climbed into taxis and set out for the house with the broken window. They assembled in the living-room, men and women both, and they sat around in a circle on the sofas and armchairs, smoking cigarettes and sipping sherry and debating what on earth should be done now with the baby upstairs, the orphan Lexington.

It soon became apparent that none of the relatives was particularly keen to assume responsibility for the child, and the discussions and arguments continued all through the day. Everybody declared an enormous, almost an irresistible desire to look after him, and would have done so with the greatest of pleasure were it not for the fact that their apartment was too small, or that they already had one baby and couldn't possibly afford another, or that they wouldn't know what to do with the poor little thing when they went abroad in the summer, or that they were getting on in years, which surely would be most unfair to the boy when he grew up, and so on and so forth. They all knew, of course, that the father had been heavily in debt for a long time and that the house was mortgaged and that consequently there would be no money at all to go with the child.

They were still arguing like mad at six in the evening when suddenly, in the middle of it all, an old aunt of the deceased father (her name was Glosspan) swept in from Virginia, and without even removing her hat and coat, not even pausing to sit down, ignoring all offers of a martini, a whisky, a sherry, she announced firmly to the assembled relatives that she herself intended to take sole charge of the infant boy from then on. What was more, she said, she would assume full financial responsibility on all counts, including education, and everyone else could go back home where they belonged and give their consciences a rest. So saying, she trotted upstairs to the nursery and snatched Lexington from his cradle and swept out of the house with the baby clutched tightly in her arms, while the relatives simply sat and stared and smiled and looked relieved, and McPottle the nurse stood stiff with disapproval at the head of the stairs, her lips compressed, her arms folded across her starchy bosom.

And thus it was that the infant Lexington, when he was thirteen days old, left the City of New York and travelled southward to live with his Great Aunt Glosspan in the State of Virginia.

## 3

Aunt Glosspan was nearly seventy when she became guardian to Lexington, but to look at her you would never have guessed it for one minute. She was as sprightly as a woman half her age, with a small, wrinkled, but still quite beautiful face and two lovely brown eyes that sparkled at you in the nicest way. She was also a spinster, though you would never have guessed that either, for there was nothing spinsterish about Aunt Glosspan. She was never bitter or gloomy or irritable; she didn't have a moustache; and she wasn't in the least bit jealous of other people, which in itself is something you can seldom say about either a spinster or a virgin lady, although of course it is not known for certain whether Aunt Glosspan qualified on both counts.

But she was an eccentric old woman, there was no doubt about that. For the past thirty years she had lived a strange isolated life all by herself in a tiny cottage high up on the slopes of the Blue Ridge Mountains, several miles from the nearest village. She had five acres of pasture, a plot for growing vegetables, a flower garden, three cows, a dozen hens, and a fine cockerel.

And now she had little Lexington as well.

She was a strict vegetarian and regarded the consumption of animal flesh as not only unhealthy and disgusting, but horribly cruel. She lived upon lovely clean foods like milk, butter, eggs, cheese, vegetables, nuts, herbs, and fruit, and she rejoiced in the conviction that no living creature would be slaughtered on her account, not even a shrimp. Once, when a brown hen of hers passed away in the prime of life from being eggbound, Aunt Glosspan was so distressed that she nearly gave up egg-eating altogether.

She knew not the first thing about babies, but that didn't worry her in the least. At the railway station in New York, while waiting for the train that would take her and Lexington back to Virginia, she bought six feeding-bottles, two dozen diapers, a box of safety pins, a carton of milk for the journey, and a small paper-covered book called *The Care of Infants*. What more could anyone want? And when the train got going, she fed the baby some milk, changed its nappies after a fashion, and laid it down on the seat to sleep. Then she read *The Care of Infants* from cover to cover.

'There is no problem here,' she said, throwing the book out of the window. 'No problem at all.'

And curiously enough there wasn't. Back home in the cottage everything went just as smoothly as could be. Little Lexington drank his milk and belched and yelled and slept exactly as a good baby should, and

Aunt Glosspan glowed with joy whenever she looked at him and showered him with kisses all day long.

## 4

By the time he was six years old, young Lexington had grown into a most beautiful boy with long golden hair and deep blue eyes the colour of cornflowers. He was bright and cheerful, and already he was learning to help his old aunt in all sorts of different ways around the property, collecting the eggs from the chicken house, turning the handle of the butter churn, digging up potatoes in the vegetable garden, and searching for wild herbs on the side of the mountain. Soon, Aunt Glosspan told herself, she would have to start thinking about his education.

But she couldn't bear the thought of sending him away to school. She loved him so much now that it would kill her to be parted from him for any length of time. There was, of course, that village school down in the valley, but it was a dreadful-looking place, and if she sent him there she just knew they would start forcing him to eat meat the very first day he arrived.

'You know what, my darling?' she said to him one day when he was sitting on a stool in the kitchen watching her make cheese. 'I don't really see why I shouldn't give you your lessons myself.'

The boy looked up at her with his large blue eyes, and gave her a lovely trusting smile. 'That would be nice,' he said.

'And the very first thing I should do would be to teach you how to cook.'

'I think I would like that, Aunt Glosspan.'

'Whether you like it or not, you're going to have to learn some time,' she said. 'Vegetarians like us don't have nearly so many foods to choose from as ordinary people, and therefore they must learn to be doubly expert with what they have.'

'Aunt Glosspan,' the boy said, 'what *do* ordinary people eat that we don't?'

'Animals,' she answered, tossing her head in disgust.

'You mean *live* animals?'

'No,' she said. 'Dead ones.'

The boy considered this for a moment.

'You mean when they die they *eat* them instead of *burying* them?'

'They don't wait for them to die, my pet. They kill them.'

'How do they kill them, Aunt Glosspan?'

'They usually slit their throats with a knife.'

'But what *kind* of animals?'

'Cows and pigs mostly, and sheep.'

'Cows!' the boy cried. 'You mean like Daisy and Snowdrop and Lily?'

'Exactly, my dear.'

'But *how* do they eat them, Aunt Glosspan?'

'They cut them up into bits and they cook the bits. They like it best when it's all red and bloody and sticking to the bones. They love to eat lumps of cow's flesh with the blood oozing out of it.'

'Pigs too?'

'They adore pigs.'

'Lumps of bloody pig's meat,' the boy said. 'Imagine that. What else do they eat, Aunt Glosspan?'

'Chickens.'

'Chickens!'

'Millions of them.'

'Feathers and all?'

'No, dear, not the feathers. Now run along outside and get Aunt Glosspan a bunch of chives, will you, my darling?'

Shortly after that, the lessons began. They covered five subjects, reading, writing, geography, arithmetic, and cooking, but the latter was by far the most popular with both teacher and pupil. In fact, it very soon became apparent that young Lexington possessed a truly remarkable talent in this direction. He was a born cook. He was dextrous and quick. He could handle his pans like a juggler. He could slice a single potato into twenty paper-thin slivers in less time than it took his aunt to peel it. His palate was exquisitely sensitive, and he could taste a pot of strong onion soup and immediately detect the presence of a single tiny leaf of sage. In so young a boy, all this was a bit bewildering to Aunt Glosspan, and to tell the truth she didn't quite know what to make of it. But she was proud as proud could be, all the same, and predicted a brilliant future for the child.

'What a mercy it is,' she said, 'that I have such a wonderful little fellow to look after me in my dotage.' And a couple of years later, she retired from the kitchen for good, leaving Lexington in sole charge of all household cooking. The boy was now ten years old, and Aunt Glosspan was nearly eighty.

## 5

With the kitchen to himself, Lexington straight away began experimenting with dishes of his own invention. The old favourites no longer interested him. He had a violent urge to create. There were hundreds of fresh ideas in his head. 'I will begin,' he said, 'by devising a chestnut soufflé.' He made it and served it up for supper that very night. It was terrific. 'You are a genius!' Aunt Glosspan cried, leaping up from her chair and kissing him on both cheeks. 'You will make history!'

From then on, hardly a day went by without some new delectable creation being set upon the table. There was Brazilnut soup, hominy cutlets, vegetable ragout, dandelion omelette, cream-cheese fritters, stuffed-cabbage surprise, stewed foggage, shallots *à la bonne femme*, beetroot mousse piquant, prunes Stroganoff, Dutch rarebit, turnips on horseback, flaming spruce-needle tarts, and many many other beautiful compositions. Never before in her life, Aunt Glosspan declared, had she tasted such food as this; and in the mornings, long before lunch was due, she would go out on to the porch and sit there in her rocking-chair, speculating about the coming meal, licking her chops, sniffing the aromas that came wafting out through the kitchen window.

'What's that you're making in there today, boy?' she would call out.

'Try to guess, Aunt Glosspan.'

'Smells like a bit of salsify fritters to me,' she would say, sniffing vigorously.

Then out he would come, this ten-year-old child, a little grin of triumph on his face, and in his hands a big steaming pot of the most heavenly stew made entirely of parsnips and lovage.

'You know what you ought to do,' his aunt said to him, gobbling the stew. 'You ought to set yourself down this very minute with paper and pencil and write a cooking-book.'

He looked at her across the table, chewing his parsnips slowly.

'Why not?' she cried. 'I've taught you how to write and I've taught you how to cook and now all you've got to do is put the two things together. You write a cooking-book, my darling, and it'll make you famous the whole world over.'

'All right,' he said. 'I will.'

And that very day, Lexington began writing the first page of that monumental work which was to occupy him for the rest of his life. He called it *Eat Good and Healthy*.

## 6

Seven years later, by the time he was seventeen, he had recorded over nine thousand different recipes, all of them original, all of them delicious.

But now, suddenly, his labours were interrupted by the tragic death of Aunt Glosspan. She was afflicted in the night by a violent seizure, and Lexington, who had rushed into her bedroom to see what all the noise was about, found her lying on her bed yelling and cussing and twisting herself up into all manner of complicated knots. Indeed, she was a terrible sight to behold, and the agitated youth danced around her in his pyjamas, wringing his hands, and wondering what on earth he should do. Finally, in an effort to cool her down, he fetched a bucket of water from the pond in the cow field and tipped it over her head, but this only intensified the paroxysms, and the old lady expired within the hour.

'This is really too bad,' the poor boy said, pinching her several times to make sure that she was dead. 'And how sudden! How quick and sudden! Why only a few hours ago she seemed in the very best of spirits. She even took three large helpings of my most recent creation, devilled mushroomburgers, and told me how succulent it was.'

After weeping bitterly for several minutes, for he had loved his aunt very much, he pulled himself together and carried her outside and buried her behind the cowshed.

The next day, while tidying up her belongings, he came across an envelope that was addressed to him in Aunt Glosspan's handwriting. He opened it and drew out two fifty-dollar bills and a letter.

> Darling boy [the letter said,] I know that you have never yet been down the mountain since you were thirteen days old, but as soon as I die you must put on a pair of shoes and a clean shirt and walk down to the village and find the doctor. Ask the doctor to give you a death certificate to prove that I am dead. Then take this certificate to my lawyer, a man called Mr Samuel Zuckermann, who lives in New York City and who has a copy of my will. Mr Zuckermann will arrange everything. The cash in this envelope is to pay the doctor for the certificate and to cover the cost of your journey to New York. Mr Zuckermann will give you more money when you get there, and it is my earnest wish that you use it to further your researches into culinary and vegetarian matters, and that you continue to work upon that great book of yours until you are satisfied that it is complete in every way. Your loving aunt – Glosspan

Lexington, who had always done everything his aunt told him, pocketed the money, put on a pair of shoes and a clean shirt, and went down the mountain to the village where the doctor lived.

'Old Glosspan?' the doctor said. 'My God, is *she* dead?'

'Certainly she's dead,' the youth answered. 'If you will come back home with me now I'll dig her up and you can see for yourself.'

'How deep did you bury her?' the doctor asked.

'Six or seven feet down, I should think.'

'And how long ago?'

'Oh, about eight hours.'

'Then she's dead,' the doctor announced. 'Here's the certificate.'

## 7

Our hero now sets out for the City of New York to find Mr Samuel Zuckermann. He travelled on foot, and he slept under hedges, and he lived on berries and wild herbs, and it took him sixteen days to reach the metropolis.

'What a fabulous place this is!' he cried as he stood at the corner of Fifty-seventh Street and Fifth Avenue, staring around him. 'There are no cows or chickens anywhere, and none of the women looks in the least like Aunt Glosspan.'

As for Mr Samuel Zuckermann, he looked like nothing that Lexington had ever seen before.

He was a small spongy man with livid jowls and a huge magenta nose, and when he smiled, bits of gold flashed at you marvellously from lots of different places inside his mouth. In his luxurious office, he shook Lexington warmly by the hand and congratulated him upon his aunt's death.

'I suppose you knew that your dearly beloved guardian was a woman of considerable wealth?' he said.

'You mean the cows and the chickens?'

'I mean half a million bucks,' Mr Zuckermann said.

'How much?'

'Half a million dollars, my boy. And she's left it all to you.' Mr Zuckermann leaned back in his chair and clasped his hands over his spongy paunch. At the same time, he began secretly working his right forefinger in through his waistcoat and under his shirt so as to scratch the skin around the circumference of his navel – a favourite exercise of his, and one that gave him a peculiar pleasure. 'Of course, I shall have to deduct fifty per cent for my services,' he said, 'but that still leaves you with two hundred and fifty grand.'

'I am rich!' Lexington cried. 'This is wonderful! How soon can I have the money?'

'Well,' Mr Zuckermann said, 'luckily for you, I happen to be on rather cordial terms with the tax authorities around here, and I am confident that I shall be able to persuade them to waive all death duties and back taxes.'

'How kind you are,' murmured Lexington.

'I should naturally have to give somebody a small honorarium.'

'Whatever you say, Mr Zuckermann.'

'I think a hundred thousand would be sufficient.'

'Good gracious, isn't that rather excessive?'

'Never undertip a tax inspector or a policeman,' Mr Zuckermann said. 'Remember that.'

'But how much does it leave for me?' the youth asked meekly.

'One hundred and fifty thousand. But then you've got the funeral expenses to pay out of that.'

'*Funeral* expenses?'

'You've got to pay the funeral parlour. Surely you know that?'

'But I buried her myself, Mr Zuckermann, behind the cowshed.'

'I don't doubt it,' the lawyer said. 'So what?'

'I never used a funeral parlour.'

'Listen,' Mr Zuckermann said patiently. 'You may not know it, but there is a law in this State which says that no beneficiary under a will may receive a single penny of his inheritance until the funeral parlour has been paid in full.'

'You mean that's a *law*?'

'Certainly it's a law, and a very good one it is, too. The funeral parlour is one of our great national institutions. It must be protected at all costs.'

Mr Zuckermann himself, together with a group of public-spirited doctors, controlled a corporation that owned a chain of nine lavish funeral parlours in the city, not to mention a casket factory in Brooklyn and a postgraduate school for embalmers in Washington Heights. The celebration of death was therefore a deeply religious affair in Mr Zuckermann's eyes. In fact, the whole business affected him profoundly, almost as profoundly, one might say, as the birth of Christ affected the shopkeeper.

'You had no right to go out and bury your aunt like that,' he said. 'None at all.'

'I'm very sorry, Mr Zuckermann.'

'Why, it's downright subversive.'

'I'll do whatever you say, Mr Zuckermann. All I want to know is how much I'm going to get in the end, when everything's paid.'

There was a pause. Mr Zuckermann sighed and frowned and continued secretly to run the tip of his finger around the rim of his navel.

'Shall we say fifteen thousand?' he suggested, flashing a big gold smile. 'That's a nice round figure.'

'Can I take it with me this afternoon?'

'I don't see why not.'

So Mr Zuckermann summoned his chief cashier and told him to give Lexington fifteen thousand dollars out of the petty cash, and to obtain a receipt. The youth, who by this time was delighted to be getting anything at all, accepted the money gratefully and stowed it away in his knapsack. Then he shook Mr Zuckermann warmly by the hand, thanked him for all his help, and went out of the office.

'The whole world is before me!' our hero cried as he emerged into the street. 'I now have fifteen thousand dollars to see me through until my book is published. And after that, of course, I shall have a great deal more.' He stood on the pavement, wondering which way to go. He turned left and began strolling slowly down the street, staring at the sights of the city.

'What a revolting smell,' he said, sniffing the air. 'I can't stand this.' His delicate olfactory nerves, tuned to receive only the most delicious kitchen aromas, were being tortured by the stench of the diesel-oil fumes pouring out of the backs of the buses.

'I must get out of this place before my nose is ruined altogether,' he said. 'But first, I've simply got to have something to eat. I'm starving.' The poor boy had had nothing but berries and wild herbs for the past two weeks, and now his stomach was yearning for solid food. I'd like a nice hominy cutlet, he told himself. Or maybe a few juicy salsify fritters.

He crossed the street and entered a small restaurant. The place was hot inside, and dark and silent. There was a strong smell of cooking-fat and cabbage water. The only other customer was a man with a brown hat on his head, crouching intently over his food, who did not look up as Lexington came in.

Our hero seated himself at a corner table and hung his knapsack on the back of his chair. This, he told himself, is going to be most interesting. In all my seventeen years I have tasted only the cooking of two people, Aunt Glosspan and myself – unless one counts Nurse McPottle, who must have heated my bottle a few times when I was an infant. But I am now about to sample the art of a new chef altogether, and perhaps, if I am lucky, I may pick up a couple of useful ideas for my book.

A waiter approached out of the shadows at the back, and stood beside the table.

'How do you do,' Lexington said. 'I should like a large hominy cutlet please. Do it twenty-five seconds each side, in a very hot skillet with sour cream, and sprinkle a pinch of lovage on it before serving – unless of course your chef knows of a more original method, in which case I should be delighted to try it.'

The waiter laid his head over to one side and looked carefully at his customer. 'You want the roast pork and cabbage?' he asked. 'That's all we got left.'

'Roast what and cabbage?'

The waiter took a soiled handkerchief from his trouser pocket and shook it open with a violent flourish, as though he were cracking a whip. Then he blew his nose loud and wet.

'You want it or don't you?' he said, wiping his nostrils.

'I haven't the foggiest idea what it is,' Lexington replied, 'but I should love to try it. You see, I am writing a cooking-book and . . .'

'One pork and cabbage!' the waiter shouted, and somewhere in the back of the restaurant, far away in the darkness, a voice answered him.

The waiter disappeared. Lexington reached into his knapsack for his personal knife and fork. These were a present from Aunt Glosspan, given him when he was six years old, made of solid silver, and he had never eaten with any other instruments since. While waiting for the food to arrive, he polished them lovingly with a piece of soft muslin.

Soon the waiter returned carrying a plate on which there lay a thick greyish-white slab of something hot. Lexington leaned forward anxiously to smell it as it was put down before him. His nostrils were wide open now to receive the scent, quivering and sniffing.

'But this is absolute heaven!' he exclaimed. 'What an aroma! It's tremendous!'

The waiter stepped back a pace, watching his customer carefully.

'Never in my life have I smelled anything as rich and wonderful as this!' our hero cried, seizing his knife and fork. 'What on earth is it made of?'

The man in the brown hat looked around and stared, then returned to his eating. The waiter was backing away towards the kitchen.

Lexington cut off a small piece of the meat, impaled it on his silver fork, and carried it up to his nose so as to smell it again. Then he popped it into his mouth and began to chew it slowly, his eyes half closed, his body tense.

'This is fantastic!' he cried. 'It is a brand-new flavour! Oh, Glosspan, my beloved Aunt, how I wish you were here with me now so you could taste this remarkable dish! Waiter! Come here at once! I want you!'

The astonished waiter was now watching from the other end of the room, and he seemed reluctant to move any closer.

'If you will come and talk to me I will give you a present,' Lexington said, waving a hundred-dollar bill. 'Please come over here and talk to me.'

The waiter sidled cautiously back to the table, snatched away the money, and held it up close to his face, peering at it from all angles. Then he slipped it quickly into his pocket.

'What can I do for you, my friend?' he asked.

'Look,' Lexington said. 'If you will tell me what this delicious dish is made of, and exactly how it is prepared, I will give you another hundred.'

'I already told you,' the man said. 'It's pork.'

'And what exactly is pork?'

'You never had roast pork before?' the waiter asked, staring.

'For heaven's sake, man, tell me what it is and stop keeping me in suspense like this.'

'It's pig,' the waiter said. 'You just bung it in the oven.'

'*Pig!*'

'All pork is pig. Didn't you know that?'

'You mean *this* is *pig's* meat?'

'I guarantee it.'

'But ... but ... that's impossible,' the youth stammered. 'Aunt Glosspan, who knew more about food than anyone else in the world, said that meat of any kind was disgusting, revolting, horrible, foul, nauseating, and beastly. And yet this piece that I have here on my plate is without doubt the most delicious thing that I have ever tasted. Now how on earth do you explain that? Aunt Glosspan certainly wouldn't have told me it was revolting if it wasn't.'

'Maybe your aunt didn't know how to cook it,' the waiter said.

'Is that possible?'

'You're damned right it is. Especially with pork. Pork has to be very well done or you can't eat it.'

'Eureka!' Lexington cried. 'I'll bet that's exactly what happened! She did it wrong!' He handed the man another hundred-dollar bill. 'Lead me to the kitchen,' he said. 'Introduce me to the genius who prepared this meat.'

Lexington was at once taken into the kitchen, and there he met the cook who was an elderly man with a rash on one side of his neck.

'This will cost you another hundred,' the waiter said.

Lexington was only too glad to oblige, but this time he gave the money to the cook. 'Now listen to me,' he said. 'I have to admit that I am really rather confused by what the waiter has just been telling me. Are you quite positive that the delectable dish which I have just been eating was prepared from pig's flesh?'

The cook raised his right hand and began scratching the rash on his neck.

'Well,' he said, looking at the waiter and giving him a sly wink, 'all I can tell you is that I *think* it was pig's meat.'

'You mean, you're not sure?'

'One can't ever be sure.'

'Then what else could it have been?'

'Well,' the cook said, speaking very slowly and still staring at the waiter. 'There's just a chance, you see, that it might have been a piece of human stuff.'

'You mean a man?'

'Yes.'

'Good heavens.'

'Or a woman. It could have been either. They both taste the same.'

'Well – now you really do surprise me,' the youth declared.

'One lives and learns.'

'Indeed one does.'

'As a matter of fact, we've been getting an awful lot of it just lately from the butcher's in place of pork,' the cook declared.

'Have you really?'

'The trouble is, it's almost impossible to tell which is which. They're both very good.'

'The piece I had just now was simply superb.'

'I'm glad you liked it,' the cook said. 'But to be quite honest, I think that was a bit of pig. In fact, I'm almost sure it was.'

'You are?'

'Yes, I am.'

'In that case, we shall have to assume that you are right,' Lexington said. 'So now will you please tell me – and here is another hundred dollars for your trouble – will you please tell me precisely how you prepared it?'

The cook, after pocketing the money, launched out upon a colourful description of how to roast a loin of pork, while the youth, not wanting to miss a single word of so great a recipe, sat down at the kitchen table and recorded every detail in his notebook.

'Is that all?' he asked when the cook had finished.

'That's all.'

'But there must be more to it than that, surely?'

'You got to get a good piece of meat to start off with,' the cook said. 'That's half the battle. It's got to be a good hog and it's got to be butchered right, otherwise it'll turn out lousy whichever way you cook it.'

'Show me how,' Lexington said. 'Butcher me one now so I can learn.'

'We don't butcher pigs in the kitchen,' the cook said. 'That lot you just ate came from a packing-house over in the Bronx.'

'Then give me the address!'

The cook gave him the address, and our hero, after thanking them both many times for all their kindness, rushed outside and leapt into a taxi and headed for the Bronx.

## 8

The packing-house was a big four-storey brick building, and the air around it smelled sweet and heavy, like musk. At the main entrance gates, there was a large notice which said VISITORS WELCOME AT ANY TIME, and thus encouraged, Lexington walked through the gates and entered a cobbled yard which surrounded the building itself. He then followed a series of signposts (THIS WAY FOR THE GUIDED TOURS), and came eventually to a small corrugated-iron shed set well apart from the main building (VISITORS' WAITING-ROOM). After knocking politely on the door, he went in.

There were six other people ahead of him in the waiting-room. There was a fat mother with her two little boys aged about nine and eleven. There was a bright-eyed young couple who looked as though they might be on their honeymoon. And there was a pale woman with long white gloves, who sat very upright, looking straight ahead, with her hands folded on her lap. Nobody spoke. Lexington wondered whether they were all writing cooking-books, like himself, but when he put this question to them aloud, he got no answer. The grown-ups merely smiled mysteriously to themselves and shook their heads, and the two children stared at him as though they were seeing a lunatic.

Soon, the door opened and a man with a merry pink face popped his head into the room and said, 'Next, please.' The mother and the two boys got up and went out.

About ten minutes later, the same man returned. 'Next, please,' he said again, and the honeymoon couple jumped up and followed him outside.

Two new visitors came in and sat down – a middle-aged husband and a middle-aged wife, the wife carrying a wicker shopping-basket containing groceries.

'Next, please,' said the guide, and the woman with the long white gloves got up and left.

Several more people came in and took their places on the stiff-backed wooden chairs.

Soon the guide returned for the third time, and now it was Lexington's turn to go outside.

'Follow me, please,' the guide said, leading the youth across the yard towards the main building.

'How exciting this is!' Lexington cried, hopping from one foot to the other. 'I only wish that my dear Aunt Glosspan could be with me now to see what I am going to see.'

'I myself only do the preliminaries,' the guide said. 'Then I shall hand you over to someone else.'

'Anything you say,' cried the ecstatic youth.

First they visited a large penned-in area at the back of the building where several hundred pigs were wandering around. 'Here's where they start,' the guide said. 'And over there's where they go in.'

'Where?'

'Right there.' The guide pointed to a long wooden shed that stood against the outside wall of the factory. 'We call it the shackling-pen. This way, please.'

Three men wearing long rubber boots were driving a dozen pigs into the shackling-pen just as Lexington and the guide approached, so they all went in together.

'Now,' the guide said, 'watch how they shackle them.'

Inside, the shed was simply a bare wooden room with no roof, but there was a steel cable with hooks on it that kept moving slowly along the length of one wall, parallel with the ground, about three feet up. When it reached the end of the shed, this cable suddenly changed direction and climbed vertically upwards through the open roof towards the top floor of the main building.

The twelve pigs were huddled together at the far end of the pen, standing quietly, looking apprehensive. One of the men in rubber boots pulled a length of metal chain down from the wall and advanced upon the nearest animal, approaching it from the rear. Then he bent down and quickly looped one end of the chain around one of the animal's hind legs. The other end he attached to a hook on the moving cable as it went by. The cable kept moving. The chain tightened. The pig's leg was pulled up and back, and then the pig itself began to be dragged backwards. But it didn't fall down. It was rather a nimble pig, and somehow it managed to keep its balance on three legs, hopping from foot to foot and struggling against the pull of the chain, but going back and back all the time until at the end of the pen where the cable changed direction and went vertically upwards, the creature was suddenly jerked off its feet and borne aloft. Shrill protests filled the air.

'Truly a fascinating process,' Lexington said. 'But what was the funny cracking noise it made as it went up?'

'Probably the leg,' the guide answered. 'Either that or the pelvis.'

'But doesn't that matter?'

'Why should it matter?' the guide asked. 'You don't eat the bones.'

The rubber-booted men were busy shackling the rest of the pigs, and one after another they were hooked to the moving cable and hoisted up through the roof, protesting loudly as they went.

'There's a good deal more to this recipe than just picking herbs,' Lexington said. 'Aunt Glosspan would never have made it.'

At this point, while Lexington was gazing skywards at the last pig to go up, a man in rubber boots approached him quietly from behind and looped one end of a chain around the youth's own ankle, hooking the other end to the moving belt. The next moment, before he had time to realize what was happening, our hero was jerked off his feet and dragged backwards along the concrete floor of the shackling-pen.

'Stop!' he cried. 'Hold everything! My leg is caught!'

But nobody seemed to hear him, and five seconds later, the unhappy young man was jerked off the floor and hoisted vertically upwards through the open roof of the pen, dangling upside down by one ankle, and wriggling like a fish.

'Help!' he shouted. 'Help! There's been a frightful mistake! Stop the engines! Let me down!'

The guide removed a cigar from his mouth and looked up serenely at the rapidly ascending youth, but he said nothing. The men in rubber boots were already on their way out to collect the next batch of pigs.

'Oh, save me!' our hero cried. 'Let me down! Please let me down!' But he was now approaching the top floor of the building where the moving belt curled over like a snake and entered a large hole in the wall, a kind of doorway without a door; and there, on the threshold, waiting to greet him, clothed in a dark-stained yellow rubber apron, and looking for all the world like Saint Peter at the Gates of Heaven, the sticker stood.

Lexington saw him only from upside down, and very briefly at that, but even so he noticed at once the expression of absolute peace and benevolence on the man's face, the cheerful twinkle in the eyes, the little wistful smile, the dimples in his cheeks – and all this gave him hope.

'Hi there,' the sticker said, smiling.

'Quick! Save me!' our hero cried.

'With pleasure,' the sticker said, and taking Lexington gently by one ear with his left hand, he raised his right hand and deftly slit open the boy's jugular vein with a knife.

The belt moved on. Lexington went with it. Everything was still upside down and the blood was pouring out of his throat and getting into his eyes, but he could still see after a fashion, and he had a blurred impression of being in an enormously long room, and at the far end of the room there was a great smoking cauldron of water, and there were dark figures, half hidden in the steam, dancing around the edge of it, brandishing long poles. The conveyor-belt seemed to be travelling right over the top of the cauldron, and the pigs seemed to be dropping down one by one into the boiling water, and one of the pigs seemed to be wearing long white gloves on its front feet.

Suddenly our hero started to feel very sleepy, but it wasn't until his good strong heart had pumped the last drop of blood from his body that he passed on out of this, the best of all possible worlds, into the next.

# Robbie

*Mary Danby*

'Of course, her boy's found himself a job down the bakery,' said Mrs Coppard.

'Has he?' Evelyn was removing the pins from the pink plastic rollers in Mrs Coppard's pale brown hair. If you half-closed your eyes it looked as though her head was covered with sausage rolls.

'He wanted to get into the police, but he failed the medical. Eczema.'

Evelyn tutted. 'Shame.' She ran her fingers through the hair, lifting the fat brown rolls away from the scalp, then she carefully began to brush out the curls, using the side of her hand to arrange them in layers.

Mrs Coppard looked at herself in the mirror, which was propped on the top of Evelyn's twin-tub washing-machine. 'D'you think I should try a rinse?' she asked.

'Something on the red side, d'you mean?'

'Mm. Or highlights, perhaps. Blonde streaks.'

Evelyn held up a hand mirror so that Mrs Coppard could see the back of her head, then she untied the nylon cape and helped her up from the kitchen chair. A glance at the clock made her start. Nearly half past three.

'I shall have to get a move on,' she told her client. 'Robbie's bus is due in.'

Mrs Coppard searched in her purse for the right change. 'Getting on all right, is he, at that school?' she asked. 'Here we are.' She handed some money over to Evelyn, who put it into a canister marked 'Sugar'.

'Thanks. Yes, he seems fine.'

Mrs Coppard went out into the passage and opened the front door. 'He's a dear little chap.' She bit her lip. 'Oops, I shouldn't say that, I suppose. But you always *think* of him as little, don't you? Human nature being what it is.'

When she had gone, Evelyn quickly tidied away the rollers and pins then set off down the farm track that led from her cottage to the road beyond. She had hardly been waiting a minute when the blue mini-bus came round the corner and drew up alongside her. Half a dozen faces pressed against the windows as the door slid back and Robbie climbed out. One of the faces left a dribble of saliva behind on the pane.

'Ho, Mumma!' said Robbie, butting her with his head and hugging her thin waist with a lack of self-consciousness unusual in a boy of eleven.

She took his hand and looked up at the lady driving the mini-bus. 'Wave goodbye to Mrs Gladwell, Robbie.'

'Bye, Mrs Gladweb!' called Robbie as the bus drew away. He hopped and skipped at the end of Evelyn's arm as they made their way back to the cottage.

'Mark Williams wet himself today,' he told her. 'There was a puddle on the floor. Mr Warner made him clean it up himself.'

'Oh no, Robbie, surely not,' said Evelyn. After all, these children couldn't help it. They didn't choose to be anti-social.

'He did,' confirmed Robbie, jumping forward with both feet and nearly pulling Evelyn's arm out.

She didn't think she believed him, but you never knew.

Before they went into the house, they visited Bella and her puppies in the shed that stood on the other side of the muddy yard that was their garden. Ted, Evelyn's husband, would have liked to have had the puppies into the house, but she knew they would have been into everything, making messes. In any case, they were quite happy in the shed. They had a big, cosy box to sleep in, and there would be plenty of room for them to move around in when they were older. At the moment they were still at the half-blind, bumbling stage.

'Billy . . . Goldie . . . Jason,' said Robbie, doing the roll-call. 'Meg . . . Scruffy.' He chuckled delightedly. 'Scruffy bit me,' he said, 'without his teeth.'

Bella was some kind of retriever cross, and her pups might have had a bit of red setter in them. They were a fair mixture of colours, and at this stage it was difficult to see what shape they would turn out to be. Their mother, lying on an old grey blanket, turned to look at Evelyn and Robbie, and thumped her tail against the side of the box.

'Booby loo, Bella,' said Robbie meaninglessly.

In a little while they left the shed and went towards the house. Robbie went ahead of Evelyn, taking four steps in all directions for every one of hers. He was a big child, plumpish, with short, stocky arms and legs and a round face. His features were squashy-looking, so that they were hard to remember when he wasn't present. But he possessed a marvellous gaiety and an optimism rarely found in those with a sharper awareness of their situation. He was clumsy, with uncoordinated movements, so that he appeared sometimes to limp or hobble. He moved ahead with little skips and lollops, heavy and ungainly, yet with a certain grace.

Like the puppies, thought Evelyn. As they went into the house, he said conversationally: 'Had yer snap?'

This was his latest expression. If it was anything like the last one, it could go on for months. Robbie was hard to fathom. If he had just been backward, it would have been easier: he could simply have been treated as a child of four of five – which was how he appeared most of the time. But every now and then his brain seemed to slip out of gear, and he would do or say something quite nonsensical. He would find a phrase that appealed to him, then repeat it over and over again, for weeks, sometimes. Last time it had been 'Catch a kitty', which he had said to everyone he came across, exploring all the different tones of voice he could use, until Ted and Evelyn had been driven nearly mad. Evelyn thought 'Had yer snap?' might prove to be even more exasperating than 'Catch a kitty'.

'Are you going to watch "Playschool"?' she asked, turning on the television as Robbie settled himself into a chair in the living-room. 'I've got a lady coming for a trim in a minute, then I'll do your tea.' Robbie put his fingers in his mouth and hugged his elbows eagerly to his body as he heard the familiar music and saw the title appear on the screen.

That was twenty minutes' peace, anyway. He loved to watch children's programmes and became totally absorbed in them, joining in all the counting songs and finger games, clapping in time (or nearly in time) to the music. He knew all the nursery rhymes. In a little while Evelyn heard him singing: 'Oh, the wheels on the bus go round and round, round and round, round and round . . .' – not very tunefully.

The lady in need of a trim was nearly half an hour late, and fussed for ages about whether or not her fringe was straight. When she finally left, it was five o'clock, and Evelyn hadn't even begun to prepare their tea. She put her head around the living-room door to check on Robbie and found him huddled in a corner, puffing and grunting.

'What on earth. . .?'

He had become bored with television after a while, had taken a length of tape from her sewing basket and had somehow managed to tie himself up. He had done this before, though not for some months.

'Oh, you silly boy,' she said, cutting him free. 'I can't leave you for a minute, can I.'

Robbie returned to his chair and applied himself intently to a soap opera on the television. He seemed happy to concentrate once more.

Evelyn was peeling the potatoes when Ted arrived home and hung up his dairyman's white coat in the passage.

'Got my tea ready?' he asked, coming into the kitchen.

'Hello, Ted,' she said, thinking how nice it would be if he were to behave like a husband in a magazine story, and kiss her before thinking of his stomach.

He was a solid, rough-skinned man, not tall, but giving an impression of largeness. He made her own pallor and wispiness seem even more pronounced, by contrast.

'Not done the potatoes yet?' he asked, peering into the sink. 'Heavens, woman, I've been *working*.'

'I know, Ted, I know,' Evelyn said in a tired voice. 'I have too.' She went on with the peeling.

Ted hunched his shoulders. 'Hairdressing, I suppose. You know I don't like it. We rent this place to live in, not as a business premises. You'll get us chucked out.'

Evelyn filled a saucepan with cold water. 'I only do it to oblige, Ted. I always say to them. I say, "I'm only doing it to oblige".'

'But they pay you. You can't say it's to oblige if they pay.'

'Oh, come on,' said Evelyn. 'You know it takes care of our summer holidays. Where would we be without it come September?' They were going to Devon for a week, to a self-catering bungalow, taking Robbie with them.

Ted opened the breadbin. 'Looks like we'll be having tea at midnight,' he said, 'so I may as well make myself a sandwich.'

Robbie appeared in the doorway and swung on the handle. 'Ho, Dad. Had yer snap? Had yer snap?' he said brightly.

'That's just the bloody trouble,' said Ted. 'I bloody haven't.'

'No need to take it out on the boy,' Evelyn told him, cutting a potato into four.

Robbie took a few seconds to size up the situation, then he ran to the biscuit tin and took out two custard creams. He held them up eagerly, right in front of his father's face.

'What're you *doing*, boy?' Ted asked irritably. 'I don't want those.' He pushed Robbie's arm aside and took a loaf from the breadbin. 'A man wants more than a couple of biscuits when he's had a hard day's work.' He placed a square of cheese between two slices of bread and took a large bite, then, still chewing on the sandwich, he asked: 'What you do today, then, Robbie? Had a nice day at school, did you?'

'Mark Williams wet himself,' said Robbie. 'I had to clear it up.'

Later that evening, Ted, wearing striped pyjamas and about to get into bed, said to Evelyn: 'Is that true, what Robbie said about mopping up after that boy?'

She tidied her clothes away in the wardrobe. 'No, I shouldn't think so. Earlier on he said the boy'd had to do it himself.'

'Oh.' Ted frowned. 'Tells a lot of lies, doesn't he.'

'Not *lies*, Ted. He doesn't really know the difference. He doesn't see things right or wrong like we do.'

Ted was often puzzled by his son. In his younger days he had dreamt of a sturdy young fellow, 'My boy', who could be taught how to wire a plug, put up a shelf, change the wheel of a car. And what had he got? An only son who was possessed of a sweet smile and a good deal of charm, but precious little else on the plus side. Where was the boy who would win the form prize up at the Comprehensive, or be chosen to play football for his school, or make his own tree house? Ted was a bitter man, and all the more so because Evelyn always refused to consider trying again. One day he'd throw away those blessed pills of hers, and they'd take their chance like anyone else.

The summer holidays arrived, and Robbie, denied the company of his schoolmates, spent his days mooching listlessly around. He was allowed to wander about the farm, and he took to towing behind him a cardboard box on a piece of string. He called it his go-kart. Evelyn had told him to keep out of the way of the men who worked on the farm, but he would hang around up by the barn, hoping to be given a ride on a tractor. Usually, though, he had to make do with a wave as they went busily past. He wasn't allowed in the milking parlour, where his father worked, but he would stand on the rails outside the shed, listening to the steady, rhythmic clank-swish of the machines and watching the big Friesians as they plodded back to their field. Once, he had tried to help herd them, but had found himself hemmed in between a cow and the side of the hayshed. He had felt her steamy breath on his face and smelt her milky smell. Sometimes he woke in the night, sweating at the memory of it.

There were some free-range chickens, and he was allowed to collect their eggs and place them carefully in trays. When he did this, the wife of one of the farmworkers sometimes gave him an egg to take home for his tea. He knew about baby chicks growing inside eggs. He had seen a dead thing that came out of a broken egg. He had touched it and it was slimy. It had a tiny beak. He didn't think it would be nice to eat.

Big chickens were. When Robbie's mother wanted a chicken to cook, Bill Johnson up at the farm would take one of the birds and wring its neck, and hand it to her by its feet, with its head hanging down, glassy-eyed, mouth open in mid-cackle.

Robbie liked to watch his mother preparing food. She would clear the kitchen table and roll up her sleeves, and open the drawer in the end of the table where she kept her knives and other implements. One day, early in the holidays, he saw a plucked chicken lying on the draining-board and he felt its funny soft skin. It was still quite warm. His mother came in and slapped it onto the table.

'Roast chicken for your dinner today, Robbie,' she said, sharpening a small cleaver, pulling it back and forth across a carving steel, criss-cross, criss-cross, like some weird native dance.

'Don't stand too close,' she warned, 'or I might cut off your nose.'

Robbie put a hand up to his face as if to reassure himself that it was still intact, and Evelyn laughed. 'That's right. You hang on to it,' she said, testing the sharpness of the cleaver against her thumb. She laid out the chicken in front of her and took hold of its head in her left hand. Suddenly there was a bang which made Robbie jump, and the head was severed. There was blood on the table. Robbie crouched down until his eyes were on a level with the chicken's. 'Had ... yer ... snap?' he asked it, very solemnly. 'It's got a tongue,' he told his mother.

She was tugging at the neck-skin now, rolling it back and exposing a lumpy, gristly-looking stump of neck. Another bang, and the cleaver sliced through the base of it. The neck rolled away across the table. Robbie picked it up and examined it.

'Haven't you got anything to do?' asked his mother, pushing a strand of hair back from her face. 'Wouldn't you like to play outside?'

Robbie placed the chicken's neck carefully against the base of the chicken's head, as if fitting together a jigsaw. 'I've done all *my* things,' he said dejectedly. 'I need someone else.'

It was so difficult to find anyone for him to play with. Occasionally one or two of the more good-hearted children in the village would come and spend some time with him, but they soon tired of their altruism and drifted away, leaving Robbie so frustrated and hurt that Evelyn sometimes felt it would be better if they left him alone.

'Why don't you take Bella for a walk?' Evelyn suggested. 'The puppies will be all right for a little while. You could go and visit Mrs Biggins.' This was an old lady who lived in another of the farm cottages.

'Mrs Biggins is a stealer,' Robbie said with a sly look. 'Mrs Biggins stole my cowboy hat.'

Evelyn sighed. 'What nonsense. You know perfectly well I gave it to her for her little grandson. It was far too small for you.'

Robbie turned and looked away, out of the window. 'Had yer snap?' he said lightly, as if to change the subject.

When he turned back, his mother had her fingers in the hole where the chicken's neck had been. Slowly she drew out the crop and windpipe, then wiped her hand on a cloth.

'I wish I had a proper go-kart,' said Robbie. 'Or wheels on my box. Its bottom is going all soft and muddy.'

Evelyn, preparing to cut off the chicken's feet, said: 'I expect Daddy could make you one. Why don't you ask him?'

Robbie studied the rough-looking yellow legs with their curled-up claws. He wouldn't want feet like that. His own were pink and soft to touch.

'Daddy's always too busy,' he complained. 'Couldn't you make me one?'

Wham! The feet jumped away across the table, as if still capable of propelling themselves. Robbie caught them and added them to the discard pile. 'Five things,' he said, counting.

'Six,' corrected his mother. 'I don't think I'm very good at making things, Robbie. They always seem to go wrong, somehow.' She made a careful slit, then plunged her hand into the bird, looking towards the ceiling, as if better to concentrate her sense of touch. In a few moments she withdrew her hand, and it was red with blood. Cupped in her fingers was a clutch of intestines, and the heart, liver and gizzard, which slipped onto the table, glistening, primitive.

Robbie put out a finger and pushed at them. 'Don't do that,' said Evelyn. In two weeks he would be going to the seaside for the weekend with a group of kind volunteers from the Blue Skies organization. He would be happy with other children around. It wasn't natural for a boy to spend his summer holidays like this. Even a boy like Robbie.

When Ted came home at noon, Evelyn took the chicken from the oven and made gravy with the stock from the giblets while Ted and Robbie went to look at the puppies.

They were quite big now, and pushed their way out of the shed as soon as the door was opened. They tumbled around for a while, like a troupe of circus acrobats, occasionally breaking off to come and sniff Ted's ankles, or lick Robbie's outstretched hand.

'They 'stand me,' he told his father. 'They know what I say.'

They were developing their own characteristics now. Goldie had a longer tail than the others, Scruffy had a rougher coat. Meg had one ear that was permanently cocked. Billy was the gentle one. Jason was the most inquisitive, for ever waddling off on his own and having to be fetched back by Bella.

'Aren't they great, eh?' said Ted, in the tender, quiet voice he used with the cows. 'Little smashers.' He made a grab for the nearest, Meg, and lifted her up. She scrambled out of his arms and rolled over on the ground, her soft, pale belly uppermost, waiting to be scratched. Bella came over then, her teats swinging heavily beneath her, and nuzzled the puppy upright.

'Did you bring her food?' Ted asked Robbie.

'I'll get it. I'll get it, Dad,' Robbie said eagerly. He skipped back to the house and fetched the bowl, which he placed inside the door of the shed. Bella headed firmly towards it, with the five puppies bounding behind, their tails straight up behind them like Dodgem posts.

'They won't need her milk for much longer,' said Ted. 'Then we'll have to decide what to do with them.'

'I'll keep them,' Robbie said with earnest enthusiasm. 'I'll look after them.'

''Fraid not, boy,' said Ted. 'We'll have to try and find homes for them. Can't have six dogs around the place. Be impossible, that. Besides, we're going on holiday soon. Can't take 'em with us.'

'Don't want them, anyway,' Robby said airily, turning suddenly to aim an imaginary revolver at a passing butterfly.

'But just a moment ago you said ...' Ted began, then he compressed his lips and sighed. There was no understanding the boy. He could be as normal as tea and biscuits one minute, silly as all-get-out the next. 'Get on in and wash your hands for lunch,' he said, unable to keep the exasperation out of his voice.

They had their meal in the kitchen, and Ted carved the chicken at the table. Robbie studied the crisp, gold skin and watched the juices run from the carving knife into the dish.

'Where's its head?' he asked.

Evelyn dished up roast potatoes and carrots. 'In the dustbin,' she said. 'You saw me cut it off.'

Robbie rocked on his chair. 'We could have kept it,' he said in a disappointed voice.

'Don't be soft,' his father said scornfully, and Evelyn asked: 'What for?'

'Just to keep,' Robbie said.

'Get on with your food,' muttered Ted. 'You shouldn't let him watch you doing chickens,' he said to Evelyn. 'It makes him silly'.

They ate in silence for a while, then Robbie, his mouth full of bread sauce, said: 'Puppies are going.'

'Not with your mouth full,' said his father. 'And hold your fork properly.'

Evelyn shot him a glance. Leave him, Ted, it warned.

'If the puppies go, they can't play with me,' Robbie went on, helping himself to more gravy and spilling some on the table. 'Everything goes.'

'Not everything, Robbie,' said his mother. 'Daddy and I are always here.'

'Everything to play with goes,' corrected Robbie.

Evelyn looked at Ted. 'Perhaps Daddy will find time this afternoon to make you that go-kart you wanted.'

'Oh . . . yes, yes, sure,' Ted mumbled. 'If I've got time.'

Robbie gave him a knowing look. 'Had yer snap?' he said, and deliberately poured the remains of his orange squash into the carrots.

Evelyn stood up. 'That was *very* naughty, Robbie. Why did you do that?'

Robbie looked penitent. 'Sorry. Sorry, Mumma,' he said, meaning it.

'Oh well.' She began to clear the table, and Robbie jumped up to help her, piling the plates with a clatter that made Ted wince.

Robbie behaved perfectly for the rest of the meal and afterwards helped his mother to make a pot of tea and carry the cups through to the living-room, where Ted half-sat, half-lay in an armchair, watching the Saturday afternoon racing on the television.

In a little while, Evelyn said: 'You won't forget that go-kart, Ted . . .'

Robbie looked up from where he lay full-length on the floor, reading a comic. 'I'd rather have a brother than a go-kart,' he said. 'A little brother to do games with.'

His father gave a short laugh and said: 'Think we should make you one of those, do you?'

Evelyn blushed. 'Really, Ted,' she remonstrated.

'Sorry, son,' went on Ted. He glanced at Evelyn. 'Your mum's not much good at making things,' he said with a hint of a sneer.

'I would really like a baby brother,' Robbie persisted. 'I could give him walks and show him my caterpillars. I've got a hundred and ninety-one.'

Evelyn, who had inspected his collection, numbering three, smiled. 'He wouldn't be able to walk at first,' she explained. 'He'd just be a little baby. There again, you might not get a brother at all – it could be a sister instead.'

Robbie looked cross. 'No,' he said. 'Don't make a sister.'

That night, Ted climbed into bed beside Evelyn and moved very close to her, so that she could feel the warmth of him through her nightdress. He put his arm around her shoulders, and she rested her head against the brick-hardness of his chest.

'Hello, Evie,' he said, using the pet name he liked to call her by when he was feeling romantic.

'Ted,' she acknowledged comfortably.

He stroked her shoulder. ''Bout what Robbie was saying. Another child. Eh?'

She squirmed in the bed, irritated. 'You know what I think, Ted. Not another. I couldn't cope with that.'

'But it needn't be,' he insisted, shifting his position so that he could see her thin, watchful face. 'The doctors said so. There's no reason to think we'd have another one like – well, like Robbie.'

Robbie. The happy months of waiting. The joy at his birth. Then the 'Could I just have a word with you?' and the tests, and the tears, and the great gaping hole of awfulness. Ted could never quite believe that Robbie was his own child, that he could have sired this being whose mind and body in no way seemed to connect with his own. Another scene: 'Yes, you have a fine, healthy boy.' Immediate recognition in the eyes. Daddy. Hello, son. 'He's ever so like you, isn't he. Going to grow up to be like his daddy, this one.'

'Please, Evie.'

'No, Ted.' She shifted away from him. 'We're not going through all that again. I couldn't stand it, not knowing. Let's just be content with what we've got, and leave it at that.'

'They can tell beforehand, now,' said Ted. 'They know when there's something wrong. They put a tube in.'

Evelyn turned away and put her head down on the pillow. 'Let them put tubes in you, then,' she said. 'You have the baby.'

The next day was Sunday, and they all went over to Ted's parents' house, where Robbie disgraced himself by having a tantrum, lying on his back and drumming his heels on the floor and refusing to get up. There appeared to be no particular reason for this sudden performance, and it was over in minutes, but they left early all the same, before tea, because Ted felt embarrassed.

'It doesn't matter,' Evelyn reassured him. 'Everyone understands. You should just ignore him, like you would a naughty toddler. It doesn't help, getting annoyed at him.'

'He's getting worse,' Ted said.

The following morning, Robbie decided to be specially helpful, as if to make up. His father had to be at work very early, and usually made his own breakfast, but this time Robbie was waiting for him in the kitchen with a plate of toast and a lukewarm pot of tea. The toast was a little burnt, and Ted got up to scrape it into the sink, but Robbie was not disheartened. When Ted was ready to go, Robbie held out his newly-laundered dairy coat for him. 'Here, Daddy.' But his father snatched it from him, saying: 'For God's sake, Robbie!' When the boy's face fell, he repented. 'Oh, come on,' he said. 'Let's go and see the puppies before I go.'

Jason was out of the shed almost before they had opened the door, and Robbie chased him around the yard, stumbling uselessly behind the agile leaping and bounding of the puppy. When Jason allowed himself to be caught, Robbie held him for a moment, laughing, then casually threw him away, as if he were a football. The puppy yelped as it hit the ground, then ran away, its tail tucked defensively between its legs.

'Robbie!' His father, furious, shook the boy by the shoulders. 'You treat those puppies roughly and you can expect a bit of rough treatment from me, right?' Robbie was gazing about the yard. 'And look at me when I'm talking to you.' Robbie obeyed, and his expression was disconcertingly mild.

'We'll shut the puppies up, now, and you're not to go near them again until I say so. Is that clear?'

'Had yer snap, Goldie? Had yer snap, Scruffy?' said Robbie.

'Bedlam, bloody bedlam,' Ted swore to himself as he mounted his bicycle and set off up the track. 'The boy ought to be shut away somewhere.'

Later that morning, Evelyn was busy at the washing line when Robbie came up to her, pulling his cardboard box behind him. It was empty, and bumped over the ground. 'I'm going to collect things,' he told her.

'Why not see if you can find some wood and some old pram wheels,' advised Evelyn. 'Then you and Daddy could make that go-kart.'

Mrs Foster came at ten-thirty for a shampoo and blow-dry.

'I see you've got your boy home,' she said. 'Holidays, is it? You must have your hands full.'

Evelyn smiled. 'Oh, he's not too bad. I'm used to him.'

'Well,' said Mrs Foster, wriggling her neck, 'if any of mine got into that sort of state I wouldn't be so calm about it.'

'What do you mean?' Evelyn stood poised, holding a bottle of shampoo in one hand.

'You know that old pond down by the pig-runs?' said Mrs Foster with relish. 'The one they call the duck pond, only there aren't any ducks now? I saw him grubbing about down there as I came past.'

'Oh no,' Evelyn sighed. 'He's not supposed to go there. Covered in mud, is he?'

'Hah!' Mrs Foster gave a high, unpleasant laugh. 'Walking mud pie, more like.'

Evelyn wearily put down the shampoo and opened the back door. 'Robbie!' she called. 'Robbie!'

In the distance she saw a dark, dishevelled figure towing a cardboard box. 'Just you come in here!' she shouted, then she went back in to Mrs Foster. 'D'you want the herbal or the medicated?' she asked in a controlled, refined way, as if trying to keep her end up.

Robbie's eyes were blue glass baubles in a filthy face.

'And where have you been?' asked Evelyn.

He smiled, and his teeth were a slice of whiteness. 'In the pond, collecting,' he told her.

'Collecting what, dear?' asked Mrs Foster, and Evelyn noticed that she couldn't quite hide her disdain.

'Secret,' said Robbie.

'Don't you bring those shoes in here,' Evelyn said sharply, as he began to step onto her clean kitchen floor. 'Take them off outside, then go on into the bathroom and get out of those wet clothes. I'll be along in a minute to give you a good scrub. No – your box can stay outside, thank you. I don't want to see your secrets today. I'm cross with you.'

As Robbie went through to the bathrom he threw a casual 'Had yer snap?' at Mrs Foster and shambled off, singing to himself: 'This ole man, he play one, he play nick-nack on my dum . . .'

'I don't know how you manage,' said Mrs Foster. 'I'd be a bag of nerves.'

After lunch, Evelyn felt one of her migraines coming on. 'Don't bother me, Robbie,' she said. 'I've got a headache. I'm going to lie down.'

'Mumma . . .' Robbie was all concern. He stroked her forehead with a damp, paw-like hand and said 'Better soon' in a soothing voice. After a while, he tired of being a nurse and went outside.

'You can play with the pups, but don't go out of the yard, Robbie,' Evelyn called after him, making her head throb with the effort. Then she took a couple of pills and went upstairs to lie down. He couldn't come to much harm, pottering about the yard, and she'd only be half an hour or so.

When she awoke it was to the sound of Ted's voice shouting for her. He was outside the back door. Quickly, she tidied herself at her dressing-table and went down to the kitchen. Her head was still like a furnace. Please let him not mind corned beef for tea again.

'Evelyn? Where are you? What's going on? What's Bella tied up for?'

She went out into the yard and saw the dog sitting at the end of a long piece of string, gently whining. She looked around. 'Robbie?' she called.

'Has he been with the puppies?' asked Ted. 'I specifically told him not to.'

Evelyn searched for Robbie with her eyes. 'Oh dear,' she said, confused. 'I said he could.'

'Oh, for God's sake,' said Ted, untying the dog.

Bella went straight to the door of the shed and sat before it, making a strange, throaty noise and scratching at the door.

'What is it, girl?' said Ted in his soft, animal-loving voice. 'What's the matter, eh?' He stood with his hand on the latch, suddenly fearful, then opened the door of the shed. He looked in, and quickly stepped back a pace. 'God,' he said. 'Oh God, no.'

Evelyn came running over but he put out an arm and held her back. 'Don't go in,' he said. 'There's been . . . an accident.'

He stepped forward into the shed, avoiding the cleaver on the floor. Bella pushed past him and nosed among her dead and dying puppies, among the blood and pain, crying over them, trying to push them back to life.

Ted bent down. 'Billy,' he whispered, touching the head of the nearest, seeing the eyes at that moment glaze over and die. There was so much blood he couldn't tell what had happened. Jason and Scruffy lay together, red and twitching. Meg . . . Goldie . . . He couldn't go on looking. Choking back his sobs he stood up, and it was then that he heard Evelyn cry out.

'Robbie!' she gasped.

The boy was clumping around the side of the shed, holding in his arms his precious cardboard box. His hands and broadly-grinning face were heavily streaked with blood.

'Ho, Mumma,' he said cheerfully. 'We can make it now. I've got all the things.'

Ted emerged from the shed, shaking and incoherent. 'What . . . what the . . .'

'But the blood, Robbie . . .' Evelyn was saying weakly. 'Are you hurt? Have you cut yourself?'

'The things for making the little brother,' Robbie went on. 'You know. I'm helping Daddy. I've got the things.'

Ted stared at the boy. He turned to where the tormented Bella was whimpering in the shed, then looked back at the squat, bedraggled, soiled figure whose fatuous smile was just beginning to fade. This figure that called itself his son. 'You bloody silly little moron,' he said coldly. 'You pathetic little god-forsaken cretin!' His voice rose to a shout, and he stormed over to Robbie and swept the box from his hands so that it fell on its side and the contents were scattered. 'Bloody maniac!' moaned Ted, collapsing miserably against the side of the shed. 'Bloody, bloody maniac.'

Evelyn was kneeling on the ground, gazing in disbelief at Robbie's spilt treasures. She spoke in a high, hysterical way, as if reality were yet to take hold. 'Frogs,' she said, putting out a hand towards a squashed, greenish-brown object, 'and snails . . .' One was still alive, and poked its soft horns out from under its shell. 'Frogs and snails and . . . and p-p-puppy dogs' . . .' she recited, touching something slim and furry and wet with warm blood, '. . . tails,' she finished, in a voice so faint it could hardly be heard.

Robbie stood a few paces away, twisting his clumsy hands together, a couple of fat tears sliding down his broad, dirty cheeks. When he spoke, his voice was hoarse with dismay.

'I wanted us to call him Terry . . .'

# The Extra Passenger

*August Derleth*

Mr Arodias had worked a long time on his plan to kill his eccentric uncle, and he was very proud of it. But then, Mr Arodias was a very clever man; he had lived by his wits for so many years that it had never been necessary for him to kill Uncle Thaddeus before. Only, now that Mr Arodias was getting along towards middle age, and his fingers were no longer so nimble as they had once been, the time came. He began by thinking that he ought not to be deprived of his inheritance any longer, and ended up by working out the perfect crime which he defied Scotland Yard to solve.

Like all such plans, it was almost absurdly simple, and Mr Arodias indulged in many a self-congratulatory chuckle when he contemplated the bumbling efforts of the CID to solve it. Uncle Thaddeus, who was a recluse, lived on the edge of Sudbury, which was on the Aberdeen line from London. Three squares from his tree-girt house lived another solitary who owned a fast car and kept it carelessly in an unlocked shed some distance from his house. Thirty miles from Sudbury, where the night train to Aberdeen stopped, lay the hamlet of East Chelmly, the next stop, rather in a curving line from Sudbury, so that it was farther by rail than by highway. It would be a simple matter to take off for Aberdeen from London on the slow night train, slip out of his compartment at Sudbury, 'take care' of Uncle Thaddeus, then appropriate his neighbour's fast car, and arrive in East Chelmly in adequate time to slip back onto his train, with none the wiser. A perfect alibi! Ah, what chuckle-heads he would make of the laddies from the Yard!

Moreover, it worked like a charm. True, the old man had recognized him and had muttered something about coming after him before the light in his crafty eyes went out and his battered head fell forward – but it was just a matter of moments; the whole thing had been rehearsed in Mr Arodias's mind so often that he knew just what to do, and flattered himself by thinking that he could have done it blindfolded. The old dodderer nearby had left his car plentifully supplied with petrol, too, as if he had been an accomplice, and it took Mr Arodias to East Chelmly in the dead of night, never meeting anyone on the long road, never seeing anyone in the little hamlets through which he passed. He arrived in East Chelmly in excellent time, and like a shadow he slipped around to the station and into his compartment with no one seeing.

No one, that is, except the extra passenger.

For at this point in his perfect crime, Mr Arodias came face to face with a factor for which he had made no provision. He had left his compartment empty, save for his bags and golf-clubs; he came back to find huddled in the opposite seat, with his hat well down over his face, an extra passenger. It was possible that the fellow had not marked Mr Arodias's entrance, but, much to his annoyance, Mr Arodias could not be sure.

'Sorry to disturb you,' he said genially. 'I have been in the lavatory.'

No answer.

Mr Arodias hawked once or twice.

No sign of life.

Mr Arodias settled back, relieved, feeling very comfortable and secure. This pleasant feeling of security did not last, however. In a few moments he was asking himself where in the devil the extra passenger had come from? There had been no stop between Sudbury and East Chelmly. The compartment was in one of the through coaches, not a local. It was barely possible that a passenger from one of the other compartments had mistaken Mr Arodias's for his own in the dark, and now occupied it by mistake. For it was still dark, being somewhat past midnight, and the lights in the corridor were dim.

But this explanation did not satisfy Mr Arodias, and he was possessed of a normal dislike of unsatisfactory matters. This was all the more true when the matter in question represented a potential flaw in what he felt was a very perfect plan. His fellow-traveller, however, was apparently oblivious of his growing perturbation; he continued to huddle there without movement other than that of the train rushing through the night. This troubled Mr Arodias; he expected nothing less than a full account explaining the extra passenger's presence.

Failing this, he began to imagine all kinds of things, and he took every opportunity to examine his companion in the light of passing stations. He wore heavy, almost loutish shoes. Obviously a countryman. His hands, which did not seem clean, were those of an old man. His hat had seen much roughing. Of his face, Mr Arodias saw nothing. How long, he wondered, had he been sleeping? If he had just simply blundered into the compartment and settled down and dozed right off, all would be well. But if he had not done so, he might well be in a position to ask annoying questions about what kept Mr Arodias in the lavatory for time enough to enable the train to put close to sixty or seventy miles behind from the time he had entered the lavatory – which was, of course, presumably at the same hour the extra passenger had entered Mr Arodias's compartment.

This thought needled Mr Arodias with desperation. Already he had visions of some officious bumpkin plodding to the police station in Aberdeen and solemnly deposing that Mr Arodias's late entrance was a suspicious circumstance. He could see it in cold print. '*Sudbury Victim's Heir Questioned*,' the headline would read. And this unwelcome stranger, huddled there like a tangible threat to his security, would have put all his suspicions down. "'E come late into 'is seat, an' I could na 'elp wonderin' where the zur kep' 'imself all that time. A good hour, 't was. Nor did 'e 'ave the look of a zick man about 'im.'

Mr Arodias could hardly contain himself. He coughed loudly. Fancying that he saw a movement about his fellow-traveller not inspired by the train, he said hastily, 'Forgive me. I didn't mean to awaken you.'

But there was no answer.

Mr Arodias bit his lip. 'I say,' he said firmly.

Silence.

The sounds of the train filled the compartment – the whistle up ahead, the rush of steam, the clicking of the drivers – filled the room and rolled around in it, swelling and growing. It was grotesque. It made such a sound that it would have awakened the dead, thought Mr Arodias. Yet the extra passenger slept calmly through it, huddled there like someone lost in the deepest dream.

He leaned forward and tapped the fellow on the knee.

'Look here, this is my compartment, you know.'

No answer.

Oh, it was maddening! Especially so for a man of Mr Arodias's temperament, and most particularly since this was happening just after he had brought off what was certain to come out in the end as his most successful *coup* in a career of successes. This confounded extra passenger was by his very presence, however innocuous he might be, taking the edge of enjoyment off his pleasure in his accomplishment of that night.

Mr Arodias considered shaking the fellow.

But this he dismissed from his mind within a few moments. There was, after all, no good in antagonizing him. There was no reason to believe that he had seen a single thing which might make him suspicious. Indeed, he might leave the compartment at any place along the line without realizing that he sat in the same train with the heir to the Sudbury recluse. No, there was absolutely no good in unnecessarily attracting attention to himself.

He felt frustrated, and he redoubled his efforts to examine his fellow traveller. He took the trouble to take out his pipe, fill it, and strike a match, rather more for the purpose of examining the extra passenger in its flickering light than for that of lighting his pipe. Then for the first time he observed that the fellow had no baggage of any kind. Manifestly then, he had stumbled into the wrong compartment. The shoes were country shoes, all right. Clod-hopperish. Mud on them, too. And on his hands. Uncouth fellow.

*Or was it mud?* The match went out.

Mr Arodias was afraid to light another. For one cataclysmic moment, the stuff on his fellow traveller's hands and shoes had looked like blood! Mr Arodias swallowed and told himself that he was having hallucinations stemming from some rudimentary conscience which had not died with the rest of it in that long ago time when he had entered upon his life of dubious practices and crime.

He sat for a long moment in silence. The hour was now past two in the morning. He busied himself for a little while peering out of the window, trying to ascertain just where the train was at the moment. Approaching the Scottish border, he decided. He closed his eyes and tried to think how he must act when they found him in Aberdeen and told him his Uncle Thaddeus was dead, slain by an unknown assailant in the night, while he was on his way to Scotland under the protection of such a perfect alibi. But there was nothing to be gained in thinking about this; he had decided upon his course of action right up to the moment he actually took possession of his inheritance – he had decided upon that long ago; it was all an integral part of his plan. Indeed, the only incident which was not integral in his plan was this extra passenger.

He turned to him again, hawked once more, coughed loudly, knocked his pipe out on the windowsill, and looked hopefully over through the darkness of the compartment at that huddled old fellow in the corner of his seat.

No movement.

'This has gone far enough,' he said aloud, becoming vexed.

Silence.

He leaned over once more and tapped his companion on the knee, with some persistence. 'Look here, you're in the wrong compartment, sir.'

This time he got an answer. It was a muttered, sleepy, 'No.'

The voice was guttural, broken. Mr Arodias was slightly disconcerted but in one way relieved.

'I'm sorry,' he said, in a more pleasant tone, 'but I believe you got into my compartment by mistake.'

'No,' said his companion again.

Instantly annoyed once more, Mr Arodias wondered why the fellow insisted on talking from beneath his hat.

'Where did you get on the train?' he asked with some asperity.

'In Sudbury.'

Sudbury! Of course! That could have been. Why had he not thought of that? He had been in such a hurry to get off the train he had not thought that someone might get on. He was about to speak again when his companion added a catastrophic afterthought.

'Where you got off,' he said.

After but a moment of cold shock, Mr Arodias rallied. 'Yes, I stepped out for a breath of air, and then went to the lavatory when I got back.'

'I thought,' the old man went on with a burr of dialect in his voice, just as Mr Arodias had imagined, 'you might have gone to see your uncle.'

Mr Arodias sat quite still. Faced with this challenge, his mind worked with the speed of lightning. Within ten seconds Mr Arodias decided that, whoever he was, the extra passenger must never leave the night train alive. He might know nothing at all of the crime, but he nevertheless knew enough to hang Mr Arodias. He knew enough, indeed; he knew Mr Arodias, he knew he had got off at Sudbury, and no doubt he knew he had reappeared in his compartment in the vicinity of East Chelmly. That was enough to doom one of them, and Mr Arodias, having got this far, had no intention of being doomed.

Mr Arodias needed time, and he was now quite willing to spar for it until he had evolved some plan for eliminating this menacing old fellow and dumping his body somewhere along the route.

'You know my uncle?' he asked in a strained voice.

'Ay, quite well.'

'I don't know him too well myself. I'm a Londoner, and he keeps to his own place in the country.'

'Ay. He has reasons, you might say.'

Mr Arodias pricked up his ears. 'What reasons?' he asked bluntly.

'A pity you don't know.'

'I don't,' said Mr Arodias, irritated.

'A pity you didn't know a bit more.'

'If there's something about my uncle I ought to know, I would like to hear it.'

'Ay, you shall. Your uncle's a mage.'

'A mage?' Mr Arodias was mystified.

'A warlock, then, if you like that better.'

Mr Arodias was amazed. He was also touched with a kind of macabre amusement. He did not know why the fact that the old man's fellow villagers regarded him as a warlock should amuse him; yet it did. Even in his amusement he did not lose sight of his decision that this prying old man must die, and he was contemplating whether he should despatch him with a quick blow or two or whether he should stifle his outcries and strangle him. The important thing, of course, was to prevent the guard from hearing anything suspicious. Meanwhile, he must carry on. Best to humour the extra passenger.

'Warlock, eh? And no doubt he has some special talents?' He caught himself just in time to prevent his saying 'had'; it would never do to refer to Uncle Thaddeus in the past tense – just in case something went wrong and his curious fellow-traveller got away after all.

'Ay, that he had.'

'Foretold the weather, no doubt.'

'That any gibbering fool could do.'

'Told fortunes, then?'

'A gipsy's trade! Not he! But then, you always did underrate him.'

'Did I, now?'

'Ay.'

'What was so wonderful about his being a warlock – if he was?'

'Oh, he was. Never a doubt about that. He had his familiar, too – on wings.'

'Wings?'

'Ay. He brought me to the train.'

Mr Arodias looked askance. A kind of premonitory tingle crept up his spine. He blinked and wished the light were a little stronger. There was beginning to be something uncomfortably challenging about his chosen victim; Mr Arodias did not like it.

'And he could send about a lich or two, if he had a mind to.'

'A lich?' said Mr Arodias in a dry voice. 'What the devil's that?'

'You don't know?'

'I wouldn't ask you if I did.'

'It's a corpse, that's what.'

'Send it about? What are you talking about?' demanded Mr Arodias, feeling a chill along his arms.

'Ay – for a special purpose. Oh, your uncle was a great one for things like that.'

'Special purpose,' repeated Mr Arodias, and at that moment his foot touched upon a sturdy weight which had the feel of a sashweight, and he bent to take it in his hand. Yes, it would do; it would do very well; and it was getting to be high time that he used it, because there was something horrible and terrible about that huddled figure.

'A special purpose,' said the extra passenger. 'Like this one.'

Mr Arodias was suddenly aware that his travelling companion had been speaking of his uncle for the past few minutes in the past tense. A kind of constriction seized upon his throat; but his fingers tightened upon the weight in his hand. The extra passenger knew or guessed far too much; whatever the risk, he must die now – quickly. He leaned forward, stealthily, as if he thought that the old fellow could see him despite the darkness and the hat over his face.

Then he snatched the hat away, and aimed his first blow.

It did not fall.

The head under that hat was hardly half a head – smashed in, and with the blood run down all over the face – the head of his Uncle Thaddeus! A scream rose and died in Mr Arodias's throat.

The eyes in that battered head were looking at him, and they were shining as if lit by the fires of hell.

No word, no sound passed Mr Arodias's lips; he was incapable of speech, of movement. A power, a force beyond Mr Arodias's comprehension emanated from the thing on the seat opposite. The eyes held him, the eyes encompassed him, the eyes drew him. Mr Arodias shrank together and slipped from the seat to his knees on the floor of the compartment. As in a dream he heard the sounds of the train, coming as if from very far away.

'Come to me, Simon,' said the thing that had been his Uncle Thaddeus.

And Simon Arodias crept across the floor and grovelled.

'Bring your face closer, Simon.'

And Simon Arodias raised his head, with a harsh whimpering sound struggling for utterance in his throat. Powerless to move, he watched one of the thick bloody hands of the extra passenger come down like a vice upon his face. Then he saw nothing more, and heard the sound of the night train like the sound of doom thundering in his ears.

The guard who found Mr Arodias collapsed from shock.

The medical examiner at Aberdeen was upset for a week. Nevertheless despite the condition of Mr Arodias's face – what was left of it – it was ascertained that he had been suffocated – 'by person or persons unknown'. Circumstances notwithstanding, Mr Arodias could not have committed suicide.

As for those fumbling chuckle-heads at Scotland Yard – they had already found the gloves which Mr Arodias had discarded on his way from the stolen car abandoned in East Chelmly to the station, the gloves which were to lead them all in good time to the little plot of ground where Mr Arodias was enjoying, not his Uncle Thaddeus's money, but his own just due.

# The Witch's Bone

*William Croft Dickinson*

Michael Elliott, MA, LLD, FSA (Scot.), frowned at the letter which had come from the Honororary Curator of the local Museum. It was quite a short letter and quite a simple one: merely asking him if he would allow the Museum to borrow his 'Witch's Bone' for a special exhibition covering Folk Beliefs and Customs. But Michael Elliott found the letter far from welcome. Short and simple as it was, it revived and increased all the fearful troubles of his mind. More than that, dare he now let the 'Bone' pass out of his own keeping – even if only for a little while?

Every day, for the last week, that witch's bone had preoccupied his mind to the exclusion of all else. The witch's bone that had brought to an end all his quarrels with Mackenzie Grant. The witch's bone that had possibly given him a revenge far more terrible than anything he had sought or expected. In a fit of anger he had thought only of testing its efficacy, never really believing it would work. And now he knew that the bone had worked only too well. Or had it? Had he indeed compassed Grant's death? All he knew was that Grant had died and that now he found it hard to recover his peace of mind.

Of course, he had only himself to blame. He had shown the bone at the last meeting of their local Antiquarian Society, just after he had acquired it; and, pleased with himself, he had expatiated upon its awful power. Mackenzie Grant had contradicted him – as usual. Grant had always treated his theories with contempt. There was his paper on lake-dwellings, and, after that, his paper on the iron-age forts in the Central Highlands. Upon both occasions Grant had stood up and pooh-poohed everything he had said. At meetings of the Council, too, the man could be relied upon to speak against anything he proposed. But all that was past history. Grant had poured scorn upon his story of the bone. And now Grant was dead. Yet how unbounded would be the relief to his tortured mind if Grant had been right, and if the story of the bone were 'stuff and nonsense' and nothing more. The very night that Grant had ridiculed his story he had put the bone to the test, directing its malevolent powers against Mackenzie Grant. And Grant had died a horrible death a few hours later. But could it not have been a ghastly coincidence in which the bone had played no part at all?

It was only a short piece of bone – probably sheep-bone – about six inches long, with a narrow ring of black bog-oak tightly encircling it near its centre. He had acquired it during his recent holiday in Sutherland. An old woman had died in a remote glen, and, because she had been reputed to be a witch, and had been feared as such, no one would bear her to burial. The local minister had called upon him, beseeching his help. 'The poor body was no witch at all,' the minister had said. 'She was just old and ill-favoured. I have had a coffin made of about the right size – at any rate it will be large enough – and if you could just drive me to the old body's hut, with the coffin in the rear of your estate-wagon, maybe we could manage to coffin her and give her a Christian burial.'

A strange request to make of any man! But the minister had won him over, and his reward had been the witch's bone.

They had found it on a shelf in the old woman's hut. The minister had seen it first, and had prodded it gently with his finger. 'So,' he had said softly. 'The witch's bone. I have been told of it. There are those of my people who say that she would utter her curse upon some man or woman, and then would make a wax figure and stick a pin into it. Then they say that if this bone rattled on its shelf, she knew that her curse had taken effect and that the person portrayed in the wax would be seized with pains in that part of the body which corresponded with the place of the pin in the wax. Some have even said that she could kill by sticking her pin in the heart or the head. For the power is in the bone. It can wound or kill any who are cursed by its possessor. And never are they spared.'

He had listened and looked with astonishment until, suddenly, the minister's face had changed and he had cried out: 'But what am I saying to you? There is no Witch of Endor in Sutherland. Indeed there is not. No such devilry is possible. I am not believing one word of it.' And the minister had boldly picked up the bone and had offered it to him. 'Take it with you,' he had said. 'It may interest some of your friends in the south.' And, wondering, he had taken it.

Yes; it had interested some of his friends. But Mackenzie Grant had laughed at him. 'A witch's bone!' he had said, contemptuously. 'Stuff and nonsense. Anyone can see by just looking at it that it's a handle, and nothing more. That ring round its centre simply means that, when it is grasped, two fingers go on one side of the ring, and two fingers on the other. Any boy, flying a kite, grasps a piece of wood in exactly the same way at the end of his string. A witch's bone, indeed. I believe, Elliott, I could persuade you that a handkerchief with a hole in it is a witch's veil to be worn at meetings of her coven. And the hole, of course, would be symbolic, indicative of her lapse from the Christian faith.' And so the man had gone on. Laughing at him before his friends.

He had kept down the anger which had surged within him; but, when he had returned home, and had taken the bone from his pocket, all his pent-up feelings had broken their bounds. He had marched straight into his study and, placing the bone upon a bookshelf near the fireplace, had resolved to prove its power to hurt. Aloud and deliberately he had cursed Mackenzie Grant; but, searching for sealing-wax, could find none. Then he had recalled the photograph of Mackenzie Grant in a recent volume of the Transactions of their Society. He had recalled, too, his aversion to destroying any photograph. To tear up a photograph had always seemed to him to be akin to tearing the living flesh and bones. So much the better. Mackenzie Grant should be torn asunder with a vengeance.

He had ripped the full-page photograph from the book and had deliberately torn it to pieces. In the fury of his task he had, for the moment, forgotten the bone. But, as the torn pieces had multiplied between his hands, suddenly there had come a rattling sound from the nearby shelf. And, at that, his heart had turned to ice. Fearfully he had looked at the bone; but it lay exactly where he had placed it, and it lay inert and still. He remembered assuring himself that he had simply imagined that rattle. He was overwrought. Yes, it was imagination and nothing more.

Yet, the next morning, when reading the *Scotsman* at breakfast-time, again a chill had struck his heart and his whole body had numbed with fear. For the paper announced with regret that a distinguished antiquary, Mr Mackenzie Grant, had been killed in a road accident. According to the announcement, Mr Grant, when driving home about midnight, after having dined with a friend, had unaccountably run head-on into a heavy lorry that had stopped for some minor adjustment on the opposite side of the road. It was a bad accident. Grant's car had been completely telescoped. But, in the opinion of the doctors, he must have been killed instantaneously, for their examination showed that he had suffered multiple injuries and that practically every bone in his body was broken.

No wonder his mind was ill at ease. He had striven to persuade himself that it was pure coincidence. That those multiple injuries had naught to do with a photograph torn into many shreds. He had laboured to free himself from a haunting burden of guilt. Yet the torturing thought was still there. Had the bone indeed the power of killing those who were cursed by its possessor?

Since then he had locked it up in his coin-cabinet. He had even been afraid to open the cabinet to make certain it was still there. And now the Museum had asked to be allowed to borrow it, to put it on display.

To say he had lost it, or had destroyed it, would be childish. Yet dare he lend it? Dare he allow it to pass out of his own keeping?

These were but some of the thoughts that troubled the mind of Dr Michael Elliott as he sat with a letter that lay before him on his desk.

About nine o'clock in the evening of the same day, when Sir Stephen Rowandson, CIE, the Honorary Curator of the Museum, was deep in a detective story, his housekeeper knocked on his study door and announced: 'Dr Michael Elliott.'

Somewhat surprised, Rowandson put down his book and rose to greet his visitor.

'Come in, Elliott. Come in. This is an unexpected pleasure.'

Michael Elliott entered the room slowly and hesitantly.

'Man, but you do look tired,' continued Rowandson, as Elliott came into the light. 'It's these cold nights. Take that chair by the fire and warm yourself. I'll get you a whisky.'

Elliott took the proffered chair and sank down in it. If, indeed, he was looking tired, he knew full well that it was not due to the coldness of the night.

'I've called about your letter, asking for the loan of my witch's bone,' he said, turning to his host and gratefully accepting the whisky which had been poured out for him. 'I thought I'd sooner bring it to you personally at your home, rather than give it to you, or leave it for you, at the Museum.'

'Why, certainly,' replied Rowandson, concealing his surprise. 'You think I might possibly leave it lying about in the Museum, and it might fall into the wrong hands?'

Rowandson spoke with a smile. But Elliott coloured slightly.

'You have guessed correctly. It may be more dangerous than we know.'

Rowandson looked more closely at his visitor. Did Elliott really believe that this bit of bone could exert occult force? He had been one of those standing by when Mackenzie Grant had poured scorn upon it; and although he had not heard Elliott's account of its supposed malignant power, he knew full well that the man was apt to be too credulous. But perhaps he had better humour him.

'You are right,' he conceded, gravely. 'I have seen some strange things myself in India. We must be careful. Would it make you happier if I promised that when I do put it on display I will put it in a locked case?'

Elliott's relief was too apparent to be disguised.

'I was hoping for something like that,' he said, taking the bone from his breast pocket. 'It is good of you to go to so much trouble; but I should feel reassured if it was under lock and key.'

'You can rely on me,' returned Rowandson. 'I will keep it safely here, in the house, until I have a locked case ready for it. And I will tell no one it is here.'

Once more Elliott's relief was so obvious that Rowandson, taking the bone from him, ostentatiously looked around his study for a safe keeping-place. Not finding one, he placed the bone on his desk. 'I'll find a safe place for it later,' he assured Elliott. 'You can rely on me. And I will certainly keep it here until I take it personally to the Museum and myself place it in a display case that can be securely locked.'

Thereafter, for some ten minutes or so, Sir Stephen Rowandson strove in vain to find some topic of conversation which would interest his visitor. But Elliott answered only in monosyllables, while his eyes constantly strayed to the witch's bone lying on the Curator's desk, and his only thought was whether he should warn Rowandson of its dangerous power, or whether that would merely make him look foolish and at the same time make Rowandson less responsive and also more careless.

'Well,' said Rowandson, as he wearied of his task. 'I mustn't keep you too late. And don't worry about your bone. It will be quite safe.'

Elliott rose heavily to his feet. 'Thank you,' he said. 'I am sorry to be so fussy, but, you know, I do believe it may be a witch's bone and not, as . . . as . . . Mackenzie Grant maintained, simply a handle of some kind.'

The last words had come out with difficulty, and Rowandson thought he understood.

'Yes, poor fellow. We shall miss his sceptical comments. We were all his victims at one time or another.'

Elliott winced. Again his eyes strayed to the witch's bone.

'You won't leave it there, will you?' he asked.

'No, no,' replied Rowandson, quickly. 'I'll find a safe place for it all right.'

Seemingly reassured, Elliott moved towards the door of the room. Rowandson opened it and, conducting his visitor through the hall, let him out of the house. For a minute or two he watched the retreating figure. 'There goes one of the most distinguished classical scholars in Europe,' he said to himself, 'and yet with more antiquarian bees in his bonnet than any man I know. A witch's bone, indeed. It may be. But, even so, what harm can it do to anyone?'

He returned to his study and, picking up the bone from his desk, examined it under the reading-lamp. But his examination made him no wiser.

'Well, well. Old Elliott was certainly mighty concerned about it, and I'd better do what I said. But where shall I put the wretched thing? I haven't a safe, and there isn't a drawer in the whole house that would defeat a ten-year-old.'

Moving about the room with the bone in his hand, Rowandson finally stopped in front of an old-fashioned knick-knack stand which bore on its shelves a medley of flints, cylindrical seals, Roman nails, and other small archaeological objects of varying periods and kinds. 'The very place,' he muttered. 'Not so much Poe's idea in *The Purloined Letter* as Chesterton's idea of hiding a leaf in a forest.'

By moving some of the specimens closer to one another he cleared a small space on one of the shelves and placed the bone there. Stepping back, he surveyed the result and found it good.

Two days later, as Sir Stephen Rowandson entered his study after a frugal breakfast, he was feeling thoroughly disgruntled. His housekeeper, summoned yesterday afternoon to nurse a sister who had suddenly been taken ill, had left him to fend for himself; and Sir Stephen Rowandson was not accustomed to domestic work. He had managed to prepare his coffee, toast and marmalade for breakfast; but now the dead ashes in his study fire-place mocked him. He would have to rake out those ashes and lay the fire himself. Unwillingly he began his task. As he busied himself with paper and firewood, his mind turned to the Museum and to his forthcoming exhibition. And his thoughts made him more disgruntled still. Why should everything go wrong at one and the same time? For, yesterday morning, when one or two members of the Society had come to the Museum to help with the final preparations, and when, in accordance with his promise, he had arranged for a place in one of the two locked cases to be reserved for Michael Elliott's witch bone, the interfering and officious Colonel Hogan had actually presumed to give contrary orders, even asserting that the bone wasn't worth a place in the exhibition anywhere. He had had trouble with the Colonel before. The man seemed to think he was in command of everything. But this time there had followed an unseemly wrangle in which he had completely lost his temper. More than that, in defending his promise to Elliott, he had hotly argued that the bone might be more dangerous than any of them realized. That heated altercation had made him look foolish; and he remembered, to his annoyance, the glances that had been exchanged. The word would now go round that he was becoming as credulous as Elliott himself. But if Elliott hadn't been so fussy, the argument would never have started at all.

'I could curse the old fool,' he muttered angrily, as he thrust the sticks of firewood among the paper which he had crushed up and laid in the hearth. 'Damn Michael Elliott, and damn his bone.'

He finished laying the fire and rose up from his task when, as he did so, he heard a strange rattle which seemed to come from somewhere within the room. Startled, he looked round. But nothing had fallen;

nothing seemed to be out of place. 'Probably a bird fluttered against the window,' he said, dubiously. 'But it didn't sound like it. It was a queer sound. Never heard anything like it before.'

Well, what now? He could go to the Museum and work there; then he could lunch at his Club; back to the Museum again; dinner at the Club; and perhaps he could even collect together a bridge-four for the evening. Yes, he could manage without his housekeeper for a day or two. But he hoped it wouldn't be longer than that.

Everything had worked according to plan, and Sir Stephen Rowandson was feeling much happier. He had put in a good morning's work; he had had an excellent lunch at his Club – and had even arranged a bridge-four; he had carried on with his exhibition in the afternoon; and, to his great relief, the members who had dropped in to help had given no indication that yesterday's wrangle had affected them in any way at all. It was nearly five o'clock, and he was thinking of giving up for the day, when he heard the bell ring. That was unusual. Who could be ringing the bell? The door was open, and people just walked in. Somewhat puzzled, he went to the door and found there a young man.

'Sir Stephen Rowandson?'

'Yes.'

'My name is Robert Reid, sir. You won't know me, but I'm the local representative of the *Scotsman* and I was told you might be able to help me.'

Sir Stephen Rowandson led his visitor into the main room of the Museum.

'And what can I do to help you?' he asked.

'I'm anxious to trace a photograph of Dr Michael Elliott. The paper wishes to carry one tomorrow. I do not like to call at his house, and it was suggested to me that probably you would have one here since, or so I gather, Dr Elliott was a prominent member of your Society.'

'But why can't you call at his house?'

The young man looked up quickly.

'But of course, how stupid of me. You cannot have heard.' Then, in a slightly lower voice, he continued: 'I'm very sorry to tell you, sir, that Dr Michael Elliott is dead. He was killed in a bad accident in Edinburgh, about half-past eleven this morning. And, as you will understand, we must carry a fairly long obituary notice. We would also like a photograph, if possible.'

'Michael Elliott dead,' repeated Rowandson, dully.

'Yes, sir. Apparently he was walking along the pavement by a site where a new building is going up when, for some unknown reason, a steel girder that was being lifted by a crane slipped from the chains which were holding it. Hitting the side of the building, it slewed round and, by sheer bad luck, fell on Dr Elliott and crushed him to death.'

'How horrible!'

'Yes, sir. But we are told that death must have been instantaneous. For not only was Dr Elliott badly crushed but also the girder, in falling, broke down a wooden screen which was shielding the site and, according to doctors, drove a wedge of broken wood from the screen straight through Dr Elliott's heart.'

For a brief space Sir Stephen Rowandson remained silent.

'It comes to all of us, sooner or later,' he said at last. 'But I wish it could have come in a way different from this. A photograph? Yes, I think I can help. There was a photograph of Dr Elliott in our local paper, the *Standard*, only the other day. Come up to my house and I'll show it to you. Then, if you think it suitable, I'm sure the *Standard* people will be only too glad to lend you the block.'

Sir Stephen Rowandson led the newspaper-man into his study, where, almost at once, he apologized for the coldness of the room.

'I'm sorry to offer you such a chilly reception,' he said. 'But my housekeeper is away and I am looking after myself. However, we'll soon have a fire, and then I'll hunt for that photograph.'

Although the young man held out a restraining hand, Rowandson struck a match, and lit the fire. Then, crossing to a pile of newspapers on a small table by his desk, he began to turn over the papers one by one. But the *Standard* which he wanted was not there.

'Queer,' he said, 'I could have sworn it was in this pile. But warm yourself at what fire there is while I have a look in the dining-room. I sometimes leave the paper there.'

He went out of the room, and the young man looked ruefully at the fire. The edges of the paper had burned, but nothing more. As one last wisp of smoke curled up towards the chimney, the fire was out.

'I can't find it anywhere,' growled Rowandson, coming back into the room. Once more he went through the pile of papers on the table, and still without success. Then he saw the dead hearth.

'Oh, I am sorry,' he cried. 'The fire has gone out. I must have packed it too tightly. Stupid of me. But it's years since I laid a fire.'

Then a new thought came to him.

'And I'm willing to bet that the *Standard* I'm looking for is there, at the bottom of my wretched fire. I just took the first paper that came to hand. I really am sorry. But look! If you go to the offices of the *Standard*, in the High Street, they'll willingly show you the issue, and then you can ask about the block. Say I sent you. Really, I should have taken you there in the first place.'

With many apologies for troubling the Honorary Curator of the Museum, the young newspaper-man left. Sir Stephen Rowandson returned to his study and there looked balefully at the dead fire.

'I suppose I shall have to re-lay the damned thing,' he muttered to himself. 'I'd better do it now, and have done with it.'

Kneeling down in front of the hearth, he removed the coal, then the firewood, and finally the paper. Yes, he had packed it too tightly. But he had learned his lesson. Straightening out a piece of the crushed-up paper, he saw it was the *Standard* for which he had been looking. He might have guessed he would use the one newspaper that was wanted. Ah! here was the page that bore poor Elliott's photograph. He straightened the page. It was still a good likeness, even though the photograph was badly crushed, and a splinter from the rough firewood had pierced it in the very heart.

But all that held no significance for Sir Stephen Rowandson. He re-laid the fire, went to his bathroom, and there – washed his hands.

# The Four-Fifteen Express

*Amelia B. Edwards*

The events which I am about to relate took place between nine and ten years ago. Sebastopol had fallen in the early spring, the peace of Paris had been concluded since March, our commercial relations with the Russian empire were but recently renewed; and I, returning home after my first northward journey since the war, was well pleased with the prospect of spending the month of December under the hospitable and thoroughly English roof of my excellent friend, Jonathan Jelf, Esq., of Dumbleton Manor, Clayborough, East Anglia. Travelling in the interests of the well-known firm in which it is my lot to be a junior partner, I had been called upon to visit not only the capitals of Russia and Poland, but had found it also necessary to pass some weeks among the trading ports of the Baltic; whence it came that the year was already far spent before I again set foot on English soil, and that, instead of shooting pheasants with him, as I had hoped, in October, I came to be my friend's guest during the more genial Christmas-tide.

My voyage over, and a few days given up to business in Liverpool and London, I hastened down to Clayborough with all the delight of a school-boy whose holidays are at hand. My way lay by the Great East Anglian line as far as Clayborough station, where I was to be met by one of the Dumbleton carriages and conveyed across the remaining nine miles of country. It was a foggy afternoon, singularly warm for the 4th of December, and I had arranged to leave London by the 4.15 express. The early darkness of winter had already closed in; the lamps were lighted in the carriages; a clinging damp dimmed the windows, adhered to the door-handles, and pervaded all the atmosphere; while the gas-jets at the neighbouring book-stand diffused a luminous haze that only served to make the gloom of the terminus more visible. Having arrived some seven minutes before the starting of the train, and, by the connivance of the guard, taken sole possession of an empty compartment, I lighted my travelling-lamp, made myself particularly snug, and settled down to the undisturbed enjoyment of a book and a cigar. Great, therefore, was my disappointment when, at the last moment, a gentleman came hurrying along the platform, glanced into my carriage, opened the locked door with a private key, and stepped in.

It struck me at the first glance that I had seen him before – a tall, spare man, thin-lipped, light-eyed, with an ungraceful stoop in the shoulders, and scant grey hair worn somewhat long upon the collar. He carried a light waterproof coat, an umbrella, and a large brown japanned deed-box, which last he placed under the seat. This done, he felt carefully in his breast-pocket, as if to make certain of the safety of his purse or pocket-book, laid his umbrella in the netting overhead, spread the waterproof across his knees, and exchanged his hat for a travelling-cap of some Scotch material. By this time the train was moving out of the station and into the faint grey of the wintry twilight beyond.

I now recognized my companion. I recognized him from the moment when he removed his hat and uncovered the lofty, furrowed, and somewhat narrow brow beneath. I had met him, as I distinctly remembered, some three years before, at the very house for which, in all probability, he was now bound, like myself. His name was Dwerrihouse, he was a lawyer by profession, and, if I was not greatly mistaken, was first cousin to the wife of my host. I knew also that he was a man eminently 'well-to-do', both as regarded his professional and private means. The Jelfs entertained him with that sort of observant courtesy which falls to the lot of the rich relation, the children made much of him, and the old butler, albeit somewhat surly 'to the general', treated him with deference. I thought, observing him by the vague mixture of lamplight and twilight, that Mrs Jelf's cousin looked all the worse for the three years' wear and tear which had gone over his head since our last meeting. He was very pale, and had a restless light in his eye that I did not remember to have observed before. The anxious lines, too, about his mouth were deepened, and there was a cavernous, hollow look about his cheeks and temples which seemed to speak of sickness or sorrow. He had glanced at me as he came in, but without any gleam of recognition in his face. Now he glanced again, as I fancied, somewhat doubtfully. When he did so for the third or fourth time I ventured to address him.

'Mr John Dwerrihouse, I think?'

'That is my name,' he replied.

'I had the pleasure of meeting you at Dumbleton about three years ago.'

'I thought I knew your face,' he said; 'but your name, I regret to say –'

'Langford – William Langford. I have known Jonathan Jelf since we were boys together at Merchant Taylors', and I generally spend a few weeks at Dumbleton in the shooting season. I suppose we are bound for the same destination.'

'Not if you are on your way to the manor,' he replied. 'I am travelling upon business – rather troublesome business, too – while you, doubtless, have only pleasure in view.'

'Just so. I am in the habit of looking forward to this visit as to the brightest three weeks in all the year.'

'It is a pleasant house,' said Mr Dwerrihouse.

'The pleasantest I know.'

'And Jelf is thoroughly hospitable.'

'The best and kindest fellow in the world!'

'They have invited me to spend Christmas week with them,' pursued Mr Dwerrihouse, after a moment's pause.

'And you are coming?'

'I cannot tell. It must depend on the issue of this business which I have in hand. You have heard perhaps that we are about to construct a branch line from Blackwater to Stockbridge.'

I explained that I had been for some months away from England, and had therefore heard nothing of the contemplated improvement.

Mr Dwerrihouse smiled complacently.

'It *will* be an improvement,' he said, 'a great improvement. Stock-bridge is a flourishing town, and needs but a more direct railway communication with the metropolis to become an important centre of commerce. This branch was my own idea. I brought the project before the board, and have myself superintended the execution of it up to the present time.'

'You are an East Anglian director, I presume?'

'My interest in the company,' replied Mr Dwerrihouse, 'is threefold. I am a director, I am a considerable shareholder, and, as head of the firm of Dwerrihouse, Dwerrihouse and Craik, I am the company's principal solicitor.'

Loquacious, self-important, full of his pet project, and apparently unable to talk on any other subject, Mr Dwerrihouse then went on to tell of the opposition he had encountered and the obstacles he had overcome in the cause of the Stockbridge branch. I was entertained with a multitude of local details and local grievances. The rapacity of one squire, the impracticability of another, the indignation of the rector whose glebe was threatened, the culpable indifference of the Stockbridge townspeople, who could *not* be brought to see that their most vital interests hinged upon a junction with the Great East Anglian line; the spite of the local newspaper, and the unheard-of difficulties attending the Common question, were each and all laid before me with a circum-stantiality that possessed the deepest interest for my excellent fellow-traveller, but none whatever for myself. From these, to my despair, he went on to more intricate matters: to the approximate expenses of construction per mile; to the estimates sent in by different contractors; to the probable traffic returns of the new line; to the provisional clauses of the new act as enumerated in Schedule D of the company's last half-yearly report; and so on and on and on, till my head ached and my attention flagged and my eyes kept closing in spite of every effort that I made to keep them open. At length I was roused by these words:

'Seventy-five thousand pounds, cash down.'

'Seventy-five thousand pounds, cash down,' I repeated, in the liveliest tone I could assume. 'That is a heavy sum.'

'A heavy sum to carry here,' replied Mr Dwerrihouse, pointing significantly to his breast-pocket, 'but a mere fraction of what we shall ultimately have to pay.'

'You do not mean to say that you have seventy-five thousand pounds at this moment upon your person?' I exclaimed.

'My good sir, have I not been telling you so for the last half-hour?' said Mr Dwerrihouse, testily. 'That money has to be paid over at half-past eight o'clock this evening, at the office of Sir Thomas's solicitors, on completion of the deed of sale.'

'But how will you get across by night from Blackwater to Stockbridge with seventy-five thousand pounds in your pocket?'

'To Stockbridge!' echoed the lawyer. 'I find I have made myself very imperfectly understood. I thought I had explained how this sum only carries us as far as Mallingford – the first stage, as it were, of our journey – and how our route from Blackwater to Mallingford lies entirely through Sir Thomas Liddell's property.'

'I beg your pardon,' I stammered. 'I fear my thoughts were wandering. So you only go as far as Mallingford tonight?'

'Precisely. I shall get a conveyance from the Blackwater Arms. And you?'

'Oh, Jelf sends a trap to meet me at Clayborough! Can I be the bearer of any message from you?'

'You may say, if you please, Mr Langford, that I wished I could have been your companion all the way, and that I will come over, if possible, before Christmas.'

'Nothing more?'

Mr Dwerrihouse smiled grimly. 'Well,' he said, 'you may tell my cousin that she need not burn the hall down in my honour *this* time, and that I shall be obliged if she will order the blue-room chimney to be swept before I arrive.'

'That sounds tragic. Had you a conflagration on the occasion of your last visit to Dumbleton?'

'Something like it. There had been no fire lighted in my bedroom since the spring, the flue was foul, and the rooks had built in it; so when

I went up to dress for dinner I found the room full of smoke and the chimney on fire. Are we already at Blackwater?'

The train had gradually come to a pause while Mr Dwerrihouse was speaking, and, on putting my head out of the window, I could see the station some few hundred yards ahead. There was another train before us blocking the way, and the guard was making use of the delay to collect the Blackwater tickets. I had scarcely ascertained our position when the ruddy-faced official appeared at our carriage door.

'Tickets, sir!' said he.

'I am for Clayborough,' I replied, holding out the tiny pink card.

He took it, glanced at it by the light of his little lantern, gave it back, looked, as I fancied, somewhat sharply at my fellow-traveller, and disappeared.

'He did not ask for yours,' I said, with some surprise.

'They never do,' replied Mr Dwerrihouse; 'they all know me, and of course I travel free.'

'Blackwater! Blackwater!' cried the porter, running along the platform beside us as we glided into the station.

Mr Dwerrihouse pulled out his deed-box, put his travelling-cap in his pocket, resumed his hat, took down his umbrella, and prepared to be gone.

'Many thanks, Mr Langford, for your society,' he said, with old-fashioned courtesy. 'I wish you a good-evening.'

'Good-evening,' I replied, putting out my hand.

But he either did not see it or did not choose to see it, and, slightly lifting his hat, stepped out upon the platform. Having done this, he moved slowly away and mingled with the departing crowd.

Leaning forward to watch him out of sight, I trod upon something which proved to be a cigar-case. It had fallen, no doubt, from the pocket of his waterproof coat, and was made of dark morocco leather, with a silver monogram upon the side. I sprang out of the carriage just as the guard came up to lock me in.

'Is there one minute to spare?' I asked, eagerly. 'The gentleman who travelled down with me from town has dropped his cigar-case; he is not yet out of the station.'

'Just a minute and a half, sir,' replied the guard. 'You must be quick.'

I dashed along the platform as fast as my feet could carry me. It was a large station, and Mr Dwerrihouse had by this time got more than half-way to the farther end.

I, however, saw him distinctly, moving slowly with the stream. Then, as I drew nearer, I saw that he had met some friend, that they were talking as they walked, that they presently fell back somewhat from the crowd and stood aside in earnest conversation. I made straight for the spot where they were waiting. There was a vivid gas-jet just above their heads, and the light fell upon their faces. I saw both distinctly – the face of Mr Dwerrihouse and the face of his companion. Running, breathless, eager as I was, getting in the way of porters and passengers, and fearful every instant lest I should see the train going on without me, I yet observed that the newcomer was considerably younger and shorter than the director, that he was sandy-haired, moustachioed, small-featured, and dressed in a close-cut suit of Scotch tweed. I was now within a few yards of them. I ran against a stout gentleman, I was nearly knocked down by a luggage-truck, I stumbled over a carpet-bag; I gained the spot just as the driver's whistle warned me to return.

To my utter stupefaction, they were no longer there. I had seen them but two seconds before – and they were gone! I stood still; I looked to right and left; I saw no sign of them in any direction. It was as if the platform had gaped and swallowed them.

'There were two gentlemen standing here a moment ago,' I said to a porter at my elbow; 'which way can they have gone?'

'I saw no gentlemen, sir,' replied the man.

The whistle shrilled out again. The guard, far up the platform, held up his arm, and shouted to me to 'come on!'

'If you're going on by this train, sir,' said the porter, 'you must run for it.'

I did run for it, just gained the carriage as the train began to move, was shoved in by the guard, and left, breathless and bewildered, with Mr Dwerrihouse's cigar-case still in my hand.

It was the strangest disappearance in the world; it was like a transformation trick in a pantomime. They were there one moment – palpably there, talking, with the gaslight full upon their faces – and the next moment they were gone. There was no door near, no window, no staircase; it was a mere slip of barren platform, tapestried with big advertisements. Could anything be more mysterious?

It was not worth thinking about, and yet, for my life, I could not help pondering upon it – pondering, wondering, conjecturing, turning it over and over in my mind, and beating my brains for a solution of the enigma. I thought of it all the way from Blackwater to Clayborough. I thought of it all the way from Clayborough to Dumbleton, as I rattled along the smooth highway in a trim dog-cart, drawn by a splendid black mare and driven by the silentest and dapperest of East Anglian grooms.

We did the nine miles in something less than an hour, and pulled up before the lodge-gates just as the church clock was striking half-past seven. A couple of minutes more, and the warm glow of the lighted hall was flooding out upon the gravel, a hearty grasp was on my hand, and a clear jovial voice was bidding me 'welcome to Dumbleton.'

'And now, my dear fellow,' said my host, when the first greeting was over, 'you have no time to spare. We dine at eight, and there are people coming to meet you, so you must just get the dressing business over as quickly as may be. By the way, you will meet some acquaintances; the Biddulphs are coming, and Prendergast (Prendergast of the Skirmishers) is staying in the house. Adieu! Mrs Jelf will be expecting you in the drawing-room.'

I was ushered to my room – not the blue room, of which Mr Dwerrihouse had made disagreeable experience, but a pretty little bachelor's chamber, hung with a delicate chintz and made cheerful by a blazing fire. I unlocked my portmanteau. I tried to be expeditious, but the memory of my railway adventure haunted me. I could not get free of it; I could not shake it off. It impeded me, it worried me, it tripped me up, it caused me to mislay my studs, to mistie my cravat, to wrench the buttons off my gloves. Worst of all, it made me so late that the party had all assembled before I reached the drawing-room. I had scarcely paid my respects to Mrs Jelf when dinner was announced, and we paired off, some eight or ten couples strong, into the dining-room.

I am not going to describe either the guests or the dinner. All provincial parties bear the strictest family resemblance, and I am not aware that an East Anglian banquet offers any exception to the rule. There was the usual country baronet and his wife; there were the usual country parsons and their wives; there was the sempiternal turkey and haunch of venison. *Vanitas vanitatum*. There is nothing new under the sun.

I was placed about midway down the table. I had taken one rector's wife down to dinner, and I had another at my left hand. They talked across me, and their talk was about babies; it was dreadfully dull. At length there came a pause. The entrées had just been removed, and the turkey had come upon the scene. The conversation had all along been of the languidest, but at this moment it happened to have stagnated altogether. Jelf was carving the turkey; Mrs Jelf looked as if she was trying to think of something to say; everybody else was silent. Moved by an unlucky impulse, I thought I would relate my adventure.

'By the way, Jelf,' I began, 'I came down part of the way today with a friend of yours.'

'Indeed!' said the master of the feast, slicing scientifically into the breast of the turkey. 'With whom, pray?'

'With one who bade me tell you that he should, if possible, pay you a visit before Christmas.'

'I cannot think who that could be,' said my friend, smiling.

'It must be Major Thorp,' suggested Mrs Jelf.

I shook my head.

'It was not Major Thorp,' I replied; 'it was a near relation of your own, Mrs Jelf.'

'Then I am more puzzled than ever,' replied my hostess. 'Pray tell me who it was.'

'It was no less a person than your cousin, Mr John Dwerrihouse.'

Jonathan Jelf laid down his knife and fork. Mrs Jelf looked at me in a strange, startled way, and said never a word.

'And he desired me to tell you, my dear madam, that you need not take the trouble to burn the hall down in his honour this time, but only to have the chimney of the blue room swept before his arrival.'

Before I had reached the end of my sentence I became aware of something ominous in the faces of the guests. I felt I had said something which I had better have left unsaid, and that for some unexplained reason my words had evoked a general consternation. I sat confounded, not daring to utter another syllable, and for at least two whole minutes there was dead silence round the table. Then Captain Prendergast came to the rescue.

'You have been abroad for some months, have you not, Mr Langford?' he said, with the desperation of one who flings himself into the breach. 'I heard you had been to Russia. Surely you have something to tell us of the state and temper of the country after the war?'

I was heartily grateful to the gallant Skirmisher for this diversion in my favour. I answered him, I fear, somewhat lamely; but he kept the conversation up, and presently one or two others joined in, and so the difficulty, whatever it might have been, was bridged over – bridged over, but not repaired. A something, an awkwardness, a visible constraint remained. The guests hitherto had been simply dull, but now they were evidently uncomfortable and embarrassed.

The dessert had scarcely been placed upon the table when the ladies left the room. I seized the opportunity to select a vacant chair next Captain Prendergast.

'In Heaven's name,' I whispered, 'what was the matter just now? What had I said?'

'You mentioned the name of John Dwerrihouse.'

'What of that? I had seen him not two hours before.'

'It is a most astounding circumstance that you should have seen him,' said Captain Prendergast. 'Are you sure it was he?'

'As sure as of my own identity. We were talking all the way between London and Blackwater. But why does that surprise you?'

'*Because*,' replied Captain Prendergast, dropping his voice to the lowest whisper – '*because John Dwerrihouse absconded three months ago with seventy-five thousand pounds of the company's money, and has never been heard of since.*'

John Dwerrihouse had absconded three months ago – and I had seen him only a few hours back! John Dwerrihouse had embezzled seventy-five thousand pounds of the company's money, yet told me that he carried that sum upon his person! Were ever facts so strangely incongruous, so difficult to reconcile? How should he have ventured again into the light of day? How dared he show himself along the line? Above all, what had he been doing throughout those mysterious three months of disappearance?

Perplexing questions these – questions which at once suggested themselves to the minds of all concerned, but which admitted of no easy solution. I could find no reply to them. Captain Prendergast had not even a suggestion to offer. Jonathan Jelf, who seized the first opportunity of drawing me aside and learning all that I had to tell, was more amazed and bewildered than either of us. He came to my room that night, when all the guests were gone, and we talked the thing over from every point of view; without, it must be confessed, arriving at any kind of conclusion.

'I do not ask you,' he said, 'whether you can have mistaken your man. That is impossible.'

'As impossible as that I should mistake some stranger for yourself.'

'It is not a question of looks or voice, but of facts. That he should have alluded to the fire in the blue room is proof enough of John Dwerrihouse's identity. How did he look?'

'Older, I thought; considerably older, paler, and more anxious.'

'He has had enough to make him look anxious, anyhow,' said my friend, gloomily, 'be he innocent or guilty.'

'I am inclined to believe that he is innocent,' I replied. 'He showed no embarrassment when I addressed him, and no uneasiness when the guard came round. His conversation was open to a fault. I might almost say that he talked too freely of the business which he had in hand.'

'That again is strange, for I know no one more reticent on such subjects. He actually told you that he had the seventy-five thousand pounds in his pocket?'

'He did.'

'Humph! My wife has an idea about it, and she may be right –'

'What idea?'

'Well, she fancies – women are so clever, you know, at putting themselves inside people's motives – she fancies that he was tempted, that he did actually take the money, and that he has been concealing himself these three months in some wild part of the country, struggling possibly with his conscience all the time, and daring neither to abscond with his booty nor to come back and restore it.'

'But now that he has come back?'

'That is the point. She conceives that he has probably thrown himself upon the company's mercy, made restitution of the money, and, being forgiven, is permitted to carry the business through as if nothing whatever had happened.'

'The last,' I replied, 'is an impossible case. Mrs Jelf thinks like a generous and delicate-minded woman, but not in the least like a board of railway directors. They would never carry forgiveness so far.'

'I fear not; and yet it is the only conjecture that bears a semblance of likelihood. However, we can run over to Clayborough tomorrow and see if anything is to be learned. By the way, Prendergast tells me you picked up his cigar-case.'

'I did so, and here it is.'

Jelf took the cigar-case, examined it by the light of the lamp, and said at once that it was beyond doubt Mr Dwerrihouse's property, and that he remembered to have seen him use it.

'Here, too, is his monogram on the side,' he added – 'a big J transfixing a capital D. He used to carry the same on his note-paper.'

'It offers, at all events, a proof that I was not dreaming.'

'Ay, but it is time you were asleep and dreaming now. I am ashamed to have kept you up so long. Goodnight.'

'Goodnight, and remember that I am more than ready to go with you to Clayborough or Blackwater or London or anywhere, if I can be of the least service.'

'Thanks! I know you mean it, old friend, and it may be that I shall put you to the test. Once more, goodnight.'

So we parted for that night, and met again in the breakfast-room at half-past eight next morning. It was a hurried, silent, uncomfortable meal; none of us had slept well, and all were thinking of the same subject. Mrs Jelf had evidently been crying, Jelf was impatient to be off, and both Captain Prendergast and myself felt ourselves to be in the painful position of outsiders who are involuntarily brought into a domestic trouble. Within twenty minutes after we had left the breakfast-table the dog-cart was brought round, and my friend and I were on the road to Clayborough.

'Tell you what it is, Langford,' he said, as we sped along between the wintry hedges, 'I do not much fancy to bring up Dwerrihouse's name at Clayborough. All the officials know that he is my wife's relation, and the subject just now is hardly a pleasant one. If you don't much mind, we will take the 11.10 to Blackwater. It's an important station, and we shall stand a far better chance of picking up information there than at Clayborough.'

So we took the 11.10, which happened to be an express, and, arriving at Blackwater about a quarter before twelve, proceeded at once to prosecute our inquiry.

We began by asking for the station-master, a big, blunt, businesslike person, who at once averred that he knew Mr John Dwerrihouse perfectly well, and that there was no director on the line whom he had seen and spoken to so frequently. 'He used to be down here two or three times a week about three months ago,' said he, 'when the new line was first set afoot; but since then, you know, gentlemen –'

He paused significantly.

Jelf flushed scarlet.

'Yes, yes,' he said, hurriedly; 'we know all about that. The point now to be ascertained is whether anything has been seen or heard of him lately.'

'Not to my knowledge,' replied the station-master.

'He is not known to have been down the line any time yesterday, for instance?'

The station-master shook his head.

'The East Anglian, sir,' said he, 'is about the last place where he would dare to show himself. Why, there isn't a station-master, there isn't a guard, there isn't a porter, who doesn't know Mr Dwerrihouse by sight as well as he knows his own face in the looking-glass, or who wouldn't telegraph for the police as soon as he had set eyes on him at any point along the line. Bless you, sir! there's been a standing order out against him ever since the 25th of September last.'

'And yet,' pursued my friend, 'a gentleman who travelled down yesterday from London to Clayborough by the afternoon express testifies that he saw Mr Dwerrihouse in the train, and that Mr Dwerrihouse alighted at Blackwater station.'

'Quite impossible, sir,' replied the station-master, promptly.

'Why impossible?'

'Because there is no station along the line where he is so well known or where he would run so great a risk. It would be just running his head into the lion's mouth; he would have been mad to come nigh Blackwater station; and if he had come he would have been arrested before he left the platform.'

'Can you tell me who took the Blackwater tickets of that train?'

'I can, sir. It was the guard, Benjamin Somers.'

'And where can I find him?'

'You can find him, sir, by staying here, if you please, till one o'clock. He will be coming through with the up express from Crampton, which stays at Blackwater for ten minutes.'

We waited for the up express, beguiling the time as best we could by strolling along the Blackwater road till we came almost to the outskirts of the town, from which the station was distant nearly a couple of miles. By one o'clock we were back again upon the platform and waiting for the train. It came punctually, and I at once recognized the ruddy-faced guard who had gone down with my train the evening before.

'The gentlemen want to ask you something about Mr Dwerrihouse, Somers,' said the station-master, by way of introduction.

The guard flashed a keen glance from my face to Jelf's and back again to mine.

'Mr John Dwerrihouse, the late director?' said he, interrogatively.

'The same,' replied my friend. 'Should you know him if you saw him?'

'Anywhere, sir.'

'Do you know if he was in the 4.15 express yesterday afternoon?'

'He was not, sir.'

'How can you answer so positively?'

'Because I looked into every carriage and saw every face in that train, and I could take my oath that Mr Dwerrihouse was not in it. This gentleman was,' he added, turning sharply upon me. 'I don't know that I ever saw him before in my life, but I remember *his* face perfectly. You nearly missed taking your seat in time at this station, sir, and you got out at Clayborough.'

'Quite true, guard,' I replied; 'but do you not also remember the face of the gentleman who travelled down in the same carriage with me as far as here?'

'It was my impression, sir, that you travelled down alone,' said Somers, with a look of some surprise.

'By no means. I had a fellow-traveller as far as Blackwater, and it was in trying to restore him the cigar-case which he had dropped in the carriage that I so nearly let you go on without me.'

'I remember your saying something about a cigar-case, certainly,' replied the guard; 'but –'

'You asked for my ticket just before we entered the station.'

'I did, sir.'

'Then you must have seen him. He sat in the corner next the very door to which you came.'

'No, indeed; I saw no one.'

I looked at Jelf. I began to think the guard was in the ex-director's confidence, and paid for his silence.

'If I had seen another traveller I should have asked for his ticket,' added Somers. 'Did you see me ask for his ticket, sir?'

'I observed that you did not ask for it, but he explained that by saying –' I hesitated. I feared I might be telling too much, and so broke off abruptly.

The guard and the station-master exchanged glances. The former looked impatiently at his watch.

'I am obliged to go on in four minutes more, sir,' he said.

'One last question, then,' interposed Jelf, with a sort of desperation. 'If this gentleman's fellow-traveller had been Mr John Dwerrihouse, and he had been sitting in the corner next the door by which you took the tickets, could you have failed to see and recognize him?'

'No, sir; it would have been quite impossible.'

'And you are certain you did *not* see him?'

'As I said before, sir, I could take my oath I did not see him. And if it wasn't that I don't like to contradict a gentleman, I would say I could also take my oath that this gentleman was quite alone in the carriage the whole way from London to Clayborough. Why, sir,' he added, dropping his voice so as to be inaudible to the station-master, who had been called away to speak to some person close by, 'you expressly asked me to give you a compartment to yourself, and I did so. I locked you in, and you were so good as to give me something for myself.'

'Yes; but Mr Dwerrihouse had a key of his own.'

'I never saw him, sir; I saw no one in that compartment but yourself. Beg pardon, sir; my time's up.'

And with this the ruddy guard touched his cap and was gone. In another minute the heavy panting of the engine began afresh, and the train glided slowly out of the station.

We looked at each other for some moments in silence. I was the first to speak.

'Mr Benjamin Somers knows more than he chooses to tell,' I said.

'Humph! do you think so?'

'It must be. He could not have come to the door without seeing him; it's impossible.'

'There is one thing not impossible, my dear fellow.'

'What is that?'

'That you may have fallen asleep and dreamed the whole thing.'

'Could I dream of a branch line that I had never heard of? Could I dream of a hundred and one business details that had no kind of interest for me? Could I dream of the seventy-five thousand pounds?'

'Perhaps you might have seen or heard some vague account of the affair while you were abroad. It might have made no impression upon you at the time, and might have come back to you in your dreams, recalled perhaps by the mere names of the stations on the line.'

'What about the fire in the chimney of the blue room – should I have heard of that during my journey?'

'Well, no; I admit there is a difficulty about that point.'

'And what about the cigar-case?'

'Ay, by Jove! there is the cigar-case. That *is* a stubborn fact. Well, it's a mysterious affair, and it will need a better detective than myself, I fancy, to clear it up. I suppose we may as well go home.'

A week had not gone by when I received a letter from the secretary of the East Anglian Railway Company, requesting the favour of my attendance at a special board meeting not then many days distant. No reasons were alleged and no apologies offered for this demand upon my time, but they had heard, it was clear, of my inquiries anent the missing director, and had a mind to put me through some sort of official examination upon the subject. Being still a guest at Dumbleton Hall, I had to go up to London for the purpose, and Jonathan Jelf accompanied me. I found the direction of the Great East Anglian line represented by a party of some twelve or fourteen gentlemen seated in solemn conclave round a huge green baize table, in a gloomy boardroom adjoining the London terminus.

Being courteously received by the chairman (who at once began by saying that certain statements of mine respecting Mr John Dwerrihouse had come to the knowledge of the direction, and that they in consequence desired to confer with me on those points), we were placed at the table, and the inquiry proceeded in due form.

I was first asked if I knew Mr John Dwerrihouse, how long I had been acquainted with him, and whether I could identify him at sight. I was then asked when I had seen him last. To which I replied, 'On the 4th of this present month, December, 1856.' Then came the inquiry of where I had seen him on that fourth day of December; to which I replied that I met him in a first-class compartment of the 4.15 down express, that he got in just as the train was leaving the London terminus, and that he alighted at Blackwater station. The chairman then inquired whether I had held any communication with my fellow-traveller; whereupon I related, as nearly as I could remember it, the whole bulk and substance of Mr John Dwerrihouse's diffuse information respecting the new branch line.

To all this the board listened with profound attention, while the chairman presided and the secretary took notes. I then produced the cigar-case. It was passed from hand to hand, and recognized by all. There was not a man present who did not remember that plain cigar-case with its silver monogram, or to whom it seemed anything less than entirely corroborative of my evidence. When at length I had told all that I had to tell, the chairman whispered something to the secretary; the secretary touched a silver hand-bell, and the guard, Benjamin Somers, was ushered into the room. He was then examined as carefully as myself. He declared that he knew Mr John Dwerrihouse perfectly well, that he could not be mistaken in him, that he remembered going down with the 4.15 express on the afternoon in question, that he remembered me, and that, there being one or two empty first-class compartments on that especial afternoon, he had, in compliance with my request, placed me in a carriage by myself. He was positive that I remained alone in that compartment all the way from London to Clayborough. He was ready to take his oath that Mr Dwerrihouse was neither in that carriage with me, nor in any compartment of that train. He remembered distinctly to have examined my ticket at Blackwater; was certain that there was no one else at that time in the carriage; could not have failed to observe a second person, if there had been one; had that second person been Mr John Dwerrihouse, should have quietly double-locked the door of the carriage and have at once given information to the Blackwater station-master. So clear, so decisive, so ready, was Somers with this testimony, that the board looked fairly puzzled.

'You hear this person's statement, Mr Langford,' said the chairman. 'It contradicts yours in every particular. What have you to say in reply?'

'I can only repeat what I said before. I am quite as positive of the truth of my own assertions as Mr Somers can be of the truth of his.'

'You say that Mr Dwerrihouse alighted at Blackwater, and that he was in possession of a private key. Are you sure that he had not alighted by means of that key before the guard came round for the tickets?'

'I am quite positive that he did not leave the carriage till the train had fairly entered the station, and the other Blackwater passengers alighted. I even saw that he was met there by a friend.'

'Indeed! Did you see that person distinctly?'

'Quite distinctly.'

'Can you describe his appearance?'

'I think so. He was short and very slight, sandy-haired, with a bushy moustache and beard, and he wore a closely fitting suit of grey tweed. His age I should take to be about thirty-eight or forty.'

'Did Mr Dwerrihouse leave the station in this person's company?'

'I cannot tell. I saw them walking together down the platform, and then I saw them standing aside under a gas-jet, talking earnestly. After that I lost sight of them quite suddenly, and just then my train went on, and I with it.'

The chairman and secretary conferred together in an undertone. The directors whispered to one another. One or two looked suspiciously at the guard. I could see that my evidence remained unshaken, and that, like myself, they suspected some complicity between the guard and the defaulter.

'How far did you conduct that 4.15 express on the day in question, Somers?' asked the chairman.

'All through, sir,' replied the guard, 'from London to Crampton.'

'How was it that you were not relieved at Clayborough? I thought there was always a change of guards at Clayborough.'

'There used to be, sir, till the new regulations came in force last midsummer, since when the guards in charge of express trains go the whole way through.'

The chairman turned to the secretary.

'I think it would be as well,' he said, 'if we had the day-book to refer to upon this point.'

Again the secretary touched the silver hand-bell, and desired the porter in attendance to summon Mr Raikes. From a word or two dropped by another of the directors I gathered that Mr Raikes was one of the under-secretaries.

He came, a small, slight, sandy-haired, keen-eyed man, with an eager, nervous manner, and a forest of light beard and moustache. He just showed himself at the door of the board-room, and, being requested to bring a certain day-book from a certain shelf in a certain room, bowed and vanished.

He was there such a moment, and the surprise of seeing him was so great and sudden, that it was not till the door had closed upon him that I found voice to speak. He was no sooner gone, however, than I sprang to my feet.

'That person,' I said, 'is the same who met Mr Dwerrihouse upon the platform at Blackwater!'

There was a general movement of surprise. The chairman looked grave and somewhat agitated.

'Take care, Mr Langford,' he said; 'take care what you say.'

'I am as positive of his identity as of my own.'

'Do you consider the consequences of your words? Do you consider that you are bringing a charge of the gravest character against one of the company's servants?'

'I am willing to be put upon my oath, if necessary. The man who came to that door a minute since is the same whom I saw talking with Mr Dwerrihouse on the Blackwater platform. Were he twenty times the company's servant, I could say neither more nor less.'

The chairman turned again to the guard.

'Did you see Mr Raikes in the train or on the platform?' he asked.

Somers shook his head.

'I am confident Mr Raikes was not in the train,' he said, 'and I certainly did not see him on the platform.'

The chairman turned next to the secretary.

'Mr Raikes is in your office, Mr Hunter,' he said. 'Can you remember if he was absent on the 4th instant?'

'I do not think he was,' replied the secretary, 'but I am not prepared to speak positively. I have been away most afternoons myself lately, and Mr Raikes might easily have absented himself if he had been disposed.'

At this moment the under-secretary returned with the day-book under his arm.

'Be pleased to refer, Mr Raikes,' said the chairman, 'to the entries of the 4th instant, and see what Benjamin Somers's duties were on that day.'

Mr Raikes threw open the cumbrous volume, and ran a practised eye and finger down some three or four successive columns of entries. Stopping suddenly at the foot of a page, he then read aloud that Benjamin Somers had on that day conducted the 4.15 express from London to Crampton.

The chairman leaned forward in his seat, looked the under-secretary full in the face, and said, quite sharply and suddenly:

'Where were *you*, Mr Raikes, on the same afternoon?'

'*I*, sir?'

'You, Mr Raikes. Where were you on the afternoon and evening of the 4th of the present month?'

'Here, sir, in Mr Hunter's office. Where else should I be?'

There was a dash of trepidation in the under-secretary's voice as he said this, but his look of surprise was natural enough.

'We have some reason for believing, Mr Raikes, that you were absent that afternoon without leave. Was this the case?'

'Certainly not, sir. I have not had a day's holiday since September. Mr Hunter will bear me out in this.'

Mr Hunter repeated what he had previously said on the subject, but added that the clerks in the adjoining office would be certain to know. Whereupon the senior clerk, a grave, middle-aged person in green glasses, was summoned and interrogated.

His testimony cleared the under-secretary at once. He declared that Mr Raikes had in no instance, to his knowledge, been absent during office hours since his return from his annual holiday in September.

I was confounded. The chairman turned to me with a smile, in which a shade of covert annoyance was scarcely apparent.

'You hear, Mr Langford?' he said.

'I hear, sir; but my conviction remains unshaken.'

'I fear, Mr Langford, that your convictions are very insufficiently based,' replied the chairman, with a doubtful cough. 'I fear that you "dream dreams", and mistake them for actual occurrences. It is a dangerous habit of mind, and might lead to dangerous results. Mr Raikes here would have found himself in an unpleasant position had he not proved so satisfactory an alibi.'

I was about to reply, but he gave me no time.

'I think, gentlemen,' he went on to say, addressing the board, 'that we should be wasting time to push this inquiry further. Mr Langford's evidence would seem to be of an equal value throughout. The testimony of Benjamin Somers disproves his first statement, and the testimony of the last witness disproves his second. I think we may conclude that Mr Langford fell asleep in the train on the occasion of his journey to Clayborough, and dreamed an unusually vivid and circumstantial dream, of which, however, we have now heard quite enough.'

There are few things more annoying than to find one's positive convictions met with incredulity. I could not help feeling impatience at the turn that affairs had taken. I was not proof against the civil sarcasm of the chairman's manner. Most intolerable of all, however, was the quiet smile lurking about the corners of Benjamin Somers's mouth, and the half-triumphant, half-malicious gleam in the eyes of the under-secretary. The man was evidently puzzled and somewhat alarmed. His looks seemed furtively to interrogate me. Who was I? What did I want? Why had I come here to do him an ill turn with his employers? What was it to me whether or not he was absent without leave?

Seeing all this, and perhaps more irritated by it than the thing deserved, I begged leave to detain the attention of the board for a moment longer. Jelf plucked me impatiently by the sleeve.

'Better let the thing drop,' he whispered. 'The chairman's right enough; you dreamed it, and the less said now the better.'

I was not to be silenced, however, in this fashion. I had yet something to say, and I would say it. It was to this effect: that dreams were not usually productive of tangible results, and that I requested to know in what way the chairman conceived I had evolved from my dream so substantial and well-made a delusion as the cigar-case which I had had the honour to place before him at the commencement of our interview.

'The cigar-case, I admit, Mr Langford,' the chairman replied, 'is a very strong point in your evidence. It is your *only* strong point, however, and there is just a possibility that we may all be misled by a mere accidental resemblance. Will you permit me to see the case again?'

'It is unlikely,' I said, as I handed it to him, 'that any other should bear precisely this monogram, and yet be in all other particulars exactly similar.'

The chairman examined it for a moment in silence, and then passed it to Mr Hunter. Mr Hunter turned it over and over, and shook his head.

'This is no mere resemblance,' he said. 'It is John Dwerrihouse's cigar-case to a certainty. I remember it perfectly; I have seen it a hundred times.'

'I believe I may say the same,' added the chairman; 'yet how account for the way in which Mr Langford asserts that it came into his possession?'

'I can only repeat,' I replied, 'that I found it on the floor of the carriage after Mr Dwerrihouse had alighted. It was in leaning out to look after him that I trod upon it, and it was in running after him for the purpose of restoring it that I saw, or believed I saw, Mr Raikes standing aside with him in earnest conversation.'

Again I felt Jonathan Jelf plucking at my sleeve.

'Look at Raikes,' he whispered; 'look at Raikes!'

I turned to where the under-secretary had been standing a moment before, and saw him, white as death, with lips trembling and livid, stealing towards the door.

To conceive a sudden, strange, and indefinite suspicion, to fling myself in his way, to take him by the shoulders as if he were a child, and turn his craven face, perforce, towards the board, were with me the work of an instant.

'Look at him!' I exclaimed. 'Look at his face! I ask no better witness to the truth of my words.'

The chairman's brow darkened.

'Mr Raikes,' he said, sternly, 'if you know anything you had better speak.'

Vainly trying to wrench himself from my grasp, the under-secretary stammered out an incoherent denial.

'Let me go,' he said. 'I know nothing – you have no right to detain me – let me go!'

'Did you, or did you not, meet Mr John Dwerrihouse at Blackwater station? The charge brought against you is either true or false. If true, you will do well to throw yourself upon the mercy of the board and make full confession of all that you know.'

The under-secretary wrung his hands in an agony of helpless terror.

'I was away!' he cried. 'I was two hundred miles away at the time! I know nothing about it – I have nothing to confess – I am innocent – I call God to witness I am innocent!'

'Two hundred miles away!' echoed the chairman. 'What do you mean?'

'I was in Devonshire. I had three weeks' leave of absence – I appeal to Mr Hunter – Mr Hunter knows I had three weeks' leave of absence! I was in Devonshire all the time; I can prove I was in Devonshire!'

Seeing him so abject, so incoherent, so wild with apprehension, the directors began to whisper gravely among themselves, while one got quietly up and called the porter to guard the door.

'What has your being in Devonshire to do with the matter?' said the chairman. 'When were you in Devonshire?'

'Mr Raikes took his leave in September,' said the secretary, 'about the time when Mr Dwerrihouse disappeared.'

'I never even heard that he had disappeared till I came back!'

'That must remain to be proved,' said the chairman. 'I shall at once put this matter in the hands of the police. In the meanwhile, Mr Raikes, being myself a magistrate and used to deal with these cases, I advise you to offer no resistance, but to confess while confession may yet do you service. As for your accomplice –'

The frightened wretch fell upon his knees.

'I had no accomplice!' he cried. 'Only have mercy upon me – only spare my life, and I will confess all! I didn't mean to harm him! I didn't mean to hurt a hair of his head! Only have mercy upon me, and let me go!'

The chairman rose in his place, pale and agitated. 'Good heavens!' he exclaimed, 'what horrible mystery is this? What does it mean?'

'As sure as there is a God in heaven,' said Jonathan Jelf, 'it means that murder has been done.'

'No! no! no!' shrieked Raikes, still upon his knees, and cowering like a beaten hound. 'Not murder! No jury that ever sat could bring it in murder. I thought I had only stunned him – I never meant to do more than stun him! Manslaughter – manslaughter – not murder!'

Overcome by the horror of this unexpected revelation, the chairman covered his face with his hand and for a moment or two remained silent.

'Miserable man,' he said at length, 'you have betrayed yourself.'

'You made me confess! You urged me to throw myself upon the mercy of the board!'

'You have confessed to a crime which no one suspected you of having committed,' replied the chairman, 'and which this board has no power either to punish or forgive. All that I can do for you is to advise you to submit to the law, to plead guilty, and to conceal nothing. When did you do this deed?'

The guilty man rose to his feet, and leaned heavily against the table. His answer came reluctantly, like the speech of one dreaming.

'On the 22nd of September!'

On the 22nd of September! I looked in Jonathan Jelf's face, and he in mine. I felt my own paling with a strange sense of wonder and dread. I saw his blanch suddenly, even to the lips.

'Merciful heaven!' he whispered. *'What was it, then, that you saw in the train?'*

What was it that I saw in the train? That question remains unanswered to this day. I have never been able to reply to it. I only know that it bore the living likeness of the murdered man, whose body had then been lying some ten weeks under a rough pile of branches and brambles and rotting leaves, at the bottom of a deserted chalk-pit about half-way between Blackwater and Mallingford. I know that it spoke and moved and looked as that man spoke and moved and looked in life; that I heard, or seemed to hear, things related which I could never otherwise have learned; that I was guided, as it were, by that vision on the platform to the identification of the murderer; and that, a passive instrument myself, I was destined, by means of these mysterious teachings, to bring about the ends of justice. For these things I have never been able to account.

As for that matter of the cigar-case, it proved, on inquiry, that the carriage in which I travelled down that afternoon to Clayborough had not been in use for several weeks, and was, in point of fact, the same in which poor John Dwerrihouse had performed his last journey. The case had doubtless been dropped by him, and had lain unnoticed till I found it.

Upon the details of the murder I have no need to dwell. Those who desire more ample particulars may find them, and the written confession of Augustus Raikes, in the files of *The Times* for 1856. Enough that the under-secretary, knowing the history of the new line, and following the negotiation step by step through all its stages, determined to waylay Mr Dwerrihouse, rob him of the seventy-five thousand pounds, and escape to America with his booty.

In order to effect these ends he obtained leave of absence a few days before the time appointed for the payment of the money, secured his passage across the Atlantic in a steamer advertised to start on the 23rd, provided himself with a heavily loaded 'life-preserver', and went down to Blackwater to await the arrival of his victim. How he met him on the platform with a pretended message from the board, how he offered to conduct him by a short cut across the fields to Mallingford, how, having brought him to a lonely place, he struck him down with the life-preserver, and so killed him, and how, finding what he had done, he dragged the body to the verge of an out-of-the-way chalk-pit, and there flung it in and piled it over with branches and brambles, are facts still fresh in the memories of those who, like the connoisseurs in De Quincey's famous essay, regard murder as a fine art. Strangely enough, the murderer, having done his work, was afraid to leave the country. He declared that he had not intended to take the director's life, but only to stun and rob him; and that, finding the blow had killed, he dared not fly for fear of drawing down suspicion upon his own head. As a mere robber he would have been safe in the States, but as a murderer he would inevitably have been pursued and given up to justice. So he forfeited his passage, returned to the office as usual at the end of his leave, and locked up his ill-gotten thousands till a more convenient opportunity. In the meanwhile he had the satisfaction of finding that Mr Dwerrihouse was universally believed to have absconded with the money, no one knew how or whither.

Whether he meant murder or not, however, Mr Augustus Raikes paid the full penalty of his crime, and was hanged at the Old Bailey in the second week in January, 1857. Those who desire to make his further acquaintance may see him any day (admirably done in wax) in the Chamber of Horrors at Madame Tussaud's exhibition, in Baker Street. He is there to be found in the midst of a select society of ladies and gentlemen of atrocious memory, dressed in the close-cut tweed suit which he wore on the evening of the murder, and holding in his hand the identical life-preserver with which he committed it.

# The Haunted Haven

*A. E. Ellis*

Attention all shipping. The Meteorological Office issued the following gale warning at 1600 hours: south-westerly gale, force eight, imminent in sea areas Irish Sea, Lundy, and Fastnet.

In the south-eastern angle of St Bride's Bay, sheltered from the south-west winds by the projecting tongue of land that ends in Wooltack Point, nestles the little fishing village of Ticklas Haven, which consists of an inn, a compact group of cottages, a stout jetty partly fashioned out of the living rock, and two snug little coves or havens, one on each side of the jetty. In the more northerly of these tiny bays ten or a dozen fishing smacks may usually be seen riding at their moorings, or lying in lopsided idleness at ebb tide. In the other cove, although it appears more sheltered and suitable in every way for use as a harbour, never a boat will be seen, nor any signs of human occupation, such as the lobster-pots, coils of rope, nets and tarpaulins, which litter the foreshore of the north cove.

Four steep roads converge upon the village, two from the landward side and two from the coast to the north and the south-west. About a furlong up the more southerly of the landward roads, a hundred and fifty feet above the cluster of cottages in the haven, stands a ruined house, still known in the village as the Doctor's House, although now deserted for some thirty years. Little remains of this once imposing and substantial dwelling, a mansion in comparison with the fishermen's cottages it dominates, save the ivy-grown walls, through which the Atlantic gales shriek and wail, and the heavy wooden gate, which creaks and bangs in the wind like demoniac artillery.

For a quiet and restful summer resort Ticklas Haven is hard to beat, and I congratulated myself on my good fortune in not only discovering so cosy a nook, but in securing comfortable lodging at the inn. The landlord was a kindly and intelligent man, some fifty years of age, and his wife a cheerful and competent housewife and an excellent cook. My days were mostly spent fishing for mackerel in the bay, taking long tramps up and down the rugged coast, or simply lolling amongst the soft lush grass on the cliff-tops, drinking in the glorious panorama of St Bride's Bay, as it sweeps round in a majestic curve from Ramsey Island in the north to the Isle of Skomer in the south. When the weather was too boisterous for outdoor pursuits, there was the snug bar-parlour of the inn, and the rough but genial society of the fishermen who frequented it. It was there that I was sitting one August evening when the radio in the bar gave utterance to that ominous gale warning.

At the mention of south-westerly gales, I perceived a sudden start amongst the fishermen present, and apprehensive glances were exchanged. Several boats were to be seen fishing in the bay, and one or two of the men walked to the door and peered out anxiously at the distant smacks.

'Glad I'm not out there now,' muttered one old salt.

'Hope my son William'll get in before dark,' said another.

This display of alarm was surprising, for the bay is sheltered to a great extent from the south-west wind, and in any case the boats were all near enough in to make harbour before being overtaken by the oncoming gale, of which the sky was already giving ample warning. I remarked as much to the innkeeper, who agreed that the boats were in no real danger, but added that nobody in Ticklas Haven would willingly be out in the bay, or even in the neighbourhood of the harbour, after nightfall, when the wind blew strongly from the south-west: it amounted to a fixed tradition with them. I at once became eager to learn the origin of this strange superstition, and besought the landlord to enlighten me further.

'Well, it's a strange story,' replied the innkeeper, 'and I can best begin by showing you a picture that a painter who stayed here many years ago gave to my grandfather, when he was landlord of this inn.'

So saying, he led the way into a back parlour and pointed to an oil-painting hanging on the wall in a dark corner. I took it down and carried it to the window, and saw that it represented the harbour at Ticklas Haven as seen from the beach at low tide. Although about eighty years old, the painting might almost have been done yesterday, for everything was depicted much as it is now, with one striking exception. The north haven, where now all the boats are kept, was in the picture practically deserted, except for some children at play on the sand, whilst the south haven presented just such a scene of activity as would be expected in so excellent a harbour. Half a dozen fishing-boats lay high and dry at its entrance, while on the shingle sat a group of fishermen mending sails and nets. Two or three women were carrying baskets of fish up towards the village, and the usual litter of gear was scattered over the foreshore. In fact the two little inlets presented an aspect just the reverse of their present-day appearance.

'Why is it,' I asked, 'that the south haven, which seems so clearly the better of the two, has now been abandoned in favour of the other, which was apparently in use in your grandfather's day?'

'That is precisely what I am about to tell you,' replied the landlord.

### The Innkeeper's Story

When I was a lad that south haven was still used, as you see it in that picture, and very few boats put into the north haven, which is, as you observe, less sheltered and convenient.

There lived in the village in those days three brothers, who worked for their uncle, the owner of a fishing-boat and gear. They were tall, strong young fellows, these three brothers, but of a morose disposition, and mixed little with other folk in the village. They were very hardy and fearless and would put to sea in all but the most tempestuous weather, usually accompanied by their uncle, who was a first-rate seaman and could handle a craft in all seas. He was a grasping old ruffian, however, and on the strength of his ownership of the boat he appropriated most of the profits of the fishing and allowed his nephews barely enough to live upon, with the understanding that on his death they would inherit his property. His niggardliness was a source of much discontent amongst the brothers, who bore their uncle no affection and only continued to work for him in the expectation of some day possessing his wealth, which, owing to economy and judicious investment was pretty considerable for a man in his position.

One spring night – I was seventeen at the time – the four put to sea, although it was beginning to blow up a gale from the south-west and the crews of none of the other boats would venture out. We watched them beating out past the Stack Rocks till they were hidden by the rain and darkness, and some of us wondered whether we should ever see them again.

Early next morning the boat returned, with no fish, and without the uncle. The brothers' story was that he had been carried overboard by a huge wave and had at once disappeared. It was useless to search for him and they were themselves in great peril. They had a very rough time getting back and the boat and gear were badly damaged. The three brothers seemed more upset about the accident than one might have expected, considering the unfriendly relations existing between them and their uncle, by whose death they now became comparatively well off. They were loud in their expressions of grief at their loss and repeatedly cursed their folly in putting to sea on such a night.

Two days later the uncle's body was washed ashore in the south haven, where it was found by a fisherman in the early morning actually caught on the anchor of his own boat. The body was carried up to the quay, where it was noticed that there was a long, livid bruise across the right temple. The doctor, who lived in that big house, now a ruin, up the hill, examined the corpse, and at the inquest expressed the opinion that the bruise had been inflicted before death and had been caused by a severe blow from some blunt instrument, such as a club – or perhaps a tiller.

The coroner looked up sharply at this, and asked if the bruise might not equally well have been caused by the deceased striking his head against the mast or the gunwale of the boat in falling overboard. The doctor agreed that that might have been the cause of the injury, but added that he could not believe that such a severe blow could have been inflicted in such a manner.

The eldest brother was then re-examined as to what precisely took place, and deposed that his uncle had been knocked overboard by the boom suddenly swinging over and striking him on the head. This fresh testimony was corroborated by the other brothers, although previously they had all repeatedly affirmed that their uncle was simply washed overboard by a wave and had made no mention of the boom. The jury, however, brought in a verdict of 'death by misadventure'. The coroner was later criticized for not excluding two of the brothers from the court while the first was giving evidence. The deceased was buried next day in the churchyard at Walwyn's Castle. That was near the end of April.

In the last week of May the youngest of the three brothers slipped on the jetty when landing from the boat one dark night, there being a heavy sea running due to a strong south-west wind, and broke his neck on the rocks in the south haven below.

Towards the end of June the eldest brother, being harbour-bound by a south-westerly gale, was gathering mussels and limpets on the rocks at the far side of the south haven, when a large stone fell from the cliff above and smashed in his skull.

Within a month the surviving brother was overtaken by a sudden squall, coming up from the south-west, while fishing out by Grassholm, and was washed ashore, together with the wreck of his boat, about a week later, at almost the indentical spot where his uncle's body had been found. The boat, so battered as to be no longer seaworthy, was hauled up on the shingle and left there to rot.

The violent deaths of these three brothers, following so regularly one after the other, considered together with the suspicious circumstances attending their uncle's death, gave cause for much gossip amongst the village folk, and what had at first been but a vague uneasiness developed into a general conviction that there had been foul play.

Some nine months after the death of the last of the brothers, we had a spell of very rough weather, with strong gales from the south-west, and the fishermen were idle for weeks on end. A large amount of driftwood was cast up during these storms and the men employed themselves in gathering and storing this for firewood. There was one old man in particular, now too infirm ever to go out fishing, who was to be seen early and late collecting this wood, and at low tide was always hobbling about the haven like some ungainly sea-bird, leaving off only when it grew too dark to see.

One stormy night the old man failed to return home and a search was made at daybreak. We had not far to look: his body was found wedged among the rocks in the south haven, with a ragged cut across the forehead. On his face was such a look of horror as I pray I may never see again. The doctor said that in his opinion the old man had received a bad fright and had started to run away, but had tripped over a boulder and stunned himself. He had then been drowned by the incoming tide. What on earth could have so terrified him was a mystery.

Some three months later, when the wind was again blowing strongly from the south-west, a girl of fifteen, daughter of one of the fishermen, went over to the rocks beyond the south haven to collect shellfish. She stayed too long and was cut off by the flowing tide, but her parents were not worried, for she was quite safe and had taken some food with her, and would be able to get back when the tide was low again about ten p.m. The sea was too rough for a boat to approach the rocks, and there was no way up the cliff, so she was just left to wait.

At half-past ten that night the girl suddenly burst into her home, screaming wildly and clearly crazed with terror. She had gone completely out of her mind and howled and raved like a maniac. Her cries soon attracted a crowd to the cottage and someone went and fetched the doctor. He could do nothing to calm the child, however, and had to put her under sedation. After being left under observation for a day or two she was taken away to the asylum, where she died soon afterwards without recovering her reason.

The most extraordinary feature of this sad case was what the poor child kept repeating in her insane ravings. It was all about 'dead men': 'the four dead men,' she would screech, 'the dead men in the boat!', and could utter nothing but incoherent phrases about 'the dead men'.

This second case of severe fright, following so soon after the death of the old wood-gatherer, and in the same place, namely the south haven, created a considerable stir amongst the villagers, and their fears were further increased by a peculiar occurrence which had been noticed several times and by many witnesses, including myself, namely that on the morning following a south-westerly gale tracks were seen in the sand leading down to the sea from the derelict boat, as if it had been launched and beached again during the night. This was humanly impossible, as the brothers' boat could not have floated for a single minute, but there the tracks always were at dawn after a high wind from the south-west, provided they had not been obliterated by the flowing tide.

One evening, shortly after the death of the poor demented girl, the doctor came into the bar-parlour here and asked to have a few words with my father in private. They came into this back room and the doctor told my father that he had been all around the village endeavouring to persuade someone to spend a night with him by the wrecked fishing-boat in the south haven when next the south-west wind blew a gale, in order to try and solve the mystery of those tracks in the sand, but not a man would go near the place after dark for love or money. The doctor then asked my father if he would watch with him, for otherwise he would go alone, and it was desirable to have more than one witness of whatever took place. My father, though not at all liking the job, eventually undertook to keep the doctor company.

It was not until the autumn equinoctial gales began that a suitable opportunity for the investigation occurred, but at last the wind blew so strongly from the south-west that the boats were unable to put to sea. At about ten o'clock one cloudy night the doctor called in for my father and the pair of them went down to the south haven. They found a sheltered corner amongst the rocks in full view of the wrecked boat, where they made themselves as comfortable as they could and began their watch. My father afterwards said that he had experienced only one thing in his life more unpleasant than the beginning of that vigil, and that was its end.

The wind, now blowing a whole gale, sent dense masses of black clouds hurtling across the moon, which intermittently shone forth upon as wild a scene as could be imagined. Even in this sheltered corner of the bay the breakers were dashing high up the rocks, while, farther out, the sea seemed to have gone mad and was foaming in tempestuous fury like a living thing in torment. No fishing-boat could have weathered such a storm for a moment.

So fiercely magnificent was the view across the bay that the two watchers became absorbed in contemplating it and forgot about the boat on which they were supposed to be keeping an eye. Suddenly my father's gaze was diverted by a movement on the sand below and he grasped the doctor's arm and pointed. There, half way between its normal resting place and the edge of the surf, was the wreck of the fishing-smack, while four men, two on each side, were hauling it down the beach!

The doctor gave a shout and began to clamber down from his perch on the rocks, but the men at the boat seemed not to hear the cry; they rapidly dragged the derelict down to the sea, launched it, and climbed aboard. Two of the men put out oars and started to row, one took the helm, while the fourth stationed himself in the bows. Then the old tub, with great rents in her sides and a hole in the bottom that a man could have crawled through, put out to sea and was quickly lost to view.

My father and the doctor stood by the edge of the sea like men thunderstruck until the incoming tide wet their legs and recalled them to themselves. They then went up the beach to make sure that it was the wreck that had thus been miraculously launched, and found that it was indeed gone. There could be no shadow of doubt that four men had put to sea in a near hurricane with a boat which would not normally have floated for ten seconds. There was nothing for it but to await the possible return of these uncanny mariners, so the two men returned to their former position on the rocks and kept a tireless watch upon the stormy sea.

Shortly after two o'clock in the morning their vigilance was rewarded by the sight of a boat approaching from the direction of the Stack Rocks. It drew rapidly inshore, and proved to be the old fishing-boat with her mysterious crew, who appeared quite unaffected by the mountainous seas and beached the boat as easily as if it had been a dead calm. The four men then dragged the boat up to its habitual place on the shingle and moved off in single file towards the village.

The doctor immediately jumped down and ran across the beach so as to intercept them, followed by my father. These two reached the foot of the quay where they waited for the four men to come up. On they came, walking stiffly in line, until they were abreast of the watchers, when the clouds covering the moon blew away and there was revealed a spectacle that sent my father tearing blindly across the beach and turned the doctor sick and faint where he stood.

Those four men were the long dead and buried brothers and their uncle!

The doctor, rallying from the first shock, continued to gaze in horror as they passed. In front, marching with no movement beyond a mechanical swinging of the legs, was the old man, a great, livid weal across the side of his forehead. Behind him, with the same mechanical gait, stalked his three nephews, the first with his head all crushed and bloody, the next swollen and bloated and covered with a tangle of seaweed, and the third with his head hanging on one side at a horrible angle. So the four dead men walked up from the sea, and the doctor, overcome with dreadful nausea, collapsed in a dead faint.

The spray blowing over the jetty brought the doctor round from his fainting fit and he tottered to his feet. The ghastly procession had vanished, so he went in search of my father, whom he found lying insensible on the shingle in the north haven, having fallen and struck his head on the prow of a boat. Help was summoned and my father was carried home, but it was many days before he was sufficiently recovered to attend to business and he never altogether got over the shock he received on that awful night. Meanwhile the doctor resolved to have the old fishing-boat destroyed, in the hope of putting a stop to these supernatural proceedings. Not a soul in the place would now go near it, so the doctor, single-handed, built up a pile of brushwood around the wreck and set it alight. The whole thing was soon consumed and the ashes were cast into the sea so that not a trace remained.

At eleven o'clock that very night, as I was shutting up the inn, four men passed up the street, walking stiffly in single file. I hastily closed and locked the door and ran up to my bedroom, the window of which overlooked the street. It was too dark to see much, but something about the figures filled me with dread, and the rearmost carried his head at an unnatural angle. I watched them until they turned up the hill leading to the doctor's house, and then went to bed. A little later I fancied I heard a scream coming from the hill, but it was not repeated and may merely have been a seagull crying.

Next day the woman who used to 'do' for the doctor came back to the village in great distress, saying that she had found the door open and the doctor gone. Search was made along the shore and all over the neighbourhood, but without success. A few days later the doctor's body was washed ashore by a high tide in the south haven and was deposited on the very spot where he had burnt the boat.

So now you can understand why we at Ticklas Haven avoid that south haven and fear the south-west wind.

'But do the dead men still haunt the haven when the sou'wester blows?' I asked.

'Nobody ever goes there to see,' replied the innkeeper.

# The Sexton's Adventure

## *J. Sheridan Le Fanu*

Those who remember Chapelizod a quarter of a century ago, or more, may possibly recollect the parish sexton. Bob Martin was held in much awe by truant boys who sauntered into the churchyard on Sundays, to read the tombstones, or play leap frog over them, or climb the ivy in search of bats or sparrows' nests, or peep into the mysterious aperture under the eastern window, which opened a dim perspective of descending steps losing themselves among profounder darkness, where lidless coffins gaped horribly among tattered velvet, bones, and dust, which time and mortality had strewn there. Of such horribly curious, and otherwise enterprising juveniles, Bob was, of course, the special scourge and terror. But terrible as was the official aspect of the sexton, and repugnant as his lank form, clothed in rusty, sable vesture, his small, frosty visage, suspicious grey eyes, and rusty, brown scratch-wig, might appear to all notions of genial frailty; it was yet true, that Bob Martin's severe morality sometimes nodded, and that Bacchus did not always solicit him in vain.

Bob had a curious mind, a memory well stored with 'merry tales' and tales of terror. His profession familiarized him with graves and goblins, and his tastes with weddings, wassail, and sly frolics of all sorts. And as his personal recollections ran back nearly three score years into the perspective of the village history, his fund of local anecdote was copious, accurate, and edifying.

As his ecclesiastical revenues were by no means considerable, he was not unfrequently obliged, for the indulgence of his tastes, to arts which were, at the best, undignified.

He frequently invited himself when his entertainers had forgotten to do so; he dropped in accidentally upon small drinking parties of his acquaintance in public houses, and entertained them with stories, queer or terrible, from his inexhaustible reservoir, never scrupling to accept an acknowledgement in the shape of hot whiskey-punch, or whatever else was going.

There was at that time a certain atrabilious publican, called Philip Slaney, established in a shop nearly opposite the old turnpike. This man was not, when left to himself, immoderately given to drinking; but being naturally of a saturnine complexion, and his spirits constantly requiring a fillip, he acquired a prodigious liking for Bob Martin's company. The sexton's society, in fact, gradually became the solace of his existence, and he seemed to lose his constitutional melancholy in the fascination of his sly jokes and marvellous stories.

This intimacy did not redound to the prosperity or reputation of the convivial allies. Bob Martin drank a good deal more punch than was good for his health, or consistent with the character of an ecclesiastical functionary. Philip Slaney, too, was drawn into similar indulgences, for it was hard to resist the genial seductions of his gifted companion; and as he was obliged to pay for both, his purse was believed to have suffered even more than his head and liver.

Be that as it may, Bob Martin had the credit of having made a drunkard of 'black Phil Slaney' – for by this cognomen was he distinguished; and Phil Slaney had also the reputation of having made the sexton, if possible, a 'bigger bliggard' than ever. Under these circumstances, the accounts of the concern opposite the turnpike became somewhat entangled; and it came to pass one drowsy summer morning, the weather being at once sultry and cloudy, that Phil Slaney went into a small back parlour, where he kept his books, and which commanded, through its dirty window-panes, a full view of a dead wall, and having bolted the door, he took a loaded pistol, and clapping the muzzle in his mouth, blew the upper part of his skull through the ceiling.

This horrid catastrophe shocked Bob Martin extremely; and partly on this account, and partly because having been, on several late occasions, found at night in a state of abstraction, bordering on insensibility, upon the high road, he had been threatened with dismissal; and, as some said, partly also because of the difficulty of finding anybody to 'treat' him as poor Phil Slaney used to do, he for a time forswore alcohol in all its combinations, and became an eminent example of temperance and sobriety.

Bob observed his good resolutions, greatly to the comfort of his wife, and the edification of the neighbourhood, with tolerable punctuality. He was seldom tipsy, and never drunk, and was greeted by the better part of society with all the honours of the prodigal son.

Now it happened, about a year after the grisly event we have mentioned, that the curate having received, by the post, due notice of a funeral to be consummated in the churchyard of Chapelizod, with certain instructions respecting the site of the grave, despatched a summons for Bob Martin, with a view to communicate to that functionary these official details.

It was a lowering autumn night: piles of lurid thunderclouds, slowly rising from the earth, had loaded the sky with a solemn and boding canopy of storm. The growl of the distant thunder was heard afar off upon the dull, still air, and all nature seemed, as it were, hushed and cowering under the oppressive influence of the approaching tempest.

It was past nine o'clock when Bob, putting on his official coat of seedy black, prepared to attend his professional superior.

'Bobby, darlin',' said his wife, before she delivered the hat she held in her hand to his keeping, 'sure you won't, Bobby, darlin' – you won't – you know what.'

'I *don't* know what,' he retorted, smartly, grasping at his hat.

'You won't be throwing up the little finger, Bobby, acushla?' she said, evading his grasp.

'Arrah, why would I, woman? there, give me my hat, will you?'

'But won't you promise me, Bobby darlin' – won't you, alanna?'

'Ay, ay, to be sure I will – why not? – there, give me my hat, and let me go.'

'Ay, but you're not promisin', Bobby, mavourneen; you're not promisin' all the time.'

'Well, divil carry me if I drink a drop till I come back again,' said the sexton, angrily; 'will that do you? And *now* will you give me my hat?'

'Here it is, darlin',' she said, 'and God send you safe back.'

And with this parting blessing she closed the door upon his retreating figure, for it was now quite dark, and resumed her knitting till his return, very much relieved; for she thought he had of late been oftener tipsy than was consistent with his thorough reformation, and feared the allurements of the half dozen 'publics' which he had at that time to pass on his way to the other end of the town.

They were still open, and exhaled a delicious reek of whiskey, as Bob glided wistfully by them; but he stuck his hands in his pockets and looked the other way, whistling resolutely, and filling his mind with the image of the curate and anticipations of his coming fee. Thus he steered his morality safely through these rocks of offence, and reached the curate's lodging in safety.

He had, however, an unexpected sick call to attend, and was not at home, so that Bob Martin had to sit in the hall and amuse himself with the devil's tattoo until his return. This, unfortunately, was very long delayed, and it must have been fully twelve o'clock when Bob Martin set out upon his homeward way. By this time the storm had gathered to a pitchy darkness, the bellowing thunder was heard among the rocks and hollows of the Dublin mountains, and the pale, blue lightning shone upon the staring fronts of the houses.

By this time, too, every door was closed; but as Bob trudged homeward, his eye mechanically sought the public-house which had once belonged to Phil Slaney. A faint light was making its way through the shutters and the glass panes over the door-way, which made a sort of dull, foggy halo about the front of the house.

As Bob's eyes had become accustomed to the obscurity by this time, the light in question was quite sufficient to enable him to see a man in a sort of loose riding-coat seated upon a bench which, at that time, was fixed under the window of the house. He wore his hat very much over his eyes, and was smoking a long pipe. The outline of a glass and a quart bottle were also dimly traceable beside him; and a large horse saddled, but faintly discernible, was patiently awaiting his master's leisure.

There was something odd, no doubt, in the appearance of a traveller refreshing himself at such an hour in the open street; but the sexton accounted for it easily by supposing that, on the closing of the house for the night, he had taken what remained of his refection to the place where he was now discussing it al fresco.

At another time Bob might have saluted the stranger as he passed with a friendly 'good night'; but, somehow, he was out of humour and in no genial mood, and was about passing without any courtesy of the sort, when the stranger, without taking the pipe from his mouth, raised the bottle, and with it beckoned him familiarly, while, with a sort of lurch of the head and shoulders, and at the same time shifting his seat to the end of the bench, he pantomimically invited him to share his seat and his cheer. There was a divine fragrance of whiskey about the spot, and Bob half relented; but he remembered his promise just as he began to waver, and said:

'No, I thank you, sir, I can't stop tonight.'

The stranger beckoned with vehement welcome, and pointed to the vacant space on the seat beside him.

'I thank you for your polite offer,' said Bob, 'but it's what I'm too late as it is, and haven't time to spare, so I wish you a goodnight.'

The traveller jingled the glass against the neck of the bottle, as if to intimate that he might at least swallow a dram without losing time. Bob was mentally quite of the same opinion; but, though his mouth watered, he remembered his promise, and shaking his head with incorruptible resolution, walked on.

The stranger, pipe in mouth, rose from his bench, the bottle in one hand, and the glass in the other, and followed at the sexton's heels, his dusky horse keeping close in his wake.

There was something suspicious and unaccountable in this importunity.

Bob quickened his pace, but the stranger followed close. The sexton began to feel queer, and turned about. His pursuer was behind, and still inviting him with impatient gestures to taste his liquor.

'I told you before,' said Bob, who was both angry and frightened, 'that I would not taste it, and that's enough. I don't want to have anything to say to you or your bottle; and in God's name,' he added, more vehemently, observing that he was approaching still closer, 'fall back and don't be tormenting me this way.'

These words, as it seemed, incensed the stranger, for he shook the bottle with violent menace at Bob Martin; but, notwithstanding this gesture of defiance, he suffered the distance between them to increase. Bob, however, beheld him dogging him still in the distance, for his pipe shed a wonderful red glow, which duskily illuminated his entire figure like the lurid atmosphere of a meteor.

'I wish the devil had his own, my boy,' muttered the excited sexton, 'and I know well enough where you'd be.'

The next time he looked over his shoulder, to his dismay he observed the importunate stranger as close as ever upon his track.

'Confound you,' cried the man of skulls and shovels, almost beside himself with rage and horror, 'what is it you want of me?'

The stranger appeared more confident, and kept wagging his head and extending both glass and bottle toward him as he drew near, and Bob Martin heard the horse snorting as it followed in the dark.

'Keep it to yourself, whatever it is, for there is neither grace nor luck about you,' cried Bob Martin, freezing with terror; 'leave me alone, will you?'

And he fumbled in vain among the seething confusion of his ideas for a prayer or an exorcism. He quickened his pace almost to a run; he was now close to his own door, under the impending bank by the river side.

'Let me in, let me in, for God's sake; Molly, open the door,' he cried, as he ran to the threshold, and leant his back against the plank. His pursuer confronted him upon the road; the pipe was no longer in his mouth, but the dusky red glow still lingered round him. He uttered some inarticulate cavernous sounds, which were wolfish and indescribable, while he seemed employed in pouring out a glass from the bottle.

The sexton kicked with all his force against the door, and cried at the same time with a despairing voice:

'In the name of God Almighty, once and for all, leave me alone.'

His pursuer furiously flung the contents of the bottle at Bob Martin; but instead of fluid it issued out in a stream of flame, which expanded and whirled round them, and for a moment they were both enveloped in a faint blaze; at the same instant a sudden gust whisked off the stranger's hat, and the sexton beheld that his skull was roofless. For an instant he beheld the gaping aperture, black and shattered, and then he fell senseless into his own doorway, which his affrighted wife had just unbarred.

I need hardly give my reader the key to this most intelligible and authentic narrative. The traveller was acknowledged by all to have been the spectre of the suicide, called up by the Evil One to tempt the convivial sexton into a violation of his promise, sealed, as it was, by an imprecation. Had he succeeded, no doubt the dusky steed, which Bob had seen saddled in attendance, was destined to have carried back a double burden to the place from whence he came.

As an attestation of the reality of this visitation, the old thorn tree which overhung the doorway was found in the morning to have been blasted with the infernal fires which had issued from the bottle, just as if a thunder-bolt had scorched it.

# The Black Ferry

## *John Galt*

I was then returning from my first session at college. The weather had
for some time before been uncommonly wet, every brook and stream
was swollen far beyond its banks, the meadows were flooded, and the
river itself was increased to a raging Hellespont, insomuch that the ferry
was only practicable for an hour before and after high tide.

The day was showery and stormy, by which I was detained at the inn
until late in the afternoon, so that it was dark before I reached the ferry-
house, and the tide did not serve for safe crossing until midnight. I was
therefore obliged to sit by the fire and wait the time, a circumstance
which gave me some uneasiness, for the ferryman was old and infirm,
and Dick his son, who usually attended the boat during the night,
happened to be then absent, the day having been such that it was not
expected any travellers would seek to pass over that night.

The presence of Dick was not, however, absolutely necessary, for the
boat swung from side to side by a rope anchored in the middle of the
stream, and, on account of the strong current, another rope had been
stretched across by which passengers could draw themselves over without
assistance, an easy task to those who had the sleight of it, but it was not
so to me, who still wore my arm in a sling.

While sitting at the fireside conversing with the ferryman and his wife,
a smart, good-looking country lad, with a recruit's cockade in his hat,
came in, accompanied by a young woman who was far advanced in
pregnancy. They were told the state of the ferry, and that unless the
recruit undertook to conduct the boat himself, they must wait the return
of Dick.

They had been only that day married, and were on their way to join
a detachment of the regiment in which Ralph Nocton, as the recruit was
called, had that evening enlisted, the parish officers having obliged him
to marry the girl. Whatever might have been their former love and
intimacy, they were not many minutes in the house when he became
sullen and morose towards her; nor was she more amiable towards him.
He said little, but he often looked at her with an indignant eye, as she
reproached him for having so rashly enlisted to abandon her and his

unborn baby, assuring him that she would never part from him while life and power lasted.

Though it could not be denied that she possessed both beauty and an attractive person, there was yet a silly vixen humour about her ill calculated to conciliate. I did not therefore wonder to hear that Nocton had married her with reluctance; I only regretted that the parish officers were so inaccessible to commiseration, and so void of conscience as to be guilty of rendering the poor fellow miserable for life to avert the hazard of the child becoming a burden on the parish.

The ferryman and his wife endeavoured to reconcile them to their lot; and the recruit, who appeared to be naturally reckless and generous, seemed willing to be appeased; but his weak companion was capricious and pettish. On one occasion, when a sudden shower beat hard against the window, she cried out, with little regard to decorum, that she would go no farther that night.

'You may do as you please, Mary Blake,' said Nocton, 'but go I must, for the detachment marches tomorrow morning. It was only to give you time to prepare to come with me that the Captain consented to let me remain so late in the town.'

She, however, only remonstrated bitterly at his cruelty in forcing her to travel in her condition, and in such weather. Nocton refused to listen to her, but told her somewhat doggedly, more so than was consistent with the habitual cheerful cast of his physiognomy, 'that although he had already been ruined by her, he trusted she had not yet the power to make him a deserter.'

He then went out, and remained some time alone. When he returned, his appearance was surprisingly changed; his face was of an ashy paleness; his eyes bright, febrile, and eager, and his lip quivered as he said:

'Come, Mary, I can wait no longer; the boat is ready, the river is not so wild, and the rain is over.'

In vain she protested; he was firm; and she had no option but either to go or to be left behind. The old ferryman accompanied them to the boat, saw them embark, and gave the recruit some instructions how to manage the ropes, as it was still rather early in the tide. On returning into the house, he remarked facetiously to his wife:

'I can never see why young men should be always blamed, and all pity reserved for the damsels.'

At that moment a rattling shower of rain and hail burst like a platoon of small shot on the window, and a flash of vivid lightning was followed by one of the most tremendous peals of thunder I have ever heard.

'Hark!' cried the old woman startling, 'was not that a shriek?' We listened, but the cry was not repeated; we rushed to the door, but no other sound was heard than the raging of the river, and the roar of the sea-waves breaking on the bar.

Dick soon after came home, and the boat having swung back to her station, I embarked with him, and reached the opposite inn, where I soon went to bed. Scarcely had I laid my head on the pillow when a sudden inexplicable terror fell upon me; I shook with an unknown horror; I was, as it were, conscious that some invisible being was hovering beside me, and could hardly muster fortitude enough to refrain from rousing the house. At last I fell asleep; it was perturbed and unsound; strange dreams and vague fears scared me awake, and in them were dreadful images of a soldier murdering a female, and open graves, and gibbet-irons swinging in the wind. My remembrance has no parallel to such another night.

In the morning the cloud on my spirit was gone, and I rose at my accustomed hour, and cheerily resumed my journey. It was a bright morning, all things were glittering and fresh in the rising sun, the recruit and his damsel were entirely forgotten, and I thought no more of them.

But when the night came round again next year, I was seized with an unaccountable dejection; it weighed me down; I tried to shake it off, but was unable, the mind was diseased, and could no more by resolution shake off its discomfort, than the body by activity can expel a fear. I retired to my bed greatly distressed, but nevertheless I fell asleep. At midnight, however, I was summoned awake by a hideous and undefinable terror; it was the same vague consciousness of some invisible visitor being near that I had once before experienced, as I have described, and I again recollected Nocton and Mary Blake in the same instant; I saw – for I cannot now believe that it was less than apparitional – the unhappy pair reproaching one another.

As I looked, questioning the integrity of my sight, the wretched bride turned round and looked at me. How shall I express my horror, when, for the ruddy beauty which she once possessed, I beheld the charnel visage of a skull; I started up and cried aloud with such alarming vehemence, that the whole inmates of the house, with lights in their hands, were instantly in the room – shame would not let me tell what I had seen, and, endeavouring to laugh, I accused the nightmare of the disturbance.

This happened while I was at a watering-place on the west coast. I was living in a boarding-house with several strangers; among them was a tall pale German gentleman, of a grave impressive physiognomy. He was the most intelligent and shrewdest observer I have ever met with, and he had to a singular degree the gift of a discerning spirit. In the morning when we rose from the breakfast-table, he took me by the arm, and led me out upon the lawn in front of the house, and when we were at some distance from the rest of the company, said:

'Excuse me, sir, for I must ask an impertinent question. Was it indeed the dream or the nightmare that alarmed you last night?'

'I have no objection to answer you freely; but tell me first, why you ask such a question?'

'It is but reasonable. I had a friend who was a painter; none ever possessed an imagination which discerned better how nature in her mysteries should appear. One of his pictures was the scene of Brutus when his evil genius summoned him to Philippi, and, strange to tell, you bear some resemblance to the painted Brutus. When, with the others, I broke into your room last night, you looked so like the Brutus in his picture, that I could have sworn you were amazed with the vision of a ghost.'

I related to him what I have done to you.

'It is wonderful,' said he; 'what inconceivable sympathy hath linked you to the fate of these unhappy persons. There is something more in this renewed visitation than the phantasma of a dream.'

The remark smote me with an uncomfortable sensation of dread, and for a short time my flesh crawled as it were upon my bones. But the impression soon wore off, and was again entirely forgotten.

When the anniversary again returned, I was seized with the same heaviness and objectless horror of mind; it hung upon me with bodings and auguries until I went to bed, and then after my first sleep I was a third time roused by another fit of the same inscrutable panic. On this occasion, however, the vision was different. I beheld only Nocton, pale and wounded, stretched on a bed, and on the coverlet lay a pair of new epaulettes, as if just unfolded from a paper.

For seven years I was thus annually afflicted. The vision in each was different, but I saw no more of Mary Blake. On the fourth occasion, I beheld Nocton sitting in the uniform of an aide-de-camp at a table, with the customary tokens of conviviality before him; it was only part of a scene, such as one beholds in a mirror.

On the fifth occasion, he appeared to be ascending, sword in hand, the rampart of a battery; the sun was setting behind him, and the shadows and forms of a strange land, with the domes and pagodas of an oriental country, lay in wide extent around: it was a picture, but far more vivid than painting can exhibit.

On the sixth time, he appeared again stretched upon a couch; his complexion was sullen, not from wounds, but disease, and there appeared at his bedside the figure of a general officer, with a star on his breast, with whose conversation he appeared pleased, though languid.

But on the seventh and last occasion on which the horrors of the visions

The Black Ferry 317

were repeated, I saw him on horseback in a field of battle; and while I looked at him, he was struck on the face by a sabre, and the blood flowed down upon his regimentals.

Years passed after this, during which I had none of these dismal exhibitions. My mind and memory resumed their healthful tone. I recollected, without these intervening years of oblivion, Nocton and Mary Blake, occasionally, as one thinks of things past, and I told my friend of the curious periodical returns of the visitations to be as remarkable metaphysical phenomena. By an odd coincidence, it so happened that my German friend was always present when I related my dreams. He in the intervals sometimes spoke to me of them, but my answers were vague, for my reminiscences were imperfect. It was not so with him. All I told he distinctly recorded and preserved in a book wherein he wrote down the minutest thing that I had witnessed in my visions. I do not mention his name, because he is a modest and retiring man, in bad health, and who has long sequestered himself from company. His rank, however, is so distinguished, that his name could not be stated without the hazard of exposing him to impertinent curiosity. But to proceed.

Exactly fourteen years – twice seven it was – I remember well, because for the first seven I had been haunted as I have described, and for the other seven I have been placed in my living. At the end of that period of fourteen years, my German friend paid me a visit here. He came in the forenoon, and we spent an agreeable day together, for he was a man of much recondite knowledge. Never have I seen one so wonderfully possessed of all sort of occult learning.

He was an astrologer of the true kind, for in him it was not a pretence but a science; he scorned horoscopes and fortune-tellers with the just derision of a philosopher, but he had a beautiful conception of the reciprocal dependencies of nature. He affected not to penetrate to causes, but he spoke of effects with a luminous and religious eloquence. He described to me how the tides followed the phases of the moon; but he denied the Newtonian notion that they were caused by the procession of the lunar changes. He explained to me that when the sun entered Aries, and the other signs of the zodiac, how his progression could be traced on this earth by the development of plants and flowers, and the passions, diseases, and affections of animals and man; but that the stars were more than the celestial signs of these terrestrial phenomena he ridiculed as the conceptions of the insane theory.

His learning in the curious art of alchemy was equally sublime. He laughed at the fancy of an immortal elixir, and his notion of the mythology of the philosopher's stone was the very essence and spirituality of ethics. The elixir of immortality he described to me as an allegory, which, from its component parts, emblems of talents and virtues, only showed that perseverance, industry, goodwill, and gift from God, were the requisite ingredients necessary to attain renown.

His knowledge of the philosopher's stone was still more beautiful. He referred to the writings of the Rosicrucians, whose secrets were couched in artificial symbols, to prove that the sages of that sect were not the fools that the lesser wise of later days would represent them. The self-denial, the patience, the humility, and trusting in God, the treasuring of time by lamp and calculation which the venerable alchemists recommended, he used to say, were only the elements which constitute the conduct of the youth that would attain to riches and honour; and these different stages which are illuminated in the alchemical volumes as descriptive of stages in the process of making the stone, were but hieroglyphical devices to explain the effects of well applied human virtue and industry.

To me it was amazing to what clear simplicity he reduced all things, and on what a variety of subjects his bright and splendid fancy threw a fair and affecting light. All those demi-sciences – physiognomy – palmistry –scaileology, etc., even magic and witchcraft, obtained from his interpretations a philosophical credibility.

In disquisitions on these subjects we spent the anniversary. He had by then enlarged the periphery of my comprehension; he had added to my knowledge, and inspired me with a profounder respect for himself.

He was an accomplished musician, in the remotest, if I may use the expression, depths of the art. His performance on the piano-forte was simple, heavy, and seemingly the labour of an unpractised hand, but his expression was beyond all epithet exquisite and solemn; his airs were grave, devotional, and pathetic, consisting of the simplest harmonic combinations; but they were wonderful; every note was a portion of an invocation; every melody the voice of a passion or a feeling supplied with elocution.

We had spent the day in the fields, where he illustrated his astrological opinions by appeals to plants, and leaves, and flowers, and other attributes of the season, with such delightful perspicuity that no time can efface from the registers of my memory the substance of his discourses. In the evening he delighted me with his miraculous music, and, as the night advanced, I was almost persuaded that he was one of these extraordinary men who are said sometimes to acquire communion with spirits and dominion over demons.

Just as we were about to sit down to our frugal supper, literally or philosophically so, as if it had been served for Zeno himself, Dick, the son of the old ferryman, who by this time was some years dead, came to the door, and requested to speak with me in private. Of course I obeyed, when he informed me that he had brought across the ferry that night a gentleman officer, from a far country, who was in bad health, and whom he could not accommodate properly in the ferry-house.

'The inn,' said Dick, 'is too far off, for he is lame, and has an open wound in the thigh. I have therefore ventured to bring him here, sure that you will be glad to give him a bed for the night. His servant tells me that he was esteemed the bravest officer in all the service in the Mysore of India.'

It was impossible to resist this appeal. I went to the door where the gentleman was waiting, and with true-heartedness expressed how great my satisfaction would be if my house could afford him any comfort.

I took him with me to the room where my German friend was sitting. I was much pleased with the gentleness and unaffected simplicity of his manners.

He was a handsome middle-aged man – his person was robust and well formed – his features had been originally handsome, but they were disfigured by a scar, which had materially changed their symmetry. His conversation was not distinguished by any remarkable intelligence, but after the high intellectual excitement which I had enjoyed all day with my philosophical companion, it was agreeable and gentlemanly.

Several times during supper, something came across my mind as if I had seen him before, but I could neither recollect when nor where; and I observed that more than once he looked at me as if under the influence of some research in his memory. At last, I observed that his eyes were dimmed with tears, which assured me that he then recollected me. But I considered it a duty of hospitality not to inquire aught concerning him more than he was pleased to tell himself.

In the meantime, my German friend, I perceived, was watching us both, but suddenly he ceased to be interested, and appeared absorbed in thought, while good manners required me to make some efforts to entertain my guest. This led on to some inquiry concerning the scene of his services, and he told us that he had been many years in India.

'On this day eight years ago,' said he, 'I was in the battle of Borupknow, where I received the wound which has so disfigured me in the face.'

At that moment I accidentally threw my eyes upon my German friend – the look which he gave me in answer, caused me to shudder from head to foot, and I began to ruminate of Nocton the recruit, and Mary Blake, while my friend continued the conversation in a light desultory manner, as it would have seemed to any stranger, but to me it was awful and oracular. He spoke to the stranger on all manner of topics, but ever and anon he brought him back, as if without design, to speak of the accidents of fortune which had befallen him on the anniversary of that day, giving it as a reason for his curious remarks, that most men observed anniversaries, time and experience having taught them to notice, that there were curious coincidences with respect to times, and places, and individuals – things, which of themselves form part of the great demonstration of the wisdom and skill displayed in the construction, not only of the mechanical, but the mortal world, showing that each was a portion of one and the same thing.

'I have been,' said he to the stranger, 'an observer and recorder of such things. I have my book of registration here in this house; I will fetch it from my bed-chamber, and we shall see in what other things, as far as your fortunes have been concerned, how it corresponds with the accidents of your life on this anniversary.'

I observed that the stranger paled a little at this proposal, and said, with an affection of carelessness while he was evidently disturbed, that he would see it in the morning. But the philosopher was too intent upon his purpose to forbear. I know not what came upon me, but I urged him to bring the book. This visibly disconcerted the stranger still more, and his emotion became, as it were, a motive which induced me, in a peremptory manner, to require the production of the book, for I felt that strange horror, so often experienced, returning upon me; and was constrained, by an irresistible impulse, to seek an explanation of the circumstances by which I had for so many years suffered such an eclipse of mind.

The stranger seeing how intent both of us were, desisted from his wish to procrastinate the curious disclosure which my friend said he could make; but it was evident he was not at ease. Indeed he was so much the reverse, that when the German went for his book, he again proposed to retire, and only consented to abide at my jocular entreaty, until he should learn what his future fortunes were to be, by the truth of what would be told him of the past.

My friend soon returned with the book. It was a remarkable volume, covered with vellum, shut with three brazen clasps, secured by a lock of curious construction. Altogether it was a strange, antique, and necromantic-looking volume. The corner was studded with knobs of brass, with a small mirror in the centre, round which were inscribed in Teutonic characters, words to the effect, 'I WILL SHOW THEE THYSELF'. Before unlocking the clasp, my friend gave the book to the stranger, explained some of the emblematic devices which adorned the cover, and particularly the words of the motto that surrounded the little mirror.

Whether it was from design, or that the symbols required it, the explanations of my friend were mystical and abstruse; and I could see that they produced an effect on the stranger, so strong that it was evident he could with difficulty maintain his self-possession. The colour entirely faded from his countenance; he became wan and cadaverous, and his hand shook violently as he returned the volume to the philosopher, who, on receiving it back, said:

'There are things in this volume which may not be revealed to every eye, yet to those who may not discover to what they relate, they will seem trivial notations.'

He then applied the key to the lock, and unclosed the volume. My stranger guest began to breathe hard and audibly. The German turned over the vellum leaves searchingly and carefully. At last he found his record and description of my last vision, which he read aloud. It was not only minute in the main circumstances in which I had seen Nocton, but it contained an account of many things, the still life, as it is called, of the picture, which I had forgotten, and among other particulars a picturesque account of the old General whom I saw standing at the bedside.

'By all that's holy,' cried the stranger, 'it is old Cripplington himself – the queue of his hair was, as you say, always crooked, owing to a habit he had of pulling it when vexed – where could you find the description of all this?'

I was petrified; I sat motionless as a statue, but a fearful vibration thrilled through my whole frame.

My friend looked back in his book, and found the description of my sixth vision. It contained the particulars of the crisis of battle in which, as the stranger described, he had received the wound in his face. It affected him less than the other, but still the effect upon him was impressive.

The record of the fifth vision produced a more visible alarm. The description was vivid to an extreme degree – the appearance of Nocton, sword in hand, on the rampart – the animation of the assault, and the gorgeous landscape of domes and pagodas, was limned with words as vividly as a painter could have made the scene. The stranger seemed to forget his anxiety, and was delighted with the reminiscences which the description recalled.

But when the record of the fourth vision was read, wherein Nocton was described as sitting in the regimentals of an aide-de-camp, at a convivial table, he exclaimed, as if unconscious of his words:

'It was on that night I had first the honour of dining with the German general.'

The inexorable philosopher proceeded, and read what I had told him of Nocton, stretched pale and wounded on a bed, with new epaulettes spread on the coverlet, as if just unfolded from a paper. The stranger started from his seat, and cried with a hollow and tearful voice:

'This is the book of life.'

The German turned over to the second vision, which he read slowly and mournfully, especially the description of my own feelings, when I beheld the charnal visage of Mary Blake. The stranger, who had risen from his seat, and was panting with horror, cried out with a shrill howl, as it were:

'On that night as I was sitting in my tent, methought her spirit came and reproached me.'

I could not speak, but my German friend rose from his seat, and holding the volume in his left hand, touched it with his right, and looking sternly at the stranger, said:

'In this volume, and in your own conscience, are the evidences which prove that you are Ralph Nocton and that on this night, twice seven years ago, you murdered Mary Blake.'

The miserable stranger lost all self-command, and cried in consternation:

'It is true, the waters raged; the rain and the hail came; she bitterly upbraided me; I flung her from the boat; the lightning flashed, and the thunder – Oh! it was not so dreadful as her drowning execrations.'

Before any answer could be given to this confession, he staggered from the spot, and almost in the same instant fell dead upon the floor.

# Friends

## *Catherine Gleason*

'Brendon, old chap, is your flat OK for this lunchtime?'

It was a question often heard in the sprawling offices of Jenkins Bros. & Smith. Brendon simply smiled and handed over his spare keys.

'Many thanks, old chap. Leave it as we found it and all that, eh?' Bob Johnson grinned, laying a finger alongside his nose, and closed the door carefully behind him.

Brendon Joyce reflected that Bob must be off to a good start with his girl-friend Felicity, the new secretary. This was the third time in a fortnight he had borrowed Brendon's flat. He felt rather pleased, as it was he who had introduced them. The flat-lending was something of a joke. In his wide and widening circle of friends, Brendon's continuous hospitality was a byword, and included providing accommodation for those people, mainly married, who were engaged in liaisons. Whether his motivation was universal benevolence or prurient gratification was never questioned, because Brendon was nice: even people who didn't like him admitted that. Handsome, young, pleasant-natured and social, he was a successful estate agent who owned a spotless modern flat which everyone invariably described as 'super'. For hobbies he cooked Cordon Bleu recipes, grew pot plants and collected people. As an old friend remarked, he would make someone a lovely wife one day, but the gender of that someone was anybody's guess. For Brendon was one of that perhaps lucky minority, or, as the more maliciously inclined put it, a freak of nature, who was sexually neutral.

He worked away through the morning, until towards noon there was a light tap on his door and a tall thin figure came in. Brendon started when he saw it was Mr Malochie, who had been auditing at the firm for the past month.

'Good morning, Mr Joyce,' said Malochie formally. He was notorious throughout the company for his reserve, and had barely exchanged a greeting with Brendon before. He looked like an undertaker with his sober dress and dour expression.

'Er – good morning,' replied Brendon, recovering from his surprise. He smiled into his visitor's face and rose, extending his hand.

The other's eyes slid away and he ignored or did not notice the gesture.

'Well, now, what can I do for you? Or did you just drop in for a chat?' Brendon used his easiest manner. Having seen how isolated the man was, he had decided that Malochie was the product of a childhood as lonely as his own and, forbidding as the auditor was, he felt sympathetic towards him.

'I understand,' said Malochie in his clipped, monotonous voice, 'that you sometimes lend out your flat at lunchtimes.'

'That's right.'

'Then I wonder,' continued Malochie precisely, 'if you would consider lending it to me, if ever I should have occasion to need it in the future.'

'Why, certainly,' said Brendon, taken aback. 'Open house to my friends. I don't believe in personal property, you know, and –'

'Thank you,' Malochie cut in. 'On the question of payment . . . ?'

'Oh, no, no.' Brendon waved his hands in embarrassment. 'No need for that at all, I assure you.'

The man stared at Brendon, or, rather, through him.

'That is very kind.'

'Not at all. In fact, why not have a look at the place tomorrow – I'm having a party, if you'd care to come.'

Malochie made no answer, but his lips twisted into an attempt at a smile, though it looked like a leer of triumph; then he turned and walked out. A most unfortunate character, thought Brendon. Much too shy and tense.

Over sandwiches in a pub, Brendon eagerly recounted Malochie's visit to some friends.

'You're highly honoured,' observed Irene, the MD's secretary. 'He's been working next door to us for weeks now and never a word has he spoken, except about the bookkeeping. He listens a lot, though.'

'He doesn't have much contact even with the other auditors, poor bloke,' put in Jim, the accountant.

'That's a pity. Mind you, I was amazed when he asked to borrow the flat.'

'I can't somehow imagine him with a girl-friend,' said Irene.

'Oh, I don't know. He's very good-looking,' said little Mary from the typing pool, and blushed.

'*Chacun à son goût*,' said Irene, grinning.

The staff of Jenkins Brothers were mostly young, intelligent, and liberal to a fault, and would have found excuses for Dr Crippen if need be, but none of them really like Malochie. 'Terrifically repressed sort of chap' was the nearest they came to criticism. Felicity had been the most explicit: 'He gives me the creeps,' she said.

.        .        .

Over the chink of glasses and party chatter, Brendon explained cheerfully, 'I should have made a splendid pimp, you know.' A circle of friends exploded with laughter. 'No, really – my true talent lies in bringing people together, and match-making, or perhaps even organizing clandestine associations in high places. I wonder if there are any jobs going in the Diplomatic Corps arranging entertainment for visiting statesmen? Nothing vulgar like orgies, you understand, but discreetly throwing the right people together. That's my true vocation.'

'You could get twenty years, Brendon!'

In his element, Brendon circulated, joining groups and introducing people, making sure nobody was bored, pressing his guests to try dishes from the cold buffet, adjusting the flattering lights and the music level on his stereo, replenishing drinks. He drifted over to a group sitting on the open stairs of his split-level flat, who were discussing Malochie.

'I invited him this evening, but I shouldn't think he'll turn up,' remarked Brendon.

'What age would you say he was?' Mary asked.

'Malochie, oh, mid-twenties, I should think.'

'What? Nearer forty, you mean.'

'Oh, older than that, surely.'

They paused, surprised.

'It really is difficult to tell that man's age,' said Felicity.

'Yes, he has one of those faces . . .'

'One really can't tell.'

'Talk of the devil,' murmured Jim. Someone had opened the door to Malochie, who stood on the threshold, looking round for his host.

'Excuse me – Malochie, don't stand there, come in. Can I get you a drink?'

Brendon bustled away, and Malochie simply stood in a corner, surveying the scene coolly and making no attempt to join in. He brought a cold atmosphere with him; the party seemed to grow quieter. Malochie now looked like an undertaker off-duty in his dark sweater and narrow black trousers, thought Brendon despairingly, pouring a scotch. Perhaps the whisky would thaw him out.

On impulse he whispered to Mary, 'Do go over and talk to him, love. You never know, he might have hidden depths.'

Mary shrugged, but duly trotted over to the saturnine guest with his drink.

Gradually the party recovered its pace, and to Brendon's surprise, when he looked over later, Mary and Malochie were deep in conversation in the corner. Mary's pretty face was flushed and she was talking seriously, and Malochie was staring into space, cradling his untouched drink. When Brendon walked over to offer them food they seemed surprised, almost annoyed, by the interruption.

'You've done it again, old man,' slurred Bob, nodding in the direction of the unlikely couple. 'Such inspiration!'

'Well, I don't like it,' said Felicity unexpectedly. 'I hope she's going to be all right with that man. Bob, you're drunk.'

Bob tried to get up, unsuccessfully. 'Merely indisposed, darling.'

'Indisposed as a newt,' muttered Felicity through her teeth. 'He can't drive like this. We'll have to get a taxi, Brendon.'

'No problem, I ordered a couple earlier on.'

'We were going to give Mary a lift,' said Felicity, anxiously glancing across the room.

As it happened, Malochie took Mary home.

The following Tuesday morning, Malochie came into Brendon's office and, in his usual dry and rigid manner, asked if he could borrow the flat keys regularly every Tuesday. Brendon was surprised and delighted.

He tried to analyse Malochie's peculiar repellent quality, but he could find no explanation for it. Finally he decided that it was the man's eyes which, though cold and blank as a reptile's, held a strange reddish glow when they flickered over his. Perhaps, thought Brendon, it was this accident of nature that made Malochie avoid looking directly at people.

On reflection, Brendon felt a little uneasy that Malochie had asked to borrow the flat before he had met Mary. After all, he could not possibly have known what would happen. Could he? Nor could he have known about Saturday's party, unless of course he had overheard people talking about it. For a moment Brendon played with the idea of Malochie having predicted his reactions and planned the whole sequence of events, then he laughed at the notion. The main thing was that they were all friends, now that Malochie was thawing out.

Round at Irene and Michael's for a drink one evening, he could not resist boasting a little about his match-making success, though, as Brendon observed his usual rule of not gossiping in detail about his friends' habits, and as neither Mary nor Malochie had told anyone about their visits to the flat, the rest of the firm knew only vaguely about their relationship. Michael, in fact, had never met them.

'Don't you think Malochie is becoming more pleasant and outgoing, and well, more friendly and human, as it were?'

'No,' said Irene. She was glued to a Dracula play on television.

'Well, I think Mary's looking brighter,' persisted Brendon. 'And I'm sure Malochie's got an awful lot of good qualities underneath it all.'

'Hidden extremely well,' suggested Bob wryly.

'He has a most unpleasant effect on me,' said Felicity, repressing a shudder. 'Sort of cold and slimy, like –'

'That's not fair.' Brendon flushed angrily. 'The poor chap's only human, after all. If you don't give people like him a chance they just get more shy and introverted. Honestly, you lot ought to know better than to talk about him like that.'

There was an awkward pause after this outburst. They were all much too fond of Brendon to upset him.

'Oh, look,' said Irene brightly. 'This play's got it all wrong – he couldn't come into her home like that. They have to be invited, you know,' she explained to Brendon who, still annoyed, had only half his mind on the fantasy violence.

'Who do?' he asked vaguely.

'Oh – vampires, succubi, incubi, ghouls, things that go bump in the night. Irene loves this stuff,' her husband chuckled.

'Succ – what?' asked Brendon automatically, wishing the play was over so they could talk instead. He did not like television much.

'Succubi. Demons in the mythology of the good old Middle Ages that manifested themselves in female form, slept with men, turned into males or incubi and impregnated women with devil children. Corruption of the soul by means of the body, you see.'

'Ghastly idea. A dreadful period altogether,' said Brendon.

'Right. The only good thing about mediaevalism was its architecture, don't you agree –'

'Do shut up while this is on, Michael. You can talk as much as you want afterwards.'

'Blow that,' said Michael cheerfully. 'Brendon and Bob and I are going to the pub for a pint. Follow us on later, girls.'

Off they went, arguing about architecture.


Brendon was finicky and houseproud, and every Tuesday he was always rather surprised to find the flat so tidy after Malochie's visits; everything was invariably exactly as he had left it in the morning. He was used to discretion, but this was ridiculous. What did they do? And where did they do it? He found himself wishing he could have the place bugged for Tuesday lunchtimes. Did they actually use the place at all? There was a thought. He remembered reading a James Bond book in which the hero stuck a hair across the opening of a drawer so that he would know if anyone had searched his room. Painstakingly, Brendon got down on his knees and pulled out a hair, which he carefully moistened and spread against the front door and the wall. The hair fell off. He tried again, and it still fell off. Obviously, he wasn't trained for this sort of thing. Disgruntled, Brendon gave up and went to bed. Perhaps Bond used glue?

It was six weeks later that Malochie and Mary vanished. They borrowed his keys as usual on Tuesday morning, and neither returned to work that afternoon. Brendon was annoyed about his keys, and positively angry when he came home that evening and found that his trunk was missing. It was dark blue with brass fittings and it lived against the wall beside the sofa. He used it to store bedding, and it served as a handy table top and even as a seat when the flat was crowded. Brendon missed it. Like everyone else, he assumed that Mary and Malochie had eloped, as Mary was barely sixteen, and he supposed that they must have needed the trunk to carry their belongings. Still, they might have left a note.

Mary's distracted parents went to the police, who interviewed her friends and family. Brendon said nothing about their borrowing his flat and his trunk, as he did not think either particularly relevant. Photographs of Mary were circulated in the newspapers, but the police gave up in exasperation their attempt to obtain a coherent idea of Malochie. No two people gave similar, much less coinciding, descriptions of the man, though they were unanimous on his qualities and the effect he produced.

'They can't even agree on his blasted height,' grumbled the officer in charge, 'and you can't make an identikit picture out of a word like "sinister".' Malochie's firm of accountants were highly embarrassed to find that his personnel file had unaccountably gone missing on the day of his disappearance.

It was three weeks later that the news broke. Brendon overslept that morning, owing to the amount of wine he had put away the night before. He walked into an atmosphere of gloom in the main office.

'Somebody died?' he asked cheerfully.

Nobody spoke. Irene began sobbing and ran out of the room.

'It's Mary,' said Bob. 'She's been murdered.'

Brendon grabbed the proffered newspaper. A girl identified as Mary had been found mutilated and dismembered in the luggage compartment of a train heading north. She was wrapped in a plastic sheet, and had been dead for three weeks. White-faced and sickened, Brendon threw the paper down. He had no wish to read the details.

'They think it was Malochie,' said Jim flatly.

Most of the day was taken up with more police interviews. Brendon did not tell them any more than they knew, because he knew it would look bad for him; not only had he introduced the pair, virtually, but he had concealed evidence. He was glad when the nightmarish day was over and he could make his way wearily back home.

At his front door, Brendon stopped short, halted by a sense of unease. What if Malochie had come back to his flat? He still had the key. He might want to confess, or to make sure Brendon did not talk. Oh, don't be so bloody dramatic, he told himself, thrusting the key in the lock. You've been watching too many mysteries. But if Malochie had been waiting for him he could hardly have had a greater shock when he walked in and saw that his trunk had been returned. There it stood as it always had, and the hairs at the back of his neck tingled as he stared at it.

He fought down an impulse to rush straight outside again, and examined the trunk. It was clean and empty. Then he looked around the flat, which was the same.

Brendon sat down, poured a drink, and wondered what to do. There seemed no point in going to the police at this stage; there was nothing untoward in or on the trunk. He went out to have a chat with his neighbours, but, curiously, none of them had seen or heard it delivered. Still, he would not bother the police about it, though it was all rather fishy. Probably a red herring, thought Brendon whimsically.

That night Brendon seemed to wake sharply from a troubled sleep. Slowly he became aware of a heavy, stifling scent. Surely it was the perfume Mary used to wear? He distinctly remembered, for he had not liked it. This smell was the same, but flat and stale. He propped himself up on one elbow, rubbing his sleepy eyes, and was reaching to turn on the bedside lamp when he tensed, sensing a movement in the twin bed next to his own. Brendon froze and strained his senses, his eyes gradually becoming used to the dark.

Dimly he discerned a struggle which he realized was a kind of attempted rape. A girl's voice – Mary's? – pleaded incoherently and constantly for his aid, but the paralysis of nightmare was upon him and he could not stir. The figures grappled painfully until the girl sank moaning under the other's grip. The victor roughly dragged the inert body from the bed and towards the open stairs. As the dreadful figures approached, Brendon saw that the upright shadow was half-concealed in tattered black drapery, and that its long body was thin, skeletally thin, the white bones almost showing through the pale, hirsute skin.

The foul presence of the thing, its gloating evil, inspired Brendon with such a sense of heart-stopping panic that he suddenly knew death to be possible from sheer fear; for the terror that furled its tendrils in his brain and confronted his breath was suffocating him, and, as the black form paused from hauling away its ghastly burden and looked down at him, he knew even as the glowing red eyes in the dark animal face perceived him that the thing that was Malochie wanted him, too.

Brendon screamed. Malochie stood watching his terror. One emaciated arm slowly lifted in the sickening travesty of a reassuring gesture, while the brutish face seemed to grin at him with malicious, mocking intimacy.

Brendon heard the sound of the body being dragged downstairs. Trembling and drenched in sweat he got out of bed and staggered to the balcony rail which ran round the upper floor. One glance was enough. Below was a scene of carnage as Malochie wreaked a horrible vengeance on the girl, tearing the body to pieces with a maniac's hands. Nausea rose in his throat as Brendon shrank back to his bed. Then the wolfish sounds below ceased, and he heard sharp clicking noises which his fear-bemused brain automatically identified with the fastenings of his trunk. He felt, rather than heard, the shuffling footsteps advancing slowly below, towards the stairs. It's my turn now, he thought wildly, as he saw a long black shadow cast on the wall and heard the sinister creak of the stairs.

He was aware of a tall shape standing by his bed. Terror nearly disappeared in amazement as he realized it was the form of a statuesque girl. She was clothed in a diaphanous black robe. His eyes travelled slowly upwards over the perfect body, which aroused no carnal respons in him, to the beautiful lips parted in a lascivious smile. He met the apparition's gaze, and then waves of blackness flooded his brain to unconsciousness. For the eyes were reptilian, and glowing red, and they were the eyes of Malochie.

The next morning Brendon awoke late. He swung out of bed, thankful it was Saturday. God, what a dream! Firmly, he repressed the memory of it. Sometimes he regretted living alone. Still, his dinner party tonight should cheer him up. Social occasions always did. Let's see, steak for five with an Elizabeth David sauce ... he noticed the twin bed. Surely he couldn't have got out of his own bed into the other? He had never done such a thing before. Yet he must have done, for the blankets and sheets were warm and twisted into knots, like his own.

His sense of unease increased when he went downstairs and saw that the trunk was wide open. He had locked it yesterday.

After breakfast, Brendon allowed his imagination to run riot. What if the dream were some kind of warning? His mother had been very superstitious. Or it could have been an invitation – or a threat. He shuddered at the thought. What was it Michael had been going on about that time? Corruption of the soul by means of the body, or some such. Well, he was safe enough from that. But what about Mary?

Supposing she had been subject to a dark attack of that kind. Perhaps she had resisted temptation and lost her life in consequence, her soul intact, her body destroyed. What if Malochie was some kind of black magic fanatic, or worse? What if it hadn't been a dream at all, but real . . .

Brendon emitted a totally mirthless giggle through cold and chattering teeth.

'Rubbish,' he squeaked, then cleared his throat and tried again.

'Rubbish,' he said in his normal voice. His own guilt feelings over Mary's death, imagination and sleepwalking were the only evils here.

Having rationalized his fear, Brendon was determined to forget it. Ten thirty – heavens, he would be late for the blasted shops.

While he was out he bought some tall white candles, thinking it would be something pleasantly different to have the place lit only by candles.

By nine o'clock he had dusted the flat, done amazing things to the steak and arranged his candles artistically around the room. Irene and her husband arrived first, followed closely by Felicity and Bob. The atmosphere was cosy and the conversation civilized, helped by the flowing burgundy. This gave rise to some ribbing about the state of Bob at Brendon's last party.

'Well, he wasn't the only one,' said Michael, coming to Bob's aid. 'That poor girl who got murdered was well away, sitting in the corner chattering to herself.'

'Mary? She was talking to Malochie,' said Brendon.

'Not at all, she was by herself, except when you spoke to her.'

'But you must have seen Malochie,' protested Bob. 'Tall, thin bloke with dark hair.'

'She was alone,' Michael insisted, 'in that corner there, and she was talking to an empty chair. I saw her.'

'It rather sounds as if someone else was well into the booze.' Felicity broke the uneasy pause with attempted gaiety.

'Oh no,' said Irene defensively. 'Michael was driving. He only drank tonic that evening.'

'More salad, anyone?' Brendon's hand shook slightly as he offered the dish.

'I never understood what Mary saw in him anyway,' remarked Felicity as she helped herself. 'He wasn't exactly attractive, Malochie, was he?'

'Good Lord, no – more like an animated corpse,' laughed Irene.

'Everyone finished? – I made some raspberry parfait if you'd care to risk it.' Brendon hastily cleared the table, refusing anyone's help.

'I love the candles, Brendon,' Felicity called into the kitchen. 'Except those two are a bit weird. Different, though,' she added kindly.

'Which two?' Brendon came back into the room, carefully carrying a bowl of raspberry parfait.

'Those on the trunk,' said Felicity.

There was a fruity splodge as Brendon's masterpiece hit the Axminster. The candles, dripping over their wine bottles on the trunk, were burning with a dim blue flame, and they had turned completely black.

Brendon had a classic hangover. It was Sunday morning, and he was huddled miserably in a chair sipping coffee. Every time his body moved his head threatened to fall off, and every time his thoughts moved he gave a deep inner groan, remembering how last night he had almost hysterically accused his friends of playing tricks on him by switching the candles, and how, even as he spoke, he knew they hadn't. They had been very concerned and reasonable about his upset, but they obviously didn't know what he was talking about and the evening was marred; the party broke up early. Suddenly afraid of being alone, Brendon had switched on every light in the flat, gathered up all the candles and thrown them in the dustbin, and then proceeded to drink himself into a stupor with the remaining wine and brandy.

It was half past twelve. Feeling slightly better, he went out to a friend's for lunch.

He returned towards evening, and entered the flat warily. Was it imagination, or were there shadows in its white-painted corners? Why was the air so cold, and the atmosphere hostile?

It was harder, here, to dismiss all that had happened over the last two days as imagination. He could find no rational explanation for the candles. If Mary really had been murdered here, perhaps some evil had lingered on to trouble him with nightmares and phenomena. After all, he and Mary had been the only ones to approach Malochie directly. Brendon shuddered. If his wild speculations were right, then the flat was haunted. But that was all superstitious nonsense. Wasn't it?

Still, to be on the safe side, he decided that if anything odd happened again he would call in a priest to purify the place. He had seen *The Exorcist*; it was wonderful what they could do these days.

Thus comforted, Brendon relaxed. He walked over to the window and glanced out at the garden. Winter was approaching and the nights were drawing in; he felt an odd reluctance to close the curtains.

Suddenly Brendon felt a cold, prickling sensation down his spine. He shuddered violently, as if a centipede had crawled up his back. Turning into the room, his eyes slowly registered a stealthy movement on the upper floor. Something or someone was up there; he heard the faint creak of bedsprings. It has to be burglars, Brendon forced himself to think, and to his eternal credit he walked deliberately up the stairs to see for himself. There was nothing and nobody. And yet – the covers on the twin bed had been slightly disturbed. It was me, thought Brendon, though he hardly believed it. I must have moved them before I went out this morning.

Once downstairs, waves of relief engulfed him. He switched on the lights and went to get a stiff drink, his head aching and throbbing as the tension ebbed from his racked nerves. His trembling fingers could hardly hold the bottle straight. But no sooner had he swallowed his drink than he jerked round, pierced as if shot by a great crash, followed by a low, agonized moaning. He scarcely registered the heavy, stale stench of perfume, for his eyes were riveted to the trunk at the opposite side of the room. The top had flown open, banging against the wall, and the groans issued from within; and Brendon almost fainted at the sight of the blood which seeped and trickled from its wooden seams to drench the carpet beneath.

With a supreme effort, Brendon gained control and, steeling himself against the shock, began to walk slowly over to the trunk. He had not taken two paces before the lights in the room dimmed, and the air turned ice-cold. From out of the trunk there emerged a feeble hand, the fingers crawling spider-fashion out of the box, the arm dripping with blood.

Brendon, sick and shaking, ran for the door. It would not open to his grasp. He shook it insanely, while terror massed behind him. Then it gave; in his panic he had not fully turned the handle. Rushing outside, he saw a dark shape bent over a hedge. Frantically he grasped the outstretched arm:

'Come quickly! Please, you must come and see –'

Slowly the man turned. Brendon all but dragged him up the steps to his flat, and got him inside. The light revealed the puzzled face of the housing estate's gardener.

'Over there. In the trunk.' Brendon leaned against the wall, covering his face. There was a long pause.

'Er . . . what exactly was it you were wanting, sir?'

'In the trunk . . . the – the noises, the . . .'

Brendon uncovered his eyes and forced them across the room. The trunk was still open, but there was no sign of blood.

'Noises, you say? Ah, yes, sir, that'll be the mice, that will. We have 'em next door, we do.'

The gardener peered curiously over his shoulder as Brendon stood over the empty trunk, glanced back to the open whisky bottle, and drew his own conclusions.

Brendon began slowly to refasten the trunk. He did not lock it. There was no point.

The man coughed politely. 'Nasty little buggers, sir, better set a trap.'
Brendon stared at him hopelessly.

'They can't hurt you, sir,' said the gardener, edging towards the door.
'Not unless they're rats,' he added helpfully. 'Well – I'll be on my way.
Good-night, sir.'

The door closed behind the man. Brendon knew that he was not alone
in the flat, but he felt quite calm; the pattern had finally emerged, and
it was of his own weaving. He knelt down to unfasten the trunk, and as
he knelt a thin black shadow fell over him and onto the wall. He turned
to encounter the beautiful girl, with the eyes that held the fires of hell.
Women aroused no response in him, or he might have been lost for ever.
He gazed unmoved, past all terror, but did not pause to watch the
exquisite, smooth face crumble into the raging, rotting animal-skull of
Malochie, and the white hands turning skeletal; he slowly turned back
to the open trunk, and he was almost grateful for the furious dead fingers
that grasped his throat, that choked and tore him into eternal oblivion.

For, in his final living moments, Brendon knew at last who it was he
had befriended.

# The Circus

## *Winston Graham*

It was Gareth Purdy's first visit for over twenty years and he was pleased to be back in the Old Country for a short time, even though he felt he owed it nothing either in sentiment or esteem. Everything he was and had become he owed to Australia, and that was where his family and his life was. Yet England, especially at this time of year when the trees were just budding, was an eye-catching place, he'd never realized how beautiful, how soft and gentle the countryside was, how warm the people were, how cultured the life. It had all looked different when you were a lad and no money and you stood shivering at a street corner – there wasn't much warmth then.

His first week-end he thought to spend in London looking round the old haunts but his business friend, Jock Munster, invited him down to his country house in Sussex, and when it came to the point this seemed so much more attractive a proposition that he accepted, and they drove to Fontain Manor on the Friday evening.

It was a lovely small manor house, weathered and mellowed by two hundred years and set in a few acres of ground in which beech trees were just unfolding lovely shot-silk feathery caterpillars of leaf. A level green lawn, bluebells, flowering cherries, daphnes, brooms and other plants he did not know gave a profusion of gentle colour which seemed far removed from the sub-tropical rigours of the district where he had made his life.

His host had a charming wife and two pretty daughters, the elder of whom willingly made a four at bridge for them, and they played till midnight, whereupon he retired to bed in a comfortable aura of well-cooked food, brandy and cigar smoke and slept for eight hours without stirring – something he had not done for many years. Soon after he woke a light breakfast was brought in for him by a maid, and he ate it, bathed, shaved and dressed and was up and walking about the house by nine-thirty. Jock had arranged a game of golf for eleven, but the only member of the family at present to be seen was the younger daughter, Phyllida, who chatted to him briskly about horses for a few minutes, and then he wandered out into the garden.

It was a superb morning. Remembering the drab, damp, cheerless days of his youth, he cocked a suspicious eye at the palely cloudless sky and wondered if there was a catch somewhere. It was put on for his benefit, no doubt, just to convince him that all those sour memories were mistaken. He was not to be deceived; but in the meantime . . .

In the far corner of the garden a gardener was planting out some bedding plants and nearby a heated greenhouse was thick with tomatoes just beginning to ripen. These rich Englishmen, he thought, still did themselves well in a way it was more difficult to do back home. The tradition of employing servants, for instance; living-in servants too. The fact that you could still *find* them. They were scarce here too, no doubt, but they were still *obtainable* and willing to do this work. Oh well, old feudal habits died hard. He'd seen nothing of this when *he* was in England – but it still persisted in spite of all.

He walked across the lawn, hands in pockets, confident, free, well-to-do, wondering if his swing would be in the groove this morning, wondering if the two men who were going to make up the foursome were anything in the same way of business as Jock and himself. As he passed the gardener he stopped a minute watching the man working, and his shadow fell across the soil. The gardener looked up and said, 'Good morning, sir.'

'Morning. Those wallflowers you're putting in?'

'No. Antirrhinums for – for summer . . . flowering . . .'

The man had straightened up, his voice hesitating, and he was staring. Fiftyish, tall, bony, thick upthrust greying hair, heavy jaw. They stared at each other. Gareth Purdy said:

'Good cripes! It's not . . . it's not Tom? . . .'

'Gareth? Is it Gareth? Yes, I can see it is! If there wasn't any other way I'd know . . .'

'How?'

'By the scar on your chin! When you fell off that bike you borrowed from Bill Carter . . .'

'Good *cripes*! . . . Tom!' Gareth held out his hand.

Tom wiped his hand down the side of his denims and they clasped hands.

'This is a bloody coincidence if ever there was one!' Gareth said. 'I'm only over for a couple of weeks and I thought I'd spend this week-end strolling round the old parts, maybe looking up one or two chums if I could find them; then Jock Munster invites me here for the week-end, and by God if I don't find my own brother digging his garden!'

Tom looked at the younger man, narrowing his eyes as if to see, but what he was trying to see was the boy whom he had not set eyes on for twenty-five years. 'I can't believe it,' he said. 'Mr Munster often has guests for the week-end, but I never thought ... How *are* you, lad? You look well. Put on a bit of weight but it suits. Doing well? You look prosperous.'

'Yes ... yes. I'm prosperous. And thanking God every day that I emigrated. I'm in the wool export business. Doing very nicely: wife and two kids; fine house outside Adelaide, drive a Cadillac, kids go to good schools ...' Gareth's round, high complexioned, energetic face clouded a little. 'You? This doesn't look too good. Pity we lost touch ...'

'Oh, I do well enough,' Tom said shortly. 'I was never the one with the brains. This suits me nicely –'

'Brains? I don't know about that! When I was a tiny kid I thought you knew everything – especially after Dad died. I know you found things a bit hard, but then we all did. You had Mum to consider – and you only eleven, was it?'

'Yes. Near twelve. And you six. Seems a long time ago.'

'Look, we must have a talk sometime. I'm playing golf later this morning, but after lunch – you'll be here then?'

'No, I knock off at twelve. But I'm just down the lane. First cottage. I'll be there all afternoon. Make some excuse –'

'Excuse hell! I'll tell them I'm going to meet my brother! It fair kills me, this meeting, out of the blue. It's a small world. I couldn't have believed it!'

Tom scraped some mud off his boot. 'Make an excuse. It's easier. And more comfortable all round.'

'What d'you mean? Why should I –'

'I mean you're a guest of theirs. Business too, I expect: the Munsters are in wool. It would make 'em feel awkward to think they were employing your brother in their garden.'

'Hell! What do I care? There's too much bloody snobbery in the world, lad –'

'I care, Gareth.'

'What? What d'you mean.'

'I like this job. Had it for four years. Munster's a decent bloke – we get on very well. But we live in separate worlds. I never ask him personal questions – he never asks me. If you've been in Australia, maybe you don't understand this, but I'd rather it stayed that way. Maybe you think it's wrong to have a master/servant relationship in the seventies; but it *works*, see. It works for him and it works for me.'

Gareth stared. 'OK, Tom. Whatever you say. But it seems a pity – Anyway, I'll be along this afternoon. We can talk about old times. God damn it, it's a fantastic coincidence, I might have looked for you for weeks!'

'Would you?' Tom asked.

'Would I? – don't know. Anyway, I wouldn't have had the *time*. I'm only here for fifteen days. Now we *have* met we must at least have an afternoon together!'

It was an easy foursome, for which Gareth Purdy was thankful because his swing didn't settle into its groove all morning. He developed a wicked hook which brought his normal length down by fifty yards and often landed him in the rough. His partner, tall and easy-going, was not at all put out, and they won by 2 and 1. But his idea of spending an hour or so in the cottage down the lane was frustrated by his host: they stayed at the golf club for lunch and played another round, then when they got home there were people in for drinks and dinner, so it was Sunday before the chance came. He walked round about eleven and found Tom in his small garden tying up some climbing thing.

'Sorry about yesterday, lad.' He explained. 'They've gone to church now. To *church*! I didn't believe anybody ever still did – but I said I'd rather take a walk and here I am.'

Tom took his pipe out of his mouth and looked at his younger brother quizzically. Indeed, they eyed each other. Tom was smart this morning, the smarter of the two, a good grey herringbone suit, white shirt, blue tie: a good-looking, bony, big man with a taut skin and light blue-grey eyes. Gareth had a flannel check shirt, a brown pull-over, fine quality wool slacks gone baggy with wear – half a head the shorter with a risk of becoming overweight. His face was as open as his shirt, Tom's more inward-looking, reserved, brooding.

They went in. Gareth admired, saying Tom had done nicely for himself, while all the time seeing the tiny cottage, the restricted life. Gareth took out photographs: the wife, the kids, that's me at Rapid Bay; Joyce sunbathing; that's up in the Mount Lofty range. Did you ever marry, Tom?'

'No . . . I never found the right one. Somehow I got put off early. Your wife – she's not a blonde? I never liked blondes.'

'No, brown hair. But blue eyes. You'd like her. Look. I've been thinking: why don't you come out there and join us? Make a new life. There's still plenty of opportunity.'

They talked about it while Tom made coffee. You're only forty-seven, Gareth said, forty-eight next month: I know. You could start something. I could set you up. They wrangled, but amiably. Tom said no. He was set here. It wouldn't do. It wouldn't work. I couldn't leave English gardens. Been growing things on and off for years. Suppose it's been ever since we came down from Lancashire. Remember that time? Gareth shook his head.

'Well you were only five. I was eleven. Dad was out of work – had

been three years. More than two million unemployed in those days.
Then he got this chance to move to London on a building site, so he
jumped at it. Somehow he scraped together enough to bring the family.
Remember the place in London?'

'Oh, yes. Top of the world. How long were we there? Two years?
Three?'

'Three. I suppose it had been a rich merchant's house once, but when
we were there there were different families living on each floor and one
WC for the whole house. Remember the O'Haras?'

'That lot that made a kitchen of the bathroom? Yep. What went
wrong with you there, Tom?'

Tom stared. 'Who said anything had? Did you notice?'

'Yep. I used to look up to you in those days. I noticed things. You
kept getting into trouble. Was it because of Dad dying?'

'No ... nothing to do with that. Anyway I never got into much
trouble.'

'We had the probation officer round, I remember. Breaking and
entering or something, wasn't it?'

Tom stirred the coffee. 'You remember too much. No, it was nothing
to do with Dad. Did you know ...'

'Know what?'

'Oh, never mind. Sugar?'

'Thanks.'

They sat and talked of domestic things, how their lives had gone since
they had separated, Gareth of his early struggles in Australia, his early
marriage, the luck that seemed to bring: he'd never looked back; Tom
of two years' national service – 'never did take much to discipline' –
casual labour, factory work – 'you get so bored you'd do anything for a
kick' – two brushes with the police but never inside, bound over, gardener
in a London park, garage foreman in Brighton, then this job. 'Suits fine.
I get a lot of fun. Shan't stay here all my life but maybe another couple
of years. I've a fancy for Scotland – west coast. Good gardens there.'

Gareth said, 'What were you going to say just now?'

'When?'

'I thought you were going to say something about when we were kids
in that top-floor flat.'

'Yes, I was. Well, yes, I was.'

Tom sipped his coffee and blew the steam away with his breath.
Outside a bird was trilling as if it was early morning He said: 'D'you
remember that other flat? D'you remember it looked out over the
Common? It was quite a thrill to me, coming from a back-to-back in
Gorton, coming from the provinces like that into the centre of the largest
city in the world and – and you moved into the *country*? House and traffic

all round, of course, but plane trees and beeches and Norway maples, and all the birds: robins, sparrows, finches. And thrushes singing just like that one now!'

'I remember the sloping ceiling,' Gareth said. 'From my bunk I could reach up and touch the rafters without even sitting up in bed.'

'Did you know,' Tom said, 'that I saw a murder?'

Gareth stared. 'What? When? In that house?'

Tom was silent for a while. 'Nay,' he said at length, 'not in the house. Outside . . . I've never told anyone this before . . .'

'Good cripes! Why didn't you? When was it? Was I there?'

'You were there – asleep.'

There was another silence. 'Here, have one of mine,' Gareth said, as he saw his brother groping for his pipe.

Tom waved away the cheroots. 'Thanks, no.' He fumbled with his tobacco pouch. 'When we got to that house I tell you I was taken by being almost in the country, overlooking that Common. I'd often sit there after school – sit on a stool looking through the low window – watching the traffic and kids kicking a ball about on the worn grass, and courting couples, and young marrieds pushing prams, and dogs bounding about and lifting their legs, and birds fluttering and fighting, and once in a while an aeroplane in the sky. It was as good as a free entertainment.'

'Hadn't you been sick?'

'Oh, you remember that. Yes, I'd had polio – you'd never think it to look at me these days – but that time I was just getting over it and my legs were weak. So I didn't play much. I used to sit and watch and dream. You know how kids dream – think they're going to be tops in some world: cricket or football, or a sea captain or a daring aviator. Those were the days when people still made records with solo flights . . . I was a romantic. Remember the circus?'

Gareth narrowed his eyes. 'No.'

'That's where it began. The circus that came to the Common. Of course I'd seen the posters stuck on telegraph poles, and there'd been talk of it at school, but I hardly believed it until I saw it for real. It came every year, the lads said, sometimes oftener, and it was a big circus not just a little travelling job. I'd never seen a circus until then, not in real life, though I'd seen one once on the movies. It came twice while we were there. You don't remember it at all?'

'Think I have a vague recollection.' Gareth watched his brother's fingers, grown big and clumsy with their daily work, pushing the tobacco down into the old pipe.

'One day just before Christmas I came home from school and found they'd that moment arrived. I banged and clattered up three flights of stairs and saw them assembling right in the bare patch of ground among the trees almost just across the street from our house. It was great watching, that evening. The big smart caravans and decorated trailers crawling in one by one, making a circle like a – like a well-drilled army of snails. Then inside – in the centre of the circle – up went the big top, up it went, up and up. And through the night I stayed awake listening to the thump and bang of hammers, the beat of the engines, the rattle of chains, the shouts of men. Every now and then I'd slip out of bed and take another look. And sure enough there'd be something fresh to see, another pole up, another spread of canvas luffed out like a sail in the wind . . .

'Dad had a proper pinched look – d'you remember it? I suppose you'd hardly remember *him*, would you?'

'Oh, yes, I do.'

'His look wasn't just from not eating enough but it was a sort of Labour Exchange look, a look a lot of men had in those days; of course he was a sick man then, and he hadn't much time for me and my enthusiasms. Going to the circus? We hadn't a penny to spare, let alone sixpence like the cheapest seats were.'

Tom struck a match. 'I didn't much care. Because I saw it all from the window – free. Once or twice I lifted you up, but usually you were too hungry to stay long – you had a rare appetite in those days. Mum said there was no filling you.'

'Just the same now. But now I have to watch it!'

'From that window I could see all the animals in their cages, and the horses, all the brown and white horses marked like maps. I used to think, if I could learn geography that way!' . . . Tom's face appeared out of a cloud of smoke. 'And there were four elephants standing in a line with chains on their feet; they were exercised daily, of course, and taken in for performances, but most of the time they stood there just rocking back and forth, all together. They never moved their feet much but just swayed in unison like, like four rubber dolls. Next to them, in the cages, were the lions and the tigers and the chimpanzees. Along the other side were the camels and the Shetland ponies, and of course the seals. Even when it was dark you could still watch because of the lights they used. Sometimes early morning they'd put on an unrehearsed show – it might have been for my benefit . . .'

Tom struck another match and held it to his pipe. His pale grey eyes were far gone in reminiscence.

'You were saying about a murder –'

'You could see the clowns, ready made up so far as the top half went, but still in sandals and grey flannel trousers. And the tightrope walker in her sequins emptying a pail of slops. And the cowboys playing cards.

And when the show began all the piebald horses would come out and form into a line without a word and go into the tent as if they were soldiers at a drill. But the best thing of all, lad, was seeing the seals go in. They'd all come out of their cages, flopping down the wooden steps, and go hobbling across clapping their flippers. There was one always had to sing a song accompanied by the band, and I'd wait at night for the noise because you could hear it all over the place and this would be a sign their turn was over. And the very first night, lad, I fell in love.'

Gareth finished his coffee and waved away an offer of more. 'You, Tom? Then? Why –'

'Oh, I know it sounds daft, and daft it no doubt was, at my age then. But from the distance of our attic she looked hardly more than a kid herself. Her name was Tilly and she rode two of the piebald horses bareback. It was a turn called Rita and Tilly, and the other was much older; I thought it was probably mother and daughter. She was blonde, this girl, with long fair hair usually done in pigtails; but for her turn she wore it loose, and it fell amost to her waist and spread out like a fan when she swung on and off the horses. She'd got blue eyes and a short nose and long beautiful legs that made her look like a colt herself. Every day I watched her practising, and to me, you know, she was like a fairy out of another world, infinitely beautiful and infinitely remote. I got to see her in the end.'

'D'you mean in the ring?'

'Yes. I stole some sweets in Bray's sweetshop and sold 'em at school – I made ninepence altogether. I went the first Saturday – they stayed two weeks that time because of Christmas. When I actually saw her in the ring, doing the things I'd watched her practising – and a lot of other things besides, under the arc lights, twisting and turning and jumping and balancing, all my romantic notions were boosted to the limit. She really did look young, terribly young to have so much cleverness and poise; she was *very* pretty; she became a sort of dream girl. A dream girl. You all right here or shall we go back in the garden?'

'I'm OK.'

'Rita was nothing – did a few tricks but often as not just directed the horses for Tilly. Tilly was the star. And after watching for a few days from the window I changed my mind about Rita being the mother. Tilly had her own caravan. Rita lived in another caravan with the ringmaster and two little boys, so I reckoned they were a married family and Tilly was on her own. But that was where the trouble began. Two men were courting Tilly. At least two, but maybe more. It was two I noticed. But she was very popular, see, and everybody liked her. One or another would always be coming to talk at her doorway. She was always flitting around teasing or jollying people. But these two. One was a clown, big, heavy, clumsy, did a lot of falling about in the ring, but when he took the white off his face he wasn't a bad looking bloke, fair-haired, bit German looking. The other was one of the tightrope walkers, slim, dark, elegant like, fancied himself, you know. They'd been at odds more than once. Tilly didn't seem to have any preference, seemed to laugh at them both. But then she laughed at most things.

Then this night, it was the second Monday, the show was over, everybody'd eaten and cleaned up and the arc lights were out and most of the lights were going out in the caravans, and I was just sitting at the window in my overcoat and thick stockings watching the single light in Tilly's caravan and wondering whether I should ever see her close to – I mean really close, because the sixpenny seats had been at the back. And suddenly there was this commotion in there.'

'In her caravan?'

'Yes. I think it was more a change in the light at first, more than actual noise. In fact, there wasn't really *ever* much noise, I suppose, but almost at once the door burst open and two men tumbled down the steps fighting. It was these two. And it was real fighting – to hurt, to kill – you hardly ever see that. And Tilly came to the door and stood there with her hand to her mouth watching them. It couldn't have lasted more than two–three minutes. If that. It was like an explosion, *see*. The big clown was winning, I thought, laying into the dark bloke, got him on the ground. Then they rolled over and a knife flashed, and suddenly it was over. And the clown was flat on his back, writhing like in slow motion and the tightrope man got up with the knife still in his hand. And nothing moved for about twenty seconds, and then the clown lay still and the tightrope man dropped his knife and Tilly skimmed down the steps and into his arms . . .'

Tom took his pipe out of his mouth and looked at the stem. Then he wiped either side of his hand with it and put the pipe back.

'In another half minute there were six or seven standing round – those that had been wakened by the struggle: the ringmaster, Rita, two clowns, a dwarf, the fat woman. A couple of them bent down looking at the clown. Pretty soon they straightened up: there was nothing to be done. The ringmaster took charge, just like he did in the ring. He turned on Tilly and the tightrope man, demanding an explanation. At least, that's what it looked like, and I could see Tilly defending the tightrope man, gesturing towards her caravan, you could almost see what she was saying: the clown forced himself in there, tightrope came to protect me. They must have talked for half an hour. Two others joined them – the lion tamer who'd been wakened because his lions were restless, the tightrope man's partner.

'There was a lot of angry talk one way or the other, angry accusations and angry denials, but you could see the ringmaster all the time holding up his hand to keep their voices down. He didn't want the whole circus roused. And now and then he'd glance up at the windows of the houses, wondering if anyone had seen. I'd no idea what he was going to do. At first I couldn't believe the clown was dead – it was too easy, killing someone like that – I expected him to sit up and join in the quarrel. Then when he didn't and I saw he really wasn't going to I waited for them to call the police. But they didn't do that either. It was cold in that bedroom and I was shivering, but maybe it wasn't all just the cold. I thought several times of waking you to come and look, but I knew you were too young and would only wail and whimper.' Tom stopped. 'Ah, well, it was a long time ago. Telling you brings it all back. What time is it?'

'Time? Now? Er – half eleven.'

'Oh, there's plenty of time then. They'll not be back till after twelve. Sure you won't have more coffee?'

'Well maybe yes. Thanks. What did you do? What did they do?'

'The circus folk? With the clown? They buried him.'

'Where?'

'Right there. On the spot. It must have taken them another hour to decide and then to do it, but I couldn't leave that window. They dug a grave in the common, right at the side of one of the caravans. The two clowns and the ringmaster and the tightrope walker. They dug a hole and put him in and filled the hole in again, and presently – it must have been near one in the morning – they cleared up the mess. The ringmaster took the knife, the tightrope man went off with his partner. Rita drove a weeping Tilly back into her caravan and stayed the night with her, the fat lady swilled water on the grass to make the blood less obvious. D'you know what they did next day? They moved the elephants. It was only a few yards, but they moved the elephants over the new dug grave. That way the ground was pressed down hard before they left . . .'

Gareth took his second cup of coffee. 'You never told anybody?'

'Never till this minute. Not for thirty-five years. I don't know why I'm telling you now, except that you're my brother and we've not met for so long and may not meet for as long again.'

'Oh, come, that's not likely now we've made contact –'

'I *thought* of going to the police. I *thought* of telling Mum. After all, they might have pooh-poohed and said I'd dreamt it, but the proof was *there*. I only had to take them to the spot. But Tilly – I was still in love with Tilly. I knew if the police were once involved she would get dragged in, even though she was entirely innocent. Anyway, I wasn't too keen on the police in those days . . . So I stayed quiet . . . Of course you can see their point of view. I suppose everybody in the circus would have to know in the end – but no one outside. It's a closed community. Nobody'd miss one clown, see. But if they got the police in it means not only a scandal, which would have been bad for them publicitywise, but the loss of another man, and a very valuable one. So they all stayed quiet and just moved on. And I stayed quiet with them.'

'Well.' Gareth stretched his legs. They were a bit stiff from 36 holes yesterday. Getting out of condition. 'It's a queer tale . . . Fascinating . . . And I suppose you never saw them again? You know –'

'Oh, yes, I did. They came back the following October.'

'Did they, by God? And was . . .'

'It's funny,' said Tom, staring out of the window with his pale absent eyes. 'All that year I hugged my secret. Once the circus had gone, of course the Common was itself again. Kids kicking a ball, courting couples, young marrieds with prams, dogs sniffing and scratching. I used to wonder if some day a dog would scratch something up. But they'd been damned clever, they'd made sure of putting the clown just deep enough. I used to walk over in the long days and stare at the spot, wondering, wondering, thinking, "I know something nobody else knows." Hugging the thought to myself. Of course there wasn't any difficulty in picking out the spot, the grass grew during the summer, and it was that much thicker and greener where the clown was.'

'Good cripes. Because *he* was there?'

'Oh, yes. I wonder someone didn't tumble, but I suppose no one ever thought.'

'Well I wouldn't have *known*.'

'I think I grew up a lot that year, Gareth. You remember Dad died in the May. It wasn't so much what was wrong with him, I thought, as if he suddenly decided the whole thing was beyond him and he was opting out. It left us in a real mess. Public assistance and so on. Then Mum got evening work washing up at a hotel, and we were able to stay on, but I more or less had to look after things while she was out, like the head of the house. At twelve to be the head of the house. God help us all.'

'Well, He did in a way.'

'Not much, lad, not much. You got the best end . . . Often during that year I dreamed about Tilly, wondering where she was, what she was thinking, wishing *I'd* been that tightrope walker so I could rescue her from a villainous clown who tried to take advantage of her. You know how it is when your mind feeds on dreams . . .'

Gareth stared at his brother's taut shiny face. 'You saw *her* again?'

'Oh, yes. And how. In the October, coming home from school, there was a man pasting a bill round a telegraph post. I nearly got run over crossing the street to see, because I'd recognized the blue and yellow notice.'

Tom said, 'As a matter of fact, though my thoughts ran on ahead of me, they didn't run quite far enough, you know, because seven days later when the circus arrived and pitched its big top again right under our windows there was something I absolutely hadn't bargained for. Never entered my head. The trees were all in leaf and I could hardly see a damned thing ...

'At the time it was a major tragedy – really was – something I'd never *dreamed* of. Although Rita and Tilly were billed and I knew they were there and caught tantalizing glimpses of them, I couldn't really see Tilly at all – except by hanging round the gate like a lot of other kids, hoping to see her if she went in or out. The trees were everywhere, you know, dense. I could never see her practising or sitting on the steps of her caravan picking at a seam in her tights, I could never see her washing or brushing her hair or watch her riding into the tent to begin her act. And all the other things too: the clowns kicking a football about and sometimes clowning for the fun of the thing; the lions fed; the fat lady eating her supper, the elephants going for their daily walk.'

'I guess I remember that visit now. Vaguely. I remember the elephants. I remember staring through the railings.'

'Yes, well, above all I wanted to know what they'd done, if anything, about the place where the clown had been buried. I watched as best I could, and I *thought* they'd pitched them in the same place, those elephants, over where they had been put before, but it was hard to be sure. And I couldn't see whether Tilly or anyone went and looked at the spot. I could only suppose they must have, just to make sure he was undisturbed ... The circus was only here for a week this second time, see, and so I had to make a big effort right away, and I got in with another lad from school on the Thursday matinee – sweets stolen from the same shop – second crime of my career. Tilly was just as marvellous as ever, and just as remote. The tightrope walker who'd done the deed was still performing. It was all wonderful – and unbearably frustrating. All Friday it was going over and over in my mind at school. Somehow I had to get nearer to her, perhaps even speak to her, even let her know if necessary that I knew her secret but that her secret was utterly safe with me. Mum had talked of going back North to live with Grandfather and Grandmother in Gorton, and I couldn't bear the thought that after Saturday I would never see Tilly ever in my life again. So the Friday evening ...'

'Did you go in?'

'Yes ... yes, but it wasn't easy making up my mind. After all, I was only just going on thirteen, and in awe of the whole set up. But it got to a stage of frustration where – Mother never got back till half-eleven, so there was plenty of time, see. I heard the end of the show and heard the animals being fed, and presently I reckoned they'd be all settling down but not yet asleep. I left you asleep in bed and hoped you wouldn't wake up.

'The circus entrance was opposite Titus Street – you remember that – and at the side of it a big car park had been made so that people didn't block the roads in their cars (not much of a traffic problem in those days). A fence had been put up round the circus to keep out the non-paying public; but with all their hammerings and uprootings some of the stakes were pretty shaky, and the wire here and there was rusted and broken. So it wasn't too hard to climb through. But a couple of the lads from school had got in on the Monday and both had been caught and given a tanning, so it wasn't the sort of thing to try on just for fun.

'I wormed a way through in a dark patch at the back, and the farthest place from the big tent, and then I made for the elephants. I realized as soon as I got in that I'd left it a bit late, because most of the things had closed up for the night. Everybody'd eaten pretty quickly, and as it was a chilly night nearly everyone was indoors. Of course it made it safer for me – but it made it that much less likely I should catch a glimpse of Tilly.

'Anyway I went first for the elephants. They *had* been pitched over the grave, as before. The lush green grass was stamped down into a dusty desert. The elephants were still munching a few vegetables. You could hear the regular creak and rattle of the chains as they rocked on their feet all together. In a cage nearby some other animal was making a scuffling gobbling noise. Couldn't tell what. There wasn't anything more I could do. I made for Tilly's caravan.'

Tom stopped and got up. His pipe had gone out and he knocked the burnt tobacco into the empty grate. Then he put the pipe in his pocket, frowned out of the window.

'I recall I had a couple of narrow escapes on the way. There were those two small dogs on the loose that I was afraid would latch on to me. Then I crawled on hands and knees round a corner made by two caravans and almost into a dwarf and a negro with tattoos on his face and a bearded woman, who were all sitting eating scrambled eggs or something. But I just ducked away in time. What I thought to do when I got to Tilly's caravan I never quite decided, but the door was shut and a light burned inside. So I just squatted down and looked and looked, hoping she might come out.

'But she didn't. And I sat. And a few people moved around here and there. And some monkeys chattered. And a lion coughed. And I began to get cold. So I went up to the caravan and crept up the three steps and looked in the window. She was in there all right. With a man. They were both naked. Their arms and legs were twined like they were an octopus or something. I suppose it was just the moment – the moment of completion. You hear about folk being rooted to the ground. Well, I was rooted. I could no more have moved away than gone in. Of course I wasn't exactly ignorant, but I'd never seen it before. This was a strange man – that slowly registered – and with my angel, my princess, my idol, see. I suppose I felt sick. I couldn't move. Then suddenly someone gripped me round the neck and by the arm and dragged me down the steps and started shouting and bashing into me.'

Tom's face was tight and grim. 'Ah, well, you see, it wasn't such a happy end to my circus.'

'Did you get a tanning?'

'Sort of. Sort of. But it was interrupted. It was this big dwarf who caught me – he was supposed to be a funny boy but he was a grown man when you saw him close to. We must have made too much noise because presently the caravan door opened and Tilly and the man put their heads out – discreet dressing-gowns by then. The dwarf said he'd caught a Peeping Tom. Tilly giggled. Let's see him, she said. The dwarf had been grinding my face in the dirt but when I stood up and she saw how young I was she laughed and said: "Reckon he's trying to pick up a few hints . . ."'

A long silence followed. The sun had gone behind a cloud and the cottage room had become as grey and lifeless as Tom's voice.

'That the end?' Gareth asked, somehow knowing it wasn't.

'Yes. Well, I reckon so. It's enough for a fine morning. Let's go outside.'

They went out. With a cloud overhead there was a nip in the air.

'I was a big lad,' Tom said. 'Even then. Maybe you remember.'

'You always looked big to me.'

'Maybe I looked big to her. I expect she thought I was about sixteen. I know when her boy friend had gone grumbling off she just stood there looking at me, and she put her arms up to push back her hair and her dressing-gown sleeves fell back and her arms were like long pale swans. And she said to the dwarf: "Fetch him in. If he wants a lesson I'll give him one."'

They walked slowly round the small garden. Two riders in black coats and bowler hats were coming slowly up the hill.

'What a thing,' said Gareth.

'I wasn't right for it, not really,' said Tom. 'Being just that bit too young and still half scared.' His face was pale in the cloud and his lips very tight as if they would hardly open. 'She was – a lot older than I thought – twenty-eight or nine probably – beautiful, oh, I'll grant you, but a devil. You hear of an older woman and a young man being the right way for it to happen. But it has to be an understanding older woman, not a devil, sniggering, taunting. She was that all right. What a baby, she kept sniggering, what a baby. Try this way. Try this other way. And so on. When I left, when at last I got away I felt as if I'd been – befouled, dragged through filth, eternally corrupted, like. I was sick three times before I got home. Mum – I don't know what she thought but all her anger seemed to go when she saw my face. I was laid up for three or four days after that, in bed. D'you remember?'

'No.'

'I never saw the circus go. I heard the hammering and the shouts and the creaking of waggons, but I never saw it go and I never saw Tilly again. Maybe it was just as well. It's best not to see your temple after it's – after it's turned into a sewer. They didn't come again while we were there – and of course about nine months later Mum took me north, and you, lucky devil, went to live with Uncle Ted . . .'

The riders had reached the cottage and as they passed Tom gave them a civil good morning. After they had passed Gareth said: 'Did you ever say anything to this Tilly about the clown you'd seen murdered?'

'No . . . It wasn't – that sort of a meeting . . .'

'Just as well.'

'Why?'

'She might have tried to shut you up for good, her and her mates.'

'Oh, I don't know . . .'

'Don't be too sure. After that night you might have been fertilizing a bit more of the common. People *can* disappear, even those with proper homes to go to.'

'Oh, I know that too well. But I didn't think of it at the time. But maybe she did kill something in me – something, I don't know what, a sense of the ideal – or – or a sense of love.'

They were silent. 'I remember well how difficult you were that last year in London. I do remember that. Think it triggered it off, like?'

'What off?'

'All that argy-bargy with the police. *I* could never please you either. Nor Mum. Like a dog that's sat on an ant's nest. It was chronic. So that when the family broke up I was desperate about losing her but glad enough I wouldn't have much to do with you.'

'Nor did you.'

'Nor did I.' Gareth looked up at his brother. 'But that's no reason why we shouldn't now. Think it over, man. There's a new life out there if you want to pick it up.'

Tom shook his head. 'I – make my own bed. And lie on it. It's time you were getting back, Gareth, they'll be out of church soon.'

'To hell with that. As if I cared.'

'I do. As I've told you.'

They talked for a few minutes more and then drifted to the gate. As he opened it Gareth said: 'I think you should have told the police. You know. After that bitch had treated you like that. What was stopping you?'

'I didn't care. I was too messed up to care. After they'd gone, when I'd got a bit better, I went and looked at the patch again. Often during the winter I often used to go and stare at it. It was like – looking at something of myself. That sound fanciful? Maybe. But it felt that way. Next summer the patch was green again. It taught me something about organic matter anyway – and too much about life, something maybe I've never been able to unlearn.'

Sunday lunch was finished and Jock Munster suggested they should go for a walk. This they did, the whole family, and a white terrier and a brown airedale and a young man attaching himself to the elder of the girls. It was a pleasant outing for Gareth, though it was long years since he had done anything quite like it. After they returned they had tea, and he and Jock stood smoking at the open French windows, talking business and arranging the deal that had almost been completed in London.

Out of the blue, his mind moving wilfully away from what they had been talking about, Gareth said suddenly: 'You've really got a great garden here. I met your gardener yesterday morning. Interesting bloke. He must be good.'

'Oh, Tom Preston. Yes ... He's more than good. Been here several years now. You ought to hear Eve talk about him. After the dismal procession we had before. Good gardeners are scarcer than gold.'

'Tom *Preston*, did you say?'

'Yes. He wins nearly all the prizes for us at the local show. The kitchen garden particularly *never* did anything before he came. Soil too clayey, they said. He gets fantastic results. Costs me a fortune in manures and fertilizers. Great believer in compost. What he puts in that heap of his is nobody's business. Look Gareth, about forward dates, in the present climate, with rates of exchange as they are ...'

Presently they went in as the air grew chilly, still talking business. The drawing room was a happy family scene. The elder daughter had gone out with her boy friend but Eve Munster was sitting beside the small bright fire doing tapestry, Phyllida was lying on her stomach reading the Sunday papers; one dog curled beside her, the other slept asthmatically on the rug before the fire. Gareth had a moment's nostalgia for an England he had never known. Then he thrust it away from him.

'Have you had him long?' he said, again irrelevantly.

'Who? Oh, Preston. Eve, I was telling Gareth what a find Preston was. Yes, we've had him over four years. Came alone out of the blue, no particular references, but after all gardeners don't really need them. Very honest, we find him, a bit John Blunt, but nobody minds that these days. And *such* a good gardener.'

'Miracles, what he's done,' said Eve, staring at her pattern. 'Particularly the kitchen garden, but really almost everything. Everybody says what wonderful soil you must have, but we haven't really. I daren't tell them it's all Preston's doing for they might try to steal him.'

Gareth Purdy went to look at some coffee table books near the window. He turned over several of them without seeing the pictures.

Into the enduring peaceful silence, Phyllida said:

'I see they haven't found that girl from Hailsham yet.'

'What girl?' asked her mother.

'Oh, that dizzy blonde, you remember. Went out the weekend before last and hasn't been seen since.'

Her mother said: 'Young people move around too much these days. They go off without even a hint to their parents.'

Phyllida said: 'The police are linking it with another girl, who disappeared from Eastbourne this time last year. And there was one the year before, the paper says, from Bexhill. They were all about twenty-two and all blonde, but I don't know if there's any other connection.'

Gareth did not get eight hours' sleep that night. In the morning they left early to avoid the traffic, but he saw the tall figure of Tom Purdy bent over his border. He did not go to speak to him. When he reached London Gareth hurriedly tidied up a number of outstanding matters and then rang Jock Munster to thank him for a delightful weekend and to say that circumstances had arisen which made it necessary for him to return to Australia at once.

# Where the Woodbine Twineth
## *Davis Grubb*

It was not that Nell hadn't done everything she could. Many's the windy, winter afternoon she had spent reading to the child from *Pilgrim's Progress* and Hadley's *Comportment for Young Ladies* and from the gilded, flowery leaves of *A Spring Garland of Noble Thoughts*. And she had countless times reminded the little girl that we must all strive to make ourselves useful in this Life and that five years old wasn't too young to begin to learn. Though none of it had helped. And there were times when Nell actually regretted ever taking in the curious, gold-haired child that tragic winter when Nell's brother Amos and his foolish wife had been killed. Eva stubbornly spent her days dreaming under the puzzle-tree or sitting on the stone steps of the ice-house making up tunes or squatting on the little square carpet stool in the dark parlour whispering softly to herself.

Eva! cried Nell one day, surprising her there. Who are you talking to?

To my friends, said Eva quietly, Mister Peppercorn and Sam and –

Eva! cried Nell. I will not have this nonsense any longer! You know perfectly well there's no one in this parlour but you!

They live under the davenport, explained Eva patiently. And behind the Pianola. They're very small so it's easy.

Eva! Hush that talk this instant! cried Nell.

You never believe me, sighed the child, when I tell you things are real.

They aren't real! said Nell. And I forbid you to make up such tales any longer! When I was a little girl I never had time for such mischievous nonsense. I was far too busy doing the bidding of my fine God-fearing parents and learning to be useful in this world!

Dusk was settling like a golden smoke over the willows down by the river shore when Nell finished pruning her roses that afternoon. And she was stripping off her white linen garden gloves on her way to the kitchen to see if Suse and Jessie had finished their Friday baking. Then she heard Eva speaking again, far off in the dark parlour, the voice quiet at first and then rising curiously, edged with terror.

Eva! cried Nell, hurrying down the hall, determined to put an end to the foolishness once and for all. Eva! Come out of that parlour this very instant!

Eva appeared in the doorway, her round face streaming and broken with grief, her fat, dimpled fist pressed to her mouth in grief.

*You* did it! the child shrieked. *You* did it!

Nell stood frozen, wondering how she could meet this.

They *heard* you! Eva cried, stamping her fat shoe on the bare, thin carpet. They heard you say you didn't want them to stay here! And now they've all gone away! *All* of them – Mister Peppercorn and Mingo and Sam and Popo!

Nell grabbed the child by the shoulders and began shaking her, not hard but with a mute, hysterical compulsion.

Hush up! cried Nell, thickly. Hush, Eva! Stop it this very instant!

You did it! wailed the golden child, her head lolling back in a passion of grief and bereavement. My *friends!* You made them go away!

All that evening Nell sat alone in her bedroom trembling with curious satisfaction. For punishment Eva had been sent to her room without supper and Nell sat listening now to the even, steady sobs far off down the hall. It was dark and on the river shore a night bird tried its note cautiously against the silence. Down in the pantry, the dishes done, Suse and Jessie, dark as night itself, drank coffee by the great stove and mumbled over stories of the old times before the War. Nell fetched her smelling salts and sniffed the frosted stopper of the flowered bottle till the trembling stopped.

Then, before the summer seemed half begun, it was late August. And one fine, sharp morning, blue with the smoke of burning leaves, the steamboat *Samantha Collins* docked at Cresap's Landing. Eva sat, as she had been sitting most of that summer, alone on the cool, worn steps of the ice-house, staring moodily at the daisies bobbing gently under the burden of droning, golden bees.

Eva! Nell called cheerfully from the kitchen window. Someone's coming today!

Eva sighed and said nothing, glowering mournfully at the puzzle-tree and remembering the wonderful stories that Mingo used to tell.

Grandfather's boat landed this morning, Eva! cried Nell. He's been all the way to New Orleans and I wouldn't be at all surprised if he brought his little girl a present!

Eva smelled suddenly the wave of honeysuckle that wafted sweet and evanescent from the tangled blooms on the stone wall and sighed, recalling the high, gay lilt to the voice of Mister Peppercorn when he used to sing her his enchanting songs.

Eva! called Nell again. Did you hear what Aunt Nell said? Your grandpa's coming home this afternoon!

Yes'm, said Eva lightly, hugging her fat knees and tucking her plain little skirt primly under her bottom.

And supper that night had been quite pleasant. Jessie made raspberry cobblers for the Captain and fetched in a prize ham from the meat-house, frosted and feathery with mould, and Suse had baked fresh that forenoon till the ripe, yeasty smell of hot bread seemed everywhere in the world. Nobody said a word while the Captain told of his trip to New Orleans and Eva listened to his stern old voice and remembered Nell's warnings never to interrupt when he was speaking and only to speak herself when spoken to. When supper was over the Captain sat back and sucked the coffee briskly from his white moustache. Then rising without a word he went to the chair by the crystal umbrella stand in the hallway and fetched back a long box wrapped in brown paper.

Eva's eyes rose slowly and shone over the rim of her cup.

I reckon this might be something to please a little girl, said the old man gruffly, thrusting the box into Eva's hands.

For me? whispered Eva.

Well now! grunted the Captain. I didn't fetch this all the way up the river from N'Orleans for any other girl in Cresap's Landing!

And presently string snapped and paper rustled expectantly and the cardboard box lay open at last and Eva stared at the creature which lay within, her eyes shining and wide with sheerest disbelief.

Numa! she whispered.

What did you say, Eva? said Nell. Don't mumble your words!

It's Numa! cried the child, searching both their faces for the wonder that was hers. They told me she'd be coming but I didn't know Grandpa was going to bring her! Mister Peppercorn said –.

Eva! whispered Nell.

Eva looked gravely at her grandfather, hoping not to seem too much of a tattle-tale, hoping that he would not deal too harshly with Nell for the fearful thing she had done that summer day.

Aunt Nell made them all go away, she began.

Nell leaned across the table clutching her linen napkin tight in her white knuckles.

Father! she whispered. Please don't discuss it with her! She's made up all this nonsense and I've been half out of my mind all this summer! First it was some foolishness about people who live under the davenport in the parlour –.

Eva sighed and stared at the gas-light winking brightly on her grandfather's watch chain and felt somewhere the start of tears.

It's really true, she said boldly. She never believes me when I tell her things are real. She made them all go away. But one day Mister Peppercorn came back. It was just for a minute. And he told me they were sending me Numa instead!

And then she fell silent and simply sat, heedless of Nell's shrill voice trying to explain. Eva sat staring with love and wonder at the Creole doll with the black, straight tresses and the lovely coffee skin.

Whatever the summer had been, the autumn, at least, had seemed the most wonderful season of Eva's life. In the fading afternoons of that dying Indian Summer she would sit by the hour, not brooding now, but holding the dark doll in her arms and weaving a shimmering spell of fancy all their own. And when September winds stirred, sharp and prescient with new seasons, Eva, clutching her dark new friend would tiptoe down the hallway to the warm, dark parlour and sit by the Pianola to talk some more.

Nell came down early from her afternoon nap one day and heard Eva's excited voice far off in the quiet house. She paused with her hand on the newel post, listening, half-wondering what the other sound might be, half-thinking it was the wind nudging itself wearily against the old white house. Then she peered in the parlour door.

Eva! said Nell. What are you doing?

It was so dark that Nell could not be certain of what she saw.

She went quickly to the window and threw up the shade.

Eva sat on the square carpet stool by the Pianola, her blue eyes blinking innocently at Nell and the dark doll staring vacuously up from the cardboard box beside her.

Who was here with you? said Nell. I distinctly heard two voices.

Eva sat silent, staring at Nell's stiff high shoes. Then her great eyes slowly rose.

You never believe me, the child whispered, when I tell you things are real.

Old Suse, at least, understood things perfectly.

How's the scampy baby doll grandpappy brought you, lamb? the old Negro woman said that afternoon as she perched on the high stool by the pump, paring apples for a pie. Eva squatted comfortably on the floor with Numa and watched the red and white rind curl neatly from Suse's quick, dark fingers.

Life is hard! Eva sighed philosophically. Yes oh yes! Life is hard! That's what Numa says!

Such talk for a youngster! Suse grunted, plopping another white quarter of fruit into the pan of spring water. What you studyin' about Life for! And you only five!

Numa tells me, sighed Eva, her great blue eyes far away. Oh yes! She really does! She says if Aunt Nell ever makes her go away she'll take me with her!

Take you! chuckled Suse, brushing a blue-bottle from her arm. Take you where?

Where the woodbine twineth, sighed Eva.

Which place? said Suse, cocking her head.

Where the woodbine twineth, Eva repeated patiently.

I declare! Suse chuckled. I never done heard tell of *that* place!

Eva cupped her chin in her hands and sighed reflectively.

Sometimes, she said presently. We just talk. And sometimes we play.

What y'all play? asked Suse, obligingly.

Doll, said Eva. Oh yes, we play doll. Sometimes Numa gets tired of being doll and I'm the doll and she puts me in the box and plays with me!

She waved her hand casually to show Suse how really simple it all was.

Suse eyed her sideways with twinkling understanding, the laughter struggling behind her lips.

She puts *you* in that little bitty box? said Suse. And *you*'s a doll?

Yes oh yes! said Eva. She really does! May I have an apple, Suse?

When she had peeled and rinsed it, Sue handed Eva a whole, firm Northern Spy.

Don't you go and spoil your supper now, lamb! she warned.

Oh! cried Eva. It's not for me. It's for Numa!

And she put the dark doll in the box and stumped off out the back door to the puzzle-tree.

Nell came home from choir practice at five that afternoon and found the house so silent that she wondered for a moment if Suse or Jessie had taken Eva down to the landing to watch the evening Packet pass. The kitchen was empty and silent except for the thumping of a pot on the stove and Nell went out into the yard and stood listening by the rose arbour. Then she heard Eva's voice. And through the falling light she saw them then, beneath the puzzle-tree.

Eva! cried Nell. Who is that with you!

Eva was silent as Nell's eyes strained to piece together the shadow and substance of the dusk. She ran quickly down the lawn to the puzzle-tree. But only Eva was there. Off in the river the evening Packet blew dully for the bend. Nell felt the wind, laced with autumn, stir the silence round her like a web.

Eva! said Nell. I distinctly saw another child with you! Who was it?

Eva sighed and sat cross-legged in the grass with the long box and the dark doll beside her.

You never believe me –, she began softly, staring guiltily at the apple core in the grass.

Eva! cried Nell, brushing a firefly roughly from her arm so that it left a smear of dying gold. I'm going to have an end to this nonsense right now!

And she picked up the doll in the cardboard box and started towards the house. Eva screamed in terror.

Numa! she wailed.

You may cry all you please, Eva! said Nell. But you may not have your doll until you come to me and admit that you don't really believe all this nonsense about fairies and imaginary people!

Numa! screamed Eva, jumping up and down in the grass and beating her fists against her bare, grass-stained knees, Numa!

I'm putting this box on top of the Pianola, Eva, said Nell. And I'll fetch it down again when you confess to me that there was another child playing with you this afternoon. I cannot countenance falsehoods!

Numa said, screamed Eva, that if you made her go away –!

I don't care to hear another word! said Nell, walking ahead of the wailing child up the dark lawn towards the house.

But the words sprang forth like Eva's very tears. – She'd take me away with her! she screamed.

Not another word! said Nell. Stop your crying and go up to your room and get undressed for bed!

And she went into the parlour and placed the doll box on top of the Pianola next to the music rolls.

A week later the thing ended. And years after that autumn night Nell, mad and simpering, would tell the tale again and stare at the pitying, doubting faces in the room around her and she would whimper to them in a parody of the childish voice of Eva herself: You never believe me when I tell you things are real!

It was a pleasant September evening and Nell had been to a missionary meeting with Nan Snyder that afternoon and she had left Nan at her steps and was hurrying up the tanbark walk by the ice-house when she heard the prattling laughter of Eva far back in the misty shadows of the lawn. Nell ran swiftly into the house to the parlour – to the Pianola. The doll box was not there. She hurried to the kitchen door and peered out through the netting into the dusky river evening. She did not call to Eva then but went out and stripped a willow switch from the little tree by the stone wall and tip-toed softly down the lawn. A light wind blew from the river meadows, heavy and sweet with wetness, like the breath of cattle. They were laughing and joking together as Nell crept soundlessly upon them, speaking low as children do, with wild, delicious intimacy, and then bubbling high with laughter that cannot be contained. Nell approached silently, feeling the dew soak through to her ankles, clutching the switch tightly in her hand. She stopped and listened for a moment, for suddenly there was but one voice now, a low and wonderfully lyric sound that was not the voice of Eva. Then Nell stared wildly down through the misshapen leaves of the puzzle-tree and saw the dark child sitting with the doll box in its lap.

So! cried Nell, stepping suddenly through the canopy of leaves. You're the darkie child who's been sneaking up here to play with Eva!

The child put the box down and jumped to its feet with a low cry of fear as Nell sprang forward, the willow switch flailing furiously about the dark ankles.

Now scat! cried Nell. Get on home where you belong and don't ever come back!

For an instant the dark child stared in horror first at Nell and then at the doll box, its sorrowing, somnolent eyes brimming with wild words and a grief for which it had no tongue, its lips trembling as if there were something Nell should know that she might never learn again after that autumn night was gone.

Go on, I say! Nell shouted, furious.

The switch flickered about the dark arms and legs faster than ever. And suddenly with a cry of anguish the dark child turned and fled through the tall grass towards the meadow and the willows on the river shore. Nell stood trembling for a moment, letting the rage ebb slowly from her body.

Eva! she called out presently. Eva!

There was no sound but the dry steady racket of the frogs by the landing.

Eva! cried Nell. You're going to get a good switching for this!

A night bird in the willow tree by the stone wall cried once and started up into the still, affrighted dark. Nell did not call again for, suddenly, like the mood of the autumn night, the very sound of her voice had begun to frighten her. And when she was in the kitchen Nell screamed so loudly that Suse and Jessie, long asleep in their shack down below the ice-house, woke wide and stared wondering into the dark. Nell stared for a long moment after she had screamed, not believing, really, for it was at once so perfect and yet so unreal. Trembling violently Nell ran back out onto the lawn.

Come back! screamed Nell hoarsely into the tangled far off shadows by the river. Come back! Oh please! Please come back!

But the dark child was gone forever. And Nell, creeping back at last to the kitchen, whimpering and slack-mouthed, looked again at the lovely little dreadful creature in the doll box: the gold-haired, plaster Eva with the eyes too blue to be real.

# Waking or Sleeping

*Willis Hall*

Breakfast-times had been getting progressively more difficult for some months now, and Emily knew, instinctively, that this morning would prove no exception. Reggie accepted the bowl of cornflakes without a word, splashed fresh milk all over them, and then sat staring at the bowl without even bothering to pick up his spoon. A few moments later he pushed the bowl of cereal away. Emily was not at all annoyed, but sat staring at her husband, sympathetically, over the teapot.

'It happened again then, last night?' she said.

Reggie nodded his head, slowly, without looking up.

'Why don't you call in and see Doctor Attercliffe on your way home from the office tonight?' asked Emily.

This time, Reggie Wormald shook his head, forced a wry smile, and selected a piece of medium-brown toast from the chromium toastrack. He buttered the toast, nibbled along one edge, pensively, and then that too was put to one side along with the cornflakes.

'Was it the same as always?' said Emily.

'It's *always* the same as always.' Reggie's temper was short and he spoke pettishly. 'It's the same bad dream – *exactly* the same – every night.'

'You didn't have it the night before last, dear,' Emily pointed out.

'No. But I had it the night before that, *and* the night before that.'

'And last night again?'

'*Yes!*'

'Oh, dear!' Emily's voice expressed concern. 'Was it *exactly* the same as the other times? Were you locked up in that awful cage again? In that horrible cellar?'

'It's a sort of dungeon. I've told you often enough. It's a medieval dungeon – not just a cellar.' Mr Wormald chewed at his lower lip, suffering the memory.

'I really think it *would* be a good idea if you popped into the doctor's this evening, Reggie.'

'And tell him what?'

'Why, tell him the truth. Tell him about the dreadful dream you keep on having. Tell him you've lost your appetite; tell him you're losing weight. Goodness, I should think he'll only need to look at you to know that *something's* wrong. You're so drawn – *and* peaky.'

Reggie Wormald 'harrumphed' non-committally and thought to himself that 'peaky' was hardly the adjective that he would use to describe the mental torture he suffered during his sleeping hours. But he kept the thought to himself. 'And what do you think Doctor Attercliffe will be able to do for me?' he said aloud.

'Why, prescribe something,' said Emily. 'Something to take – probably a tonic.'

'I *don't want* a tonic.'

'You most certainly need *something*,' said Emily, pursuing her theme relentlessly. 'Doctor Attercliffe will diagnose what's wrong with you, and give you something for it.'

'I *know* what's wrong with me,' said Reggie. He paused and let out a deeply-felt long-suffering sigh, before continuing: 'And I can hardly take up the valuable time of an extremely busy general practitioner, simply because I'm suffering from nightmares.'

'Night*mare*, dear,' Emily Wormald corrected her husband. 'The same horrid nightmare almost every night of the week. It's obviously something . . . well, something in your mind, Reggie. Doctor Attercliffe will probably think that it might be good for you to see a . . . a specialist.'

Mr Wormald clattered his cup noisily in his saucer and blew out his cheeks. 'What absolute rubbish, Emily,' he said. 'The fact that I'm having a recurring bad dream is not necessarily a sign that I'm ready for the nut-hatch.'

'I didn't say it was, dear.'

'You said that I needed a psychiatrist.'

'No, I didn't, Reggie – '

'Yes, you did – '

'*No*,' Emily's voice was firm though quiet. 'I said "specialist". All I said was that there's obviously *something* wrong with you.'

'Most probably indigestion,' said Reggie.

Emily, taking her husband's last remark as an intended slight upon her own cooking, rose from the table, and maintained a dignified silence.

The subject was considered closed.

Mr Wormald left for the office a few minutes later. He did not call in and see Doctor Attercliffe on his way home. That same evening, Mrs Wormald cooked the lightest of meals: steamed halibut and a milk pudding.

Mr Wormald ate the food without once referring to the nightmares or even to his digestion. The meal passed almost in silence. After dinner, Reggie decided against watching the television news – for fear that some disaster might have taken place that could set his subconscious thoughts racing. He went up to bed just after ten-thirty, taking with him a P. G. Wodehouse novel and, with only the slightest feeling of trepidation, he switched off his bedside lamp at a quarter to eleven.

A beam of moonlight stole into the bedroom through a gap in the curtains. Reggie Wormald paused only to cast a resentful glance at Emily, who lay sleeping soundly at his side, and then he put his balding head on the pillow and tried to channel his mind into thinking comfortable thoughts.

It was well over an hour before he fell into a restless sleep.

*He started, fearfully, aware that he was waking yet again from a fitful and uncomfortable doze. How long, he wondered, had his eyes been closed? An hour? A minute? Less than a minute? Certainly not more than an hour – for in the narrow confines of the metal cage, complete sleep was utterly impossible.*

*At first, as always, as consciousness returned, he was aware only of the chill and clammy damp that seemed to seep from the rags he was wearing through his flesh and into the very marrow of his bones. He held his breath and bit his lip in terror and foreboding of the pain that he knew was yet to come. And then it came, the cramp biting into his body like ugly, jagged knife-cuts. A scream shrilled out in the darkness and it occurred to him that it was his mouth that was open and that the scream was coming from somewhere at the back of his own throat. The only light came from the flickering torch on the wall. Not that he needed light. For in those awful, painful waking moments, his world consisted only of the narrow cage in which he was contained and he was fully aware of every single metal strip that formed the cage – for each and every one gnawed at his flesh. And he knew, by now, that in time the unbearable pain would become bearable and when it did, mercifully, that he might even doze again.*

*He tried to stretch his neck. It was an instinctive movement, for he knew full well by dint of long experience that the cage was far too small for him to hold his head upright. He was imprisoned in the cage with his knees tucked tight up against his chest and his head, locked, permanently it seemed, slightly to one side. His head, in fact, had grown almost accustomed to this awkward position – although the throbbing cramp in his neck was there all the time. Except, of course, for those precious moments, or minutes, or hours, during which he dozed. He had not the faintest idea how long he had been in the cage – apart from knowing that it had been a long time – but he did not know whether that time stretched into months or years.*

Sometimes, in the still of the night, he would awaken from his dream. Not for long, but long enough for him to become aware of familiar sounds in the darkness of the room and beyond. The fretful whisper of the electric clock on his bedside table. The oh-so-regular breathing of Emily, sound asleep at his side. The faint sigh of the night wind in the branches of the cedar tree outside the bedroom window. And sometimes, should he remain awake long enough, he began to distinguish familiar objects, too, as his eyes became accustomed to the dark. The dark grey line that was the window-ledge. A pale streak of light caught in the full-length wall mirror on moonlit nights. But then he would be sucked back into sleep again; pulled back in at the edges of his constant dream . . .

*With extreme difficulty, he could move his rump a couple of inches on the rusting strips of metal that formed the base of the cage. Not that it gave him pleasure to move, for each time he did so it was as if a thousand needle-points gouged at his skin. But only by moving occasionally, by proving that he could shift himself no matter how slightly, was he able to convince himself that he was actually still alive.*

*And every time he moved, the cage swung an inch or two, groaning a complaint on the rusty hook which was attached to the length of chain that disappeared in the darkness up above his head where he sensed, rather than saw, the dank, vaulted ceiling that formed the farthest edges of his universe. Beneath the cage, some three feet away, lay the damp, glistening, cold slab dungeon floor.*

*In addition to being able to shift his backside slightly, he could also raise his hands sufficiently to get them to his mouth, albeit with difficulty. It was good that he could do this, for otherwise it would not be possible for him to feed himself whenever the old woman brought him food. Thinking of food gave him a gnawing pain in the tight hollow that had once been his stomach and the thought also brought saliva to his mouth.*

*He tried to concentrate his mind on the old woman herself, and not on the scraps of food she brought with her. He wondered how long it was since the old woman had last been and, much more important, how long it would be before she came again? He had never been able to make up his mind as to whether she paid her visits to him regularly or irregularly. If she came to him regularly, how long was it between her visits? Two days? Three days, even? And if she visited him irregularly, how long was the longest period she had left him alone with the pain and the dreadful thought that she was never coming back again? Four days? Five days? Even a week?*

*He did not know. He did not know who she was or where she came from or if she fed other prisoners out there in the dark corridors beyond the pale circle of light from the flickering torch. What language did she speak? Was it the same as the one that he had once used himself? And, if so, what language was that? For he had been hunched in the cage for so long now that he had no longer any use for words, or any recollection of a previous life before the cage. Occasionally, he made sounds. He grunted with pleasure when the old woman arrived with her scraps. He whimpered with sorrow sometimes whenever some of those same scraps fell from his clumsy fingers through the bottom of the cage on to the floor beneath, to be seized upon, almost immediately, by the scuttling, scuffling rats.*

*The old woman was the only contact that he had with the outside world – if there was an outside world. But in all the time that he had been in the cage, he had never had any communication of any sort with the crone. In all the years of his imprisonment, she had never so much as offered him one word, either in kindness or in anger. She had never once looked into his eyes.*

*In that dark part of his mind that contained the past, he seemed to recollect, vaguely, that there had been a time when he* had *tried to communicate with the old woman. But, if his memory did not play him false, it seemed that she had never so much as intimated, in any way, that she had even* heard, *let alone understood.*

*He wondered too, occasionally, why it was that the old woman brought him his scraps and filled his leather mug with water? He had never heard of a woman jailor. Sometimes, he even wondered if she was his jailor? Perhaps she was a benefactress? For without the scraps she brought him, he would surely die. Perhaps she had taken the task upon herself? Perhaps she was just an old, old woman, without the means to free him from his cage, but who brought him the scraps she garnered from somewhere whenever she was able? Perhaps this was the only kindness she was capable of bestowing in the entire world?*

*And then again, on the other hand, could it be counted as a kindness to keep him alive in all this wretchedness? No, it was not a kindness. The old woman was not a friend, she was his jailor right enough. If she were a friend, the only possible act of kindness would be for her never to come to him again ...* He didn't mean it! *His cramped, pained body cried out to God, denying the lie. And, please, dear God, let her bring him the scraps soon! His belly ached for food and his parched, white lips were cracked in a dozen places for the want of water.*

*He shifted again and the harsh metal bars of the floor of the cage jarred through the thin layer of rump-flesh and grated along his bones.*

Sometimes, in the middle quiet of the night, he found himself in that half-sleeping, half-waking world where dreams and reality were mingled. He was in the cage, but it was not the old woman that brought him food, but the comforting figure of Emily, in a rose pink nightgown, sitting beside him in the cage and holding a polished wood tray, covered with a snow white cloth, and containing buttered toast and a pot of tea for one, neatly arranged with milk jug and sugar bowl and a starched white napkin in his own, familiar napkin ring. Or, again, he was stretched out cosily in his own warm bed but it was the old crone standing over him, with the greasy scraps of food in one hand and the cracked filthy water jug in the other. And sometimes, on such occasions, he woke to the slow recognition of his bedroom, with the quiet whirring of the electric clock and the reassuring regularity of Emily's breathing. On other more cruel occasions though, he did not wake, but drifted back into the awful dream world of the rusty chain groaning above his head and the shrilly whispering rats below his cage ...

*The sound of tiny feet scampering off into the darkness brought him out of his reverie and back into the awareness of the pain of the cage, but his heart rose in his skinny frame because he knew that the old woman was coming. A few seconds later, he heard the shuffle of her rag-bound feet across the dungeon floor. His dry, parched mouth was swelling up from the back of his throat at the thought of food.*

*He struggled to control his shaking hands, forcing them to obey the warning signals that his brain was sending out. He scrabbled urgently at the bottom of the cage for the leather mug and the bony fingers of one hand clutched at its handle. He willed his thin, scarecrow arm to raise the mug up, chest-high, before the old woman arrived. He jerked his other hand up past his body and his fingers spread out, slowly, awkwardly, instinctively after years of practice, into the position that was exactly the right one in which to catch the scraps of food – not too wide apart or the scraps would tumble through the gaps between; not too close together or some of the precious crumbs might spill over the side of his palm and out through the cage, on to the floor, to be snapped up hungrily by the scavenging rats.*

*The old woman arrived. He could just make out the lank tangle of grey greasy hair that fell over her face. He could dimly see the threadbare rags – no better than his own in fact – that hung from her grimy, wrinkled shoulders. He knew that he was whimpering quietly, like a helpless animal, but he could not stop himself even though he was ashamed. As always, the old woman paid him not the slightest attention.*

*The manner in which the old crone gave him his food was always the same. First, she thrust the neck of the jug between the bars of the cage, tipped it up, and filled the leather mug in his shaking hand. Next, she pushed her own leathery fist, containing the scraps of food, between the bars and then dropped them into his open palm. It was a routine that they had played out together countless times, a routine that never varied, and yet on each and every occasion that it took place, it proved a terrifying and nerve-wracking experience for him.*

*Supposing the hand that held the mug was shaking so much the contents spilled over and trickled to the floor before he could raise them to his lips? What if he were to misjudge the width of the spaces between his outstretched fingers, or supposing the scraps of food were smaller than usual – either of these instances might easily result in him losing precious pieces of the only sustenance that would come his way for a couple of days at least, much longer perhaps.*

*But on this occasion, everything went according to plan. In one shaking hand he held a mug full of water; in his other fist he clutched the greasy scraps of food. The old woman shuffled away as silently as she had come. He was left to consider the treasure she had given him, and to decide in which way he would dispose of it. It was always a difficult decision, but one that he thoroughly enjoyed deliberating over. Whether to wolf down the scraps immediately and sip the water afterwards, slowly; or should he gulp down the water first, leaving the scraps in his lap to be nibbled at leisure? He usually chose the latter course, for it was easier to safeguard the scraps than it was to hold the mug of water on his trembling lap.*

*Settling himself gradually, keenly anticipating the feast to come, he held the mug close to his chest protectively with one hand, while he lowered the other and carefully placed the bits of food between his hunched legs. He sat as still as he was able for several moments, enjoying the possession of his hoard with miserly greed. Then, unable to hold back any longer, he slowly lifted the mug of water to his mouth and allowed the contents to dribble down his throat.*

*It was in this moment that disaster struck.*

*A single cunning rat, it seemed, had not scuttled off across the floor with its fellows when the old woman had arrived, but had hugged the wall, silently waiting its chance. The scent of food had drifted down from the prisoner's lap and crept into the rat's twitching nostrils. Now, suddenly, twisting and arching its body as it rose in an attempt to force itself clean through the bars at the bottom of the cage, the rat leapt upwards and its hard snout struck him at the back of his thigh. It was by no means the first time that a rat had attempted its way into the cage, but on this occasion it was totally unexpected.*

*He flinched, jerked at his leg, and the precious food-scraps spilled from his lap and tumbled on to the bottom of the cage, some of them falling straight to the floor, others rolling on the metal bars before slipping through, beyond his reach. He let out a wild, strangled cry that pierced the darkness of the dungeon. Then, as he scrabbled in desperation with his free hand in an attempt to retrieve what food-scraps he could, the trembling hand that held the mug loosed its hold and his water spilled to the ground.*

*There was an ever-tightening knot in the pit of his stomach; his tongue was thick and dry and clung to the roof of his mouth. A moment ago he had owned both food and water, and now he had neither. Nothing. Nothing at all. It would be days – an eternity, it seemed – before the old woman came again.*

*Beneath the cage, the rat had dropped to the ground again and, to add to his hunger and frustration, he could hear the razor-teeth shearing into his food. The rat was attempting to devour all the scraps before the rest of the rat-pack returned. Already there was the brisk if tentative patter of needle-sharp claws across the slab floor.*

*His head sank even further on to his chest and his whole body shook with self-pity. Had there been moisture to spare inside his head there would have been tears running down the hollows of his cheeks. He gave himself entirely to the despair that had been at his shoulder, it seemed, since time began.*

'Reggie? . . . Reggie?'

He opened his eyes, blinked, and closed them again against the unexpected glare of sunlight.

'Are you sure you're all right, dear?' said Emily.

He opened his eyes again, narrower this time. Emily's face swam into focus. She was sitting in bed beside him, fiddling with the automatic tea-maker and looking down at him anxiously. He darted his glance about the room, taking in familiar objects, returning to reality, trying hard to dispel the terror that he knew was still visible in his face.

'I couldn't wake you, Reggie.' There was an accusatory note to Emily's voice. 'I couldn't – really I couldn't. I tried. You were making horrid noises, sort of in your throat – and sobbing. I tried three times to wake you, but it was no use.'

'I'm all right now,' he said, but the voice did not sound like his own.

'It was that nightmare again, wasn't it?'

'Yes.'

'It's no good, you know, Reggie,' Emily said, firmly. 'You really will have to see someone about it.'

He nodded, shivered at a sudden vivid recollection of the dream, and pulled himself up in bed. 'I'll call in at the doctor's on my way home from the office tonight,' he said.

'Not before time,' said Emily, handing him a cup of tea in a gold-rimmed teacup. 'It *is* sweetened, but not stirred.'

Doctor Attercliffe beamed at Mr Wormald across his surgery roll-top desk. 'Nightmares, eh? Well, well, well. We must put a stop to those chappies, mustn't we?'

'It's a night*mare*, doctor,' said Mr Wormald. 'It's always the same one. I'm suspended in a sort of medieval cage and –'

'Mmmm, mmmm,' said Doctor Attercliffe, scribbling illegibly on a prescription form; frowning slightly at the chatter that was coming up from the fifteen to twenty other patients that were still needing attention in the waiting room. 'That's not at all unusual, to keep on having the same bad dream, you know.'

'But it's so – *vivid*,' said Mr Wormald.

'Mmmm, mmmm,' muttered Doctor Attercliffe, handing the prescription to Mr Wormald. 'Those little beggars should do the trick. Take one at night, fifteen minutes before you go to bed. I've put you down for a dozen, but don't complete the course if you find that two or three nights of them have put you back in top form.'

Mr Wormald looked down at the prescription he was holding. 'I don't really have trouble in getting to sleep,' he said.

'Course you don't – course you don't,' said Doctor Attercliffe. 'But what you need is the right *kind* of sleep. Those little devils will put your spark out. Give me a ring at the end of the week, let me know how you're suited. Ask the next poor benighted blighter to come in, on your way out, would you?'

Mr Wormald had egg mayonnaise, green salad, and stewed apples and custard for dinner that night.

At ten-fifteen he took one of the red pills that Doctor Attercliffe had prescribed, and at half past ten he was in bed.

'What did the doctor say those pills would do for you?' asked Emily who, as usual, was in bed before her husband.

'He said they'd put my spark out,' said Reggie.

'Good,' said Emily. 'I'm sure the doctor knows best.' And she placed her woman's magazine on her bedside table and switched off her bedside lamp.

Mr Wormald switched off his light too, and settled his head on the pillow, hopefully but not entirely without doubts.

*The prisoner in the cage awoke, shivering violently. As always, he prepared himself for the violent cramp that he knew would bite into his body almost at once. But, after all these years, he was ready for it – used to it, in fact. He had dozed and awakened; dozed and awakened; day in, day out; month after week and year after month until now there was nothing that mattered beyond the narrow, rusting metal strips that made up the cage in which he ate and slept and lived. He no longer cared particularly about the old woman – if she came, all well and good; but if she seemed to stay away for days on end, he was prepared to wait. After all, what else was there to do but wait?*

He no longer awakened from the dream. There were no more brief night-time excursions into that bedroom and the bed he had once shared – ages ago – with the woman called Emily. All that was in the far distant past.

*The prisoner shifted, slightly, on the bottom of the cage, causing the whole metal structure to groan, complainingly, on the hook and chain by which it hung from the vaulted ceiling.*

*Beneath the cage, across the dungeon floor, he could hear the urgent, familiar pit-pat of tiny claws and the shrill whispers of the rat-pack. But he had long since ceased to care about the rats. He had grown too wily over the years to allow them to steal his food and his existence and theirs were two entirely separate things. They lived outside the cage; he belonged within. He moved his backside again, half an inch at the most, for, with time, he had finally come to terms with living in the cage. The man who owns a forty acre park may take great pleasure in walking across his domain – the man who lives inside a cage experiences supreme joy in shifting his backside an inch, even though it may also cause excruciating pain.*

He never returned again now to that half-sleeping, half-waking world where dreams and reality were mingled.

The cage was reality.

Somehow, at some time, the dream had become reality. Reality had become the dream, and the dream had long since ceased to exist. No matter. He was not even aware that there ever had been any other world than the narrow one he lived in.

*He was in the cage. The cage was his world. He would remain there for ever and all time. He sat quite still, gazing out at the darkness that was his sky. He smiled to himself. Things, after all, were not too bad. For the next couple of hours, he decided, he would think about the old woman, and after that – yes, why not? – he would shift his backside one half inch.*

# Someone in the Lift

## L.P. Hartley

'There's someone coming down in the lift, Mummy!'

'No, my darling, you're wrong, there isn't.'

'But I can see him through the bars – a tall gentleman.'

'You think you can, but it's only a shadow. Now you'll see, the lift's empty.'

And it always was.

This piece of dialogue, or variations of it, had been repeated at intervals ever since Mr and Mrs Maldon and their son Peter had arrived at the Brompton Court Hotel, where, owing to a domestic crisis, they were going to spend Christmas. New to hotel life, the little boy had never seen a lift before and he was fascinated by it. When either of his parents pressed the button to summon it he would take up his stand some distance away to watch it coming down.

The ground floor had a high ceiling so the lift was visible for some seconds before it touched floor level and it was then, at its first appearance, that Peter saw the figure. It was always in the same place, facing him in the left-hand corner. He couldn't see it plainly, of course, because of the double grille, the gate of the lift and the gate of the lift-shaft, both of which had to be firmly closed before the lift would work.

He had been told not to use the lift by himself – an unnecessary warning, because he connected the lift with the things that grown-up people did, and unlike most small boys he wasn't over anxious to share the privileges of his elders: he was content to wonder and admire. The lift appealed to him more as magic than as mechanism. Acceptance of magic made it possible for him to believe that the lift had an occupant when he first saw it, in spite of the demonstrable fact that when it came to rest, giving its fascinating click of finality, the occupant had disappeared.

'If you don't believe me, ask Daddy,' his mother said.

Peter didn't want to do this, and for two reasons, one of which was easier to explain than the other.

'Daddy would say I was being silly,' he said.

'Oh no, he wouldn't, he never says you're silly.'

This was not quite true. Like all well-regulated modern fathers, Mr Maldon was aware of the danger of offending a son of tender years: the psychological results might be regrettable. But Freud or no Freud, fathers are still fathers, and sometimes when Peter irritated him Mr Maldon would let fly. Although he was fond of him, Peter's private vision of his father was of someone more authoritative and awe-inspiring than a stranger, seeing them together, would have guessed.

The other reason, which Peter didn't divulge, was more fantastic. He hadn't asked his father because, when his father was with him, he couldn't see the figure in the lift.

Mrs Maldon remembered the conversation and told her husband of it. 'The lift's in a dark place,' she said, 'and I dare say he does see something, he's so much nearer to the ground than we are. The bars may cast a shadow and make a sort of pattern that we can't see. I don't know if it's frightening him, but you might have a word with him about it.'

At first Peter was more interested than frightened. Then he began to evolve a theory. If the figure only appeared in his father's absence, didn't it follow that the figure might be, could be, must be, his own father? In what region of his consciousness Peter believed this it would be hard to say; but for imaginative purposes he did believe it and the figure became for him 'Daddy in the lift'. The thought of Daddy in the lift did frighten him, and the neighbourhood of the lift-shaft, in which he felt compelled to hang about, became a place of dread.

Christmas Day was drawing near and the hotel began to deck itself with evergreens. Suspended at the foot of the staircase, in front of the lift, was a bunch of mistletoe, and it was this that gave Mr Maldon his idea.

As they were standing under it, waiting for the lift, he said to Peter:

'Your mother tells me you've seen someone in the lift who isn't there.'

His voice sounded more accusing than he meant it to, and Peter shrank.

'Oh, not now,' he said, truthfully enough. 'Only sometimes.'

'Your mother told me that you always saw it,' his father said, again more sternly than he meant to. 'And do you know who I think it may be?'

Caught by a gust of terror Peter cried, 'Oh, please don't tell me!'

'Why, you silly boy,' said his father reasonably. 'Don't you want to know?'

Ashamed of his cowardice, Peter said he did.

'Why, it's Father Christmas, of course!'

Relief surged through Peter.

'But doesn't Father Christmas come down the chimney?' he asked.

'That was in the old days. He doesn't now. Now he takes the lift!'

Peter though a moment.

'Will you dress up as Father Christmas this year,' he asked, 'even though it's an hotel?'

'I might.'

'And come down in the lift?'

'I shouldn't wonder.'

After this Peter felt happier about the shadowy passenger behind the bars. Father Christmas couldn't hurt anyone, even if he was (as Peter now believed him to be) his own father. Peter was only six but he could remember two Christmas Eves when his father had dressed up as Santa Claus and given him a delicious thrill. He could hardly wait for this one, when the apparition in the corner would at last become a reality.

Alas, two days before Christmas Day the lift broke down. On every floor it served, and there were five (six counting the basement), the forbidding notice 'Out of Order' dangled from the door-handle. Peter complained as loudly as anyone, though secretly, he couldn't have told why, he was glad that the lift no longer functioned; and he didn't mind climbing the four flights to his room, which opened out of his parents' room but had its own door too. By using the stairs he met the workmen (he never knew on which floor they would be) and from them gleaned the latest news about the lift crisis. They were working overtime, they told him, and were just as anxious as he to see the last of the job. Sometimes they even told each other to put a jerk into it. Always Peter asked them when they would be finished, and they always answered, 'Christmas Eve at latest.'

Peter didn't doubt this. To him the workmen were infallible, possessed of magic powers capable of suspending the ordinary laws that governed lifts. Look how they left the gates open, and shouted to each other up and down the awesome lift-shaft, paying as little attention to the other hotel visitors as if they didn't exist! Only to Peter did they vouchsafe a word.

But Christmas Eve came, the morning passed, the afternoon passed, and still the lift didn't go. The men were working with set faces and a controlled hurry in their movements; they didn't even return Peter's 'Good night' when he passed them on his way to bed. Bed! He had begged to be allowed to stay up this once for dinner; he knew he wouldn't go to sleep, he said, till Father Christmas came. He lay awake, listening to the urgent voices of the men, wondering if each hammer-stroke would be the last; and then, just as the clamour was subsiding, he dropped off.

Dreaming, he felt adrift in time. Could it be midnight? No, because his parents had after all consented to his going down to dinner. Now was the time. Averting his eyes from the forbidden lift he stole downstairs. There was a clock in the hall, but it had stopped. In the dining-room there was another clock; but dared he go into the dining-room alone, with no one to guide him and everybody looking at him?

He ventured in, and there, at their table, which he couldn't always pick out, he saw his mother. She saw him, too, and came towards him, threading her way between the tables as if they were just bits of furniture, not alien islands under hostile sway.

'Darling,' she said, 'I couldn't find you – nobody could, but here you are!' She led him back and they sat down. 'Daddy will be with us in a minute.' The minutes passed; suddenly there was a crash. It seemed to come from within, from the kitchen perhaps. Smiles lit up the faces of the diners. A man at a nearby table laughed and said, 'Something's on the floor! Somebody'll be for it!' 'What is it?' whispered Peter, too excited to speak aloud. 'Is anyone hurt?' 'Oh, no, darling, somebody's dropped a tray, that's all.'

To Peter it seemed an anti-climax, this paltry accident that had stolen the thunder of his father's entry, for he didn't doubt that his father would come in as Father Christmas. The suspense was unbearable. 'Can I go into the hall and wait for him?' His mother hesitated and then said yes.

The hall was deserted, even the porter was off duty. Would it be fair, Peter wondered, or would it be cheating and doing himself out of a surprise, if he waited for Father Christmas by the lift? Magic has its rules which mustn't be disobeyed. But he was there now, at his old place in front of the lift; and the lift would come down if he pressed the button.

He knew he mustn't, that it was forbidden, that his father would be angry if he did; yet he reached up and pressed it.

But nothing happened, the lift didn't come, and why? Because some careless person had forgotten to shut the gates – 'monkeying with the lift,' his father called it. Perhaps the workmen had forgotten, in their hurry to get home. There was only one thing to do – find out on which floor the gates had been left open, and then shut them.

On their own floor it was, and in his dream it didn't seem strange to Peter that the lift wasn't there, blocking the black hole of the lift-shaft, though he daren't look down it. The gates clicked to. Triumph possessed him, triumph lent him wings; he was back on the ground floor, with his finger on the button. A thrill of power such as he had never known ran through him when the machinery answered to his touch.

But what was this? The lift was coming up from below, not down from above, and there was something wrong with its roof – a jagged hole that let the light through. But the figure was there in its accustomed corner, and this time it hadn't disappeared, it was still there, he could see it through the mazy criss-cross of the bars, a figure in a red robe with white fur edges, and wearing a red cowl on its head: his father, Father Christmas, Daddy in the lift. But why didn't he look at Peter, and why was his white beard streaked with red?

The two grilles folded back when Peter pushed them. Toys were lying at his father's feet, but he couldn't touch them for they too were red, red and wet as the floor of the lift, red as the jag of lightning that tore through his brain . . .

# The Peculiar Case of
# Mrs Grimmond

## Dorothy K. Haynes

Now, at last, I am able to concentrate on Nicky. When he first came, there was Deil to consider, Deil, my cat. He was jealous, and though I didn't love him any less, I probably neglected him, because Nicky, at that time, was a novelty.

He isn't a novelty any more. He has become a burden. However, he is all I have left. Deil is gone, the baby is dead, and her parents will never forgive me. The neighbours hardly spoke from one week's end to another, so that is no great loss, but there were girls, pretty girls from a youth club, who used to call occasionally. I enjoyed their visits; but they turned on me, after the baby died, and said horrible things.

'She was like a witch,' they said, 'a witch, with her black cat beside her.' I thought all that bigotry had gone out with the Middle Ages. That was how they treated silly old women who cherished a pet instead of a child, lonely souls who were glad of an animal for company. I loved Deil; but I would have liked children better; and I'm not a silly old woman. I used to be a schoolteacher; I've been to University.

Maybe I've let myself go a little. It's difficult when you're old. My teeth don't stay clean, my hair keeps tumbling out of its pins, and I wear thick stockings to hide the veins on my legs; but my mind is clear. They know me at the library, and I talk sensibly. I'd enjoy intelligent conversation, if I'd anyone to talk to.

The place where I lived before they brought me here wasn't all that it should be, but you know what rents are like nowadays. That's one reason why I didn't try harder to make friends. I could never have asked anyone in – except the girls, of course, and I suppose they enjoyed the idea of slumming. I'd only a bed-sitting-room with too much furniture in it, stuff I couldn't bear to part with when my husband died and I sold the house. The bed was too large, there was nowhere to store food, and dust got into everything when I poked the fire. A coal fire is company when you're alone.

I don't know what I'd have done without Deil. I'd had him since he

was a kitten, and every night he slept on my bed. He went out at the
same time every morning; a clean, obedient cat ... but he brought in
mice. That was the only thing I didn't like about him. I rescued them,
whenever I could. The neighbours used to shake their heads when they
saw me running down the stairs with a quivering mouse in my hand,
but I couldn't bear to see them suffer.

One morning, Deil brought in something that wasn't a mouse. I was
lighting the fire when I heard squeals and hisses on the landing, and
there was Deil bouncing something that screamed and scuttled in circles.
It shot into the room, so I held off the cat with one foot, shut the door,
and grabbed the thing just as it was heading for the fire.

It lay in my hands, very cold, and so still that at first I thought I had
crushed it. Carefully, I loosened my fingers to look. Heavens, what was
it? It was no mouse, it was like nothing I had ever seen, black, very black,
all curly like a poodle, but harder, without the warmth of flesh; bright
eyes, sharp teeth, and a curious curl like a spring on top of its head. As
the pressure of my hand lightened, it sat up on little haunches, and stared
at me with its cold jet eyes; and suddenly it began to yelp, a thin yapping
sound that set my teeth on edge like the scrape of a knife.

What was it? I thought of dragons and salamanders, but it was none
of those. There was something fierce about it, something frightening,
but it sat still enough, for all its yelping. It went on and on, till I couldn't
hear myself think, and then Deil began yowling at the door. I grasped
the black thing firmly, so that he couldn't get at it, and then, when he
came questing in, I held my hand close to his face. He jumped back,
spitting. The thing had made a dab at him, and from then on he knew
not to touch it.

'What'll I call you?' I said to myself. 'You're as black as old Nick. I'll
call you Nicky.' There was an old birdcage on top of the wardrobe,
among bags and hatboxes, and I stood on a chair, took it down, and
blew the dust off. It would do, meantime. I slipped Nicky in, wiped my
hand, and watched him pattering about, and then I poured out a saucer
of milk for Deil.

I put the cage back on top of the wardrobe when I went out. Deil had
to be fed, and Nicky too; but what would a thing like that eat? I got
some fish, to make up to Deil for taking away his prey, but he was in the
huff, and wouldn't be petted. He ate the fish, and then stalked out, and
I was almost relieved to see him go. It meant that I could take Nicky
out and see what he wanted.

The latch was stiff, I remember, and the beast was just out of reach,
watching me. He kept quiet till I manoeuvred my wrist through the
door and grabbed him, and then he twisted and bit me. In my fright, I
loosened my fingers, but he didn't escape. He hung on, nuzzling my

wrist, sucking at the thick blue vein. I was so startled that I couldn't move. I just sat and watched him, till he gave a funny little sound, between a slurp and a squeak, and sat back on his haunches again.

Slightly sickened, I stared at him. My wrist oozed and clotted. So that was how he fed? Put him out, put him away *now*, I thought. But what was a drop or two of blood? People give blood every day, and are no worse off. Surely I could spare enough to nourish this quaint and fascinating new pet?

So I kept him. Most of the time he stayed in the birdcage, running back and forwards, and yelping on and on; but at times I took him out, and when he had satisfied himself, I would seat him on my hand, staring at him, trying to coax him into some kind of tameness.

The black thing would not tame. He was docile enough, he didn't run away, but he gave neither affection nor recognition. The eyes, bright as ball bearings, stared coldly, and there was antagonism in the hard tight fur, the claws and tail and the wiry whirl on his head.

Gradually, Deil became afraid of him. When he was in he took to cowering against me, glancing over his shoulder, anywhere but at the yapping miniature on my hand. And I was too taken up with my new pet to notice him. Only sometimes, when I had shut the cage door, and the yelping had quietened for a while, I would stroke the cat and hold the aching spot on my wrist, and give a little shudder, as if something frightened me. As if I had made a decision which sometime, somehow, I would regret.

It was the day when the three girls visited me. I had the place tidied for them, and they came trooping in, filling the room with scent and fresh air. One had a fur hood, one had high leather boots, and they all wore long scarves twisted round their necks. They weren't so very different, after all, to the girls I used to teach in my day.

Deil was asleep on the bed, and they stroked him and petted him because they were still not quite sure of themselves. I found seats for them, and they all sat round the fire, grinning with goodwill.

Suddenly, in his corner, the thing started to yelp and scurry. The cat arched his back, and the girls stared curiously. 'What's that, Mrs Grimmond?'

'It's a – a rare breed of animal,' I said. 'It gets a bit noisy sometimes.'

Of course, they wanted to look at it. 'Is that it up there in the cage?' they asked.

'Yes,' I said. 'I wouldn't go near it, if I were you. It isn't used to people yet.'

'It sounds like a puppy.'

'Yes. I've just thought,' I said, 'would you go down to the dairy, all of you, and get me a pint of milk? I'll make a cup of tea while you're away.'

I hustled them out, and as soon as they were gone, I lifted the thing out and let him suck. He was savage this time, mauling me as he drank, and I drew in my breath as I dabbed my scarred wrist. At least, he would be quiet now, and maybe, when they came back, the girls would have forgotten about him.

They didn't mention him. They sat for a while, telling me about their club, and their activities and their homes, and I would have enjoyed it if I had been able to concentrate. My mind was taken up with the cage in the corner, my ears strained for the first rustle which would attract attention again. I had no idea why I was so sensitive about Nicky. Maybe it was because of the way he fed? I was glad when the girl in the high boots said, 'Well . . .' and signed that it was time to go. 'We'll call again,' she said, and I said, 'Yes, well . . .' hurrying them out before the thing could yelp.

Next day I had a visit from one of my neighbours. I had never spoken to her, but she wondered if she could ask a favour. Her mother had taken ill, and her husband was away all day. Could I possibly look after the baby for an afternoon?

'She's very good,' she said. 'She sleeps all the time. I could leave you her bottle all made up.'

Flustered, excited, I accepted the baby in her carrycot. 'No, Deil,' I said, as the cat stood on his hind legs to look, 'that's not for pussy cats. That's a baby for me to look after.'

I was happier than I had been for years. Maybe after all, the animal thing was bringing me luck. Now here was a baby in the house, with all the things belonging to it, nappies and milk and talcum. I put the carrycot by the window, and sat down to watch the child asleep.

At two o'clock she wakened for her feed. Carefully, I held her in my arms, stiff and inexperienced. I had never had any children of my own. Deil brushed by with a stiff tail, and I drew a deep breath and put the bottle between the soft pink lips.

And suddenly, the thing in the cage began to yelp.

The baby jerked away from the bottle, puckered her face, and cried, and I joggled her about clumsily. 'Be quiet!' I ordered, and the baby began to cry louder. 'Not you, pet!' I pleaded. I began to panic, forcing the bottle into her mouth to silence her, shaking her, and screaming at the thing in the cage. At last I laid the child down in the carrycot, my whole body faint and sweating.

I would have to get my priorities right. The child came first, obviously, but I couldn't feed her with all that noise going on. It upset both me and the baby. I went over, angrily, to the cage, and took out the fiend thing, holding him like a bird.

I did not want to feed him. I had to screw myself up now to endure the first savage bite, and I was beginning to resent his gluttony. I would have liked to open the door and chase him out and wash away all traces of his presence, but somehow I could not bring myself to do it. He was company for me in the long hours when Deil was out about his own business. And besides, in some queer way he belonged to me now – or was it that I belonged to him? Sometimes, when I balanced him on my hand, I had the feeling that I was the servant receiving orders from the thorny black tongue.

I could not bear to let him touch my sore wrist. He would have to take the other. But the creature was so voracious that he bit more deeply than usual, and I cried out in pain. I was sobbing as he sucked, sobbing helplessly, and above the sound of my sobs came the cries of the baby, louder, hysterical, as she clenched her fists and screamed from a wide round mouth.

It was too much. I would have to have silence. Silence! I stood up as if to crash down an imaginary cane on a desk, and the thing jerked off my arm, yammering for more. Any minute now, he would add to the noise. I looked round, my hands going to my head, ready to add my own screams to the screams which deaved me; then the noise quietened to a choke, a snuffle, a moment's frenzied heaving and struggle, and it was quiet, quiet. The clock ticked with a gobble in its voice, the cat padded over the floor, and I found my arms aching with pressure. I dropped the cushion I must have lifted, and the baby's face stared back, silent, suffocated, her eyes very blue, staring – oh pet, don't stare like that, I didn't mean it, I didn't, I didn't, it was only the noise . . .

Sitting in the dead afternoon, with the coal falling and the clock ticking, I waited for them all to come. I folded my hands on my lap, the window darkened, the room grew cold; and then, all at once, everyone was there, in a bubble of voices and sobs. I could not answer them. It was only when I saw Deil beaten out of the room that my throat loosened, and I cried out.

'Leave him! Don't hurt him!'

'Don't *hurt* him? My God – !'

I shook my head. Deil had been lying on the baby's chest, but he hadn't done any harm. Only, his claws had caught when they –

'He wasn't hurting her. I wouldn't allow – '

'What happened, then?' asked a policeman, licking a scratch on his knuckle. Funny how I felt safer with the police than with the neighbours.

My voice quivered when I tried to explain.

'I'm not used to babies. It was the noise. I couldn't feed them both at once, and they were both yelling – '

'Who? The cat?'

'No, no. The baby, and – I don't know what you call it. It's in the cage,' I said, pointing to the table where I had placed it. 'You'd better take it away. I should never have kept it.'

There was nothing there. It must have escaped when I shook it off my arm. There was only the old cage, empty, and needing a clean. The policeman looked queerly at me; but neither of us could look at the young mother, or at the father who kept saying, 'Why did you let her? For God's sake, look at her!' As if it mattered now!

Later, a car came and took me to the police station, all confused and dishevelled. I grew more confused as I tried to make them understand. A black thing, I said, a dragon, a poodle, a devil – how could I explain? 'Where did you get it?' asked a man in plain clothes, and I told the truth. 'The cat brought it in. Deil, my cat.'

They looked at each other, furtive, meaning glances – I saw them – and shook their heads. I tried to explain why I had kept it, a lonely old woman with only her cat for company, a cat which went out often and left her. Maybe it would grow tame, I had thought, another friend. I told how he had yapped to be fed.

'What did you feed it on?' said the man, who seemed to be trying to trap me.

'It sucked my blood.' I held up my red and festered wrists, and they crowded round, touching and turning them. 'I didn't like it. But it kept yapping, and with the baby crying . . .'

'So you let the cat smother the baby while you were feeding this . . . pet of yours?'

'Oh, no, it wasn't the cat. *I* smothered . . . I must have done. I didn't mean it. All I wanted was quiet.'

'Why didn't you kill the animal thing, instead of the baby?'

I didn't know. I didn't remember doing the killing. All I remember was the noise, and afterwards, putting down the pillow. I had never even said I was sorry. To be really sorry I would have had to remember it more clearly – and I didn't want to remember.

They took me back to the house after that, to the gaunt stone building, the echoing stairs, my own door up at the top. There was my room, still littered, the fire only grey feathers, and the child's bottle standing on the hearth. I knew they would never come back for the bottle.

They looked at the cage, at the few black turds mixed with the gravel at the bottom. 'Birds' droppings?' they hinted. I said no. They asked me to prove that I had had something there, to name witnesses. I told them about the girls, the friendly girls who had come to visit, who had wanted to help in any way they could.

It was then that they said that about me. 'She was like a witch, with her black cat beside her.' You could hear the youth and relish in their voices. As for the thing in the cage, they had heard it, but what did that prove? They had seen nothing. 'She wouldn't let us look,' they said accusingly. 'She acted funny. She wanted us out of the house.'

It didn't matter. I knew, I admitted, I was responsible for the baby's death, and I couldn't understand why they didn't take my word for it. They still don't believe me. Criminal negligence, they charged me with, but with diminished responsibility; that meant that I had let Deil smother her, and it was all wrong. I wouldn't have let Deil harm a hair of her head. But they kicked him to death, my poor pet that never hurt anyone in his life, and somehow I felt that worse than what had happened to the baby.

It seems that, all along, it is the innocent who have to suffer. Since they brought me here I have been thinking a lot about those poor old women who went to the stake for witchcraft. In another age, it could have been me. People don't change. The papers printed what the girls said about me being like a witch, and quite a few people believed it. 'Look what she called her cat. Maybe it was the devil. Maybe it was her familiar spirit.' But witches don't have ordinary animals for familiars. They have stranger things, according to what I have read, three-legged kids, talking toads, cockroaches . . .

And I had Nicky.

I see it now. These grotesque creatures suckled on the blood of those who cared for them, and Nicky fed on me. Oddly, the idea doesn't shock me. If I *am* a witch, then Nicky was sent on purpose, to cling to me, to belong to me, and be, in his own peculiar way, a friend.

He brought me nothing but sorrow. The old days have gone, my home, my cat, the hope that some day, someone would come and stay a while. Almost, I find myself yearning now for what I had started to hate, the cause of it all, the small frightened thing that sat on my hand and yapped at me.

He is here again! I don't know where he came from. He is just *here*, in answer to my desire, and he is ravenous. I would thrust my hand out, willingly, for him to feed, but I have to be careful. They watch me too closely. They don't believe what I told them about the scars on my wrists, and I mustn't do anything to make them suspicious, or they might treat Nicky as they treated Deil.

So now I have to smuggle him in, secretly, and feed him, each time from a different spot. It hurts – God, how it hurts! – but I suckle him often, so that he will not yelp, and when he is sated, he sits quietly on my hand, staring at me. But for all my longing, there is no love in the cold eyes, no yielding in the hard horny flesh; and as I stare at him, my hand goes down to my side to caress the emptiness where my cat used to sit, and comfort me, and cower from what I know now is evil.

# The Trapdoor

## C. D. Heriot

It was two months before John Staines – under doctor's orders – found suitable accommodation. He must build up his system, the doctor said, by fresh air and quiet at the week-ends after the strain and stress of his office work.

So John explored the home counties; and then, one Sunday late in April, he stopped to drink at an isolated beer house, the Fernahan Arms, on the eastern edge of Hertfordshire, not far from the main road to Cambridge. It was quiet, sheltering behind a larchwood on the edge of a hill; it seemed clean and spacious within; and in the pale gold of the spring sunshine it looked a friendly place.

The landlady was dark and stout, and the very fact that her gaze, when she brought his beer, was completely – almost carefully – devoid of interest, made him decide that the Fernahan Arms might prove to be the solution of his difficulties.

'Thank you,' he said, taking the mug. 'Do you have many people staying here during the summer?'

'No,' said the landlady.

'You seem to have a pretty large place. I suppose it's rather off the beaten track to catch many casual visitors.'

''Tis,' said the landlady.

'I was wondering,' he continued, 'whether – you see, I'm looking for some place where I could come down at the week-ends – Saturday to Monday morning – and I was wondering whether we couldn't come to some arrangement. I – I like this place,' he added lamely. The landlady was not being very helpful. She looked at him for a minute or two.

'Yes,' she said again.

'Well, now –' there was a shade of impatience in his voice – 'what are your terms?'

As if she had been waiting to make quite sure that he was in earnest, the woman became a little more communicative. Her name, it appeared, was Mrs Palethorpe. They arranged that he should have a room to the front at the top of the house overlooking the road. Yes, she understood that he was after quiet and rest. She assured him that it would be quiet.

There was hardly any traffic on the road and none at night. He would have his meals brought up to him. Would he like to see the room?

It was light and airy and looked across the road over a pleasant vista of wood and meadow. It was furnished with dressing-table and washstand to match, two heavy dining-room chairs upholstered in faded moss-green plush and an immense mahogany commode crowned with an empty carafe upon a mat of crochet in high relief. The pattern of the linoleum was even more astonishing than that of the wallpaper.

It suited John, however, and the following Saturday afternoon found him exploring the place in sunlight. The village was pleasant without being picturesque, and only a chimney here or a patch of stonework there hinted at its antiquity. There were prehistoric remains of some sort in the meadow beyond the church; but these, he decided, would keep until Sunday before he examined them. In the meantime the sun was low and the breeze had freshened into a decidedly chilly wind. He would return to the inn.

Outside he paused to examine it. It was uncompromisingly square in outline, and the shallow windows and mean proportions of sill and doorway seemed to emphasize its bareness. On the other side of the road stood the sign, as if trying to dissociate itself from the house. The road itself seemed to twist past the house with an air of haste and plunged down the hill in an abrupt curve, hiding itself between thick hawthorn hedges until it reached the calmer levels below. Above, the roof sloped steeply upwards, black against the sunset, surmounted by two chimney stacks with pots of different heights, like irregular teeth.

And with a slight shock John was aware of a resemblance between the house and its mistress, Mrs Palethorpe. Both had that blankly disinterested expression and that power of altering their appearance according to their mood. At this moment the Fernahan Arms was chilly – and looked it. How different from the bland invitation it had given him on his first arrival!

That evening he sat in the bar with the gamekeeper from the Big House, a couple of farm labourers, and an old-age pensioner in a corduroy suit. He learned quite a lot about the Fernahan Arms.

As he had suspected, it had not always been a public house. In the happy days before the war, the house had been inhabited by a man of the name of Weedon with his wife and father-in-law – a very old man he was, and dead these twenty year.

'Thirty,' said Mrs Palethorpe from behind the bar.

The pensioner became confused in calculating the exact number of years. Mrs Palethorpe retired to the parlour and the keeper took up the history.

After the old man died – Wright his name was – Mr and Mrs Weedon lived on there till the war came. Then he joined up and was terribly badly wounded and came back and died, and then she moved and *his* cousin's husband, Mr Palethorpe, took it over and opened a pub because t'other was closed during the war, see! and when he died Mrs Palethorpe she kept it on and made a good thing of it she did, being the only place for two mile around.

'Whose cousin's husband?' asked John, vainly attempting to connect the relationship of so many pronouns.

'Why, Weedon, of course. Weedon was Mrs Palethorpe's cousin . . .'

That lady suddenly reappeared, and with a guilty feeling of having been overheard discussing her affairs, John ordered another couple of drinks. Her face was as expressionless as usual, but John was conscious of her annoyance. It emanated from her so strongly that the atmosphere seemed almost to darken and turn chill. She turned her back and began to add figures in an account book. Conversation stopped except for a few unintelligible noises from the labourers. A clock intruded its precise, monotonous voice. Mrs Palethorpe let it have its way for several minutes before she turned again.

'Time,' she said, with an air of snubbing them all. Mugs were emptied and replaced with furtive scrapes. The door was opened and remained so, letting in the cold night wind to puff the calendars from the wall and draw the lamp flame cornerwise up its chimney until the last of the heavy boots had rasped and clumped its way out. The evening was over.

'I think I'll go right up now,' said John.

'Here's your candle,' said Mrs Palethorpe, pointing to the dresser with her left hand as she unhooked the lamp.

She preceded him upstairs and along the passage. He watched the shadows fly from them as they approached, scattering circles and curves of light on walls and ceiling. He noticed, for the first time, just outside his room, a trapdoor in the ceiling.

'What's up there?' he asked.

She stopped.

'The loft,' she said.

'Anything in it?'

'Nothing,' she replied and walked on into his room.

Next morning appeared in a flurry of cloud and sunshine. As John dressed, a sudden shower drenched the shivering fields and hurried away across the hill to give place to a pale rainbow that planted a tentative foot in a hedge opposite his window and arched up out of sight round to the front of the house, gathering strength as he watched it. He went into the passage to get a better view and followed its shining curve to the zenith with a comforting sense of peace and fulfilment. Scarcely focusing

his gaze upon it, he stood, his head thrown back, delighting in the spring
and the rain and the sunshine, and the fact that he was John Staines.
And as he stood there, his eye was caught by the trapdoor and followed
its edge to the bolt. It was shot fast; but what riveted his attention was
the fact that the handle had been filed or sawn away so that it would be
exceedingly difficult to withdraw. He gazed at it for some moments
speculating upon the reason for this. Mr Wright perhaps, or his son-in-
law, had wished to prevent the trapdoor from being opened. But, if so,
why not a padlock? Anybody with patience and a pair of pliers could
stand on a step-ladder and draw back the bar. The hinges on the opposite
side indicated that the cover opened inward. One would have to push
upward and then . . .

'Here's your breakfast,' said Mrs Palethorpe, behind him.

John blushed. Once again he experienced a guilty feeling of having
been caught investigating her private affairs. It was absurd, but he found
himself explaining matters.

'I was looking at the rainbow, and I noticed the trap-door,' he said.

'That's the loft,' she said.

'I know, but I noticed that the handle of the bolt's missing – and it
seemed queer, somehow . . .'

Mrs Palethorpe stepped past him into his room, bearing the tray. She
set it on the table near the window.

'There's only the loft up there,' she said. 'It's never used.'

'I suppose not,' he replied. 'It would be fairly difficult to open now.
What happens when you want to mend the roof?'

'They climbs up by the washhouse.' She turned at the door and looked
at him. 'There's nothing up there as I knows of, and no cause to go and
look. The bolt was that way before we come here.'

He found himself returning to the point.

'But who filed off the handle?' he asked.

She was almost tart. 'How should I know?'

'Mr Weedon, perhaps?'

'Mr Weedon wouldn't have done such a foolish thing – not as *I* knows,'
she said. 'Mr Weedon was a respectable man. He took the house as his
poor father-in-law left it and lived quiet. And if you want to know,' she
added angrily, 'Mr Wright was an invalid . . . so it wasn't him.'

With that she turned and went out.

John ate his breakfast hastily. Why had she been so annoyed? Damn
it! He had only looked at the blessed trapdoor. And as he passed under
it on his way out, he looked at it again, defiantly. She was right; it
certainly had not been used for a long time. The paint lay in scales and
blisters that the least touch would have dislodged. The apparent cause
of her annoyance was cobwebbed and rusty. It was firm in its socket.

Pincers would definitely be necessary. Oil, perhaps, to soften the rust. But why, he asked himself abruptly, was he bothering about bolts and trap-doors? He was here to get out into the fresh air. There were prehistoric earthworks to explore. Hertfordshire awaited him. Away with dust and cobwebs! Out into the sunshine!

On his return to the bar that evening he was greeted as an old acquaintance by the pensioner who took up the conversation at exactly the point where he had left off the previous day. 'She were wrong,' he announced triumphantly. 'It were twenty-five year come twenty-seventh of this month that old Wright died. I asked my daughter, and she calculated it were twenty-five year exactly.'

'Really,' said John, with a wary eye for Mrs Palethorpe's appearance. 'Did Mr Wright have a long illness?'

'No, he did not. Why, he was as strong and 'ealthy as I be till he was took sudden-like. One day he was a-sitting sunnin' hisself and the next took to 'is bed and no one to set eyes on him till his corpse were a-carried out near six months after.'

'But six months is a long time for a man to be ill,' said John.

'My Edith she were bad three year,' said the pensioner, with conclusive emphasis. 'Mortal agony all the time she was. No – six months isn't so very long. Why, we 'ad the doctor every day for the last year and an narf. *And* a distrik nurse. It were 'er legs,' he added confidentially. 'Old Wright he weren't in no pain as it were. Mr Weedon called it a decline.'

'And what did the doctor call it?' asked John.

'Ah! 'E wouldn't have no doctor. That was just it. Many's the time Mr Weedon 'e would come an' tell us how he'd begged on his bended knee to 'ave the doctor, but old Wright, he was stubborn, he was. Couldn't abide the sight of a doctor, he couldn't Mr Weedon said. Just wasted away. 'Is coffin was as light as light. Just wasted right away. He were a cross-grained old chap, he were, and a tongue on him. Always creating about something or other, he were.'

At this point Mrs Palethorpe returned to the bar. The pensioner turned a bright eye on her.

'This young gentleman was asking about old Wright's illness,' he remarked, to John's embarrassment. 'I said he just wasted away, right away.'

'Mr Staines doesn't need to be interested in sickness. He's here for his health.' Her voice carried a warning.

John laughed. 'He was calculating the exact date of Mr Wright's death before I came in,' he said. 'I only –'

Mrs Palethorpe interrupted him.

'What does it matter,' she said, 'twenty, thirty, forty years ago – it's all over now. He's dead.'

'That's right,' said the pensioner.

'Very well, then. There's no call for you all to be discussing it. Death's not such a pleasant subject for an old man, nor yet a young one.'

John looked at his feet.

The pensioner, hurt, mumbled incoherently and finished his beer. The tension was only broken by the entrance of two or three other customers.

But late that night he lay in bed remembering her voice and expression.

'Death's not such a pleasant subject for an old man, nor yet a young one.'

And the subject haunted his dreams.

Indeed, it was the culmination of a nightmare of hurrying footsteps and hushed voices in a low room, and it made him start awake and lie breathless for a moment, staring at the grey square of the window and trying to rationalize the panic fears that swooped and fluttered in his mind.

Then, as he lay, the swirling terrors of his dream stopped short and coalesced into one anguished dread that settled on him and chilled his drowsy consciousness into sharp awakening.

From the ceiling above his head came a soft, irregular thumping. Somebody was up there in the dark loft, knocking on the trapdoor!

He listened. The noise continued for a little while, then stopped; and just as he was beginning to enjoy a glow of reassurance that his nightmare was over and the normal world was real and solid about him, it began again.

It was no dream.

So real, so urgent a knocking that he was out of bed and at the door in automatic reaction to the appeal before he became conscious of this sudden transference from one strangeness to another. Why should anyone knock at such an hour in such a house? There was no other sound. Outside the window deep greyness dragged on the fields and lifted them to an unfamiliar horizon where a few dull stars sparked feebly in the cloud-rift. The land was cold and empty and indifferent. Inside was a tepid darkness faintly odorous of cloth and cooking. It, too, was unhelpful. And still resounded above him – but fainter now – the knocking that had hammered wakefulness into his dreams.

Once – twice – twice again – and then silence, a quite absolute silence that rang in John's ears. A small drowsy doubt arose. What a fool he was to stand bemused in the darkness listening to problematic noises! There was no noise now. Had there ever been a noise in this dark grey world? Ashamed and sleepy, he stumbled back to bed. Nevertheless before he left for the early bus next morning he had gazed for a long time at the trapdoor and satisfied the rational half of his mind that the bolt was really rusted into its socket and that no sane person would ever desire to use it as an exit from the loft if there was any other way of doing so. He determined to discover if there were when next he came to the Fernahan Arms.

And, of course, there was not. While Mrs Palethorpe presided, safely out of the way, at the bar, he prowled inside and out, and finally, with a half-ashamed sense of the fantasy of his action, furtively climbed the stairs that led to a loft at the back of the house. There, behind barriers of chicken-food in sacks and the last remnants of winter apples, he passed through an inner door and found that the greater part of the main loft had been partitioned off uncompromisingly with wood and plaster, and that there was no evidence of aperture or entrance.

With full realization, even the thick stuffiness of sunlight upon stagnant air was not warm enough to prevent a shudder over him. For suddenly he knew that the knocking in the night *had* been real, and it had come from a dark prison under the roof that had been unopened for years. And he did not like to think of the time when he must try to sleep in the room beneath.

He went to view the earthworks after that. But a shower drenched him, and a sudden wind wheeped mournfully through the surrounding thicket. Common sense fought losing battles with his uneasiness all the way home, till at last he decided, as he watched his soles steaming before the fire in Mrs Palethorpe's room, that he must solve the mystery of the trapdoor before darkness arrived with its panic reinforcements.

But it was dusk before he had thought of a suitable excuse for borrowing a pair of pliers – to extract a nail from his shoe, he said; and then the house was full of footsteps and movements – so full of watchful noise that it seemed like a challenge to finish matters that evening, however late. He waited, therefore, until the bar was open, and even loitered over a half pint, after his supper, in company with the pensioner and one or two men from the farms. Then, just after nine o'clock, he sauntered into the back room and through towards the staircase and the darkness of the upper floors. The window showed grey. Outside on the road lay an ochreish splash of light from a lower window; and a bat or a bird, swooping suddenly across the sky, seemed only to emphasize the stillness and immobility of the landscape. Very faintly came a murmur from the bar. Up here the quiet silence lay like midnight along the walls – but a night tense with storm.

Quietly and not without a tingling of half-frightened excitement John brought a chair from his room and placed it in the passage below the trapdoor. Standing on it he discovered that he could easily reach the bolt, but it would be tiring to work on it above his head.

He listened.

There was no other sound save the distant intermittent noise of voices in the bar. He was quite alone up here, with little fear of interruption.

Emboldened, he put back the chair and with infinite precaution edged the heavy commode across the linoleum. When he stood on it his shoulders were thrust against the ceiling with his head bowed like a caryatid's.

He flashed a pocket torch and began to twist the rusty bolt with his pliers.

It was very stiff. The grind of metal on metal sent little rustling tremors across the wood. Flakes of long-dried paint fell and spun round in the thick air, and queer reverberations echoed from within the loft.

The bolt turned. Slowly he forced it back, twisting this way and that, and always with one ear strained, as it were, for the least likelihood of disturbance from downstairs. Once he heard a door shut, and as he stopped and turned, his pliers must have struck the trapdoor with a blow that made him start and caused his heart to beat faster with the remembrance of that interior knocking of the previous night. Sweating, he turned his eyes to the grey circle of woodwork lit by his torch. It was not yet too late. The bolt was not yet free. He could still leave things as they were – get down – put away all evidence of his curiosity and descent to light and warmth and normality. But, swinging back, came the memory of his nightmare (if it had been a nightmare) and the necessity of satisfying himself on that point once and for all.

With a dismal sense of compulsion and an almost despairing reckless-ness, he twisted the bar through the final quarter of an inch, but the ultimate cessation of noise was no relief.

For a moment he hesitated, then with a sudden push he raised the trapdoor. It was lighter than he had anticipated and flew upwards, balancing for one perilous instant while his torch streamed upwards into dusty emptiness, before it fell back on to the floor of the loft with a crash so loud that for a moment John's unfocused fears were centred round the embarrassment and shame of his discovery by Mrs Palethorpe.

Instinctively he switched off his torch and stood motionless, his head and shoulders inside the loft, looking down at the greyness of the carpet beneath.

A tense and absolute silence succeeded the noise of the falling trapdoor. But it did not last for long. With a slithering rustle something moved in the blackness and descended upon his head, resolving itself into a pair of hands, thin and damp, covering his face and groping in a blind, brutish fashion about his mouth and eyes.

An old and filthy smell was in his nostrils. He cried out gaspingly, terror and disgust arching his body in a rigid convulsion. But his strangled shouts were muffled in a frenzied pressure. Weakly he sagged and fell clumsily to the ground.

Mrs Palethorpe, it appeared, had found him and dragged him into another room. Her masterful personality did not desert her, though there is no evidence as to how she explained away her lodger's screams to a bar full of interested countrymen. A doctor came and attended to cuts and bruises occasioned by John's fall. He also prescribed something for his shuddering state of collapse and communicated the necessary information to John's place of business that he was unwell and would need a long holiday. He was a discreet man who asked few questions, and it was probably due to him that Mrs Palethorpe's letter was not despatched for several months.

'DEAR MR STAINES' (it ran), 'I am sending you some things you left behind. I dont wish to be rude, dear sir, but you ought to have minded your business or this would never have happened. Still I suppose you could not have helped it though I could have told you that nothing would have happened if you had left things as they were. It was always only the knocks and they dont do nobody any harm, but it don't like being disturbed, thats why the bolt was cut, only I did not want to tell you, it being a scandal in the family as you might say. Nothing was ever proved only old Wright, he was a terror, always nagging and too old to be good for much, and Weedon was slow to anger and long put it by, there's no denying. Dear sir, I havent ever said anything to anybody about this before, so please will you keep mum too, because it would do my place a lot of harm; but the fact was, they did not give the old man enough to eat, and its my belief they kept him up in the loft till he died. The doctor said he were thin when he signed the certificate, but Weedon said he would not eat and he believed it. Nothing ever has happened except the knocks, but the rap was always like that since before we came, and it's like that now again. Please do not say a word about this to anybody, only it was right you should know. I hope you are feeling quite well again and got over it all. – Yours truly,

ALICE PALETHORPE.'

John burned the letter and did his best to forget its contents. But he now lives in a first-floor mansion flat and has a marked distaste for old-fashioned country pubs.

# The Day of Reckoning

## Patricia Highsmith

John took a taxi from the station, as his uncle had told him to do in case they weren't there to meet him. It was less than two miles to Hanshaw Chickens, Inc. as his Uncle Ernie Hanshaw now called his farm. John knew the white two-storey house well, but the long grey barn was new to him. It was huge, covering the whole area where the cow barn and the pigpens had been.

'Plenty of wishbones in that place!' the taxi driver said cheerfully as John paid him.

John smiled. 'Yes, and I was just thinking – not a chicken in sight!'

John carried his suitcase towards the house. 'Anybody home?' he called, thinking Helen would probably be in the kitchen now, getting lunch.

Then he saw the flattened cat. No, it was a kitten. Was it real or made of paper? John set his suitcase down and bent closer. It was real. It lay on its side, flat and level with the damp reddish earth, in the wide track of a tyre. Its skull had been crushed and there was blood there, but not on the rest of the body which had been enlarged by pressure, so that the tail looked absurdly short. The kitten was white with patches of orange, brindle and black.

John heard a hum of machinery from the barn. He put his suitcase on the front porch, and hearing nothing from the house, set off at a trot for the new barn. He found the big front doors locked, and went round to the back, again at a trot, because the barn seemed to be a quarter of a mile long. Besides the machine hum, John heard a high-pitched sound, a din of cries and peeps from inside.

'Ernie?' John yelled. Then he saw Helen. '*Hello*, Helen!'

'John! Welcome! You took a taxi? We didn't hear any car!' She gave him a kiss on the cheek. 'You've grown another three inches!'

His uncle climbed down from a ladder and shook John's hand. 'How're you, boy?'

'Okay, Ernie. What's going on here?' John looked up at moving belts which disappeared somewhere inside the barn. A rectangular metal container, nearly as big as a boxcar, rested on the ground.

Ernie pulled John closer and shouted that the grain, a special mixture, had just been delivered and was being stored in the factory, as he called the barn. This afternoon a man would come to collect the container.

'Lights shouldn't go on now, according to schedule, but we'll make an exception so you can see. Look!' Ernie pulled a switch inside the barn door, and the semi-darkness changed to glaring light, bright as full sun.

The cackles and screams of the chickens augmented like a siren, like a thousand sirens, and John instinctively covered his ears. Ernie's lips moved, but John could not hear him. John swung around to see Helen. She was standing farther back, and waved a hand, shook her head and smiled, as if to say she couldn't bear the racket. Ernie drew John farther into the barn, but he had given up talking and merely pointed.

The chickens were smallish and mostly white, and they all shuffled constantly. John saw that this was because the platforms on which they stood slanted forward, inclining them towards the slowly moving feed troughs. But not all of them were eating. Some were trying to peck the chickens next to them. Each chicken had its own little wire coop. There must have been forty rows of chickens on the ground floor, and eight or ten tiers of chickens went up to the ceiling. Between the double rows of back-to-back chickens were aisles wide enough for a man to pass and sweep the floor, John supposed, and just as he thought this, Ernie turned a wheel, and water began to shoot over the floor. The floor slanted towards various drain holes.

'*All automatic! Somethin', eh?*'

John recognized the words from Ernie's lips, and nodded appreciatively. 'Terrific!' But he was ready to get away from the noise.

Ernie shut off the water.

John noticed that the chickens had worn their beaks down to blunt stubs, and their white breasts dripped blood where the horizontal bar supported their weight. What else could they do but eat? John had read a little about battery chicken farming. These hens of Ernie's, like the hens he had read about, couldn't turn around in their coops. Much of the general flurry in the barn was caused by chickens trying to fly upward. Ernie cut the lights. The doors closed after them, apparently also automatically.

'Machine farming has really got me over the jump,' Ernie said, still talking loudly. 'I'm making good money now. And just imagine, one man – me – can run the whole show!'

John grinned. 'You mean you won't have anything for me to do?'

'Oh, there's plenty to do. You'll see. How about some lunch first? Tell Helen I'll be in in about fifteen minutes.'

John walked towards Helen. 'Fabulous.'

'Yes. Ernie's in love with it.'

They went on towards the house, Helen looking down at her feet, because the ground was muddy in spots. She wore old tennis shoes, black corduroy pants, and a rust-coloured sweater. John purposely walked between her and where the kitten lay, not wanting to mention it now.

He carried his suitcase up to the square, sunny corner room which he had slept in since he was a boy of ten, when Helen and Ernie had bought the farm. He changed into blue jeans, and went down to join Helen in the kitchen.

'Would you like an old-fashioned? We've got to celebrate your arrival,' Helen said. She was making two drinks at the wooden table.

'Fine. – Where's Susan?' Susan was their eight-year-old daughter.

'She's at a – Well, sort of summer school. They'll bring her back around four-thirty. Helps fill in the summer holidays. They make awful clay ashtrays and fringed money-purses – you know. Then you've got to praise them.'

John laughed. He gazed at his aunt-by-marriage, thinking she was still very attractive at – what was it? Thirty-one, he thought. She was about five feet four, slender, with reddish blonde curly hair and eyes that sometimes looked green, sometimes blue. And she had a very pleasant voice. 'Oh, thank you.' John accepted his drink. There were pineapple chunks in it, topped with a cherry.

'Awfully good to see you, John. How's college? And how're your folks?'

Both those items were all right. John would graduate from Ohio State next year when he would be twenty, then he was going to take a post-graduate course in government. He was an only child, and his parents lived in Dayton, a hundred and twenty miles away.

Then John mentioned the kitten. 'I hope it's not yours,' he said, and realized at once that it must be, because Helen put her glass down and stood up. Who else could the kitten have belonged to, John thought, since there was no other house around?

'Oh, Lord! Susan's going to be –' Helen rushed out of the back door.

John ran after her, straight for the kitten which Helen had seen from a distance.

'It was that big truck this morning,' Helen said. 'The driver sits so high up he can't see what's –'

'I'll help you,' John said, looking around for a spade or a trowel. He found a shovel and returned, and prised the flattened body up gently, as if it were still alive. He held it in both his hands. 'We ought to bury it.'

'Of course. Susan musn't see it, but I've got to tell her. – There's a fork in back of the house.'

John dug where Helen suggested, a spot near an apple tree behind the house. He covered the grave over, and put some tufts of grass back so it would not catch the eye.

'The times I've brought that kitten in the house when the damned trucks came!' Helen said. 'She was barely four months, wasn't afraid of anything, just went trotting up to cars as if they were something to play with, you know?' She gave a nervous laugh. 'And this morning the truck came at eleven, and I was watching a pie in the oven, just about to take it out.'

John didn't know what to say. 'Maybe you should get another kitten for Susan as soon as you can.'

'What're you two doing?' Ernie walked towards them from the back door of the house.

'We just buried Beansy,' Helen said. 'The truck got her this morning.'

'Oh.' Ernie's smile disappeared. 'That's too bad. That's really too bad, Helen.'

But at lunch Ernie was cheerful enough, talking of vitamins and antibiotics in his chicken feed, and his produce of one and a quarter eggs per day per hen. Though it was July, Ernie was lengthening the chicken's 'day' by artificial light.

'All birds are geared to spring,' Ernie said. 'They lay more when they think spring is coming. The ones I've got are at peak. In October they'll be under a year old, and I'll sell them and take on a new batch.'

John listened attentively. He was to be here a month. He wanted to be helpful. 'They really do eat, don't they? A lot of them have worn off their beaks, I noticed.'

Ernie laughed. 'They're de-beaked. They'd peck each other through the wire, if they weren't. Two of 'em got loose in my first batch and nearly killed each other. Well, one did kill the other. Believe me, I de-beak 'em now, according to instructions.'

'And one chicken went on eating the other,' Helen said. 'Cannibalism.' She laughed uneasily. 'Ever hear of cannibalism among chickens, John?'

'No.'

'Our chickens are insane,' Helen said.

Insane. John smiled a little. Maybe Helen was right. Their noises had sounded pretty crazy.

'Helen doesn't much like battery farming,' Ernie said apologetically to John. 'She's always thinking about the old days. But we weren't doing so well then.'

That afternoon, John helped his uncle draw the conveyor belts back into the barn. He began learning the levers and switches that worked things. Belts removed eggs and deposited them gently into plastic containers. It was nearly 5 p.m. before John could get away. He wanted to say hello to his cousin Susan, a lively little girl with hair like her mother's.

As John crossed the front porch, he heard a child's weeping, and he remembered the kitten. He decided to go ahead anyway and speak to Susan.

Susan and her mother were in the living-room – a front room with flowered print curtains and cherrywood furniture. Some additions, such as a bigger television set, had been made since John had seen the room last. Helen was on her knees beside the sofa on which Susan lay, her face buried in one arm.

'Hello, Susan,' John said. 'I'm sorry about your kitten.'

Susan lifted a round, wet face. A bubble started at her lips and broke. 'Beansy –'

John embraced her impulsively. 'We'll find another kitten. I promise. Maybe tomorrow. Yes?' He looked at Helen.

Helen nodded and smiled a little. 'Yes, we will.'

The next afternoon, as soon as the lunch dishes had been washed, John and Helen set out in the station wagon for a farm eight miles away belonging to some people called Ferguson. The Fergusons had two female cats that frequently had kittens, Helen said. And they were in luck this time. One of the cats had a litter of five – one black, one white, three mixed – and the other cat was pregnant.

'White?' John suggested. The Fergusons had given them a choice.

'Mixed,' Helen said. 'White is all good and black is – maybe unlucky.'

They chose a black and white female with white feet.

'I can see this one being called Bootsy,' Helen said, laughing.

The Fergusons were simple people, getting on in years, and very hospitable. Mrs Ferguson insisted they partake of a freshly baked coconut cake along with some rather powerful home-made wine. The kitten romped around the kitchen, playing with great rolls of dust that she dragged out from under a big cupboard.

'That ain't no battery kitten!' Frank Ferguson remarked, and drank deep.

'Can we see your chickens, Frank?' Helen asked. She slapped John's knees suddenly. 'Frank has the most *wonderful* chickens, almost a hundred!'

'What's wonderful about 'em?' Frank said, getting up on a stiff leg. He opened the back screen door. 'You know where they are, Helen.'

John's head was buzzing pleasantly from the wine as he walked with Helen out to the chicken yard. Here were Rhode Island Reds, big white Leghorns, roosters strutting and tossing their combs, half-grown speckled chickens, and lots of little chicks about six inches high. The ground was covered with claw-scored watermelon rinds, tin bowls of grain and mush,

and there was much chicken dung. A wheel-less wreck of a car seemed
to be a favourite laying spot: three hens sat on the back of the front seat
with their eyes half closed, ready to drop eggs which would surely break
on the floor behind them.

'It's such a wonderful *mess*!' John shouted, laughing.

Helen hung by her fingers in the wire fence, rapt. 'Like the chickens
I knew when I was a kid. Well, Ernie and I had them too, till about –'
She smiled at John. 'You know – a year ago. Let's go in!'

John found the gate, a limp thing made of wire that fastened with a
wooden bar. They went in and closed it behind them.

Several hens drew back and regarded them with curiosity, making
throaty, sceptical noises.

'They're such stupid darlings!' Helen watched a hen fly up and perch
herself in a peach tree. 'They can see the sun! They can fly!'

'And scratch for worms – and eat watermelon!' John said.

'When I was little, I used to dig worms for them at my grandmother's
farm. With a hoe. And sometimes I'd step on their droppings, you know –
well, on purpose – and it'd go between my toes. I loved it. Grandma
always made me wash my feet under the garden hydrant before I came
in the house.' She laughed. A chicken evaded her outstretched hand
with an *'Urrr-rrk!'* 'Grandma's chickens were so tame, I could touch
them. All bony and warm with the sun, their feathers. Sometimes I want
to open all the coops in the barn and open the doors and let ours loose,
just to see them walking on the grass for a few minutes.'

'Say, Helen, want to buy one of these chickens to take home? Just for
fun? A couple of 'em?'

'No.'

'How much did the kitten cost? Anything?'

'No, nothing.'

Susan took the kitten into her arms, and John could see that the
tragedy of Beansy would soon be forgotten. To John's disappointment,
Helen lost her gaiety during dinner. Maybe it was because Ernie was
droning on about his profit and loss – not loss really, but outlay. Ernie
was obsessed, John realized. That was why Helen was bored. Ernie
worked hard now, regardless of what he said about machinery doing
everything. There were creases on either side of his mouth, and they
were not from laughing. He was starting to get a paunch. Helen had
told John that last year Ernie had dismissed their handyman Sam, who'd
been with them seven years.

'Say,' Ernie said, demanding John's attention. 'What d'you think of
the idea? Start a battery chicken farm when you finish school, and hire

*one man* to run it. You could take another job in Chicago or Washington or wherever, and you'd have a steady *separate* income for life.'

John was silent. He couldn't imagine owning a battery chicken farm.

'Any bank would finance you – with a word from Clive, of course.'

Clive was John's father.

Helen was looking down at her plate, perhaps thinking of something else.

'Not really my life-style, I think' John answered finally. 'I know it's profitable.'

After dinner, Ernie went into the living-room to do his reckoning, as he called it. He did some reckoning almost every night. John helped Helen with the dishes. She put a Mozart symphony on the record-player. The music was nice, but John would have liked to talk with Helen. On the other hand, what would he have said, exactly? *I understand why you're bored. I think you'd prefer pouring slop for pigs and tossing grain to real chickens, the way you used to do.* John had a desire to put his arms around Helen as she bent over the sink, to turn her face to his and kiss her. What would Helen think if he did?

That night, lying in bed, John dutifully read the brochures on battery chicken farming which Ernie had given him.

> ... The chickens are bred small so that they do not eat so much, and they rarely reach more than $3\frac{1}{2}$ pounds ... Young chickens are subjected to a light routine which tricks them into thinking that a day is 6 hours long. The objective of the factory farmer is to increase the original 6-hour day by leaving the lights on for a longer period each week. Artificial Spring Period is maintained for the hen's whole lifetime of 10 months ... There is no real falling off of egg-laying in the natural sense, though the hen won't lay quite so many eggs towards the end ... (Why, John wondered. And wasn't 'not quite so many' the same as 'falling off'?) At 10 months the hen is sold for about 30c a pound, depending on the market ...

And below:

> Richard K. Schultz of Poon's Cross, Pa., writes: 'I am more than pleased and so is my wife with the modernization of my farm into a battery chicken farm operated with Muskeego-Ryan Electric equipment. Profits have quadrupled in a year and a half and we have even bigger hopes for the future ...'
>
> Writes Henry Vliess of Farnham, Kentucky: 'My old farm was barely breaking even. I had chickens, pigs, cows, the usual. My friends used to laugh at my hard work combined with all my tough luck. Then I ...'

John had a dream. He was flying like Superman in Ernie's chicken barn, and the lights were all blazing brightly. Many of the imprisoned chickens looked up at him, their eyes flashed silver, and they were struck blind. The noise they made was fantastic. They wanted to escape, but could no longer see, and the whole barn heaved with their efforts to fly upward. John flew about frantically, trying to find the lever to open the coops, the doors, anything, but he couldn't. Then he woke up, startled to find himself in bed, propped on one elbow. His forehead and chest were damp with sweat. Moonlight came strong through the window. In the night's silence, he could hear the steady high-pitched din of the hundreds of chickens in the barn, though Ernie had said the barn was absolutely sound-proofed. Maybe it was 'day-time' for the chickens now. Ernie said they had three more months to live.

John became more adept with the barn's machinery and the fast artificial clocks, but since his dream he no longer looked at the chickens as he had the first day. He did not look at them at all if he could help it. Once Ernie pointed out a dead one, and John removed it. Its breast, bloody from the coop's barrier, was so distended, it might have eaten itself to death.

Susan had named her kitten 'Bibsy', because it had a white oval on its chest like a bib.

'Beansy and now Bibsy,' Helen said to John. 'You'd think all Susan thinks about is food!'

Helen and John drove to town one Saturday morning. It was alternately sunny and showery, and they walked close together under an umbrella when the showers came. They bought meat, potatoes, washing powder, white paint for a kitchen shelf, and Helen bought a pink-and-white striped blouse for herself. At a pet shop, John acquired a basket with a pillow to give Susan for Bibsy.

When they got home, there was a long dark grey car in front of the house.

'Why, that's the doctor's car!' Helen said.

'Does he come by just to visit?' John asked, and at once felt stupid, because something might have happened to Ernie. A grain delivery had been due that morning, and Ernie was always climbing about to see that everything was going all right.

There was another car, dark green, which Helen didn't recognize beside the chicken factory. Helen and John went into the house.

It was Susan. She lay on the living-room floor under a plaid blanket, only one sandalled foot and yellow sock visible under the fringed edge. Dr Geller was there, and a man Helen didn't know. Ernie stood rigid and panicked beside his daughter.

Dr Geller came towards Helen and said, 'I'm sorry, Helen. Susan was dead by the time the ambulance got here. I sent for the coroner.'

'What *happened*?' Helen started to touch Susan, and instinctively John caught her.

'Honey, I didn't see her in time,' Ernie said. 'She was just chasing under that damned container after the kitten just as it was lowering.'

'Yeah, it bumped her on the head,' said a husky man in tan work-clothes, one of the delivery men. 'She was running out from under it, Ernie said. My *gosh*, I'm sorry, Mrs Hanshaw!'

Helen gasped, then she covered her face.

'You'll need a sedative, Helen,' Dr Geller said.

The doctor gave Helen a needle in her arm. Helen said nothing. Her mouth was slightly open, and her eyes stared straight ahead. Another car came and took the body away on a stretcher. The coroner took his leave then too.

With a shaky hand, Ernie poured whiskies.

Bibsy leapt about the room, and sniffed at the red splotch on the carpet. John went to the kitchen to get a sponge. It was best to try to get it up, John thought, while the others were in the kitchen. He went back to the kitchen for a saucepan of water, and scrubbed again at the abundant red. His head was ringing, and he had difficulty keeping his balance. In the kitchen, he drank off his whisky at a gulp and it at once burnt his ears.

'Ernie, I think I'd better take off,' the delivery man said solemnly. 'You know where to find me.'

Helen went up to the bedroom she shared with Ernie, and did not come down when it was time for dinner. From his room, John heard floorboards creaking faintly, and knew that Helen was walking about in the room. He wanted to go in and speak to her, but he was afraid he would not be capable of saying the right thing. Ernie should be with her, John thought.

John and Ernie gloomily scrambled some eggs, and John went to ask Helen if she would come down or would prefer him to bring her something. He knocked on the door.

'Come in,' Helen said.

He loved her voice, and was somehow surprised to find that it wasn't any different since her child had died. She was lying on the double bed, still in the same clothes, smoking a cigarette.

'I don't care to eat, thanks, but I'd like a whisky.'

John rushed down, eager to get something that she wanted. He brought ice, a glass, and the bottle on a tray. 'Do you just want to go to sleep?' John asked.

'Yes.'

She had not turned on a light. John kissed her cheek, and for an instant she slipped her arm around his neck and kissed his cheek also. Then he left the room.

Downstairs the eggs tasted dry, and John could hardly swallow even with sips of milk.

'My God, what a day,' Ernie said. 'My God.' He was evidently trying to say more, looked at John with an effort at politeness, or closeness.

And John, like Helen, found himself looking down at his plate, wordless. Finally, miserable in the silence, John got up with his plate and patted Ernie awkwardly on the shoulder. 'I am sorry, Ernie.'

They opened another bottle of whisky, one of the two bottles left in the living-room cabinet.

'If I'd known this would happen, I'd never have started this damned chicken farm. You know that. I meant to earn something for my family – not go limping along year after year.'

John saw that the kitten had found the new basket and gone to sleep in it on the living-room floor. 'Ernie, you probably want to talk to Helen. I'll be up at the usual time to give you a hand.' That meant 7 a.m.

'Okay. I'm in a daze tonight. Forgive me, John.'

John lay for nearly an hour in his bed without sleeping. He heard Ernie go quietly into the bedroom across the hall, but he heard no voices or even a murmur after that. Ernie was not much like Clive, John thought. John's father might have given way to tears for a minute, might have cursed. Then with his father it would have been all over, except for comforting his wife.

A raucous noise, rising and falling, woke John up. The chickens, of course. What the hell was it now? They were louder than he'd ever heard them. He looked out of the front window. In the pre-dawn light, he could see that the barn's front doors were open. Then the lights in the barn came on, blazing out onto the grass. John pulled on his tennis shoes without tying them, and rushed into the hall.

'*Ernie! – Helen!*' he yelled at their closed door.

John ran out of the house. A white tide of chickens was now oozing through the wide front doors of the barn. What on earth had happened? 'Get *back*!' he yelled at the chickens, flailing his arms.

The little hens might have been blind or might not have heard him at all through their own squawks. They kept on flowing from the barn, some fluttering over the others, and sinking again in the white sea.

John cupped his hands to his mouth. 'Ernie! The *doors*!' He was shouting into the barn, because Ernie must be there.

John plunged into the hens and made another effort to shoo them back. It was hopeless. Unused to walking, the chickens teetered like drunks, lurched against each other, stumbled forward, fell back on their tails, but they kept pouring out, many borne on the backs of those who walked. They were pecking at John's ankles. John kicked some aside and moved towards the barn doors again, but the pain of the blunt beaks on his ankles and lower legs made him stop. Some chickens tried to fly up to attack him, but had no strength in their wings. *They are insane*, John remembered. Suddenly frightened, John ran towards the clearer area at the side of the barn, then on towards the back door. He knew how to open the back door. It had a combination lock.

Helen was standing at the corner of the barn in her bathrobe, where John had first seen her when he arrived. The back door was closed.

'What's *happening*?' John shouted.

'I opened the coops,' Helen said.

'Opened them – why? – Where's Ernie?'

'He's in there.' Helen was oddly calm, as if she were standing and talking in her sleep.

'Well, what's he *doing*? Why doesn't he close the place?' John was shaking Helen by the shoulders, trying to wake her up. He released her and ran to the back door.

'I've locked it again,' Helen said.

John worked the combination as fast as he could, but he could hardly see it.

'Don't open it! Do you want them coming *this* way?' Helen was suddenly alert, dragging John's hands from the lock.

Then John understood. Ernie was being killed in there, being pecked to death. Helen wanted it. Even if Ernie was screaming, they couldn't have heard him.

A smile came over Helen's face. 'Yes, he's in there. I think they will finish him.'

John, not quite hearing over the noise of chickens, had read her lips. His heart was beating fast.

Then Helen slumped, and John caught her. John knew it was too late to save Ernie. He also thought that Ernie was no longer screaming.

Helen straightened up. 'Come with me. Let's watch them,' she said, and drew John feebly, yet with determination, along the side of the barn towards the front doors.

Their slow walk seemed four times as long as it should have been. He gripped Helen's arm. 'Ernie *in* there?' John asked, feeling as if he were dreaming, or perhaps about to faint.

'In there.' Helen smiled at him again, with her eyes half closed. 'I came down and opened the back door, you see – and I went up and woke Ernie. I said, "Ernie, something's wrong in the factory, you'd better come down." He came down and went in the back door – and I opened the coops with the lever. And then – I pulled the lever that opens the front door. He was – in the middle of the barn then, because I started a fire on the floor.'

'A fire?' Then John noticed a pale curl of smoke rising over the front door.

'Not much to burn in there – just the grain,' Helen said. 'And there's enough for them to eat outdoors, don't you think?' She gave a laugh.

John pulled her faster towards the front of the barn. There seemed to be not much smoke. Now the whole lawn was covered with chickens, and they were spreading through the white rail fence onto the road, pecking, cackling, screaming, a slow army without direction. It looked as if snow had fallen on the land.

'Head for the house!' John said, kicking at some chickens that were attacking Helen's ankles.

They went up to John's room. Helen knelt at the front window, watching. The sun was rising on their left, and now it touched the reddish roof of the metal barn. Grey smoke was curling upward from the horizontal lintel of the front doors. Chickens paused, stood stupidly in the doorway until they were bumped by others from behind. The chickens seemed not so much dazzled by the rising sun – the light was brighter in the barn – as by the openness around them and above them. John had never before seen chickens stretch their necks just to look up at the sky. He knelt beside Helen his arm around her waist.

'They're all going to – go away,' John said. He felt curiously paralysed.

'Let them.'

The fire would not spread to the house. There was no wind, and the barn was a good thirty yards away. John felt quite mad, like Helen, or the chickens, and was astonished by the reasonableness of his thought about the fire's not spreading.

'It's all over,' Helen said, as the last, not quite the last chickens wobbled out of the barn. She drew John closer by the front of his pyjama jacket.

John kissed her gently, then more firmly on the lips. It was strange, stronger than any kiss he had ever known with a girl, yet curiously without further desire. The kiss seemed only an affirmation that they were both alive. They knelt facing each other, tightly embracing. The cries of the hens ceased to sound ugly, and sounded only excited and puzzled. It was like an orchestra playing, some members stopping, others resuming instruments, making a continuous chord without a tempo. John did not know how long they knelt like that, but at last his knees hurt, and he stood up, pulling Helen up, too. He looked out of the window and said:

'They must be all out. And the fire isn't any bigger. Shouldn't we –' But the obligation to look for Ernie seemed far away, not at all pressing on him. It was as if he dreamed this night or this dawn, and Helen's kiss, the way he had dreamed about flying like Superman in the barn. Were they really Helen's hands in his now?

She slumped again, and plainly she wanted to sit on the carpet, so he left her and pulled on his blue jeans over his pyjama pants. He went down and entered the barn cautiously by the front door. The smoke made the interior hazy, but when he bent low, he could see fifty or more chickens pecking at what he knew must be Ernie on the floor. Bodies of chickens overcome by smoke lay on the floor, like little white puffs of smoke themselves, and some live chickens were pecking at these, going for the eyes. John moved towards Ernie. He thought he had braced himself, but he hadn't braced himself enough for what he saw: a fallen column of blood and bone to which a few tatters of pyjama cloth still clung. John ran out again, very fast, because he had breathed once, and the smoke had nearly got him.

In his room, Helen was humming and drumming on the windowsill, gazing out at the chickens left on the lawn. The hens were trying to scratch in the grass, and were staggering, falling on their sides, but mostly falling backwards, because they were used to shuffling to prevent themselves from falling forward.

'Look!' Helen said, laughing so, there were tears in her eyes. 'They don't know what grass is! But they like it!'

John cleared his throat and said, 'What're you going to say? – What'll we say?'

'Oh – say.' Helen seemed not at all disturbed by the question. 'Well – that Ernie heard something and went down and – he wasn't completely sober, you know. And – maybe he pulled a couple of wrong levers. – Don't you think so?'

# An Invitation to the Hunt

*George Hitchcock*

His first impulse upon receiving it had been to throw it in the fire. They did not travel in the same social set and he felt it presumptuous of them, on the basis of a few words exchanged in the shopping centre and an occasional chance meeting on the links, to include him in their plans. Of course, he had often seen them – moving behind the high iron grillework fence that surrounded their estates, the women in pastel tea-gowns serving martinis beneath the striped lawn umbrellas and the men suave and bronzed in dinner jackets or sailing togs – but it had always been as an outsider, almost as a Peeping Tom.

'The most charitable interpretation,' he told Emily, 'would be to assume that it is a case of mistaken identity.'

'But how could it be?' his wife answered holding the envelope in her slender reddened fingers. 'There is only one Fred Perkins in Marine Gardens and the house number is perfectly accurate.'

'But there's no earthly reason for it. Why *me* of all people?'

'I should think,' said Emily helping him on with his coat and fitting the two sandwiches neatly wrapped in aluminium foil into his pocket, 'that you would be delighted. It's a real step upward for you. You've often enough complained of our lack of social contacts since we moved out of the city.'

'It's fantastic,' Perkins said, 'and of course I'm not going,' and he ran out of his one-storey shingled California ranch cottage to join the car pool which waited for him at the kerb.

All the way to the city, like a dog with a troublesome bone, he worried and teased at the same seemingly insoluble problem: how had he attracted their notice? What was there in his appearance or manner which had set him apart from all the rest? There had been, of course, that day the younger ones had come in off the bay on their racing cutter, when by pure chance (as it now seemed) he had been the one man on the pier within reach of the forward mooring line. He recalled the moment with satisfaction – the tanned, blonde girl leaning out from the bowsprit with a coil of manilla in her capable hand. 'Catch!' she had cried and at the same instant spun the looping rope towards him through

the air. He had caught it deftly and snubbed it about the bitt, easing the
cutter's forward motion. 'Thanks!' she had called across the narrowing
strip of blue water, but there had been no sign of recognition in her eyes,
nor had she when a moment later the yacht was securely tied to the
wharf invited him aboard or even acknowledged his continuing presence
on the pier. No, that could hardly have been the moment he sought.

Once at the Agency and there bedded down in a day of invoices, he
tried to put the problem behind him, but it would not rest. At last, victim
of a fretful pervasive anxiety which ultimately made concentration
impossible, he left his desk and made his way to the hall telephone (years
ago a written reproof from Henderson had left him forever scrupulous
about using the Agency phone for private business) where he deposited
a dime and rang his golf partner, Bianchi.

'They met for lunch at a quiet restaurant on Maiden Lane. Bianchi
was a young man recently out of law school and still impressed by the
improbable glitter of society. This will give him a thrill, Perkins thought.
He's a second generation Italian and it isn't likely that he's ever laid eyes
on one of these.

'The problem is,' he said aloud, 'that I'm not sure why they invited
me. I hardly know them. At the same time I don't want to do anything
that might be construed as – well – as –'

'Defiance?' Bianchi supplied.

'Perhaps. Or call it unnecessary rudeness. We can't ignore their
influence.'

'Well, first let's have a look at it,' Bianchi said finishing his vermouth.
'Do you have it with you?'

'Of course.'

'Well, let's see it.'

Poor Bianchi! It was obvious that he was dying for an invitation
himself and just as obvious from his slurred, uncultivated English and
his skin acne that he would never receive one. Perkins took the envelope
from his note-case and extracted the stiff silver-edged card which he laid
face up on the table.

'It's engraved,' he pointed out.

'They always are,' Bianchi said putting on his shell-rimmed reading
glasses, 'but that doesn't prove a thing. They aren't the real article
without the watermark.' He held the envelope up against the table lamp
hoping, Perkins imagined, that the whole thing would prove fraudulent.

'It's there,' he admitted, 'by God, it's there.' And Perkins detected a
note of grudging respect in his voice as he pointed out the two lions
rampant and the neatly quartered shield. 'It's the real McCoy and no
mistake.'

'But what do I do now?' Perkins asked with a hint of irriation.

'First let's see the details.' Bianchi studied the engraved Old English script:

The pleasure of your company at the hunt
is requested
on August sixteenth of this year
R.S.V.P.                              Appropriate attire ob.

'The "ob",' he explained, is for "obligatory".'
'I know that.'
'Well?'
'The problem is,' Perkins said in an unnecessarily loud voice, 'that I have no intention of going.'
He was aware that Bianchi was staring at him incredulously but this merely strengthened his own stubbornness.
'It's an imposition. I don't know them and it happens I have other plans for the sixteenth.'
'All right, all right,' Bianchi said soothingly, 'no need to shout. I can hear you perfectly well.'
With a flush of embarrassment Perkins looked about the restaurant and caught the reproving gaze of the waiters. Obviously he had become emotionally involved in his predicament to the extent of losing control; he hastily reinserted the invitation in its envelope and returned it to his note-case. Bianchi had arisen and was folding his napkin.
'Do as you like,' he said, 'but I know a dozen men around town who would give their right arm for that invitation.'
'But I don't hunt!'
'You can always learn,' Bianchi said coldly and, signalling for the water, paid his bill and left.
Meanwhile, word of the invitation had apparently got around the Agency, for Perkins noticed that he was treated with new interest and concern. Miss Nethersole, the senior librarian, accosted him by the water-cooler in deep thrush-like tones.
'I'm so thrilled for you, Mr Perkins! There is no one else in the whole office who deserves it more.'
'That's very sweet of you,' he answered attempting to hide his embarrassment by bending over the faucet, 'but the truth is I'm not going.'
'Not going?' The rich pearshaped tones (the product of innumerable diction lessons) broke into a cascade of rippling laughter. 'How can you say that with a straight face? Have you seen the rotogravure section?'
'No,' Perkins said shortly.
'It's all there. The guests, the caterers, even a map of the course. I should give anything to be invited!'

No doubt you would. Perkins thought, looking at her square masculine breastless figure, it's just the sort of sport which would entertain you, but aloud he merely said, 'I have other commitments,' and went back to his desk.

After lunch he found the rotogravure section stuck under the blotter of his desk. Aware that every eye in the office was secretly on him he did not dare unfold it but stuck it in his coat pocket and only later, after he had arisen casually and strolled down the long row of desks to the men's room, did he in the privacy of a locked cubicle and with trembling hands spread it out on his knees. Miss Nethersole had been right: the guest list was truly staggering. It filled three columns of six-point type; titles gleamed like diamonds in the newsprint; there were generals, statesmen, manufacturers and university presidents; editors of great magazines, movie queens and polar explorers; radio-casters, regents, prize-winning novelists – but Perkins could not begin to digest the list. His eyes ferreted among the jumbled syllables and at last with a little catch of delight he came upon the one he had unconsciously sought: 'Mr Fred Perkins'. That was all, no identification, no Ll.D. nor Pres. Untd. Etc. Corp. He read his one name over four times and then neatly folded the paper and put it back in his pocket.

'Well,' he said with a thin-lipped smile, 'I'm not going and that's that.'

But apparently Emily, too, had seen the paper.

'The phone has been ringing all day,' she informed him as soon as he entered the house and deposited his briefcase on the cane-bottomed chair by the TV set. 'Of course everyone is furiously envious but they don't dare admit it so I've been receiving nothing but congratulations.'

She helped him off with his coat.

'Come into the dining-room,' she said mysteriously, 'I've a little surprise for you.' The telephone rang. 'No, wait, you mustn't go in without me. I will only be a minute.'

He stood uneasily shifting from one foot to the other until she returned.

'It was the Corrigans,' she announced. 'Beth wants us to come to a little dinner party on the seventeenth. Naturally,' she added, 'the date isn't accidental. They expect to pump you for all the details before anyone else in the subdivision hears about it. Now come on –' and like a happy child on Christmas morning she took his hand and led him into the dining-room.

Perkins followed her with mumbled protestations.

'Isn't it gorgeous?'

There, spread out on the mahogany table (not yet fully paid for) were a pair of tan whipcord breeches, a tattersall vest and a bright pink coat with brass buttons. In the centre of the table where the floral piece usually stood was a gleaming pair of boots.

'And here's the stock,' she said waving a bright bit of yellow silk under his eyes. 'You can wear one of my stick-pins, the one with the onyx in the jade setting I think would be best. And I've ordered a riding crop with a silver handle, it's to be delivered tomorrow.'

'You're taking a great deal for granted,' Perkins said. He picked up the boots and felt the soft pliable waxed leather. 'They must be very expensive. Where did you get the money for them?'

Emily laughed. 'They're on credit, silly, we have twelve months to pay.'

'I'll look ridiculous in that coat.'

'No, you won't. You're a very handsome man and I've always said you would cut a fine figure anywhere.'

'Well,' said Perkins hesitantly, 'I suppose we can send them back if I decide not to go.'

After dinner Bianchi drove by in his old Studebaker and obviously a bit fuzzy from too many cocktails. Emily opened the door for him.

'Fred is in the bedroom trying on his new hunting outfit,' she said, 'he'll be out in a moment.'

'Who is it?' Perkins shouted and when she answered he hastily took off the pink coat (which was a bit tight under the arms anyway) and slipped on his smoking-jacket. He remembered the scene in the restaurant and felt ashamed to let Bianchi see that his resolution was wavering.

'Look, Fred,' Bianchi said when they were seated in the living-room over their Old Fashioneds, 'I hope you've finally changed your mind – about –' He glanced at Emily to see how much she knew of the invitation.

'Go ahead. I've told her everything,' Perkins said.

'Well, you can certainly decline if you feel strongly about it,' said Bianchi in his best legal manner, 'but I don't advise it. If they once get the idea you're snubbing them they can make things pretty unpleasant for you – and in more ways than one.'

'But this is ridiculous!' Emily interrupted. 'He is not going to decline. Are you, darling?'

'Well,' Perkins said.

She caught the indecision in his voice and went on vehemently, 'This is the first social recognition you've ever had, Fred, you can't think of declining. Think what it will mean for the children! In a few years they'll be ready for college. And you know what that means. And do you seriously plan to remain in this house for the rest of your life?'

'There's nothing wrong with this house,' Perkins said defensively, reflecting that the house was not yet paid for but already Emily was finding fault with it.

'Suppose the invitation was a mistake,' Emily continued. 'I'm not saying that it was, but suppose it just for a minute. Is that any the less reason why you shouldn't accept?'

'But I don't like hunting,' Perkins interjected weakly, 'And I'll look ridiculous on a horse.'

'No more ridiculous than ninety per cent of the other guests. Do you suppose Senator Gorman will exactly look like a centaur? And what about your boss, Mr Henderson? He's certainly no polo player.'

'Is he going?' Perkins asked in surprise.

'He certainly is. If you had paid the slightest attention to the guest list you would have noticed it.'

'All right, all right,' Perkins said, 'then I'll go.'

'I think that's the wisest course,' said Bianchi with a slightly blurry attempt at the judicial manner.

He wrote his acceptance that evening, in pen and ink on a plain stiff card with untinted edges.

'It's all right for them to use silvered edges,' Emily pointed out, 'but they're apt to think it shows too much swank if you do.' She phoned a messenger service – explaining, 'it's not the sort of thing you deliver by mail' – and the next morning a uniformed messenger dropped his acceptance off at the gatekeeper's lodge.

The ensuing week passed swiftly. Emily fitted the pink coat and the tan breeches, marked them with chalk and sent them out for alterations. The yellow stock, she decided, would not do after all – 'a bit too flashy,' she observed – so it was replaced by one in conservative cream. The alteration necessitated a change in stickpin and cuff-links to simple ones of hammered silver which she selected in the village. The expense was ruinous but she over-rode his objections. 'So much depends upon your making a good impression and after all if it goes well you will be invited again and can always use the same clothes. And the cuff-links will be nice with a dinner jacket,' she added as an afterthought.

At the Agency he found that he basked in a new glow of respect. On Monday Mr Presby, the office manager, suggested that he might be more comfortable at a desk nearer the window.

'Of course, with air-conditioning it doesn't make as much difference as it did in the old days, but still there's a bit of a view and it helps break the monotony.'

Perkins thanked him for his thoughtfulness.

'Not at all,' Presby answered, 'it's a small way of showing it, but we appreciate your services here, Mr Perkins.'

And on Friday afternoon Henderson himself, the Agency chief and reputedly high in the councils of Intercontinental Guaranty & Trust, stopped by his desk on his way home. Since in a dozen years he had received scarcely a nod from Henderson, Perkins was understandably elated.

'I understand we'll be seeing each other tomorrow,' Henderson said resting one buttock momentarily on the corner of Perkins' desk.

'Looks like it,' Perkins said noncommittally.

'I damn well hope they serve whisky,' Henderson said. 'I suppose hot punch is strictly in the old hunting tradition but it gives me gas.'

'I think I'll take a flask of my own,' said Perkins as if it were his longstanding habit at hunts.

'Good idea,' Henderson said getting up. And as he left the office he called back over his shoulder, 'Save a nip for me, Fred!'

After dinner that evening Emily put the children to bed and the two of them then strolled to the edge of Marine Gardens and gazed across the open fields towards the big houses behind their iron grilles. Even from that distance they could see signs of bustle and activity. The driveway under the elms seemed full of long black limousines and on the spreading lawns they could make out the caterer's assistants setting up green tables for the morrow's breakfast. As they watched, an exercise boy on a chestnut mare trotted by outside the fence leading a string of some forty sleek brown and black horses towards the distant stables.

'The weather will be gorgeous,' Emily said as they turned back. 'There's just a hint of autumn in the air already.'

Perkins did not answer her. He was lost in his own reflections. He had not wanted to go, part of him still did not want to go. He realized that he was trembling with nervous apprehension; but of course that might have been expected – the venture into new surroundings, the fear of failure, of committing some social gaffe, of not living up to what they must certainly expect of him – these were causes enough for his trembling hands and the uneven palpitation of his heart.

'Let's go to bed early,' Emily said, 'you'll need a good night's sleep.'

Perkins nodded and they went into their house. But despite the obvious necessity, Perkins slept very little that night. He tossed about envisaging every conceivable social humiliation until his wife at last complained, 'you kick and turn so that I can't get a bit of sleep,' and took her pillow and a blanket and went into the children's room.

He had set the alarm for six – an early start was called for – but it was long before that when he was awakened.

'Perkins? Fred Perkins?'

He sat bolt upright in bed.

'Yes?'

It was light but the sun had not yet risen. There were two men standing in his bedroom. The taller of them, he who had just shaken his shoulder, was dressed in a black leather coat and wore a cap divided into pie-shaped slices of yellow and red.

'Come on, get up!' the man said.

'Hurry along with it,' added the second man, shorter and older but dressed also in leather.

'What is it?' Perkins asked. He was fully awake now and the adrenalin charged his heart so that it pumped with a terrible urgency.

'Get out of bed,' said the larger man and seizing the covers with one hand jerked them back. As he did so Perkins saw the two lions rampant and the quartered shield stamped in gilt on the breast of his leather coat. Trembling, and naked except for his shorts, he rose from his bed into the cool, crisp morning.

'What is it?' he repeated senselessly.

'The hunt, the hunt, it's for the hunt,' said the older man.

'Then let me get my clothes,' Perkins stammered and moved towards the dressing-table where in the dim light he could see the splendid pink coat and whipcord breeches spread out awaiting his limbs. But as he turned he was struck a sharp blow by the short taped club which he had not observed in the large man's hand.

'You won't be needing them,' his attacker laughed, and out of the corner of his eye Perkins saw the older man pick up the pink coat and holding it by the tails rip it up the centre.

'Look here!' he began but before he could finish the heavy man in black leather twisted his arm sharply behind his back and pushed him out of the french doors into the cold clear sunless air. Behind him he caught a glimpse of Emily in her nightclothes appearing suddenly in the door, heard her terrified scream and the tinkle of glass from one of the panes which broke as the short man slammed the door shut. He broke loose and ran in a frenzy across the lawn but the two gamekeepers were soon up with him. They seized him under the armpits and propelled him across the street to the point where Marine Gardens ended and the open country began. There they threw him onto the stubbled ground and the short one drew out a whip.

'Now run! you son of a bitch, run!' screamed the large man.

Perkins felt the sharp agony of the whip across his bare back. He stumbled to his feet and began to lope across the open field. The grass cut his bare feet, sweat poured down his naked chest and his mouth was filled with incoherent syllables of protest and outrage, but he ran, he ran, he ran. For already across the rich summery fields he heard the hounds baying and the clear alto note of the huntsman's horn.

# Taboo

## *Geoffrey Household*

I had this story from Lewis Banning, the American; but as I also know Shiravieff pretty well and have heard some parts of it from him since, I think I can honestly reconstruct his own words.

Shiravieff had asked Banning to meet Colonel Romero, and after lunch took them, as his habit is, into his consulting-room; his study, I should call it, for there are no instruments or white enamel to make a man unpleasantly conscious of the workings of his own body, nor has Shiravieff, among the obscure groups of letters that he is entitled to write after his name, any one which implies a medical degree. It is a long, restful room, its harmony only broken by sporting trophies. The muzzle of an enormous wolf grins over the mantelpiece, and there are fine heads of ibex and aurochs on the opposite wall. No doubt Shiravieff put them there deliberately. His patients from the counties came in expecting a quack doctor but at once gained confidence when they saw he had killed wild animals in a gentlemanly manner.

The trophies suit him. With his peaked beard and broad smile, he looks more the explorer than the psychologist. His unvarying calm is not the priestlike quality of the doctor; it is the disillusionment of the traveller and exile, of one who has studied the best and the worst in human nature and discovered that there is no definable difference between them.

Romero took a dislike to the room. He was very sensitive to atmosphere, though he would have denied it indignantly.

'A lot of silly women,' he grumbled obscurely, 'pouring out emotions.'

They had, of course, poured out plenty of emotions from the same chair that he was occupying; but, since Shiravieff made his reputation on cases of shell-shock, there must have been a lot of silly men too. Romero naturally would not mention that. He preferred to think that hysteria was confined to the opposite sex. Being a Latin in love with England, he worshipped and cultivated our detachment.

'I assure you that emotions are quite harmless once they are out of the system,' answered Shiravieff, smiling. 'It's when they stay inside that they give trouble.'

'*Cá!* I like people who keep their emotions inside,' said Romero. 'It is why I live in London. The English are not cold – it is nonsense to say they are cold – but they are well bred. They never show a sign of what hurts them most. I like that.'

Shiravieff tapped his long forefinger on the table in a fast, nervous rhythm.

'And what if they *must* display emotion?' he asked irritably. 'Shock them – shock them, you understand, so that they must! They can't do it, and they are hurt for life.'

They had never before seen him impatient. Nobody had. It was an unimaginable activity, as if your family doctor were to come and visit you without his trousers. Romero had evidently stirred up the depths.

'I've shocked them, and they displayed plenty of emotion,' remarked Banning.

'Oh, I do not mean their little conventions,' said Shiravieff slowly and severely. 'Shock them with some horrid fact that they can't blink away, something that would outrage the souls of any of us. Do you remember de Maupassant's story of the man whose daughter was buried alive – how she returned from the grave and how all his life he kept the twitching gesture with which he tried to push her away? Well, if that man had shrieked or thrown a fit or wept all night he mightn't have suffered from the twitch.'

'Courage would have saved him,' announced the colonel superbly.

'No!' shouted Shiravieff. 'We're all cowards, and the healthiest thing we can do is to express fear when we feel it.'

'The fear of death –' began Romero.

'I am not talking about the fear of death. It is not that. It is our horror of breaking a taboo that causes shock. Listen to me. Do either of you remember the Zweibergen case in 1926?'

'The name's familiar,' said Banning. 'But I can't just recall . . . was it a haunted village?'

'I congratulate you on your healthy mind,' said Shiravieff ironically. 'You can forget what you don't want to remember.'

He offered them cigars and lit one himself. Since he hardly ever smoked it calmed him immediately. His grey eyes twinkled as if to assure them that he shared their surprise at his irritation. Banning had never before realized, so he said, that the anti-smoke societies were right, that tobacco was a drug.

'I was at Zweibergen that summer. I chose it because I wanted to be alone. I can only rest when I am alone,' began Shiravieff abruptly. 'The eastern Carpathians were remote ten years ago – cut off from the tourists by too many frontiers. The hungarian magnates who used to shoot the forests before the war had vanished, and their estates were sparsely settled. I didn't expect any civilized company.

'I was disappointed to find that a married couple had rented the old shooting-box. They were obviously interesting, but I made no advances to them beyond passing the time of day whenever we met on the village street. He was English and she American – one of those delightful women who are wholly and typically American. No other country can fuse enough races to produce them. Her blood, I should guess, was mostly Slav. They thought me a surly fellow, but respected my evident desire for privacy – until the time when all of us in Zweibergen wanted listeners. Then the Vaughans asked me to dinner.

'We talked nothing but commonplaces during the meal, which was, by the way, excellent. There were a joint of venison and some wild strawberries, I remember. We took our coffee on the lawn in front of the house, and sat for a moment in silence – the mountain silence – staring out across the valley. The pine forest, rising tier upon tier, was very black in the late twilight. White, isolated rocks were scattered through it. They looked as if they might move on at any minute – like the ghosts of great beasts pasturing upon the treetops. Then a dog howled on the alp above us. We all began talking at once. About the mystery, of course.

'Two men had been missing in that forest for nearly a week. The first of them belonged to a little town about ten miles down the valley; he was returning after nightfall from a short climb in the mountains. He might have vanished into a snowdrift or ravine, for the paths were none too safe. There were no climbing clubs in that district to keep them up. But it seemed to be some less common accident that had overtaken him. He was out of the high peaks. A shepherd camping on one of the lower alps had exchanged a goodnight with him, and watched him disappear among the trees on his way downwards. That was the last that had been seen or heard of him.

'The other was one of the search party that had gone out on the following day. The man had been posted as a stop, while the rest beat the woods towards him. It was the last drive, and already dark. When the line came up to his stand he was not there.

'Everybody suspected wolves. Since 1914 there had been no shooting over the game preserves, and animal life of all sorts was plentiful. But the wolves were not in pack, and the search parties did not find a trace of blood. There were no tracks to help. There was no sign of a struggle. Vaughan suggested that we were making a mystery out of nothing – probably the two men had become tired of a domestic routine, and taken the opportunity to disappear. By now, he expected, they were on their way to the Argentine.

'His cool dismissal of tragedy was inhuman. He sat there, tall, distant, and casually strong. His face was stamped ready-made out of that pleasant upper-class mould. Only his firm mouth and thin sensitive nostrils showed that he had any personality of his own. Kyra Vaughan looked at him scornfully.

'"Is that what you really think?" she asked.

'"Why not?" he answered. "If those men had been killed it must have been by something prowling about and waiting for its chance. And there isn't such a thing."

'"If you want to believe the men aren't dead, believe it!" Kyra said.

'Vaughan's theory that the men had disappeared of their own free will was, of course, absurd; but his wife's sudden coldness to him seemed to me to be needlessly impatient. I understood when I knew them better. Vaughan – your reserved Englishman, Romero! – was covering up his thoughts and fears, and chose, quite unconsciously, to appear stupid rather than to show his anxiety. She recognized the insincerity without understanding its cause, and it made her angry.

'They were a queer pair, those two; intelligent, cultured, and so interested in themselves and each other that they needed more than one life to satisfy their curiosity. She was a highly strung creature, with swift brown eyes and a slender, eager body that seemed to grow like a flower from the ground under her feet. And natural! I don't mean she couldn't act. She could – but when she did, it was deliberate. She was defenceless before others' suffering and joy, and she didn't try to hide it.

'Lord! She used to live through enough emotions in one day to last her husband for a year!

'Not that he was unemotional. Those two were very much alike, though you'd never have guessed it. But he was shy of tears and laughter, and he had armed his whole soul against them. To a casual observer he seemed the calmer of the two, but at bottom he was an extremist. He might have been a poet, a Saint Francis, a revolutionary. But was he? No! He was an Englishman. He knew he was in danger of being swayed by emotional ideas, of giving his life to them. And so? And so he balanced every idea with another, and secured peace for himself between the scales. She, of course, would always jump into one scale or the other. And he loved her for it. But his non-committal attitudes got on her nerves.'

'She could do no wrong in your eyes,' said Romero indignantly. His sympathies had been aroused on behalf of the unknown Englishman. He admired him.

'I adored her,' said Shiravieff frankly. 'Everybody did. She made one live more intensely. Don't think I undervalued him, however. I couldn't help seeing how his wheels went round, but I liked him thoroughly. He was a man you could trust, and good company as well. A man of action. What he did had little relation to the opinions he expressed.

'Well, after that dinner with the Vaughans I had no more desire for a lonely holiday; so I did the next best thing, and took an active interest in everything that was going on. I heard all the gossip, for I was staying in the general clearing-house, the village inn. In the evenings I often joined the district magistrate as he sat in the garden with a stein of beer in front of him and looked over the notes of the depositions which he had taken that day.

'He was a very solid functionary – a good type of man for a case like that. A more imaginative person would have formed theories, found evidence to fit them, and only added to the mystery. He did not want to discuss the case. No, he had no fear of an indiscretion. It was simply that he had nothing to say, and was clear-headed enough to realize it. He admitted that he knew no more than the villagers whose depositions filled his portfolio. But he was ready to talk on any other subject – especially politics – and our long conversations gave me a reputation for profound wisdom among the villagers. Almost I had the standing of a public official.

'So, when a third man disappeared, this time from Zweibergen itself, the mayor and the village constable came to me for instructions. It was the local grocer who was missing. He had climbed up through the forest in the hope of bagging a blackcock at dusk. In the morning the shop did not open. Only then was it known that he had never returned. A solitary shot had been heard about ten-thirty p.m., when the grocer was presumably trudging homewards.

'All I could do, pending the arrival of the magistrate, was to send out search parties. We quartered the forest, and examined every path. Vaughan and I, with one of the peasants, went up to my favourite place for blackcock. It was there, I thought, that the grocer would have gone. Then we inspected every foot of the route which he must have taken back to the village. Vaughan knew something about tracking. He was one of those surprising Englishmen whom you may know for years without realizing that once there were coloured men in Africa or Burma or Borneo who knew him still better, and drove game for him, and acknowledged him as someone juster than their gods, but no more comprehensible.

'We had covered some four miles when he surprised me by suddenly showing interest in the undergrowth. Up to then I had been fool enough to think that he was doing precisely nothing.

'"Someone has turned aside from the path here," he said. "He was in a hurry, I wonder why."

'A few yards from the path there was a white rock about thirty feet high. It was steep, but projecting ledges gave an easy way up. A hot spring at the foot of it bubbled out of a cavity hardly bigger than a fox's earth. When Vaughan showed me the signs, I could see that the scrub which grew between the rocks and the path had been roughly pushed aside. But I pointed out that no one was likely to dash off the path through that thicket.

'"When you know you're being followed, you like to have a clear space around you," Vaughan answered. "It would be comforting to be on top of that rock with a gun in your hands – if you got there in time. Let's go up."

'The top was bare stone, with clumps of creeper and ivy growing from the crannies. Set back some three yards from the edge was a little tree, growing in a pocket of soil. One side of its base was shattered into slivers. It had received a full charge of shot at close quarters. The peasant crossed himself. He murmured:

'"They say there's always a tree between you and it."

'I asked him what "it" was. He didn't answer immediately, but played with his stick casually, and as if ashamed, until the naked steel point was in his hand. Then he muttered:

'"The werewolf."

'Vaughan laughed and pointed to the shot marks six inches from the ground.

'"The werewolf must be a baby one, if it's only as tall as that," he said. "No, the man's gun went off as he fell. Perhaps he was followed too close as he scrambled up. About there is where his body would have fallen."

'He knelt down to examine the ground.

'"What's that?" he asked me. "If it's blood, it has something else with it."

'There was only a tiny spot on the bare rock. I looked at it. It was undoubtedly brain tissue. I was surprised that there was no more of it. It must, I suppose, have come from a deep wound in the skull. Might have been made by an arrow, or a bird's beak, or perhaps a tooth.

'Vaughan slid down the rock, and prodded his stick into the sulphurous mud of the stream bed. Then he hunted about in the bushes like a dog.

'"There was no body dragged away in that direction," he said.

'We examined the farther side of the rock. It fell sheer, and seemed an impossible climb for man or beast. The edge was matted with growing things. I was ready to believe that Vaughan's eyes could tell if anything had passed that way.

'"Not a sign!" he said. "Where the devil has his body gone to?"

'The three of us sat on the edge of the rock in silence. The spring bubbled and wept beneath, and the pines murmured above us. There was no need of a little particle of human substance, recognizable only to a physiologist's eye, to tell us that we were on the scene of a kill. Imagination? Imagination is so often only a forgotten instinct. The man who ran up that rock wondered in his panic why he gave way to his imagination.

'We found the magistrate in the village when we returned and reported our find to him.

'"Interesting! But what does it tell us?" he said.

'I pointed out that at least we knew the man was dead or dying.

'"There's no certain proof. Show me his body. Show me any motive for killing him."

'Vaughan insisted that it was the work of an animal. The magistrate disagreed. If it were wolf, he said, we might have some difficulty in collecting the body, but none in finding it. And as for bear – well, they were so harmless that the idea was ridiculous.

'Nobody believed in any material beast, for the whole countryside had been beaten. But tales were told in the village – the old tales. I should never have dreamed that those peasants accepted so many horrors as fact if I hadn't heard those tales in the village inn. The odd thing is that I couldn't say then, and I can't say now, that they were altogether wrong. You should have seen the look in those men's eyes as old Weiss, the game warden, told how time after time his grandfather had fired point-blank at a grey wolf whom he met in the woods at twilight. He had never killed it until he loaded his gun with silver. Then the wolf vanished after the shot, but Heinrich the cobbler was found dying in his house with a beaten silver dollar in his belly.

'Josef Weiss, his son, who did most of the work on the preserves and was seldom seen in the village unless he came down to sell a joint or two of venison, was indignant with his father. He was a heavily built, sullen fellow, who had read a little. There's nobody so intolerant of superstition as your half-educated man. Vaughan, of course, agreed with him – but then capped the villagers' stories with such ghastly tales from native folklore and mediaeval literature that I couldn't help seeing he had been brooding on the subject. The peasants took him seriously. They came and went in pairs. No one would step out into the night without a companion. Only the shepherd was unaffected. He didn't disbelieve, but he was a mystic. He was used to passing to and fro under the trees at night.

'"You've got to be a part of those things, sir," he said to me, "Then you'll not be afraid of them. I don't say a man can turn himself into a wolf – the Blessed Virgin protect us!– but I know why he'd want to."

'That was most interesting.

'"I think I know too," I answered. "But what does it feel like?"

'"It feels as if the woods had got under your skin, and you want to walk wild and crouch at the knees."

'"He's perfectly right," said Vaughan convincingly.

'That was the last straw for those peasants. They drew away from Vaughan, and two of them spat into the fire to avert his evil eye. He seemed to them much too familiar with the black arts.

'"How do you explain it?" asked Vaughan, turning to me.

'I told him it might have a dozen different causes, just as fear of the dark has. And physical hunger might also have something to do with it.

'I think our modern psychology is inclined to give too much importance to sex. We forget that man is, or was, a fleet-footed hunting animal equipped with all the necessary instincts.

'As soon as I mentioned hunger, there was a chorus of assent – though they really didn't know what I or the shepherd or Vaughan was talking about. Most of those men had experienced extreme hunger. The innkeeper was reminded of a temporary famine during the war. The shepherd told us how he had once spent a week stuck on the face of a cliff before he was found. Josef Weiss, eager to get away from the supernatural, told his experiences as a prisoner of war in Russia. With his companions he had been forgotten behind the blank walls of a fortress while their guards engaged in revolution. Those poor devils had been reduced to very desperate straits indeed.

'For a whole week Vaughan and I were out with the search parties day and night. Meanwhile Kyra wore herself out trying to comfort the womenfolk. They couldn't help loving her – yet half suspected that she herself was at the bottom of the mystery. I don't blame them. They couldn't be expected to understand her intense spirituality. To them she was like a creature from another planet, fascinating and terrifying. Without claiming any supernatural powers for her, I've no doubt that Kyra could have told the past, present, and future of any of those villagers much more accurately than the travelling gipsies.

'On our first day of rest I spent the afternoon with the Vaughans. He and I were refreshed by twelve hours' sleep, and certain that we could hit on some new solution to the mystery that might be the right one. Kyra joined in the discussion. We went over the old theories again and again, but could make no progress.

'"We shall be forced to believe the tales they tell in the village," I said at last.

'"Why don't you?" asked Kyra Vaughan.

'We both protested. Did she believe them, we asked.

'"I'm not sure," she answered. "What does it matter? But I know that evil has come to those men. Evil . . ." she repeated.

'We were startled. You smile, Romero, but you don't realize how that atmosphere of the uncanny affected us.

'Looking back on it, I see how right she was. Women – good Lord, they get hold of the spiritual significance of something, and we take them literally!

'When she left us I asked Vaughan whether she really believed in the werewolf.

'"Not exactly," he explained. "What she means is that our logic isn't getting us anywhere – that we ought to begin looking for something which, if it isn't a werewolf, has the spirit of the werewolf. You see, even if she saw one, she would be no more worried than she is. The outward form of things impresses her so little."

'Vaughan appreciated his wife. He didn't know what in the world she meant, but he knew that there was always sense in her parables, even if it took one a long time to make the connection between what she actually said and the way in which one would have expressed the same thing oneself. That, after all, is what understanding means.

'I asked what he supposed she meant by evil.

'"Evil?" he replied. "Evil forces – something that behaves as it has no right to behave. She means almost – possession. Look here! Let's find out in our own way what she means. Assuming it's visible, let's see this thing."

'It was, he still thought, an animal. Its hunting had been successful, and now that the woods were quiet it would start again. He didn't think it had been driven away for good.

'"It wasn't driven away by the first search parties," he pointed out. "They frightened all the game for miles around, but this thing simply took one of them. It will come back, just as surely as a man-eating lion comes back. And there's only one way to catch it – bait!"

'"Who's going to be the bait?" I asked.

'"You and I."

'I suppose I looked startled. Vaughan laughed. He said that I was getting fat, that I would make most tempting bait. Whenever he made jokes in poor taste, I knew that he was perfectly serious.

'"What are you going to do?" I asked. "Tie me to a tree and watch out with a gun?"

'"That's about right, except that you needn't be tied up – and as the idea is mine you can have first turn with the gun. Are you a good shot?"

'I am and so was he. To prove it, we practised on a target after dinner, and found that we could trust each other up to fifty yards in clear moonlight. Kyra disliked shooting. She had a horror of death. Vaughan's excuse didn't improve matters. He said that we were going deer-stalking the next night and needed some practice.

'"Are you going to shoot them while they are asleep?" she asked disgustedly.

'"While they are having their supper, dear."

'"Before, if possible," I added.

'I disliked hurting her by jokes that to her were pointless, but we chose that method deliberately. She couldn't be told the truth, and now she would be too proud to ask questions.

'Vaughan came down to the inn the following afternoon, and we worked out a plan of campaign. The rock was the starting-point of all our theories, and on it we decided to place the watcher. From the top there was a clear view of the path for fifty yards on either side. The watcher was to take up his stand, while covered by the ivy, before sunset, and at a little before ten the bait was to be on the path and within shot. He should walk up and down, taking care never to step out of sight of the rock, until midnight, when the party would break up. We reckoned that our quarry, if it reasoned, would take the bait to be a picket posted in that part of the forest.

'The difficulty was getting home. We had to go separately in case we were observed, and hope for the best. Eventually we decided that the man on the path, who might be followed, should go straight down to the road as fast as he could. There was a timber slide quite close, by which he could cut down in ten minutes. The man on the rock should wait awhile and then go home by the path.

'"Well, I shall not see you again until to-morrow morning," said Vaughan as he got up to go. "You'll see me but I shan't see you. Just whistle once, very softly, as I come up the path, so that I know you're there."

'He remarked that he had left a letter for Kyra with the notary in case of accidents, and added, with an embarrassed laugh, that he supposed it was silly.

'I thought it was anything but silly, and said so.

'I was on the rock by sunset. I wormed my legs and body back into the ivy, leaving head and shoulders free to pivot with the rifle. It was a little .300 with a longish barrel. I felt certain that Vaughan was as safe as human science and a steady hand could make him.

'The moon came up, and the path was a ribbon of silver in front of me. There's something silent about moonlight. It's not light. It's a state of things. When there was sound it was unexpected, like the sudden shiver on the flank of a sleeping beast. A twig cracked now and then. An owl hooted. A fox slunk across the pathway, looking back over his shoulder. I wished that Vaughan would come. Then the ivy rustled behind me. I couldn't turn round. My spine became very sensitive, and a point at the back of my skull tingled as if expecting a blow. It was no good my telling myself that nothing but a bird could possibly be behind me – but of course it was a bird. A nightjar whooshed out of the ivy, and my body became suddenly cold with sweat. That infernal fright cleared all vague fears right out of me. I continued to be uneasy, but I was calm.

'After a while I heard Vaughan striding up the path. Then he stepped within range, a bold, clear figure in the moonlight. I whistled softly, and he waved his hand from the wrist in acknowledgment. He walked up and down, smoking a cigar. The point of light marked his head in the shadows. Wherever he went, my sights were lined a yard or two behind him. At midnight he nodded his head towards my hiding-place and trotted rapidly away to the timber slide. A little later I took the path home.

'The next night our rôles were reversed. It was my turn to walk the path. I found that I preferred to be the bait. On the rock I had longed for another pair of eyes, but after an hour on the ground I did not even want to turn my head. I was quite content to trust Vaughan to take care of anything going on behind me. Only once was I uneasy. I heard, as I thought, a bird calling far down in the woods. It was a strange call, almost a whimper. It was like the little frightened exclamation of a woman. – Birds weren't popular with me just then. I had a crazy memory of some Brazilian bird which drives a hole in the back of your head and lives on brains. I peered down through the trees, and caught a flicker of white in a moonlit clearing below. It showed only for a split second, and I came to the conclusion that it must have been a ripple of wind in the silver grass. When the time was up I went down the timber slide and took the road home to the inn. I fell asleep wondering whether we hadn't let our nerves run away with us.

'I went up to see the Vaughans in the morning. Kyra looked pale and worried. I told her at once that she must take more rest.

'"She won't," said Vaughan. "She can't resist other people's troubles."

'"You see, I can't put them out of my mind as easily as you," she answered provocatively.

'"Oh Lord!" Vaughan exclaimed. "I'm not going to start an argument."

'"No – because you know you're in the wrong. Have you quite forgotten this horrible affair?"

'I gathered up the reins of the conversation, and gentled it into easier topics. As I did so, I was conscious of resistance from Kyra; she evidently wanted to go on scrapping. I wondered why. Her nerves, no doubt, were overstrained, but she was too tired to wish to relieve them by a quarrel. I decided that she was deliberately worrying her husband to make him admit how he was spending his evenings.

'That was it. Before I left, she took me apart on the pretext of showing me the garden and pinned the conversation to our shooting expeditions.

Please God I'm never in the dock if the prosecuting counsel is a woman! As it was, I had the right to ask questions in my turn, and managed to slip from under her cross-examination without allowing her to feel it. It hurt. I couldn't let her know the truth, but I hated to leave her in that torment of uncertainty. She hesitated an instant before she said good-bye to me. Then she caught my arm, and cried:

'"Take care of him!"'

'I smiled and told her that she was overwrought, that we were doing nothing dangerous. What else could I say?

'That night, the third of the watching, the woods were alive. The world which lives just below the fallen leaves – mice and moles and big beetles – was making its surprising stir. The night birds were crying. A deer coughed far up in the forest. There was a slight breeze blowing, and from my lair on top of the rock I watched Vaughan trying to catch the scents it bore. He crouched down in the shadows. A bear ambled across the path up wind, and began to grub for some succulent morsel at the roots of a tree. It looked as woolly and harmless as a big dog. Clearly neither it nor its kind were the cause of our vigil. I saw Vaughan smile, and knew that he was thinking the same thought.

'A little after eleven the bear looked up, sniffed the air, and disappeared into the black bulk of the undergrowth as effortlessly and completely as if a spotlight had been switched off him. One by one the sounds of the night ceased. Vaughan eased the revolver in his pocket. The silence told its own tale. The forest had laid aside its business, and was watching like ourselves.

'Vaughan walked up the path to the far end of his beat. I looked away from him an instant, and down the path through the trees my eyes caught that same flicker of white. He turned to come back, and by the time that he was abreast of the rock I had seen it again. A bulky object it seemed to be, soft white, moving fast. He passed me, going towards it, and I lined my sights on the path ahead of him. Bounding up through the woods it came, then into the moonlight, and on to him. I was saved only by the extreme difficulty of the shot. I took just a fraction of a second longer than I needed, to make very sure of not hitting Vaughan. In that fraction of a second, thank God, she called to him! It was Kyra. A white ermine coat and her terrified running up the path had made of her a strange figure.

'She clung to him while she got her breath back. I heard her say:

'"I was frightened. There was something after me. I know it."

'Vaughan did not answer, but held her very close and stroked her hair. His upper lip curled back a little from his teeth. For once his whole being was surrendered to a single emotion: the desire to kill whatever had frightened her.

'"How did you know I was here?" he asked.

'"I didn't. I was looking for you. I looked for you last night, too."

'"You mad, brave girl!" he said.

'"But you mustn't, mustn't be alone. Where's Shiravieff?"

'"Right there." He pointed to the rock.

'"Why don't you hide yourself, too?"

'"One of us must show himself," he answered.

'She understood instantly the full meaning of his reply.

'"Come back with me!" she cried. "Promise me to stop it!"

'"I'm very safe, dear," he answered. "Look!"

'I can hear his tense voice right now, and remember their exact words. Those things eat into the memory. At the full stretch of his right arm he held out his handkerchief by two corners. He did not look at me, nor alter his tone.

'"Shiravieff," he said, "make a hole in that!"

'It was just a theatrical bit of nonsense, for the handkerchief was the easiest of easy marks. At any other time I would have been as sure as he of the result of the shot. But what he didn't know was that I had so nearly fired at another white and much larger mark – I was trembling so that I could hardly hold the rifle. I pressed the trigger. The hole in the handkerchief was dangerously near his hand. He put it down to bravado rather than bad shooting.

'Vaughan's trick had its effect. Kyra was surprised. She did not realize how easy it was, any more than she knew how much harder to hit is a moving mark seen in a moment of excitement.

'"But let me stay with you," she appealed

'"Sweetheart, we're going back right now. Do you think I'm going to allow my most precious possession to run wild in the woods?"

'"What about mine?" she said, and kissed him.

'They went away down the short cut. He made her walk a yard in front of him, and I caught the glint of moonlight on the barrel of his revolver. He was taking no risks.

'I myself went back by the path – carelessly, for I was sure that every living thing had been scared away by the voices and the shot. I was nearly down when I knew I was being followed. You've both lived in strange places – do you want me to explain the sensation? No? Well then, I knew I was being followed. I stopped and faced back up the path. Instantly something moved past me in the bushes, as if to cut off my retreat. I'm not superstitious. Once I heard it, I felt safe, for I knew where it was. I was sure I could move faster down that path than anything in the undergrowth – and if it came out into the open, it would have to absorb five steel explosive bullets. I ran. So far as I could hear, it didn't follow.

'I told Vaughan the next morning what had happened.

'"I'm sorry," he said, "I had to take her back. You understand, don't you?"

'"Of course," I answered in surprise. "What else could you do?"

'"Well, I didn't like leaving you alone. We had advertised our presence pretty widely. True, we should have frightened away any animal – but all we know about this animal is that it doesn't behave like one. There was a chance of our attracting instead of frightening it. We're going to get it to-night," he added savagely.

'I asked if Kyra would promise to stay at home.

'"Yes. She says we're doing our duty, and that she won't interfere. Do you think this is our duty?"

'"No!" I said.

'"Nor do I. I never feel anything which I enjoy can possibly be my duty. And, by God, I enjoy this now!"

'I think he did enjoy it as he waited on the rock that night. He wanted revenge. There was no reason to believe that Kyra had been frightened by anything more than night and loneliness, but he was out against the whole set of circumstances that had dared to affect her. He wanted to be the bait instead of the watcher – I believe, with some mad hope of getting his hands on his enemy. But I wouldn't let him. After all, it was my turn.

'Bait! As I walked up and down the path, the word kept running through my mind. There wasn't a sound. The only moving thing was the moon which passed from tree-top to tree-top as the night wore on. I pictured Vaughan on the rock, the foresight of his rifle creeping backwards and forwards in a quarter-circle as it followed my movements. I visualized the line of his aim as a thread of light passing down and across in front of my eyes. Once I heard Vaughan cough. I knew that he had seen my nervousness and was reassuring me. I stood by a clump of bushes some twenty yards away, watching a silver leaf that shook as some tiny beast crawled up it.

'Hot breath on the back of my neck – crushing weight on my shoulders – hardness against the back of my skull – the crack of Vaughan's rifle – they were instantaneous, but not too swift for me to know all the terror of death. Something leapt away from me and squirmed into the springhead beneath the rock.

'"Are you all right?" shouted Vaughan, crashing down through the ivy.

'"What was it?"

'"A man. I've winged him. Come on! I'm going in after him!"

'Vaughan was berserk mad. I've never seen such flaming disregard of danger. He drew a deep breath, and tackled the hole as if it were a man's ankles. Head and shoulders, he sloshed into the mud of the cavity, emptying his Winchester in front of him. If he couldn't wriggle forward swiftly without drawing breath he would be choked by the sulphur fumes or drowned. If his enemy were waiting for him, he was a dead man. He disappeared and I followed. No, I didn't need any courage. I was covered by the whole length of Vaughan's body. But it was a vile moment. We'd never dreamed that anything could get in and out through that spring. Imagine holding your breath, and trying to squirm through hot water, using your hips and shoulders like a snake, not knowing how you would return if the way forward was barred. At last I was able to raise myself on my hands and draw a breath. Vaughan had dragged himself clear and was on his feet, holding a flashlight in front of him.

'"Got him!" he said.

'We were in a low cave under the rock. There was air from the cracks above us. The floor was of dry sand, for the hot stream flowed into the cave close to the hole by which it left. A man lay crumpled up at the far end of the hollow. We crossed over to him. He held a sort of long pistol in his hand. It was a spring humane-killer. The touch of that wide muzzle against my skull is not a pleasant memory. The muzzle is jagged, you see, so that it grips the scalp while the spike is released.

'We turned the body over – it was Josef Weiss. Werewolf? Possession? I don't know. I would call it an atavistic neurosis. But that's a name, not an explanation.

'Beyond the body there was a hole some six feet in diameter, as round as if it had been bored by a rotary drill. The springs which had forced that passage had dried up, but the mottled-yellow walls were smooth as marble with the deposit left by the water. Evidently Weiss had been trying to reach that opening when Vaughan dropped him. We climbed that natural sewer pipe. For half an hour the flashlight revealed nothing but the sweating walls of the hole. Then we were stopped by a roughly hewn ladder which sprawled across the passage. The rungs were covered with mud, and here and there were dark stains on the wood. We went up. It led to a hollow evidently dug out with spade and chisel. The roof was of planks, with a trap-door at one end. We lifted it with our shoulders, and stood up within the four walls of a cottage. A fire was smouldering on the open hearth, and as we let in the draught of air, a log burst into flame. A gun stood in the ingle. On a rack were some iron traps and a belt of cartridges. There was a table in the centre of the room with a long knife on it. That was all we saw with our first glance. With our second we saw a lot more. Weiss had certainly carried his homicidal mania to extremes. I imagine his beastly experiences as a prisoner of war had left a kink in the poor devil's mind. Then, digging out a cellar or repairing the floor, he had accidentally discovered the dry channel beneath the cottage, and followed it to its hidden outlet. That turned his secret desires into action. He could kill and remove his victim without any trace. And so he let himself go.

'At dawn we were back at the cottage with the magistrate. When he came out, he was violently, terribly sick. I have never seen a man be so sick. It cleared him. No, I'm not being humorous. It cleared him mentally. He needed none of those emotional upheavals which we have to employ to drive shock out of our system. Didn't I tell you he was unimaginative? He handled the subsequent inquiry in a masterly fashion. He accepted as an unavoidable fact the horror of the thing, but he wouldn't listen to tales which could not be proved. There was never any definite proof of the extra horror in which the villagers believed.'

There was an exclamation from Lewis Banning.

'Ah – you remember now. I thought you would. The press reported that rumour as a fact, but there was no definite proof, I tell you.

'Vaughan begged me to keep it from his wife. I was to persuade her to go away at once before a breath of it could reach her. I was to tell her that he might have received internal injuries, and should be examined without delay. He himself believed the tale that was going round, but he was very conscious of his poise. I suspect that he was feeling a little proud of himself – proud that he was unaffected. But he dreaded the effect of the shock on his wife.

'We were too late. The cook had caught the prevailing fever, and told that unpleasant rumour to Kyra. She ran to her husband, deadly pale, desperate, instinctively seeking protection against the blow. He could protect himself, and would have given his life to be able to protect her. He tried, but only gave her words and more words. He explained that, looking at the affair calmly, it didn't matter; that no one could have know; that the best thing was to forget it; and so on. It was absurd. As if anyone who believed what was being said could look at the affair calmly!

'Sentiments of that kind were no comfort to his wife. She expected him to show his horror, not to isolate himself as if he had shut down a lid, not to leave her spiritually alone. She cried out at him that he had no feeling and rushed to her room. Perhaps I should have given her a sedative, but I didn't. I knew that the sooner she had it out with herself, the better, and that her mind was healthy enough to stand it.

'I said so to Vaughan, but he did not understand. Emotion, he thought, was dangerous. It mustn't be let loose. He wanted to tell her again not to "worry". He didn't see that he was the only person within ten miles who wasn't "worried".

'She came down later. She spoke to Vaughan scornfully, coldly, as if she had found him unfaithful to her. She said to him:

'"I can't see the woman again. Tell her to go, will you?"'

'She meant the cook. Vaughan challenged her. He was just obstinately logical and fair.

'"It's not her fault," he said. "She's an ignorant woman, not an anatomist. We'll call her in, and you'll see how unjust you are."

'"Oh no!" she cried – and then checked herself.

'"Send for her then!" she said.

'The cook came in. How could she know, she sobbed – she had noticed nothing – she was sure that what she had bought from Josef Weiss was really venison – she didn't think for a moment . . . Well, blessed are the simple!

'"My God! Be quiet!" Kyra burst out. "You all of you think what you want to think. You all lie to yourselves and pretend and have no feelings!"

'I couldn't stand any more. I begged her not to torture herself and not to torture me. It was the right note. She took my hands and asked me to forgive her. Then the tears came. She cried, I think, till morning. At breakfast she had a wan smile for both of us, and I knew that she was out of danger – clear of the shock for good. They left for England the same day.

'I met them in Vienna two years ago, and they dined with me. We never mentioned Zweibergen. They still adored one another, and still quarrelled. It was good to hear them talk and watch them feeling for each other's sympathy.

'Vaughan refused his meat at dinner, and said that he had become a vegetarian.

'"Why?" I asked deliberately.

'He answered that he had recently had a nervous breakdown – could eat nothing, and had nearly died. He was all right now, he said; no trace of the illness remained but his distaste for meat . . . it had come over him quite suddenly . . . he could not think why.

'I tell you the man was absolutely serious. He could *not* think why. Shock had lain hidden in him for ten years, and then had claimed its penalty.'

'And you?' asked Banning. 'How did you get clear of shock? You had to control your emotions at the time.'

'A fair question,' said Shiravieff. 'I've been living under a suspended sentence. There have been days when I thought I should visit one of my colleagues and ask him to clean up the mess. If I could only have got the story out of my system, it would have helped a lot – but I couldn't bring myself to tell it.'

'You have just told it,' said Colonel Romero solemnly.

# Guests from Gibbet Island

*Washington Irving*

Whoever has visited the ancient and renowned village of Communipaw may have noticed an old stone building of most ruinous and sinister appearance. The doors and window-shutters are ready to drop from their hinges; old clothes are stuffed in the broken panes of glass; while legions of half-starved dogs prowl about the premises, and rush out and bark at every passer-by; for your beggarly house in a village is most apt to swarm with profligate and ill-conditioned dogs. What adds to the sinister appearance of this mansion is a tall frame in front, not a little resembling a gallows, and which looks as if waiting to accommodate some of the inhabitants with a well-merited airing. It is not a gallows, however, but an ancient signpost; for this dwelling in the golden days of Communipaw was one of the most orderly and peaceful of village taverns, where public affairs were talked and smoked over. In fact, it was in this very building that Oloffe the Dreamer, and his companions, concerted that great voyage of discovery and colonization, in which they explored Buttermilk Channel, were nearly shipwrecked in the Strait of Hell-gate, and finally landed on the Island of Manhattan, and founded the great city of New Amsterdam.

Even after the province had been cruelly wrested from the sway of their High Mightinesses by the combined forces of the British and the Yankees, this tavern continued its ancient loyalty. It is true, the head of the Prince of Orange disappeared from the sign, a strange bird being painted over it, with the explanatory legend of *Die Wilde Gans*, or The Wild Goose; but this all the world knew to be a sly riddle of the landlord, the worthy Teunis Van Gieson, a knowing man in a small way, who laid his finger beside his nose and winked when any one studied the signification of his sign and observed that his goose was hatching, but would join the flock whenever they flew over the water; an enigma which was the perpetual recreation and delight of the loyal but fat-headed burghers of Communipaw.

Under the sway of this patriotic, though discreet and quiet publican, the tavern continued to flourish in primeval tranquillity, and was the resort of true-hearted Nederlanders, from all parts of Pavonia, who met here quietly and secretly to smoke and drink the downfall of Briton and Yankee, and success to Admiral Van Tromp.

The only drawback on the comfort of the establishment was a nephew of mine host, a sister's son, Yan Yost Vanderscamp by name, and a real scamp by nature. This unlucky whipster showed an early propensity to mischief, which he gratified in a small way by playing tricks upon the frequenters of the Wild Goose: putting gunpowder in their pipes, or squibs in their pockets, and astonishing them with an explosion, while they sat nodding round the fireplace in the bar-room; and if perchance a worthy burgher from some distant part of Pavonia lingered until dark over his potation, it was odds but young Vanderscamp would slip a brier under his horse's tail, as he mounted, and send him clattering along the road in neck-or-nothing style, to the infinite astonishment and discomfiture of the rider.

It may be wondered at that mine host of the Wild Goose did not turn such a graceless varlet out of doors, but Teunis Van Gieson was an easy-tempered man, and having no child of his own, looked upon his nephew with almost parental indulgence. His patience and good nature were doomed to be tried by another intimate of his mansion. This was a cross-grained curmudgeon of a negro, named Pluto, who was a kind of enigma in Communipaw. Where he came from, nobody knew. He was found one morning, after a storm, cast like a sea-monster on the strand in front of the Wild Goose, and lay there, more dead than alive. The neighbours gathered round, and speculated on this production of the deep; whether it were fish or flesh, or a compound of both, commonly yclept a merman. The kind-hearted Teunis Van Gieson, seeing that he wore the human form, took him into his house, and warmed him into life. By degrees, he showed signs of intelligence, and even uttered sounds very much like language, but which no one in Communipaw could understand. Some thought him a negro just from Guinea, who had either fallen overboard, or escaped from a slave-ship. Nothing, however, could ever draw from him any account of his origin. When questioned on the subject, he merely pointed to Gibbet Island, a small rocky islet, which lies in the open bay, just opposite Communipaw, as if that were his native place, though everybody knew it had never been inhabited.

In the process of time, he acquired something of the Dutch language, that is to say, he learnt all its vocabulary of oaths and maledictions, with just words sufficient to string them together. 'Donder en blicksem!' (thunder and lightning), was the gentlest of his ejaculations. For years he kept about the Wild Goose, more like one of those familiar spirits or household goblins we read of, than like a human being. He acknowledged allegiance to no one, but performed various domestic offices, when it suited his humour: waiting occasionally on the guests; grooming the horses; cutting wood; drawing water; and all this without being ordered. Lay any command on him, and the stubborn sea-urchin was sure to rebel. He was never so much at home, however, as when on the water, plying about in skiff or canoe, entirely alone, fishing, crabbing, or grabbing for oysters, and would bring home quantities for the larder of the Wild Goose, which he would throw down at the kitchen-door with a growl. No wind nor weather deterred him from launching forth on his favourite element: indeed, the wilder the weather, the more he seemed to enjoy it. If a storm was brewing, he was sure to put off from shore; and would be seen far out in the bay, his light skiff dancing like a feather on the waves, when sea and sky were in a turmoil, and the stoutest ships were fain to lower their sails. Sometimes on such occasions he would be absent for days together. How he weathered the tempest, and how and where he subsisted, no one could divine, nor did any one venture to ask, for all had an almost superstitious awe of him. Some of the Communipaw oystermen declared they had more than once seen him suddenly disappear, canoe and all, as if plunged beneath waves, and after a while come up again, in quite a different part of the bay; whence they concluded that he could live under water like that notable species of wild duck, commonly called the hell-diver. All began to consider him in the light of a foul-weather bird, like the Mother Carey's Chicken, or petrel; and whenever they saw him putting far out in his skiff, in cloudy weather, made up their minds for a storm.

The only being for whom he seemed to have any liking, was Yan Yost Vanderscamp, and him he liked for his very wickedness. He in a manner took the boy under his tutelage, prompted him to all kinds of mischief, aided him in every wild harum-scarum freak, until the lad became the complete scapegrace of the village: a pest to his uncle, and to everyone else. Nor were his pranks confined to the land; he soon learned to accompany old Pluto on the water. Together these worthies would cruise about the broad bay, and all the neighbouring straits and rivers; poking around in skiffs and canoes; robbing the set nets of the fishermen; landing on remote coasts, and laying waste orchards and water-melon patches; in short, carrying on a complete system of piracy, on a small scale. Piloted by Pluto, the youthful Vanderscamp soon became acquainted with all the bays, rivers, creeks, and inlets of the watery world around him; could navigate from the Hook to Spiting-Devil on the darkest night, and learned to set even the terrors of Hell-gate at defiance.

At length, negro and boy suddenly disappeared, and days and weeks elapsed, but without tidings of them. Some said they must have run away and gone to sea; others jocosely hinted that old Pluto, being no other than his namesake in disguise, had spirited away the boy to the nether regions. All, however, agreed in one thing, that the village was well rid of them.

In the process of time, the good Teunis Van Gieson slept with his fathers, and the tavern remained shut up, waiting for a claimant, for the next heir was Yan Yost Vanderscamp, and he had not been heard of for years. At length, one day, a boat was seen pulling for shore, from a long, black, rakish-looking schooner that lay at anchor in the bay. The boat's crew seemed worthy of the craft from which they debarked. Never had such a set of noisy, roistering, swaggering varlets landed in peaceful Communipaw. They were outlandish in garb and demeanour, and were headed by a rough, burly, bully ruffian, with fiery whiskers, a copper nose, a scar across his face, and a great Flaundrish beaver slouched on one side of his head, in whom, to their dismay, the quiet inhabitants were made to recognize their early pest, Yan Yost Vanderscamp. The rear of this hopeful gang was brought up by old Pluto, who had lost an eye, grown grizzly-headed, and looked more like a devil than ever. Vanderscamp renewed his acquaintance with the old burghers, much against their will, and in a manner not at all to their taste. He slapped them familiarly on the back, gave them an iron grip of the hand, and was hail fellow well met. According to his own account, he had been all the world over; had made money by bags full; had ships in every sea, and now meant to turn the Wild Goose into a country-seat, where he and his comrades, all rich merchants from foreign parts, might enjoy themselves in the interval of their voyages.

Sure enough, in a little while there was a complete metamorphose of the Wild Goose. From being a quiet, peaceful Dutch public house, it became a most riotous, uproarious private dwelling; a complete rendezvous for boisterous men of the seas, who came here to have what they called a 'blow out' on dry land, and might be seen at all hours, lounging about the door, or lolling out of the windows, swearing among themselves, and cracking rough jokes on every passer-by. The house was fitted up, too, in so strange a manner: hammocks slung to the walls, instead of bedsteads; odd kinds of furniture, of foreign fashion: bamboo couches, Spanish chairs; pistols, cutlasses, and blunderbusses, suspended on every peg, silver crucifixes on the mantel-pieces, silver candlesticks and porringers on the tables, contrasting oddly with the pewter and Delft ware of the original establishment. And then the strange amusements of these sea-monsters! Pitching Spanish dollars, instead of quoits; firing blunderbusses out of the window; shooting at a mark, or at any unhappy dog, or cat, or pig, or barn-door fowl, that might happen to come within reach.

The only being who seemed to relish their rough waggery was old

Pluto; and yet he led but a dog's life of it, for they practised all kinds of manual jokes upon him: kicked him about like a football, shook him by his grizzly mop of wool; and never spoke to him without coupling a curse by way of adjective to his name, and consigning him to the infernal regions. The old fellow, however, seemed to like them better, the more they cursed him, though his utmost expression of pleasure never amounted to more than the growl of a petted bear, when his ears are rubbed.

Old Pluto was the ministering spirit at the orgies of the Wild Goose; and such orgies as took place there! Such drinking, singing, whooping, swearing; with an occasional interlude of quarrelling and fighting. The noisier grew the revel, the more old Pluto plied the potations, until the guests would become frantic in their merriment, smashing everything to pieces, and throwing the house out of the windows. Sometimes, after a drinking bout, they sallied forth and scoured the village, to the dismay of the worthy burghers, who gathered their women within doors, and would have shut up the house. Vanderscamp, however, was not to be rebuffed. He insisted on renewing acquaintance with his old neighbours, and on introducing his friends, the merchants, to their families; swore he was on the look-out for a wife, and meant, before he stopped, to find husbands for all their daughters. So, will-ye, nill-ye, sociable he was; swaggered about their best parlours, with his hat on one side of his head; sat on the good wife's nicely-waxed mahogany table, kicking his heels against the carved and polished legs; kissed and tousled the young vrouws; and if they frowned and pouted, gave them a gold rosary, or a sparkling cross, to put them in good humour again.

Sometimes nothing would satisfy him, but he must have some of his old neighbours to dinner at the Wild Goose. There was no refusing him, for he had the complete upper hand of the community, and the peaceful burghers all stood in awe of him. But what a time would the quiet, worthy men have, among these rakehells, who would delight to astound them with the most extravagant gunpowder tales, embroidered with all kinds of foreign oaths; clink the can with them; pledge them in deep potations; bawl drinking songs in their ears, and occasionally fire pistols over their heads, or under the table, and then laugh in their faces, and ask them how they liked the smell of gunpowder.

Thus was the little village of Communipaw for a time like the unfortunate wight possessed with devils; until Vanderscamp and his brother merchants would sail on another trading voyage, when the Wild Goose would be shut up, and everything relapse into a quiet, only to be disturbed by his next visitation.

The mystery of all these proceedings gradually dawned upon the tardy intellects of Communipaw. These were the times of the notorious Captain Kidd, when the American harbours were the resorts of piratical adventurers of all kinds, who, under pretext of mercantile voyages, scoured the West Indies, made plundering descents upon the Spanish Main, visited even the remote Indian Seas, and then came to dispose of their booty, have their revels, and fit out new expeditions, in the English colonies.

Vanderscamp had served in this hopeful school, having risen to importance among the buccaneers, had pitched upon his native village, and early home, as a quiet, out-of-the-way, unsuspected place, where he and his comrades, while anchored at New York, might have their feasts, and concert their plans, without molestation.

At length the attention of the British government was called to these piratical enterprises, that were becoming so frequent and outrageous. Vigorous measures were taken to check and punish them. Several of the most noted freebooters were caught and executed, and three of Vanderscamp's chosen comrades, the most riotous swashbucklers of the Wild Goose, were hanged in chains on Gibbet Island, in full sight of their favourite resort. As to Vanderscamp himself, he and his man Pluto again disappeared, and it was hoped by the people of Communipaw that he had fallen in some foreign brawl, or been swung on some foreign gallows.

For a time, therefore, the tranquillity of the village was restored, the worthy Dutchmen once more smoked their pipes in peace, eyeing, with peculiar complacency, their old pests and terrors, the pirates dangling and drying in the sun, on Gibbet Island.

This perfect calm was doomed at length to be ruffled. The fiery persecution of the pirates gradually subsided. Justice was satisfied with the examples that had been made, and there was no more talk of Kidd, and the other heroes of like kidney. On a calm summer evening, a boat, somewhat heavily laden, was seen pulling into Communipaw. What was the surprise and disquiet of the inhabitants to see Yan Yost Vanderscamp seated at the helm, and his man Pluto tugging at the oar! Vanderscamp, however, was apparently an altered man. He brought home with him a wife, who seemed to be a shrew, and to have the upper hand of him. He no longer was the swaggering, bully ruffian, but affected the regular merchant, and talked of retiring from business, and settling down quietly, to pass the rest of his days in his native place.

The Wild Goose mansion was again opened, but with diminished splendour, and no riot. It is true, Vanderscamp had frequently nautical visitors, and the sound of revelry was occasionally overheard in his house; but everything seemed to be done under the rose; and old Pluto was the

only servant that officiated at these orgies. The visitors, indeed, were by
no means of the turbulent stamp of their predecessors; but quiet,
mysterious traders, full of nods, and winks, and hieroglyphic signs, with
whom, to use their cant phrase, 'everything was snug'. Their ships
came to anchor at night, in the lower bay; and on a private signal,
Vanderscamp would launch his boat, and accompanied solely by his
man Pluto, would make them mysterious visits. Sometimes boats pulled
in at night, in front of the Wild Goose, and various articles of merchandise
were landed in the dark, and spirited away, nobody knew whither. One
of the more curious of the inhabitants kept watch, and caught a glimpse
of the features of some of these night visitors, by the casual glance of a
lantern, and declared that he recognized more than one of the freebooting
frequenters of the Wild Goose in former times; whence he concluded
that Vanderscamp was at his old game, and that this mysterious
merchandise was nothing more or less than piratical plunder. The
more charitable opinion, however, was that Vanderscamp and his
comrades, having been driven from their old line of business by the
'oppressions of government', had resorted to smuggling to make both
ends meet.

Be that as it may: I come now to the extraordinary fact, which is the
butt-end of this story. It happened late one night, that Yan Yost
Vanderscamp was returning across the broad bay, in his light skiff,
rowed by his man Pluto. He had been carousing on board of a vessel
newly arrived, and was somewhat obfuscated in intellect by the liquor
he had imbibed. It was a still, sultry night; a heavy mass of lurid clouds
was rising in the west, with the low muttering of distant thunder.
Vanderscamp called on Pluto to pull lustily that they might get home
before the gathering storm. The old negro made no reply, but shaped
his course so as to skirt the rocky shores of Gibbet Island. A faint creaking
overhead caused Vanderscamp to cast up his eyes, when to his horror
he beheld the bodies of three pot companions and brothers in iniquity
dangling in the moonlight, their rags fluttering, and their chains creaking, as they were slowly swung backward and forward by the rising
breeze.

'What do you mean, you blockhead!' cried Vanderscamp, 'by pulling
so close to the island?'

'I thought you'd be glad to see your old friends once more,' growled
the negro: 'you were never afraid of a living man, what do you fear from
the dead?'

'Who's afraid?' hiccupped Vanderscamp, partly heated by liquor,
partly nettled by the jeer of the negro; 'who's afraid! Hang me, but I
would be glad to see them once more, alive or dead at the Wild Goose.

Come, my lads in the wind!' continued he, taking a draught, and flourishing the bottle above his head, 'here's fair weather to you in the other world; and if you should be walking the rounds tonight, odds fish! but I'll be happy if you will drop in to supper.'

A dismal creaking was the only reply. The wind blew loud and shrill, and as it whistled round the gallows, and among the bones, sounded as if they were laughing and gibbering in the air. Old Pluto chuckled to himself, and now pulled home. The storm burst over the voyagers, while they were yet far from shore. The rain fell in torrents, the thunder crashed and pealed, and the lightning kept up an incessant blaze. It was stark midnight before they landed in Communipaw.

Dripping and shivering, Vanderscamp crawled homeward. He was completely sobered by the storm; the water soaked from without having diluted and cooled the liquor within. Arrived at the Wild Goose, he knocked timidly and dubiously at the door, for he dreaded the reception he was to receive from his wife. He had reason to do so. She met him at the threshold, in a precious ill-humour.

'Is this a time,' said she, 'to keep people out of their beds, and to bring home company, to turn the house upside down?'

'Company?' said Vanderscamp, meekly; 'I have brought no company with me, wife.'

'No, indeed! they have got here before you, but by your invitation; and blessed-looking company they are, truly!'

Vanderscamp's knees smote together. 'For the love of heaven, where are they, wife?'

'Where? – why in the blue-room, upstairs; making themselves as much at home as if the house were their own.'

Vanderscamp made a desperate effort, scrambled up to the room, and threw open the door. Sure enough, there, at a table, on which burned a light as blue as brimstone, sat the three guests from Gibbet Island, with halters round their necks, and bobbing their cups together, as they were hob-a-nobbing, and trolling the old Dutch freebooters' glee, since translated into English:

> For three merry lads be we,
> And three merry lads be we:
> I on the land, and thou on the sand,
> And Jack on the gallows-tree.

Vanderscamp saw and heard no more. Starting back with horror, he missed his footing on the landing-place, and fell from the top of the stairs to the bottom. He was taken up speechless, and, either from the fall or the fright, was buried in the yard of the little Dutch church at Bergen on the following Sunday.

From that day forward, the fate of the Wild Goose was sealed. It was pronounced a *haunted house*, and avoided accordingly. No one inhabited it but Vanderscamp's shrew of a widow, and old Pluto, and they were considered but little better than its hobgoblin visitors. Pluto grew more and more haggard and morose, and looked more like an imp of darkness than a human being. He spoke to no one, but went about muttering to himself, or, as some hinted, talking with the devil, who, though unseen, was ever at his elbow. Now and then he was seen pulling about the bay alone in his skiff in dark weather, or at the approach of nightfall: nobody could tell why, unless on an errand to invite more guests from the gallows. Indeed it was affirmed that the Wild Goose still continued to be a house of entertainment for such guests, and that on stormy nights, the blue chamber was occasionally illuminated, and sounds of diabolical merriment were overheard, mingling with the howling of the tempest. Some treated these as idle stories, until on one such night, it was about the time of the equinox, there was a horrible uproar in the Wild Goose, that could not be mistaken. It was not so much the sound of revelry, however, as strife, with two or three piercing shrieks that pervaded every part of the village. Nevertheless, no one thought of hastening to the spot. On the contrary, the honest burghers of Communipaw drew their nightcaps over their ears, and buried their heads under the bedclothes, at the thought of Vanderscamp and his gallows companions.

The next morning, some of the bolder and more curious undertook to reconnoitre. All was quiet and lifeless at the Wild Goose. The door yawned wide open, and had evidently been open all night, for the storm had beaten into the house. Gathering more courage from the silence and apparent desertion, they gradually ventured over the threshold. The house had indeed the air of having been possessed by devils. Everything was topsy-turvy; trunks had been broken open, and chests of drawers and corner cupboards turned inside out, as in a time of general sack and pillage; but the most woeful sight was the widow of Yan Yost Vanderscamp, with the marks of a deadly gripe on the windpipe.

All now was conjecture and dismay at Communipaw; and the disappearance of old Pluto, who was nowhere to be found, gave rise to all kinds of wild surmises. Some suggested that the negro had betrayed the house to some of Vanderscamp's buccaneering associates, and that they had decamped together with the booty; others surmised that the negro was nothing more nor less than a devil incarnate, who had now accomplished his ends, and made off with his dues.

Events, however, vindicated the negro from this last imputation. His skiff was picked up, drifting about the bay, bottom upward, as if wrecked in a tempest; and his body was found, shortly afterwards, by some

Communipaw fishermen, stranded among the rocks of Gibbet Island, near the foot of the pirates' gallows. The fishermen shook their heads, and observed that old Pluto had ventured once too often to invite guests from Gibbet Island.

# The Book

*Margaret Irwin*

On a foggy night in November, Mr Corbett, having guessed the murderer by the third chapter of his detective story, arose in disappointment from his bed and went downstairs in search of something more satisfactory to send him to sleep.

The fog had crept through the closed and curtained windows of the dining-room and hung thick on the air, in a silence that seemed as heavy and breathless as the fog.

The dining-room bookcase was the only considerable one in the house and held a careless unselected collection to suit all the tastes of the household, together with a few dull and obscure old theological books that had been left over from the sale of a learned uncle's library. Cheap red novels bought on railway stalls by Mrs Corbett, who thought a journey the only time to read, were thrust in like pert undersized intruders among the respectable nineteenth-century works of culture, chastely bound in dark blue or green, which Mr Corbett had considered the right thing to buy during his Oxford days; beside these there swaggered the children's large, gaily bound story-books and collections of fairy tales in every colour.

From among this neat new cloth-bound crowd there towered here and there a musty sepulchre of learning, brown with the colour of dust rather than leather, with no trace of gilded letters, however faded, on its crumbling back to tell what lay inside. A few of these moribund survivors from the Dean's library were inhospitably fastened with rusty clasps; all remained closed, and appeared impenetrable, their blank forbidding backs uplifted above their frivolous surroundings with the air of scorn that belongs to a private and concealed knowledge.

It was an unusual flight of fancy for Mr Corbett to imagine that the vaporous and fog-ridden air that seemed to hang more thickly about the bookcase was like a dank and poisonous breath exhaled by one or other of these slowly rotting volumes.

He hurriedly chose a Dickens from the second shelf as appropriate to a London fog, and had returned to the foot of the stairs when he decided that his reading tonight should by contrast be of blue Italian skies and white statues, in beautiful rhythmic sentences. He went back for a Walter Pater.

He found *Marius the Epicurean* tipped sideways across the gap left by his withdrawal of *The Old Curiosity Shop*.

It was a very wide gap to have been left by a single volume, for the books on that shelf had been closely wedged together. He put the Dickens back into it and saw that there was still space for a large book. He said to himself, in careful and precise words: 'This is nonsense. No one can possibly have gone into the dining-room and removed a book while I was crossing the hall. There must have been a gap before in the second shelf.' But another part of his mind kept saying, in a hurried, tumbled torrent: 'There was no gap in the second shelf.'

He snatched at both the *Marius* and *The Old Curiosity Shop* and went to his room in a haste that was unnecessary and absurd.

Tonight, Dickens struck him in a different light. Beneath the author's sentimental pity for the weak and helpless he could discern a revolting pleasure in cruelty and suffering, while the grotesque figures of the people in Cruikshank's illustrations revealed too clearly the hideous distortions of their souls. What had seemed humorous now appeared diabolic, and in disgust at these two old favourites he turned to Walter Pater for the repose and dignity of a classic spirit.

But presently he wondered if this spirit were not in itself of a marble quality, frigid and lifeless, contrary to the purpose of nature. 'I have often thought,' he said to himself, 'that there is something evil in the austere worship of beauty for its own sake.' He had never thought so before, but he liked to think that this impulse of fancy was the result of mature consideration, and with this satisfaction he composed himself for sleep.

He woke two or three times in the night, an unusual occurrence, but he was glad of it, for each time he had been dreaming horribly of these blameless Victorian works. Sprightly devils in whiskers and peg-top trousers tortured a lovely maiden and leered in delight at her anguish; the gods and heroes of classic fable acted deeds whose naked crime and shame Mr Corbett had never appreciated in Latin and Greek Unseens.

When he had wakened in a cold sweat from the spectacle of the ravished Philomel's torn and bleeding tongue, he decided there was nothing for it but to go down and get another book that would turn his thoughts in some more pleasant direction. But his increasing reluctance to do this found a hundred excuses. The recollection of the gap in the shelf now recurred to him with a sense of unnatural importance; in the troubled dozes that followed, this gap between two books seemed the most hideous deformity, like a gap between the front teeth of some grinning monster.

But in the clear daylight of the morning Mr Corbett came down to the pleasant dining-room, its sunny windows and smell of coffee and toast, and ate an undiminished breakfast with a mind chiefly occupied in self-congratulation that the wind had blown the fog away in time for his Saturday game of golf. Whistling happily, he was pouring out his final cup of coffee when his hand remained arrested in the act, as his glance, roving across the bookcase, noticed that there was now no gap at all in the second shelf. He asked who had been at the bookcase already, but neither of the girls had, nor Dicky, and Mrs Corbett was not yet down. The maid never touched the books. They wanted to know what book he missed in it, which made him look foolish, as he could not say.

'I thought there was a gap in the second shelf,' he said, 'but it doesn't matter.'

'There never is a gap in the second shelf,' said little Jean brightly. 'You can take out lots of books from it, and when you go back the gap's always filled up. Haven't you noticed that? I have.'

Nora, the middle one in age, said Jean was always being silly; she had been found crying over the funny pictures in the *Rose and the Ring*, because she said all the people in them had such wicked faces.

Mr Corbett did not like to think of such fancies for his Jeannie. She retaliated briskly by saying Dicky was just as bad, and he was a big boy. He had kicked a book across the room and said, 'Filthy stuff,' just like that. Jean was a good mimic; her tone expressed a venom of disgust, and she made the gesture of dropping a book as though the very touch of it were loathsome. Dicky, who had been making violent signs at her, now told her she was a beastly little sneak, and he would never again take her for rides on the step of his bicycle. Mr Corbett was disturbed as he gravely asked his son how he had got hold of this book.

'Took it out of that bookcase, of course,' said Dick furiously.

It turned out to be the *Boy's Gulliver's Travels* that Granny had given him, and Dicky had at last to explain his rage with the devil who wrote it to show that men were worse than beasts and the human race a wash-out.

Mr Corbett, with some annoyance, advised his son to take out a nice bright modern boy's adventure story that could not depress anybody. It appeared, however, that Dicky was 'off reading just now', and the girls echoed this.

Mr Corbett soon found that he, too, was 'off reading'. Every new book seemed to him weak, tasteless, and insipid, while his old and familiar books were depressing or even, in some obscure way, disgusting. Authors must all be filthy-minded; they probably wrote what they dared not express in their lives.

His taste for reading revived as he explored with relish the hidden infirmities of minds that had been valued by fools as great and noble. He saw Jane Austen and Charlotte Brontë as two unpleasant examples of spinsterhood: the one as a prying, sub-acid busybody in everyone else's flirtations, the other as a raving, craving mænad seeking self-immolation on the altar of her frustrated passions.

These powers of penetration astonished him. With a mind so acute and original he should have achieved greatness yet he was a mere solicitor and not prosperous at that. If he had but the money he might do something with those ivory shares, but it would be a pure gamble, and he had no luck. His natural envy of his wealthier acquaintances now mingled with a contempt for their stupidity that approached loathing. The digestion of his lunch in the City was ruined by meeting sentimental yet successful dotards, whom he had once regarded as pleasant fellows. The very sight of them spoiled his game of golf, so that he came to prefer reading alone in the dining-room even on sunny afternoons.

He discovered also, and with a slight shock, that Mrs Corbett had always bored him. Dicky he began actively to dislike as an impudent blockhead, and the two girls were as insipidly alike as white mice; it was a relief when he abolished their tiresome habit of coming in to say goodnight.

In the now unbroken silence and seclusion of the dining-room he read with feverish haste, as though he were seeking for some clue to knowledge, some secret key to existence which would quicken and inflame it.

He even explored the few decaying remains of his uncle's theological library. One of these books had diagrams and symbols in the margin, which he took to be mathematical formulae of a kind he did not know. He presently discovered that they were drawn, not printed, and that the book was in manuscript, in a very neat, crabbed black writing that resembled black letter printing. It was, moreover, in Latin, a fact that gave Mr Corbett a shock of unreasoning disappointment. For while examining the signs on the margin he had been filled with an extraordinary exultation, as though he knew himself to be on the edge of a discovery that should alter his whole life. But he had forgotten his Latin.

With a secret and guilty air, which would have looked absurd to anyone who knew his harmless purpose, he stole to the schoolroom for Dicky's Latin dictionary and grammar, and hurried back to the dining-room, where he tried to discover what the book was about with an anxious industry that surprised himself. There was no name to it, nor of the author. Several blank pages had been left at the end, and the writing ended at the bottom of a page, with no flourish nor superscription, as though the book had been left unfinished. From what sentences he could translate it seemed to be a work on theology.

There were constant references to the Master, to his wishes and

442 Realms of Darkness

injunctions, which appeared to be of a complicated kind. Mr Corbett began by skipping these as mere accounts of ceremonial, but a word caught his eye as one unlikely to occur in such an account. He read this passage attentively looking up each word in the dictionary, and could hardly believe the result of his translation.

'Clearly,' he decided, 'this book must be by some early missionary, and the passage I have just read the account of some horrible rite practised by a savage tribe of devil-worshippers.' Though he called it 'horrible', he reflected on it, committing each detail to memory. He then amused himself by copying the signs in the margin near it and trying to discover their significance. But a sensation of sickly cold came over him, his head swam, and he could hardly see the figures before his eyes. He suspected a sudden attack of influenza and went to ask his wife for medicine.

They were all in the drawing-room, Mrs Corbett helping Nora and Jean with a new game, Dicky playing the pianola, and Mike, the Irish terrier, who had lately deserted his accustomed place on the dining-room hearth-rug, stretched by the fire.

He thought how like sheep they looked and sounded, nothing in his appearance in the mirror struck him as odd: it was their gaping faces that were unfamiliar. He then noticed the extraordinary behaviour of Mike, who had sprung from the hearth-rug and was crouched in the farthest corner uttering no sound, but with his eyes distended and foam round his bared teeth. Under Mr Corbett's glance he slunk towards the door, whimpering in a faint and abject manner, and then as his master called him he snarled horribly, and the hair bristled on the scruff of his neck.

'What *can* be the matter with Mike?' asked Mrs Corbett.

Her question broke a silence that seemed to have lasted a long time. Jean began to cry. Mr Corbett said irritably that he did not know what was the matter with any of them.

Then Nora asked: 'What is that red mark on your face?'

He looked again in the glass and could see nothing.

'It's quite clear from here,' said Dicky. 'I can see the lines in the finger-print.'

'Yes, that's what it is,' said Mrs Corbett in her brisk staccato voice: 'the print of a finger on your forehead. Have you been writing in red ink?'

Mr Corbett precipitately left the room for his own, where he sent down a message that he was suffering from headache and would have his dinner in bed. He wanted no one fussing round him. By next morning he was amazed at his fancies of influenza, for he had never felt so well in his life.

No one commented on his looks at breakfast, so that he concluded the mark had disappeared. The old Latin book he had been translating on the previous night had been moved from the writing bureau, although Dicky's grammar and dictionary were still there. The second shelf was, as always in the daytime, closely packed; the book had, he remembered, been in the second shelf. But this time he did not ask who put it back.

That day he had an unexpected stroke of luck in a new client of the name of Crab, who entrusted him with large sums of money; nor was he irritated by the sight of his more prosperous acquaintances; but with difficulty refrained from grinning in their faces, so confident was he that his remarkable ability must soon place him higher than any of them. At dinner he chaffed his family with what he felt to be the gaiety of a schoolboy.

In spite of this new alertness, he could not attend to the letters he should have written that evening, and drifted to the bookcase for a little light distraction, but found that for the first time there was nothing he wished to read. He pulled out a book from above his head at random, and saw that it was the old Latin book in manuscript.

As he turned over its stiff and yellow pages, he noticed with pleasure the smell of corruption that had first repelled him in these decaying volumes, a smell, he now thought, of ancient and secret knowledge.

This idea of secrecy seemed to affect him personally, for on hearing a step in the hall he hastily closed the book and put it back in its place. He went to the schoolroom where Dicky was doing his homework and told him he required his Latin grammar and dictionary again for an old law report. To his annoyance he stammered and put his words awkwardly; he thought that the boy looked oddly at him and he cursed him in his heart for a suspicious young devil, though of what he should be suspicious he could not say. Nevertheless, when back in the dining-room, he listened at the door and then softly turned the lock before he opened the books on the writing bureau.

The script and Latin seemed much clearer than on the previous evening and he was able to read at random a passage relating to a trial of a German midwife in 1620 for the murder and dissection of 783 children.

It appeared to be an account of some secret society whose activities and ritual were of a nature so obscure, and when not, so vile and terrible, that Mr Corbett would not at first believe that this could be a record of any human mind.

He read until far later than his usual hour for bed, and when at last he rose, it was with the book in his hands. To defer his parting with it, he stood turning over the pages until he reached the end of the writing, and was struck by a new peculiarity.

The ink was much fresher and of a far poorer quality than the thick rusted ink in the bulk of the book; on close inspection he would have said that it was of modern manufacture and written quite recently, were it not for the fact that it was in the same crabbed late seventeenth-century handwriting.

This, however, did not explain the perplexity, even dismay and fear he now felt as he started at the last sentence. It ran: *Continue te in perennibus studiis*, and he had at once recognized it as a Ciceronian tag that had been dinned into him at school. He could not understand how he had failed to notice it yesterday.

Then he remembered that the book had ended at the bottom of a page. But now, the last two sentences were written at the very top of a page. However long he looked at them, he could come to no other conclusion than that they had been added since the previous evening.

He now read the sentence before the last: *Re imperfecta mortuus sum*, and translated the whole as 'I died with my purposes unachieved. Continue, thou, the never-ending studies.'

With his eyes still fixed upon it, Mr Corbett replaced the book on the writing bureau and stepped back from it to the door, his hand outstretched behind him, groping and then tugging at the door handle. As the door failed to open, his breath came in a faint, hardly articulate scream. Then he remembered that he had himself locked it, and he fumbled with the key in frantic ineffectual movements until at last he opened it and banged it after him as he plunged backwards into the hall.

For a moment he stood there looking at the door handle; then with a stealthy, sneaking movement, his hand crept out towards it, touched it, began to turn it, when suddenly he pulled his hand away and went up to his bedroom, three steps at a time.

There he hid his face in the pillow, cried and raved in meaningless words, repeating: 'Never, never, never. I will never do it again. Help me never to do it again.' With the words 'Help me,' he noticed what he was saying – they reminded him of other words, and he began to pray aloud.

But the words sounded jumbled, they persisted in coming into his head in a reverse order so that he found he was saying his prayers backwards, and at this final absurdity he suddenly began to laugh very loud. He sat up on the bed, delighted at this return to sanity, common sense and humour, when the door leading into Mrs Corbett's room opened, and he saw his wife staring at him with a strange, grey, drawn face that made her seem like the terror-stricken ghost of her usually smug and placid self.

'It's not burglars,' he said irritably. 'I've come to bed late, that is all, and must have wakened you.'

'Henry,' said Mrs Corbett, and he noticed that she had not heard him: 'Henry, didn't you hear it?'

'What?'

'That laugh.'

He was silent, an instinctive caution warning him to wait until she spoke again. And this she did, imploring him with her eyes to reassure her.

'It was not a human laugh. It was like the laugh of a devil.'

He checked his violent inclination to laugh again. It was wiser not to let her know that it was only his laughter she had heard. He told her to stop being fanciful, and Mrs Corbett gradually recovered her docility.

The next morning, Mr Corbett rose before any of the servants and crept down to the dining-room. As before, the dictionary and grammar alone remained on the writing bureau; the book was back on the second shelf. He opened it at the end. Two more lines had been added, carrying the writing down to the middle of the page. They ran:

> *Ex auto canceris*
> *In dentem elephantis.*

Which translated as:

> Out of the money of the crab
> Into the tooth of the elephant.

From this time on, his acquaintances in the City noticed a change in the mediocre, rather flabby and unenterprising 'old Corbett'. His recent sour depression dropped from him; he seemed to have grown twenty years younger, strong, brisk, and cheerful, and with a self-confidence in business that struck them as lunacy. They waited with a not unpleasant excitement for the inevitable crash, but his every speculation, however wild and hare-brained, turned out successful.

He never stayed in town for dinners or theatres, for he was always now in a hurry to get home, where, as soon as he was sure of being undisturbed, he would take down the manuscript book from the second shelf of the dining-room and turn to the last pages.

Every morning he found that a few words had been added since the evening before, and always they formed, as he considered, injunctions to himself. These were at first only with regard to his money transactions, giving assurance to his boldest fancies, and since the brilliant and unforeseen success that had attended his gamble with Mr Crab's money in African ivory, he followed all such advice unhesitatingly.

But presently, interspersed with these commands, were others of a meaningless, childish, yet revolting character, such as might be invented by a decadent imbecile.

He at first paid no attention to these directions, but found that his new speculations declined so rapidly that he became terrified not merely for his fortune but for his reputation and even safety, since the money of various of his clients was involved. It was made clear to him that he must follow the commands in the book altogether or not at all, and he began to carry out their puerile and grotesque blasphemies with a contemptuous amusement, which, however, gradually changed to a sense of their monstrous significance. They became more capricious and difficult of execution, but he now never hesitated to obey blindly, urged by a fear that he could not understand.

By now he understood the effect of this book on the others near it and the reason that had impelled its mysterious agent to move the books into the second shelf, so that all in turn should come under the influence of that ancient and secret knowledge.

In respect to it, he encouraged his children, with jeers at their stupidity, to read more, but he could not observe that they ever now took a book from the dining-room bookcase. He himself no longer needed to read, but went to bed early and slept soundly. The things that all his life he had longed to do when he should have enough money now seemed to him insipid. His most exciting pleasure, was the smell and touch of these mouldering pages, as he turned them to find the last message inscribed to him.

One evening it was in two words only: *Canem occide*.

He laughed at this simple and pleasant request to kill the dog, for he bore Mike a grudge for his change from devotion to slinking aversion. Moreover, it could not have come more opportunely, since in turning out an old desk he had just discovered some packets of rat poison bought years ago and forgotten. He whistled light-heartedly as he ran upstairs to rummage for the packets, and returned to empty one in the dog's dish of water in the hall.

That night the household was awakened by terrified screams proceeding from the stairs. Mr Corbett was the first to hasten there, prompted by the instinctive caution that was always with him these days. He saw Jean, in her nightdress, scrambling up on to the landing on her hands and knees, clutching at anything that afforded support and screaming in a choking, tearless, unnatural manner. He carried her to the room she shared with Nora, where they were quickly followed by Mrs Corbett.

Nothing coherent could be got from Jean. Nora said that she must have been having her old dream again: when her father demanded what this was, she said that Jean sometimes woke in the night, crying, because she had dreamed of a hand passing backwards and forwards over the dining-room bookcase, until it found a certain book and took it out of the shelf. At this point she was always so frightened that she woke up.

On hearing this, Jean broke into fresh screams, and Mrs Corbett would have no more explanations. Mr Corbett went out onto the stairs to find what had brought the child there from her bed. On looking down into the lighted hall he saw Mike's dish overturned. He went down to examine it and saw that the water he had poisoned must have been upset and absorbed by the rough doormat, which was quite wet.

He went back to the little girls' room, told his wife that she was tired and must go to bed, and he would now take his turn at comforting Jean. She was now much quieter. He took her on his knee, where at first she shrank from him. Mr Corbett remembered with an awed sense of injury that she never now sat on his knee, and would have liked to pay her out for it by mocking and frightening her. But he had to coax her into telling him what he wanted, and with this object he soothed her, calling her by pet names that he thought he had forgotten, telling her that nothing could hurt her now he was with her. He listened to what he had at last induced her to tell him.

She and Nora had kept Mike with them all the evening and taken him to sleep in their room for a treat. He had lain at the foot of Jean's bed and they had all gone to sleep. Then Jean began her old dream of the hand moving over the books in the dining-room bookcase; but instead of taking out a book it came across the dining-room and out onto the stairs. It came up over the banisters and to the door of their room, and turned their door handle very softly and opened it. At this point she jumped up, wide awake, and turned on the light, calling to Nora. The door, which had been shut when they went to sleep, was wide open, and Mike was gone.

She told Nora that she was sure something dreadful would happen to him if she did not go and bring him back, and ran down into the hall, where she saw him just about to drink from his dish. She called to him and he looked up, but did not come, so she ran to him and began to pull him along with her when her nightdress was clutched from behind and then she felt a hand seize her arm.

She fell down and then clambered upstairs as fast as she could, screaming all the way.

It was now clear to Mr Corbett that Mike's dish must have been upset in the scuffle. She was again crying, but this time he felt himself unable to comfort her. He retired to his room, where he walked up and down in an agitation he could not understand.

'I am not a bad man,' he kept saying to himself. 'I have never done anything actually wrong. My clients are none the worse for my speculations, only the better.'

Presently he added: 'It is not wrong to try and kill a dog, an ill-tempered brute. It turned against me. It might have bitten Jeannie.'

He noticed that he had thought of her as Jeannie which he had not done for some time; it must have been because he had called her that tonight. He must forbid her ever to leave her room at night; he could not have her meddling. It would be safer for him if she were not there at all.

Again that sick and cold sensation of fear swept over him; he seized the bed-post as though he were falling, and held onto it for some minutes. 'I was thinking of a boarding school,' he told himself, and then, 'I must go down and find out – find out –' He would not think what it was he must find out.

He opened his door and listened. The house was quiet. He crept onto the landing and along to Nora's and Jean's door, where again he stood, listening. There was no sound, and at that he was again overcome with unreasonable terror. He imagined Jean lying very still in her bed, too still. He hastened away from the door, shuffling in his bedroom slippers along the passage and down the stairs.

A bright fire still burned in the dining-room grate. A glance at the clock told him it was not yet twelve. He stared at the bookcase. On the second shelf was a gap which had not been there when he had left. On the writing bureau lay a large open book. He knew that he must cross the room and see what was written in it. Then, as before, words that he did not intend came sobbing and crying to his lips, muttering 'No, no, not that. Never, never, never.' But he crossed the room and looked down at the book. As last time, the message was in only two words: '*Infantem occide.*'

He slipped and fell forwards against the bureau. His hands clutched at the book, lifted it as he recovered himself, and with his finger he traced out the words that had been written. The smell of corruption crept into his nostrils. He told himself that he was not a snivelling dotard but a man stronger and wiser than his fellows, superior to the common emotions of humanity, who held in his hands the sources of ancient and secret power.

He had known what the message would be. It was after all the only safe and logical thing to do. Jean had acquired dangerous knowledge. She was a spy, an antagonist. That she was so unconsciously, that she was eight years old, his youngest and favourite child, were sentimental appeals that could make no difference to a man of sane reasoning power such as his own.

Jean had sided with Mike against him. 'All that are not for me are against me,' he repeated softly. He would kill both dog and child with the white powder that no one knew to be in his possession.

He laid down the book and went to the door. What he had to do he would do quickly, for again that sensation of deadly cold was sweeping over him. He wished he had not to do it tonight; last night it would have been easier, but tonight she had sat on his knee and made him afraid. He imagined her lying very still in her bed, too still.

He held onto the door-handle but his fingers seemed to have grown numb, for he could not turn it. He clung to it, crouched and shivering, bending over it until he knelt on the ground, his head beneath the handle which he still clutched with upraised hands. Suddenly the hands were loosened and flung outwards with the frantic gesture of a man falling from a great height, and he stumbled to his feet.

He seized the book and threw it on the fire. A violent sensation of choking overcame him, he felt he was being strangled, as in a nightmare he tried again and again to shriek aloud, but his breath would make no sound. His breath would not come at all. He fell backwards heavily down on the floor, where he lay very still.

In the morning the maid who came to open the dining-room windows found her master dead. The sensation caused by this was scarcely so great in the City as that given by the simultaneous collapse of all Mr Corbett's recent speculations. It was instantly assumed that he must have had previous knowledge of this and so committed suicide.

The stumbling-block of this theory was that the medical report defined the cause of Mr Corbett's death as strangulation of the windpipe by the pressure of a hand which had left the marks of its fingers on his throat.

# The Three Sisters

## *W. W. Jacobs*

Thirty years ago on a wet autumn evening the household of Mallett's Lodge was gathered round the death-bed of Ursula Mallow, the eldest of the three sisters who inhabited it. The dingy moth-eaten curtains of the old wooden bedstead were drawn apart, the light of a smoking oil-lamp falling upon the hopeless countenance of the dying woman as she turned her dull eyes upon her sisters. The room was in silence except for an occasional sob from the youngest sister, Eunice. Outside the rain fell steadily over the streaming marshes.

'Nothing is to be changed, Tabitha,' gasped Ursula to the other sister, who bore a striking likeness to her, although her expression was harder and colder; 'this room is to be locked up and never opened.'

'Very well,' said Tabitha brusquely; 'though I don't see how it can matter to you then.'

'It does matter,' said her sister with startling energy. 'How do you know, how do I know that I may not sometimes visit it? I have lived in this house so long I am certain that I shall see it again. I *will* come back. Come back to watch over you both and see that no harm befalls you.'

'You are talking wildly,' said Tabitha, by no means moved at her sister's solicitude for her welfare. 'Your mind is wandering; you know that I have no faith in such things.'

Ursula sighed, and beckoning to Eunice, who was weeping silently at the bedside, placed her feeble arms around her neck and kissed her.

'Do not weep, dear,' she said feebly. 'Perhaps it is best so. A lonely woman's life is scarce worth living. We have no hopes, no aspirations; other women have had happy husbands and children, but we in this forgotten place have grown old together. I go first, but you must soon follow.'

Tabitha, comfortably conscious of only forty years and an iron frame, shrugged her shoulders and smiled grimly.

'I go first,' repeated Ursula in a new and strange voice as her heavy eyes slowly closed, 'but I will come for each of you in turn, when your lease of life runs out. At that moment I will be with you to lead your steps whither I now go.'

As she spoke the flickering lamp went out suddenly as though extinguished by a rapid hand, and the room was left in utter darkness. A strange suffocating noise issued from the bed, and when the trembling women had relighted the lamp, all that was left of Ursula Mallow was ready for the grave.

That night the survivors passed together. The dead woman had been a firm believer in the existence of that shadowy borderland which is said to form an unhallowed link between the living and the dead, and even stolid Tabitha, slightly unnerved by the events of the night, was not free from certain apprehensions that she might have been right.

With the bright morning their fears disappeared. The sun stole in at the window, and seeing the poor earthworn face on the pillow so touched it and glorified it that only its goodness and weakness were seen, and the beholders came to wonder how they could ever have felt any dread of aught so calm and peaceful. A day or two passed, and the body was transferred to a massive coffin long regarded as the finest piece of work of its kind ever turned out of the village carpenter's workshop. Then a slow and melancholy cortège headed by four bearers wound its solemn way across the marshes to the family vault in the grey old church, and all that was left of Ursula was placed by the father and mother who had taken that self-same journey some thirty years before.

To Eunice as they toiled slowly home the day seemed strange and Sabbath-like, the flat prospect of marsh wilder and more forlorn than usual, the roar of the sea more depressing. Tabitha had no such fancies. The bulk of the dead woman's property had been left to Eunice, and her avaricious soul was sorely troubled and her proper sisterly feelings of regret for the deceased sadly interfered with in consequence.

'What are you going to do with all that money, Eunice?' she asked as they sat at their quiet tea.

'I shall leave it as it stands,' said Eunice slowly. 'We have both got sufficient to live upon, and I shall devote the income from it to supporting some beds in a children's hospital.'

'If Ursula had wished it to go to a hospital,' said Tabitha in her deep tones, 'she would have left the money to it herself. I wonder you do not respect her wishes more.'

'What else can I do with it then?' inquired Eunice

'Save it,' said the other with gleaming eyes, 'save it.'

Eunice shook her head.                               .

'No,' said she, 'it shall go to the sick children, but the principal I will not touch, and if I die before you it shall become yours and you can do what you like with it.'

'Very well,' said Tabitha, smothering her anger by a strong effort; 'I don't believe that was what Ursula meant you to do with it, and I don't believe she will rest quietly in the grave while you squander the money she stored so carefully.'

'What do you mean?' asked Eunice with pale lips. 'You are trying to frighten me; I thought that you did not believe in such things.'

Tabitha made no answer, and to avoid the anxious inquiring gaze of her sister, drew her chair to the fire and, folding her gaunt arms, composed herself for a nap.

For some time life went on quietly in the old house. The room of the dead woman, in accordance with her last desire, was kept firmly locked, its dirty windows forming a strange contrast to the prim cleanliness of the others. Tabitha, never very talkative, became more taciturn than ever, and stalked about the house and the neglected garden like an unquiet spirit, her brow roughened into the deep wrinkles suggestive of much thought. As the winter came on, bringing with it the long dark evenings, the old house became more lonely than ever, and an air of mystery and dread seemed to hang over it and brood in its empty rooms and dark corridors. The deep silence of night was broken by strange noises for which neither the wind nor the rats could be held accountable. Old Martha, seated in her distant kitchen, heard strange sounds upon the stairs, and once, upon hurrying to them, fancied she saw a dark figure squatting upon the landing, though a subsequent search with candle and spectacles failed to discover anything. Eunice was disturbed by several vague incidents, and, as she suffered from a complaint of the heart, rendered very ill by them. Even Tabitha admitted a strangeness about the house but, confident in her piety and virtue, took no heed of it, her mind being fully employed in another direction.

Since the death of her sister all restraint upon her was removed, and she yielded herself up entirely to the stern and hard rules enforced by avarice upon its devotees. Her house-keeping expenses were kept rigidly separate from those of Eunice and her food limited to the coarsest dishes, while in the matter of clothes the old servant was by far the better dressed. Seated alone in her bedroom this uncouth, hard-featured creature revelled in her possessions, grudging even the expense of the candle-end which enabled her to behold them. So completely did this passion change her that both Eunice and Martha became afraid of her, and lay awake in their beds night after night trembling at the chinking of the coins at her unholy vigils.

One day Eunice ventured to remonstrate. 'Why don't you bank your money, Tabitha?' she said; 'it is surely not safe to keep such large sums in such a lonely house.'

'Large sums!' repeated the exasperated Tabitha, 'large sums; what nonsense is this? You know well that I have barely sufficient to keep me.'

'It's a great temptation to housebreakers,' said her sister, not pressing the point. 'I made sure last night that I heard somebody in the house.'

'Did you?' said Tabitha, grasping her arm, a horrible look on her face. 'So did I. I thought they went to Ursula's room, and I got out of bed and went on the stairs to listen.'

'Well?' said Eunice faintly, fascinated by the look on her sister's face.

'There was *something* there,' said Tabitha slowly. 'I'll swear it, for I stood on the landing by her door and listened; something scuffling on the floor round and round the room. At first I thought it was the cat, but when I went up there this morning the door was still locked, and the cat was in the kitchen.'

'Oh, let us leave this dreadful house,' moaned Eunice.

'What!' said her sister grimly; 'afraid of poor Ursula? Why should you be? Your own sister who nursed you when you were a babe, and who perhaps even now comes and watches over your slumbers.'

'Oh!' said Eunice, pressing her hand to her side, 'if I saw her I should die. I should think that she had come for me as she said she would. O God! have mercy on me, I am dying.'

She reeled as she spoke, and before Tabitha could save her, sank senseless to the floor.

'Get some water,' cried Tabitha, as old Martha came hurrying up the stairs. 'Eunice has fainted.'

The old woman, with a timid glance at her, retired, reappearing shortly afterwards with the water, with which she proceeded to restore her much-loved mistress to her senses. Tabitha, as soon as this was accomplished, stalked off to her room, leaving her sister and Martha sitting drearily enough in the small parlour, watching the fire and conversing in whispers.

It was clear to the old servant that this state of things could not last much longer, and she repeatedly urged her mistress to leave a house so lonely and mysterious. To her great delight Eunice at length consented, despite the fierce opposition of her sister, and at the mere idea of leaving gained greatly in health and spirits. A small but comfortable house was hired in Morville, and arrangements made for a speedy change.

It was the last night in the old house, and all the wild spirits of the marshes, the wind and the sea seemed to have joined forces for one supreme effort. When the wind dropped, as it did at brief intervals, the sea was heard moaning on the distant beach, strangely mingled with the desolate warning of the bell-buoy as it rocked to the waves. Then the wind rose again, and the noise of the sea was lost in the fierce gusts which, finding no obstacle on the open marshes, swept with their full fury upon the house by the creek. The strange voices of the air shrieked in its chimneys, windows rattled, doors slammed, and even the very curtains seemed to live and move.

Eunice was in bed, awake. A small night-light in a saucer of oil shed a sickly glare upon the worm-eaten old furniture, distorting the most innocent articles into ghastly shapes. A wilder gust than usual almost deprived her of the protection afforded by that poor light, and she lay listening fearfully to the creakings and other noises on the stairs, bitterly regretting that she had not asked Martha to sleep with her. But it was not too late even now. She slipped hastily to the floor, crossed to the huge wardrobe, and was in the very act of taking her dressing-gown from its peg when an unmistakable footfall was heard on the stairs. The robe dropped from her shaking fingers, and with a quickly beating heart she regained her bed.

The sounds ceased and a deep silence followed, which she herself was unable to break although she strove hard to do so. A wild gust of wind shook the windows and nearly extinguished the light, and when its flame had regained its accustomed steadiness she saw that the door was slowly opening, while the huge shadow of a hand blotted the papered wall. Still her tongue refused its office. The door flew open with a crash, a cloaked figure entered and, throwing aside its coverings, she saw with a horror past all expression the napkin-bound face of the dead Ursula smiling terribly at her. In her last extremity she raised her faded eyes above for succour, and then as the figure noiselessly advanced and laid its cold hand upon her brow, the soul of Eunice Mallow left its body with a wild shriek and made its way to the Eternal.

Martha, roused by the cry, and shivering with dread, rushed to the door and gazed in terror at the figure which stood leaning over the bedside. As she watched, it slowly removed the cowl and the napkin and exposed the fell face of Tabitha, so strangely contorted between fear and triumph that she hardly recognized it.

'Who's there?' cried Tabitha in a terrible voice as she saw the old woman's shadow on the wall.

'I thought I heard a cry,' said Martha, entering. 'Did anybody call?'

'Yes, Eunice,' said the other, regarding her closely. 'I, too, heard the cry, and hurried to her. What makes her so strange? Is she in a trance?'

'Aye,' said the old woman, falling on her knees by the bed and sobbing bitterly, 'the trance of death. Ah, my dear, my poor lonely girl, that this should be the end of it! She has died of fright,' said the old woman, pointing to the eyes, which even yet retained their horror. 'She has seen something *devilish*.'

Tabitha's gaze fell. 'She has always suffered with her heart,' she muttered; 'the night has frightened her; it frightened me.'

She stood upright by the foot of the bed as Martha drew the sheet over the face of the dead woman.

'First Ursula, then Eunice,' said Tabitha, drawing a deep breath. 'I can't stay here. I'll dress and wait for the morning.'

She left the room as she spoke, and with bent head proceeded to her own. Martha remained by the bedside, and gently closing the staring eyes, fell on her knees and prayed long and earnestly for the departed soul. Overcome with grief and fear, she remained with bowed head until a sudden sharp cry from Tabitha brought her to her feet.

'Well,' said the old woman, going to the door.

'Where are you?' cried Tabitha, somewhat reassured by her voice.

'In Miss Eunice's bedroom. Do you want anything?'

'Come down at once. Quick! I am unwell.'

Her voice rose suddenly to a scream. 'Quick! For God's sake! Quick, or I shall go mad. *There is some strange woman in the house.*'

The old woman stumbled hastily down the dark stairs. 'What is the matter?' she cried, entering the room. 'Who is it? What do you mean?'

'I saw it,' said Tabitha, grasping her convulsively by the shoulder. 'I was coming to you when I saw the figure of a woman in front of me going up the stairs. Is it – can it be Ursula come for the soul of Eunice, as she said she would?'

'Or for yours?' said Martha, the words coming from her in some odd fashion, despite herself.

Tabitha, with a ghastly look, fell cowering by her side, clutching tremulously at her clothes. 'Light the lamps,' she cried hysterically. 'Light a fire, make a noise; oh, this dreadful darkness! Will it never be day!'

'Soon, soon,' said Martha, overcoming her repugnance and trying to pacify her. 'When the day comes you will laugh at these fears.'

'I murdered her,' screamed the miserable woman, 'I killed her with fright. Why did she not give me the money? 'Twas no use to her. Ah! *Look there!*'

Martha, with a horrible fear, followed her glance to the door, but saw nothing.

'It's Ursula,' said Tabitha, from between her teeth. 'Keep her off! Keep her off!'

The old woman, who by some unknown sense seemed to feel the presence of a third person in the room, moved a step forward and stood before her. As she did so Tabitha waved her arms as though to free herself from the touch of a detaining hand, half-rose to her feet, and without a word fell dead before her.

At this the old woman's courage forsook her, and with a great cry she rushed from the room, eager to escape from this house of death and mystery. The bolts of the great door were stiff with age, and strange voices seemed to ring in her ears as she strove wildly to unfasten them. Her brain whirled. She thought that the dead in their distant rooms called to her, and that a devil stood on the step outside laughing and holding the door against her. Then with a supreme effort she flung it open, and heedless of her night-clothes passed into the bitter night. The path across the marshes was lost in the darkness, but she found it; the planks over the ditches slippery and narrow, but she crossed them in safety, until at last, her feet bleeding and her breath coming in great gasps, she entered the village and sank down more dead than alive on a cottage doorstep.

# The Haunted Dolls' House

## M. R. James

'I suppose you get stuff of that kind through your hands pretty often?' said Mr Dillet, as he pointed with his stick to an object which shall be described when the time comes: and when he said it, he lied in his throat, and knew that he lied. Not once in twenty years – perhaps not once in a lifetime – could Mr Chittenden, skilled as he was in ferreting out the forgotten treasures of half a dozen counties, expect to handle such a specimen. It was collectors' palaver, and Mr Chittenden recognized it as such.

'Stuff of that kind, Mr Dillet! It's a museum piece, that is.'

'Well, I suppose there are museums that'll take anything.'

'I've seen one, not as good as that, years back,' said Mr Chittenden thoughtfully. 'But that's not likely to come into the market: and I'm told they 'ave some fine ones of the period over the water. No: I'm only telling you the truth, Mr Dillet, when I say that if you was to place an unlimited order with me for the very best that could be got – and you know I 'ave facilities for getting to know of such things, and a reputation to maintain – well, all I can say is, I should lead you straight up to that one and say, "I can't do no better for you than that, sir."'

'Hear, hear!' said Mr Dillet, applauding ironically with the end of his stick on the floor of the shop. 'How much are you sticking the innocent American buyer for it, eh?'

'Oh, I shan't be over hard on the buyer, American or otherwise. You see, it stands this way, Mr Dillet – if I knew just a bit more about the pedigree –'

'Or just a bit less,' Mr Dillet put in.

'Ha, ha! you will have your joke, sir. No, but as I was saying, if I knew just a little more than what I do about the piece – though anyone can see for themselves it's a genuine thing, every last corner of it, and there's not been one of my men allowed to so much as touch it since it came into the shop – there'd be another figure in the price I'm asking.'

'And what's that: five and twenty?'

'Multiply that by three and you've got it, sir. Seventy-five's my price.'

'And fifty's mine,' said Mr Dillet.

The point of agreement was, of course, somewhere between the two, it does not matter exactly where – I think sixty guineas. But half an hour later the object was being packed, and within an hour Mr Dillet had called for it in his car and driven away. Mr Chittenden, holding the cheque in his hand, saw him off from the door with smiles, and returned, still smiling, into the parlour where his wife was making the tea. He stopped at the door.

'It's gone,' he said.

'Thank God for that!' said Mrs Chittenden, putting down the teapot. 'Mr Dillet, was it?'

'Yes, it was.'

'Well, I'd sooner it was him than another.'

'Oh, I don't know; he ain't a bad feller, my dear.'

'Maybe not, but in my opinion he'd be none the worse for a bit of a shake up.'

'Well, if that's your opinion, it's my opinion he's put himself into the way of getting one. Anyhow, *we* shan't have no more of it, and that's something to be thankful for.'

And so Mr and Mrs Chittenden sat down to tea.

And what of Mr Dillet and of his new acquisition? What it was, the title of this story will have told you. What it was like, I shall have to indicate as well as I can.

There was only just room enough for it in the car, and Mr Dillet had to sit with the driver: he had also to go slow, for though the rooms of the Dolls' House had all been stuffed carefully with soft cottonwool, jolting was to be avoided, in view of the immense number of small objects which thronged them; and the ten-mile drive was an anxious time for him, in spite of all the precautions he insisted upon. At last his front door was reached, and Collins, the butler, came out.

'Look here, Collins, you must help me with this thing – it's a delicate job. We must get it out upright, see? It's full of little things that mustn't be displaced more than we can help. Let's see, where shall we have it? (After a pause for consideration.) Really, I think I shall have to put it in my own room, to begin with at any rate. On the big table – that's it.'

It was conveyed – with much talking – to Mr Dillet's spacious room on the first floor, looking out on the drive. The sheeting was unwound from it, and the front thrown open, and for the next hour or two Mr Dillet was fully occupied in extracting the padding and setting in order the contents of the rooms.

When this thoroughly congenial task was finished, I must say that it would have been difficult to find a more perfect and attractive specimen of a Dolls' House in Strawberry Hill Gothic than that which now stood on Mr Dillet's large kneehole table, lighted up by the evening sun which came slanting through three tall sash-windows.

It was quite six feet long, including the Chapel or Oratory which flanked the front on the left as you faced it, and the stable on the right. The main block of the house was, as I have said, in the Gothic manner: that is to say, the windows had pointed arches and were surmounted by what are called ogival hoods, with crockets and finials such as we see on the canopies of tombs built into church walls. At the angles were absurd turrets covered with arched panels. The Chapel had pinnacles and buttresses, and a bell in the turret and coloured glass in the windows. When the front of the house was open you saw four large rooms, bedroom, dining-room, drawing-room and kitchen, each with its appropriate furniture in a very complete state.

The stable on the right was in two storeys, with its proper complement of horses, coaches and grooms, and with its clock and Gothic cupola for the clock bell.

Pages, of course, might be written on the outfit of the mansion – how many frying-pans, how many gilt chairs, what pictures, carpets, chandeliers, four-posters, table linen, glass, crockery and plate it possessed; but all this must be left to the imagination. I will only say that the base or plinth on which the house stood (for it was fitted with one of some depth which allowed of a flight of steps to the front door and a terrace, partly balustraded) contained a shallow drawer or drawers in which were neatly stored sets of embroidered curtains, changes of raiment for the inmates, and, in short, all the materials for an infinite series of variations and refittings of the most absorbing and delightful kind.

'Quintessence of Horace Walpole, that's what it is: he must have had something to do with the making of it.' Such was Mr Dillet's murmured reflection as he knelt before it in a reverent ecstasy. 'Simply wonderful! this is my day and no mistake. Five hundred pound coming in this morning for that cabinet which I never cared about, and now this tumbling into my hands for a tenth, at the very most, of what it would fetch in town. Well, well! It almost makes one afraid something'll happen to counter it. Let's have a look at the population, anyhow.'

Accordingly, he set them before him in a row. Again, here is an opportunity, which some would snatch at, of making an inventory of costume: I am incapable of it.

There were a gentleman and lady, in blue satin and brocade respectively. There were two children, a boy and a girl. There was a cook, a nurse, a footman, and there were the stable servants, two postilions, a coachman, two grooms.

'Anyone else? Yes, possibly.'

The curtains of the four-poster in the bedroom were closely drawn round all four sides of it, and he put his finger in between them and felt in the bed. He drew the finger back hastily, for it almost seemed to him as if something had – not stirred, perhaps, but yielded – in an odd live way as he pressed it. Then he put back the curtains, which ran on rods in the proper manner, and extracted from the bed a white-haired old gentleman in a long linen night-dress and cap, and laid him down by the rest. The tale was complete.

Dinner-time was now near, so Mr Dillet spent but five minutes in putting the lady and children into the drawing-room, the gentleman into the dining-room, the servants into the kitchen and stables, and the old man back into his bed. He retired into his dressing-room next door, and we see and hear no more of him until something like eleven o'clock at night.

His whim was to sleep surrounded by some of the gems of his collection. The big room in which we have seen him contained his bed: bath, wardrobe, and all the appliances of dressing were in a commodious room adjoining: but his four-poster, which itself was a valued treasure, stood in the large room where he sometimes wrote, and often sat, and even received visitors. To-night he repaired to it in a highly complacent frame of mind.

There was no striking clock within earshot – none on the staircase, none in the stable, none in the distant church tower. Yet it is indubitable that Mr Dillet was startled out of a very pleasant slumber by a bell tolling One.

He was so much startled that he did not merely lie breathless with wide-open eyes, but actually sat up in his bed.

He never asked himself, till the morning hours, how it was that, though there was no light at all in the room, the Dolls' House on the kneehole table stood out with complete clearness. But it was so. The effect was that of a bright harvest moon shining full on the front of a big white stone mansion – a quarter of a mile away it might be, and yet every detail was photographically sharp. There were trees about it, too – trees rising behind the chapel and the house. He seemed to be conscious of the scent of a cool still September night. He thought he could hear an occasional stamp and clink from the stables, as of horses stirring. And with another shock he realized that, above the house, he was looking, not at the wall of his room with its pictures, but into the profound blue of a night sky.

There were lights, more than one, in the windows, and he quickly saw that this was no four-roomed house with a movable front, but one of many rooms, and staircases – a real house, but seen as if through the wrong end of a telescope. 'You mean to show me something,' he muttered to himself, and he gazed earnestly on the lighted windows. They would in real life have been shuttered or curtained, no doubt, he thought; but, as it was, there was nothing to intercept his view of what was being transacted inside the rooms.

Two rooms were lighted – one on the ground floor to the right of the door, one upstairs, on the left – the first brightly enough, the other rather dimly. The lower room was the dining-room: a table was laid, but the meal was over, and only wine and glasses were left on the table. The man of the blue satin and the woman of the brocade were alone in the room, and they were talking very earnestly, seated close together at the table, their elbows on it: every now and again stopping to listen, as it seemed. Once *he* rose, came to the window and opened it and put his head out and his hand to his ear. There was a lighted taper in a silver candlestick on a sideboard. When the man left the window he seemed to leave the room also; and the lady, taper in hand, remained standing and listening. The expression on her face was that of one striving her utmost to keep down a fear that threatened to master her – and succeeding. It was a hateful face, too; broad, flat and sly. Now the man came back and she took some small thing from him and hurried out of the room. He, too, disappeared, but only for a moment or two. The front door slowly opened and he stepped out and stood on the top of the *perron*, looking this way and that; then turned towards the upper window that was lighted, and shook his fist.

It was time to look at that upper window. Through it was seen a four-post bed: a nurse or other servant in an arm-chair, evidently sound asleep; in the bed an old man lying: awake, and, one would say, anxious, from the way in which he shifted about and moved his fingers, beating tunes on the coverlet. Beyond the bed a door opened. Light was seen on the ceiling, and the lady came in: she set down her candle on a table, came to the fireside and roused the nurse. In her hand she had an old-fashioned wine bottle, ready uncorked. The nurse took it, poured some of the contents into a little silver saucepan, added some spice and sugar from casters on the table, and set it to warm on the fire. Meanwhile the old man in the bed beckoned feebly to the lady, who came to him, smiling, took his wrist as if to feel his pulse, and bit her lip as if in consternation. He looked at her anxiously, and then pointed to the window, and spoke. She nodded, and did as the man below had done; opened the casement and listened – perhps rather ostentatiously: then drew in her head and shook it, looking at the old man, who seemed to sigh.

By this time the posset on the fire was steaming, and the nurse poured it into a small two-handled silver bowl and brought it to the bedside. The old man seemed disinclined for it and was waving it away, but the lady and the nurse together bent over him and evidently pressed it upon him. He must have yielded, for they supported him into a sitting position, and put it to his lips. He drank most of it, in several draughts, and they laid him down. The lady left the room, smiling goodnight to him, and took the bowl, the bottle and the silver saucepan with her. The nurse returned to the chair, and there was an interval of complete quiet.

Suddenly the old man started up in his bed – and he must have uttered some cry, for the nurse started out of her chair and made but one step of it to the bedside. He was a sad and terrible sight – flushed in the face, almost to blackness, the eyes glaring whitely, both hands clutching at his heart, foam at his lips.

For a moment the nurse left him, ran to the door, flung it wide open, and, one supposes, screamed aloud for help, then darted back to the bed and seemed to try feverishly to soothe him – to lay him down – anything. But as the lady, her husband, and several servants, rushed into the room with horrified faces, the old man collapsed under the nurse's hands and lay back, and the features, contorted with agony and rage, relaxed slowly into calm.

A few moments later, lights showed out to the left of the house, and a coach with flambeaux drove up to the door. A white-wigged man in black got nimbly out and ran up the steps, carrying a small leather trunk-shaped box. He was met in the doorway by the man and his wife, she with her handkerchief clutched between her hands, he with a tragic face, but retaining his self-control. They led the newcomer into the dining-room, where he set his box of papers on the table, and, turning to them, listened with a face of consternation at what they had to tell. He nodded his head again and again, threw out his hands slightly, declined, it seemed, offers of refreshment and lodging for the night, and within a few minutes came slowly down the steps, entering the coach and driving off the way he had come. As the man in blue watched him from the top of the steps, a smile not pleasant to see stole slowly over his fat white face. Darkness fell over the whole scene as the lights of the coach disappeared.

But Mr Dillet remained sitting up in the bed: he had rightly guessed that there would be a sequel. The house front glimmered out again before long. But now there was a difference. The lights were in other windows, one at the top of the house, the other illuminating the range of coloured windows of the chapel. How he saw through these is not quite obvious, but he did. The interior was as carefully furnished as the rest of the establishment, with its minute red cushions on the desks, its Gothic stall-canopies, and its western gallery and pinnacled organ with gold pipes. On the centre of the black and white pavement was a bier: four tall candles burned at the corners. On the bier was a coffin covered with a pall of black velvet.

As he looked the folds of the pall stirred. It seemed to rise at one end: it slid downwards: it fell away, exposing the black coffin with its silver handles and name-plate. One of the tall candlesticks swayed and toppled over. Ask no more, but turn, as Mr Dillet hastily did, and look in at the lighted window at the top of the house, where a boy and girl lay in two truckle-beds, and a four-poster for the nurse rose above them. The nurse was not visible for the moment; but the father and mother were there, dressed now in mourning, but with very little sign of mourning in their demeanour. Indeed, they were laughing and talking with a good deal of animation, sometimes to each other, and sometimes throwing a remark to one or other of the children, and again laughing at the answers. Then the father was seen to go on tiptoe out of the room, taking with him as he went a white garment that hung on a peg near the door. He shut the door after him. A minute or two later it was slowly opened again, and a muffled head poked round it. A bent form of sinister shape stepped across to the truckle-beds, and suddenly stopped, threw up its arms and revealed, of course, the father, laughing. The children were in agonies of terror, the boy with the bedclothes over his head, the girl throwing herself out of bed into her mother's arms. Attempts at consolation followed – the parents took the children on their laps, patted them, picked up the white gown and showed there was no harm in it, and so forth; and at last putting the children back into bed, left the room with encouraging waves of the hand. As they left it, the nurse came in, and soon the light died down.

Still Mr Dillet watched immovable.

A new sort of light – not of lamp or candle – a pale ugly light, began to dawn around the door-case at the back of the room. The door was opening again. The seer does not like to dwell upon what he saw entering the room: he says it might be described as a frog – the size of a man – but it had scanty white hair about its head. It was busy about the truckle-beds, but not for long. The sound of cries – faint, as if coming out of a vast distance – but, even so, infinitely appalling, reached the ear.

There were signs of a hideous commotion all over the house: lights moved along and up, and doors opened and shut, and running figures passed within the windows. The clock in the stable turret tolled one, and darkness fell again.

It was only dispelled once more, to show the house front. At the bottom of the steps dark figures were drawn up in two lines, holding flaming torches. More dark figures came down the steps, bearing, first one, then another small coffin. And the lines of torch-bearers with the coffins between them moved silently onward to the left.

The hours of night passed on – never so slowly, Mr Dillet thought.

Gradually he sank down from sitting to lying in his bed – but he did not close an eye: and early next morning he sent for the doctor.

The doctor found him in a disquieting state of nerves, and recommended sea-air. To a quiet place on the East Coast he accordingly repaired by easy stages in his car.

One of the first people he met on the sea front was Mr Chittenden, who, it appeared, had likewise been advised to take his wife away for a bit of a change.

Mr Chittenden looked somewhat askance upon him when they met: and not without cause.

'Well, I don't wonder at you being a bit upset, Mr Dillet. What? yes, well, I might say 'orrible upset, to be sure, seeing what me and my poor wife went through ourselves. But I put it to you, Mr Dillet, one of two things: was I going to scrap a lovely piece like that on the one 'and, or was I going to tell customers: "I'm selling you a regular picture-palace-dramar in reel life of the olden time, billed to perform regular at one o'clock a.m."? Why, what would you 'ave said yourself? And next thing you know, two Justices of the Peace in the back parlour, and pore Mr and Mrs Chittenden off in a spring cart to the County Asylum and everyone in the street saying, "Ah, I thought it 'ud come to that. Look at the way the man drank!" – and me next door, or next door but one, to a total abstainer, as you know. Well, there was my position. What? Me 'ave it back in the shop? Well, what do *you* think? No, but I'll tell you what I will do. You shall have your money back, bar the ten pound I paid for it, and you make what you can.'

Later in the day, in what is offensively called the 'smoke-room' of the hotel, a murmured conversation between the two went on for some time.

'How much do you really know about the thing, and where it came from?'

'Honest, Mr Dillet, I don't know the 'ouse. Of course, it came out of the lumber room of a country 'ouse – that anyone could guess. But I'll go as far as say this, that I believe it's not a hundred miles from this place. Which direction and how far I've no notion. I'm only judging by guess-work. The man as I actually paid the cheque to ain't one of my regular men, and I've lost sight of him; but I 'ave the idea that this part of the country was his beat, and that's every word I can tell you. But now, Mr Dillet, there's one thing that rather physicks me. That old chap,– I suppose you saw him drive up to the door – I thought so: now, would he have been the medical man, do you take it? My wife would have it so, but I stuck to it that was the lawyer, because he had papers with him, and one he took out was folded up.'

'I agree,' said Mr Dillet. 'Thinking it over, I came to the conclusion that was the old man's will, ready to be signed.'

'Just what I thought,' said Mr Chittenden, 'and I took it that will would have cut out the young people, eh? Well, well! It's been a lesson to me, I know that. I shan't buy no more dolls' houses, nor waste no more money on the pictures – and as to this business of poisonin' grandpa, well, if I know myself, I never 'ad much of a turn for that. Live and let live: that's bin my motto throughout life, and I ain't found it a bad one.'

Filled with these elevated sentiments, Mr Chittenden retired to his lodgings. Mr Dillet next day repaired to the local Institute, where he hoped to find some clue to the riddle that absorbed him. He gazed in despair at a long file of the Canterbury and York Society's publications of the Parish Registers of the district. No print resembling the house of his nightmare was among those that hung on the staircase and in the passages. Disconsolate, he found himself at last in a derelict room, staring at a dusty model of a church in a dusty glass case: *Model of St. Stephen's Church, Coxham. Presented by J. Merewether, Esq, of Ilbridge House, 1877. The work of his ancestor James Merewether, d. 1786.* There was something in the fashion of it that reminded him dimly of his horror. He retraced his steps to a wall map he had noticed, and made out that Ilbridge House was in Coxham Parish. Coxham was, as it happened, one of the parishes of which he had retained the name when he glanced over the file of printed registers, and it was not long before he found in them the record of the burial of Roger Milford, aged seventy-six, on the 11th of September, 1757, and of Roger and Elizabeth Merewether, aged nine and seven, on the 19th of the same month. It seemed worth while to follow up this clue, frail as it was; and in the afternoon he drove out to Coxham. The east end of the north aisle of the church is a Milford chapel, and on its north wall are tablets to the same persons; Roger, the elder, it seems, was distinguished by all the qualities which adorn 'the Father, the Magistrate, and the Man': the memorial was erected by his attached daughter Elizabeth, 'who did not long survive the loss of a parent ever solicitous for her welfare, and of two amiable children.' The last sentence was plainly an addition to the original inscription.

A yet later slab told of James Merewether, husband of Elizabeth, 'who in the dawn of life practised, not without success, those arts which, had he continued their exercise, might in the opinion of the most competent judges have earned for him the name of the British Vitruvius: but who, overwhelmed by the visitation which deprived him of an affectionate partner and a blooming offspring, passed his Prime and Age in a secluded yet elegant Retirement: his grateful Nephew and Heir indulges a pious sorrow by this too brief recital of his excellences.'

The children were more simply commemorated. Both died on the night of the 12th of September.

Mr Dillet felt sure that in Ilbridge House he had found the scene of his drama. In some old sketch-book, possibly in some old print, he may yet find convincing evidence that he is right. But the Ilbridge House of today is not that which he sought; it is an Elizabethan erection of the forties, in red brick with stone quoins and dressings. A quarter of a mile from it, in a low part of the park, backed by ancient, stag-horned, ivy-strangled trees and thick undergrowth, are marks of a terraced platform overgrown with rough grass. A few stone balusters lie here and there, and a heap or two, covered with nettles and ivy, of wrought stones with badly-carved crockets. This, someone told Mr Dillet, was the site of an older house.

As he drove out of the village, the hall clock struck four, and Mr Dillet started up and clapped his hands to his ears. It was not the first time he had heard that bell.

Awaiting an offer from the other side of the Atlantic, the dolls' house still reposes, carefully sheeted, in a loft over Mr Dillet's stables, whither Collins conveyed it on the day when Mr Dillet started for the sea coast.

# The Yellow Cat

## *Michael Joseph*

It all began when Grey was followed home, inexplicably enough, by the strange, famished yellow cat. The cat was thin with large, intense eyes which gleamed amber in the forlorn light of the lamp on the street corner. It was standing there as Grey passed, whistling dejectedly, for he had had a depressing run of luck at Grannie's tables, and it made a slight piteous noise as it looked up at him. Then it followed at his heels, creeping along as though it expected to be kicked unceremoniously out of the way.

Grey did, indeed, make a sort of half-threatening gesture when, looking over his shoulder, he saw the yellow cat behind.

'If you were a black cat,' he muttered, 'I'd welcome you – but get out!'

The cat's melancholy amber eyes gleamed up at him, but it made no sign and continued to follow. This would have annoyed Grey in his already impatient humour, but he seemed to find a kind of savage satisfaction in the fact that he was denied even the trifling consolation of a good omen. Like all gamblers, he was intensely superstitious, although he had had experience in full measure of the futility of all supposedly luck-bringing mascots. He carried a monkey's claw sewn in the lining of his waistcoat pocket, not having the courage to throw it away. But this wretched yellow cat that ought to have been black did not irritate him as might have been expected.

He laughed softly; the restrained, unpleasant laugh of a man fighting against misfortune.

'Come on, then, you yellow devil; we'll sup together.'

He took his gloveless hand from his coat pocket and beckoned to the animal at his heels; but it took as little notice of his gesture of invitation as it had of his menacing foot a moment before. It just slid along the greasy pavement, covering the ground noiselessly, not deviating in the slightest from the invisible path it followed, without hesitation.

It was a bitterly cold, misty night, raw and damp. Grey shivered as he thrust his hand back into the shelter of his pocket and hunched his shoulders together underneath the thin coat that afforded but little protection against the cold.

With a shudder of relief he turned into the shelter of the courtyard which lay between the icy street and the flight of stairs which led to his room. As he stumbled numbly over the rough cobblestones of the yard he suddenly noticed that the yellow cat had disappeared.

He was not surprised and gave no thought whatever to the incident until, a few minutes later, at the top of the ramshackle stairs, the feeble light of a hurricane lamp revealed the creature sitting, or rather lying, across the threshold of his door.

He took an uncertain step backward. He said to himself: 'That's odd.' The cat looked up at him impassively with brooding, sullen eyes. He opened the door, stretching over the animal to turn the crazy handle.

Silently the yellow cat rose and entered the shadowy room. There was something uncanny, almost sinister in its smooth, noiseless movements. With fingers that shook slightly, Grey fumbled for matches, struck a light and, closing the door behind him, lit the solitary candle.

He lived in this one room, over a mews which had become almost fashionable since various poverty-stricken people, whose names still carried some weight with the bourgeois tradesmen of this Mayfair backwater, had triumphantly installed themselves; and Grey turned it skilfully to account when he spoke with casual indifference of 'the flat' he occupied, 'next to Lady Susan Tyrrell's'.

Grey, although he would never have admitted it, was a cardsharper and professional gambler. But even a cardsharper needs a little ordinary luck. Night after night he watched money pass into the hands of 'the pigeons', ignorant, reckless youngsters, and foolish old women who, having money to burn, ought by all the rules of the game to have lost. Yet when playing with him, Grey, a man respected even among the shabby fraternity of those who live by their wits, they won. He had turned to roulette, but even with a surreptitious percentage interest in the bank he had lost. His credit was exhausted. Grannie herself had told him he was a regular Jonah. He was cold, hungry and desperate. Presently his clothes, the last possession, would betray him, and no longer would he be able to borrow the casual trifle that started him nightly in his desperate bout with fortune.

His room contained a wooden bed and a chair. A rickety table separated them. The chair served Grey as a wardrobe; on the table stood a candle with a few used matches which he used to light the cheap cigarettes he smoked in bed; the grease had a habit of adhering to the tobacco when the candle was used, and Grey was fastidious. The walls were bare save for a cupboard, a pinned-up *Sporting Life* Racing Calendar and two cheap reproductions of Kirchner's midinettes. There was no carpet on the floor. A piece of linoleum stretched from the empty grate to the side of the bed.

At first Grey could not see the cat, but the candle, gathering strength, outlined its shadow grotesquely against the wall. It was crouched on the end of the bed.

He lighted one of the used matches and lit the small gas-ring which was the room's sole luxury. Gas was included in the few shillings he paid weekly for rent; consequently Grey used it for warmth. He seldom used it to cook anything, as neither whisky (which he got by arrangement with one of Grannie's waiters), bread nor cheese, which formed his usual diet, require much cooking.

The cat moved and, jumping noiselessly on to the floor, cautiously approached the gas-ring, by the side of which it stretched its lean yellowish body. Very softly but plaintively it began to mew.

Grey cursed it. Then he turned to the cupboard and took out a cracked jug. He moved the bread on to his own plate and poured out the little milk it contained in the shallow bread-plate.

The cat drank, not greedily but with the fierce rapidity which betokens hunger and thirst. Grey watched it idly as he poured whisky into a cup. He drank, and refilled the cup. He then began to undress, carefully, in order to prolong the life of his worn dinner-jacket.

The cat looked up. Grey, taking off his shirt, beneath which, having no vest, he wore another woollen shirt, became uncomfortably aware of its staring yellow eyes. Seized with a crazy impulse, he poured the whisky from his cup into the remainder of the milk in the plate.

'Share and share alike,' he cried. 'Drink, you –'

Then the yellow cat snarled at him; the vilest, loathsome sound; and Grey for a moment was afraid. Then he laughed, as if at himself for allowing control to slip, and finished undressing, folding the garments carefully, and hanging them on the chair.

The cat went back to its place at the foot of the bed, its eyes gleaming warily in Grey's direction. He restrained his impulse to throw it out of the room and clambered between the rough blankets without molesting it.

By daylight the cat was an ugly misshapen creature. It had not moved from the bed. Grey regarded it with amused contempt.

Usually the morning found him profoundly depressed and irritable. For some unaccountable reason he felt now almost light-hearted.

He dressed, counted his money and decided to permit himself the luxury of some meagre shopping in the adjacent Warwick Market, which supplied the most expensive restaurant proprietors with the cheapest food. Nevertheless, it was an accommodating spot for knowledgeable individuals like Grey.

The cat, still crouching on the bed, made no attempt to follow him, and he closed the door as softly as its erratic hinges would allow, aware that the cat's eyes still gazed steadily in his direction.

In the market, he obeyed an impulse to buy food for the cat, and at the cost of a few pence added a portion of raw fish to his purchases. On the way home he cursed himself for a fool, and would have thrown the fish away, the clumsy paper wrapping having become sodden with moisture, when he was hailed by a voice he had almost forgotten.

'Grey! Just the man I want to see!'

Grey greeted him with a fair show of amiability, although, if appearance were any indication, the other was even less prosperous than himself. He, too, had been an *habitué* of Grannie's in the old days, but had long since drifted out on the sea of misfortune. Despite his shabby appearance, he turned to Grey and said:

'You'll have a drink?' Then, noting Grey's dubious glance, he laughed and added: 'It's on me all right. I've just touched lucky.'

A little later Grey emerged from the public-house on the corner the richer by five pounds, which the other had insisted on lending him in return for past favours. What exactly the past favours had been, Grey was too dazed to inquire; as far as he could recollect he had always treated the man with scant courtesy. He did not even remember his name.

He was still trying to remember who the man was when he climbed the stairs. He knew him well enough, for Grey was the type who never forgets a face. It was when his eyes alighted on the yellow cat that he suddenly remembered.

The man was Felix Mortimer. And Felix Mortimer had shot himself during the summer!

At first Grey tried to assure himself that he had made a mistake. Against his better judgment he tried to convince himself that the man merely bore a strong resemblance to Felix Mortimer. But at the back of his mind *he knew*.

Anyway, the five-pound note was real enough.

He methodically placed the fish in a saucepan and lit the gas-ring.

Presently the cat was eating, in that curious, deliberate way it had drunk the milk the night before. Its emaciated appearance plainly revealed that it was starving; yet it devoured the fish methodically, as though now assured of a regular supply.

Grey, turning the five-pound note in his hand, wondered whether the cat had after all changed his luck. But his thoughts kept reverting to Felix Mortimer . . .

The next few days left him in no doubt. At Grannie's that night fortune's pendulum swung back unmistakably. He won steadily. From roulette he turned to *chemin de fer*, elated to find that his luck held good.

'Your luck's changed – with a vengeance!' said one of the 'regulars' of the shabby genteel saloon.

'With a vengeance,' echoed Grey, and paused; wondering with the superstition of the born gambler if there were significance in the phrase.

He left Grannie's the richer by two hundred odd pounds.

His success was the prelude to the biggest slice of luck, to use his own phrase, that he had ever known. He gambled scientifically, not losing his head, methodically banking a proportion of his gains each morning; planning, scheming, striving to reach that high-water mark at which, so he told himself with the gambler's time-worn futility, he would stop and never gamble again.

Somehow he could not make up his mind to leave the poverty-stricken room in the fashionable mews. He was terribly afraid it would spell a change of luck. He tried to improve it, increase its comfort, but it was significant that he bought first a basket and a cushion for the yellow cat.

For there was no doubt in his mind that the cat was the cause of his sudden transiton from poverty to prosperity. In his queer, intensely superstitious mind, the yellow cat was firmly established as his mascot.

He fed it regularly, waiting on it himself as though he were its willing servant. He made a spasmodic attempt to caress it, but the cat snarled savagely at him and, frightened, he left it alone. If the cat ever moved from the room he never saw it go; whenever he went in or came out the cat was there, watching him with its gleaming amber eyes.

He accepted the situation philosophically enough. He would talk to the cat of himself, his plans for the future, the new people he met – for money had speedily unlocked more exalted doors than Grannie's – all this in the eloquence derived from wine and solitude, he would pour out into the unmoved ears of the cat, crouching at the foot of the bed. And then, without daring to speak of it, he would think of Felix Mortimer and the gift that had proved the turning-point of his fortunes.

The creature watched him impassively, contemptuously indifferent to his raving or his silence. But the weird *ménage* continued, and Grey's luck held good.

The days passed and he became ambitious. He was now within reach of that figure which he fondly imagined would enable him to forsake his precarious existence. He told himself that he was now, to all intents and purposes, safe. And he decided to move into more civilized and appropriate surroundings.

Nevertheless, he himself procured an expensive wicker contraption to convey the yellow cat from the garret to his newly acquired and, by contrast, luxurious maisonnette. It was furnished in abominable taste, but the reaction from sheer poverty had its effect. And then he had begun to drink more than was good for a man who required a cool head and a steady nerve for at least part of a day which was really night.

One day he had cause to congratulate himself on his new home. For he met, for the first time in his thirty odd years of life, a woman. Now Grey divided women into two classes. There were 'the regulars' – soulless creatures with the gambler's fever and crook's alphabet – and 'pigeons', foolish women, some young, most of them old, who flourished their silly but valuable plumage to be plucked by such as he.

But Elise Dyer was different. She stirred his pulses with a strange, exquisite sensation. Her incredible fair hair, flaxen as waving corn, her fair skin, her deep violet eyes and her delicate carmine mouth provoked him into a state of unaccustomed bewilderment.

They talked one night of mascots. Grey, who had never mentioned the yellow cat to a soul, whispered that he would, if she cared, show her the mascot that had brought him his now proverbial good luck. The girl agreed, with eager enthusiasm, to his diffident suggestion to go with him to his flat; and he, in his strange simplicity, stammered that she would do him honour. He had forgotten that Elise Dyer knew him for a rich man.

Elated by his triumph, he paid her losses and called for champagne. The girl plied him skilfully with wine, and presently he was more drunk than he had been since the beginning of his era of prosperity.

They took a cab to the flat. Grey felt that he had reached the pinnacle of triumph. Life was wonderful, glorious! What did anything matter now?

He switched on the light and the girl crossed his threshold. The room which they entered was lavishly illuminated, the lights shaded into moderation by costly fabrics. The room, ornate and over-furnished, reflected money. The girl gave a gasp of delight.

For the first time the cat seemed aware of something unusual. It stretched itself slowly and stood up, regarding them with a fierce light in its eyes.

The girl screamed.

'For God's sake take it away!' she cried. 'I can't bear it! I can't be near it. Take that damned cat away!' And she began to sob wildly, piteously, retreating towards the door.

At this Grey lost all control and, cursing wildly, shouting bestial things at the oncoming animal, seized it by the throat.

'Don't – don't cry, dearie,' panted Grey, holding the cat; 'I'll settle this swine soon enough. Wait for me!' And he staggered through the open door.

Grey ran through the deserted streets. The cat had subsided under the clutch of his fingers and lay inert, its yellowish fur throbbing. He scarcely knew where he was going. All he realized was an overwhelming desire to be rid of the tyranny of this wretched creature he held by the throat.

At last he knew where he was going. Not far from Grey's new establishment ran the Prince's canal, that dark sluggish stream that threads its way across the fashionable residential district of the outlying west. To the canal he ran; and without hesitation he threw the yellow cat into the water.

The next day he realized what he had done. At first he was afraid, half hoping that the superstitious spasm of fear would pass. But a vivid picture swam before his eyes, the broken surface of a sluggish dream. . .

'You're a coward,' she taunted him. 'Why don't you act like a man? Go to the tables and see for yourself that you can still win in spite of your crazy cat notions!'

At first he refused, vehemently; but it gradually dawned on him that therein lay his chance of salvation. Once let him throw down the gauntlet *and win* and his peace of mind would be assured.

That night he received a vociferous welcome on his return to the Green Baize Club.

It was as he feared. He lost steadily.

Then suddenly an idea came to him. Supposing the cat were still alive? Why hadn't he thought of that before? Why, there was a saying that every cat had nine lives! For all he knew it might have swum safely to the bank and got away.

His feverish impulse crystallized into action. He hurriedly left the club and beckoned urgently to a passing taxicab.

After what seemed interminable delay he reached the spot where he had madly flung the cat away from him. The stillness of the water brought home to him the futility of searching for the animal here. This was not the way to set to work.

The thing preyed on his mind in the days that followed. Exhaustive inquiries failed to discover the least trace of the yellow cat.

Night after night he went to the tables, lured there by the maddening thought that if only he could win he would drug the torment and be at peace. But he lost. . .

And then a strange thing happened.

One night, returning home across a deserted stretch of the park, he experienced a queer, irresistible impulse to lift his feet from the grass and make for the gravel path. He resented the impulse, fought against it; he was cold and worn out, and by cutting across the grass he would save many minutes of weary tramping. But the thing – like a mysterious blind instinct – persisted, and in the end he found himself running, treading gingerly on the sodden grass.

He did not understand why this had happened to him.

The next day Grey did not get out of his bed until late in the afternoon.

He crossed the room in search of his dressing-gown and caught sight of himself in the glass of his wardrobe. Only then did he realize that he was clambering over the floor with his head near the carpet, his hands outstretched in front of him. He stood upright with difficulty and reached a shaking hand for brandy.

It took him two hours to struggle into his clothes, and by the time he was ready to go out it was nearly dark. He crept along the street. The shops were closing. He saw nothing of them until he reached the corner where he halted abruptly, with a queer sensation of intense hunger. On the cold marble before him lay unappetizing slabs of raw fish. His body began to quiver with suppressed desire. Another moment and nothing could have prevented him seizing the fish in his bare hands, when the shutters of the shop dropped noisily across the front of the sloping marble surface.

Grey knew that something had happened, that he was very ill. Now that he could not see the vision of the yellow cat, his mind was a blank. Somehow he retraced his footsteps and got back to his room.

The bottle of brandy stood where he had left it. He had not turned on the light, but he could see it plainly. He dragged it to his lips.

With a crash it went to the floor, while Grey leapt into the air, savage with nausea. He felt that he was choking. With an effort he pulled himself together, to find that it was beyond his power to stop the ghastly whining sound that issued from his lips. He tried to lift himself on to the bed, but in sheer exhaustion collapsed on the floor, where he lay still in an attitude not human.

The room lightened with the dawn and a new day passed before the thing on the floor moved. Something of the clarity of vision which comes to starving men now possessed him. He stared at his hands.

The fingers seemed to have withered; the nails had almost disappeared, leaving a narrow streak of hornish substance forming in their place. He tore himself frantically towards the window. In the fading light he saw that the backs of his hands were covered with a thin, almost invisible surface of coarse, yellowish fur.

Unimaginable horrors seized him. He knew now that the scarlet thread of his brain was being stretched to breaking-point. Presently it would snap...

Unless – unless. The yellow cat alone could save him. To this last human thought he clung, in an agony of terror.

Unconscious of movement, he crept swiftly into the street, his shapeless eyes peering in the darkness which surrounded him. He groped his way stealthily towards the one place which the last remnant of his brain told him might yield the secret of his agony.

Down the silent bank he scrambled headlong, towards the still water. The dawn's pale radiance threw his shadow into a grotesque pattern. On the edge of the canal he halted, his hands embedded in the sticky crumbling earth, his head shaking, his eyes searching in agonized appeal, into the depths of the motionless water.

There he crouched, searching, searching ...

And there in the water he saw the yellow cat.

He stretched out the things that were his arms, while the yellow cat stretched out its claws to enfold him in the broken mirror of the water.

# The Reaper's Image

## *Stephen King*

'We moved it last year, and quite an operation it was, too,' Mr Carlin said as they mounted the stairs. 'Had to move it by hand, of course. No other way. We insured it against accident with Lloyd's before we even took it out of the case in the drawing-room. Only firm that would insure for the sum we had in mind.'

Spangler said nothing. The man was a fool. Johnson Spangler had learned a long time ago that the only way to talk to a fool was to ignore him.

'Insured it for a quarter of a million dollars,' Mr Carlin resumed when they reached the second-floor landing. His mouth quirked in a half-bitter, half-humorous line. 'And a pretty penny it cost, too.' He was a little man, not quite fat, with rimless glasses and a bald head that shone like a varnished volleyball. A suit of armour, guarding the mahogany shadows of the second-floor corridor, stared at them impassively.

It was a long corridor, and Spangler eyed the walls and hangings with a cool professional eye. Samuel Claggert had bought in copious quantities, but he had not bought well. Like so many of the self-made industry emperors of the late 1800s, he had been little more than a pawnshop rooter masquerading in collector's clothing, a connoisseur of canvas monstrosities, trashy novels and poetry collections in expensive cowhide bindings, and atrocious pieces of sculpture, all of which he considered Art.

Up here the walls were hung – festooned was perhaps a better word – with imitation Moroccan drapes, numberless (and, no doubt, anonymous) Madonnas holding numberless haloed babes while numberless angels flitted hither and hither in the background, grotesque scrolled candelabra, and one monstrous and obscenely ornate chandelier surmounted by a salaciously grinning nymphet.

Of course the old pirate had come up with a few interesting items; the law of averages demanded it. And if the Samuel Claggert Memorial Private Museum (Guided Tours on the Hour – Admission $1.00 Adults, $.50 Children – nauseating) was ninety-eight per cent blatant junk, there was always that other two per cent, things like the Coombs long rifle over the hearth in the kitchen, the strange little *camera obscura* in the parlour, and of course the –

'The DeIver looking-glass was removed after a rather unfortunate . . . incident,' Mr Carlin said abruptly, motivated apparently by a ghastly glaring portrait of no one in particular at the base of the next staircase. 'There have been others, harsh words, wild statements, but this was an attempt to actually destroy the mirror. The woman, a Miss Sandra Bates, came in with a rock in her pocket. Fortunately her aim was bad and she only cracked a corner of the case. The mirror was unharmed. The Bates girl had a brother –'

'No need to give me the dollar tour,' Spangler said quietly. 'I'm conversant with the history of the DeIver glass.'

'Fascinating, isn't it?' Carlin cast him an odd, oblique look. 'There was that English duchess in 1709 . . . and the Pennsylvania rug-merchant in 1746 . . . not to mention –'

'I'm conversant with the history,' Spangler repeated quietly. 'It's the workmanship I'm interested in. And then, of course, there's the question of authenticity –'

'Authenticity!' Mr Carlin chuckled, a dry sound, as if bones had stirred in the cupboard below the stairs. 'It's been examined by experts, Mr Spangler.'

'So was the Lemlier Stradivarius.'

'So true,' Mr Carlin said. 'But no Stradivarius ever had quite the . . . the unsettling effect of the DeIver glass.'

'Yes, quite,' Spangler said in his softly contemptuous voice. 'Quite.'

They climbed the third and fourth flights of stairs in silence. As they drew closer to the roof of the rambling structure, it became oppressively hot in the dark upper galleries. With the heat came a creeping stench that Spangler knew well, for he had spent all his adult life working in it – the smell of long-dead flies in shadowy corners, of wet rot and creeping wood lice behind the plaster. The smell of age. It was a smell common only to museums and mausoleums. He imagined much the same smell might arise from the grave of a virginal young girl, forty years dead.

Up here the relics were piled helter-skelter in true junkshop profusion; Mr Carlin led Spangler through a maze of statuary, frame-splintered portraits, pompous gold-plated birdcages, the dismembered skeleton of an ancient tandem bicycle. He led him to the far wall where a stepladder had been set up beneath a trapdoor in the ceiling. A dusty padlock hung from the trap.

Off to the left, an imitation Adonis stared at them pitilessly with blank pupil-less eyes. One arm was outstretched, and a yellow sign hung on the wrist which read: ABSOLUTELY NO ADMITTANCE.

Mr Carlin produced a keyring from his jacket pocket, selected one, and mounted the stepladder. He paused on the third rung, his bald head gleaming faintly in the shadows. 'I don't like that mirror,' he said. 'I never did. I'm afraid to look into it. I'm afraid I might look into it one day and see . . . what the rest of them saw.'

'They saw nothing but themselves,' Spangler said.

Mr Carlin began to speak, stopped, shook his head, and fumbled above him, craning his neck to fit the key properly into the lock. 'Should be replaced,' he muttered. 'It's – damn!' The lock sprung suddenly and swung out of the hasp. Mr Carlin made a fumbling grab for it, and almost fell off the ladder. Spangler caught it deftly and looked up at him. He was clinging shakily to the top of the stepladder, face white in the brown semi-darkness.

'You *are* nervous about it, aren't you?' Spangler said in a mildly wondering tone.

Mr Carlin said nothing. He seemed paralysed.

'Come down,' Spangler said. 'Please.'

Carlin descended the ladder slowly, clinging to each rung like a man tottering over a bottomless chasm. When his feet touched the floor he began to babble, as if the floor contained some current that had turned him on, like an electric light.

'A quarter of a million,' he said. 'A quarter of a million dollars' worth of insurance to take that . . . *thing* from down there to up here. That goddamn *thing*. They had to rig a special block and tackle to get it into the gable store-room up there. And I was hoping – almost praying – that someone's fingers would be slippery . . . that the rope would be the wrong test . . . that the thing would fall and be shattered into a million pieces –'

'Facts,' Spangler said. 'Facts, Carlin. Number one: John DeIver was an English craftsman of Norman descent who made mirrors in what we call the Elizabethan period of England's history. He lived and died uneventfully. No pentacles scrawled on the floor for the housekeeper to rub out, no sulphur-smelling documents with a splotch of blood on the dotted line. Number two: His mirrors have become collectors' items due principally to fine craftsmanship and to the fact that a form of crystal was used that has a mildly magnifying and distorting effect upon the eye of the beholder – a rather distinctive trademark. Number three: Only five DeIvers remain in existence, to our present knowledge – two of them in America. They are priceless. Number four: This DeIver and one other that was destroyed in the London Blitz have gained a rather spurious reputation due largely to falsehood, exaggeration, and coincidence –'

'Number five,' Mr Carlin said. 'Supercilious bastard, aren't you?'

Spangler looked with mild detestation at the blind-eyed Adonis.

'I was guiding the tour that Sandra Bates's brother was a part of when he got his look into your precious mirror, Spangler. He was perhaps sixteen, part of a high-school group. I was going through the history of the glass and had just got to the part *you* would appreciate – extolling the flawless craftsmanship, the perfection of the glass itself, when the boy raised his hand. "But what about that black splotch in the upper left-hand corner?" he asked. "That looks like a mistake."

'And one of his friends asked him what he meant, so the Bates boy started to tell him, then stopped. He looked at the mirror very closely, pushing right up to the red velvet guard-rope around the case – *then he looked behind him as if what he had seen had been the reflection of someone – of someone in black – standing at his shoulder*. "It looked like a man," he said. "But I couldn't see the face. It's gone now." And that was all.'

'Go on,' Spangler said. 'You're itching to tell me it was the Reaper – I believe that is the common explanation, isn't it? That occasional chosen people see the Reaper's image in the glass? Get it out of your system, man. Tell me about the horrific consequences and defy me to explain it. Was he later hit by a car? Jump out of a window? What?'

Mr Carlin chuckled a forlorn little chuckle. 'You should know better, Spangler. Haven't you told me twice that you are ... ah ... conversant with the history of the DeIver glass? There were no horrific consequences. There never have been. That's why the DeIver glass isn't Sunday supplementized like the Koh-i-Noor Diamond or the curse on King Tut's tomb. It's mundane compared to those. You think I'm a fool, don't you?'

'Yes,' Spangler said. 'Can we go up now?'

'Certainly,' Mr Carlin said passionlessly. He climbed the ladder and pushed the trapdoor. There was a clickety-clickety-bump as it was drawn up into the shadows by a counter-weight, and then Mr Carlin disappeared into the shadows. Spangler followed. The blind Adonis stared unknowingly after them.

The gable-room was explosively hot, lit only by one cobwebby, many-angled window that filtered the hard outside light into a dirty milky glow. The DeIver looking-glass was propped at an angle to the light, catching most of it and reflecting a pearly patch onto the far wall. It had been bolted securely into a wooden frame. Mr Carlin was not looking at it. Quite studiously not looking at it.

'You haven't even put a dust-cloth over it,' Spangler said, visibly angered for the first time.

'I think of it as an eye,' Mr Carlin said. His voice was still drained, perfectly empty. 'If it's left open, always open, perhaps it will go blind.'

Spangler paid no attention. He took off his jacket, folded the buttons carefully in, and with infinite gentleness he wiped the dust from the convex surface of the glass itself. Then he stood back and looked at it.

It was genuine. There was no doubt about it, never had been, really. It was a perfect example of DeIver's particular genius. The cluttered room behind him, his own reflection, Carlin's half-turned figure – they were all clear, sharp, almost three-dimensional. The faint magnifying effect of the glass gave everything a slightly curved effect that added an almost fourth-dimensional distortion. It was –

His thought broke off, and he felt another wave of anger.

'Carlin.'

Carlin said nothing.

'Carlin, you damned fool, I thought you said that girl didn't harm the mirror.'

No answer.

Spangler stared at him icily in the glass. 'There is a piece of friction tape in the upper left-hand corner. Did she crack it? For God's sake, man, speak up!'

'You're seeing the Reaper,' Carlin said. His voice was deadly and without passion. 'There's no friction tape on the mirror. Put your hand over it . . . dear God . . .'

Spangler wrapped the upper sleeve of his coat carefully around his hand, reached out, and pressed it gently against the mirror. 'You see? Nothing supernatural. It's gone. My hand covers it.'

'Covers it? Can you feel the tape? Why don't you pull it off?'

Spangler took his hand away carefully and looked into the glass. Everything in it seemed a little more distorted; the room's odd angles seemed to yaw crazily as if on the verge of sliding off into some unseen eternity. There was no dark spot in the mirror. It was flawless. He felt a sudden unhealthy dread rise in him and despised himself for feeling it.

'It looked like him, didn't it?' Mr Carlin asked. His face was very pale, and he was looking directly at the floor. A muscle twitched spasmodically in his neck. 'Admit it, Spangler. It looked like a hooded figure standing behind you, didn't it?'

'It looked like friction tape masking a short crack,' Spangler said very firmly. 'Nothing more, nothing less –'

'The Bates boy was very husky,' Carlin said rapidly. His words seemed to drop into the hot, still atmosphere like stones into a quarry full of sullen dark water. 'Like a football player. He was wearing a letter sweater and dark green chinos. We were halfway to the upper hall exhibits when –'

'The heat is making me feel ill,' Spangler said a little unsteadily. He had taken out a handkerchief and was wiping his neck. His eyes searched the convex surface of the mirror in small, jerky movements.

'When he said he wanted a drink of water ... a drink of water, for God's sake!'

Carlin turned and stared wildly at Spangler. 'How was I to know? How was I to know·'

'Is there a lavatory? I think I'm going to –'

'His sweater ... I just caught a glimpse of his sweater going down the stairs ... then ...'

'– be sick.'

Carlin shook his head, as if to clear it, and looked at the floor again. 'Of course. Third door on your left, second floor, as you go towards the stairs.' He looked up appealingly. 'How was I to *know?*'

But Spangler had already stepped down onto the ladder. It rocked under his weight and for a moment Carlin thought – hoped – that he would fall. He didn't. Through the open square in the floor Carlin watched him descend, holding his mouth lightly with one hand.

'Spangler –?'

But he was gone.

Carlin listened to his footfalls fade to echoes, then die away. When they were gone, he shivered violently. He tried to move his own feet to the trapdoor, but they were frozen. Just that last, hurried glimpse of the boy's sweater ... God! ...

It was as if huge invisible hands were pulling his head, forcing it up. Not wanting to look, Carlin stared into the glimmering depths of the Delver looking-glass.

There was nothing there.

The room was reflected back to him faithfully in its glimmering confines. A snatch of a half-remembered Tennyson poem occurred to him, and he muttered it aloud: ' "I'm half-sick of shadows," said the Lady of Shalott ...'

And still he could not look away, and the breathing stillness held him. Behind the mirror a moth-eaten buffalo head peered at him with flat obsidian eyes.

The boy had wanted a drink of water, and the fountain was in the first-floor lobby. He had gone downstairs and –

And had never come back.

Ever.

Anywhere.

Like the duchess who had paused after primping before her glass for a soirée and decided to go into the sitting-room for her pearls. Like the rug-merchant who had gone for a carriage ride and had left behind him only an empty carriage and two close-mouthed horses.

And the DeIver glass had been in New York from 1897 until 1920, had been there when Judge Crater –

Carlin stared as if hypnotized into the shallow depths of the mirror. Below, the blind-eyed Adonis kept watch.

He waited for Spangler much like the Bates family must have waited for their son, much like the duchess's coachman must have waited for his mistress to return from the sitting-room. He stared into the mirror and waited.

And waited.

And waited.

# Soldier Key

## *Sterling E. Lanier*

Everyone in the club, even those who disliked him, agreed that Brigadier ('not Brigadier General, please') Donald Ffellowes, RA, ret, could tell a good yarn when he chose. He seemed to have been in the British Army, the Colonial Police and MI5 as well at one time or another, and to have served all over the globe.

People who loathed him and the English generally, said all his tales were lies, that he was a remittance man, and that his gift for incredible stories was a direct inheritance from Sir John Mandeville, the medieval rumourmonger. Still even those who denounced his stories the most loudly never left once he started on them. If Ffellowes was a liar, he was an awfully good one.

Mason Williams, who was one of those who resented Ffellowes as both British and overbearing, had instantly ordered stone crab when he saw it on the club's menu. Of the eight others present at the big table that day, only one besides Williams had ever had stone crab, but we all decided to try it, that is, except Ffellowes.

'No, thank you,' he repeated coldly, 'I'll have the sweetbreads. I don't eat crab or any crustacean, for that matter. I used to love it,' he went on, 'in fact I ate crab, lobster, langouste, crawfish and shrimp with the best of you at one time. Until 1934 to be exact. An unpleasant and perhaps peculiar set of circumstances caused me to stop. Perhaps you would care to hear why?

'Now, I couldn't get it past my mouth, and if I did I couldn't swallow it. You see, something happened . . .'

His voice trailed away into silence, and we could all see that his thoughts were elsewhere. He stared at the snowy tablecloth for a moment and then looked up with an apologetic smile. We waited, and not even Williams seemed anxious to interrupt.

'I've never told anyone about this, but I suppose I ought, really. It's a quite unbelievable story, and not a very nice one. Yet, if you'd like to hear it?' he queried again.

An instant chorus of affirmation rose from around the table. We were all men who had travelled and seen at least something of life, but none of our tales ever matched what we extracted from Ffellowes at long intervals.

'Wait until after dinner,' was all he would say. 'I need a good meal under my belt and some coffee and a cigar before this one.'

The rest of us looked at one another rather like boys who have been promised a treat, as indeed we had. Williams grunted something, but made no objection. His denunciations of the British always came *after* Ffellowes' stories, I noticed.

When we were settled in our leather chairs in an alcove of the huge library, with cigars drawing and coffee and brandy beside us, Ffellowes began.

'Did any of you ever sail the Caribbean in the pre-War period? I don't mean on a cruise ship, although that's fun. I mean actually sailed, in a small boat or yacht, touching here and there, calling at ports when you felt like it and then moving on? If not, you've missed something.

'The dawns were fantastic and the sunsets better. The food from the galley, fresh fish we'd caught ourselves, usually, was superb, and the salt got into our skin, baked there by the sun.

'Islands rose up out of the sea, sometimes green and mountainous like Jamaica, sometimes low and hidden by mangroves and reefs like the Caymans or Inagua.

'We called at funny little ports and gave drinks to local officials who came aboard and got tight and friendly and told us astonishing scandals and implausible state secrets, and finally staggered off, swearing eternal friendship.

'And then at dawn, we hoisted anchor, set sail and checked our charts, and off we went to see what was over the next horizon, because there was always another island.'

He paused and sipped his coffee, while we waited in silence.

'I had three months' leave on half pay at the time due to a mix-up; so Joe Chapin and I (he's dead a long time, poor fellow, killed at Kohima) chartered an island schooner at Nassau and hired two coloured men to help us work her and cook. They were from Barbados and wanted to get back there, and that suited us. Badians were good seamen and good men, too. One, the older, was called Maxton, the other, Oswald, and I've forgotten their last names. We told them to call us Joe and Don, but it was always "Mistah Don, Sah" to me, and "Cap'n" to Joe, because he was officially captain on the papers.

'Well, we sailed along south for a month or so, calling here and there, picking up news and having fun at this port or that, until we got to Basse-Terre on Guadeloupe. We were ashore having a few rums in the bar with the port officials when we first heard of Soldier Key.

'Any of you ever heard of it? Well, you won't now because it's gone.

The people are, anyway. The big hurricane of 1935 smashed it more than flat, and I'm told the few people left were moved by the British government. I checked up later on and found they went first to Dominica and then elsewhere, but there weren't many left.

'At any rate, the French customs officer we were drinking with suggested we look in at Soldier Key if we wanted an unusual, what you call "offbeat", place to visit.

'"Messieurs," he told us, "this is a very strange place. You will not, I think, call twice, because few do, but I do not think you will be bored. These people are British like yourselves, and yet the island has no British official in residence, which is odd. They have an agreement with the government of Dominica that they govern themselves. Twice a year comes an inspection, but otherwise they are alone, with none to disturb them. Curious, is it not?"

'We agreed it sounded mildly strange, but asked why we should bother going at all?

'"As to that," he said, "you must suit yourselves. But you English always seek new things, and this place is a strange one. The people are, how you say it, *forgot* by everyone. They trade little, selling only *langouste* (the spiny lobster) and the meat of green turtle. They are good seamen, but they offer few ports and avoid other fishing boats. For some reason they never sell the turtle shell, although they could catch all the shell turtles they wish. I cannot tell you more, except I once called there for water when on a cruise and the place made me feel discomfortable." He paused and tried to convey what he meant. 'Look, these Key of the Soldier people all belong to one church, not mine or yours either. To them, all who are not of this communion are damned eternally, and when they look at you, you feel they wish to speed the process. A funny place, Messieurs, but interesting."

'He finished his rum and stood up to go. "And another thing, Messieurs," he said, "all people of colour dislike this place, and there are none of them who live there. Again, interesting, eh? Why not try it? You may be amused."

'Well, after we got back to the boat, we hauled out our charts and looked for Soldier Key. It was there all right, but it was quite easy to see how one could miss it. It lay about two days' sail west by northwest of Dominica, and it looked like a pretty small place indeed. The copy of the *Mariner's Guide* we had wasn't really new, and it gave the population as five hundred (approximately) with exports limited to lobster and imports nil. A footnote said it was settled in 1881 by the Church of the New Revelation. This, of course, must be the church to which our little customs official had been referring, but I'd never heard of it, nor had

Joe. Still, there are millions of sects all over the place; so that meant nothing, really.

'Finally, before we turned in, Joe had an idea. "I'm certain someone has some reference books in town," he said. "I'll have a dekko tomorrow morning, first thing, shall I?"

'Well, he did, and about noon, when I was considering the day's first drink in the same waterfront bar as the night before, he came in with a small volume, very worn-looking, in his hand.

'"Look at this," he said, "I found it in the local library; been there for ever, I should think."

'What he had in his hand was a slim black book, written in English, cheaply bound and very tattered, with brown pages crumbling at the edges. It was dated London, 1864, and was written by someone who called himself the Opener of the Gate, Brother A. Poole. The title of the book was *The New Revelation Revealed to the Elect*.

'"One of those island people must have left it here on their way through," I said, "or perhaps some fisherman lost it. Have you looked at it?"

'We read it aloud in turn, as much as we could stand, that is, because it was heavy going, and it was really a very boring book. A good bit of it came from Revelation and also the nastier bits of the Old Testament, and practically all of it was aimed at warning Those Who Transgressed.

'But there were stranger parts of it, based apparently on Darwin, of all people, and even some Jeremy Bentham. All in all, a weirder hodgepodge was never assembled even by your Aimee Semple McPherson or our own Muggletonians.

'The final summing up of the hundred pages or so, was a caution, or rather summons, to the Faithful, to withdraw from the world to a Secluded Spot at the first opportunity. Judging from what we heard, Soldier Key was the Secluded Spot.

'"It would be fascinating to find out what a gang like this has done in seventy years of isolation, don't you think?" said Joe. I agreed. I sounded like giving a new twist to our trip.

'Well, we weighed anchor that afternoon, after a farewell drink with our customs friend, and his last words intrigued us still more.

'"Have you any weapons on board?"

'I answered that we had a shark rifle, a 30-30 Winchester carbine, and a Colt .45 automatic pistol.

'"Good. I think less well today than I did last night of having directed you to this place. There are strange rumours among les Noirs of Soldier Key. Send me a card from your next port, as a favour, eh?"

'We promised and then said goodbye. Once clear of the harbour, we plotted a course and then told the two crewmen where we were going. The reaction was intriguing.

'Maxton, the older, looked rather glum, but Oswald, who was a six-foot black Hercules, actually forgot his usual respectful terms of address.

'"Mon, what you go theah fo'? They not good people theah; wery bad people on Soljah Cay, Mon!"

'When Joe and I pressed them to say why exactly they disliked the place, they could not, or would not, give us any answers, except that no one went there from other islands and that the folk were unfriendly, especially to coloured people.

'"Come, come, Oswald," said Joe finally, "there surely must be something you are not telling us."

'The man stared at the deck and finally mumbled something about "Duppies".

'Well, you know, this made us laugh, and that was an error. Duppies are West Indian ghosts, evil spirits, and are objects of fear among all British West Indian Negroes from Jamaica to Trinidad. When we joshed these two men about them, they shut up like oysters! Not one further word could we get out of them about Soldier Key. No, that's not right, I got one more thing a day later.

'Oswald was fishing with a hand line from the stern at a time when I had the helm. I had asked him idly what he was using for bait.

'He reached into a metal pail beside him and pulled out a huge black and grey snail's shell about six inches across. "Soljah, Mistah Don, Sah." I noticed he held it gingerly, and I suddenly saw why. The owner of the shell was not the original snail at all, but a weird-looking crab, with great orange and purple claws, too large for its size, beady eyes on stalks and a mass of red spiky legs. In fact, it was the northern hermit crab, simply grown huge and aggressive in the tropics. Its claws snapped and clicked as it tried to reach his fingers, and then he dropped it back into the pail.

'"They are many of thom where we go, Mistah Don, Sah, wery many of the Soljahs."

'So here was the reason for the name of the island! I had been speculating to myself as to whether the British had ever had a fort there, but the explanation was much simpler. Hermit Crab Island! Under this new name, it made all the vague warnings of our French friend seem quite silly, and when I told Joe about it later when we changed watch, he rather agreed.

'We made our landfall in a trifle under three days, due mostly to light airs, you know. The island was flat, only about seven miles long and two wide; so it would not have been a hard place to miss, actually. We came steadily in from the East, took down sail and started the auxiliary engine, because there was a circular reef marked on the charts as extending almost completely around the island and it only had a few navigable openings.

'It was evening, and the sun was on the horizon when we saw the first lights of the island's only town. There was a hundred-yard passage through the reef, marked clearly as showing seven fathoms opposite the town; so we brought the schooner in until we were no more than fifty or so yards off-shore.

'The town lay in a semicircle about a shallow bay. There was a broken beach, with bits of low cliff about five feet above the water, which we could just dimly make out. I saw dimly because it was now completely dark and there was no moon, only Caribbean starlight, although that's pretty bright.

'We switched off the engine, anchored and watched the town because it was the oddest-appearing port we had ever seen. There wasn't a sound. A few dimmish lights, perhaps half a dozen, burned in windows at wide intervals, but no dogs barked, no rooster crowed, no noise of voices came over the water. There was a gentle breeze in our rigging and the lapping of wavelets on the hull, and that was all.

'Against the sky at one point to the left, we could see the loom of some tall building, and we thought that this might be a church, but what we were to make of this silence baffled us. Night, especially the evening, is a lively time in the tropics, in fact the liveliest. Where were the people?

'We debated going ashore and decided against it. I saw "we", but I assure you our crew wasn't debating. They had made it quite plain earlier that they were not going even if ordered, not even in daylight.

'"This is a bad place, Cap'n," said Oswald to Joe. "We do not wish to discommode you, Sah, but we don't go on thot land, at all, Sah, no!"

'And that was that. So, we set anchor watch and turned in. A few mosquitoes came out from shore but not many, and we fell asleep with no trouble at all, determined to solve the mystery of the quiet in the morning.

'I was awakened by a hand on my arm. I blinked because it was still pitch-black out, and I looked at my watch. It was two a.m. Against the stars I could see Joe's head as he stooped over me.

'"Come on deck, Don," he said, "and listen." Even as he spoke, I was conscious that the night was no longer completely quiet.

'On deck, the four of us, for the two crewmen were up too, crouched in the cockpit, and we all strained our ears.

'The sound we were hearing was quite far off, a mile at the very least from the volume, but it was unmistakably the sound of many human voices singing. To us, it sounded like a hymn, but the tune was not a familiar one.

'After what seemed about twenty-three stanzas, it stopped, and we listened in the silent night again. Then, there came a distant shout, somewhat sustained, and again silence for a moment. Then the rhythmic mass cry again, but longer this time and seeming to go up and down. It went on this way for about ten minutes, first the silence and then the noise of human voices, and I tried without success to make out what was going on. Joe got the clue first.

'"Responses," he said, and of course, that was it. We were listening to something very like a psalm, chanted by a lot of people, a long way off, and naturally we couldn't hear the minister at all, but only the antiphony.

'After a bit, it stopped, and after fifteen minutes or so we turned in again. Now we knew why the town was quiet. All the people, apparently including the babies, were celebrating a church service somewhere inland. The Church of the New Revelation seemed to go in for midnight services.

'Well, we woke at six a.m. to a typical blazing Caribbean morning and also a visitor. Standing on the edge of the deck coaming was the hatless figure of a man, staring down at Joe and myself out of pale blue eyes.

'He was about sixty from his looks, clean-shaven and sallow, with thick white hair and a gaunt, peaked face. Not especially impressive until you studied the eyes. Ice blue they were, and so cold they gave me a chill even in the ninety-plus heat on deck.

'"What do you want here?" he said, with no other introduction at all. "We seek no visitors. This island is dedicated to the Lord."

'I introduced Joe and myself, but he paid no attention. I noticed his shabby but clean white suit and tieless stiff collar as he stepped down into the cockpit. Behind him, I saw a little skiff tied to the stern in which he had rowed himself out.

'"Look!" he said suddenly, an expression of disgust crossing his features. "You are bringing pollution with you. You slay the helpless creatures of the Lord!" With that he reached down and seized the bait bucket and emptied Oswald's bait, three of the big purple hermit crabs, over the side in one convulsive heave.

'"Now, I say, just a moment, now," said Joe, letting annoyance show through. "Exactly who are you, and what's this all about? We've tried to be polite, but there are limits . . ."

'The cold grey eyes swept over us again, and their nasty glint deepened. "I am Brother Poole, son of the Founder. You would call me the Pastor, I suppose. The government of this blessed place is in my keeping. Once again, I say, who are you and what do you want?"

'Joe answered peaceably enough and re-introduced us, but he had obviously been doing some thinking while he listened to Poole.

'"We just wanted to get some water and a little food," said Joe, "and some fresh fruit, before we go to Dominica. No law against you going ashore on your island, is there?" He added, "Isn't this British territory? Doesn't the Dominican governor ever allow people ashore here?"

'It was quite obvious that he had given Brother Poole something to chew on, you know. Whatever Poole's powers were on the island, he wasn't used to having them challenged. And it was evident from his hesitation that he didn't care for the remarks about the British or Crown government. You could see his bony face working as he grappled with the problem. Finally, something he must have thought was a smile struggled to get through. Frankly, I preferred his previous expression. A sanctimonious whine also crept into his hard voice.

'"I regret my sharpness, gentlemen. We have so few visitors, mostly fishermen of loose morals. I am the guardian of our little Eden here, and I have to think of my flock. Of course, you may come ashore, and buy what you need. I only ask that you kill nothing, do no fishing while here, out of respect to our law."

'We stated we had no intention of killing anything and said we'd come ashore after we cleaned up and had breakfast. He climbed back into his boat, but before he cast off, turned back to us.

'"Please see that those two black heathens stay on your schooner. Their presence is not wanted on our island, where they might corrupt our people." A good share of the original venom had come back into his speech.

'As he pulled away, I turned to Maxton and Oswald to apologize, but it was unnecessary. Their faces were immobile, but also, it seemed to me, a shade paler under their natural darkness. Before I could say anything, Maxton spoke.

'"Don't worry about us, Sah. We hov no desiah to enter in thot place. It is of the utmost dislike to us, I ossuah you, Sah."

'Well, Joe and I shaved, and put on clean clothes, and then rowed our dinghy into the empty dock. There was only one, and that one small. A lot of fishing boats, all under twenty feet, were moored to buoys and also pulled up the sloping beach, where it existed, that is.

'The town lay before me to observe, as Joe was doing the rowing, and I had a full view from the stern. It looked pretty small, perhaps fifty houses all told, plus the one church we had spotted the night before, a steepled white thing with something metallic, not a cross, on the steeple, which caught the sunlight and reflected it blindingly.

'The houses were all white stucco, mostly palm-thatch-roofed, but a few with rusting tin instead, and all set on short stilts a foot or so off the ground. You could have duplicated them on any other island in the Caribbean.

'A few coco palms grew here and there and some shortish trees, mostly in the yards of the houses. Behind the town, a low green scrub rolled away, the monotonous outline broken only by a few of the taller thatch palms. The whole place lay shimmering in the heat, because not a breath of air moved.

'And neither did anything else. A white figure on the end of the dock was Brother Poole, identifiable at long range as waiting for us. But behind him the town lay silent and still. Not so much as a dog or chicken crossed a yard or disturbed the dust of the white roads. It was, if anything, more eerie than the night before.

'We nosed into the dock, and Poole leaned down to catch the painter Joe flung up to him. We climbed up as he was securing it to a post. Then he stood up and faced us.

'"Welcome to Soldier Key, gentlemen," he said. "I hope I did not appear too unfriendly earlier, but I have a precious duty here, guarding my flock. Although you are not of the Elect, I know you would not wish to bring disturbance to a pious community, which has cut itself off from the dross and vanity of the world." He turned to lead us down the dock without waiting for an answer and threw another remark over his shoulder. "The governor of Dominica has given me magistrate's powers."

'The carrot and the stick, eh! Joe and I exchanged glances behind his back.

'At the foot of the dock, Poole turned again, the cold eyes gleaming in the sunlight. "I presume you wish to see our little town? You will find it quiet. This is a festival of our church, and all of our people rest during the day to prepare for the evening service, by fasting and by prayer. I would be doing so too, but for the duties of hospitality, which are paramount."

'I had been trying to analyse his very odd accent since I'd first heard it. It was not West Indian, but a curiously altered Cockney, flat and nasal, something like the worst sort of Australian, what they call "Stryne". I thought then, and still think, that I know exactly how Uriah Heep must have sounded.

'As we walked up the silent main street, which lay dreaming in the white heat, our feet kicking up tiny clouds of coral dust, I suddenly saw something move in the shadow of a house. At first I thought it was a cat, then a large rat, but as it moved, it came momentarily into a patch of sunlight, and I stopped to stare.

'It was a soldier, a hermit crab, but enormous in size, at least a foot long, its naked body hidden in and carrying a huge conch shell as it scuttled clumsily along. As we came abreast of it, its stalked eyes seemed to notice us, and to my surprise, instead of retreating, it ran towards us and stopped only a foot away. Its great orange and purple claws looked capable of severing one's wrist or a finger, at any rate.

'Poole had stopped too, and then, reaching into his pocket, he pulled out a linen bag from which he extracted a strip of dried meat. He leaned down, do you know, and placed it in front of the crab. It seized it and began to shred it in the huge claws, passing bits back to its mouth, where other small appendages chewed busily. It was as thoroughly nasty a sight as I'd ever glimpsed. Also, I wondered at the meat.

'"That's a monster," I said. "How on earth do you tame them? I had no idea they grew so big. And I thought you ate no meat?"

'"They are not *tame*, as you in the gross world think of it," said Poole sharply. "They are our little brothers, our friends, as much a part of life as we are, and all units of the great chain live here in peace, some higher, some lower, but all striving to close the great circle which holds us to the material earth, at peace, yet in competition, the lower sinking, failing, the higher mastering the lower, then aiding. It is all part of –" His whining voice rose as he spoke, but suddenly stopped as he realized that our expressions were baffled, unmoved by the exposition of his extraordinary creed. "You would not understand," he finished lamely, and pocketing the still unexplained meat, he turned to lead us on. We followed, glancing at one another. Behind us, the huge crab still crunched on its dainty, clicking and mumbling.

'Wrapped in thought about Poole and his religion, I really didn't notice that we had come to the town square, until I almost ran into Joe, who had stopped in front of me.

'Before us now stood the church we had glimpsed earlier, a massive, white-stuccoed structure with a pointed spire. As I looked up, I could see by squinting that the shiny object on the steeple was, indeed, not a cross. It was a huge crab claw, gilded and gleaming in the sunlight!

'My jaw must have dropped, because Poole felt it incumbent on himself to explain. "We have abandoned the more obvious Christian symbols," he said. "And since our friends, the soldiers, are the commonest local inhabitants, we chose to symbolize the unity of all life by placing their limb on our little place of worship."

'"Rather! I can see it's their church," said Joe pointing. "Look there, Donald."

'As he spoke, I saw what he had seen first, that the shadows around the base of the church were moving and alive – with the great hermit crabs.

'Large, small, and a few immense, they rustled and clanked in and around the coral blocks which formed the base, and the scrubby bushes which flanked the blocks, a sea of shells, claws, spiny legs and stalked eyes.

'Poole must have seen that we were revolted, because he moved on abruptly, leaving us no choice except to follow him. As we moved, I heard a distant human sound break the hot silence for the first time that morning, the sound of hammering. It came from our right, towards the edge of town, and peering down a sandy street in that direction, I thought I could identify the source – a long shedlike structure, about a third of a mile away.

'"I thought everyone had retired to pray?" said Joe at the same moment. "What's that hammering?"

'Poole looked annoyed. I never met a man less good at disguising his feelings, but since he normally never had to while on his island, it must have been quite hard to learn. Finally his face cleared and the spurious benevolence gained control.

'"A few of the men are working on religious instruments," he said. "We have a festival coming: we call it the Time of the Change, so there is a dispensation for them. Would you like to see them at work?"

'Since the silent town had so far yielded nothing of interest except the soldiers, which we loathed, we said yes.

'We came at length to one end of the long building, and Poole held aside a rattan screen door, so that we could go in first. A blast of frightful heat hit us in the face as we entered.

'Inside, the building was one long open shed, lit by vents in the walls, and by a fire which blazed in a trench running half the length of the structure. Several giant metal cauldrons bubbled over the fire, with huge pieces of some horn-like material sticking out of them.

'Over against one wall were several long benches, and at these, a number of bronzed white men, stripped to tattered shorts, were furiously hammering at some pieces of the horny substance, flattening it and bending it, forcing it into huge wooden clamps and vices and pegging it together.

'As we watched, several of them stopped work and seized a huge piece of the stuff, and dragging it to the fire, dumped it into one of the giant pots. No one paid us the slightest attention, but simply kept working as though driven by some frantic need, some internal pressure. The whole affair was most mysterious.

'I stepped close to one of the pots to see if I could learn what it was they were working on, and as I looked I saw, to my amazement, it was a tortoise shell.

'Now, a hawksbill sea turtle, the only known source of shell, seldom grows one much over a yard long, you know. The pieces these men were working on must have been made with many dozens of them at least. What on earth were they doing?

'Poole, who had been surveying our bewilderment with a sardonic smile, decided to mystify us further. Tapping Joe on the shoulder and pointing, he started walking down the length of the long shed, skirting the fires and the workmen, but ignoring them.

'His goal was the far left-hand corner, which we now saw had a palm-thatch curtain extending from floor to ceiling, masking what lay behind.

'With the air of a second-rate showman on his unpleasant face he pulled on a rope and drew the high brown curtain aside. "Behold our aim, gentlemen. Here is a fitting offering that we make for the altar of the Most High!"

'What we saw was certainly worth more than a little showmanship. Before us, poised on seven or eight large sawhorses, was a giant, gleaming shell, as if some colossal and quite improbable snail had been washed up from the deeps of the sea. Golden, mottled and semi-translucent, it towered over our heads, and must have been at least twelve feet in diameter from the great opening in the base to the peak of the spiral tip. As we drew closer we saw that the whole marvellous object was artificial, being made of plates of overlapping tortoise shell pegged so cunningly that it was hard to see any joint. At one place on the side, a large gap showed where the work was not yet complete. Obviously, this was why the silent, half-naked workers were toiling so industriously. It was a very beautiful and awe-inspiring sight, if still a mysterious one.

'Poole drew the curtain closed and stood with his hands in his coat pockets smiling at our amazement. "That's one of the most beautiful things I've ever seen," I said, quite honestly. "May I ask what you do with it when it's finished?"

'Some strong emotion flashed for a second across his face, to be replaced by a bland expression of benignity. "We set it afloat on a large raft, surrounded by offerings of fruit and flowers," he said. "An offering to God, to be swept where He wills by the waves and winds."

'Seeing our incomprehension at the idea of so much hard work going to waste, he elaborated, still smiling in his sneering way. "You see, it takes a long time to make the shell. The whole community, our whole little island, participates. Men must catch turtles. Then they must be killed, as mercifully as possible, the shell cured in a special manner and so on, right up until the final work. Then, when we gather at the ceremony of departure, all our people share in the delight of speeding it forth. We feel that we send our sins with it and that our long labour and offering to God may help our souls to Paradise. A naïve idea to you cultivated men of the great, outside world, no doubt, but very dear to us. My father, of blessed memory, the Founder, devised the whole idea."

'Actually, you know, the idea was a lovely and reverent one. It reminded me of the Doge of Venice marrying the Sea, and other ceremonies of a similar nature. Brother Poole must have spent some time indeed on the composition of his tale, for it was quite the pleasantest thing we had heard about the island.

'While he had been speaking, we had passed out of the shed into the glaring sunlight, which seemed cool after the inferno we had left behind us.

'As we stood blinking in the sun, Poole turned to us with the false benignity now vanished from his face. "So, gentlemen, you have seen all there is to see of our little town. There is an important religious festival tonight, the launching of our offering. I must ask you to purchase such supplies as you need and leave before this evening, since non-believers are not permitted here during our holy night and day, which is tomorrow. I can sell you any supplies you may need."

'Well, we had no reason to linger. Personally, as I said earlier, I had taken a profound dislike to the whole town and particularly to Brother Poole, who seemed to embody it, as well as actually to direct it. We walked to the wharf, discussing what we needed on the way. Poole seemed ready to sell fruit, bananas, mangoes and papayas, as well as bread, at perfectly honest prices, and offered us fresh water free of any charge at all.

'Only once did any hardness come back into his voice, and that was then I asked if any spiny lobsters, *langouste*, were for sale.

'"We do not take life here," he said. "I told you earlier of our rule."

'Joe could not help breaking in with an obvious point, although he should have known better when dealing with a fanatic.

'"What about turtles? You kill them for their shells and presumably eat the meat? And what about the fish you catch?"

'Poole looked murderous. "We do not eat meat," he snapped. "You would not understand, being heretics, unaware of the Divine Revelation, but the turtles' deaths are allowable, since we beautify our offering to God with their shells. The greater cause is served through a smaller fault. Also, the fish are set aside to us as our portion, though a sinful one. But what is the use of explaining these holy things to you, since you have not seen the Light."

'After this, he declined to say anything else at all, except to wish us a good journey in a furious voice and to add that our purchases and water would be on the dock in an hour. With that, he stalked off and disappeared around the corner of the street. Upon his departure, all movement ceased, and the town dreamed on, neither sound nor movement breaking the noon silence. Yet we both had the feeling that eyes watched us from behind every closed shutter and each blank, sealed window.

'We rowed back to our schooner in silence. Only when we climbed aboard, to be greeted by Maxton and Oswald, did our voices break out together, as if pent up.

'"Appalling character, he was! What a perfectly hellish place! Did you feel the eyes on your back?" et cetera.

'Only after settling down and disposing of lunch, which the men had thoughtfully made in our absence, did we seriously talk. The conclusion we reached was that the British government and local administration in Dominica needed a good jolt about this place, and that it ought to be thoroughly investigated to find out just how happy the locals really were about Brother Poole and his hermit crab church. Other than that, we decided the sooner we left, the better.

'During lunch we had seen some of the locals, all whites, manhandling a cart down on the dock, and unloading it. We now rowed ashore and found two large, covered baskets of fruit, half a dozen loaves of new bread, and an old oil drum of water, which looked and tasted clean and fresh. We also found Poole, who seemed to appear out of the air and accepted the previously agreed-on payment for the food. When that was over and we promised to return the water drum after putting the water in our tank, he came to his official business again.

'"Now that you have water, you can leave, I suppose," he said. "There is no further reason for interrupting our holy festivities?" His arrogant whine, half command and half cringe, was on the upsurge. It annoyed Joe as well as me, and his answer to the order, on the face of it, was quite natural, really.

'"We'll probably use the land breeze this evening," said Joe. "Of course, we may decide not to. Your bay is so pretty. We like to look at it."

'"Yes," I added, picking up his cue. "You know how we yachtsmen are, passionate lovers of scenery. Why, we may decide to stay a week."

'Of course we were only trying to get a rise out of Reverend Poole, but he had absolutely no sense of humour. Yet he realized that we disliked him quite as much as he did us. His eyes blazed with sudden rage, and he half-lifted one hand, as though to curse us. But another expression crossed his face first, and the mask dropped again. He must have suddenly realized that he didn't have a pair of his co-religionists to deal with.

'Without another word, he turned on his heel and left, leaving us sitting in our rowboat staring at one another.

'We got the water, bread and fruit out, and I rowed back and left the empty oil drum on the dock. The town still lay as quiet as ever in the

sun, and no breeze disturbed the few coco palms. From the pier, I could
see no sign of any movement farther in, and the harbour was like a
mirror, on the reflection of which our schooner and the small, anchored
fishing boats hung motionless in the heat.

'Back aboard again, I conferred with Joe, and then we told the two
crewmen we would leave on the evening land breeze. The harbour was
deep enough so that tide made no difference. We could have used our
engine, of course, but we hated to do so when sails would do the work.
Aside from disliking engines, as all who sail for pleasure do, we always
thought of emergencies, when the fuel might be desperately needed.

'Oswald and Maxton brightened up when we said we were going, and
had we left right then, I'm sure they would have offered to row, or swim,
for that matter. Their dislike of Soldier Key had never been plainer.

'The afternoon drifted on, and again the tropical night came quickly,
with no real evening. But there was no wind. The expected land breeze
simply didn't appear. When this happens, one can usually expect it to
come around midnight or a little after in these waters, although I have
no idea why. We'd had it happen before, however, so we waited. Since
we had anchor lights on, we were perfectly visible from shore, but tonight
no lights at all showed there. There was no moon, but brilliant starlight,
and we could see the outline of the shore and the loom of the buildings
behind, as silent as ever.

'We decided to leave one man awake to look for wind, and the rest
would turn in all standing, that is, dressed, not that we wore much but
shorts. We could raise sail in no time. Oswald said he was not sleepy,
and so he got the job.

'I don't know why I should have wakened at midnight. There was
still no wind, and we had all been sleeping on deck. I looked at my
watch, cast my eye along the deck to Maxton's and Joe's sleeping forms
and then went aft to find Oswald. He wasn't there, so I looked forward
again. No sign of him, and the starlight was clear enough to see from
bow to stern. There was no use waking the others on a false alarm. I got
up and dropped into the cabin, gave it a quick once-over, and then came
out of the forward hatch and went quickly aft to the stern. No Oswald.

'I woke the others quietly, and explained the situation in a few words.
From the moment I spoke, none of us had any doubt as to what had
happened. Oswald had never left voluntarily. Someone, or something,
with human motivation, had plucked him off the schooner as easily as
you gaff a fish and even more quietly, and the purpose and the strength
had come from the silent town, from Soldier Key.

'We discovered afterwards that it had been easy for them. Several
swimmers approached as silently as sharks and one of them had clipped
Oswald over the head with a club as he sat with his back to the rail.

Then, without a sound, he had been lowered into the bay and towed back to shore. Why they had left the rest of us I shall never know, but I suspect that they simply had got cold feet. Or perhaps Poole thought that we'd be reluctant to report our loss. By the time we got back with help, he could always plead ignorance and say that we had done the poor chap in ourselves. He of course would have his whole island to back him up. As a second purpose, I think he wanted us out of there and this was perhaps a last warning. Well, if that were so, he had made a mistake.

'Without anyone's having to speak, all three of us went below and began to gather weapons. I took the big Colt automatic pistol, because it was my own, Joe the .30-30 carbine, and Maxton simply tucked his cane knife, a big machete, without which most West Indians feel undressed, in his belt. Then we collected ammunition and went aft to our dinghy. I hauled the painter in without even looking until the cut end came into my hand! I had not noticed its absence on my earlier check, but the Key men had cut it adrift.

'However, this actually didn't put us back a bit. Still without speaking, but all three purposeful, we began to rig a float for the weapons out of small line and four life preservers. We had it done and ready to move in less than two minutes and were about to slip over the side when Maxton suddenly caught us by the arms and put a hand to his ear.

'As we listened in the quiet dark, a noise, almost a vibration, began to come over the water. It was a sound we couldn't identify, a strange sort of muffled rustling or shuffling sound, and Joe and I looked at each other in the starlight, absolutely baffled. Maxton whispered in our ears.

'"Dot is feet. Dey move somewheah."

'Of course he was quite right. We were listening to the whole town on the move, the rustle of hundreds of feet scuffing through the coral dust of the streets. Where they were going we didn't know, but we began to drop into the water, because this silent march almost certainly meant no good to Oswald. We all three knew *that*, somehow. I took the lead, carrying the pistol out of water, so that we should be armed upon landing. Behind me, Joe and Maxton swam, pushing the little raft with the rifle, the spare ammo, our shoes, and two canteens. Joe had added something else, but I didn't find that out until later.

'I swam for the edge of town way over on the left, well away from the dock or boats, since I had to assume that if they had posted a sentry, he would be placed at that point. It apparently was quite unnecessary, but we had to try to outguess them at every point, and we still thought these people rational. I tried not to think of sharks, which I dislike.

'As we swam, I listened for the sound of footsteps, but it had died away, and this lent new urgency to our efforts. In a very short time, my feet grated on the coral beach, and keeping the pistol poised, I waded ashore, the other two behind me. Joe had the rifle at the ready now, and Maxton had drawn his machete.

'There was no sign of movement. We had landed just on the outer edge of town, the last house looming about two hundred feet to our right. Not a sound broke the silence but faint insect humming and the splash of ripples breaking on the narrow beach.

'After listening a minute, we put on our shoes, then divided the ammunition and the canteens. I saw Joe stick something else in his belt, but I was concentrating so hard on listening that it really didn't register.

'We placed the life preservers above the high-water mark under a bush and moved into the town, guns at the ready. If the town were quiet by day, it was dead that night. This was a town presumably inhabited by living people, but not a murmur of life came from any of the shuttered houses. At each corner, we stopped and listened, but we could hear nothing. Nothing human, that is. Twice I almost fired at rustling shadows and faint clanking noises, only to realize that it was only the hideous crabs from which the island took its name.

'The church was our goal, by unspoken agreement, but when we reached the square, it loomed silent and unlit in front of us. The central door was wide open, and we could hear no movement from the black interior. Wherever the people were, it was not there.

'Moving on, we struck a broader street, one which led away inland from the water. As we paused in the shadow of a tamarind tree, Maxton suddenly held up a hand and dropped to his knees. I couldn't make out what he was doing, but he stood up in a second.

'"This dust has been kicked up wery recent. I think the people come this way, many people."

'I couldn't smell anything, but Joe and I knew we didn't have his perceptions, and we had no other clues anyway. Besides, we had heard the marching feet, and they had gone somewhere, and then there was the singing of the previous night, too.

'Keeping to the edge of the road, we went inland, walking quickly, but very much on the alert. The road left the town, which wasn't too big, remember, after about two hundred yards and cut straight into the scrub, in the direction of the centre of the island, as near as we could make out. At about fifteen minutes' walk from the town, we learned that Maxton was right. We were deep in the shadowy scrub now, not a jungle, but the thick, low thorn bush of most West Indian islands. The road still ran straight and smooth ahead of us, a dim, white ribbon under the stars. Only insect noises broke the silence.

'Suddenly, we all halted. Not far off, a half mile at a guess, a sound erupted into the night. We had heard it before, not so loud, on the previous night and recognized it at once for the mass chorus of human voices in a chant. It came from ahead of us and to one side, the left.

'Our pace quickened to a trot, and as we ran we listened, trying to pinpoint the noise. It was some sort of service, because we could hear the sound die into silence and then start again. As we drew closer to the source, we began to hear the single voice which led the chant, high and faint, and then the muffled roar that followed from the congregation.

'It was only the voices that saved us from missing the path. The trees had increased in height, and shadowed the road a good deal, so that we should have overshot the left fork if we hadn't been watching for it. Even then, Maxton was the only one to spot it, and he suddenly signalled us to turn into what looked like a dense bush. Following him, we broke through a screen of vegetation, which gave way so easily that we realized that it must have been dragged there after cutting. And there was a road again, narrower but still plain and well-trodden. Some old habit of caution must have led them so to mask their path. We now moved at an increased speed.

'Ahead of us, the voices swelled in another chant, but we could not as yet distinguish words. The single voice was silent. As the noise increased, so did our caution, and we slowed our pace, since we had no wish to burst unexpectedly into the middle of some gathering of goodness knows what.

'All at once, we could see light ahead through the trees, a flickering, reddish glow which lit the path far better than the dim starlight. We eased down to a slow walk and advanced cautiously.

'The light grew continually stronger as we went on, reflected back from our faces and the boles and leaves of the thorn bushes and palmettoes. The sound of voices was almost deafening now, but we were searching so hard for a sight of a guard or sentry, we paid no attention to the words, which were blurred in any case.

'The trees suddenly thinned before us, and stooping low, the three of us crawled abreast of their edge and peered into the open, keeping well behind the screening branches, and off the road, which suddenly appeared to vanish. When we reached the last line of bushes, it was easy to see why. We were gazing down into an immense pit.

'We were on one edge of an enormous hole in the ground, quite round and perhaps seventy feet deep. It was rimmed with greyish limestone rock, level at the edges, to which point the bushes grew, all around.

'At our feet, the path, now very narrow, wound down a steep slope to the smooth floor of white sand below. One side of the natural amphitheatre, for such it was, was banked up into lines of crude seats, sloping to the open floor of packed sand. The width of the whole place must have been at least two hundred yards in diameter, if not more.

'The entire population of Soldier Key, now silent, was sitting on the banked seats of this private arena, gazing at the scene before them with rapt attention. We had an excellent view of them, which made up in completeness for what we had missed earlier. Every man, woman and child, perhaps two hundred or more, was stark naked, clothed only in garlands of flowers and flower necklaces. Every single living soul on the island must have been there, and not a sound came from even the smallest baby at its mother's breast, or the oldest crone. I could see no coloured people, but only whites. Apparently the creed of the New Revelation was not valid for any but Caucasians.

'Inching forward to get a better look, we were able to see what held their attention. Two great bonfires burned on the floor of the pit, and between them Brother Poole, the Shepherd of his people, was moving about. As naked as his flock, his scrawny white body gleaming as if oiled, he was capering in a strange way around three objects on the sand, between the fires.

'In the centre, golden in the firelight, lay the immense shell we had seen earlier in the workshed in town. No holes now marred its perfection, and it lay gleaming and wonderful on one of its sides, the opening facing us as we watched.

'On either side of the shell, dwarfed by its bulk, were two bound human bodies! One was Oswald. He was not only bound but gagged. As far away as we were, we could see his eyes roll and the muscles under his dark skin strain as he tried to break his bonds. The other figure was that of a white girl, perhaps fifteen or so from her build. She lay silent and unmoving, but I could see that her eyes were open. Around the three, the shell and the bodies, Brother Poole danced and waved his hands, as if in some maniac's parody of a benediction. Although he was otherwise quite nude, he wore a strange necklace, of some hard, purplish objects, which bounded and shook as he moved. So silent were the people that even as high as we were lying, I could hear the click and rattle of them. The sound jogged my memory, until I suddenly realized why it was familiar. He was wearing a necklace of hermit crab claws and the noise was just as if some of them were scuttling about.

'I stated that the pit was circular. The floor was level, sloping up on one side to the packed earth seats of the people, and on the other side to the limestone walls. Nothing grew on these smooth walls, excepting only in one place, directly opposite the seats, where dense canopies of some creeper hung down, half obscuring a great triangular opening or cleft in the rock, about twenty feet in height and at least that wide near the base. Pressed against the cliff to one side of the hole, was a massive, now open door or gate, made of bulky timbers in a heavy frame. It was hung on great iron hinges driven into the rock. Could this be the Gate of which

Poole claimed to be the Opener, I wondered? In front of the hole, and a little to one side, there was a still pool of water, probably a spring. Directly across from us, a path similar to that below us wound up the cliff face and vanished into the dark fringe of foliage at the top.

'Brother Poole suddenly ceased his capering and raised both hands. He was now facing the dark opening across the arena, and to this he addressed his invocation. I cannot at this date give it word for word, but roughly it went rather like this:

"Oh, Lord of Majesty, Incarnation of Survival, Manifestation of Nature and its struggle, Devourer of Sin and the Flesh, have mercy upon us."

'Behind him a roar arose as the crowd repeated the last line, ". . . have mercy upon us." He continued:

"Have mercy, Oh Thou, Shelled in Adamant. Of Thy mercy, accept our offerings, a new home for Thy greatness, new life for Thy limbs, new viands for Thy table. Enter upon Thy new home and partake of Thine offerings."

'This rather unpleasant parody of a communion service seemed extraordinarily unreal, it was so fantastic.

'In the red light, Poole's gaunt face, now drooling slightly, assumed an air of repellent majesty. Much as he disgusted me, the creature did have a certain hypnotic power at that moment. He believed in what he was doing. Behind his back, his audience sat rapt and expectant, all of them, old and young, leaning forward in the same tense pause of anticipation. As he ceased to speak, time almost seemed to stop, and he held his hands out, facing the opening in the rock wall.

'Joe broke the spell, pushing the rifle at me and snatching the Colt from my limp hand.

'"Stay here and cover us," he hissed. "Maxton and I are going down."

'The two of them moved like cats, breaking from the scrub and racing down the path below me with driving steps. My brain cleared and I aimed the loaded rifle at Poole. If anybody went, he certainly would be the first.

'Maxton and Joe were on the sandy floor of the pit before anyone even noticed them. Joe had a clasp knife in one hand and the pistol in the other, and he flashed behind Poole's back and stopped to cut the girl's bonds. Behind him, Maxton was doing the same for Oswald with the edge of his machete.

'A chorus of screams from the crowd announced that not all of them were in a trance, but none of them moved. I refocused on Poole, but he still faced the cave, apparently lost to the actual world, entranced in an ecstasy of religion.

'Then, I caught a flicker of movement from the corner of my right eye and risked a glance in that direction. What I saw made my rifle fall with a thud to the earth.

'Framed in the entrance to the cleft was Horror incarnate. Poised on giant stalked legs, monstrous, incredible, gleaming in the firelight, stood the Soldier of Soldier Key, the Living God of Brother Poole and his awful church.

'The giant purple and orange claws, the larger of the two at least six feet long, were held in front of the mass of clicking, grinding mouth parts. From the stalked eyes held out ten feet above the ground, to the great, red-pointed legs, jointed and barbed with three-inch spines, there stood complete and perfect a hermit crab that must have weighed not less than a thousand pounds.

'As it moved slowly forward from the mouth of its private cave, the dragging shell which covered its soft body and rear end became visible, and I saw the true reason for the labour of the whole island. It, the shell, was made of tortoise shell, still recognizable though dirty and scarred, and although enormous, it was obviously too small. The soft body bulging from the opening must have desperately needed more room. The purpose of the new and larger shell, which lay sparkling on the sand, was now clear. The god was to have a new house.

'As all this flashed through my mind, I recovered my wits and snatched up the rifle again. It was as well I did, because now things were starting to break down on the pit floor.

'Emerging from his trance, Poole had turned around and had seen before his dumbfounded eyes his sacrifices no longer neatly tied up but actually escaping. Joe had the limp body of the girl over one shoulder, and Maxton was aiding Oswald to follow in the direction of the foot of the nearer path, just beneath my own position.

'With a shriek, Poole summoned his nude worshippers to the assault. "Blasphemy! Slay the desecrators of the shrine! Kill them, in the sight of the Living God!"

'With a roar, the whole mob poured off its earth benches and rushed for the three figures which ran slowly across the sand. Poole stood where he was, his hand raised in a curse, his face now wholly evil, working with madness in the firelight. Behind him some few yards, that unbelievable crustacean had paused, immobile, like a bizarre statue, motionless save for the moving, twitching mouth parts.

'I think to this day we would have been dead men, but for two factors. Joe, heavily burdened, Maxton and Oswald were still thirty feet from the path's entrance. Behind them, the horde of frantic, raving islanders were no more than a hundred paces. I had begun to shoot, forgetting Poole, firing at the foremost men instead, and hitting at once, but it did no real good. Those behind simply leapt over the prostrate bodies and came on. One rifle simply could not stop this gibbering animal horde. But something else could.

'Above the howling of the pack and the bark of my rifle rang out a scream so awful and agonized that I can still hear it in my sleep. No one could have ignored that dreadful cry. With three exceptions, everyone halted to see the cause.

'Brother Poole had momentarily forgotten his god, but his god had not forgotten him. As he stood there launching curses and hellfire, the monster, irritated no doubt by all the noise and movement, had come from behind and now clutched him in its titanic, larger claw, as firmly as its little brothers would hold a grasshopper. Suddenly, with no apparent effort, it simply closed the claw, and before our eyes, the two halves of the screaming Shepherd of the Island fell to the sand in a fountain of blood.

'The three below, however, had not halted nor seen this sight, but were now steadily coming up the path. I resumed my ineffective rifle practice, for with fresh screams of rage, the mob of worshippers surged forward again, and began to gain. But Joe changed that.

'He halted and allowed Oswald and Maxton to run past. Dumping the girl, who had never moved at all, to the ground, he reached for his belt and pulled out a bulky metallic object which I now saw for the first time in the firelight. It was the schooner's flare pistol.

'Aiming at the centre of the oncoming crowd, he fired straight into them, and then the flare exploded somewhere in the mass in a blast of white incandescence. At the same instant, I had a stroke of genius, and almost without thinking, I shifted my sights and squeezed off a shot at that incredible horror, the Soldier, aiming directly for the centre of the head, and just over the grinding mouth parts.

'In the twin lights of the flare and the still-blazing fires, I caught a glimpse of Hell. Blackened figures writhed in agony on the ground, and others, their hair ablaze, ran aimlessly about shrieking in pain and fright. But this was not all. My bullet must have wounded the Soldier in its tenderest parts. Raising its great shell off the ground and snapping its giant claws, it rushed at the nearest humans in a frenzy, not gripping and holding, but instead slashing and flailing about with its colossal pincers. That a creature of its bulk could move with speed was a revelation to me, of an unsought kind. I remember seeing a screaming child crushed flat by a great leg.

'I was no longer firing, but simply watching the base of the path with one eye and the terrible scene below with the other. In only a few seconds,

Maxton's and Oswald's heads appeared just before me, as they climbed panting from the inferno below.

'A little behind them came Joe, reloading as he ran and checking his backtrail as he paused at the bend in the path. The girl was gone.

'I rose and covered the path behind them as they reached level ground. "That lunatic girl got up and ran back into the crowd," gasped Joe. "To hell with her. Let's get out of here."

'With me to the rear covering the retreat, we stumbled off down the track to the main road. In a minute the edge of the cliff was lost to view, and only the red glow on the leaves and the appalling sounds remained to tell us of what we had left behind. Breathless with shock and fright, we ran on at our best speed under the stars and trees until we reached the road and only a far-off wailing came to our ears.

'As we ran, I tried to make some sense out of what I had seen. In only a few moments, a maze of jumbled thoughts poured through me. How had that incredible thing been grown? How long had it lived? How many people had died to feed it? As the sound of anguished voices died away, my brain simply gave up, and I devoted myself to breathing and moving. Thinking back now, I believe that somehow, through their insane religion, the islanders had created a miracle of biology, taking a tiny animal and forcing its size somehow until no natural sea shell could contain it, and then building artificial ones to house its increased growth. But now, of course, no one will ever know the answers.

'There was no pursuit, I may say. The whole population of the island had been in that shambles of a pit, and we simply walked, for we could no longer run, back to the town and along the beach to our piled and tied life preservers. Within an hour of leaving the Amphitheatre of the Crab, we were climbing wearily over the side of the schooner. It took us only a few minutes to start the engine and get in the anchor, and then we were underway. Checking my watch, I found it was four-thirty a.m., although it seemed that a week had gone by.

'At blazing dawn, the island was only a faint blur on the horizon, which soon sank into the sea, leaving us feeling that we had been in a bad dream.

'Now, we never called at Dominica. The four of us talked it over and decided not to.

'Look here, you fellows, we had probably killed, at a minimum, twenty or so souls, directly by flare or gunfire, and more still through the agency of the Soldier. By the time any representatives of the law arrived, what evidence would they find in our favour? Whatever governing group or person took over from Poole would have the whole island behind him or it. Who would believe our story? No one.

'No, we did nothing, at least at the time. We sent an anonymous letter

to the Colonial Office and a copy to the Dominican Administrator later
on, saying nothing at all about giant crabs, but demanding an inquiry
into voodoo murders and local affairs generally. I have never heard that
anything came of it, and as I told you earlier, the people were almost
wiped out by the hurricane of the following year.

'But I don't eat lobster or crab. It came too close to being the other
way round, you see? Anyone care for bridge?'

Williams managed to grunt. We would hear from him later on, no
doubt.

# The Sanguivites

## *Kay Leith*

'Employ him,' urged Mrs Reckitt. 'All he needs is baccy money. How's your drink?'

'We don't really need a gardener for our half-acre,' said John, drinking up and handing his glass over. 'Thanks. I mean, we don't really need Mrs Bittoms either, with Meg working from home, but she gave us practically no choice.'

His hostess laughed knowingly. 'Oh, you'll find that the locals always get their own way, either by doing nothing, or by downright sabotage. If you don't take on old Gelder, he'll probably put a spell on your chrysanthemums, or persuade all the weeds in Ashton-Carvel to seed on your land. I wouldn't risk it if I were you. Only, don't let him touch your mower, darling. It'll probably fall apart in his hands!'

John didn't want to have to point out that finance was at the root of his disinclination to take on Gelder. They'd committed themselves to a mortgage which didn't allow for any frills, and a gardener was just an outrageous luxury – especially one that was mechanically illiterate.

He took his merry leave of the Reckitts, hopped the fence into his own ground, and walked through his own front door nearly an hour after his train had arrived. He noted on the way the weeds that had sprouted since the weekend. Everywhere he looked things needed to be done.

'You're late,' said Meg, coming out of the kitchen in sunsuit and bare feet.

'Met Reckitt at the station and he insisted I come in for a drink. From the looks of you, it's just as well I persuaded him that you'd be too busy to join us.'

'Yes,' agreed Meg. 'Just as well. I spent all afternoon working like a maniac, and all I want to do now is eat and collapse.'

'They were on about that old gardener chap . . .'

'You mean Gelder?' Meg turned, lips pursed, and went back into the kitchen. 'Oh, Mrs Bittoms brought him round this morning, poor old soul, so I took him on.'

'You what?' John snatched at his wife's arm and made her face him. 'You did *what*? Are you mad? We can't afford him.'

Meg's eyes blazed, but only briefly. 'Oh, don't get uptight about it. He's only going to cost us the price of a few packets of cigarettes and the same number of cups of tea, and if you're worried about that, I've decided to cut my smoking in half, and it's about time you did too – that and your evening guzzles.'

John wanted to slap her. She was always making remarks about that. God knows, he needed a couple in the evening after the kind of day he put in – an eleven-hour stretch from eight a.m. till seven p.m. Having gone in for their dream cottage in the country, was *he* ever going to get the chance to enjoy it? It was all very well for *her*, comfily getting her nest together . . .

'You know he can't bloody well use the mower, don't you?' he said, not bothering to conceal his irritation.

'Oh, don't worry,' said Meg, shovelling food into serving dishes. '*I'll* cut the grass.' Then she stopped and turned. 'But you realize, I hope, that with all the decorating and one thing and another, I'm getting precious little time to do any of my own work.'

'Well, why did you take on the old fool?'

'Because the old fool, as you call him, will at least keep down the weeds for me.' She dabbed the beads of sweat on her upper lip and spread her hands, palms up. 'Look at my godawful hands, John. I can hardly hold the paintbrush steady any more with the beating my muscles are taking nowadays. The illustrations I promised Harmers aren't even half-finished.'

Chastened, John went over and took Meg's hands, raising them to his lips. 'I know. I'm sorry. I know. If this place is going to be too much for us, then the only sensible thing to do is to get rid of it.'

Meg stiffened. 'Over my dead body! At least I've got dear old Mrs Bittoms to do the laundry.' She busied herself with the dinner preparations again. 'If you've forgotten what it used to be like before we came here, I haven't. It'll take more than sore hands to put *me* off! When I've finished putting the paper on the lounge walls I won't feel quite so beleaguered. After all, we've been here only six weeks . . .'

And Meg was right: it took more than sore hands to put her off Larch Cottage. It also took more than a miscarriage she had two months later – brought on, the doctor said, by trying to lay a path of stone slabs up to the shed where the mower was kept. Gelder just hadn't wanted to know.

Following her disappointment, depression – something she had never been subject to – set in as winter approached. She forced herself to execute her various commissions, but she couldn't find the energy to follow up the other things that needed to be done – like whitewashing the inside of the laundry room, cementing in the odd stone that had fallen out of the wall separating their garden and the field on the right, and hacking down the briar that smothered the wall at the far end beyond the mower shed.

Gelder did just certain things. Other things he forgot to do, or just waited until he thought *she* had forgotten them. She contained her occasional fury: after all, he was an old man and he must at times have felt tired.

But there was something Meg had always wanted – a warm, delicious memory out of her childhood – an apple tree trained against a wall. Ideally, it ought to go at the end of the garden where the thicket of briar now was. Why anybody had let it get to such impenetrable proportions was astonishing.

She explained it all patiently to Gelder. 'It would be an ideal place, Harry. If you start today, I can buy a tree and get it in before there's any danger of frost.'

The old man took his pipe out of his mouth as if to answer. Meg nodded encouragingly. But all he did was to push the stem of the pipe in and out between his glazed lips, all the while regarding her with a vacant, faintly worried stare.

What was his difficulty? Meg wondered, becoming more and more determined that in her garden things were going to be done her way.

'Come on, Harry,' she coaxed. 'I'll show you what to do.'

That approach usually worked the oracle, and he'd stand watching her for a minute or two and then take over, nodding his head and then shaking it, and sighing. Occasionally he'd tut-tut, but he managed to make it sound very much like a gurgle from his pipe.

But this time, when she'd reached the end of the stone path and grabbed a branch of bramble, she looked back to see that the stubborn old man was still standing where she'd left him.

'Oh, come on, Harry!' she called. 'It won't hurt your hands if you're careful and wear the gloves I gave you.'

He remained where he was, pushing his pipe in and out of his mouth like some sort of non-return valve. Several times he looked back at the kitchen window as though he expected Mrs Bittoms to come out and help him.

'All right,' fumed Meg. 'If I have to do it myself, I will!'

She snicked and dragged out the loops of thorny, vicious vegetation for several minutes, aware that Gelder was still standing, undecided.

'If you don't want to co-operate,' Meg said, turning, 'at least clear away the bits and burn them.'

Slowly he put his pipe into his pocket and, eyes rolling, joined her. 'I'll do it, Mizz,' he wheezed. 'Leave it be, an' I'll do it.'

'Oh ... Well, thanks very much.' Meg allowed her sarcasm to show. 'Don't bother with any of the other jobs until you've dealt with this.'

Gelder didn't turn up for work next morning. Mrs Bittoms said that he'd caught a chill and would have to stay in bed. He returned to Larch Cottage five days later, wrapped up to the gills in scarves and smelling of wintergreen. He'd just set foot on Meg's stone path, laden with pipe, billhook and secateurs, when the heavens opened up. It wasn't an ordinary downpour; it went on all day.

Meg had the feeling that the old man had known exactly when the rain would start and had timed his return to work to coincide with it. It kept raining.

Irritably, she told Gelder that if he wanted something to do that would keep him under cover, he could start clearing out the laundry room and whitewashing it. Surprisingly, he agreed, but he was very slow, and he kept interrupting her to ask if he should throw away this thing and what should he do with that thing. A simple job that should only have taken, at most, a day, became a major operation.

The rain went on for three days, and at the end of it Gelder had whitewashed one wall. On the fourth day, a Saturday, it ceased and, gum-booted and thick-gloved, Meg marched forth to set about the still-existing briar. Without the disapproving stare of Harry Gelder she went ahead with furious abandon.

The wall itself was about ten feet high, and Meg chose to continue along from right to left. She was handicapped in that she had to drag away and stack in a corner the branches, which were still wet and unburnable; therefore it was not until her second stint on Sunday morning that she broke through to find to her mild astonishment that there was a paved area in front of the wall. Perhaps someone had had a greenhouse there at one time.

As the thicket thinned, something blue caught her eye. Spurred on, she hacked and dragged until she was able to get through to the clear, paved space, which she found to be well-worn stones forming a half-circle under the blue thing that had caught her eye.

It was a niche set into the old, lichen-encrusted wall, about two feet by one foot, with a blue frame and some odd, indistinct bas-relief images in it. The images were milky and opaque: a group of people standing before a table – at least, that is what she thought it was. It looked very old.

She dashed in to find John, who had started to re-wire the house that weekend.

'Is it all that important?' Covered with dust and cobwebs, he looked through the ceiling trapdoor. 'I can't come down right now.'

'I don't know. It's a sort of ... Heavens, I don't know – a shrine or ikon, or something. Religious, I think. Must be terribly old. Never mind. Have a look at it later.'

By mid-afternoon Meg had cleared the paving stones in front of her 'shrine'.

'Gosh! It's quite exciting,' she told John over a cup of tea. 'I don't know anything about semi-precious stones, but it looks as if it might be worth something. The blue colour is so vivid ...'

'Stuck in an old wall and covered by briar?' John scoffed. Meg was inclined to get carried away by the oddest notions. He imagined that it might be her artistic temperament. For instance, all her ups and downs with Gelder who, admittedly, was a bone-headed old cuss. But, then, a lot of that could have been the result of losing the baby. Funnily, he hadn't thought he'd care much if they had a child, but now he wanted one even more than Meg did. It would add something to their lives. He hoped she wouldn't do something silly and lose the one she was carrying.

He followed her out to examine the thing, more to humour her than anything else. He was silent for several seconds as he peered closely at the blue frame and the raised figures in the niche.

'I don't know, I'm sure ...' He scraped lightly at it with his screwdriver and peered again. 'Might be lapis lazuli – the blue is so deep. As for the figures, I don't know.' He licked a finger and wiped it on the milky part. Then he peered, thunderstruck.

'I say, look at that! Opal – or chalcedony. The wet has brought the colours up!' He turned to his wife excitedly, then back again to the wall. 'Darling, this must be worth a bomb! It must be centuries old, and priceless! Let's get somebody down from London who might know about this sort of thing!'

By the time they went to bed, after a celebration drink, they'd decided very broadly what they were going to do with the fortune they were sure they'd get for the shrine, or ikon. First, they would build on a nursery; then they'd put in a decent central heating system – on top, of course, of having some really efficient help around the cottage and garden, and getting a second car so that they wouldn't be forever having spats about whose need was the greater. This money was going to be the answer to all their difficulties.

Just before they finally went to sleep John sat up. 'I say, Meg. Will it be safe enough out there? I mean, suppose people get to know ...'

'Don't worry, dear,' Meg said comfortingly. 'I piled the briar back in front of the thing. If it has remained safe this long, it's hardly likely to be stolen now. It's pretty deeply embedded in that wall, and in any case nobody knows about it but us.'

And that is where Meg was disastrously wrong. Had they treated their find as an amusing curiosity and planted a tree in front of it, as she'd wanted to do originally, or allowed the thicket of briar to grow again, nothing more might have happened. They'd probably have sold Larch Cottage in a few years' time, made a whacking profit on it, bought a place by the sea – which Meg was already beginning to dream about – and lived happily ever after.

These things didn't come to pass because Meg and John were deprived of their right to shape their own future. Even had they been told what would happen, it wouldn't have stopped their plans to sell the shrine. Had the doubt entered their minds, they would have rationalized it by saying that it was too old to have any trace of archaic and menacing connotation still lurking about it.

Mrs Bittoms and Gelder stood silently before the shrine for several minutes. Then they walked back to the kitchen, where the old woman put on the kettle. Gelder never came into the house when Meg was there, but she had taken John to the station and had then gone on to the shops.

'She's two months gone,' said Mrs Bittoms.

'Oh, yes? Did she tell you, Martha?'

The woman scoffed. 'I don't need to be told things like that.'

'You're a witch, Martha.'

Mrs Bittoms shuddered. 'I'd rather you didn't call me that, Harry – not even in a joke. You and me, we ain't getting any younger, an' we've no kin to carry on. An' I been thinking – what if the masters think we ain't done our job proper, letting her find the thing?'

Harry Gelder paled, and he poked the stem of his pipe in and out of his mouth agitatedly. 'Oh, don't say such things, Martha. We always done our best – always! 'Tweren't our fault these two came. An', er – well, when she gets an idee into 'er 'ead, ain't much I can do 'bout it.'

Meg spent much more than she ought to have done, but it would have been a remarkable woman who, with a lot of money coming her way, wouldn't have anticipated it somewhat. It had been silly to buy dresses that in a few months' time wouldn't fit her – might never fit her if she didn't get her figure back after the baby came – and which, in any case, would be out of fashion by then.

She'd just felt she had to let off steam, and it had been a long time since she'd been able to think about anything except how existing resources were going to stretch to cover essentials.

Meg met John off the train, and in spite of the cold evening, wore the new white dress with the plunging front. John hardly noticed it. He was too full of the chappie from the museum who was coming down to see the shrine.

'He couldn't credit that I was telling the truth. Said he'd heard of only one other of the same type, and that had been found in Hungary and was damaged anyway. He said it would be priceless, if it's genuine.'

'Did he say what it is supposed to be?' asked Meg, yawning. Her pre-lunch sherry was making her feel tired, and somewhat deflated.

'Oh, a shrine or ikon of some obscure sect. He mentioned ... what was it now? ... Sanguivites, or something like that.'

Before he sat down to eat, John had to go and check that their treasure was still there. He had to try to figure out how to get it out of the wall without damaging it. Perhaps it would be better to leave that to the museum chappie. John was certain that he wouldn't know a night's peace until it was in a safe place – or they'd got the money for it and its safety had become the concern of others.

Meantime Meg had taken off the white dress – which couldn't have been very stunning, since it had made no impression whatsoever on John – and had donned a risqué black chiffon which was practically see-through.

'Wow!' he goggled as he sat down to eat. 'That dress makes me forget I'm starving!'

Meg laughed, pleased, and opened a bottle of wine. 'Let's eat first. I can't understand why nobody who lived here before ever found the shrine.'

'Well, it was a retired couple, darling – nobody who wanted to be clever, like you, and plant an apple tree!'

Meg had just cleared away when a tall young man in a dinner suit came up the front path. Meg was nearest to the door and opened it.

'Oh!' The young man was incredibly handsome. His long-lashed, dark blue eyes looked at her face and body with open delight and admiration. The impact of his gaze took her breath away.

'It's the kind of mistake I wish I could make all the time,' he said at last, expelling a long, soundless whistle. 'I'm congratulating myself that I have come to the wrong door.'

'Do come in ...' Meg stepped back, feeling her wits draining out of the tips of her fingers. She could only gesture weakly towards the lounge, praying that he wouldn't decide to go away.

'John, this gentleman seems to have got lost ...'

Meg could have spent the rest of her life just looking at Martin Sardin. He was not only physically perfect, he had a voice the like of which she had never heard before, and his manners were impeccable.

Something she'd always wondered about came back to her: does a girl marry the man she loves, or just grows to love the man she knows she can have. She knew then that she'd never really loved John – not the way she could love this man. And yet she also knew that one woman could never hope to possess him.

He was describing, with frequent flashing glances in Meg's direction, how he'd been invited to some party and had lost the address, when a young man and woman walked up the path. John rose quickly. Seen even from that distance, the girl was a stunner.

'Why, Martin!' The blonde had on the simplest, most understated little dress of pale blue linen. Meg felt frippery and contrived. 'If we hadn't seen your car up the road, we'd have become completely lost!'

Her eyes flicked at John sultrily, and he didn't feel quite so miffed about the attention Meg was getting from the big chap.

'I discovered these delightful people all by myself,' said Martin. 'I'm not sure I want to share them with you.'

'Would you like a drink?' asked Meg, who felt she had to do something to break the excruciating and thrilling spell of Martin's eyes.

'Oh, how lovely! Yes, please.'

'Very civilized . . .'

'What a lovely place you have here.'

Several more people arrived, all outstandingly good-looking, superbly dressed and culturally polished. One or two had faint accents. They all gave the impression that they lived on a plane that ordinary mortals couldn't hope to achieve, or were so international that they could never ever not feel at home.

'I say,' said Martin, looking at Meg, 'I'm enjoying it here too much to want to go. May we stay?'

There was a chorus of coaxing pleas, and Meg and John felt quite overwhelmed. The thought, just a trace, that it might be some sort of game – that in some way he and Meg were being 'sent up' – was lost whenever John looked into the incredible violet eyes of the blonde girl.

She had the endearing trick when she talked of inclining her head and shoulders towards him, as though she wished to snuggle into his arms. No doubt in bed she'd be a raver.

'Somebody ring up Mike and tell him to come over,' said Martin. 'You don't mind, do you, Meg?'

'Not at all. The more the merrier,' said Meg, and immediately regretted the common phrase. Her glance took in her husband's close proximity to the blonde. 'It gets dull around here at times. We never have any good parties. Come on, Martin,' she said daringly. 'Help me fix some snacks.'

Meg ought to have fought him off, but she didn't want to. She returned his kisses and permitted his importunities, and she couldn't have cared less if someone had come in and caught them. It didn't matter that he might think that she was only another willing female. She knew she was, and it didn't matter.

When he murmured that nobody would miss them if they went outside for half an hour, her only objection was that it might be chilly.

'I assure you, lovely girl, you won't feel cold,' he said, opening the door.

Meg would have gone to the ends of the earth, or plunged her hands into boiling oil, if he'd asked her. When they stepped through the kitchen door into the October night it seemed that a pale moon bathed sweetly-scented flowers and that some night bird was filling the air with melody.

She turned her head briefly. Some people were watching them from the lounge window. She didn't feel ashamed – just awash with adoration for the tall man whose eyes glowed into hers.

John woke up at about one-thirty, his mouth parched and unpleasant, realizing that he was still half-dressed. He looked over the bed, raised himself on his elbow, and looked again. The head on the other pillow wasn't brunette like Meg's. It wasn't blonde, either, which was what his vague recollection had hinted it ought to be.

It was grey! In the light of the moon he saw, with horror, that the head was bald, the nose long, thin and hooked, and the mouth smooth and beak-like.

He'd spent a frantic hour of sex with *that*? Oh, God, no...!

Retching, he humped himself out of bed. What ghastly lunacy was this? Where was Meg? Whose idea of a joke was it? Had they been looking for some fun and decided that he and Meg would make good victims? Idle spawn of the devil! He knew – he'd sensed – that they'd been up to no good.

He stood shuddering over the bathroom basin as the nausea abated. Uppermost in his mind came the need to get that thing out of their bed before Meg saw it. What had happened to her?

He washed his face and hands and staggered back to the bedroom, vowing that never again would he get so drunk that he didn't know what he was doing. Yet, he hadn't drunk all that much ...

The thing wasn't there. It had been there, for there were the inden-tations of a head and body ...

He started downstairs towards the lounge.

'Meg! Meg, where are you?'

At the sound of his words the air was ripped apart with a shriek of insupportable terror. Had it been Meg? Then there was a hoarse moan, which tailed off into a sigh.

'Meg!' Bursting into the lounge he snapped on the light.

They were waiting for him: things that had lost their aura of exclusive-

ness, their air of youth and beauty and breeding. They weren't pretending any more to be what they weren't.

Only centuries could have shaped them as they were: ageless, powerful,
rotten. They had no body hair; their skin was grey; their ears, like
gargoyles' ears, came to a point; their eyes were slits and had no pupils.
They were of a uniform height, thin and small, with arms and legs like
sinewy sticks. The mouths were little expressionless beaks.

Without haste they surrounded him, prodding him into the garden.
Repelled, he shrank from the touch of their claws. The eyes glowed now,
eager, in the dark. They rustled dryly as they moved, their devils' tails
up-curled, ropelike.

There seemed to be dozens of them, all crouched in front of the niche
in the wall. Gibbering excitedly, they forced John to his knees.

The blue frame was blazing out from the wall, which seemed to have
disappeared altogether. The milky-white figures shimmered, intensify-
ing, into colour. The images grew in size. There was an odd dripping
sound, and the steady throb of a weird chant.

John tried to get up, but his arms were held in vicelike talons. The
high priest, shrouded in black, his back turned, dedicated the upheld
dagger to a statue of a ram, or goat.

Something was wetting the knees of John's trousers. He looked down.
Revolted, he saw that he was kneeling in blood! It came from overflowing
bowls beneath the altar.

The high priest spread his arms, and with a collective grunt of pleasure
the Sanguivites hurried forward to dip their beaks in the bowls. Stomach
heaving, John saw that as they drank they became pink!

Slowly the priest turned and held the dagger upraised. John gasped.
It was the man who'd first arrived at the cottage. Then John became
aware that the passive, eager-eyed nude figure on the stone table was
Meg!

'Meg!' shouted John brokenly, but she didn't seem to hear him. 'Meg!'

'Listen well,' said the priest. 'I am Sardonyx. You must choose. Die
here with your woman, or agree to our terms and go free.'

Mesmerized, Meg looked up at the slowly descending knife, making
no attempt to avoid it.

'How?' whispered John.

'This shrine must be guarded. You must guard it. Agree to this and
you and this woman may go. Fail in your duty and you will die here as
these two others have done.'

The crowding acolytes split their ranks to let him see the two bodies
lying beside the altar.

'I promise,' John said, forcing the words out of his dry throat.

There was a sigh of general satisfaction. Like the invasion of sanity, the pale dawn bleached out the garish scene of carnage, the shrine slowly resumed its normal size and the images became fixed and milky. Meg rose, bewildered, from the cold ground and John darted towards her.

'Note well,' said the voice of Sardonyx. 'This is, for us, a sacred place. Do not let anything happen to it. Teach your child to do likewise. Fail and retribution will be swift.'

There was silence, but for Meg's sobs. John looked around. He was filled with the sensation that it had never happened.

They staggered back to the cottage and went inside. The empty glasses and the crushed cushions proved that they had indeed had visitors, whoever they had been.

John made a cup of tea to soothe Meg's shattered nerves. To go to bed, to sleep, was unthinkable. The cold grey day was merely a lengthening of the depressing dawn.

Haggard-eyed, Meg stirred at eight-thirty. 'Mrs Bittoms will be here soon.'

'Mrs Bittoms will never come again,' said John.

Meg focused her tired eyes. 'Oh, come on! It was only something we dreamed.'

'It was not a dream.'

'But we can't stay here *all* our lives,' she complained. 'It's not to be borne, is it? Imagine what it will mean. What about all our plans?'

'Do you want to put it to the test?' John asked, hollowly.

'No, but they can't mean for us to stay here all the time . . .'

'One of us must be here all the time . . .'

Later that week the two curiously bloodless bodies were found not far from Larch Cottage. That convinced Meg finally that it hadn't all been a wicked joke.

The months passed and the child was born. Meg decided that when her time came she was going to die in her own bed, and that her daughter was to be the one who would ensure that that came about. Above all, the child had to learn a deep sense of duty to her parents. Why, when she got older, perhaps she could be left to look after things . . .

As the months passed, John became grimmer and more taciturn – a man whose sole relaxation was drinking too much in the evening. Sometimes, before bed, he'd go out and stand swaying blearily before the thing he hated most in life, shouting a defiance that never reached his lips.

One night, he knew, when he was past caring, he'd take an axe and hack it to pieces.

# Hybrid

## *L. A. Lewis*

I have known Billy Cole, or, to give him his proper title, Dr X. W. Cole, MD, MRCS, since we were at school together. The 'X' stands for Xavier, a tradition in his family, but, of course, no one could be bothered with a mouthful like that.

He is, both in character and appearance, what one generally refers to as a 'hard case'. All doctors have to be, owing to their familiarity with pain and disease and the tragedy of their causes; but Billy is an exception even among his fraternity because most of his professional career has been spent in the capacity of a Ship's Surgeon in the Mercantile Marine.

Slight acquaintances get the impression that he is so calloused to human suffering and human vice as to be completely lacking in sympathy or sentiment, and indeed, his uncompromising, severely practical exterior supports the belief. In reality he is about the squarest and whitest soul I know, and it is only his first-hand experience of life's seamy side among most of the world's races that has developed his iron self-control. I think he could hear or witness any conceivable horror literally without turning a hair.

On the occasion of his last shore leave prior to sailing for the Orient he followed his usual custom of spending a few days at my bachelor apartments in Town, and as his arrival had been too late for me to organize a satisfactory 'night out', we were passing a quiet evening in my library over nuts and wine.

Since it will probably become self-evident later in the story, I may as well confess now to a strongly developed vein of morbid curiosity. Though I am pretty brawny in physique, I find something so uncanny in the actual spectacle of even a comparatively harmless lunatic as to give me feelings of absolute terror. At the same time maniacs and their more disgusting reactions hold me in a strange fascination.

I had been listening avidly to Billy's description of some of his most repulsive 'cases' when he concluded his recital with one about a dipsomaniac who ended his days chasing gigantic, violet wasps with a broom, and this yarn reminded me of some theories on the hallucinations accompanying 'DT's' which I had once heard in the course of an address by an eminent theosophical lecturer.

'Billy,' I asked him, without much expectation of tolerance from his pragmatic mind, 'do you think there may be anything in the occultist's notion that such monstrosities really *exist*, and are sometimes rendered visible through the medium of alcohol, drugs, and so forth?'

Much to my surprise, he accepted the suggestion without a trace of mockery, and answered with considerable gravity.

'You mean what they call breaking down the "web" that is supposed to divide the physical from the "astral". Well, when I was a student, I should have laughed like hell at any such idea. But – *experientia docet*. If you like, I'll tell you about another case that appeared to confirm that hypothesis. At all events, it had some aspects that were beyond ordinary pathological reasoning.'

'Fire away,' I invited eagerly, the morbid streak well to the fore. Billy settled himself deeper in his chesterfield and helped himself to a handful of nuts which he began cracking methodically, if absently.

'As far as I remember,' he began, 'we never had a schoolfellow named Chalmers – so I will call my "case" by that name. You see, the man in question *was* one of our contemporaries at St Egbert's, and I've no doubt you'd remember him well enough, but it wouldn't be at all fair to him – or to his admirable wife – to give away their secret.

'Chalmers was, to all outward appearances, a perfectly normal, healthy boy, good at games to an average degree, passable in his form work, though not brilliant. I'm not a bit afraid of your recognizing him from my description because he *was* so very average. He possessed one *trait*, though, of which I don't suppose anyone suspected him.

'Beneath his shell of seemingly thoughtless exuberance lay a deep strain of mysticism, all caused, so far as I could make out, by his having recurrent experiences of a singularly evil nightmare dating back to his very earliest recollections.

'I think I was his only confidant, though why he should have picked on me as recipient of his confidences I can't think. Fate, I imagine, and anyway it certainly helped me tremendously in understanding his symptoms afterwards.

'Well, as Chalmers described it, he could not recall any time in his infancy when he was not haunted by an appalling fear – the worse because it was ill-defined – of some horrible entity constantly lurking near him. The usual childish dislike of darkness was, in his case, raised to the *nth* degree, so that he positively yelled with terror whenever he was left without light for a single instant. Up to the age of nearly nine he could not be induced to go to bed without a night-light, and a nurse or someone to share his room, but at about that period the new adventure of being sent to a day school and having a lot of fresh interests seems to have forced the thing into the back of his consciousness, where it remained for so long that he was finally able to forget it almost completely.

'He became quite a normal boy, swotted his subjects reasonably, played his cricket and football, and went to bed at night healthily tired, sleeping soundly without recourse to night-lights. When his mind did, very occasionally, turn to the presence that had haunted his cradle and cot, its nature had become so indistinct that, as he told me, he could not have described it even in the vaguest terms.

'Now, I'm sure you remember the phase we all went through at about fifteen when we fell easy prey to advertisers' announcements on the covers of penny 'shockers', and were always wasting our pocket-money on dud water-pistols, electric tie-pins, et cetera. Some of us were most attracted by cheap-jack palmists and astrologers, and used to send in perfectly good half-crown postal orders together with time and place of birth in exchange for 'an astounding character delineation and outline of your future'. Chalmers belonged to this school of thought and must have spent pounds on being told to "beware of a dark woman", and all the usual bilge. He got fed up with it at last because, as he naively explained, no two forecasts corresponded.

'Now, personally, I'm inclined to think that, have he left fortune-telling alone for good, he might have grown up into an absolutely fit, sane, and unimaginative human animal, and saved himself the hell of a nasty experience later. But, as Fate would have it, a most superior sort of fair came to the town for a few days, and one of the side-shows was a booth tenanted by a self-styled lady psychometrist.'

'I remember,' I interrupted. 'Madame Caramel or Caramella or something.'

'Um. Name like that,' Billy agreed. 'Anyway, somebody persuaded Chalmers to give her a trial, and he duly paid his dollar and was taken into a dark room where the lady seated herself beside him on a divan and proceeded to hold his hand. He'd always had his fortune told by post before, and this method was a new one on him, with the result that he thought first of all she wanted him to make love to her. Being then about sixteen and unversed in the ways of the world, he was trying to decide how he ought to begin when the lady suddenly began talking at a rapid rate and squeezing his hand with a great access of muscular strength. Looking at her sharply, he saw that her eyes were shut and that her complexion had gone quite white, while beads of sweat stood out on the forehead. So greatly was he fascinated by his first experience of somebody in an apparently genuine trance that he missed quite a lot of her opening statements, but his ears were sharpened when she began telling him that his was a destiny of abysmal horror, and that his feet would walk forever in the glades of hell overshadowed by a sin-bred monster of his own begetting. He told me about the whole thing quite unexpectedly when we were out on a bird's-nesting ramble on a half-holiday, and, though he could not repeat the episode *verbatim*, the gist of it was that he had been addicted to the cult of Black Magic in a former life, and had begotten – or caused to be begotten – some dreadful hybrid, part human, part fowl, which looked to him for the continuity of its earthly existence, life by life, as he himself was reincarnate. That his "ego" had long since dropped the cult and was now concerned only with the processes of *natural* law did not free him from the responsibility for his "creature", and only by resuming his former malpractices at the cost of his own soul could he give this being its just chance of evolving through successive stages of bestiality until a wholly human vehicle could be attained.

'Well, that sort of thing at the time seemed to me the last word in tripe, apart from its degenerate aspect, and I told Chalmers so pretty bluntly. He retorted that he would certainly have thought the same, but for the fact that the psychometrist's affirmation had caused the resumption of his childish nightmares, and with greatly enhanced vividness.

'He was in a highly excitable state, and absolutely shouted down my arguments when he came to describe the thing that overshadowed him. He swore that it was the same apparition that had lurked long ago in his nursery, and described it as mainly human in shape, standing erect on legs, but entirely covered by silver-grey feathers except for the neck, which was naked and scrawny like that of a vulture. It loped rather than walked, and constantly tilted its feathered face to this or that side like a fowl when it is listening. Its eyes were jet-black and beady and filled with a febrile glee whenever they met his own. In spite of my youthful scepticism I found myself powerfully impressed by Chalmers' recital, and realized that his hallucination must, to him at any rate, be terribly existent. He became most convincing when he alluded to the creature's habit of hopping – or *fluttering* – onto his bed, and perching, with crossed legs, upon his chest. Several times, he maintained, he had dropped off to sleep through sheer weariness, awakening to find the monstrosity crouching above him, its restless, glinting orbs flickering rapidly from his head to his feet with an expression of conquering delight, as though it had, after long search, found its appointed resting-place. He went back to night-lights after that – not the old-fashioned wax wicks, but thirty-watt electric bulbs. The electric light switch in his bedroom remained depressed during the whole of his sleeping hours, and he craved for human companionship in those nocturnal stretches, though convention precluded the presence of a female nurse.

'You must understand that Chalmers was then going through a sort of private hell, and would have hated to take his people into his confidence for fear of ridicule. He could not, therefore, ask his brother to share his room, and must needs fight his own damnable destiny with his own resources.

'About twenty boys left St E's at the end of that term – so you can amuse yourself guessing at Chalmers' identity. He was numbered among the twenty, and I didn't set eyes on him again for about two years, when I happened to bump across him in Oxford. No. He wasn't an "undergrad". His parents were both dead, and had left him enough money to treat Life as a kind of prolonged "Cook's Tour". That advantage didn't seem to have helped much. He had evidently undergone a tremendous change. In that brief period all his boyhood and good-nature had dropped away from him, and left a miserable, human hulk, unable – or unwilling – to discuss any ordinary human pleasantries, such as theatres, and concerned only with an abysmal introspectivness.

'It was close to Carfax I met him, and, after listening to his sorrows as long as I thought judicious, I took him into the first licensed restaurant I could think of – it happened to be the "George" – and bought him a feed, complete with alcoholic extras. That didn't seem to do him much good, and, having ascertained that he was temporarily residing at the "Crown and Thistle" at Abingdon, I ran him home in my car. That was the last I saw of Chalmers for about twelve years, and by the time I next heard of him both the man and his delusion had pretty well faded from my memory.

'It was during one of my visits to the old people at their house near Worcester that our paths crossed again, and it happened in this way. The governor, as you know, still keeps his practice going, and we were discussing one of his invalids at a rather late hour one evening in his study.

'The housemaid presently announced a lady visitor whom she had shown into the consulting-room, and the Pater, who is very easy-going about surgery hours, went straight in to see her. He came back almost at once, however, and told me I was the doctor she wished to see.

'This surprised me a bit as, apart from giving the old man occasional advice with some difficult case, I had never been concerned in his practice and was, in fact, very rarely at liberty to go and stay with him.

'The girl who confronted me was tall and well formed, her untouched complexion testifying to a country upbringing. She introduced herself, without preamble, as Mrs Cyril Chalmers, and said how thankful she was that I happened to be on shore leave. She looked intelligent and level-headed, though her face showed lines of worry, and I noticed – it is a doctor's job to notice such things – that she was about to become a mother. Chalmers and his obsession came back to me as soon as she mentioned the name, but I quite naturally supposed that it was about her pregnancy she wished to consult me. This supposition was strengthened when she asked how soon my leave expired, and I told her I still had three weeks to go.

'"In that case," she went on, "perhaps you wouldn't mind attending to my confinement, but it's really about Cy that I've come to see you. He tells me you know all about the thing which he believes overshadows him."

'I nodded, and she gave me a look of relief. "That helps," she continued, "because, when I tell you that the thing has mastered him and turned him into a raving lunatic, you'll understand how to approach his case. He's been completely uncontrolled for months now, and the only reason I've been able to keep him at home is because he hasn't actually attacked anyone – at least not murderously. I've had to get rid of all female servants, you understand, and our staff now consists of two ex-service men, one acting as male nurse and the other as cook-general. Of course, I could quite easily get him certified and put in a mental home, only it's sometimes difficult to get a patient out again even when they are cured. Often I fear he is incurable, but you will be a better judge of that, and if there is any treatment available for such a case I'd like it done at home. Cy takes the same view, but doesn't want to be attended by anyone but yourself. He has great faith in you."

'"Oh," I interrupted, "he has lucid intervals, then?" But she shook her head vigorously. "No," came her flat denial. "He is *constantly* 'possessed'. He keeps hopping and sidling about like some horrible crow, and even in his sleep he looks only half human."

'"Then how was he able to direct you to me?" I naturally enquired, and received the astonishing reply, *"His body is mad, but his mind is sane."*

'"What the devil do you mean?" I asked sharply, for this crazy statement sounded suspiciously like a leg-pull.

'She answered in a perfectly calm voice, and I began to admire her level-headedness, though I was badly puzzled.

'"You'll understand when you see him, doctor. The fact is, he doesn't realize what has happened. All the time he is strutting and flapping about the place he can talk and answer questions in his own perfectly normal voice, but he doesn't seem to know that *his* vocal chords are uttering the words. He speaks as though he were in some other part of the room watching the antics of his own body. It is quite evident after a few moments' conversation that he has some extraordinary sense of standing outside himself and looking on. He thinks his body is the creation that haunts him!"

'I kept silent a few minutes while I tried to take this in. It was a new kind of delusion in my experience.

'"Well," I suggested at length, "you'd better tell me how the whole business started." And it was in giving the account of this that her admirable poise *did*, for a short time, desert her. I found ample excuse, though, when I'd heard the facts. The ordeal that poor girl had gone through would have driven ninety per cent of women straight off their heads.

'Apparently she and Chalmers had met at a dance about two years before and fallen in love, more or less at first sight. As he had plenty of money there was no reason for a long engagement, though Chalmers was sensible enough to tell his fiancée about his secret fear and the words of the fortune-teller before the wedding. He assured her there was no hereditary insanity in his family, and that his delusion – if delusion it was – could hurt nobody but himself, adducing the fact that no other person had ever been able to see his spectre even though it presented itself to his own perceptions in crowded places. The girl was pleased at this display of his confidence, which made her all the more eager to marry him as she believed her companionship would be a help when he thought the apparition was nearby. The ceremony was therefore hastened on, and for several months it *did* seem that the acquisition of a wife had improved Chalmers' spirits. He began to go about much more than he had done for years, taking his wife on a constant round of theatres, dances, and bridge-parties. He even voluntarily alluded to his obsession, and she realized that his choice of such a gay life was prompted by his desire for distraction from it.

'The only inconvenience she suffered was having to get used to sleeping with a light on.

'Well, they kept up a protracted honeymoon for a considerable time, travelling a lot, and staying at all the most expensive hotels. The girl – a country parson's daughter – had never lived so lavishly before, and she enjoyed every bit of it.

'At last, however, she suggested that they ought to take a house somewhere and settle down for a bit, if only to return the hospitality they had been receiving from Chalmers' wealthy acquaintances, and the place they picked was an old Victorian mansion in a Sussex village not too far from Town.

'The furnishers and decorators had it ready for them in a few weeks, and they celebrated their entrance into County life by throwing a big house-party to which a number of Bright Young People were invited. Everything seems to have gone with a swing from start to finish, the Bright Young People inventing their own amusements from day to day and thus saving host and hostess a lot of organizing.

'Mrs Chalmers, however, noticed from the outset that her husband's recent gaiety was on the decline. He entered into various round games and skylarks when he was literally cornered by his guests, but, as often as opportunity offered, he would slip out unobserved and wander off into the country for hours on end, frequently not returning till the small hours of the morning. He began to suffer badly from insomnia, but turned down all suggestions that he should try sleeping draughts. Mrs Chalmers was constantly waking up in the night to find him sitting in a chair reading, and her woman's instinct finally brought her to the realization that he was *frightened to sleep*.

'One morning when he came home after three and found her lying awake she took him to task about it. He was more fidgety and *distrait* than ever, and his eyes had a wild expression like those of something hunted.

'"Really, my dearest," she began, "You were sweet to tell me all about your trouble when we were engaged. What have I done to lose your confidence now? I could see for myself that, whatever your delusion, you weren't mad, and that was why I never hesitated to marry you. But, if you don't get a doctor to give you a sleeping mixture you'll *go* mad. What is there about this place that's upsetting you? You were all right until we came here."

'Chalmers, it seems, suddenly broke down, burst into tears, and went off into a long disjointed account of having found the monster's home.

'"I felt certain I recognized this place when I first saw it," he concluded, "and I hadn't been in it many hours before I began to get flashes of having lived here before – not in this life, but centuries ago. I remembered vaguely on the second evening of our residence some *outré* event having taken place in these very grounds, though the house wasn't there then. I think it happened in some kind of marquee bearing heraldic signs. There was much consternation among a group of priests, and something was put to death and buried in a field about a mile away. I recall being forced to march in the procession to the burial ground, and after that – it's all hopelessly confused – but I – *I think I was burnt at the stake*."

'He shivered and threw himself face down across the bed while his anxious wife soothingly stroked his hair.

'"I found the field that same night," he continued brokenly, "and the thing rose up out of the ground to meet me. Its got a hypnotic hold on me and forces me to go night after night to commune with it. As soon as it appears I fall into a kind of stupor and can see nothing clearly, though I have a dreadful remembrance after of having stood for hours on end in a rustling, *feathery* embrace. I don't know what the thing does to me, but I am falling more and more into its spell, and I have no volition to resist."

'He sobbed again convulsively, and then muttered in scarcely audible tones: "In a way I'm even beginning to *like* it! At first I felt that it was angry with me for not giving it a beastly, *hybrid* vehicle for the accomplishment of its desires. Now it seems content with our loathsome communions."

'You can well picture poor Mrs Chalmers' state of mind when she heard this confession. As she saw it, her husband was now definitely suffering from a serious dementia, but she realized how impossible it would be to get his consent to medical advice, and how futile it was to argue with him.

'She uttered no word of criticism, but quietly and firmly made up her mind to follow him to his next assignation and see for herself what he did. Their house-party was now almost broken up, and she had no great difficulty in slipping out of a side-door that evening, dressed in a dark, inconspicuous costume, and following Chalmers along a thickly hedged lane to a five-barred gate over which he proceeded to climb. He had marched all the way like a sleep-walker without once turning his head, and she now contrived to follow him into the field, where she concealed herself in the moon-shadow of a broad and leafy elm. She saw Chalmers march mechanically on and halt in the middle of the meadow, where he stood with outstretched arms as though awaiting the embrace of some invisible being. For some ten minutes he remained thus unmoving. Then all at once he seemed to divine her presence, though how he could have seen her in the shadows at such a distance, and with his back towards her, she could not fathom. She only knew that he had turned about and was dashing with unbelievable speed straight for her hiding-place. She stood rooted there, utterly paralysed with terror, for, instead of the square-shouldered, nimble sprint she had so often admired on the tennis courts, he was coming in a series of fluttering, sidelong hops instinct with the vigorous intensity of a ravening culture. Within what seemed a second of time he was upon her and, seizing her in a grip of abnormal strength, had thrown her to the ground. So, with one sinewy hand on her throat, he held her pinned, while the other, fingers crooked like talons, ripped and tore at her clothing. Her whirling senses shrieked to her that this was not her husband suddenly demented, but an entirely alien presence into which he had been transformed. Her struggles and attempts to cry out were rendered futile in that merciless grip, and she could only lie supine with eyes fast shut to keep out the terror of the metamorphosed face, while in her nostrils clung a farmyard reek, and weird croakings and twitterings assailed her ears. Then her senses left her completely.

'When she came to she was still lying in a bed of long, dewy grass in the shadow of the elm, her clothes torn to shreds and her body bruised from head to foot. Of Chalmers there was no sign. Fortunately a long silk opera cloak she had been wearing had fallen from her at the first onslaught and escaped damage. She was able to conceal the remnants of her costume beneath it, and to reach the house without exciting comment.

'Now, I think she proved herself a very courageous gentlewoman when she made her way to their bedroom by the back-stairs without seeking the aid of guests or servants. On trying the door she found it locked, but, at the rattle of the handle, her husband's voice – now absolutely normal – came from within.

' "You can't come in, dear,' he said earnestly, "the Thing has come back with me, and it won't leave."

' "Nonsense," she replied with firmness, "I *must* come. Don't you know you've hardly left a rag of clothes on me?"

' "I've *what*," he shouted incredulously, "what d'you mean? I haven't even seen you since tea!" The apparent sanity of his tone helped her courage. Chalmers must have been quite unconscious of his actions in the field.

' "I must come in," she repeated, "never mind what you've got in there with you. I must help you fight it."

'She heard the lock click and a scamper of footsteps crossing the floor. She pushed the door open, slammed it behind her, and stood leaning back against it, her frightened gaze resting on the astounding spectacle before her.

'Attired in purple pyjamas, and holding in his mouth a wriggling garden worm, Chalmers was hanging by both hands and one bare foot from the bedrail in the attitude of a parrot that clings inverted to the top of its cage.

' "You see," he remarked courteously, the worm dropping to the floor as his lips opened, "the beastly thing's got in here now and pinched a suit of my pyjamas."

'He dropped to the floor, twisting in agile fashion to alight upon his feet, and hopped upon the window-sill, where he perched with his head askew, and went on conversationally, "Now that you've seen it with your own eyes I need evade the subject no longer. Here it is – even contriving to look something like me – and here it undoubtedly means to stay unless we can think of some way to get rid of it. Two heads better than one, eh, dear?"

'He stopped for a moment, scratched the back of his ear with one big toe, and continued: "I wouldn't mind so much if the brute would keep still sometimes, but it won't. It seems imbued with an eternal energy, and keeps hopping about as you can see." As he spoke he sprang from the sill to the top of a big walnut wardrobe and perched there.

'Mrs Chalmers' face became more composed as an idea presented itself. "It's movements are so quick," she remarked, "that they distract my attention from you. Would you mind telling me where you were standing, for instance, when it made the last move?"

'Chalmers' voice sounded sulky and irritable as he answered her.

'"You little idiot! I wasn't standing. I've been sitting here on the bed ever since you came in." But the voice came from the grotesque figure on the wardrobe.

'Well, that is as much as I need tell you about the origin of Chalmers' dementia,' said Billy, mechanically shelling another nut. 'Chalmers refused to occupy the same bedroom with his wife because, as he explained, he could not get rid of his uncanny visitant, and it was not proper that she should robe and disrobe in its presence – an opinion for which the poor lady was devoutly thankful.

'We put her up for the night, and the next day I travelled with her to her Sussex home to interview the patient. He – or rather his body – was in a recalcitrant state when I was shown in. The nurse, a big brawny fellow, told me that it had been the devil's own job to prevent his escaping that morning when he heard that his wife was still away. Even primed with Mrs Chalmers' account of her husband's delusion, I will confess that it gave me an uncanny feeling to see the fellow strutting and pirouetting obscenely while his voice said in perfectly natural acccents: "Glad you could come, Cole, but take no notice of that idiot."

'"I wasn't trying to escape. It was the blasted hybrid, and, if they let it, there'll be hell popping. Not a woman in the village will be safe from what I can guess of its instincts." I noticed that Chalmers' face was heavily coated with cream and talcum powder so that he looked unpleasantly like a sex pervert.

'"Why do you –?" I began, and then hastily remembered his delusion. "Why does your hybrid put that stuff on its face?" He hopped several times from floor to bed and back again before replying.

'"It imitates me," he said, "in every little thing I do. I uses my safety razor – only it has to remove not hair, but *feathers*. I suppose it puts the cream and talcum on to hide the quills."

'I shivered a bit, and soon made a pretext to leave him.

'"Mrs Chalmers," I told his wife, as soon as we were out of earshot, "there is no need to get your husband certified, but I absolutely insist upon his leaving this house until your confinement is over. Now I've a friend – a Dr Gunter – who keeps a private nursing home not many miles from here. We shall have to drug Cyril and take him there in a closed car. Gunter will look after him until you're on your feet again, and then you can bring him back here – if you still wish to."

'To my relief, she fell in with the proposal, and that afternoon the plan was put into effect. For once Chalmers seemed to realize that he was in some way identified with his "hybrid", for he shouted at me to get to hell out of it for a treacherous hound, while I was adjusting the chloroform pad.

'I stayed on at the house to keep an eye on the wife until her time came, and then 'phoned Gunter, asking him to come over as assistant. You see, I had found out that Mrs Chalmers' pregnancy dated from the night of his metamorphosis, and had decided to administer an anaesthetic.

'It would be as well, I thought, if she *saw* nothing.

'Well, the event finally took place, and my watch told me the hour was two a.m. We removed the – er offspring to an adjoining room, where it lived only for a few hours. Confidentially, we made no very serious effort to save its life, and it was just as we had finally ascertained that the pulse had really stopped that a 'phone call came in from Gunter's Matron to say that Chalmers had suddenly recovered his sanity. One of his first acts had been to wipe the powder from his face with a handkerchief, and he had then called an attendant, to whom he expressed his satisfaction that the "hybrid" had all at once dissolved into thin air, leaving him with a greater sense of freedom and well-being than he had known for months.

'As it happened, Gunter was then washing his hands, and it was I who took the call. Something prompted me to inquire the hour at which Chalmers had been restored, and the Matron replied that, to the best of her knowledge, it was about two a.m.

'Now then, you can call me imaginative if you like, old man, but *I believe* that there *was* something from "the other side" attached to Chalmers, and that it *did* actually steal his body for a period of time. When the offspring was born its needed vehicle was to hand, and into it the non-human strain passed from Chalmers through the medium of his wife. Evidently it could not get back when the infant body died, and I think that, with Chalmers' debt of suffering paid in full, Providence may have mercifully allowed the hybrid *soul* to die too. I shall never forget the venom with which its new-born eyes looked at me while I withheld the nourishment it needed.'

Billy stopped and toook a sip of port, but my morbid streak was not yet satisfied.

'But what was the offspring *like*?' I demanded.

Billy shot me an amused glance. 'Thank God it was passably human in *shape*,' he responded, 'but we had to *pluck* it before the undertakers came.'

# The Black Druid

## *Frank Belknap Long*

Mr Stephen Benefield entered the library and hung his black chesterfield overcoat on the rack which the trustees had grudgingly provided for the accommodation of inclement and cold weather accessories. There were seven other overcoats on the rack. Mr Benefield paused to count them – he was a methodical and observing man – and passed to the reference desk. When the librarian approached him he nodded amiably.

'I wish to peruse, please, Lucian Brown's *The Cromlech Jeelos*. It is No. 3268 A. I looked it up yesterday in the catalogue.'

The librarian scowled and went in search of the book. When she returned with it Mr Benefield took it firmly between his lean, gloved hands and turned the pages until he found the passage he was seeking. 'Rutilius Namatianus affirmed that the Druids invested all contiguous objects with their peculiar evil, so that anyone who touched so much as the hem of their robes was in deadly danger of becoming a partaker of their fallen divinity.'

Closing the book Mr Benefield smiled and passed it back over the desk. 'That is the passage I was looking for,' he explained. 'I do not believe I shall need a copy of it. I thought it might be a very long passage, but it is so brief that I can remember enough of it to paraphrase it without the aid of a written copy. Thank you very much. I am Stephen Benefield, an archaeologist. I use such passages in my books.'

'They say his books are becoming frightfully obscure,' cogitated the librarian as she returned *The Cromlech Jeelos* to its prescribed niche. 'I don't wonder! How can a man who takes Lucian Brown seriously write comprehensively?'

Mr Benefield made his way solemnly back to the coat-rack and stared for a moment in chagrin at the empty hook whereon he had hung his chesterfield. 'I am sure that I hung my coat on that rack,' he ruminated. 'And where is it now?'

Feeling decidedly anxious, he began hastily to re-count the coats on the rack. There were still five garments remaining, and his anxiety did not diminish until he had completed his enumeration. Someone had deliberately – and illegitimately – lifted Mr Benefield's chesterfield from its original hook and hung it on the opposite side of the rack! He recognized it immediately by its grey silk lining and velvet collar. Taking it indignantly down he put it on and left the building.

All the way to the IRT, which was to convey Mr Benefield to his home in the Bronx, he kept muttering to himself. 'What right had anyone to tinker with my overcoat?'

Descending the subway stairs he deposited a worn nickel in the inevitable turnstile and boarded a train labelled 180th Street, Bronx Park.

The car was disagreeably crowded, but Mr Benefield darted towards and successfully captured a seat near the door which a gargantuan Italian had just previously vacated. Sinking into it with relief he crossed his legs and stared contemptuously at the passengers opposite him.

'Vulgar and stupid people,' he muttered to himself. 'What do they know of art and science and the splendour of antiquity?'

Mr Benefield was quite well informed in regard to antiquity. He had visited Egypt and explored all the ruins that are to be found in that maleficent and grievously exploited land; he was familiar with Tibet and its glamorous mountain monasteries; he had poked into forbidden volumes in the libraries of central China and climbed the Andes to stare at the colossal stone monuments left by the pre-Incas for the edification of mere superior Nordics. And incidentally, he had spent seven years at Yale and emerged with a PhD and a conviction that archaeology was a sacred science and that there were more things in it than are dreamed of in our vulgar philosophies.

But unfortunately Mr Benefield was now unhappily married and financially harassed and was no longer able to devote himself as exclusively as he might have wished to his favourite science. In fact, his personality had become distorted through suppression. He still took his archaeological researches seriously, which was commendable, but for several months now he had been interesting himself in less savoury pursuits, pursuits which intelligent men in the third decade of the twentieth century do not ordinarily approve of, and his academic colleagues had ceased to regard him with unqualified respect.

Indeed, several of Mr Benefield's recent utterances – the statement that he believed in vampires, for instance, and that Haitian voodooism was not a thing to be lightly sniffed at – had even alienated a considerable number of his *imaginative* friends. Mr Benefield had actually become, in his less lucid moments, a kind of eclectic theosophist. He did not care for the didactic and sugary mysticism of Madame Blavatsky and he despised the modern exponents of her cult, but he shared the mystical credulity of the poet Maeterlinck and the medieval, albeit not precisely the religious, bias, of such contemporary reactionaries as Chesterton and

Belloc. In brief, he believed that life is a mysterious business and that we know very little about it. Certain fragments of Aurignacian Venuses which he had diligently collected in the rock caverns of the Pyrenees had confirmed him in his hypothesis.

But now as he sat in the subway *en route* to the Bronx he was not thinking of Aurignacian Venuses. He was not even thinking of the Jeelos of the Dolmens that occupy so many fascinating pages in Lucian Brown's scholarly brochure. His mind was wholly taken up with the people opposite him. They were returning his stares with an avidness that somehow horrified him.

They were looking at him as though they were convulsed with curiosity; almost as though their eyes were being drawn from their heads in his direction by some power outside of themselves.

It is true that Mr Benefield was, in some respects, an odd-looking man. His hair was absurdly long and it descended upon his forehead in a circular, antiquated bang; his hat was two sizes too small for his immoderately large head – a brachycephalic head, although he boasted twenty generations of Saxon forebears – and his socks, which his wife had purchased for him, were of heavy wool, and, unsupported by garters, they bulged above his shoes like the elephantine folds on the torso of an Abyssinian eunuch.

But these idiosyncrasies were not, in themselves, sufficient to account for the horrified expressions on the faces of his fellow passengers. Mr Benefield wondered if by any chance he had neglected to shave before leaving home that morning. His beard was unusually prolific and one day's neglect was sufficient to render it a faintly conspicuous object. Not so conspicuous, indeed, as the fallen hose or antiquated bang, but Mr Benefield was supremely unconscious of his general ludicrousness. It was merely his beard that worried him, and to make certain that he had really shaved – his memory failed to record the act – he raised his right hand and passed it slowly over his chin.

His chin was wet and dripping! Mr Benefield snatched his hand away and stared at it in horror. Upon his palm lay a moist, black, inexplicable smudge. A gelatinous smudge.

He coughed uneasily. He had no recollection of having passed under a dirty drain, but under something of the sort he must, of necessity, have walked. 'From one of the tall buildings,' he muttered, under his breath. 'It rained yesterday and the wind has blown the filthy water out of the drain onto my face. I must be a ludicrous spectacle indeed. No wonder they are staring at me!'

His dignity would not permit him to remain in his seat after this distressing discovery. Rising hastily he passed to the rear of the car, and concealed himself in a corner of the vestibule.

There were only two other persons in the vestibule – a child of seven and its elderly nurse.

The child saw Mr Benefield first. It stared for a moment in abject terror; then it buried its frightened face in the folds of its guardian's coat. 'Black bogey man!' she screamed. 'I wanta get off!'

Instantly the nurse raised her face. For a second she gazed at Mr Benefield in sheer incredulity; then distress deepened to terror in her eyes, and with a scream she seized the child by the arm and retreated into the car.

Fortunately for Mr Benefield the car at that moment arrived at his station and he was able to elude the onrush of curious passengers that promptly ensued. Dashing wildly across the platform he ascended the stairs to the street and hurled himself into the adjacent darkness.

The darkness was soothing; it was Gilead to his impaired pride. He strode through it in silence, literally wrapped in it, his mind for a moment enjoying the quietude that precedes a storm. He hadn't dared to touch his face again.

He hadn't dared, but in a moment he would dare. The darkness was rapidly restoring his confidence and in a moment he would dare anything. He was conscious of a dim power stirring within him. But at the same time he experienced an overwhelming sense of discomfiture, of constriction. His clothes, he felt, were stifling him. It was absurd that he should be stifled by that hideous stiff thing that encircled his neck. What was it called? Ah, yes, a collar! He had almost forgotten the name of it, but remembering suddenly he ripped it off and threw it upon the pavement. Then he felt his face again. It was slimy, blubbery. His hand slid over it.

'Good God!' he gasped, and began to run. He must reach home as quickly as possible and wash from his face the unspeakable filth that had descended upon it!

He ran for fully five minutes, and arrived at the door of his lodging completely out of breath. As he fumbled hectically for his keys he experienced an overwhelming sense of horror, and of shame, which was paradoxically mingled with a wild and turbulent rebelliousness. It was as though he had suddenly, in some hideous and unnatural manner, broken the mould of humanity in which we have been cast. It was almost as though – he couldn't express it precisely – as though he had become a sharer of some esoteric and limitless divinity, and might experience every mundane emotion simultaneously; as though all the pleasures and all the agonies in a human life-span might be his in a single instant, and also pleasures and pains that have no counterparts in the world we know.

And then – Mr Benefield saw a face in the glass panel before him that defiled the exterior of the door. Instantly his whole being became flooded with an unearthly, paralysing fear, with a consuming and overpowering revulsion. The soft, fleshy feel of his face had vaguely suggested the abnormal, but this, this, *this* –! It wasn't, dear God, it wasn't even anything human that stared back at him.

*Not human. Not human.* It didn't even remotely resemble a human face. It was covered with thick dark hair and where its mouth should have been –

Mr Benefield recoiled before the awful horror of the thing. His brain had gone cold; he could not swallow. Slowly, dumbly, he raised his hands and gazed at them. It was as he had feared. The – the claws were very long. Quickly he unsheathed them in the heavy folds of flesh on his moist black palms. Almost – a stab of terror crossed his face as he made the acknowledgement in that moment of torture and doubt – almost he preferred the face. The face – had eyes. At least eyes. *His* eyes. But could he swear to that? Even now, as he stared hysterically into them they seemed to melt and merge with that awful face.

Familiar thoughts were forming in the brain that was no longer wholly his. He knew that the brain was no longer in its entirety his brain because with the phrases he recognized were mingled obscene and outlandish syllables derived from some hellish idiom that was sufficiently Gaelic in its sibilants to be perhaps very vaguely comprehensible to him. Or, if not actually comprehensible, at least damnably suggestive.

'*Ushtey Doinney! Kea! Doinney!* The overcoat! The overcoat! It isn't yours. *He* wore it. *Dei Ai. Sinthat.* Rutilius – Rutilius Namatiamus knew. *He knew.* They do not die. The coat! The coat! For God's dear sake, take it off! Don't you understand. *Doinney Ushty.* He, the *Druid* – a Vate – in the library. In America, yes, yes! They do not die.'

With a tremendous effort of will Mr Benefield seized the lapels of his overcoat and sought to take it off. But in the glass the *thing* did not approve. Its eyes shone with a malign lust and from the cavern in its dark face black saliva dripped.

'*Gush – ur!*'

Almost Mr Benefield succumbed to its obscene plea. Almost he craved to wallow in rapture unspeakable in the unclean sty where – but no, no, it was unthinkable. A voice roared within him.

'*It's damned Celtic superstition.* The Romans drove the little people into the hills; with steel and flame they slew their dark gods. They spat upon the Vates and the Bards. The Saxons and the Normans spat too! And you? Their blood is in you. Slay! Laugh! You are a scion of the invincible races! No Vate can withstand you. Slay their priests.'

There came to him then a sudden sense of power. It was as though all his forebears – Romans, Saxons, Normans, Danes – had suddenly come to life within him, and were urging him forward, shrieking into his ears:

'Fight, fight! For Caesar, for Arthur, for clean gods and brave, for valour and mercy and your very soul!'

With a shout so tremendous that it seemed scarcely even by derivation Benefieldian he tore off his outer garment and hurled it furiously from him. '*Eadem qua te insinuaveris retro via repetenda est!*' he cried. 'You – you cringing Celtic obscenity!'

He hurled the malediction directly at what he thought had become himself. But when he looked again, when he peered with angry, defiant eyes at the image in the glass he discovered that it had lost all of its loathsomeness. Whereupon his fury evaporated, as well it might, for the reflection of the original Mr Benefield was scarcely an anger-provoking object. And the original Mr Benefield it was that now stared back at him.

Mingled with the relief which he overwhelmingly experienced at this discovery was an unaccountable sensation of lassitude. He began, apparently, to exist in a kind of trance. Getting out his keys he opened the door and passed almost unconsciously through the vestibule and up two flights of stairs to his room. He wondered vaguely if his wife would reproach him for coming home so late. If she knew – but no, he would not tell her. The experience was already receding in his mind. Even now he doubted it and in time it would perhaps be forgotten even by himself. And he was so very tired – the fragmentary vestige of his reason that remained on its throne warned him that it would never do to argue with his wife or attempt to explain anything to her. Only sleep could restore his shattered psyche; and he must contrive somehow to get into his bed unobserved. It was a curious world – a very inexplicable and curious world, and if people were as intelligent as certain misguided fools believed they would not ask questions about – well, Druids, or for that matter, about anything. They would accept everything as proved, QED, and simply go to sleep – like contented, well-nourished cats.

Unfortunately Mr Benefield was not permitted to sleep uninterruptedly until ten o'clock, his usual hour for rising, on the following morning. At eight minutes to nine he was awakened by his wife, who exclaimed: 'That silly old creature across the hall, Mrs Harmone, just got me up to tell me a crazy story. She has been idiotically frightened, and she says there was a burglar in the house at about eleven o'clock last night!'

'A burglar?' inquired Mr Benefield sleepily. 'How dreadful!'

'Yes, dreadful – and very queer if true. What do you think the man did?'

'I can't hazard a guess.' Mr Benefield's emotional self was still deeply immersed in sleep, i.e., in his subconscious, and he spoke with cool intellectual detachment.

'He was tall and very, very thin and he climbed in by the parlour window. Mrs Harmone was dozing in a chair near the centre of the room and she saw him. She didn't dare scream for fear he would shoot her. She simply sat and watched him, trying not to breathe. He went right through the parlour and out into the hall. And a moment later she heard him close the front door. He came in the window and went out the door!'

'Wasn't that unusual – for a burglar?' murmured Mr Benefield.

'Mrs Harmone thought so. And as soon as he shut the door she dashed towards it, and peered through the curtain at him.

'What do you think? *The man had left his overcoat on the porch*, and he was bending over to recover it when Mrs Harmone peered out at him. While she watched him he put it on. His back was turned towards her, but she said – his head looked very queer. Nasty, she said. It gave her the shivers. He wore an English bowler hat, which covered most of it, but his ears, she said, stood out. And they were very black – and pointed!'

'Pointed!' echoed Mr Benefield. He was fully awake now, and experiencing an acute and lively horror.

'Actually – pointed. Or so she claims. And then, she said, he descended the stairs and went shuffling down the street. She went out on the porch and watched him until he turned the corner. And then, she said, she had to go in, because there was such a horrid, fearsome odour – like you smell at the Zoo, in the monkey-houses, she said. Then she frowned, and shook her head. "But it wasn't a monkey smell exactly. It was more like – more like snakes!"'

Mr Benefield groaned and clutched valiantly at a straw. 'I think,' he affirmed, 'that Mrs Harmone's nervous energy is unfortunately discharged through the efferent channels of those sensori-motor arcs which comprise what neurologists would call the focus of cortical awareness. She visions things which are scarcely present to the senses.'

'She imagines things, you mean?'

'Yes, my dear. That expresses it quite succinctly. She imagines things. Now, please do not wake me for another hour.'

Mr Benefield turned upon his side and went resolutely to sleep. But in the dream that immediately ensued he encountered the very thing that he had hoped to avoid and was obliged, perforce, to pay subconscious tribute to the veracity of Mrs Harmone. 'God's Death!' he shouted, as he tracked it to its lair in a hellish wood. 'Does a Knight of Malta fear such as you?'

# The Tomb of Sarah

## F. G. Loring

My father was the head of a celebrated firm of church restorers and decorators about sixty years ago. He took a keen interest in his work, and made an especial study of any old legends or family histories that came under his observation. He was necessarily very well read and thoroughly well posted in all questions of folk-lore and medieval legend. As he kept a careful record of every case he investigated the manuscripts he left at his death have a special interest. From among them I have selected the following, as being a particularly weird and extraordinary experience. In presenting it to the public I feel it is superfluous to apologize for its supernatural character.

### MY FATHER'S DIARY

1941, *17th June*. Received a commission from my old friend, Peter Grant, to enlarge and restore the chancel of his church at Hagarstone, in the wilds of the west country.

*5th July*. Went down to Hagarstone with my head man, Somers. A very long and tiring journey.

*7th July*. Got the work well started. The old church is one of special interest to the antiquarian, and I shall endeavour while restoring it to alter the existing arrangements as little as possible. One large tomb, however, must be moved bodily ten feet at least to the southward. Curiously enough there is a somewhat forbidding inscription upon it in Latin, and I am sorry that this particular tomb should have to be moved. It stands among the graves of the Kenyons, an old family which has been extinct in these parts for centuries. The inscription on it runs thus:

SARAH

1630

For the sake of the dead and the welfare of the
living, let this sepulchre remain untouched
and its occupant undisturbed until
the Coming of Christ.

In the name of the Father, the Son
and the Holy Ghost.

*8th July.* Took counsel with Grant concerning the 'Sarah Tomb'. We are both very loth to disturb it, but the ground has sunk so beneath it that the safety of the church is in danger; thus we have no choice. However, the work shall be done as reverently as possible under our own direction.

Grant says there is a legend in the neighbourhood that it is the tomb of the last of the Kenyons, the evil Countess Sarah, who was murdered in 1630. She lived quite alone in the old castle, whose ruins still stand three miles from here on the road to Bristol. Her reputation was an evil one even for those days. She was a witch or were-woman, the only companion of her solitude being in the shape of a huge Asiatic wolf. This creature was reputed to seize upon children, or failing these, sheep and other small animals, and convey them to the castle, where the countess used to suck their blood. It was popularly supposed that she could never be killed. This, however, proved a fallacy, since she was strangled one day by a mad peasant woman who had lost two children, she declaring that they had both been seized and carried off by the countess's familiar. This is a very interesting story, since it points to a local superstition very similar to that of the vampire, existing in Slavonic and Hungarian Europe.

The tomb is built of black marble, surmounted by an enormous slab of the same material. On the slab is a magnificent group of figures. A young and handsome woman reclines upon a couch; round her neck is a piece of rope, the end of which she holds in her hand. At her side is a gigantic dog with bared fangs and lolling tongue. The face of the reclining figure is a cruel one; the corners of the mouth are curiously lifted, showing the sharp points of long canine or dog teeth. The whole group, though magnificently executed, leaves a most unpleasant sensation.

If we move the tomb it will have to be done in two pieces, the covering slab first and then the tomb proper. We have decided to remove the covering slab tomorrow.

*9th July* 6 p.m. A very strange day.

By noon everything was ready for lifting off the covering stone, and after the men's dinner we started the jacks and pulleys. The slab lifted easily enough, though it fitted closely into its seat and was further secured by some sort of mortar or putty, which must have kept the interior perfectly air-tight.

None of us was prepared for the horrible rush of foul, mouldy air that escaped as the cover lifted clear of its seating. And the contents that gradually came into view were more startling still. There lay the fully dressed body of a woman, wizened and shrunk and ghastly pale as if from starvation. Round her neck was a loose cord, and, judging by the scars still visible, the story of death by strangulation was true enough.

The most horrible part, however, was the extraordinary freshness of the body. Except for the appearance of starvation, life might have been only just extinct. The flesh was soft and white, the eyes were wide open and seemed to stare at us with a fearful understanding in them. The body itself lay on mould, without any pretence to coffin or shell.

For several moments we gazed with horrible curiosity, and then it became too much for my workmen, who implored us to replace the covering slab. That, of course, we would not do; but I set the carpenters at work at once to make a temporary cover while we moved the tomb to its new position. This is a long job, and will take two or three days at least.

9 p.m. Just at sunset we were startled by the howling of, seemingly, every dog in the village. It lasted for ten minutes or a quarter of an hour, and then ceased as suddenly as it began. This, and a curious mist that has risen round the church, makes me feel rather anxious about the 'Sarah Tomb'. According to the best established traditions of the vampire-haunted countries, the disturbance of dogs or wolves at sunset is supposed to indicate the presence of one of these fiends, and local fog is always considered to be a certain sign. The vampire has the power of producing it for the purpose of concealing its movements near its hiding-places at any time.

I dare not mention or even hint my fears to the rector, for he is, not unnaturally perhaps, a rank disbeliever in many things that I know, from experience, are not only possible but even probable. I must work this out alone at first, and get his aid without his knowing in what direction he is helping me. I shall now watch till midnight at least.

10.15 p.m. As I feared and half expected. Just before ten there was another outburst of the hideous howling. It was commenced most distinctly by a particularly horrible and blood-curdling wail from the vicinity of the churchyard. The chorus lasted only a few minutes, however, and at the end of it I saw a large dark shape, like a huge dog, emerge from the fog and lope away at a rapid canter towards the open country. Assuming this to be what I fear, I shall see it return soon after midnight.

12.30 p.m. I was right. Almost as midnight struck I saw the beast returning. It stopped at the spot where fog seemed to commence, and, lifting up its head, gave tongue to that particularly long-drawn wail that I had noticed as preceding the outburst earlier in the evening.

Tomorrow I shall tell the rector what I have seen; and if, as I expect, we hear of some neighbouring sheepfold having been raided, I shall get him to watch with me for this nocturnal marauder. I shall also examine the 'Sarah Tomb' for something which he may notice without any previous hint from me.

*10th July.* I found the workmen this morning much disturbed in mind about the howling of the dogs. 'We doan't like it, zur,' one of them said to me – 'we doan't like it; there was summat abroad last night that was unholy.' They were still more uncomfortable when the news came round that a large dog had made a raid upon a flock of sheep, scattering them far and wide, and leaving three of them dead with torn throats in the field.

When I told the rector of what I had seen and what was being said in the village, he immediately decided that we must try and catch or at least identify the beast I had seen. 'Of course,' said he, 'it is some dog lately imported into the neighbourhood, for I know of nothing about here nearly as large as the animal you describe, though its size may be due to the deceptive moonlight.'

This afternoon I asked the rector, as a favour, to assist me in lifting the temporary cover that was on the tomb, giving as an excuse the reason that I wished to obtain a portion of the curious mortar with which it had been sealed. After a slight demur he consented, and we raised the lid. If the sight that met our eyes gave me a shock, at least it appalled Grant.

'Great God!' he exclaimed; 'the woman is alive!'

And so it seemed for a moment. The corpse had lost much of its starved appearance and looked hideously fresh and alive. It was still wrinkled and shrunken, but the lips were firm, and of the rich red hue of health. The eyes, if possible, were more appalling than ever, though fixed and staring. At one corner corner of the mouth I thought I noticed a slight dark-coloured froth, but I said nothing about it then.

'Take your piece of mortar, Harry,' gasped Grant, 'and let us shut the tomb again. God help me! Parson though I am, such dead faces frighten me!'

Nor was I sorry to hide that terrible face again; but I got my bit of mortar, and I have advanced a step towards the solution of the mystery.

This afternoon the tomb was moved several feet towards its new position, but it will be two or three days yet before we shall be ready to replace the slab.

10.15 p.m. Again the same howling at sunset, the same fog enveloping the church, and at ten o'clock the same great beast slipping silently out into the open country. I must get the rector's help and watch for its return. But precautions we must take, for if things are as I believe, we take our lives in our hands when we venture out into the night to waylay the – vampire. Why not admit it at once? For that the beast I have seen is the vampire of that evil thing in the tomb I can have no reasonable doubt.

Not yet come to its full strength, thank Heaven! after the starvation of nearly two centuries, for the present it can only maraud as wolf apparently. But, in a day or two, when full power returns, that dreadful woman in new strength and beauty will be able to leave her refuge. Then it would not be sheep merely that would satisfy her disgusting lust for blood, but victims that would yield their life-blood without a murmur to her caressing touch – victims that, dying of her foul embrace, themselves must become vampires in their turn to prey on others.

Mercifully my knowledge gives me a safeguard; for that little piece of mortar that I rescued today from the tomb contains a portion of the sacred host, and who holds it, humbly and firmly believing in virtue, may pass safely through such an ordeal as I intended to submit myself and the rector to tonight.

12.30 p.m. Our adventure is over for the present, and we are back safe.

After writing the last entry recorded above, I went off to find Grant and tell him that the marauder was out on the prowl again. 'But, Grant,' I said, 'before we start out tonight I must insist that you will let me prosecute this affair in my own way; you must promise to put yourself completely under my orders, without asking any questions as to the why and wherefore.'

After a little demur, and some excusable chaff on his part at the serious view I was taking of what he called a 'dog hunt', he gave me his promise. I then told him that we were to watch tonight and try and track the mysterious beast, but not to interfere with it in any way. I think, in spite of his jests, that I impressed him with the fact that there might be, after all, good reason for my precautions.

It was just after eleven when we stepped out into the still night.

Our first move was to try and penetrate the dense fog round the church, but there was something so chilly about it, and a faint smell so disgustingly rank and loathsome, that neither our nerves nor our stomachs were proof against it. Instead, we stationed ourselves in the dark shadow of a yew-tree that commanded a good view of the wicket entrance to the churchyard.

At midnight howling of the dogs began again, and in a few minutes we saw a large grey shape, with green eyes shining like lamps, shamble swiftly down the path towards us.

The rector started forward, but I laid a firm hand upon his arm and whispered a warming: 'Remember!' Then we both stood very still and watched as the great beast cantered swiftly by. It was real enough, for we could hear the clicking of its nails on the stone flags. It passed within a few yards of us, and seemed to be nothing more nor less than a great grey wolf, thin and gaunt, with bristling hair and dripping jaws. It stopped where the mist commenced, and turned around. It was truly a horrible sight, and made one's blood run cold. The eyes burnt like fires, the upper lip was snarling and raised, showing the great canine teeth, while round the mouth clung and dripped a dark-coloured froth.

It raised its head and gave tongue to its long wailing howl, which was answered from afar by the village dogs. After standing for a few moments it turned and disappeared into the thickest part of the fog.

Very shortly afterwards the atmosphere began to clear, and within ten minutes the mist was all gone, the dogs in the village were silent, and the night seemed to reassume its normal aspect. We examined the spot where the beast had been standing and found, plainly enough upon the stone flags, dark spots of froth and saliva.

'Well, rector,' I said, 'will you admit now, in view of the things you have seen today, in consideration of the legend, the woman in the tomb, the fog, the howling dogs, and, last but not least, the mysterious beast you have seen so close, that there is something not quite normal in it all? Will you put yourself unreservedly in my hands and help me, whatever I may do, first to make assurance doubly sure, and finally to take the necessary steps for putting an end to this horror of the night?' I saw that the uncanny influence of the night was strong upon him, and wished to impress it as much as possible.

'Needs must,' he replied, 'when the Devil drives: and in the face of what I have seen I must believe that some unholy forces are at work. Yet, how can they work in the sacred precincts of a church? Shall we not call rather upon Heaven to assist us in our needs?'

'Grant,' I said solemnly, 'that we must do, each in his own way. God helps those who help themselves, and by His help and the light of my knowledge we must fight this battle for Him and the poor lost soul within.'

We then returned to the rectory and to our rooms, though I have sat up to write this account while the scene is fresh in my mind.

*11th July.* Found the workmen again very much disturbed in their minds, and full of a strange dog that had been seen during the night by several people, who had hunted it. Farmer Stotman, who had been watching his sheep (the same flock that had been raided the night before), had surprised it over a fresh carcass and tried to drive it off, but its size and fierceness so alarmed him that he had beaten a hasty retreat for a gun. When he returned the animal was gone, though he found that three more sheep from his flock were dead and torn.

The 'Sarah Tomb' was moved today to its new position; but it was a long, heavy business, and there was not time to replace the covering slab. For this I was glad, as in the prosaic light of day the rector almost disbelieves the events of the night, and is prepared to think everything to have been magnified and distorted by our imagination.

As, however, I could not possibly proceed with my war of extermination against this foul thing without assistance, and as there is nobody else I can rely upon, I appealed to him for one more night – to convince him that it was no delusion, but a ghastly, horrible truth, which must be fought and conquered for our own sakes, as well as that of all those living in the neighbourhood.

'Put yourself in my hands, rector,' I said, 'for tonight at least. Let us take those precautions which my study of the subject tells me are the right ones. Tonight you and I must watch in the church; and I feel assured that tomorrow you will be as convinced as I am, and be equally prepared to take those awful steps which I know to be proper, and I must warn you that we shall find a more startling change in the body lying there than you noticed yesterday.'

My words came true; for on raising the wooden cover once more the rank stench of a slaughterhouse arose, making us feel positively sick. There lay the vampire, but how changed from the starved and shrunken corpse we saw two days ago for the first time! The wrinkles had almost disappeared, the flesh was firm and full, the crimson lips grinned horribly over the long pointed teeth, and a distinct smear of blood had trickled down one corner of the mouth. We set our teeth, however, and hardened our hearts. Then we replaced the cover and put what we had collected into a safe place in the vestry. Yet even now Grant could not believe that there was any real or pressing danger concealed in that awful tomb, as he raised strenuous objections to any apparent desecration of the body without further proof. This he shall have tonight. God grant that I am not taking too much on myself! If there is any truth in old legends it would be easy enough to destroy the vampire now; but Grant will not have it.

I hope for the best of this night's work, but the danger in waiting is very great.

6 p.m. I have prepared everything: the sharp knives, the pointed stake, fresh garlic, and the wild dog-roses. All these I have taken and concealed in the vestry, where we can get at them when our solemn vigil commences.

If either or both of us die with our fearful task undone, let those reading my record see that this is done. I lay it upon them as a solemn obligation. 'That the vampire be pierced through the heart with the stake, then let the burial service be read over the poor clay at last released from its doom. Thus shall the vampire cease to be, and a lost soul rest.'

*12 July.* All is over. After the most terrible night of watching and horror, one vampire at least will trouble the world no more. But how thankful should we be to a merciful Providence that that awful tomb was not disturbed by anyone not having the knowledge necessary to deal with its dreadful occupant! I write this with no feelings of self-complacency, but simply with a great gratitude for the years of study I have been able to devote to this subject.

And now to my tale.

Just before sunset last night the rector and I locked ourselves into the church, and took up our position in the pulpit. It was one of those pulpits, to be found in some churches, which is entered from the vestry, the preacher appearing at a good height through an arched opening in the wall. This gave us a sense of security (which we felt we needed), a good view of the interior, and direct access to the implements which I had concealed in the vestry.

The sun set and the twilight gradually deepened and faded. There was, so far, no sign of the usual fog, nor any howling of the dogs. At nine o'clock the moon rose, and her pale light gradually flooded the aisles, and still no sign of any kind from the 'Sarah Tomb'. The rector had asked me several times what he might expect, but I was determined that no words or thought of mine should influence him, and that he should be convinced by his own senses alone.

By half-past ten we were both getting very tired, and I began to think that perhaps after all we should see nothing that night. However, soon after eleven we observed a light mist rising from the 'Sarah Tomb'. It seemed to scintillate and sparkle as it rose, and curled in a sort of pillar or spiral.

I said nothing, but I heard the rector give a sort of gasp as he clutched my arm feverishly. 'Great Heaven!' he whispered, 'it is taking shape.'

And, true enough, in a very few moments we saw standing erect by the tomb the ghastly figure of the Countess Sarah!

She looked thin and haggard still, and her face was deadly white; but the crimson lips looked like a hideous gash in the pale cheeks, and her eyes glared like red coals in the gloom of the church.

It was a fearful thing to watch as she stepped unsteadily down the aisle, staggering a little as if from weakness and exhaustion. This was perhaps natural, as her body must have suffered much physically from her long incarceration, in spite of the unholy forces which kept it fresh and well.

We watched her to the door, and wondered what would happen; but it appeared to present no difficulty, for she melted through it and disappeared.

'Now, Grant,' I said, 'do you believe?'

'Yes,' he replied, 'I must. Everything is in your hands, and I will obey your commands to the letter, if you can only instruct me how to rid my poor people of this unnameable terror.'

'By God's help I will,' said I; 'but you shall be yet more convinced first, for we have a terrible work to do, and much to answer for in the future, before we leave the church again this morning. And now to work, for in its present weak state the vampire will not wander far, but may return at any time, and must not find us unprepared.'

We stepped down from the pulpit, and taking dog-roses and garlic from the vestry, proceeded to the tomb. I arrived first and, throwing off the wooden cover, cried: 'Look! it's empty!' There was nothing there! Nothing except the impress of the body in the loose damp mould!

I took the flowers and laid them in a circle round the tomb, for legend teaches us that vampires will not pass over these particular blossoms if they can avoid it.

Then, eight or ten feet away, I made a circle on the stone pavement, large enough for the rector and myself to stand in, and within the circle I placed the implements that I had brought into the church with me.

'Now,' I said, 'from this circle, which nothing unholy can step across, you shall see the vampire face to face, and see her afraid to cross that other circle of garlic and dog-roses to regain her unholy refuge. But on no account step beyond the holy place you stand in, for the vampire has a fearful strength not her own, and, like a snake, can draw her victim willingly to his own destruction.'

Now so far my work was done, and calling the rector, we stepped into the holy circle to await the vampire's return.

Nor was this long delayed. Presently a damp, cold odour seemed to pervade the church, which made our hair bristle and flesh creep. And then, down the aisle with noiseless feet, came That which we watched for.

I heard the rector mutter a prayer, and I held him tightly by the arm, for he was shivering violently.

Long before we could distinguish the features we saw the glowing eyes and the crimson sensual mouth. She went straight to her tomb, but stopped short when she encountered my flowers. She walked right round the tomb seeking a place to enter, and as she walked she saw us. A spasm of diabolical hate and fury passed over her face; but it quickly vanished, and a smile of love, more devilish still, took its place. She stretched out her arms towards us. Then we saw that round her mouth gathered a bloody froth and from under her lips long pointed teeth gleamed and champed.

She spoke: a soft soothing voice, a voice that carried a spell with it, and affected us both strangely, particularly the rector. I wished to test as far as possible, without endangering our lives, the vampire's power.

Her voice had a soporific effect, which I resisted easily enough, but which seemed to throw the rector into a sort of trance. More than this: it seemed to compel him to her in spite of his efforts to resist.

'Come!' she said – 'come! I give sleep and peace – sleep and peace – sleep and peace.'

She advanced a little towards us; but not far, for I noted that the sacred circle seemed to keep her back like an iron hand.

My companion seemed to become demoralized and spellbound. He tried to step forward and, finding me detain him, whispered: 'Harry, let go! She is calling me! I must! I must! Oh, help me! help me!' And he began to struggle.

It was time to finish.

'Grant!' I cried, in a loud, firm voice, 'in the name of all that you hold sacred, have done and play the man!' He shuddered violently and gasped: 'Where am I?' Then he remembered, and clung to me convulsively for a moment.

At this a look of damnable hate changed the smiling face before us, and with a sort of shriek she staggered back.

'Back!' I cried: 'back to your unholy tomb! No longer shall you molest the suffering world! Your end is near.'

It was fear that now showed itself in her beautiful face (for it was beautiful in spite of its horror) as she shrank back, back and over the circlet of flowers, shivering as she did so. At last, with a low mournful cry, she appeared to melt back again into her tomb.

As she did so the first gleams of the rising sun lit up the world, and I knew all danger was over for the day.

Taking Grant by the arm, I drew him with me out of the circle and led him to the tomb. There lay the vampire once more, still in her living death as we had a moment before seen her in her devilish life. But in the eyes remained that awful expression of hate, and cringing, appalling fear.

Grant was pulling himself together.

'Now,' I said, 'will you dare the last terrible act and rid the world for ever of this horror?'

'By God!' he said solemnly, 'I will. Tell me what to do.'

'Help me to lift her out of her tomb. She can harm us no more,' I replied.

With averted faces we set to our terrible task, and laid her out upon the flags.

'Now,' I said, 'read the burial service over the poor body, and then let us give it its release from this living hell that holds it.'

Reverently the rector read the beautiful words, and reverently I made the necessary responses. When it was over I took the stake and, without giving myself time to think, plunged it with all my strength through the heart.

As though really alive, the body for a moment writhed and kicked convulsively, and an awful heart-rending shriek woke the silent church; then all was still.

Then we lifted the poor body back; and, thank God! the consolation that legend tells is never denied to those who have to do such awful work as ours came at last. Over the face stole a great and solemn peace; the lips lost their crimson hue, the prominent sharp teeth sank back into the mouth, and for a moment we saw before us the calm, pale face of a most beautiful woman, who smiled as she slept. A few minutes more, and she faded away to dust before our eyes as we watched. We set to work and cleaned up every trace of our work, and then departed for the rectory. Most thankful were we to step out of the church, with its horrible associations, into the rosy warmth of the summer morning.

With the above end notes in my father's diary, though a few days later this further entry occurs.

*15th July.* Since the 12th everything has been quiet and as usual. We replaced and sealed up the 'Sarah Tomb' this morning. The workmen were surprised to find the body had disappeared, but took it to be the natural result of exposing it to the air.

One odd thing came to my ears today. It appears that the child of one of the villagers strayed from home the night of the 11th inst, and was found asleep in a coppice near the church, very pale and quite exhausted. There were two small marks on her throat, which have since disappeared.

What does this mean? I have, however, kept it to myself, as, now that the vampire is no more, no further danger either to that child or any other is to be apprehended. It is only those who die of the vampire's embrace that become vampires at death in their turn.

# The Skeleton Hand

*Agnes MacLeod*

I am about to relate some events which took place in the early part of this century, in a remote little fishing village on the south coast of Devonshire. The occurrences are themselves so remarkable that they have been well known to the present generation of inhabitants; but as things get altered in oral transmission through many persons, it has been thought well to place this record in writing.

Near the village of Jodziel, in a pretty little cottage on the top of the bright red sandstone cliff which overhangs the village, lived two maiden sisters, the Misses Rutson. Their father, a sea-captain, had died a year before the events I am about to relate occurred. Their mother had died in giving birth to the younger sister, Anne, who was now a most beautiful girl of eighteen. The Misses Rutson were very devotedly attached to one another, and were much beloved by the village neighbours. The hamlet being a very sequestered one, they seldom saw any one from the outer world except occasionally sailors, who would stroll along the cliff from Plymouth or from other fishing villages along the coast. In the autumn of 1813 a pressgang visited South Devon and made their headquarters for some time in the village of Jodziel. The captain, a certain Captain Sinclair by name – a coarse brutal fellow in appearance – was very much struck by the extraordinary beauty of Miss Anne. He forced himself upon her, and continued paying her the most distasteful attentions, which the gentle girl did her very utmost to check, but in vain. The day before Captain Sinclair left Jodziel, he made a formal offer of marriage to Miss Anne, which in the presence of her sister she immediately and decisively declined. Captain Sinclair flew into the most violent passion, swore he had never been thwarted yet by any woman, and that she should belong to him or never marry at all. Anne was so much upset by the terrible scene, and by Captain Sinclair's outrageous language, that her sister was very glad when an invitation from an aunt residing in London gave Anne a few weeks' much-needed change. Mrs Travers was the only near relative remaining to the Misses Rutson, and owing to various circumstances the sisters had seen but little of their aunt, though with Maurice Travers, her only son, they were better acquainted.

Maurice's regiment had been quartered for the summer of 1813 at Plymouth, and he had frequently been over to see his cousins, and many a pleasant summer day had they spent wandering along the beautiful Devonshire coast. Miss Rutson had not been slow to perceive that stronger attractions than those of mere scenery brought the young officer so constantly to their cottage, and she was not therefore very much surprised at receiving one morning, about three weeks after Anne's departure from home, a letter announcing her engagement to her cousin, Maurice Travers, and her immediate return to Jodziel. It was decided that the marriage should take place early in the following May, and I will now quote one or two passages from Miss Rutson's diary at this time.

'*May 1* – Such a horrid meeting we have just had. Anne and I had been for a stroll along the shore when we noticed a little boat which lay drawn up under a rock at some distance, and Anne's eyes, which are keener than mine, caught sight of the name painted in gold letters. "Ah, sister, come away," she cried; "it is a boat from the Raven. I thought Captain Sinclair was not to be in these waters again; he told me he was to sail for the West Indies last month." We turned, and were hurriedly retracing our steps towards the house when we heard a cry of *Stop*! I looked at Anne; she was deadly white. "Run on quick," I cried; "I will speak to him." My heart was beating so fast I could run no longer; besides, I felt it might be well to hear what Captain Sinclair had to say, so I drew myself together and waited. Presently he appeared clambering up the side of the cliff, his swarthy face purple with excitement. "Where is she?" he gasped. "I have come back to fetch her; I could not sail without her, my own beautiful Anne!" "Recollect yourself, sir," I cried indignantly. "How dare you speak of my sister in this free manner! She has told you most clearly, and that in my presence, that she looks on your pursuit of her as odious, and she begs, both for her own sake and yours, that you will never attempt to see her again." "Do you think I will be daunted by such a speech from a foolish girl?" he answered scornfully; "No, no, she shall be mine yet, whether she will or no." "You are mistaken," I replied as calmly as I could; "Next Monday she marries our first cousin, Maurice Travers, and will be at peace from your hated persecutions."

'I shall never forget his scowl of fury as he turned from me and dashed down the cliff, shouting as he did so, "She shall be mine!" When I got home, feeling very nervous and shaken, who should I find just starting to seek me but Maurice, who had come three days earlier than we expected him. An hour before I should have felt very cross at having my last quiet hours with Anne so much curtailed, but now I was only too thankful to feel we had a protector near us. He went out after hearing my story, but could see no trace of either boat or its owner.

'*May 2* – To my great relief the Raven, with Captain Sinclair on board, has left Plymouth this morning for the West Indies. Maurice had business at Plymouth, and he took the opportunity of making inquiries concerning the Raven, which was, he found, in the very act of putting to sea. I feel, oh, so thankful and relieved.

'*May 4* – How shall I ever begin to write the events of this most dreadful day! Such a brilliant sunshiny morning, quite like summer, and my darling came down looking like one of the sweet white roses which were just coming into bloom around the windows. I plucked a beautiful spray of them, and she put them in her white satin waistband just before starting for church. I have those roses by me now as I write, but, O my darling! where are you? The wedding was a very quiet one. After the ceremony we had the clergyman and doctor, with their wives and their children, to lunch, and presently Anne rose and said she would go and change her dress. I was going to follow her, but she stopped me with one of her sweet kisses and said, "Let me have a few moments alone in the old room to say goodbye to it all." I let her go – when did I ever thwart her in anything? She went, and Maurice began romping with the children, and we ladies cut slices of wedding-cake, to be taken round to village favourites next day, and still Anne did not call. Once, indeed, I had fancied I heard her voice; but when I had gone upstairs her door was locked, and she had not answered my gentle tap, so I came down again, not wishing to intrude upon her privacy. At length, however, Maurice became impatient, and said I must go and fetch her down, or they would never be in time to catch the coach at Plymouth. The door was still locked. When I got upstairs I knocked, first gently, then more loudly. I was not frightened at first, for there was a door-window in the room leading down a little flight of steps into the garden, and I thought she had gone down these to take a last look at her flowers, so I called to Maurice to run round to the garden, for she must be there. I remained listening at the bedroom door, which in a moment or two flew open and Maurice, with a very disturbed face, stood before me. "She has evidently been in the garden," he said, "for the door on to the outside steps was open; but there is no one there now." I made no answer, but flew past him into the bedroom. It needed but a glance to show my darling had gone straight through the room; her gloves and handkerchief were thrown on a chair by the window, and her pale-blue travelling-dress lay undisturbed upon the bed. I ran hastily through the room and garden, which was empty; the gate on to the cliff was ajar, and we noticed (but not till later) that there must have been a struggle at the spot, for some of the lilac boughs were torn down, as if someone had held fast by them and been dragged forcibly away. Maurice and the rest of the party followed me on to the cliff, for the alarm had now become general; for a little while we ran wildly, calling her dear name, but presently Maurice came to me, and drawing my arm within his own, led me back towards the house. "Someone must be here to receive her when she comes home," he said gently, and here his lips grew white. "It might be well to have her bed ready in case –" He was out of the room without finishing his sentence. It was needless; the same horrible fear had already seized on me. The cliff, the terrible cliff; I cannot go on writing, my heart is too heavy.

'*Twelve o'clock* – They have come back, and, O God! the only trace of her is the spray of white roses I picked for her this morning. They were found on top of the cliff about half a mile from here. I think they are a message from my darling to me, for they were not trampled on or crushed; she must have taken them carefully and purposely from her belt; they shall never, never leave me.

'*May 11* – It is a week since that dreadful day, and not the smallest clue to her disappearance. Poor Maurice is half mad with grief; he has sought for her high and low, and spent all the little sum destined for their wedding journey on these vain researches. Now he wanders along the cliff up and down, up and down, the whole of the long day, and then he comes and sits opposite to me with his elbows on his knees, till I tell him it is time for bed, when he goes without a word; but I hear him pacing his room half the night.

'*May 31* – Maurice has had to join his regiment for foreign service. I am glad: he would have gone mad had he remained inactive here.

'*Sept. 3* – I have been very ill, but Patty assures me there has not been a trace of any clue during my long time of blessed unconsciousness, and now the terrible aching void is again here. O my darling, my darling, come back!

'*Sept. 6* – Why should I go on writing? my life henceforth is only waiting.'

After this comes a long break of fully twenty years in the diary; then in an aged and trembling character occurs the following entry:

'*May 4, 1835* – I don't know, what impels me once more to pen this diary; possibly this wild hurricane of wind which is making the house rock like a boat has upset me, but I feel so glad and satisfied, as if my long waiting were nearly over. I have just been upstairs to see that all is in order for my darling. We have kept everything aired and prepared for her these thirty years, so that she should find all comfortable when she comes home at last. My poor darling, she will only find Patty and me to welcome her. Let me think, this is nearly twenty years ago since we heard of Maurice's death at Waterloo. Oh what a fearful crash! and how that rumbling noise goes on sounding as if the cliff had given way.'

Here the diary abruptly terminates; but the remainder of the tragic story is yet told in that little Devonshire village. The violence of the storm had in very truth caused a subsidence in the cliff, and in doing so had brought to light a skeleton on which yet hung some tattered remnants of what had once been white satin, and from whose bony fingers rolled a tarnished wedding-ring. The bones were collected with tender care and brought to the house of the unhappy sister. She received them without much apparent surprise, directed they should be laid on 'Miss Anne's bed upstairs,' and as soon as the men had left the house, went and laid herself upon the bed also, where her faithful maid Patty, coming to see after her an hour later, found her stone-dead, and held tight in her dead grasp was a pair of white gloves and a lace pocket-handkerchief.

The two sisters were laid to rest in one grave, and it was not till after the funeral was over that it was discovered that, through some inadvertence, one of the skeleton hands had not been placed in the coffin with the rest of the body.

At first there was some talk of reopening the grave, but the old maid Patty entreated so earnestly to be allowed to retain the hand that she at last succeeded in carrying her point. A glass case was made by Mrs Patty's order, and in it the poor hand was placed; and when Mrs Patty went down to the inn to spend her last remaining years with her daughter the landlady, the case was placed on a shelf close to the old woman's seat, and many a time would she recount the sad story to the sailors who frequented the village inn.

In the spring of 1837 a larger number than usual were gathered round the fireside of the Blue Dragon. A fearful storm, accompanied by violent gusts of hail, swept round the house. Suddenly the door burst open, and a young man entered, half dragging, half supporting an old man, bent and shrunk with age and infirmity. 'Here you are, sir,' he said to the old man; 'This is the Blue Dragon. You won't find a snugger berth between here and Plymouth'; so saying, he thrust the old man into a chair by the fire, and continued, half aside to the company. 'Found the old cove wandering about the cliffs, and thought he would be blown over, so offered to guide him here. I think he is a little –' and he tapped his forehead significantly. The rest of the party turned round curiously to gaze at the stranger, who, seeming to wake from some reverie, proceeded to order something hot both for himself and his self-constituted guide. The hot gin-and-water seemed further to rouse him, and he began asking a few questions concerning the country and neighbourhood; but in the very act of speaking his attention was suddenly arrested by the sight of the glass case and skeleton hand. He sprang from his chair with a savage cry of mingled terror and dismay. 'The hand,' he cried, 'the hand! why does it point at me? I never meant, O God!–' and he fell down in a fit, rolling and gasping on the floor, and shrieking wildly at intervals, 'The hand, the hand!' They raised the wretched man from the floor and laid him on a bed, whilst the doctor was hurriedly summoned. Meanwhile the sufferer continued disjointed mutterings, till, becoming exhausted, he sank into a stupor. On the doctor's arrival, however, he once more roused himself, and asked in a quieter and more composed manner whose the hand was. On being told, he trembled violently, but said: 'I am Captain Sinclair; I knew the wedding-day; I told my ship to sail without me from Plymouth, saying I would rejoin her at Falmouth. I meant to bring Anne with me; I hid in the garden, she came into it alone, I rushed forward, threw a shawl I had ready over her head, and carried her away; she resisted with all her might, but I was a strong man, and her cries were stifled by the shawl. Of course I could not get along very fast, and presently I heard voices of those in search of her. She heard them also, and made another frantic effort to free herself. My strength was nearly exhausted, but mad with rage and disappointment, I drew my knife from my belt and stabbed her to the heart, crying fiercely, "I have kept my oath, you shall never be another's." Then I hurled the body down the cliff, where I saw it catch in a crevice of the rock. O God!' he cried, shuddering and covering his face with his hands, 'I see it now – that dreadful scene, the blue waves dancing beneath the brilliant sunshine, and that white shapeless mass caught in the frowning cliff with one arm sticking stiffly upwards. I rolled down one or two stones, endeavouring to conceal it; and when I left the spot, all I could see was a hand pointing at me.' Here the miserable wretch broke off with a deep groan. In a moment more he sprang up with another wild shout of 'The hand, the bloody hand!' and so shrieking, his body fell lifeless to the ground. . . The skeleton hand in the adjoining room was dripping blood.

# The Man from Glasgow

## W. Somerset Maugham

It is not often that anyone entering a great city for the first time has the luck to witness such an incident as engaged Shelley's attention when he drove into Naples. A youth ran out of a shop pursued by a man armed with a knife. The man overtook him and with one blow in the neck laid him dead on the road. Shelley had a tender heart. He didn't look upon it as a bit of local colour; he was seized with horror and indignation. But when he expressed his emotions to a Calabrian priest who was travelling with him, a fellow of gigantic strength and stature, the priest laughed heartily and attempted to quiz him. Shelley says he never felt such an inclination to beat anyone.

I have never seen anything so exciting as that, but the first time I went to Algeciras I had an experience that seemed to me far from ordinary. Algeciras was then an untidy, neglected town. I arrived somewhat late at night and went to an inn on the quay. It was rather shabby, but it had a fine view of Gibraltar, solid and matter-of-fact, across the bay. The moon was full. The office was on the first floor, and a slatternly maid, when I asked for a room, took me upstairs. The landlord was playing cards. He seemed little pleased to see me. He looked me up and down, curtly gave me a number, and then, taking no further notice of me, went on with his game.

When the maid had shown me to my room I asked her what I could have to eat.

'What you like,' she answered.

I knew well enough the unreality of the seeming profusion.

'What have you got in the house?'

'You can have eggs and ham.'

The look of the hotel had led me to guess that I should get little else. The maid led me to a narrow room with whitewashed walls and a low ceiling in which was a long table laid already for the next day's luncheon. With his back to the door sat a tall man, huddled over a *brasero*, the round brass dish of hot ashes which is erroneously supposed to give sufficient warmth for the temperate winter of Andalusia. I sat down at table and waited for my scanty meal. I gave the stranger an idle glance.

He was looking at me, but meeting my eyes he quickly turned away. I waited for my eggs. When at last the maid brought them he looked up again.

'I want you to wake me in time for the first boat,' he said.

'*Si, señor.*'

His accent told me that English was his native tongue, and the breadth of his build, his strongly marked features, led me to suppose him a northerner. The hardy Scot is far more often found in Spain than the Englishman. Whether you go to the rich mines of Rio Tinto, or to the *bodegas* of Jerez, to Seville or to Cadiz, it is the leisurely speech of beyond the Tweed that you hear. You will meet Scotsmen in the olive groves of Carmona, on the railway between Algeciras and Bobadilla, and even in the remote cork woods of Merida.

I finished eating and went over to the dish of burning ashes. It was mid-winter and the windy passage across the bay had chilled my blood. The man pushed his chair away as I drew mine forwards.

'Don't move,' I said. 'There's heaps of room for two.'

I lit a cigar and offered one to him. In Spain, the Havana from Gib is never unwelcome.

'I don't mind if I do,' he said, stretching out his hand.

I recognized the singing speech of Glasgow. But the stranger was not talkative, and my efforts at conversation broke down before his monosyllables. We smoked in silence. He was even bigger than I had thought, with great broad shoulders and ungainly limbs; his face was sunburned, his hair short and grizzled. His features were hard; mouth, ears and nose were large and heavy and his skin much wrinkled. His blue eyes were pale. He was constantly pulling his grey moustache. It was a nervous gesture that I found faintly irritating. Presently I felt that he was looking at me, and the intensity of his stare grew so irksome that I glanced up expecting him, as before, to drop his eyes. He did, indeed, for a moment, but then raised them again. He inspected me from under his long, bushy eyebrows.

'Just come from Gib?' he asked suddenly.

'Yes.'

'I'm going tomorrow – on my way home. Thank God.'

He said the last two words so fiercely that I smiled.

'Don't you like Spain?'

'Oh, Spain's all right.'

'Have you been here long?'

'Too long. Too long.'

He spoke with a kind of gasp. I was surprised at the emotion my casual inquiry seemed to excite in him. He sprang to his feet and walked backwards and forwards. He stamped to and fro like a caged beast, pushing aside a chair that stood in his way, and now and again repeated the words in a groan. 'Too long. Too long.' I sat still. I was embarrassed. To give myself countenance I stirred the *brasero* to bring the hotter ashes to the top, and he stood suddenly still, towering over me, as though my movement had brought back my existence to his notice. Then he sat down heavily in his chair.

'D'you think I'm queer?' he asked.

'Not more than most people,' I smiled.

'You don't see anything strange in me?'

He leant forward as he spoke so that I might see him well.

'No.'

'You'd say so if you did, wouldn't you?'

'I would.'

I couldn't quite understand what all this meant. I wondered if he was drunk. For two or three minutes he didn't say anything and I had no wish to interrupt the silence.

'What's your name?' he asked suddenly. I told him.

'Mine's Robert Morrison.'

'Scotch?'

'Glasgow. I've been in the blasted country for years. Got any baccy?'

I gave him my pouch and he filled his pipe. He lit it from a piece of burning charcoal.

'I can't stay any longer. I've stayed too long. Too long.'

He had an impulse to jump up again and walk up and down, but he resisted it, clinging to his chair. I saw on his face the effort he was making. I judged that his restlessness was due to chronic alcoholism. I find drunks very boring, and I made up my mind to take an early opportunity of slipping off to bed.

'I've been managing some olive groves,' he went on. 'I'm here working for the Glasgow and South of Spain Olive Oil Company Limited.'

'Oh, yes.'

'We've got a new process for refining oil, you know. Properly treated, Spanish oil is every bit as good as Lucca. And we can sell it cheaper.'

He spoke in a dry matter-of-fact, business-like way. He chose his words with Scotch precision. He seemed perfectly sober.

'You know, Ecija is more or less the centre of the olive trade, and we had a Spaniard there to look after the business. But I found he was robbing us right and left, so I had to turn him out. I used to live in Seville; it was more convenient for shipping the oil. However, I found I couldn't get a trustworthy man to be at Ecija, so last year I went there myself. D'you know it?'

'No.'

'The firm has got a big estate two miles from the town, just outside the village of San Lorenzo, and it's got a fine house on it. It's the crest of a hill, rather pretty to look at, all white, you know, and straggling, with a couple of storks perched on the roof. No one lived there, and I thought it would save the rent of a place in town if I did.'

'It must have been a bit lonely,' I remarked.

'It was.'

Robert Morrison smoked on for a minute or two in silence. I wondered whether there was any point in what he was telling me.

I looked at my watch.

'In a hurry?' he asked sharply.

'Not particularly. It's getting late.'

'Well, what of it?'

'I suppose you didn't see many people?' I said, going back.

'Not many. I lived there with an old man and his wife who looked after me, and sometimes I used to go down to the village and play *tresillo* with Fernàndez, the chemist, and one or two men who met at his shop. I used to shoot a bit and ride.'

'It doesn't sound such a bad life to me.'

'I'd been there two years last spring. By God, I've never known such heat as we had in May. No one could do a thing. The labourers just lay about in the shade and slept. Sheep died and some of the animals went mad. Even the oxen couldn't work. They stood around with their backs all humped up and gasped for breath. That blasted sun beat down and the glare was so awful, you felt your eyes would shoot out of your head. The earth cracked and crumbled, and the crops frizzled. The olives went to rack and ruin. It was simply hell. One couldn't get a wink of sleep. I went from room to room; trying to get a breath of air. Of course I kept the windows shut and had the floors watered, but that didn't do any good. The nights were just as hot as the days. It was like living in an oven.

'At last I thought I'd have a bed made up for me downstairs on the north side of the house in a room that was never used because in ordinary weather it was damp. I had an idea that I might get a few hours' sleep there at all events. Anyhow it was worth trying. But it was no damned good; it was a wash-out. I turned and tossed and my bed was so hot that I couldn't stand it. I got up and opened the doors that led to the veranda and walked out. It was a glorious night. The moon was so bright that I swear you could read a book by it. Did I tell you the house was on the crest of a hill? I leant against the parapet and looked at the olive trees. It was like the sea. I suppose that's what made me think of home. I thought of the cool breeze in the fir trees and the racket of the streets in Glasgow. Believe it or not, I could smell them, and I could smell the sea. By God, I'd have given every bob I had in the world for an hour of that air. They say it's a foul climate in Glasgow. Don't you believe it. I like the rain and the grey sky and that yellow sea and the waves. I forgot that I was in Spain, in the middle of the olive country, and I opened my mouth and took a long breath as though I were breathing in the sea-fog.

'And then all of a sudden I heard a sound. It was a man's voice. Not loud, you know, low, it seemed to creep through the silence like – well, I don't know what it was like. It surprised me. I couldn't think who could be down there in the olives at that hour. It was past midnight. It was a chap laughing. A funny sort of laugh. I suppose you'd call it a chuckle. It seemed to crawl up the hill – disjointedly.'

Morrison looked at me to see how I took the odd word he used to express a sensation that he didn't know how to describe.

'I mean, it seemed to shoot up in little jerks, something like shooting stones out of a pail. I leant forward and stared. With the full moon it was almost as light as day, but I'm dashed if I could see a thing. The sound stopped, but I kept on looking at where it had come from in case somebody moved. And in a minute it started off again, but louder. You couldn't have called it a chuckle any more, it was a real belly laugh. It just rang through the night. I wondered it didn't wake my servants. It sounded like someone who was roaring drunk.

'"Who's there?" I shouted.

The only answer I got was a roar of laughter. I don't mind telling you I was getting a bit annoyed. I had half a mind to go down and see what it was all about. I wasn't going to let some drunken swine kick up a row like that on my place in the middle of the night. And then suddenly there was a yell. By God, I was startled. Then cries. The man had laughed with a deep bass voice, but his cries were – shrill, like a pig having his throat cut.

'"My God",' I cried.

'I jumped over the parapet and ran down towards the sound. I thought somebody was being killed. There was silence and then one piercing shriek. After that sobbing and moaning. I'll tell you what it sounded like, it sounded like someone at the point of death. There was a long groan and then nothing. Silence. I ran from place to place. I couldn't find anyone. At last I climbed the hill again and went back to my room.

'You can imagine how much sleep I got that night. As soon as it was light, I looked out of the window in the direction from which the row had come and I was surprised to see a little white house in a sort of dale among the olives. The ground on that side didn't belong to us and I'd never been through it. I hardly ever went to that part of the house and so I'd never seen the house before. I asked José who lived there. He told me that a madman had inhabited it, with his brother and a servant.

'Oh, was that the explanation?' I said. 'Not a very nice neighbour.'

The Scot bent over quickly and seized my wrist. He thrust his face into mine and his eyes were starting out of his head with terror.

'The madman had been dead for twenty years,' he whispered.

He let go my wrist and leant back in his chair, panting.

'I went down to the house and walked all round it. The windows were barred and shuttered and the door was locked. I knocked, I shook the handle and rang the bell. I heard it tinkle, but no one came. It was a two-storey house and I looked up. The shutters were tight closed, and there wasn't a sign of life anywhere.'

'Well, what sort of condition was the house in?' I asked.

'Oh, rotten. The whitewash had worn off the walls and there was practically no paint left on the door or the shutters. Some of the tiles off the roof were lying on the ground. They looked as though they'd been blown away in a gale.'

'Queer,' I said.

'I went to my friend Fernàndez, the chemist, and he told me the same story as José. I asked about the madman and Fernàndez said that no one ever saw him. He was more or less comatose ordinarily, but now and then he had an attack of acute mania and then he could be heard from ever so far laughing his head off and then crying. It used to scare people. He died in one of his attacks and his keepers cleared out at once. No one had ever dared to live in the house since.

'I didn't tell Fernàndez what I'd heard. I thought he'd only laugh at me. I stayed up that night and kept watch. But nothing happened. There wasn't a sound. I waited about till dawn and then I went to bed.'

'And you never heard anything more?'

'Not for a month. The drought continued and I went on sleeping in the lumber-room at the back. One night I was fast asleep, when something seemed to happen to me; I don't exactly know how to describe it, it was a funny feeling as though someone had given me a little nudge, to warn me, and suddenly I was wide awake. I lay there in my bed and then in the same way as before I heard a long, low gurgle, like a man enjoying an old joke. It came from away down in the valley and it got louder. It was a great bellow of laughter. I jumped out of bed and went to the window. My legs began to tremble. It was horrible to stand there and listen to the shouts of laughter that rang through the night. Then there was the pause, and after that a shriek of pain and that ghastly sobbing. It didn't sound human. I mean, you might have thought it was an animal being tortured. I don't mind telling you I was scared stiff. I couldn't have moved if I'd wanted to. After a time the sounds stopped, not suddenly, but dying away little by little. I strained my ears, but I couldn't hear a thing. I crept back to bed and hid my face.

'I remembered then that Fernàndez had told me that the madman's attacks only came at intervals. The rest of the time he went quite quiet. Apathetic, Fernàndez said. I wondered if the fits of mania came regularly. I reckoned out how long it had been between the two attacks I'd heard. Twenty-eight days. It didn't take me long to put two and two together; it was quite obvious that it was the full moon that set him off. I'm not a nervous man really and I made up my mind to get to the bottom of it, so I looked out in the calendar which day the moon would be full next and that night I didn't go to bed. I clasped my revolver and loaded it. I prepared a lantern and sat down on the parapet of my house to wait. I felt perfectly cool. To tell you the truth, I was rather pleased with myself because I didn't feel scared. There was a bit of wind, and it whistled about the roof. It rustled over the leaves of the olive trees like waves swishing on the pebbles of the beach. The moon shone on the white walls of the house in the hollow. I felt particularly cheery.

'At last I heard a little sound, the sound I knew, and I almost laughed. I was right; it was the full moon and the attacks came as regular as clockwork. That was all to the good. I threw myself over the wall into the olive grove and ran straight to the house. The chuckling grew louder as I came near. I got to the house and looked up. There was no light anywhere, I put my ears to the door and listened. I heard the madman simply laughing his bloody head off. I beat on the door with my fist and I pulled the bell. The sound of it seemed to amuse him. He roared with laughter. I knocked again, louder and louder, and the more I knocked the more he laughed. Then I shouted at the top of my voice.

'"Open the blasted door, or I'll break it down."

'I stepped back and kicked the latch with all my might. I flung myself at the door with the whole weight of my body. It cracked. Then I put all my strength into it and the damned thing smashed open.

'I took the revolver out of my pocket and held my lantern in the other hand. The laughter sounded louder now that the door was opened. I stepped in. The stink nearly knocked me down. I mean, just think, the windows hadn't been opened for twenty years. The row was enough to raise the dead, but for a moment I didn't know where it was coming from. The walls seemed to throw the sound backwards and forwards. I pushed open a door by my side and went into a room. It was bare and white and there wasn't a stick of furniture in it. The sound was louder and I followed it. I went into another room, but there was nothing there. I opened a door and found myself at the foot of a staircase. The madman was laughing just over my head. I walked up, cautiously, you know, I wasn't taking any risks, and at the top of the stairs there was a passage. I walked along it, throwing my light ahead of me, and I came to a room at the end. I stopped. He was in there. I was only separated from the sound by a thin door.

'It was awful to hear it. A shiver passed through me and I cursed myself because I began to tremble. It wasn't like a human being at all. By Jove, I very nearly took to my heels and ran. I had to clench my teeth to force myself to stay. But I simply couldn't bring my self to turn the handle. And then the laughter was cut, cut with a knife you'd have said, and I heard a hiss of pain. I hadn't heard that before, it was too low to carry to my place, and then a gasp.

'"Ay!" I heard the man speak in Spanish. "You're killing me. Take it away. Oh God, help me!"

He screamed. The brutes were torturing him. I flung open the door and burst in. The draught blew a shutter back and the moon streamed in so bright that it dimmed my lantern. In my ears, as clearly as I heard you speak and as close, I heard the wretched chap's groans. It was awful, moaning and sobbing, and frightful gasps. No one could survive that. He was at the point of death. I tell you I heard his broken, choking cries right in my ears. And the room was empty.'

Robert Morrison sank back in his chair. That huge solid man had strangely the look of a lay figure in a studio. You felt that if you pushed him he would fall over in a heap onto the floor.

'And then?' I asked.

He took a rather dirty handkerchief out of his pocket and wiped his forehead.

'I felt I didn't much want to sleep in that room on the north side, so, heat or no heat, I moved back to my own quarters. Well, exactly four weeks later, about two in the morning, I was waked up by the madman's chuckle. It was almost at my elbow. I don't mind telling you that my nerve was a bit shaken by then, so next time the blighter was due to have an attack, next time the moon was full, I mean, I got Fernàndez to come and spend the night with me. I didn't tell him anything. I kept him up playing cards till two in the morning, and then I heard it again. I asked him if he heard anything. "Nothing," he said. "There's somebody laughing," I said. "You're drunk, man," he said, and he began laughing too. That was too much. "Shut up, you fool," I said. The laughter grew louder and louder. I cried out. I tried to shut it out by putting my hands to my ears, but it wasn't a damned bit of good. I heard it and I heard the scream of pain. Fernàndez thought I was mad. He didn't dare say so, because he knew I'd have killed him. He said he'd go to bed, and in the morning I found he'd slunk away. His bed hadn't been slept it. He'd taken himself off when he left me.

'After that I couldn't stop in Ecija. I put a factor there and went back to Seville. I felt myself pretty safe there, but as the time came near I began to get scared. Of course I told myself not to be a damned fool, but, you know, I damned well couldn't help myself. The fact is, I was afraid the sounds had followed me, and I knew if I heard them in Seville I'd go on hearing them all my life. I've got as much courage as any man, but damn it all, there are limits to everything. Flesh and blood couldn't stand it. I knew I'd go stark staring mad. I got in such a state that I began drinking, the suspense was so awful, and I used to lie awake counting the days. And at last I knew it'd come. And it came. I heard those sounds in Seville – sixty miles away from Ecija.'

I didn't know what to say. I was silent for a while.

'When did you hear the sounds last?' I asked.

'Four weeks ago.'

I looked up quickly. I was startled.

'What d'you mean by that? It's not full moon tonight?'

He gave me a dark, angry look. He opened his mouth to speak and then stopped as though he couldn't. You would have said his vocal cords were paralysed, and it was with a strange croak that at last he answered.

'Yes, it is.'

He stared at me and his pale blue eyes seemed to shine red. I have never seen in a man's face a look of such terror. He got up quickly and stalked out of the room, slamming the door behind him.

I must admit that I didn't sleep any too well that night myself.

# The Hostelry

## *Guy de Maupassant*

At the foot of the glaciers, in those naked and rock-bound *couloirs* which indent the snow-clad ranges of the High Alps, you will find every here and there a guest house. These little hostelries are constructed of timber and are all built very much to the same pattern. The Schwarenbach Inn was one of them.

The Schwarenbach served as a refuge to travellers attempting the passage of the Gemmi. For the six summer months it remained open, with Jean Hauser's family in residence; but as soon as the early snows began to accumulate, filling the valley and rendering the descent to Loeche impracticable, Jean Hauser with his three sons and his wife and daughter quitted the house, leaving it in charge of the old guide Gaspard Hari and his companion, together with Sam, the big mountainbred dog. The two men, with the dog, lived in their prison of snow until the spring arrived. They had nothing to look at, except the vast white slopes of the Balmhorn. Pale glistening mountain peaks rose all round them. They were shut in, blockaded, by the snow; it lay on them like a shroud, growing ever deeper and deeper until the little house was enveloped, closed in, obliterated. The snow piled itself upon the roof, blinded the windows and walled up the door.

On the day on which the Hauser family took their departure for Loeche, the winter was close at hand, and the descent was becoming dangerous. The three sons set off on foot leading three mules laden with household belongings. Behind them followed the mother, Jeanne Hauser, and her daughter Louise, both riding the same mule. Next and last came the father and the two caretakers. The latter were to accompany the family as far as the beginning of the track that leads down the mountain-side to Loeche.

The party first skirted the edge of the little lake, already frozen, in its rocky hollow in front of the inn; then they proceeded along the valley, which lay before them, a white sheet of snow, with icy peaks dominating it on every side. A flood of sunshine fell across the whiteness of this frozen wilderness, lighting it up with a cold, blinding brilliance. There was no sign of life in this sea of mountains; not a movement could be seen in the limitless solitude; not a sound disturbed the profound silence.

Gradually the younger of the guides, Ulrich Kunsi, a tall long-limbed Swiss, forged ahead of the two older men and overtook the mule on which the two women were riding. The daughter saw him as he approached and there was sadness in the glance with which she summoned him to her side.

She was a little peasant girl with a complexion like milk. Her flaxen hair was so pale that one would fancy it had been bleached by prolonged residence amongst the snows and glaciers.

On overtaking the mule on which Louise and her mother were riding, Ulrich Kunsi placed his hand on the crupper and slackened his pace. The mother began talking; she expounded in infinite detail her instructions for wintering. It was the first time that Ulrich had stayed behind. Old Hari, on the other hand, had already accomplished his fourteenth hibernation, under the snow that covered the Schwarenbach Inn.

Ulrich listened, but without any appearance of grasping what was said. He never took his eyes off the daughter. Every now and then he would reply: 'Yes, Madame Hauser.' But his thoughts seemed far away, and his face remained calm and impassive.

They reached the Daubensee, which lies at the foot of the valley. Its surface was now a vast level sheet of ice. On the right, the rocks of the Daubenhorn, dark and precipitous, rose above the vast moraines of the Lemmern Glacier, and the Wildstrubel towered over all.

As they approached the Gemmi saddle, from which begins the descent to Loeche, they suddenly beheld, across the deep wide valley of the Rhone, the prodigious sky-line of the Valais Alps, a distant multitude of white peaks of unequal size, some pointed, some flattened, but all glistening in the rays of the sun.

There was the two-horned Mischabel, the majestic mass of the Weisshorn, the lumbering Brunegghorn, the lofty and fear-inspiring Cervin, which has killed so many men, and the Dent-Blanche, monstrous yet alluring. Below them, in an enormous hollow at the foot of terrifying precipices, they caught sight of Loeche, so far away from them that the houses seemed like a handful of sand, thrown down into the vast crevasse which has at one end the barrier of the Gemmi, and at the other a wide exit to the Rhone valley.

They had reached the head of a path, which winds downwards in serpentine coils, fantastic and extraordinary, along the mountainside, until it reaches the almost invisible village at the foot. The mule stopped and the two women jumped down into the snow. By this time the two older men had overtaken the rest of the party.

'Now, friends,' said old Hauser, 'we must say goodbye till next year. And keep your hearts up.'

'Till next year,' replied Hari.

The men embraced. Madame Hauser gave her cheek to be kissed and her daughter followed her example. When it was Ulrich Kunsi's turn to kiss Louise, he whispered in her ear:

'Don't forget us up on our heights.'

'No,' she replied in tones so low that he guessed, rather than heard, the word.

'Well, well, goodbye,' said old Hauser again. 'Take care of yourselves.'

He strode on past the women and led the way downwards. All three were lost to view at the first bend in the track. Gaspard and Ulrich turned back towards the Schwarenbach Inn. They walked slowly and in silence, side by side. They had seen the last of their friends. They were to be alone, with no other companionship, for four or five months.

Gaspard Hari began to tell Ulrich about the previous winter. His companion then had been Michael Carol; but accidents were likely to happen during the long solitude, and Michael had grown too old for the job. Still, they had had a pretty good time together. The secret of the whole thing was to make up your mind to it from the beginning. Sooner or later one invented distractions and games and things to while away the time.

With downcast eyes Ulrich Kunsi listened to his companion, but his thoughts were following the women, who were making their way to the village, down the zigzag path on the Gemmi mountainside.

They soon caught sight of the distant inn. It looked very tiny, like a black dot at the base of the stupendous mountain of snow. When they opened the door of the house, Sam, the great curly-haired dog, gambolled round them joyfully.

'Well, Ulrich, my boy,' said old Gaspard, 'we have no women here now. We must get dinner ready ourselves. You can set to and peel the potatoes.'

They sat down on wooden stools and began to prepare the soup. The forenoon of the following day seemed long to Ulrich Kunsi. Old Hari smoked his pipe and spat into the fireplace. The younger man looked through the window at the superb mountain, which rose in front of the house. In the afternoon he went out, and pursuing the road he had taken the previous day, he followed the tracks of the mule on which the two women had ridden. He arrived at last at the saddle of the Gemmi, and lying prone on the edge of the precipice, gazed down on Loeche. The village, nestling in its rocky hollow, had not yet been obliterated by the snow. But there was snow very near it. Its advance had been arrested by the pine forests which guarded the environs of the hamlet. Seen from a height, the low houses of the village looked like paving-stones set in a field.

Ulrich reflected that Louise Hauser was now in one of those grey cottages. Which one was it, he wondered. They were too remote to be separately distinguished. He had a yearning to go down there while it was still possible. But the sun had disappeared behind the great peak of Wildstrubel, and Ulrich turned homewards. He found Hari smoking. On Ulrich's return Hari proposed a game of cards and the two men sat down on opposite sides of the table. They played for a long time at a simple game called brisque. Then they had supper and went to bed.

Subsequent days were like the first, clear and cold, without any fresh fall of snow. Gaspard passed his days watching the eagles and other rare birds, which adventure themselves in these frozen altitudes. For his part, Ulrich went regularly to the *col* to look down at the distant village. In the evening they played cards, dice and dominoes, staking small objects to lend an interest to the game.

One morning, Hari, who had been the first to rise, called out to Ulrich. A drifting cloud of white foam, deep yet ethereal, was sinking down on them and on all around them, spreading over them slowly, silently, a cover which grew ever thicker and heavier. The snowfall lasted four days and four nights. The door and windows had to be cleared, a passage dug, and steps cut, to enable them to climb out on to the surface of powdery snow, which twelve hours of frost had made harder than the granite of the moraines.

After that, they lived as in a prison, hardly ever venturing outside their dwelling. The household tasks were divided between them and were punctually performed. Ulrich Kunsi undertook the cleaning and washing up and keeping the house neat. He also split the firewood. Hari kept the fire going and did the cooking. These necessary and monotonous tasks were relieved by long contests at dice or cards. Being both of them of calm and placid temperament, they never quarrelled. They never went even as far as to display impatience or peevishness, or to speak sharply to each other, both having determined beforehand to make the best of their wintry sojourn on the heights. Occasionally Gaspard took his gun and went out hunting chamois, and when he had the good luck to kill one, it was high day and holiday in the Schwarenbach Inn and there was great feasting on fresh meat.

One morning Hari set forth on one of these expeditions. The thermometer outside the inn showed thirty degrees of frost. Hari started before sunrise, hoping to take the chamois by surprise on the lower slopes of the Wildstrubel.

Left to himself, Ulrich remained in bed until ten o'clock. He was by nature a good sleeper, but he would not have dared to give way to this proclivity in the presence of the old guide, who was an early riser and always full of energy. He lingered over his breakfast, which he shared with Sam, who passed his days and nights sleeping in front of the fire. After breakfast he felt his spirits oppressed, and almost daunted, by the solitude, and he longed for his daily game of cards with the unconquerable craving that comes of ingrained habit. Later, he went out to meet his comrade, who was due to return at four o'clock.

The whole valley was now of a uniform level under its thick covering of snow. The crevasses were full to the top; the two lakes could no longer be distinguished; the rocks lay hid under a snowy quilt. Lying at the foot of the immense peaks, the valley was now one immense basin, symmetrical, frozen, and of a blinding whiteness.

It was three weeks since Ulrich had been to the edge of the precipice from which he looked down at the village. He thought he would go there again, before climbing the slopes that led to the Wildstrubel. The snow had now reached Loeche, and the houses were lost under their white mantle.

Turning to the right, he reached the Lemmern glacier. He walked with the mountaineer's long stride, driving his iron-pointed stick down on to the snow, which was as hard as stone. With his far-sighted eyes he sought the small black dot which he expected to see moving, in the far distance, over this vast sheet of snow. On reaching the edge of the glacier he stopped, wondering whether old Hari had really come that way. Then, with increasing anxiety and quicker steps, he began to skirt the moraines.

The sun was sinking. The snow was suffused with a tinge of pink, and over its crystalline surface swept sharp gusts of a dry and icy breeze. Ulrich tried to reach his friend with a call, shrill, vibrant, prolonged. His voice took its flight into the deathless silence, in which the mountains slept. It rang far out over the deep motionless undulations of frozen foam, like the cry of a bird over the waves of the sea. Then it died away. And there was no reply.

He walked on and on. The sun had sunk behind the peaks, and the purple glow of sunset still lingered about them, but the depths of the valley were grey and shadowy, and Ulrich was suddenly afraid. He had an idea that the silence, the cold, the solitude were taking possession of him, were about to arrest his circulation and freeze his blood, stiffen his limbs and convert him into a motionless, frozen image. With all speed he could, he ran back towards the inn. Hari, he thought, must have taken another way and reached home already. He would find him seated by the fire, with a dead chamois at his feet. He soon came in sight of the hostelry. There was no smoke issuing from the chimney. Ulrich ran yet faster, and when he opened the door of the house, Sam leaped up to greet him. But there was no Gaspard Hari.

In consternation Kunsi turned hither and thither, as though expecting to find his comrade hiding in a corner. Then he relighted the fire and made the soup, still hoping that he would look up and see the old man coming in. From time to time he went outside, in case there should be some sign of him. Night had fallen, that wan, livid night of mountains, illumined only by the slender, yellow crescent of a new moon, which was sinking towards the skyline and would soon disappear behind the ridge.

Returning to the house, Ulrich sat down by the fire and while he was warming his hands and feet, his thoughts ran on possible accidents. Gaspard might have broken a leg, or fallen into a hollow, or made a false step, which had cost him a sprained ankle. He would be lying in the snow, helpless against the benumbing cold, in agony of mind, far from any other human soul, calling out for help, shouting with all the strength of his voice in the silence of the night.

How to discover where he was? So vast and craggy was the mountain, so dangerous the approaches to it, especially in the winter, that it would take ten or twenty guides searching for a week in all directions to find a man in that immensity. None the less Ulrich made up his mind to take Sam and set forth to look for Gaspard, if he had not come back by one in the morning.

He made his preparations. He put two days' provisions into a bag, took his cramp-irons, wound round his waist a long, strong, slender rope, and inspected thoroughly his spiked stick and his ice-axes. Then he waited. The fire was burning with a clear flame; the great dog lay snoring in its warmth; the steady ticking of the clock, in its resonant wooden case, sounded like the beating of a heart. Still he waited, his ears straining to catch any distant noise. When the light breeze whispered round roof and walls, he shivered.

The clock struck the hour of midnight. Feeling chilled and nervous, he put some water on the fire to boil, so that he might have some steaming coffee before setting out. When the clock struck one, he rose, called Sam, opened the door and struck out in the direction of the Wildstrubel. He climbed for five hours continuously. He scaled the rocks with the help of his irons, and cut steps in the ice with his axe, always advancing steadily and sometimes hauling the dog after him up some steep escarpment. It was about six o'clock when he reached one of the peaks to which Gaspard often came in search of chamois. There he waited for the day to break.

The sky above became gradually paler. Then suddenly that strange radiance, which springs no one knows whence, gleamed over the great ocean of snow-clad peaks, stretching for a hundred leagues around him. The vague light seemed to arise out of the snow itself and to diffuse itself in space. One by one, the highest and farthest pinnacles were suffused by a tender rosy hue and the red sun rose from behind the great masses of the Bernese Alps. Ulrich Kunsi set forth again. Like a hunter, he went down, searching for tracks and saying to his dog:

'Seek, old man, seek.'

He was now on his way down the mountain, investigating every chasm, and sometimes sending forth a prolonged call, which quickly died away in the dumb immensity. At times he put his ear close to the ground to listen. Once he thought he heard a voice and he ran in the direction of it, shouting as he ran, but he heard nothing more, and sat down, exhausted and despairing. About mid-day he shared some food with Sam, who was as weary as himself. And again he set out on his search. When evening came, he was still walking, having accomplished fifty kilometres among the mountains. He was too far from his house to think of returning there, and too tired to drag himself along any farther. Digging a hole in the snow, he curled up in it with his dog, under cover of a blanket which he had brought with him. Man and beast lay together, each body sharing the warmth of the other, but frozen to the marrow none the less. Ulrich's mind was haunted by visions, and his limbs were shaking with cold. He could not sleep at all. When he rose, day was on the point of breaking. His legs felt as rigid as bars of iron; his resolution was so enfeebled that he almost sobbed aloud in his distress, and his heart beat so violently that he nearly collapsed with emotion whenever he fancied that he heard a sound.

The thought suddenly came to him that he too might perish of cold amidst these solitudes, and the fear of such a death whipped up his energy and roused him to fresh vigour. He was now making the descent towards the inn, and kept falling down from weariness and picking himself up again. His dog Sam, with one paw disabled, followed far behind, limping. It was four o'clock in the afternoon before they reached the Schwarenbach. Hari was not there. Ulrich lighted a fire, had something to eat, and then fell asleep, so utterly stupefied with fatigue that he could think of nothing. He slept for a long, a very long time. It seemed as if nothing could break his repose, when suddenly he heard a voice cry 'Ulrich'. He was shaken out of his profound torpor, and started up. Was it a dream? Was it one of those strange summonses that disturb the slumber of uneasy souls? No. He could hear it still. That quivering hail had pierced his ear, had taken possession of his body, right to the tips of his nervous fingers. Beyond all doubt, there had been a cry for help, an appeal for succour. Someone had called out 'Ulrich!' Then someone must be in the vicinity of the house. There could be no question about it. He opened the door and shouted with all his strength, 'Gaspard, is that you?'

There was no reply. The silence was not broken by sound, or whisper, or groan. It was night, and the snow lay all around, ghastly in its whiteness.

The wind had risen. It was that icy wind which splits the rocks and leaves nothing alive on these forsaken altitudes. It blew in sharp, withering gusts, dealing death more surely than even the fiery blasts of the desert. Again Ulrich called out:

'Gaspard, Gaspard, Gaspard!'

He waited a little, but silence still reigned on the mountainside, and he was forthwith stricken by a terror which shook him to the very bones. He leaped back into the inn, closed and bolted the door, and with chattering teeth collapsed into a chair. He was now sure that the appeal for help had come from his comrade, at the moment at which he was yielding up the ghost. He was as certain of that as one is of being alive or eating bread. For two days and three nights old Gaspard Hari had been wrestling with death in some hollow in one of those deep unsullied ravines, whose whiteness is more sinister than the darkness of underground caverns. For two days and three nights he had been dying, and at this very moment, while he lay in the article of death, his thoughts had turned to his comrade, and his soul, in the instant of gaining its freedom, had flown to the inn where Ulrich lay sleeping. It had exercised that mysterious and terrible power, possessed by the souls of the dead, to haunt the living. The voiceless spirit had called aloud in the overwrought soul of the sleeper, had uttered its last farewell, or, perhaps, its reproach, its curse on the man who had not searched diligently enough.

Ulrich felt its presence there, behind the walls of the house, behind the door, which he had just closed. The soul was prowling around. It was like a bird of night fluttering against a lighted window. Ulrich, distraught with terror, was ready to scream. He would have taken to flight, but dared not open the door. And never again, he felt, would he dare to open that door, for the spectre would be hovering, day and night, round the inn, until the corpse of the old guide had been recovered and laid in the consecrated earth of a cemetery.

When day broke, Ulrich regained a little confidence from the brilliance of the returning sun. He prepared his breakfast and made some soup for the dog, but after that he remained seated motionless in a chair. His heart was in agony; his thoughts turned ever to the old man, who was lying out there in the snow. When night again descended upon the mountains, new terrors assailed him. He paced to and fro in the smoke-blackened kitchen, by the dim light of a solitary candle. Up and down he strode, and always he was listening, for that cry which had terrified him the night before. Might it not ring out again through the mournful silence of the outer world? He felt forlorn, poor wretch; forlorn, as never a man had been, here in this vast whiteness of snow, all alone, seven thousand feet above the inhabited world, above the dwellings of men, above the excitements, the hubbub, the noise, the thrills of life; alone in the frozen sky. He was torn by a mad desire to make his escape in whatsoever direction, by whatsoever means; to descend to Loeche, even if he had to hurl himself over the precipice. But he did not dare so much as to open the door; he felt sure that that thing outside, the dead man, would bar his passage and prevent him from leaving his comrade alone upon those heights.

As midnight approached his limbs grew weary, and fear and distress overcame him. He dreaded his bed, as one dreads a haunted spot, but yielding at last to drowsiness he sank into a chair.

Suddenly his ears were pierced by the same strident cry that he had heard the previous night. It was so shrill that Ulrich stretched out his hands to ward off the ghost, and losing his balance fell backwards on to the floor. Aroused by the noise, the dog began to howl in terror, and ran hither and thither in the room, trying to find out whence the danger threatened. When he came to the door, he sniffed at the edge of it, and began howling, snorting, and snarling, his hair bristling, his tail erect. Beside himself with terror, Kunsi rose and, grasping a stool by one leg, shouted:

'Don't come in. Don't come in. Don't come in or I'll kill you.'

Excited by his menacing tones, the dog barked furiously at the invisible enemy whom his master was challenging. Gradually Sam calmed down, and went back to lie on the hearth, but he was still uneasy; his eyes were gleaming and he was baring his fangs and growling. Ulrich, too, regained his wits; but, feeling faint with terror, he took a bottle of brandy from the sideboard and drank several glasses of it in quick succession. As his mind became duller his courage rose, and a feverish heat coursed along his veins. On the following day he ate hardly anything, confining himself to the brandy, and for some days after he lived in a state of brutish intoxication. The moment the thought of Gaspard Hari crossed his mind, he began drinking and he did not leave off until he collapsed to the ground in a drunken torpor, and lay there face downwards, snoring and helpless. Hardly had he recovered from the effects of the burning and maddening liquor, when the cry 'Ulrich!' roused him, as though a bullet had penetrated his skull. He started to his feet staggering to and fro, stretching out his hands to keep himself from falling, and calling to his dog to help him. Sam, too, appeared to be seized with his master's madness. He hurled himself against the door, scratching at it with his claws, gnawing it with his long white teeth, while Ulrich, with his head thrown back, his face turned upwards, swallowed brandy in great gulps, as though he were drinking cool water after a climb. Presently his thoughts, his memory, his terror, would be drowned in drunken oblivion.

In three weeks he had finished his entire stock of spirits. But the only effect of his inebriation was to lull his terror to sleep. When the means for this were no longer available, his fears returned with fresh ferocity. His fixed idea, aggravated by prolonged intoxication, gained force continually in that absolute solitude, and worked its way, like a gimlet, ever deeper into his spirit. Like a wild beast in a cage, he paced his room, every now and then putting his ear to the door to listen for the voice of Gaspard's ghost, and hurling defiance at it through the wall. And when, in utter weariness, he lay down, he would again hear the voice and leap once more to his feet. At last, one night, with the courage of a coward driven to bay, he flung himself at the door and opened it, to see who it was who was calling him, and to compel him to silence. But the cold air struck him full in the face, and froze him to the marrow. He slammed the door to again, and shot the bolts, never noticing that his dog had dashed out into the open. Shivering, he threw some more wood on to the fire and sat down to warm himself. Suddenly he started. There was someone scratching at the wall and moaning.

'Go away,' he said, terror-stricken.

The answer was a melancholy wail.

His last remaining vestiges of reason were swept away by fear.

'Go away,' he cried again, and he turned hither and thither in an effort to find some corner in which he could hide himself. But the creature outside continued to wail, and passed along the front of the house, rubbing itself against the wall. Ulrich dashed to the oaken sideboard, which was full of provisions and crockery, and with superhuman strength dragged it across the room and set it against the door to act as a barricade. Then he took all the remaining furniture, mattresses, palliasses, chairs, and blockaded the window, as if in a state of siege. But the thing outside went on groaning dismally, and Ulrich himself was soon replying with groans not less lugubrious. Days and nights passed, and still these two continued to answer each other's howls.

The ghost, as it seemed to Ulrich, moved unceasingly round the house, scratching at the walls with its nails in a fierce determination to break a way through. Within the house, Ulrich crouched with his ear close to the masonry, following every movement of the thing outside, and answering all its appeals with horrifying shrieks. Then came a night when Ulrich heard no more sounds from without. Overcome with fatigue, he dropped into a chair and fell asleep immediately. When he awoke, his mind and memory were a blank. It was as if that sleep of prostration had swept his brain clean of everything. He felt hungry and took some food . . .

The winter was over. The passage of the Gemmi became practicable; and the Hauser family set forth on its journey to the inn. At the top of the first long acclivity, the two women clambered up on to their mule. They spoke about the two men, whom they expected presently to meet again. They were surprised that neither of them had descended a few days earlier, as soon as the Loeche road was practicable, to give them the news of their long winter sojourn. When they came in sight of the inn, which was still covered with a thick mantle of snow, they saw that the door and window were closed, but old Hauser was reassured by a thin column of smoke which was rising from the chimney. As he drew nearer, however, he saw on the outer threshold the skeleton of an animal. It was a large skeleton, lying on its side, and the flesh had been torn off the bones by eagles.

All three examined it.

'That must be Sam,' Madame Hauser said.

Then she called out for Gaspard, and from the inside of the house came a shrill cry like that of an animal. Old Hauser, too, shouted Gaspard's name. A second cry came from within. The father and his two sons thereupon endeavoured to open the door, but it resisted their efforts. They took a long beam out of an empty stable and used it as a battering-ram. They dashed it with all their strength against the door, which gave way with the shriek of splintering planks. The sideboard fell over on the floor with a great crash which shook the house, and revealed, standing behind it, a man whose hair came down to his shoulders, and whose beard touched his chest. His eyes were bright; his clothing was in rags.

Louise alone recognized him.

'Mamma!' she gasped, 'it is Ulrich.'

And the mother saw that it was indeed Ulrich, although his hair had turned white.

He suffered them to come near and touch him, but when they asked him questions he made no reply. He had to be taken down to Loeche, where the doctors certified that he was insane.

The fate of old Gaspard was never known.

During the following summer Louise Hauser came near to dying of a decline, which was attributed to the rigours of the mountain climate.

# The Phantom of the Lake

*Edmund Mitchell*

My profession is that of a barrister; but a comfortable private income and devoted love for the seclusion of my library have conduced to keep me out of the madding strife of the law courts.

My residence is in London; and when I am not in chambers, I am to be found almost certainly at Eastwood Hall, a dear old house lying in a beautifully wooded park within a few hours' journey from the Metropolis.

Eastwood was the home of my boyhood. Mrs Armitage, who was then its mistress, was my aunt, but throughout my orphaned youth she was to me as a mother. Her two sons, though some ten years younger than myself, I always looked upon as my younger brothers, and as such loved them in my own quiet way. Their father, Colonel Armitage, after a long illness contracted during foreign service, had died when Charles was about three years old, and Norman was beginning to think about cutting his first tooth.

When the great sorrow of her husband's death fell upon Mrs Armitage, I was only a boy myself. Unlike her own sons, however, I was old enough to realize what death meant; and the grief-stricken widow, her young married life blighted almost at its outset, turned to me for such sympathy and consolation as a boy can give. From that hour when the long expected end had come and she flung her arms around my neck, sobbing as if her heart would break, a new bond of affection seemed to unite us. I have always thought that in the years that followed, something of her chastened sorrow passed into my life making me thoughtful beyond my age. Be that as it may, as I grew towards manhood I came to be my aunt's adviser and counsellor in all matters relating to the boys and the property.

The years rolled by, the lads grew to man's estate, and Eastwood ceased to be my home. But my rooms were always kept ready for me at the Hall; and whenever I chose to make my appearance, there was awaiting me a warm welcome from my cousins and their mother.

Nor did I ever lose the position of family adviser. No step of any consequence was taken without my being consulted. Many a trivial little matter for discussion was made the excuse for a pressing invitation to run down to Eastwood, and was accepted by my conscience as a sufficient justification for breaking for a spell from my studies and literary work. I was unfettered by the trammels of wedlock; and was free at any moment to go whither my soul listed.

My mind often travels back to one special occasion on which I was bidden to Eastwood. My visit this time was for a good and sufficient reason. Charles's regiment was ordered rather unexpectedly to India, and he had leave of a few brief days at home before sailing. Of course I had to be at once telegraphed for, as there were a hundred and one things to discuss and arrange.

My poor aunt was in great distress at the prospect of a long parting from her son. Charles himself was in high spirits. A soldier by birth and disposition, he longed for change and adventure. After three or four busy days, the hour of parting came, and on Charles's part no less than his mother's the farewell was a sad and affecting one.

Norman and I accompanied him to Portsmouth, and saw the *Malabar* sail. The two brothers were deeply attached, and poor Norman seemed afraid to open his lips, lest he should betray tears in his voice. There were love and gratitude in Charles's grasp as he wrung my hand for the last time. We watched the vessel steam away, the young soldier standing on the deck with his comrades, his hand again and again waving an adieu. Then we turned sadly away, our faces set homeward.

I accompanied Norman back to Eastwood, and remained there a few days, comforting the mother's anxious heart as best I could. At the end of a fortnight, when I went up to London, Mrs Armitage had begun to speak cheerfully and hopefully of her absent boy.

Six months passed by, and Norman too had gone from the home nest, having entered the Diplomatic Service and become attached to a foreign Embassy. We heard regularly from Charles in India; he wrote long letters to his mother, and these, by previous arrangement, were sent by her to Norman and by Norman to me. Thus we all had the full benefit of his news and in return hardly a mail passed without each of us giving him a letter.

It was now midsummer – Charles had sailed early in the year. I had not been out of London for more than a month, and the weather was oppressively hot and sultry. For some days I had felt overcome with ennui, and disinclined for work of any kind.

At last, one morning when I looked forth, and saw that we were in for another baking day, I gave in; escaped from the hot streets and glaring pavements, and found myself speeding through green fields and over bubbling brooks towards Eastwood.

The warmest of welcomes awaited me. Now that both her sons were away, Mrs Armitage felt her life dull and cheerless, and she was grateful when I announced my intention of staying with her for at least two or three weeks. Our tête-à-tête dinner that evening was a pleasant one: our conversation all in regard to the absent ones and their letters. An Indian mail was almost due, and the news it would bring was eagerly canvassed.

Shortly after ten o'clock we retired to rest. My rooms, on the ground floor in one of the wings, had french windows opening on to the lawn. On reaching them, I flung the windows wide; and lighting a shaded lamp, set myself to read, with the cool night air caressing my forehead.

But somehow that night I could not fix my thoughts on my book. At last after one or two vain efforts, I rose, lit a cigar, turned down the lamp, and drawing the windows softly behind me, sauntered forth into the park.

One of the great attractions of Eastwood is the lake; in breadth it at no point exceeds a stone's throw, but, as it winds about, its length extends beyond a mile.

From earliest boyhood the lake had been replete with memories of boating, fishing, swimming and skating. Thither that night I bent my footsteps, sauntering slowly along. A quarter of an hour sufficed to bring me to the wooded path that followed the windings of the water. At last I came to the boat-house, in front of which the lake was at its broadest. I seated myself on a bench; and having finished my cigar, gave myself up to the luxury of meditation.

The moonlight streamed upon the water, the surface where its silvery sheen fell in bright contrast to the dark shadows thrown by the trees and by the scattered shrub-clad islets. A balmy zephyr blew down the valley, faintly rustling the leaves and rippling the water at my feet.

Seated there, I felt like one of the Lotophagi of old, filled with perfect bliss, forgetful of time past and unmindful of time to come. I heard the ripple of the water and the rustle of the leaves. I had the faint consciousness of the distant chiming of the clock in the village church tower. Ever and anon, also, the splash of a trout rising to a moth broke upon my ear; otherwise, not a sound invaded the perfect stillness of the night.

A full hour may have passed thus, when I was roused in a second from this stage of half-dreaming trance. I leaned forward, eagerly listening.

It was a strange sound to hear on a midsummer night, yet my practised ear could liken it to nothing but the rhythmical ring of a skater sweeping in long curves over an ice-bound sheet of water.

The sound for a brief space faded without dying away. I had heard the same effect a hundred times before, when on winter nights I had outstripped Charles or Norman, and had waited for them at the boat-house until they rounded the bend some hundred yards farther up. As this thought flashed through my mind, the sound again gradually grew in my ear, and now I could distinguish the sharp clang of the steel as it met the surface of the ice and the dull swish of the succeeding stroke.

Almost involuntarily I strained my eyes towards the bend, which was over-shadowed by lofty trees and bathed in inky blackness. My trained ear followed and interpreted every modulation of the sound, and my heart murmured, 'Now, he is round.'

At the same instant there shot out from the dark shadow onto the silvery surface of the moonlit water what in all truth seemed to be the form of a skater advancing with rapid, bold sweeps. Fascinated and for the moment dead to other thoughts, I watched every graceful movement. In a brief second the figure was almost abreast of the boat-house. There was a shadowy indistinctness about it, but it seemed that of a young man of noble bearing, wearing a broad-brimmed hat, a dark cloak closely muffled around him.

Soon the skater had shot up almost opposite to where I stood. Then, without warning, the arms were flung forward, there was a faint cry of alarm, and the figure seemed to sink into the water.

At that moment the boughs of the trees around me bent as if before the wind, and a wintry blast swept past me, whirling it almost seemed snowflakes in my face, and chilling me to the bone. I was conscious of a succession of wavelets leaping up and dashing against the sides of the boat-house. Then all was still; and when I shook from me the feeling of horror that froze my very heart's blood, the soft balmy midsummer night breeze was playing upon my cheek, and the waters of the lake were rippling peacefully and almost imperceptibly at my feet.

So realistic had been the vision I had seen and the sounds I had heard, that my first impulse was to take a boat, and push out to where the figure disappeared. I rushed to the boat-house door, forgetting in my eagerness that it was always locked except when someone was rowing on the lake. When I realized that I could not get at the boats, I paused to reflect.

While my mind had never given the subject anything but casual and momentary attention, I had always refused belief in the so-called supernatural. I came now to realize, however, that this night I had seen something undreamed of before in my philosophy.

As I turned from the boat-house, and made my way homeward along the tree-lined path, I felt my blood still chilled with fear. I had always considered myself a fairly strong-minded man, and incapable of conjuring up imaginary alarms, but more than once I started at my own shadow, and it was with a feeling of relief that I regained my room.

My sleep that night was fitful and broken, and by seven o'clock I had risen worn out and unrefreshed. Breakfast at the Hall was at nine o'clock. About eight I strolled forth, to see if an hour's walk would restore my spirits.

For a moment I hesitated between the path by the lake and the avenue. I chose the latter.

I had reached the main gates, and was standing looking along the high-road, uncertain whether to retrace my footsteps or prolong my walk, when a gig drove up rapidly from the direction of the village. It soon reached the spot where I stood, and the man who was driving dropped the reins and jumped to the ground. I at once recognized the village postmaster. I saw that his face was pale, and then I caught a glimpse of an ominous yellow envelope in his hand.

'What is wrong, Mr Scott?' I almost gasped.

'Thank heaven I've met you, Mr Hawthorne. I took the message myself off the wire the moment I opened the office, and came straight here.'

'What is it?'

And I took the envelope from his hand and tore it open.

The message was from Calcutta, and was very brief. It was addressed to Mrs Armitage by one of Charles's brother-officers, and told her that her son had died from fever after a six hours' illness.

That was all. 'Details by mail,' were the closing words.

My heart sank within me. For one minute everything seemed to whirl round about me. Then I realized the terrible task that lay before me. In a few seconds I had made up my mind. I jumped into the gig beside Mr Scott and he drove me rapidly into the village. I at once despatched this message to Norman in Paris: 'Come home at once; let nothing delay you.'

Then I got Scott to drive me back to the park gates. My last words to him were: 'Remember, not a whisper of this must reach Mrs Armitage till Mr Norman's return. The secret meanwhile lies with you and me.'

I was a little late for breakfast. Heaven knows how I got through the meal. I excused my absence of mind and my inability to converse on the plea of a sick headache. After rising from the table, I withdrew to my room, and eagerly consulted Bradshaw. I found that Norman could be here at six-thirty the next morning.

The day passed like a restless dream; I moved about and spoke mechanically. I was afraid to shut myself up in my room, for I wanted to be near my aunt in order that I might guard against the bare possibility of the terrible news breaking on her unexpectedly.

I was thankful when night came, and she retired to rest. As for myself, the succeeding hours were spent in sleeplessly walking to and fro. How the night dragged its slow length along!

At last daylight broke. By five o'clock I was at the little roadside station. An hour later the kind-hearted postmaster joined me. He offered to apologize for coming, but – 'You see, sir, I couldn't help it.' His voice spoke his sympathy, and without one friend to consult I was grateful for his company.

The train arrived to the minute, and Norman sprang on to the platform. His face was pale and anxious.

'What is wrong, Harry?' he asked eagerly. 'Is it my mother?'

'No,' I faltered.

'Charley then?'

In another moment he knew all.

We started for the Hall, Mr Scott undertaking to look after the luggage. I took him to my own rooms, gaining admittance by the french windows, and no one in the house knew that Norman had come home.

By eight o'clock he had recovered from his first shock of grief and was able to discuss with me the dreaded duty that awaited us, of breaking the news to his mother.

I will not attempt to describe the scene that followed. When Mrs Armitage entered the breakfast parlour, my face must have told her that some terrible trouble had fallen amongst us. I faltered out Charles's name. Thank God I had Norman at hand for her to fold to her heart. With him left, she had still someone to live for.

It was several months ere I ventured to speak to my aunt in regard to the vision I had seen on the lake the night before receiving the terrible news that Charles was dead. From the first the two events became associated in my mind, but I feared to mention the subject. But the day came when we could converse calmly and resignedly about him that was gone.

Then I learned for the first time the story of the Phantom of the Lake. It was based on a family legend that several generations back the youthful owner of Eastwood Hall had gone out to skate the very night before his marriage. It had been a severe winter, and the ice was perfectly safe, so that his friends did not seek to prevent his going, though no one felt inclined to accompany him. But on the lake that afternoon a portion of the ice had been broken to allow swimming room for the swans. No eye saw the accident; no one was at hand to render help. But next morning the body was found and the young maiden who that day should have become a bride, lost her reason when she beheld her lover's lifeless form.

Hence grew the legend that never an Armitage dies a sudden or violent death but some member of the family sees the phantom skater on the ice, and hears his last bubbling cry across the waters.

Colonel Armitage had imparted the family story to his wife, and both agreed that it would be better to let the weird legend fade into oblivion. He himself had passed away after a long and lingering illness, and there was no report of any supernatural manifestation to mark the event. So the strange story had died out, carefully concealed by the one or two who knew it, and not until now had it reached my ears.

Well, time advanced with inaudible and noiseless step, and another five or six years rolled over our heads. Norman was rising in the Diplomatic Service, and bid fair to be a future statesman. Mrs Armitage was still with us, and reigned as mistress of the Hall. I spent many months of each year with her.

Once again I was bidden to Eastwood in regard to a family matter of importance. Norman was coming home from Berlin to get married. He would start for England in about a fortnight's time.

The news was not unexpected, but it created quite a stir in the household. The next two weeks were spent in busy preparations for Norman's welcome home, and also for the event that was to follow when he would bring a bride to the old Hall.

Every arrangement had been made, and we were now expecting his arrival almost hour by hour. His last letter had stated that he would leave at the earliest possible moment, but he could not say definitely to a day when he would be released from his post.

It was early autumn, and the weather was close and sultry. The cool of the evening was the most enjoyable part of the day, and I loved to spend it on the lake, where there was nearly always a gentle breeze blowing down the valley. Not that the place was without saddest memories. I never found myself on the water but I thought of the fate of Charles. Many a time since then in the falling shades of night had I stooped and listened for the ring of the phantom skater speeding along the ice. I had never heard it again.

We had been all day on the tiptoe of expectancy, but the last train from London had arrived without bringing Norman. Having a number of important letters to write, soon after dinner I bade my aunt goodnight, and withdrew to my rooms. It was ten o'clock before I had completed my work. Rather late for a row on the lake, I thought, but I felt fagged with the heat of the day and tired with writing. So I got the key of the boat-house and started for the water-side.

Among the boats was a pretty racing gig, some twenty feet long. I got her out, and started for a good pull. Bending to my oars, I made the little craft fly through the water, leaving behind a long white track that sparkled in the bright gleam of the harvest moon.

I soon reached the head of the lake, and started on the home journey at a more leisurely stroke. When I had accomplished the distance, and just as I approached the boat-house I looked at my watch. It was ten minutes past eleven.

I was in the act of raising one oar to turn the gig round at right angles to the bank, so as to shoot her into the boat-house, when every muscle of my body seemed to become rigid.

There, away in the distance, borne faintly on the breeze, came the rhythmical ring of skates speeding over the ice!

I listened, frozen with horror. At times the sound died away, then rose again, and I seemed with my mind to follow the phantom skater as he rounded each bend or passed each clump of trees.

Now, however, the ring of the skates was sharp and clear, and on it came, nearer and nearer, mercilessly approaching.

At last the figure I had seen years before shot round the bend, and glided towards me along the glittering surface of the water.

For a moment I was paralysed. But, at last, mind and muscle acted together, and with one sweep of my still uplifted oar I turned the boat broadside to the lake, right in the way of the advancing figure.

I moved my lips, but for a time they refused to utter a sound. At last, with a supreme effort, I managed to shout out, 'Holloa! holloa!'

I heard my voice echoing down the valley, and I hardly recognized its terror-stricken tones.

At the sound the speed with which the advancing figure advanced seemed to slacken, and I could hear the grinding sound that is caused by a skater endeavouring to stop when in full career.

Twenty yards from the boat the figure came to a standstill. 'Holloa! holloa!' I again cried out, incapable of uttering any other sound.

For a moment the phantom gazed at me, my long boat barring his path; then he turned slowly round, and skated away in the direction whence he came. He disappeared round the bend, and the ring of the skates died away in the distance.

I cannot tell how I managed to get ashore. I knew where brandy was kept in the boat-house, but my trembling hand could hardly raise the glass to my lips. It was not for myself I feared. I thought of Norman.

Till break of day I watched in the boat-house, and listened with straining ear; but not again did the dreaded ring of the iron skates break upon the silence of the night. In the grey of the morning I slipped back to the Hall.

I changed my clothes, and endeavoured to calm myself. By six o'clock I was in the little village post office, having roused Mr Scott fully two hours before his time.

I telegraphed to Berlin, to Norman's address, to ascertain whether he had yet started for England, and sat down in a state of sickening agony and suspense, determined to await the reply.

Some fifteen minutes afterwards the clicking of the instrument showed that a message was on the wire. I started to my feet, never thinking that it was impossible for an answer from Berlin to have reached me yet.

'It won't be for you, sir,' said Mr Scott, advancing to the instrument. I pressed close behind him.

'Yes, it is, though,' he cried, eagerly; then, after a moment, he added: 'And it is from Mr Norman.'

The clicking of the instrument pierced my brain as the postmaster spelt out the message word by word. It was dated from Dover, and the hour of despatch was one a.m. It ran as follows: 'Accident in the Channel. Don't be alarmed. Safe, and starting for home.'

The message had lain in the London General Post Office till the office at Eastwood had opened.

I seized my hat and rushed to the station. Norman might arrive by the morning train. Such indeed was the case. How fervently I thanked God in my heart when I saw him standing before me alive and well.

I soon got from him the outline of his story. He had reached Calais just a few minutes after the English packet had left. A tug-boat that had towed in a disabled vessel was, however, on the point of starting for Dover. He had at once accepted the offer of a passage, hoping that, after all, he might catch the mail train at Dover. When the boat had almost reached its destination, a fog came on, and soon after they were run down by the very passenger steamer that Norman had missed. The smaller vessel foundered almost instantaneously and, with the exception of Norman, all on board perished.

But the most remarkable part of his story was to come. He had not felt sleepy, and had remained on deck during the whole passage. He happened to look at his watch a few minutes before the accident happened. It was a quarter to eleven o'clock. A few minutes later he found himself struggling in the water for dear life. He saw the vessel that had run them down, her way hardly checked by the collision, fade into the misty darkness.

He thinks he was in the water quite half an hour. Hope had left him, he was numbed and almost senseless, when there reached his ear, borne through the billows of fog, a faint 'Holloa! holloa!'

But, strangest of all, he thought that he recognized my voice – that it was I who was calling to him across the waters.

Nerved to make one more effort for life he struck out in the direction whence the cry came, and tried to articulate my name. But his numbed lips refused to speak.

Then again he heard my voice shouting 'Holloa! holloa!' In vain he tried to answer.

He remembered nothing more till he found himself on board the mail packet, with someone by his side moistening his lips with brandy.

A boat had been launched from the steamer without a minute's delay after the accident, and it had come back through the fog to endeavour to rescue the ill-fated vessel's crew. No one, however, was seen but Norman, and, indeed, when he was saved the rescuing party had almost given up hope. They heard him splashing in the water, and reached him not a moment too soon. He was insensible when they got him on board. He was soon brought round, and was able to proceed at once to London.

My story was told to Norman and his mother, and to this day both of them hold that to me he owes his life.

Years have rolled by, and when I visit Eastwood little forms climb my knees, and childish voices bestow upon me the loving name 'Uncle Harry'. Mrs Armitage, now descending into the vale of years – I myself have entered on the downward slope – always greets me with her blessing. Norman and his wife – the story has been told to her – are to me as brother and sister.

An artificially constructed island now marks the spot where in a bygone generation the young owner of Eastwood Hall came to his untimely end. But none of us ever refer to the legend of the Phantom of the Lake, and we endeavour, as far as possible, to forget its existence.

# The Thing in the Upper Room

## Arthur Morrison

A shadow hung ever over the door, which stood black in the depth of its arched recess, like an unfathomable eye under a frowning brow. The landing was wide and panelled, and a heavy rail, supported by a carved balustrade, stretched away in alternate slopes and levels down the dark staircase, past other doors, and so to the courtyard and the street. The other doors were dark also; but it was with a difference. That top landing was lightest of all, because of the skylight; and perhaps it was largely by reason of contrast that its one doorway gloomed so black and forbidding. The doors below opened and shut, slammed, stood ajar. Men and women passed in and out, with talk and human sounds – sometimes even with laughter or a snatch of song; but the door on the top landing remained shut and silent through weeks and months. For, in truth, the *logement* had an ill name, and had been untenanted for years. Long even before the last tenant had occupied it, the room had been regarded with fear and aversion, and the end of that last tenant had in no way lightened the gloom that hung about the place.

The house was so old that its weather-washed face may well have looked down on the bloodshed of St Bartholomew's, and the haunted room may even have earned its ill name on that same day of death. But Paris is a city of cruel history, and since the old mansion rose proud and new, the *hôtel* of some powerful noble, almost any year of the centuries might have seen the blot fall on that upper room that had left it a place of loathing and shadows. The occasion was long forgotten, but the fact remained; whether or not some horror of the *ancien régime* or some enormity of the Terror was enacted in that room was no longer to be discovered; but nobody would live there, nor stay beyond that gloomy door one second longer than he could help. It might be supposed that the fate of the solitary tenant within living memory had something to do with the matter – and, indeed, his end was sinister enough; but long before his time the room had stood shunned and empty. He, greatly daring, had taken no more heed of the common terror of the room than to use it to his advantage in abating the rent; and he had shot himself a little later, while the police were beating at his door to arrest him on a charge of murder. As I have said, his fate may have added to the general aversion from the place, though it had no in no way originated it; and now ten years had passed, and more, since his few articles of furniture had been carried away and sold; and nothing had been carried in to replace them.

When one is twenty-five, healthy, hungry and poor, one is less likely to be frightened from a cheap lodging by mere headshakings than might be expected in other circumstances. Attwater was twenty-five, commonly healthy, often hungry, and always poor. He came to live in Paris because, from his remembrance of his student days, he believed he could live cheaper there than in London; while it was quite certain that he would not sell fewer pictures, since he had never yet sold one.

It was the *concierge* of a neighbouring house who showed Attwater the room. The house of the room itself maintained no such functionary, though its main door stood open day and night. The man said little, but his surprise at Attwater's application was plain to see. Monsieur was English? Yes. The *logement* was convenient, though high, and probably now a little dirty, since it had not been occupied recently. Plainly, the man felt it to be no business of his to enlighten an unsuspecting foreigner as to the reputation of the place; and if he could let it there would be some small gratification from the landlord, though, at such a rent, of course a very small one indeed.

But Attwater was better informed than the *concierge* supposed. He had heard the tale of the haunted room, vaguely and incoherently, it is true, from the little old engraver of watches on the floor below, by whom he had been directed to the *concierge*. The old man had been voluble and friendly, and reported that the room had a good light, facing north-east – indeed, a much better light than he, engraver of watches, enjoyed on the floor below. So much so that, considering this advantage and the much lower rent, he himself would have taken the room long ago, except – well, except for other things. Monsieur was a stranger, and perhaps had no fear to inhabit a haunted chamber; but that was its reputation, as everybody in the quarter knew; it would be a misfortune, however, to a stranger to take the room without suspicion, and to undergo unexpected experiences. Here, however, the old man checked himself, possibly reflecting that too much information to inquirers after the upper room might offend his landlord. He hinted as much, in fact, hoping that his friendly warning would not be allowed to travel farther. As to the precise nature of the disagreeable manifestations in the room, who could say? Perhaps there were really none at all. People said this and that. Certainly, the place had been untenanted for many years, and he would not like to stay in it himself. But it might be the good fortune of monsieur to break the spell, and if monsieur was resolved to defy the *revenant*, he wished monsieur the highest success and happiness.

So much for the engraver of watches; and now the *concierge* of the neighbouring house led the way up the stately old panelled staircase, swinging his keys in his hand, and halted at last before the dark door in the frowning recess. He turned the key with some difficulty, pushed open the door, and stood back with an action of something not wholly deference, to allow Attwater to enter first.

A sort of small lobby had been partitioned off at some time, though except for this the *logement* was of one large room only. There was something unpleasant in the air of the place – not a smell, when one came to analyse one's sensations, though at first it might seem so. Attwater walked across to the wide window and threw it open. The chimneys and roofs of many houses of all ages straggled before him, and out of the welter rose the twin towers of St Sulpice, scarred and grim.

Air the room as one might, it was unpleasant; a sickly, even a cowed, feeling, invaded one through all the senses – or perhaps through none of them. The feeling was there, though it was not easy to say by what channel it penetrated. Attwater was resolved to admit none but a common-sense explanation, and blamed the long closing of door and window; and the *concierge*, standing uneasily near the door, agreed that that must be it. For a moment Attwater wavered, despite himself. But the rent was very low, and, low as it was, he could not afford a sou more. The light was good, though it was not a top-light, and the place was big enough for his simple requirements. Attwater reflected that he should despise himself ever after if he shrank from the opportunity; it would be one of those secret humiliations that will rise again and again in a man's memory, and make him blush in solitude. He told the *concierge* to leave door and window wide open for the rest of the day, and he clinched the bargain.

It was with something of amused bravado that he reported to his few friends in Paris his acquisition of a haunted room; for, once out of the place, he readily convinced himself that his disgust and dislike while in the room were the result of imagination and nothing more. Certainly, there was no rational reason to account for the unpleasantness; consequently, what could it be but a matter of fancy? He resolved to face the matter from the beginning, and clear his mind from any foolish prejudices that the hints of the old engraver might have inspired, by forcing himself through whatever adventures he might encounter. In fact, as he walked the streets about his business, and arranged for the purchase and delivery of the few simple articles of furniture that would be necessary, his enterprise assumed the guise of a pleasing adventure. He remembered that he had made an attempt, only a year or two ago, to spend a night in a house reputed haunted in England, but had failed to find the landlord. Here was the adventure to hand, with promise of a tale to tell in future times; and a welcome idea struck him that he might look out the ancient history of the room, and work the whole thing into a magazine article, which would bring a little money.

So simple were his needs that by the afternoon of the day following his first examination of the room it was ready for use.

He took his bag from the cheap hotel in a little street of Montparnasse, where he had been lodging, and carried it to his new home. The key was now in his pocket, and for the first time he entered the place alone. The window remained wide open; but it was still there – that depressing, choking something that entered the consciousness he knew not by what gate. Again he accused his fancy. He stamped and whistled, and set about unpacking a few canvases and a case of old oriental weapons that were part of his professional properties. But he could give no proper attention to the work, and detected himself more than once yielding to a childish impulse to look over his shoulder. He laughed at himself – with some effort – and sat determinedly to smoke a pipe, and grow used to his surroundings. But presently he found himself pushing his chair farther and farther back, till it touched the wall. He would take the whole room into view, he said to himself in excuse, and stare it out of countenance. So he sat and smoked, and as he sat his eye fell on a Malay dagger that lay on the table between him and the window. It was a murderous, twisted thing, and its pommel was fashioned into the semblance of a bird's head, with curved beak and an eye of some dull red stone. He found himself gazing on this red eye with an odd, mindless fascination. The dagger in its wicked curves seemed now a creature of some outlandish fantasy – a snake with a beaked head, a thing of nightmare, in some new way dominant, overruling the centre of his perceptions. The rest of the room grew dim, but the red stone glowed with a fuller light; nothing more was present to his consciousness. Then, with a sudden clang, the heavy bell of St Sulpice aroused him, and he started up in some surprise.

There lay the dagger on the table, strange and murderous enough, but merely as he had always known it. He observed with more surprise, however, that his chair, which had been back against the wall, was now some six feet forward, close by the table; clearly, he must have drawn it forward in his abstraction, towards the dagger on which his eyes had been fixed... The great bell of St Sulpice went clanging on, repeating its monotonous call to the Angelus.

He was cold, almost shivering. He flung the dagger into a drawer, and turned to go out. He saw by his watch that it was later than he had supposed; his fit of abstraction must have lasted some time. Perhaps he had even been dozing.

He went slowly downstairs and out into the streets. As he went he grew more and more ashamed of himself, for he had to confess that in some inexplicable way he feared that room. He had seen nothing, heard nothing of the kind that one might have expected, or had heard of in any room reputed haunted; he could not help thinking that it would have been some sort of relief if he had. But there was an all-pervading, overpowering sense of another Presence – something abhorrent, not human, something almost physically nauseous. Withal it was something more than presence; it was power, domination – so he seemed to remember it. And yet the remembrance grew weaker as he walked in the gathering dusk; he thought of a story he had once read of a haunted house wherein it was shown that the house actually was haunted – by the spirit of fear, and nothing else. That, he persuaded himself, was the case with his room; he felt angry at the growing conviction that he had allowed himself to be overborne by fancy – by the spirit of fear.

He returned that night with the resolve to allow himself no foolish indulgence. He had heard nothing and had seen nothing; when something palpable to the senses occurred, it would be time enough to deal with it. He took off his clothes and got into bed deliberately, leaving candle and matches at hand in case of need. He had expected to find some difficulty in sleeping, or at least some delay, but he was scarce well in bed ere he fell into a heavy sleep.

Dazzling sunlight through the window woke him in the morning, and he sat up, staring sleepily about him. He must have slept like a log. But he had been dreaming; the dreams were horrible. His head ached beyond anything he had experienced before, and he was far more tired than when he went to bed. He sank back on the pillow, but the mere contact made his head ring with pain. He got out of bed, and found himself staggering; it was all as though he had been drunk – unspeakably drunk with bad liquor. His dreams – they had been horrid dreams; he could remember that they had been bad, but what they actually were was now gone from him entirely. He rubbed his eyes and stared amazedly down at the table: where the crooked dagger lay, with its bird's head and red stone eye. It lay just as it had lain when he sat gazing at it yesterday, and yet he would have sworn that he had flung that same dagger into a drawer. Perhaps he had dreamed it; at any rate, he put the thing carefully into the drawer now, and, still with his ringing headache, dressed himself and went out.

As he reached the next landing the old engraver greeted him from his door with an inquiring good-day. 'Monsieur has not slept well, I fear?'

In some doubt, Attwater protested that he had slept quite soundly. 'And as yet I have neither seen nor heard anything of the ghost,' he added.

'Nothing?' replied the old man, with a lift of the eyebrows, 'nothing at all? It is fortunate. It seemed to me, here below, that monsieur was moving about very restlessly in the night; but no doubt I was mistaken. No doubt, also, I may felicitate monsieur on breaking the evil tradition. We shall hear no more of it; monsieur has the good fortune of a brave heart.'

He smiled and bowed pleasantly, but it was with something of a puzzled look that his eyes followed Attwater descending the staircase.

Attwater took his coffee and roll after an hour's walk, and fell asleep in his seat. Not for long, however, and presently he rose and left the café. He felt better, though still unaccountably fatigued. He caught sight of his face in a mirror beside a shop window, and saw an improvement since he had looked in his own glass. That indeed had brought him a shock. Worn and drawn beyond what might have been expected of so bad a night, there was even something more. What was it? How should it remind him of that old legend – was it Japanese? – which he had tried to recollect when he had wondered confusedly at the haggard apparition that confronted him? Some tale of a demon-possessed person who in any mirror, saw never his own face, but the face of the demon.

Work he felt to be impossible, and he spent the day on garden seats, at café tables, and for a while in the Luxembourg. And in the evening he met an English friend, who took him by the shoulders and looked into his eyes, shook him, and declared that he had been overworking, and needed, above all things, a good dinner, which he should have instantly. 'You'll dine with me,' he said, 'at La Perouse, and we'll get a cab to take us there. I'm hungry.'

As they stood and looked for a passing cab a man ran shouting with newspapers. 'We'll have a cab,' Attwater's friend repeated, 'and we'll take the new murder with us for conversation's sake. Hi! *Journal!*'

He bought a paper, and followed Attwater into the cab. 'I've a strong idea I knew the poor old boy by sight,' he said. 'I believe he'd seen better days.'

'Who?'

'The old man who was murdered in the Rue Broca last night. The description fits exactly. He used to hang about the cafés and run messages. It isn't easy to read in this cab; but there's probably nothing fresh in this edition. They haven't caught the murderer, anyhow.'

Attwater took the paper, and struggled to read it in the changing light. A poor old man had been found dead on the footpath of the Rue Broca, torn with a score of stabs. He had been identified – an old man

not known to have a friend in the world; also, because he was so old and
so poor, probably not an enemy. There was no robbery; the few sous the
old man possessed remained in his pocket. He must have been attacked
on his way home in the early hours of the morning, possibly by a
homicidal maniac, and stabbed again and again with inconceivable
fury. No arrest had been made.

Attwater pushed the paper way: 'Pah!' he said; 'I don't like it. I'm a
bit off colour, and I was dreaming horribly all last night; though why
this should remind me of it I can't guess. But it's no cure for the blues,
this!'

'No,' replied his friend heartily; 'we'll get that upstairs, for here we
are, on the quay. A bottle of the best Burgundy on the list and the best
dinner they can do – that's your physic. Come!'

It was a good prescription, indeed. Attwater's friend was cheerful and
assiduous, and nothing could have bettered the dinner. Attwater found
himself reflecting that indulgence in the blues was a poor pastime, with
no better excuse than a bad night's rest. And last night's dinner in
comparison with this! Well, it was enough to have spoiled his sleep, that
one-franc-fifty dinner.

Attwater left La Perouse as gay as his friend. They had sat late, and
now there was nothing to do but cross the water and walk a little in the
boulevards. This they did, and finished the evening at a café table with
half a dozen acquaintances.

Attwater walked home with a light step, feeling less drowsy than at
any time during the day. He was well enough. He felt he should soon
get used to the room. He had been a little too much alone lately, and
that had got on his nerves. It was simply stupid.

Again he slept quickly and heavily – and dreamed. But he had an
awakening of another sort. No bright sun blazed in at the open window
to lift his heavy lids, and no morning bell from St Sulpice opened his
ears to the cheerful noise of the city. He awoke gasping and staring in
the dark, rolling face-downward on the floor, catching his breath in
agonized sobs; while through the window from the streets came a clamour
of hoarse cries: cries of pursuit and the noise of running men: a shouting
and clatter wherein here and there a voice was clear among the rest – '*A
l'assassin! Arrêtez!*'

He dragged himself to his feet in the dark, gasping still. What was
this – all this? Again a dream? His legs trembled under him, and he
sweated with fear. He made for the window, panting and feeble; and
then, as he supported himself by the sill, he realized wonderingly that
he was fully dressed – that he wore even his hat. The running crowd
straggled through the outer street and away, the shouts growing fainter.

What had wakened him? Why had he dressed? He remembered his matches, and turned to grope for them; but something was already in his hand – something wet, sticky. He dropped it on the table, and even as he struck the light, before he saw it, he knew. The match sputtered and flared, and there on the table lay the crooked dagger, smeared and dripping and horrible.

Blood was on his hands – the match stuck in his fingers. Caught at the heart by the first grip of an awful surmise, he looked up and saw in the mirror before him, in the last flare of the match, the face of the Thing in the Room.

# The Tell-Tale Heart

## *Edgar Allan Poe*

True! – nervous – very, very dreadfully nervous I had been and am; but why will you say that I am mad? The disease had sharpened my senses – not destroyed – not dulled them. Above all was the sense of hearing acute. I heard all things in the heaven and in the earth. I heard many things in hell. How, then, am I mad? Hearken! and observe how healthily – how calmly I can tell you the whole story.

It is impossible to say how first the idea entered my brain; but once conceived, it haunted me day and night. Object there was none. Passion there was none. I loved the old man. He had never wronged me. He had never given me insult. For his gold I had no desire. I think it was his eye! yes, it was this! One of his eyes resembled that of a vulture – a pale blue eye, with a film over it. Whenever it fell upon me, my blood ran cold; and so by degrees – very gradually – I made up my mind to take the life of the old man, and thus rid myself of the eye for ever.

Now this is the point. You fancy me mad. Madmen know nothing. But you should have seen *me*. You should have seen how wisely I proceeded – with what caution – with what foresight – with what dissimulation I went to work! I was never kinder to the old man than during the whole week before I killed him. And every night, about midnight, I turned the latch of his door and opened it – oh, so gently! And then, when I had made an opening sufficient for my head, I put in a dark lantern, all closed, closed, so that no light shone out, and then I thrust in my head. Oh, you would have laughed to see how cunningly I thrust it in! I moved it slowly – very, very slowly, so that I might not disturb the old man's sleep. It took me an hour to place my whole head within the opening so far that I could see him as he lay upon his bed. Ha! – would a madman have been so wise as this? And then, when my head was well in the room, I undid the lantern cautiously – oh, so cautiously – cautiously (for the hinges creaked) – I undid it just so much that a single thin ray fell upon the vulture eye. And this I did for seven long nights – every night just at midnight – but I found the eye always closed; and so it was impossible to do the work; for it was not the old man who vexed me, but his Evil Eye. And every morning, when the day broke, I went boldly into the chamber, and spoke courageously to him, calling him by name in a hearty tone, and inquiring how he had passed the night. So you see he would have been a very profound old man, indeed, to suspect that every night, just at twelve, I looked in upon him while he slept.

Upon the eighth night I was more than usually cautious in opening the door. A watch's minute hand moves more quickly than did mine. Never before that night had I *felt* the extent of my own powers – of my sagacity. I could scarcely contain my feelings of triumph. To think that there I was, opening the door, little by little, and he not even to dream of my secret deeds or thoughts. I fairly chuckled at the idea; and perhaps he heard me; for he moved on the bed suddenly, as if startled. Now you may think that I drew back – but no. His room was as black as pitch with the thick darkness (for the shutters were close fastened, through fear of robbers), and so I knew that he could not see the opening of the door, and I kept pushing it on steadily, steadily.

I had my head in, and was about to open the lantern, when my thumb slipped upon the tin fastening, and the old man sprang up in the bed, crying out – 'Who's there?'

I kept quite still and said nothing. For a whole hour I did not move a muscle, and in the meantime I did not hear him lie down. He was still sitting up in the bed listening; – just as I have done, night after night, hearkening to the death watches in the wall.

Presently I heard a slight groan, and I knew it was the groan of mortal terror. It was not a groan of pain or of grief – oh, no! – it was the low stifled sound that arises from the bottom of the soul when overcharged with awe. I knew the sound well. Many a night, just at midnight, when all the world slept, it has welled up from my own bosom, deepening, with its dreadful echo, the terrors that distracted me. I saw I knew it well. I knew what the old man felt, and pitied him, although I chuckled at heart. I knew that he had been lying awake ever since the first slight noise, when he had turned in the bed. His fears had been ever since growing upon him. He had been trying to fancy them causeless, but could not. He had been saying to himself – 'It is nothing but the wind in the chimney – it is only a mouse crossing the floor,' or 'it is merely a cricket which has made a single chirp.' Yes, he has been trying to comfort himself with these suppositions; but he had found all in vain. *All in vain*; because Death, in approaching him, had stalked with his black shadow before him, and enveloped the victim. And it was the mournful influence of the unperceived shadow that caused him to feel – although he neither saw nor heard – to *feel* the presence of my head within the room.

When I had waited a long time, very patiently, without hearing him lie down, I resolved to open a little – a very, very little crevice in the lantern. So I opened it – you cannot imagine how stealthily, stealthily – until, at length, a single dim ray, like a thread of the spider, shot from out the crevice and full upon the vulture eye.

It was open – wide, wide open – and I grew furious as I gazed upon it. I saw it with perfect distinctness – all a dull blue, with a hideous veil over it that chilled the very marrow in my bones; but I could see nothing else of the old man's face or person: for I had directed the ray as if by instinct, precisely upon the damned spot.

And now have I not told you that what you mistake for madness is but over-acuteness of the senses? – now, I say, there came to my ears a low, dull, quick sound, such as a watch makes when enveloped in cotton. I knew *that* sound well too. It was the beating of the old man's heart. It increased my fury, as the beating of a drum stimulates the soldier into courage.

But even yet I refrained and kept still. I scarcely breathed. I held the lantern motionless. I tried how steadily I could maintain the ray upon the eye. Meantime the hellish tattoo of the heart increased. It grew quicker and quicker, and louder and louder every instant. The old man's terror *must* have been extreme! It grew louder, I say, louder every moment! – do you mark me well? I have told you that I am nervous: so I am. And now at the dead hour of the night, amid the dreadful silence of that old house, so strange a noise as this excited me to uncontrollable terror. Yet, for some minutes longer I refrained and stood still. But the beating grew louder, louder! I thought the heart must burst. And now a new anxiety seized me – the sound would be heard by a neighbor! The old man's hour had come! With a loud yell, I threw open the lantern and leaped into the room. He shrieked once – once only. In an instant I dragged him to the floor, and pulled the heavy bed over him. I then smiled gaily, to find the deed so far done. But, for many minutes, the heart beat on with a muffled sound. This, however, did not vex me; it would not be heard through the wall. At length it ceased. The old man was dead. I removed the bed and examined the corpse. Yes, he was stone, stone dead. I placed my hand upon the heart and held it there many minutes. There was no pulsation. He was stone dead. His eye would trouble me no more.

If still you think me mad, you will think so no longer when I describe the wise precautions I took for the concealment of the body. The night waned, and I worked hastily, but in silence. First of all I dismembered the corpse. I cut off the head and the arms and the legs.

I then took up three planks from the flooring of the chamber, and deposited all between the scantlings. I then replaced the boards so cleverly, so cunningly, that no human eye – not even *his* – could have detected any thing wrong. There was nothing to wash out – no stain of any kind – no blood-spot whatever. I had been too wary for that. A tub had caught all – ha! ha!

When I had made an end of these labors, it was four o'clock – still dark as midnight. As the bell sounded the hour, there came a knocking at the street door. I went down to open it with a light heart, – for what had I *now* to fear? There entered three men, who introduced themselves, with perfect suavity, as officers of the police. A shriek had been heard by a neighbor during the night; suspicion of foul play had been aroused; information had been lodged at the police office, and they (the officers) had been deputed to search the premises.

I smiled, – for *what* had I to fear? I bade the gentlemen welcome. The shriek, I said, was my own in a dream. The old man, I mentioned, was absent in the country. I took my visitors all over the house. I bade them search – search *well*. I led them, at length, to *his* chamber. I showed them his treasures, secure, undisturbed. In the enthusiasm of my confidence, I brought chairs into the room, and desired them *here* to rest from their fatigues, while I myself, in the wild audacity of my perfect triumph, placed my own seat upon the very spot beneath which reposed the corpse of the victim.

The officers were satisfied. My *manner* convinced them. I was singularly at ease. They sat, and while I answered cheerily, they chatted familiar things. But, ere long, I felt myself getting pale and wished them gone. My head ached, and I fancied a ringing in my ears: but still they sat and still chatted. The ringing became more distinct: – it continued and became more distinct: I talked more freely to get rid of the feeling: but it continued and gained definitiveness – until, at length, I found that the noise was *not* within my ears.

No doubt I now grew *very* pale; – but I talked more fluently, and with a heightened voice. Yet the sound increased – and what could I do? It was *a low, dull, quick sound – much such a sound as a watch makes when enveloped in cotton*. I gasped for breath – and yet the officers heard it not. I talked more quickly – more vehemently; but the noise steadily increased. I arose and argued about trifles, in a high key and with violent gesticulations, but the noise steadily increased. Why *would* they not be gone? I paced the floor to and fro with heavy strides, as if excited to fury by the observation of the men – but the noise steadily increased. Oh God! what *could* I do? I foamed – I raved – I swore! I swung the chair upon which I had been sitting, and grated it upon the boards, but the noise arose over all and continually increased. It grew louder – louder – *louder*! And still the men chatted pleasantly, and smiled. Was it possible they heard not? Almighty God! – no, no! They heard! – They suspected! – they *knew*! – they were making a mockery of my horror! – this I thought, and this I think. But any thing was better than this agony! Any thing was more tolerable than this derision! I could bear those hypocritical smiles no longer! I felt that I must scream or die! – and now – again! – hark! louder! louder! louder! *louder!* –

'Villains!' I shrieked, 'dissemble no more! I admit the deed! – tear up the planks! – here, here! – it is the beating of his hideous heart!'

# The Demon King

## J. B. Priestley

Among the company assembled for Mr Tom Burt's Grand Annual Pantomime at the old Theatre Royal, Bruddersford, there was a good deal of disagreement. They were not quite 'the jolly, friendly party' they pretended to be – through the good offices of 'Thespian' – to the readers of *The Bruddersford Herald* and *Weekly Herald Budget*. The Principal Boy told her husband and about fifty-five other people that she could work with anybody, was famous for being able to work with anybody, but that nevertheless the management had gone and engaged, as Principal Girl, the one woman in the profession who made it almost impossible for anybody to work with anybody. The Principal Girl told her friend, the Second Boy, that the Principal Boy and the Second Girl were spoiling everything and might easily ruin the show. The Fairy Queen went about pointing out that she did not want to make trouble, being notoriously easy-going, but that sooner or later the Second Girl would hear a few things that she would not like. Johnny Wingfield had been heard to declare that some people did not realize even yet that what audiences wanted from a panto was some good fast comedy work by the chief comedian, who had to have all the scope he required. Dippy and Doppy, the broker's men, hinted that even if there were two stages, Johnny Wingfield would want them both all the time.

But they were all agreed on one point, namely, that there was not a better demon in provincial panto than Mr Kirk Ireton, who had been engaged by Mr Tom Burt for this particular show. The pantomime was *Jack and Jill*, and those people who are puzzled to know what demons have to do with Jack and Jill, those innocent water-fetchers, should pay a visit to the nearest pantomime, which will teach them a lot they did not know about fairy tales. Kirk Ireton was not merely a demon, but the Demon King, and when the curtain first went up, you saw him on a darkened stage standing in front of a little chorus of attendant demons, made up of local baritones at ten shillings a night. Ireton looked the part, for he was tall and rather satanically featured and was known to be very clever with his make-up; and what was more important, he sounded the part too, for he had a tremendous bass voice, of most

demonish quality. He had played Mephistopheles in *Faust* many times
with a good touring opera company. He was, indeed, a man with a fine
future behind him. If it had not been for one weakness, pantomime
would never have seen him. The trouble was that for years now he had
been in the habit of 'lifting the elbow' too much. That was how they all
put it. Nobody said that he drank too much, but all agreed that he lifted
the elbow. And the problem now was – would there be trouble because
of this elbow-lifting?

He had rehearsed with enthusiasm, sending his great voice to the back
of the empty, forlorn gallery in the two numbers allotted to him, but at
the later rehearsals there had been ominous signs of elbow-lifting.

'Going to be all right, Mr Ireton?' the stage-manager inquired
anxiously.

Ireton raised his formidable and satanic eyebrows. 'Of course it is,' he
replied, somewhat hoarsely. 'What's worrying you, old man?'

The other explained hastily that he wasn't worried. 'You'll go well
here,' he went on. 'They'll eat those two numbers of yours. Very musical
in these parts. But you know Bruddersford, of course. You've played
here before.'

'I have,' replied Ireton grimly. 'And I loathe the dam' place. Bores
me stiff. Nothing to do in it.'

This was not reassuring. The stage-manager knew only too well Mr
Ireton was already finding something to do in the town, and his
enthusiastic description of the local golf courses had no effect. Ireton
loathed golf too, it seemed. All very ominous.

They were opening on Boxing Day night. By the afternoon, it was
known that Kirk Ireton had been observed lifting the elbow very
determinedly in the smoke-room of 'The Cooper's Arms', near the
theatre. One of the stage-hands had seen him: 'And by gow, he wor
lapping it up an' all,' said this gentleman, no bad judge of anybody's
power of suction. From there, it appeared, he had vanished, along with
several other riotous persons, two of them thought to be Leeds men –
and in Bruddersford they know what Leeds men are.

The curtain was due to rise at seven-fifteen sharp. Most members of
the company arrived at the theatre very early. Kirk Ireton was not one
of them. He was still absent at six-thirty, though he had to wear an
elaborate make-up, with glittering tinselled eyelids and all the rest of it,
and had to be on the stage when the curtain rose. A messenger was
despatched to his lodgings, which were not far from the theatre. Even
before the messenger returned, to say that Mr Ireton had not been in
since noon, the stage-manager was desperately coaching one of the local
baritones, the best of a stiff and stupid lot, in the part of the Demon
King. At six-forty-five, no Ireton; at seven, no Ireton. It was hopeless.

'All right, that fellow's done for himself now,' said the great Mr Burt, who had come to give his Grand Annual his blessing. 'He doesn't get another engagement from me as long as he lives. What's this local chap like?'

The stage-manager groaned and wiped his brow. 'Like nothing on earth except a bow-legged baritone from a Wesleyan choir.'

'He'll have to manage somehow. You'll have to cut the part.'

'Cut it, Mr Burt! I've slaughtered it, and what's left of it, he'll slaughter.'

Mr Tom Burt, like the sensible manager he was, believed in a pantomime opening in the old-fashioned way, with a mysterious dark scene among the supernaturals. Here it was a cavern in the hill beneath the Magic Well, and in these dismal recesses the Demon King and his attendants were to be discovered waving their crimson cloaks and plotting evil in good, round chest-notes. Then the Demon King would sing his number (which had nothing whatever to do with Jack and Jill or demonology either), the Fairy Queen would appear, accompanied by a white spotlight, there would be a little dialogue between them, and then a short duet.

The cavern scene was all set, the five attendant demons were in their places, while the sixth, now acting as King, was receiving a few last instructions from the stage-manager, and the orchestra, beyond the curtain, were coming to the end of the overture, when suddenly, from nowhere, there appeared on the dimly-lighted stage a tall and terrifically imposing figure.

'My God! There's Ireton,' cried the stage-manager, and bustled across, leaving the temporary Demon King, abandoned, a pitiful makeshift now. The new arrival was coolly taking his place in the centre. He looked superb. The costume, a skin-tight crimson affair touched with a baleful green, was far better than the one provided by the management. And the make-up was better still. The face had a greenish phosphorescent glow, and its eyes flashed between glittering lids. When he first caught sight of that face, the stage-manager felt a sudden idiotic tremor of fear, but being a stage-manager first and a human being afterwards (as all stage-managers have to be), he did not feel that tremor long, for it was soon chased away by a sense of elation. It flashed across his mind that Ireton must have gone running off to Leeds or somewhere in search of this stupendous costume and make-up. Good old Ireton! He had given them all a fright, but it had been worth it.

'All right, Ireton?' said the stage-manager quickly.

'All right,' replied the Demon King, with a magnificent, careless gesture.

'Well, you get back in the chorus then,' said the stage-manager to the Wesleyan baritone.

'That'll do me champion,' said the gentleman, with a sigh of relief. He was not ambitious.

'All ready?'

The violins began playing a shivery sort of music, and up the curtain went. The six attendant demons, led by the Wesleyan, who was in good voice now that he felt such a sense of relief, told the audience who they were and hailed their monarch in appropriate form. The Demon King, towering above them, dominating the scene superbly, replied in a voice of astonishing strength and richness. Then he sang the number allotted to him. It had nothing to do with Jack and Jill and very little to do with demons, being a rather commonplace bass song about sailors and shipwrecks and storms, with thunder and lightning effects supplied by the theatre. Undoubtedly this was the same song that had been rehearsed; the words were the same; the music was the same. Yet it all seemed different. It was really sinister. As you listened, you saw the great waves breaking over the doomed ships, and the pitiful little white faces disappearing in the dark flood. Somehow, the storm was much stormier. There was one great clap of thunder and flash of lightning that made all the attendant demons, the conductor of the orchestra, and a number of people in the wings, nearly jump out of their skins.

'And how the devil did you do that?' said the stage-manager, after running round to the other wing.

'That's what I said to 'Orace 'ere,' said the man in charge of the two sheets of tin and the cannon ball.

'Didn't touch a thing that time, did we, mate?' said Horace.

'If you ask me, somebody let off a firework, one o' them big Chinese crackers, for that one,' his mate continued. 'Somebody monkeying about, that's what it is.'

And now a white spotlight had found its way on to the stage, and there, shining in its pure ray, was Miss Dulcie Farrar, the Fairy Queen, who was busy waving a silver wand. She was also busy controlling her emotions, for somehow she felt unaccountably nervous. Opening night is opening night, of course, but Miss Farrar had been playing Fairy Queens for the last ten years (and Principal Girls for the ten years before them), and there was nothing in this part to worry her. She rapidly came to the conclusion that it was Mr Ireton's sudden reappearance, after she had made up her mind that he was not turning up, that had made her feel so shaky, and this caused her to feel rather resentful. Moreover, as an experienced Fairy Queen who had had trouble with demons before, she was convinced that he was about to take more than his share of the stage. Just because he had hit upon such a good make-up! And it *was* a good make-up, there could be no question about that. That greenish face, those glittering eyes – really, it was awful. Overdoing it, she called it. After all, a panto *was* a panto.

Miss Farrar, still waving her wand, moved a step or two nearer, and cried:

'I know your horrid plot, you evil thing,
And I defy you, though you are the Demon King.'

'What, you?' he roared, contemptuously, pointing a long forefinger at her.

Miss Farrar should have replied: 'Yes, I, the Queen of Fairyland,' but for a minute she could not get out a word. As that horribly long forefinger shot out at her, she had felt a sudden sharp pain and then found herself unable to move. She stood there, her wand held out at a ridiculous angle, motionless, silent, her mouth wide open. But her mind was active enough. 'Is it a stroke?' it was asking feverishly. 'Like Uncle Edgar had that time at Greenwich. Oo, it must be. Oo, whatever shall I do? Oo. Oo. Ooooo.'

'Ho-ho-ho-ho-ho.' The Demon King's sinister baying mirth resounded through the theatre.

'Ha-ha-ha-ha-ha.' This was from the Wesleyan and his friends, and was a very poor chorus of laughs, dubious, almost apologetic. It suggested that the Wesleyan and his friends were out of their depth, the depth of respectable Bruddersfordian demons.

Their king now made a quick little gesture with one hand, and Miss Farrar found herself able to move and speak again. Indeed, the next second, she was not sure that she had ever been *unable* to speak and move. That horrible minute had vanished like a tiny bad dream. She defied him again, and this time nothing happened beyond an exchange of bad lines of lame verse. There were not many of these, however, for there was the duet to be fitted in, and the whole scene had to be played in as short a time as possible. The duet, in which the two supernaturals only defied one another all over again, was early Verdi by way of the local musical director.

After singing a few bars each, they had a rest while the musical director exercised his fourteen instrumentalists in a most imposing operatic passage. It was during this halt that Miss Farrar, who was now quite close to her fellow-duettist, whispered: 'You're in great voice, tonight, Mr Ireton. Wish I was. Too nervous. Don't know why, but I am. Wish I could get it out like you.'

She received, as a reply, a flash of those glittering eyes (it really was an astonishing make-up) and a curious little signal with the long forefinger. There was no time for more, for now the voice part began again.

Nobody in the theatre was more surprised by what happened then than the Fairy Queen herself. She could not believe that the marvellously rich soprano voice that came pealing and soaring belonged to her. It was tremendous. Covent Garden would have acclaimed it. Never before, in all her twenty years of hard vocalism, had Miss Dulcie Farrar sung like that, though she had always felt that *somewhere* inside her there was a voice of that quality only waiting the proper signal to emerge and then astonish the world. Now, in some fantastic fashion, it had received that signal.

Not that the Fairy Queen overshadowed her supernatural colleague. There was no overshadowing *him*. He trolled in a diapason bass, and with a fine fury of gesture. The pair of them turned that stolen and botched duet into a work of art and significance. You could hear Heaven and Hell at battle in it. The curtain came down on a good rattle of applause. They are very fond of music in Bruddersford, but unfortunately the people who attend the first night of the pantomime are not the people who are most fond of music, otherwise there would have been a furore.

'Great stuff that,' said Mr Tom Burt, who was on the spot. 'Never mind, Jim. Let 'em take a curtain. Go on, you two, take the curtain.' And when they had both bowed their acknowledgements, Miss Farrar excited and trembling, the Demon King cool and amused, almost contemptuous, Mr Burt continued: 'That would have stopped the show in some places, absolutely stopped the show. But the trouble here is, they won't applaud, won't get going easily.'

'That's true, Mr Burt,' Miss Farrar observed. 'They take a lot of warming up here. I wish they didn't. Don't you, Mr Ireton?'

'Easy to warm them,' said the tall crimson figure.

'Well, if anything could, that ought to have done,' the lady remarked.

'That's so,' said Mr Burt condescendingly. 'You were great, Ireton. But they won't let themselves go.'

'Yes, they will.' The Demon King, who appeared to be taking his part very seriously, for he had not yet dropped into his ordinary tones, flicked his long fingers in the air, roughly in the direction of the auditorium, gave a short laugh, turned away, and then somehow completely vanished, though it was not difficult to do that in those crowded wings.

Half an hour later, Mr Burt, his manager, and the stage-manager, all decided that something must have gone wrong with Bruddersford. Liquor must have been flowing like water in the town. That was the only explanation.

'Either they're all drunk or I am,' cried the stage-manager.

'I've been giving 'em pantomimes here for five-and-twenty years,' said Mr Burt, 'and I've never known it happen before.'

'Well, nobody can say they're not enjoying it.'

'Enjoying it! They're enjoying it too much. They're going daft. Honestly, I don't like it. It's too much of a good thing.'

The stage-manager looked at his watch. 'It's holding up the show, that's certain. God knows when we're going to get through at this rate. If they're going to behave like this every night, we'll have to cut an hour out of it.'

'Listen to 'em now,' said Mr Burt. 'And that's one of the oldest gags in the show. Listen to 'em. Nay, dash it, they must be all half-seas over.'

What had happened? Why – this: that the audience had suddenly decided to let itself go in a fashion never known in Bruddersford before. The Bruddersfordians are notoriously difficult to please, not so much because their taste is so exquisite but rather because, having paid out money, they insist upon having their money's worth, and usually arrive at a place of entertainment in a gloomy and suspicious frame of mind. Really tough managers like to open a new show in Bruddersford, knowing very well that if it will go there, it will go anywhere. But for the last half-hour of this pantomime there had been more laughter and applause than the Theatre Royal had known for the past six months. Every entrance produced a storm of welcome. The smallest and stalest gags set the whole house screaming, roaring, and rocking. Every song was determinedly encored. If the people had been specially brought out of jail for the performance, they could not have been more easily pleased.

'Here,' said Johnny Wingfield, as he made an exit as a Dame pursued by a cow, 'this is frightening me. What's the matter with 'em? Is this a new way of giving the bird?'

'Don't ask me,' said the Principal Boy. 'I wasn't surprised they gave me such a nice welcome when I went on, because I've always been a favourite here, as Mr Burt'll tell you, but the way they're carrying on now, making such a fuss over nothing, it's simply ridiculous. Slowing up the show, too.'

After another quarter of an hour of this monstrous enthusiasm, this delirium, Mr Burt could be heard grumbling to the Principal Girl, with whom he was standing in that close proximity which Principal Girls somehow invite. 'I'll tell you what it is, Alice,' Mr Burt was saying. 'If this goes on much longer, I'll make a speech from the stage, asking 'em to draw it mild. Never known 'em to behave like this. And it's a funny thing, I was only saying to somebody – now who was it I said that to? – anyhow, I was only saying to somebody that I wished this audience would let themselves go a bit more. Well, now I wish they wouldn't. And that's that.'

There was a chuckle, not loud, but rich, and distinctly audible.

'Here,' cried Mr Burt. 'Who's that? What's the joke?'

It was obviously nobody in their immediate vicinity. 'It sounded like Kirk Ireton,' said the Principal Girl, 'judging by the voice.' But Ireton was nowhere to be seen. Indeed, one or two people who had been looking for him, both in his dressing-room and behind, had not been able to find him. But he would not be on again for another hour, and nobody had time to discover whether Ireton was drinking again or not. The odd thing was, though, that the audience lost its wild enthusiasm just as suddenly as it had found it, and long before the interval it had turned itself into the familiar stolid Bruddersford crowd, grimly waiting for its money's worth. The pantomime went on its way exactly as rehearsed, until it came to the time when the demons had to put in another appearance.

Jack, having found the magic water and tumbled down the hill, had to wander into the mysterious cavern and there rest awhile. At least, he declared that he would rest, but being played by a large and shapely female, and probably having that restless feminine temperament, what he did do was to sing a popular song with immense gusto. At the end of that song, when Jack once more declared that he would rest, the Demon King had to make a sudden appearance through a trap-door. And it was reported from below, where a spring-board was in readiness, that no Demon King had arrived to be shot on to the stage.

'Now where – oh, where – the devil has Ireton got to?' moaned the stage-manager, sending people right and left, up and down, to find him.

The moment arrived, Jack spoke his and her cue, and the stage-manager was making frantic signals to her from the wings.

'Ouh-wer,' screamed Jack, and produced the most realistic bit of business in the whole pantomime. For the stage directions read *Shows fright*, and Jack undoubtedly did show fright, as well he (or she) might, for no sooner was the cue spoken than there came a horrible green flash, followed by a crimson glare, and standing before her, having apparently arrived from nowhere, was the Demon King. Jack was now in the power of the Demon King and would remain in those evil clutches until rescued by Jill and the Fairy Queen. And it seemed as if the Principal Boy had suddenly developed a capacity for acting (of which nobody had ever suspected her before), or else that she was thoroughly frightened, for now she behaved like a large rabbit in tights. That unrehearsed appearance of the Demon King seemed to have upset her, and now and then she sent uneasy glances into the wings.

It had been decided, after a great deal of talk and drinks round, to introduce a rather novel dancing scene into this pantomime, in the form of a sort of infernal ballet. The Demon King, in order to show his power and to impress his captive, would command his subjects to dance – that is, after he himself had indulged in a little singing, assisted by his faithful six. They talk of that scene yet in Bruddersford. It was only witnessed in its full glory on this one night, but that was enough, for it passed into civic history, and local landlords were often called in to settle bets about it in the pubs. First, the Demon King sang his second number, assisted by the Wesleyan and his friends. He made a glorious job of it, and after a fumbled opening and a sudden glare from him, the Wesleyan six made a glorious job of it too. Then the Demon King had to call for his dancing subjects, who were made up of the troupe of girls known as Tom Burt's Happy Yorkshire Lasses, daintily but demonishly tricked out in red and green. While the Happy Yorkshire Lasses pranced in the foreground, the six attendants were supposed to make a few rhythmical movements in the background, enough to suggest that, if they wanted to dance, they could dance, a suggestion that the stage-manager and the producer knew to be entirely false. The six, in fact, could not dance and would not try very hard, being not only wooden but also stubborn Bruddersford baritones.

But now, the Happy Yorkshire Lasses having tripped a measure, the Demon King sprang to his full height, which seemed to be about seven feet two inches, swept an arm along the Wesleyan six, and commanded them harshly to dance. And they did dance, they danced like men possessed. The King himself beat time for them, flashing an eye at the conductor now and again to quicken that gentleman's baton, and his faithful six, all with the most grotesque and puzzled expressions on their faces, cut the most amazing capers, bounding high into the air, tumbling over one another, flinging their arms and legs about in an ecstasy, and all in time to the music. The sweat shone on their faces; their eyes rolled forlornly; but still they did not stop, but went on in crazier and crazier fashion, like genuine demons at play.

'All dance!' roared the Demon King, cracking his long fingers like a whip, and it seemed as if something had inspired the fourteen cynical men in the orchestral pit, for they played like madmen grown tuneful, and on came the Happy Yorkshire Lasses again, to fling themselves into the wild sport, not as if they were doing something they had rehearsed a hundred times, but as if they, too, were inspired. They joined the orgy of the bounding six, and now, instead of there being only eighteen Happy Lasses in red and green, there seemed to be dozens and dozens of them. The very stage seemed to get bigger and bigger, to give space to all these whirling figures of demoniac revelry. And as they all went spinning, leaping, cavorting crazily, the audience, shaken at last out of its stolidity, cheered them on, and all was one wild insanity.

Yet when it was done, when the King cried, 'Stop!' and all was over, it was as if it had never been, as if everybody had dreamed it, so that nobody was ready to swear that it had really happened. The Wesleyan and the other five all felt a certain faintness, but each was convinced that he had imagined all that wild activity while he was making a few sedate movements in the background. Nobody could be quite certain about anything. The pantomime went on its way; Jack was rescued by Jill and the Fairy Queen (who was now complaining of neuralgia); and the Demon King allowed himself to be foiled, after which he quietly disappeared again. They were looking for him when the whole thing was over except for that grand entry of all the characters at the very end. It was his business to march in with the Fairy Queen, the pair of them dividing between them all the applause for the supernaturals. Miss Farrar, feeling very miserable with her neuralgia, delayed her entrance for him, but as he was not to be found, she climbed the little ladder at the back alone, to march solemnly down the steps towards the audience. And the extraordinary thing was that when she was actually making her entrance, at the top of those steps, she discovered that she was not alone, that her fellow-supernatural was there too, and that he must have slipped away to freshen his make-up. He was more demonish than ever.

As they walked down between the files of Happy Yorkshire Lasses, now armed to the teeth with tinsel spears and shields, Miss Farrar whispered: 'Wish I'd arranged for a bouquet. You never get anything here.'

'You'd like some flowers?' said the fantastic figure at her elbow.

'Think I would! So would everybody else.'

'Quite easy,' he remarked, bowing slowly to the footlights. He took her hand and led her to one side, and it is a fact – as Miss Farrar will tell you, within half an hour of your making her acquaintance – that the moment their hands met, her neuralgia completely vanished. And now came the time for the bouquets. Miss Farrar knew what they would be; there would be one for the Principal Girl, bought by the management, and one for the Principal Boy, bought by herself.

'Oo, look!' cried the Second Boy. 'My gosh! – Bruddersford's gone mad.'

The space between the orchestral pit and the front row of stalls had been turned into a hothouse. The conductor was so busy passing up bouquets that he was no longer visible. There were dozens of bouquets, and all of them beautiful. It was monstrous. Somebody must have spent a fortune on flowers. Up they came, while everybody cheered, and every woman with a part had at least two or three. Miss Farrar, pink and wide-eyed above a mass of orchids, turned to her colleague among the supernaturals, only to find that once again he had quietly disappeared. Down came the curtain for the last time, but everybody remained standing there, with arms filled with expensive flowers, chattering excitedly. Then suddenly somebody cried, 'Oo!' and dropped her flowers, and others cried, 'Oo!' and dropped *their* flowers, until at last everybody who had had a bouquet had dropped it and cried, 'Oo!'

'Hot,' cried the Principal Girl, blowing on her fingers, 'hot as anything, weren't they? Burnt me properly. That's a nice trick.'

'Oo, look!' said the Second Boy, once more. 'Look at 'em all. Withering away.' And they were every one of them, all shedding their colour and bloom, curling, writhing, withering away. . .

'Message come through for you, sir, an hour since,' said the doorkeeper to the manager, 'only I couldn't get at yer. From the Leeds Infirmary, it is. Says Mr Ireton was knocked down in Boar Lane by a car this afternoon, but he'll be all right tomorrow. Didn't know who he was at first, so couldn't let anybody know.'

The manager stared at him, made a number of strange noises, then fled, signing various imaginary temperance pledges as he went.

'And another thing,' said the stage-hand to the stage-manager. 'That's where I saw the bloke last. He was there one minute and next minute he wasn't. And look at the place. All scorched.'

'That's right,' said his mate, 'and what's more, just you take a whiff— that's all, just take a whiff. Oo's started using brimstone in this the-ater? Not me nor you neither. But I've a good idea who it is.'

# Peekaboo

## *Bill Pronzini*

Roper came awake with the feeling that he wasn't alone in the house.

He sat up in bed, tense and wary, a crawling sensation on the back of his scalp. The night was dark, moonless; warm clotted black surrounded him. He rubbed sleep-mucus from his eyes, blinking, until he could make out the vague greyish outlines of the open window in one wall, the curtains fluttering in the hot summer breeze.

Ears straining, he listened. But there wasn't anything to hear. The house seemed almost graveyard still, void of even the faintest of night sounds.

What was it that had woken him up? A noise of some kind? An intuition of danger? It might only have been a bad dream, except that he couldn't remember dreaming. And it might only have been imagination, except that the feeling of not being alone was strong, urgent.

There's somebody in the house, he thought.

Or some *thing* in the house?

In spite of himself Roper remembered the story the nervous real estate agent in Whitehall had told him about this place. It had been built in the early 1900s by a local family, and when the last of them died off a generation later it was sold to a man named Lavolle who had lived in it for forty years. Lavolle had been a recluse whom the locals considered strange and probably evil; they hadn't had anything to do with him. But then he'd died five years ago, of natural causes, and evidence had been found by county officials that he'd been 'some kind of devil worshipper' who had 'practised all sorts of dark rites'. That was all the real estate agent would say about it.

Word had got out about that and a lot of people seemed to believe the house was haunted or cursed or something. For that reason, and because it was isolated and in ramshackle condition, it had stayed empty until a couple of years ago. Then a man called Garber, who was an amateur parapsychologist, leased the place and lived here for ten days. At the end of that time somebody came out from Whitehall to deliver groceries and found Garber dead. Murdered. The real estate agent wouldn't talk about how he'd been killed; nobody else would talk about it either.

Some people thought it was ghosts or demons that had murdered Garber. Others figured it was a lunatic – maybe the same one who'd killed half a dozen people in this part of New England over the past couple of years. Roper didn't believe in ghosts or demons or things that went bump in the night; that kind of supernatural stuff was for rural types like the ones in Whitehall. He believed in psychotic killers, all right, but he wasn't afraid of them; he wasn't afraid of anybody or anything. He'd made his living with a gun too long for that. And the way things were for him now, since the bank job in Boston had gone sour two weeks ago, an isolated back-country place like this was just what he needed for a few months.

So he'd leased the house under a fake name, claiming to be a writer, and he'd been here for eight days. Nothing had happened in that time: no ghosts, no demons, no strange lights or wailings or rattling chains – and no lunatics or burglars or visitors of any kind. Nothing at all.

Until now.

Well, if he *wasn't* alone in the house, it was because somebody human had come in. And he sure as hell knew how to deal with a human intruder. He pushed the blankets aside, swung his feet out of bed, and eased open the nightstand drawer. His fingers groped inside, found his .38 revolver and the flashlight he kept in there with it; he took them out. Then he stood, made his way carefully across to the bedroom door, opened it a crack, and listened again.

The same heavy silence.

Roper pulled the door wide, switched on the flash, and probed the hallway with its beam. No one there. He stepped out, moving on the balls of his bare feet. There were four other doors along the hallway: two more bedrooms, a bathroom, and an upstairs sitting room. He opened each of the doors in turn, swept the rooms with the flash, then put on the overhead lights.

Empty, all of them.

He came back to the stairs. Shadows clung to them, filled the wide foyer below. He threw the light down there from the landing. Bare mahogany walls, the lumpish shapes of furniture, more shadows crouching inside the arched entrances to the parlour and the library. But that was all: no sign of anybody, still no sounds anywhere in the warm dark.

He went down the stairs, swinging the light from side to side. At the bottom he stopped next to the newel post and used the beam to slice into the blackness in the centre hall. Deserted. He arced it around into the parlour, followed it with his body turned sideways to within a pace of the archway. More furniture, the big fieldstone fireplace at the far wall,

the parlour windows reflecting glints of light from the flash. He glanced
back at the heavy darkness inside the library, didn't see or hear any
movement over that way, and reached out with his gun hand to flick the
switch on the wall inside the parlour.

Nothing happened when the electric bulbs in the old-fashioned
chandelier came on; there wasn't anybody lurking in there.

Roper turned and crossed to the library arch and scanned the interior
with the flash. Empty bookshelves, empty furniture. He put on the
chandelier. Empty room.

He swung the cone of light past the staircase, into the centre hall –
and then brought it back to the stairs and held it there. The area beneath
them had been walled on both sides, as it was in a lot of these old houses,
to form a coat or storage closet; he'd found that out when he first moved
in and opened the small door that was set into the staircase on this side.
But it was just an empty space now, full of dust –

The back of his scalp tingled again. And a phrase from when he was
a kid playing hide-and-seek games popped into his mind.

*Peekaboo, I see you. Hiding under the stair.*

His finger tightened around the butt of the .38. He padded forward
cautiously, stopped in front of the door. And reached out with the hand
holding the flash, turned the knob, jerked the door open, and aimed the
light and the gun inside.

Nothing.

Roper let out a breath, backed away to where he could look down the
hall again. The house was still graveyard quiet; he couldn't even hear
the faint grumblings its old wooden joints usually made in the night. It
was as if the whole place was wrapped in a breathless waiting hush. As
if there was some kind of unnatural presence at work here –

Screw that, he told himself angrily. No such things as ghosts and
demons. There seemed to be presence here, all right – he could feel it
just as strongly as before – but it was a human presence. Maybe a burglar,
maybe a tramp, maybe even a goddamn lunatic. But *human.*

He snapped on the hall lights and went along there to the archway
that led into the downstairs sitting room. First the flash and then the
electric wall lamps told him it was deserted. The dining room off the
parlour next. And the kitchen. And the rear porch.

Still nothing.

Where was he, damn it? Where was he hiding?

The cellar? Roper thought.

It didn't make sense that whoever it was would have gone down there.
The cellar was a huge room, walled and floored in stone, that ran under
most of the house; there wasn't anything in it except spiderwebs and
stains on the floor that he didn't like to think about, not after the real

estate agent's story about Lavolle and his dark rites. But it was the only place left that he hadn't searched.

In the kitchen again, Roper crossed to the cellar door. The knob turned soundlessly under his hand. With the door open a crack, he peered into the thick darkness below and listened. Still the same heavy silence.

He started to reach inside for the light switch. But then he remembered that there wasn't any bulb in the socket above the stairs; he'd explored the cellar by flashlight before, and he hadn't bothered to buy a bulb. He widened the opening and aimed the flash downwards, fanning it slowly from left to right and up and down over the stone walls and floor. Shadowy shapes appeared and disappeared in the bobbing light: furnace, storage shelves, a wooden wine rack, the blackish gleaming stains at the far end, spiderwebs like tattered curtains hanging from the ceiling beams.

Roper hesitated. Nobody down there either, he thought. Nobody in the house after all? The feeling that he wasn't alone kept nagging at him – but it *could* be nothing more than imagination. All that business about devil worshipping and ghosts and demons and Garber being murdered and psychotic killers on the loose might have affected him more than he'd figured. Might have jumbled together in his subconscious all week and finally come out tonight, making him imagine menace where there wasn't any. Sure, maybe that was it.

But he had to make certain. He couldn't see all of the cellar from up here; he had to go down and give it a full search before he'd be satisfied that he really was alone. Otherwise he'd never be able to get back to sleep tonight.

Playing the light again, he descended the stairs in the same wary movements as before. The beam showed him nothing. Except for the faint whisper of his breathing, the creak of the risers when he put his weight on them, the stillness remained unbroken. The odours of dust and decaying wood and subterranean dampness dilated his nostrils; he began to breathe through his mouth.

When he came off the last of the steps he took a half-dozen strides into the middle of the cellar. The stones were cold and clammy against the soles of his bare feet. He turned to his right, then let the beam and his body transcribe a slow circle until he was facing the stairs.

Nothing to see, nothing to hear.

But with the light on the staircase, he realized that part of the wide, dusty area beneath them was invisible from where he stood – a mass of clotted shadow. The vertical boards between the risers kept the beam from reaching all the way under there.

The phrase from when he was a kid repeated itself in his mind: *Peekaboo, I see you. Hiding under the stair.*

With the gun and the flash extended at arm's length, he went diagonally to his right. The light cut away some of the thick gloom under the staircase, letting him see naked stone draped with more grey webs. He moved closer to the stairs, ducked under them, and put the beam full on the far joining of the walls.

Empty.

For the first time Roper began to relax. Imagination, no doubt about it now. No ghosts or demons, no burglars or lunatics hiding under the stair. A thin smile curved the corners of his mouth. Hell, the only one hiding under the stair was himself –

'Peekaboo,' a voice behind him said . . .

# The Black Lake

*Tony Richards*

'Listen,' said Greg Cowley.

'What? What is it?'

'Quiet, Doug! Be very quiet. Can you hear? . . . There's not a *sound*.'

Douggie Endell glanced at him and shrugged, untroubled.

The lake stretched out before them, black as tar beneath the pitiless Missouri sun. It was ringed around its entire edge with brown, decaying reeds. There was a tiny island in the middle, and a dead and withered overhanging tree which, ordinarily, might have provided shelter for teal and coots and other water birds, nesting places and perches for their land-feeding cousins. Not a single high pitched cry rang out across the lake. No frogs croaked, nothing scuttled through the reeds. There was not even, Cowley noticed, the humming of mosquitoes.

His friend, Douggie Endell, rubbed both sweaty palms together and then wiped them off against his gaudy Hawaiian shirt. 'Catfish country!' he said, grinning. 'You can almost *feel* them down there, whiskering around. Big! I'm gonna get me a big one.'

'I don't know, Doug,' Cowley said. He lit a cigarette and blew smoke against the motionless afternoon air.

There had, after all, been the strange looks they had received from the locals, in the town twenty miles back, where they'd stopped for hamburgers and fuel. And the words of the gas station attendant. *Lake up there? Yeah! But no one been near* that *lake for a long time*.

Douggie was looking at him oddly by now. 'Not sure? We'll take a vote, then. Come on.' And he began leading the way back up the dead-grass covered, shallow hill beyond which lay the trailer and the edge of the dusty road. The three married men, including Hugh Rosario, had set out at the beginning of the week on this annual hunting-and-fishing trip. They had stopped where they liked, reaped harvests of bass and pike and game. But Douggie had read, in one of his interminable magazines, that there were catfish around here which could pull a child into the water, swallow it whole. He *wanted* one of those. And Hugh Rosario *always* went along with him.

Cowley stopped at the top of the low hill and turned. Well, at least there was *one* other sign of life! Coming in swiftly from the east a bird, a swallow, was homing in on the lake, perhaps hoping to catch some insects there. It swung in very low across the water. Cowley watched it, the sun beating down on his head, sweat trickling into his eyes. The bird changed direction once, twice, lunged at something just above the surface . . .

And was gone.

Suddenly gone.

Ripples spread out across the jet black water.

'Did you see that?' he said to Douggie.

'See . . .?'

'The bird. The swallow. Disappeared.'

'Those things move so fast –' Douggie said. 'I'd get your hat on, get out of the sun. Out here, it can turn your brain to scrambled egg.'

Cowley wiped the hot, salty perspiration off his brow and out of his eyes. The back of his head, he realized, had begun to pound. 'Perhaps you're right,' he said. He followed his friend back to the trailer.

He saw the exact same thing happen again two hours later – except this time he was at close enough quarters to make out what was going on.

He and Hugh and Douggie had been busy in that time. First, they had pitched camp – he grudgingly. Then, wiry Hugh Rosario had gone down to the water with a can and used it to replenish their practically dry car radiator. Now, at long last, they had set up their rods and stout lines and were spaced two yards apart beside the black water, trying for a catfish. The sun was going down by now. Shadows lengthened in its dying rays. Cowley kept his hat on nonetheless. He felt calmer now. His brooding feeling about the lake would not entirely go away, but then, perhaps that was natural, there was always something eerie about these marshy places where the catfish dwelled. He imagined the oil-black creatures with their tiny jewel-like eyes rooting through the mud and the foulness down there, scavenging. Good to eat though. Unless, he smiled, remembering Douggie's tales about the swallowed children, they ate you first.

The swallow came winging in from the east, just like the other one. It was no more than a tiny patch of grey in the thickening gloom, with the flash of a paler grey belly. It swooped incredibly low over the surface of the lake – Cowley marvelled at how those birds could fly so very low. Then, a tiny black speck, a flying insect, detached itself from the water. The swallow swung towards it. Caught it in its beak.

And suddenly there was darkness all around it. Jet blackness. There was no sight of its flapping wings. Its pale flash of chest had disappeared. There was a splash, and ripples . . . and the bird was gone.

Cowley felt a chill spreading through his stomach. He could not bring himself to move his legs. It had all happened so fast. So *fast*! His hands clenched involuntarily. But he somehow found it in himself to speak.

'Hugh. Douggie!'

Neither of them were taking any notice of him. The tip of Douggie's fishing rod had begun gently to bounce.

What *exactly* had he seen? A bird fall in the water? Something rear out of the lake and eat the bird? The latter explanation made more sense, in its own bizarre way – but there was something he was missing, something ticking at the back of his mind. The *insect*. It was to do with the insect!

He watched with horrified fascination as the tip of Douggie's rod gave a sudden massive thump, and the man in his gaudy shirt grabbed hold of it and struck. The fibre glass bent double. Douggie let out a whoop which resounded round the lake.

'Got one! Got one!'

Cowley lunged across and grabbed him by the shoulder.

'Let it go, Doug!'

'*What?*'

'Cut the line!'

'What are you talking about, Greg Cowley?' Hugh Rosario said in that quiet voice of his.

'Something's spooking him,' Douggie interjected. 'He's been twitchy since he got here.' He went on playing the fish.

'What's up, Greg?' Hugh asked, looking genuinely concerned.

'I . . .' Cowley faltered. 'I'm not sure. Something's eaten a bird out there.'

'You're kidding?'

'I *saw* it. I think we ought to get away from here.'

'Sure,' Douggie put in again. '*When* I land this fish.'

The moon had begun to rise by now. Out on the far end of the line, thrashing with its tail, something swirled below the silvered waters of the lake.

By the end of five minutes, it was struggling feebly close to the bank. Hugh Rosario snapped out of his trance and got a gaff beneath it, then pulled, putting all his weight into the effort. Douggie's catch came flapping on to dry land. It was a catfish, perhaps thirty pounds. Big, and strong, but that was all.

'You see!' Douggie said, throwing down his rod. Black ooze trickled from his line back into the lake. 'Was that what all the fuss was about?'

He hefted a piece of deadwood and cracked the fish three times across the base of the skull. It quivered, then lay still. Cowley could not take his eyes from it. True, he had expected something more. But the uneasy feeling would not go away. There had been something wrong with the swallow's insect; there was something wrong with this fish. It was so hard to tell in the moonlight.

'Get a torch down here,' Douggie ordered Rosario. He waited till the beam was on the fish's mouth. Then he knelt down to unhook it. He made a point, at the last moment, to turn his face around and grin at Cowley.

Then he put his hand inside the fish's mouth.

And screamed.

Cowley's first thought was, *My God, it's bitten him! I thought it was dead!* But the screams were too high pitched for that. Douggie was trying to stand up, but the fish's mouth had closed around his wrist.

Collapsed tight around his wrist, Cowley realized, rooted to the spot. It was all happening so numbingly fast!

In an instant, the fish had lost its shape. It appeared like nothing so much now as an obscene length of quivering black ooze, the same dark colour as the lake. It spread up Douggie's arm towards his shoulder. From his shoulder to his face. In an instant, it had filled his eyes, covered his cheeks – and still it was spreading. Douggie gave out one final scream, inhumanly high and loud.

And then he flailed backwards, out of terror and pain. The edge of the bank crumbled under him. The black lake slid around him, muffling his splashes.

He was gone.

Silence.

Cowley stood there, one arm outstretched, watching the ripples spreading. There was not a single movement beneath the surface of the water. A drowning man, *surely*, should at least kick and flail, if only for an instant. And perhaps it was that – the knowledge that Douggie was already dead, and from something other than drowning, something to do not with the water but the entire lake *itself* – that prevented him from doing the normal thing and diving in.

Somewhere, in a drawer back at home, he had a life-saving medal from the end of his schooldays. But that was for normal circumstances, which did not apply here.

'Oh my God,' Hugh Rosario was saying, very quietly. He was still holding the torch. He angled it upwards from his face, as though noticing it for the first time in a very long while, and then shone it back at the water. Tears were already beginning to run across his whitened face. 'What *was* that? What in the name of heaven . . .?'

Cowley, somehow, got a hold of himself. They were both going into shock, he knew, but that would have to be delayed for just a little while.

What on earth were they doing standing here like idiots? He grabbed hold of Hugh Rosario's arm.

'I didn't *do* nothing,' Rosario said.

Cowley yanked at him. The torch tumbled to the ground.

'He was my friend and I didn't *do* nothing. He can't be dead. He can't be!'

Rosario was *already* in shock. He was barely capable of moving at the moment. Cowley slung the man's arm over his shoulder, gripped him tightly – and began hauling him back up the slope towards the trailer and the car. He had never realized what a dead weight a man in shock could be. Sweat began to trickle down between his shoulder blades. Despite the fear, despite the growing coldness of the night, he felt that he was burning up inside.

And all the while, Rosario kept mumbling the same things over and over again. *I didn't do nothing. He was my friend. What are we going to tell his family? He can't be dead. He can't be. I don't want him dead.* As though *wanting* could bring Douggie Endell back.

By the time they reached the top of the hill, neither of them could go any further. Cowley turned around and released his grip, letting Hugh gently down to a seated position. Then he squatted down beside him, breathing heavily. He gazed back at the lake.

It was perfectly still now, completely silent. The surface had the unflawed smoothness of a mirror; the moonlight glittered down, washing across it, and it was hard to believe that, moments ago, a man had died in there, agonized and screaming.

A gentle breeze came up from the East and began to stir the reeds around the bank.

Cowley put his arm around Rosario and felt how violently the man was trembling. Or perhaps part of the trembling was his own.

'Come on, Hugh. We've got to get back to the car.'

Hugh could not hear him. He was staring unblinkingly at the water out of his tear-stained face, and his lips were moving robotically.

'He *can't* be dead,' he was still saying. 'I don't *want* him dead. I don't *want* . . .'

He leaned forwards, stretched out his arm.

Something moved beneath the surface of the lake.

No! Cowley thought. He stood upright very slowly, not once taking his eyes from the water's surface. The movement, creating an oily black bulge, was coming from near the bank. It was the exact same place where Douggie had fallen. For an instant, Cowley had a nightmarish vision of catfish lurking down there, feeding on Douggie Endell's corpse. And then the surface tension of the water broke.

And a shape began to emerge.

A human shape.

A head and a pair of shoulders, silhouetted against the reflection of the moon.

*He's dead!* Cowley's mind screamed. *I saw him die! I saw it!*

The silhouette lifted an arm, as though it were begging for help.

And Hugh Rosario gave a loud, bewildered cry of '*Douggieee!*'. He was scrambling back down the hill before Cowley could stop him.

Cowley turned and raced back for the open door of the trailer. His mind was working furiously. A connection was being made. It was something he had read once, about certain aquatic creatures that present themselves as prey and then, when other fish get close enough, devour them, predators themselves. And what if it was not simply a fish this time? What if the entire lake –

He leaped inside the caravan, snatched up his hunting rifle, and was rushing back towards the water.

He skidded to a halt at the brow of the hill.

Down there, Hugh Rosario was trying to rescue what he thought was Douggie. He had grabbed a handful of dead brush on the bank, and was leaning out across the water, trying to reach his friend.

'*Hugh!*' Cowley yelled.

The man took no notice. But the silhouette did. It turned its dark, featureless face towards him and then looked away and began wading towards the bank. Cowley flicked the safety catch off. He raised the rifle to his shoulder. Then he froze. *What if he was wrong? What if it* was *Douggie?*

The silhouette was closer now.

'Come on, Douggie. You can make it!' Hugh Rosario was shouting.

Their hands were practically touching.

The moonlight shimmered brightly on the ripples. The reflected light began lapping up the body of the silhouette. And it must have touched its face – because, suddenly, Hugh Rosario yelled and began to pull back. He lost his balance. One foot slipped out across the water, and the silhouette grabbed hold of it.

Cowley snapped the gun to his shoulder and began firing. He emptied the entire magazine into the silhouette. It did no good at all. As though the bullets were passing through ooze ... through water.

The silhouette started to lose its human form. It became no more than a horrible amorphous mass, and began enveloping Rosario. The man screamed. He was still clinging on to the brush, struggling to pull himself free, but the lake had claimed his entire leg now and was working up his body. Rosario shrieked like a child. His hands spasmed around the clump of dead brush, as though it were his last link with the world. And then the blackness claimed his head, his face. His arms became limp. His hands released their grip. He was gone, into the water.

Cowley stood motionless on the hilltop, clutching the gun. He waited for the silhouette to come back, but it did not reappear.

Hurling the empty rifle down, he swivelled around and scrambled back for the car. He kicked the huge Dodge station wagon into life and, slamming the gearshift into place, raced off along the dusty road.

He had not even uncoupled the trailer. It swung behind him for the first half mile, smashing into trees and posts along the roadside, spilling out its contents. Finally, the coupling broke, and the last sight he had in the rearview mirror was of it spinning down the road bank like a tent in a high wind.

The Dodge moved faster now. Cowley drove like a man possessed. All he wanted to do was to get as far from that lake as possible.

It was somehow *alive*, a living creature, the whole thing, he realized. It somehow *fed*, in the same manner as those cunning predatory fish fed. The swallows had wanted insects, and the lake had provided them with what looked like insects, and then devoured them. Douggie Endell had wanted a catfish; the lake had provided him with a simulacrum of one, and swallowed him. Hugh Rosario had wanted Douggie back . . .

He could still remember those final screams. He clenched his teeth and concentrated on the road.

How many miles had he travelled now? Two? Three at the outside. Which made it still seventeen miles back to the town. God, he needed to see the lights of civilization. God, he needed to see another human face.

He had been travelling on an upward incline all the way. The motor thumped and roared.

Cowley glanced down at the dashboard and saw to his disbelief that the temperature gauge's needle was almost in the red area, the danger zone.

And then he remembered. This afternoon, Hugh Rosario had refilled the radiator with several gallons . . . from the lake! *He was carrying the water with him!*

No! *Oh God, no!*

He could only watch as the needle swung to the centre of the red zone. There was a sudden explosion as the radiator burst.

Black steam shot up before the windscreen, blinding him. He fought to regain control of the Dodge for a second, and then it slewed to the right and crashed against a tree stump. Pain seared up through Cowley, through his legs and the back of his neck. And he passed out.

It was still night when he came part way to. He was slightly delirious, he realized vaguely. The moon hung high above him through the starred windscreen, and the grasses stirred gently in the breeze. His legs were numb beneath the steering wheel. He could not feel his left arm, nor move it. The pain in his neck had spread right down his spine now, tearing him.

He managed to shift his head a little and squinted out through the intact side window. Save for the rustling grasses, there were no sounds at all. Shouldn't there at least have been the chirruping of crickets at this time of year? The black water had poured out of the radiator and was lying, cooling, all around the car.

*Come on!* Cowley thought. *I'm helpless. Come and get me!*

The water quivered slightly, but otherwise did not move.

*What are you waiting for?* Cowley thought. It should either begin its long journey back down the gradient towards the lake, or attack him. But not this motionlessness, anything but this.

Then he realized. Dimly, he understood. Some of the windows had splintered in the Dodge, but none of them had smashed, and no doors had burst open. There was no way for the water to get in.

Except that, an hour later, the pain in Cowley's back had become a miasma of agony – spreading to his brain, rendering him almost totally delirious. A dream-image began forming in his head. It was the image of a little house with all the windows brightly lit, with flowers in the porch. The door came open and, in the image, a figure stood before him. The thought took shape. *I want to see my wife again.*

He gazed out of the side window again. The black water had gone. In its place stood a familiar form, a female shape, caught in silhouette. It was so wonderful of her to come all this way to rescue him. Smiling, he opened the door to let her in.

# The Red Turret

## *Flavia Richardson*

After a lapse of nearly half a century an Erringham came once more to the home of his fathers. Roy Erringham had spent the first thirty years of his life abroad: born and bred in Canada, he never saw his old home till he walked into it by right of succession one October evening.

Jerome Erringham, his father, was dead: going abroad, a poverty-stricken younger son, he had carved his way to fame and wealth, if not fortune, by his own efforts and those of his wife. Roy, the only child, had inherited the bulk of his wealth. Ten years before, his father had come into the Erringham property, but business necessities had kept him from coming to take possession; moreover, he counted himself an outcast and a working-man – one who had but little desire to live in the lordly home of his fathers.

Now there was only one Erringham left in the world – the last of a once proud and spreading family – and that one was Roy. True, there was hope for the future, for Helen, Roy's wife of a year, was a healthy woman and there was no reason why she should not bear sons.

Together, Roy and Helen walked into the old house on the day after they landed in England.

Roy loved it. Helen hated and feared it.

'But it's beautiful,' he said, as he led her from one room to another. 'Beautiful. Can't you see it?'

She shook her head. 'I can't bear it. Roy, I don't think I can live here. It's too – too gloomy. There is something uncanny about it. The house seems to be watching us. Don't you feel it?'

He shook his head and patted her on the shoulder.

'Of course it's watching us, silly. Why not? It's the old home of the Erringhams. We've been here for centuries. It's glad we've come back. It wants to make sure that we're the right sort.'

'The right sort,' Helen repeated, with a shiver. 'Yes, Roy, but what sort does this house want?' Her voice shrilled a little.

'You're tired.' He spoke with masterful decision. 'Come and rest for a bit. We'll go over the rest of the house tomorrow.'

Away in the newer wing which the housekeeper, engaged by the lawyers, had rendered habitable, Helen felt less disturbed. She determined that, come what might, she would have her own rooms in this new and more comfortable quarter. Not for her the stone-walled grandeur of the great dining-room or the panels of the long saloon: she admitted that though she could appreciate grandeur in the abstract, she wanted modernity and comfort in real life. Tucked up on the luxurious chesterfield, a shaded electric standard at her elbow, a new magazine on the occasional-table, she felt at peace. This was home: she began to get a touch of warmth into her feeling for the old house. After all, it was only natural that so old a place should have an atmosphere.

'Perhaps it's me,' she murmured, half asleep. 'I'm the thing that's wrong. I don't belong here. I belong to Canada. I'm not really an Erringham – it thinks I'm an interloper.'

In the morning various business claimed both her and Roy. In the afternoon, neighbours, forgetful of the bother of settling into a house that had been shut up for years, insisted on coming to call.

Not till dinner was over did Roy have time to finish his tour.

'You'll come with me, darling?' he said, a little anxiously.

Helen assented. After all, it was her home; she must make it like her, must herself grow accustomed to the atmosphere.

They went through the long succession of rooms that they had seen the day before till at last they reached the picture gallery.

It ran the whole width of the house on the first floor. Above it was nothing but the roof. The high ceiling had been built to give an impression of space. The bedrooms on the floor above were all in the other wing.

Helen went to one of the long mullioned windows and looked out.

'We look down on the terrace here,' she observed, over her shoulder. Then she added: 'Roy, the door to the turret ought to be somewhere here. It's at this end of the house.'

'Of course.' He joined her at the window and took his bearings.

'That's funny,' he said, looking back into the room. 'There's no sign of a door here. Wonder where it is.'

He strolled over to the end of the room, and Helen followed him, scanning the Erringham ancestors idly as she passed. Suddenly she gave a little cry and covered her face with her hands.

'What's the matter?' Roy was beside her in an instant.

'That picture!' she cried, pointing to the corner in deepest shadow. 'It moved! I'm sure it did! . . .' Her voice rose a trifle.

'Steady on, darling!' Roy spoke reprovingly. 'You never used to have nerves like these. Of course it didn't move. Let's go over and look at it. I can't see who it is from here, it's so dark.'

He stepped to the wall to turn on the electric light, but the switch was dead, and with an exclamation of annoyance he turned back.

'I've got my flashlight with me,' he said. 'Come on, Helen. We'll kill this bogy of yours before we go downstairs.'

He pressed the button of the torch and directed the glare onto the picture in the corner.

'Great-grandfather,' he said, his eye catching the date on the frame. 'He–he – not a very pleasant-looking old bird, eh?'

Helen laughed nervously. She saw the distinctive Erringham features; saw, too, how they were reproduced in Roy. Standing there with the faint radiance on his face, he might almost have been his great-grandfather come back to life.

'I believe there was some sort of scandal about the old man,' said Roy, as he looked at the portrait again. 'I don't know what it was: Dad never mentioned it. But when I went through his papers after he was dead, I found some funny passages in some old letters that his mother sent him. She was daughter-in-law to this old man and lived here with my grandfather before he came into the property. I gather he was a bit of a queer fish, but I don't know why.'

'I don't like him,' Helen whispered. 'He looks so evil.'

'Not too prepossessing,' agreed Roy. 'Got the worst type of Erringham face, hasn't he?' He lifted the torch and looked at the picture from another angle. 'Hello,' he said, 'what's that? Do you see, a handle or something on the side of the frame. I believe it's the entrance to the door of the turret. Let's go and see.'

'Oh, don't, Roy,' Helen pleaded, urged by some instinct for which she could not account. 'Please don't. Do wait for daylight.'

'Not I,' he returned. 'The moon's coming up. The view from the turret over to the hills will be perfectly marvellous. Come along, Helen. Don't be a 'fraid cat,' he taunted.

She set her lips and waited while he pulled at the handle.

As they had expected, the whole portrait swung round and a narrow flight of steps was disclosed to view.

'I wonder why they hid it,' said Roy, as he swung the light up.

'Not much hidden, was it? We should have seen the lever at once in daylight.' Helen was determined to make the whole matter as uninteresting and commonplace as she could. Somehow she sensed that in the turret lay danger – danger not so much to herself as to Roy, and she was determined to give it no aid by preparing to be afraid.

'Perhaps,' Roy assented a little unwillingly.

He gave one glance at the portrait of his great-grandfather and then began to climb up the staircase. It wound round in a narrow spiral, evidently built in the thickness of the outer wall, while the turret itself rested on the roof of the picture gallery.

Helen followed, partly because she did not dare to trust Roy alone with what might happen, and partly because she herself did not dare to stop alone in the picture gallery with the Erringhams around. To her sensitive mind an air of repellent contempt came from the pictured faces. She knew they were not so much resentful of her as pitying, but pitying with a sneer.

Setting her teeth, she tossed her head at the lot of them and put her foot on the first stair.

The staircase was only the height of the gallery, and three or four turns took them to the door at the top which barred the way.

Roy turned the great iron handle and pushed the door ajar. It was a heavy oaken affair, clamped with metal bands and screws. No one could have passed it without immense effort had it been barred.

'Here's the turret,' said Roy, throwing the beam forward. Helen pressed to his side, and together they looked in amazement.

The turret was much larger than it looked from the ground, whence it gave the impression of being merely a pepper-box. It was deceptively built, its size running inwards along the width of the roof so that the chimney-stacks broke the line and hid much of it.

On three sides were windows, deep-set, filled with thick glass, on which strange designs had been painted, evidently by amateur hands. Helen walked over to them and looked at them closely. The moon was shining full into the little room, and its strange furnishings were clearly picked out. Roy snapped off the torch, for it was not needed, and he knew that the battery was wearing low. He would want what light he had to help them down the spiral stairs and through the picture gallery.

The moon passed behind a cloud, and for a moment the room was plunged into darkness. Before Helen could implore Roy to put on the torch, there came a strange unearthly radiance, filling the whole place and yet appearing from a source unknown.

Helen shrank back into the embrasure of the window, frightened.

Roy stood still in the middle of the room, taken unawares, yet amazed rather than scared. He knew all at once that he had dimly expected this. That as an Erringham he must be present at some strange, mysterious rite and make a choice. He waited.

Helen waited also. She grew less afraid. Her eyes roamed round the room. In the dim yet clear red of the light, it was easy to pick out the objects on the floor. In the wall that had no window was set a table. On it stood a golden plate and cup. Before it was a narrow mat, ivory white, worked in black. The light was so clear that she could distinguish the pattern of fir-cones that formed the chief feature of the scrolled design.

In the distance a clock struck ten times. The normal sound would ordinarily have reassured her, suggesting as it did a house inhabited by servants, a sane and pleasant life to which she could return at any moment if she so chose. But at the moment of the first stroke of the clock some new power seemed to fill the room.

It was so subtle, so strong, and so unexpected, that for the moment Helen was nearly overwhelmed by it. It gave her no time to prepare: it caught her, as it were, in a web of fine tissue and held her, unable to speak or move, yet conscious of all that went on.

She tried to cry out to Roy, but her voice was strangled in her throat. She tried to go to him, but her limbs seemed paralysed.

Her eyes fixed themselves on him and saw the change that came over his features. He had lost some of the wonder that had marked them when the phenomenal light began to appear. He was looking absorbed, interested, almost, Helen shuddered mentally, as if he were about to enjoy himself. He seemed to be expecting something, as if he knew what was about to happen and why.

Out of the radiance of the red light a figure seemed to materialize – the figure of an old man wearing the robes of a priest. He turned, and Helen caught sight of his mocking, sardonic face. Her head reeled, she found she could not faint. Roy's great-grandfather stood in the middle of the room, beckoning to Roy – and Roy went to him, gladly, as if it were a natural thing!

'Erringham of the Erringhams, you have come!' The words could have issued from no living mouth, yet Helen would have sworn that she heard them clearly spoken.

Roy took another step towards that strange figure clad in gold and black, with touches of white that gleamed red in the light.

'I have come,' he said, with assurance, as one who saw no cause for fear. 'What do you want?'

'Tonight you have your choice,' the strange, unearthly voice went on. 'Your father refused to choose: he died a stranger in a strange land rather than face the choice of the Erringhams. Your grandfather died: your uncle died. You have come back.'

'I am here,' Roy reiterated. 'What do I choose?'

'Whether you will eat of the Tree of Knowledge of Good and Evil, whether you will learn the control of the Life Force, whether you will be as God, even as I am, and conquer even the last great enemy, Death, that rides upon the Pale Horse and passes no one by.'

'And the price?'

'There is none. Knowledge is Power. What more do you desire? Death shall pass you by, so shall you escape the final reckoning, since only the dead can be judged by God.'

'I choose. I will follow you.'

The old man's eyes seemed to gleam more brightly, and the face he turned towards Helen was distorted with devilish glee. She tried again to scream, to warn Roy, but she could not make a sound.

'And the ritual?' Roy asked. He had not moved, but it was plain that he was beginning to suffer from suppressed excitement. His face was very pale and the sweat began to show on his forehead.

'The Service of Sacrifice shall be held tonight.'

The strange apparition went to the table built against the wall, which Helen, her heart sinking again, now recognized as an altar. He busied himself for a moment with the golden vessels. Then he bent down and touched a spring in the front of the table. It swung open, and, controlled by the same spring, a stone slab slid quietly forward, resting some six inches above the ground. On it lay a strangely shaped knife, the handle glittering with jewels.

'All is prepared,' said the man, as he drew himself up again.

In obedience to a sign, Roy came forward to the altar and flung himself on his knees.

Old Erringham stood before the stone slab and raised his arms. He began to chant, softly at first, then more loudly in that terrible room. At first Helen could not pick out the words, was only aware that they were in a strange tongue. Then gradually something familiar yet mysterious about them struck her and she realized with a further pang of horror that she was listening to that foulest of all rites, the Black Mass.

'But there should be a sacrifice. There must be blood,' she heard herself saying, able to speak for the first time, but seemingly unable to control her words.

'There shall be blood. There shall be blood and a burnt-offering. There shall be a willing sacrifice,' came back to her, chanted by the priest.

Moving in spite of herself, with no power over her limbs, walking as if hypnotized, Helen found herself crossing the floor to that terrible altar. Roy still knelt, his face buried in his hands. She tried to speak to him but could not. She could not even touch him as she went by. She must move as if in a dream.

Still without conscious volition, yet terribly aware of all that was going on, Helen found herself lying on the slab. Staring up into the face of the Erringham apostate, she was nearly rendered unconscious by the malevolence of his look. Suddenly an inner power came to her; she knew that she could only save herself by a supreme effort – still more, that only so could she save Roy.

Summoning every ounce of will power, she broke the bonds that controlled her. She found her voice. Brokenly, only half conscious of what she said, she began to recite the Pater Noster. . . At the first words, a fury seized the demon bending above her. He seized the jewelled-handled knife and thrust it into Roy's hands.

'It is the moment of the Sacrifice,' he chanted, his voice drowning Helen's feeble tones. 'It is the moment for the spilling of the blood. See, my son, I place the golden cup beneath the Stone that it may catch the precious drops as they run, that you and I may drink from them and live.'

As one in a dream, Roy rose from his knees and took the knife that was held out to him. He tested the blade against his nail, swung it in the air, and –

'Roy!' Helen screamed.

The sound startled him. He dropped the knife. It fell across his leg, gashing the shin through his sock. A little blood trickled out and across the altar-stone.

With a cry of baffled fury, mingled with desire, old Erringham bent down and tried to catch the flow in the golden chalice.

Helen, on her feet by now, caught the cup, making the Sacred Sign as she did so. There was a blinding flash of light, that seemed to come from the altar. The room was lighted up and at the same moment a crashing peal of thunder broke over the house. As it died away, came another ominous crash, and the roof of the turret started to crumble and fall in.

Helen seized Roy and dragged him to the head of the stairs. Behind them was the rumbling of falling stones and plaster, with a crash at intervals, as one of the big roof-beams came down.

Somehow they staggered down the stairs and through the picture gallery, till they roused the frightened servants to action.

The storm had been sharp and sudden: only that one flash and one crack of thunder had been heard.

In the morning they went upstairs to see the damage done. The picture gallery seemed unharmed in spite of the masonry that had fallen on its roof. But when they went to the door of the staircase Roy and Helen started back in amazement.

The picture of old Erringham, the wizard, the devotee of the Black One, had been torn from its frame and lay, a great cut in the canvas over the heart, face downwards on the floor.

They dragged it to one side and forced their way up to the turret. One wall still stood, the one against which had been built the altar-stone. For the rest, Roy and Helen stood under the sweet blue sky and the clean sunlight.

Beneath the altar was a heap of rubbish. Roy went over to examine it. He came back, his face graver than before.

'Don't go to look,' he said. 'I – I must get someone to help. They are – bones. There must have been a body buried there.'

Helen turned white. 'Your great-grandfather,' she said.

'I expect so. You remember they always said his grave was empty in the churchyard. Last night the Devil came for his own.'

Helen shivered. 'I am glad the turret has gone,' she said, and led Roy to the head of the stairs.

# Intercom

## *Agnes Short*

The Chanonry is a tranquil street of high walls, trees and quiet, professorial houses. Four hundred and fifty years ago this same Chanonry contained within its high walls and dykes (for defence in troublous times) not only the grand cathedral church with its tower and sonorous bells, but also the bishop's palace, the prebends' lodgings with their yards and glebes, the chaplains' court (or chambers) and a hospital for twelve poor men.

But the great tower fell. The Reformation stripped the ancient cathedral of its statuary and gold and reduced it to the gaunt, grey proportions of a parish church. The houses of the prebends were demolished and the houses of the gentry sold, pulled stone from stone to build up different, democratic houses for the Presbyterian middle classes. The chaplain's passageway is lost and there is a students' hall of residence where the bishop's palace stood, but somewhere under the vaulted pre-cast concrete of the modern dining hall the old-town draw-well still holds its secret and the buried bodies of men. The hospital, too, has disappeared and what remains of the chaplains' court is an ordinary private house.

Or so Margaret Ford believed until she stood on the doorstep in a night of drenching rain and looked up at the great, blank wall above her. It was a wall of dead windows: the larger blinded by shutters, the smaller by stones and cement. Bricked up how many years ago? By whom? And why? The rain glistened on the pitted quarters of a heraldic crest set into the wall above a small, barred window. The girl made out beyond the darkness the crude outline of a boar's head, castles and Latin, picked out in scraps and gold. '*Spe –*'

'Hope, lingering hopelessly on,' she thought, with unexpected sadness.

Beneath the crest there was the bricked-in crescent of what must once have been an arch, and a window embrasure at ankle level told her the walls were four feet thick. The raindrops which clung to the rough stone of the walls were dark and moist, like blood, except where the gleam from a street lamp rounded them briefly with light. The glistening street stretched on either side of her, silent and empty, between high, crenellated walls.

The only sound was the steady drip, drip of moisture from the overhanging trees and somewhere, in a far-away street, an echoing footstep which receded deliberately into silence. The girl shivered, pulled her cloak more tightly around her and rang the bell again.

The door opened and light flooded the steps.

'I'm so sorry. I hope you haven't been ringing for ages, but we can't hear the bell upstairs. Or downstairs, come to that. One of the penalties of living in a big house.'

The man was thin, with the nervous thinness of the ascetic. He was good-looking in a famished way, especially now, in dinner jacket and black tie. The girl stepped over the threshold and shook herself like a timid animal. Rain showered the hall with diamonds.

'Let me take your coat.'

Professor Adams lifted the dark cloak from her shoulders. His wife, descending the stair in her sensible black dress with the beading at the neck, felt an uncomfortable jolt of the heart when she rounded the last landing and saw them standing there. Her husband dark, thin, intense. And the girl ... she could find no words to describe the girl. In her simple, timeless gown of crimson wool, belted loosely at the waist, and her black, straight hair she was at the same time innocence and danger. Joan Adams shook away the fear and stepped briskly down the last few steps.

'I'll show you where everything is, dear,' she said with a professional smile.  She opened a door and they descended below street level to a low-beamed room of oak and brass and rough stone walls.

'We like the bare stone,' she explained. 'It's the original structure down here, all sixteenth-century. The floor's intact, too, but I'm afraid I drew the line at stone flags, even for history's sake. This is the intercom,' she went on, indicating a small box on the dresser. 'The walls are so thick it's impossible to hear them without it, so keep it switched on. Then you'll hear if one of them wakes. The kitchen is this way.'

She led the girl out of the beamed room by a second door, into an arched scullery.

'This is the old coach entrance,' Mrs Adams explained. 'They used to drive in this way to the courtyard. I expect you saw the crest on the wall outside. It really was a court in the old days, you see. Four sides of a square and four towers, one at each corner. The piece we live in is all that's left.'

'Who lived here?' asked the girl.

'Here? Originally twenty chaplains from the cathedral and a hard time they must have had, too. All sorts of rigid rules. Doors barred at eight o'clock and no women, of course. They still went in for celibacy in those days, though I expect some of them managed to get round it just the same, don't you?'

The girl didn't answer. She was looking upwards to the arched dimness of the ceiling where there was a huge iron hook.

'That's where they hung the lantern,' said Mrs Adams. 'And men too, I wouldn't wonder. Here's the kitchen,' she went on, going up three steps to the next room. 'I've left everything ready. There's coffee and sandwiches and so on when you want them. I think that's about all. I've locked the back door. In a house like this where everything is so spread out you have to be careful. You'd never hear if anyone came in uninvited. Not that they ever would,' she continued hastily – good baby-sitters were rare and precious – 'but it's best to be careful. Now I'll just show you where the children are.'

They passed back through the arch of the scullery and the low-beamed living room, up narrow stairs to the front hall and upwards again to the open doorway of a shuttered room. The girl looked quickly into the darkness – shadows, two beds, two sleeping shapes, more shadows.

'What do I do if they wake?' she whispered.

'They won't. They never do. But if by any chance something should disturb them, give them a drink of orange juice and tell them a little story. Reassure them that we'll be back soon. I've left a note of where we're going.'

As Margaret nodded, something made her glance over her shoulder. A movement? Or a stir of cold air? Behind her a shadowed corridor stretched to a short flight of steps; more doors. Stairs climbed upwards into narrow, creaking darkness. The uncurtained window of the landing showed her nothing but her own outline, a small, slim girl with flowing hair and a long dress. The dim landing lamp flickered back from the glass like candle flame against the night. Somewhere on the floor above them a board creaked, a window rattled softly in its frame.

'Is the rest of the house empty?' asked the girl, timidly.

'There's no one else in, if that's what you mean,' said Mrs Adams. 'Only you and the children. But there's nothing to worry about.'

'Joan!' called a voice from the hall. 'We'll be late!'

'Coming!' They descended to the front hall. 'I was just showing Margaret the ropes. Now,' she added, turning to the girl, 'are you sure you'll be all right?'

'There's television and so on,' said John Adams vaguely. 'Books. Help yourself. Make yourself at home.'

'Thank you, but I'm going to try and get some work done. It's so noisy in my digs and I've that essay of yours to finish.'

'Good girl,' said Adams. 'You'll find it quiet enough here and you can use any of my reference books you like. Oh and if you do hear noises, don't worry. It's only the central heating.'

Outside in the car Mrs Adams turned worriedly to her husband. 'Are you sure she's all right? She hardly spoke a word and she looks so frail. Almost unreal. That ridiculous dress and all that hair. And her eyes! She looks as if she lives in a different world.'

'She's all right. A bit tense, perhaps, but sensible enough. Things have been getting too much for her lately, that's all. Overwork, depression, end-of-term nerves, you know the sort of thing. And her digs sound pretty grim. She jumped at the chance of an evening on her own.'

'Yes, but the children . . . you do think . . .?'

'For Christ's sake, Joan, stop fussing. You want to go to the party, don't you? I thought that was the whole point and you said yourself there was no one else.'

'Yes, I know, and you did very well to find anyone at all. But she gives me the creeps. You don't think she's on drugs, do you?'

'I have not the slightest idea. Would you like me to go back and ask her?'

His wife ignored the sarcasm. 'It's her eyes, I think. When I saw her standing on the doorstep in the rain with that cloak to her feet and the hood, I had the ridiculous idea that she'd found her way into the wrong century.'

'She's certainly brilliant on sixteenth-century poetry,' agreed Adams. 'Especially the love poems, which is odd because I gather she has no time for boys.'

'Oh?' Mrs Adams pricked up her ears. 'Not girls instead?'

'Of course not!' John Adams felt unreasonably angry on the girl's behalf. 'There's nothing at all abnormal about her. In fact, she's a particularly feminine and attractive girl. I had the impression that her fellow students just don't interest her.'

'Perhaps it's you she's after?' said Joan Adams with a laugh, but her voice had an edge which made her husband jam his foot down hard on the accelerator and set his teeth. The party had better be good.

The girl stood in the middle of the room and waited until the car engine disappeared into the distance. She stood a moment longer, listening to the silence, then she began to move slowly round the room, touching the rough stone of the walls with reverent fingers, tracing the outline of the ancient beams. There was a Jacobean chest, a refectory table, and a row of leather-bound books. Campion. Lyly. Sir Philip Sidney. She took one out, opened it and read aloud at random.

'"Joy to the persone of my love".' Her voice moved like velvet in the silence. Suddenly her heart swelled and she laughed softly. She spread her skirts, dipped to the carpeted floor in a sweeping curtsy and began to pace the first stately steps of a galliard. Somewhere, far away and faint, she heard a lute pluck sweetly in time to her dance.

The girl paused, listened, but there was nothing.

'Wishful thinking,' she said aloud and sighed. 'And this won't get that essay written.'

She opened her bag and took out papers, a clip file and a sheaf of notes which she spread out in front of her on the refectory table. She turned off the main light and sat down at the table in the small golden pool of the reading lamp. She wrote a careful headline 'The Sacred and the Profane in Sixteenth-Century Poetry' and began to work.

It was some time before she noticed the music. But gradually she became aware that somewhere beyond the black and white clarity of the written word there was sound and light. Somewhere the soft, plucking beauty of a lute was stringing the darkness with gold. The girl's hand stopped and she looked up. Her eyes probed the shadows of the room, listening. The lamplight splashed the surface of the polished wood with gold but on the edge of that light the shadows held only shapes, formless and unknown. The notes dropped on, like needles now, into the silence. They were the same measured notes of the galliard. The girl's heart beat painfully fast until the crimson wool trembled over her breasts. Then a draught knifed under the ill-fitting door and the floor beneath her feet struck cold as stone. She pushed back her chair and stood up, holding her body rigid and tensing slender fingers against the oak of the table.

But the music had stopped. She listened for an endless minute until the room seemed to fill with the patter of rain on leaves and the creak of silence. But there was nothing else. Only against her cheek a puff of cold air like a dead kiss.

The girl shuddered. She straightened her papers with nervous, unseeing hands while her eyes searched the shadows.

At last she sat down and deliberately forced herself to concentrate on the carefully written page. 'The conflict of divine and human love . . . Woman on the one hand as Mary, on the other as Eve the temptress . . . the fleeting nature of beauty and human love contrasted with the permanence of heaven . . .'

Heaven in those days, she thought, was an unquestioned and coveted goal. Damnation must have seemed a very real danger, with one's own eternity at stake. Men might well have been driven to monstrous deeds to preserve that hope intact. She had made a marginal note to remind herself to follow up the point and decided to strengthen her spirits with coffee and something to eat.

She opened the second door, stepped quickly out under the vaulted arch and the hook, then up the three short steps to the kitchen.

While she waited for the kettle to boil, the girl went over and over the essay as she had written it so far. There was still, she knew, something that evaded her, but it would come. Professor Adams was good – some said brilliant – but there was an aspect of sixteenth-century literature which the girl felt had escaped even him. It was not a question of intellect or understanding or even of research. It was something more nebulous than that, something she could only describe as feeling. As she stirred the milky liquid in her cup, the girl realized with a strange sense of loneliness that she was more in tune with the period than he was.

It was then that she heard the voices. They came from the room she had left and seemed to be arguing. One pleading, the other, younger, protesting.

'It must be the intercom! The children have woken up.'

She left her cup on the dresser and hurried out of the kitchen, back to the living room. Sure enough, faint, blurred voices were coming from the intercom on the dresser. She flicked the switch to make sure and the voices stopped. She flicked it on again and the indistinguishable mumur resumed. She scurried out of the room and upstairs, but at the door of the children's room she stopped, listening, wondering how she was going to deal with these two unknowns. But she heard nothing. Until, as she stood tense and receptive, straining to hear, the sound of steady, peaceful breathing reached her ears from beyond the darkness.

'Someone talking in his sleep,' she decided and tiptoed quietly downstairs.

But she had scarcely regained the kitchen and picked up her cup when the voices resumed. Then the music. It was the same tune, but this time there were words, in a soft tenor voice which caressed the silence with persuasive sweetness.

> *Joy to the persone of my love although she me disdain*
> *Fixt are my thoughts and may not move*
> *And yet I love in vain.*

The lute played unmistakably in the background. The girl stood immobile, listening, while her eyes grew larger and darker in the pale oval of her face. She put down the cup with trembling deliberation and moved slowly towards the door. The skirts of her crimson gown brushed softly over the stone flags of the floor and her breath was like the mist in the cold air.

But the beamed room was empty. She crossed to the dresser and put out a hand. The small grid of the intercom was warm to the touch. With fumbling fingers, the girl switched it off.

She stood a long moment with her hand on the set, waiting, while the silence taunted her with shadows.

'I'll leave it switched off,' she decided. 'That will stop them.' Then Mrs Adams' voice came back to her, competent and firm. 'Keep the set switched on. Otherwise you'll never hear them.' At last, submissively, the girl's fingers moved to the switch.

This time the result was instant and unmistakable. Margaret ran into the kitchen, snatched up the phone with hands which trembled uncontrollably, and fumbled at the dial. As she waited for someone to answer she glanced over her shoulder through the open door, across the gloom of the vaulted scullery to the low-beamed silence of that other room. And the intercom . . .

'Mary? Mary, listen . . .'

'Is that you, Margaret?' The voice sounded aggrieved. 'What on earth's the matter? I was just washing my hair.'

'There's something odd,' began Margaret anxiously, glancing over her shoulder to those alien shadows.

'How do you mean, *odd*? Look, I'm dripping all over the carpet. Hang on a sec while I get a towel.'

In the waiting silence the music came clearly across the distance, but as soon as Mary spoke again, it stopped. 'Okay now. What's going on?'

'I'm not sure, but I keep hearing music that isn't there.'

There was a snort from the other end. 'You've been at the Prof's whisky!'

'No, honestly, Mary. It's true. It's coming over the intercom. A man, singing.'

'It's probably the next door neighbour in his bath.'

'With a lute accompaniment?'

'His wife, playing to him as he soaks. Who lives next door anyway?'

'But it's not that kind of music, Mary. It's personal, as if he is singing to . . . *me*.' She paused, tense and waiting. 'Yes! There it is again. Can't you hear it?'

'Not a thing,' said Mary cheerfully. 'Look, Meg. You can pick up all sorts of things on an intercom. Radio transmissions. Other people's TV. Voices in the road. Just forget it. Haven't you a book to read?'

'Yes, but . . .'

'Then why not make yourself some coffee, put your feet up and enjoy it? I'd come round to keep you company, only I'm in the middle of setting my hair.'

The girl didn't answer.

'Are you still there, Meg? You're not having one of your moods again, are you?'

'I don't think so, but . . .'

'Look, Meg. Don't worry. It's somebody's record, that's all. But if you really want me to come over, I will.'

'No, of course not,' said Margaret humbly. 'You finish your hair. I'll be all right.'

Slowly she replaced the receiver and stood, listening. Now there was nothing. Nothing at all but the huge, silken silence of the night. She picked up the cup of coffee and walked deliberately back into the living room. She put the cup carefully on the table and sat down. But she made no attempt to work. Instead she sat wary and rigid, waiting.

Five long minutes passed. At last, when nothing happened, she picked up her pen and began to read over what she had written.

She read through almost five pages before she heard the weeping; soft, insistent, heartbroken. The poor little things! They must be having a nightmare and she'd been so absorbed she hadn't even heard them. She flung back her chair and sped upstairs.

But at the door of the children's room she stopped dead. There was no sound except the steady rise and fall of breathing. Carefully she tiptoed into the room and stood looking down at the two sleeping shapes.

'A bad dream,' she told herself. 'It must have been.' She slipped out of the room and moved reluctantly downstairs.

At the door of the living room she stopped. From inside the room came the same unmistakable sound of a woman weeping. 'I can bear it no longer!' followed by a heartbroken sob.

Then a man's voice, loving, anguished. 'Do not tempt me.'

The girl's heart flipped painfully. She leaned gasping against the wall while her trembling fingers plucked at the stone for support. She must be going mad. Mad. The wooden door at her face seemed an entrance to a different world and she was incapable of moving away. A cold draught stirred the folds of her skirt and she felt the hair on the nape of her neck rise. On either side of her stretched stone-flagged floors, stone walls and silent shadows. Here stood the common hall of the chaplains four hundred years ago. Here twenty priests had eaten together in candlelight and celibacy, night after night until death. Until eternity. Margaret felt terror rising like a scream in her throat. She pressed back against the rough wall, while her eyes searched the darkness fearfully, probing, probing . . .

Shadows stirred. A draught lifted the hem of her skirt and passed coldly on. Somewhere a window rattled. From the depths of the ancient passageway came a whisper like the breath of time. 'My deireste . . .'

The girl broke away from the wall and fled. Through the living room, through the scullery, to the telephone on the kitchen wall. She clutched the instrument with wild hands and dialled the number that Mrs Adams had left her.

She heard the phone shrill on and on, regular and strident like the beat of her own heart. But there was no reply. At a successful party records and conviviality drown all sounds except their own.

After five endless minutes the girl gave in. She dropped the phone back on to its hook and stood with head and shoulders bowed while tears of despair beaded her cheeks. She could fight alone no longer. If no one would help her there was nothing for her but to give in. She moved slowly back into the living room and stood submissively beside the intercom, waiting ...

The small rectangle quivered soundlessly in the silence. The girl listened. And waited, while her fingers twisted restlessly in the strands of her belt. She heard breathing, the tiny creak of an infant turning over in bed, a childish mumble. Then, faint at first, but growing steadily closer came the swish of cloth on stone, of sandalled feet. The breathing grew louder and louder.

'Deireste ...'

'No,' gasped the girl as she felt cold breath brush her cheek, her breast. 'Please, no ... I can't bear it!'

She backed away across the room, her hands outstretched, pleading. The voice strengthened until it filled the stone-flagged hall. 'Do not tempt me!'

Later, softly, came the song.

> *Oh woe is me that ever I did see*
> *The beauty that did me bewitch ...*

The notes of the lute swelled and reverberated through the room until they seemed to soak into the very stone.

'Funny,' said Mrs Adams. 'She's not here.' They had let themselves into the house in the small hours with a careful key. 'I'll see if she's upstairs.'

Professor Adams drifted vaguely in a haze of alcoholic good humour towards the table, where his fuddled brain had recognized something he knew. An essay.

'Good girl. She's been busy. A sweet child. "Here woman is seen as the temptress who must be ..."' His smile became puzzled. The essay ended in mid-sentence. And at the foot of the page were three scrawled words, in different ink. 'Farewell my deireste ...'

His wife appeared in the doorway.

'She's not upstairs either,' she said worriedly. She pushed past him towards the kitchen. But as she opened the door to the scullery something soft brushed against her face.

'John!' she screamed. 'She's here!'

Together they looked upwards, appalled, at the crimson gown, the pale dead face and flowing hair which hung from the lantern hook by a twisted cord – a tasselled, silken cord such as was worn in olden times by a novice priest.

# Examination Day

*Henry Slesar*

The Jordans never spoke of the exam, not until their son, Dickie, was twelve years old. It was on his birthday that Mrs Jordan first mentioned the subject in his presence, and the anxious manner of her speech caused her husband to answer sharply.

'Forget about it,' he said. 'He'll do all right.'

They were at the breakfast table, and the boy looked up from his plate curiously. He was an alert-eyed youngster, with flat blond hair and a quick, nervous manner. He didn't understand what the sudden tension was about, but he did know that today was his birthday, and he wanted harmony above all. Somewhere in the little apartment there were wrapped, beribboned packages waiting to be opened, and in the tiny wall-kitchen something warm and sweet was being prepared in the automatic stove. He wanted the day to be happy, and the moistness of his mother's eyes, the scowl on his father's face, spoiled the mood of fluttering expectation with which he had greeted the morning.

'What exam?' he asked.

His mother looked at the tablecloth. 'It's just a sort of Government intelligence test they give children at the age of twelve. You'll be taking it next week. It's nothing to worry about.'

'You mean a test like in school?'

'Something like that,' his father said, getting up from the table. 'Go and read your comics, Dickie.' The boy rose and wandered towards that part of the living room which had been 'his' corner since infancy. He fingered the topmost comic of the stack, but seemed uninterested in the colourful squares of fast-paced action. He wandered towards the window, and peered gloomily at the veil of mist that shrouded the glass.

'Why did it have to rain today?' he said. 'Why couldn't it rain tomorrow?'

His father, now slumped into an armchair with the Government newspaper, rattled the sheets in vexation. 'Because it just did, that's all. Rain makes the grass grow.'

'Why, Dad?'

'Because it does, that's all.'

Dickie puckered his brow. 'What makes it green, though? The grass?'

'Nobody knows,' his father snapped, then immediately regretted his abruptness.

Later in the day, it was birthday time again. His mother beamed as she handed over the gaily-coloured packages, and even his father managed a grin and a rumple-of-the-hair. He kissed his mother and shook hands gravely with his father. Then the birthday cake was brought forth, and the ceremonies concluded.

An hour later, seated by the window, he watched the sun force its way between the clouds.

'Dad,' he said, 'how far away is the sun?'

'Five thousand miles,' his father said.

Dickie sat at the breakfast table and again saw moisture in his mother's eyes. He didn't connect her tears with the exam until his father suddenly brought the subject to light again.

'Well, Dickie,' he said, with a manly frown, 'you've got an appointment today.'

'I know, Dad. I hope –'

'Now, it's nothing to worry about. Thousands of children take this test every day. The Government wants to know how smart you are, Dickie. That's all there is to it.'

'I get good marks in school,' he said hesitantly.

'This is different. This is a – special kind of test. They give you this stuff to drink, you see, and then you go into a room where there's a sort of machine –'

'What stuff to drink?' Dickie said.

'It's nothing. It tastes like peppermint. It's just to make sure you answer the questions truthfully. Not that the Government thinks you won't tell the truth, but this stuff makes *sure*.'

Dickie's face showed puzzlement, and a touch of fright. He looked at his mother, and she composed her face into a misty smile.

'Everything will be all right,' she said.

'Of course it will,' his father agreed. 'You're a good boy, Dickie; you'll make out fine. Then we'll come home and celebrate. All right?'

'Yes, sir,' Dickie said.

They entered the Government Educational Building fifteen minutes before the appointed hour. They crossed the marble floors of the great pillared lobby, passed beneath an archway and entered an automatic lift that brought them to the fourth floor.

There was a young man wearing an insignia-less tunic, seated at a polished desk in front of Room 404. He held a clipboard in his hand,

and he checked the list down to the Js and permitted the Jordans to enter.

The room was as cold and official as a courtroom, with long benches flanking metal tables. There were several fathers and sons already there, and a thin-lipped woman with cropped black hair was passing out sheets of paper.

Mr Jordan filled out the form, and returned it to the clerk. Then he told Dickie: 'It won't be long now. When they call your name, you just go through the doorway at that end of the room.' He indicated the portal with his finger.

A concealed loudspeaker crackled and called off the first name. Dickie saw a boy leave his father's side reluctantly and walk slowly towards the door.

At five minutes to eleven, they called the name of Jordan.

'Good luck, son,' his father said, without looking at him. 'I'll call for you when the test is over.'

Dickie walked to the door and turned the knob. The room inside was dim, and he could barely make out the features of the grey-tunicked attendant who greeted him.

'Sit down,' the man said softly. He indicated a high stool beside his desk. 'Your name's Richard Jordan?'

'Yes, sir.'

'Your classification number is 600–115. Drink this, Richard.'

He lifted a plastic cup from the desk and handed it to the boy. The liquid inside had the consistency of buttermilk, tasted only vaguely of the promised peppermint. Dickie downed it, and handed the man the empty cup.

He sat in silence, feeling drowsy, while the man wrote busily on a sheet of paper. Then the attendant looked at his watch, and rose to stand only inches from Dickie's face. He unclipped a penlike object from the pocket of his tunic, and flashed a tiny light into the boy's eyes.

'All right,' he said. 'Come with me, Richard.'

He led Dickie to the end of the room, where a single wooden armchair faced a multi-dialled computing machine. There was a microphone on the left arm of the chair, and when the boy sat down, he found its pinpoint head conveniently at his mouth.

'Now just relax, Richard. You'll be asked some questions, and you think them over carefully. Then give your answers into the microphone. The machine will take care of the rest.'

'Yes, sir.'

'I'll leave you alone now. Whenever you want to start, just say "ready" into the microphone.'

'Yes, sir.'

The man squeezed his shoulder, and left.

Dickie said, 'Ready.'

Lights appeared on the machine, and a mechanism whirred. A voice said:

'Complete this sequence. One, four, seven, ten . . .'

Mr and Mrs Jordan were in the living room, not speaking, not even speculating.

It was almost four o'clock when the telephone rang. The woman tried to reach it first, but her husband was quicker.

'Mr Jordan?'

The voice was clipped; a brisk, official voice.

'Yes, speaking.'

'This is the Government Educational Service. Your son, Richard M. Jordan, Classification 600–115, has completed the Government examination. We regret to inform you that his intelligence quotient is above the Government regulation, according to Rule 84, Section 5, of the New Code.'

Across the room, the woman cried out, knowing nothing except the emotion she read on her husband's face.

'You may specify by telephone,' the voice droned on, 'whether you wish his body interred by the Government, or would you prefer a private burial place? The fee for Government burial is ten dollars.'

# The Devil's Ape

## Barnard Stacey

In the cheerful glow from a cedar fire three men sat talking in serious tones, then lapsing into silence; anxious-eyed, stern-faced, struggling with their fears.

'Was there any reason for Nickey to think he'd done it?' asked Parker suddenly.

'What – killed Hugh?' flared Wynch scornfully. 'I'll take my oath he didn't. We ate our Temple dinners together before he took up painting. I know Nickey.'

The two older men looked at him indulgently.

'So do I,' said Mason quietly, rattling his pipe stem between his teeth.

'Then you know he didn't,' pressed Wynch aggressively.

'I tell you I *don't* know,' repeated Mason doggedly. The others looked at him suspiciously and Wynch clutched the arms of his chair.

'What?' he demanded, but Mason didn't answer. Parker bent forward and cleared his throat.

'We're all friends of Nickey's here,' he said soothingly. 'Real friends; but you were the only one of us with him that evening, Mason – with him all the time. You were at the inquest, too, afterwards, on poor Hugh.'

He stopped for the emotion to clear from his voice. 'We know the coroner's verdict, but tell us frankly what *did* happen?'

The atmosphere had become strained. Mason felt their searching glances, but he didn't look up. He refilled his pipe. Then he faced them.

'Well, I'll tell you,' he said in a weary tone, 'then you can decide for yourselves. Personally, I can't, but – I must say this first to clear myself. I've built up my practice, such as it is –' he waved his KC and knighthood airily away – 'on facts converted into evidence. It's the royal road to Law – so that I'm not a man easily spoofed or spoon-fed.

'The day the Huntsby case collapsed so dramatically I found myself at six o'clock with a free evening for once. I was at a loose end, too tired to bother about dressing, so I slipped into a grill room and dined alone. It was early when I'd finished, so I strolled into the Mall wondering where to make for next, when I suddenly thought of Nickey.

'I hadn't seen him for ages, so I jumped into a taxi. You went to his rooms, didn't you, Wynch?'

Wynch nodded. 'They were in the same building as Hugh's,' he muttered.

'Yes, Hugh lived immediately above Nickey. His study was plumb over Nickey's sitting-room. Remember that: it's important. Nickey had a man with him – Charlie Somers; I hadn't seen him before. Nice chap, with a boyish smile. Well, Nickey was in great form. Apparently they'd been ragging Hugh and he'd got huffy. Threatened to complain or something – he was like that – and finally he'd turned them out and locked himself in.

'We three sat smoking and chatting about Nickey's latest picture – a modern Dante and Beatrice. He'd just bought a new lay figure; life-size thing it was, all jointed, and Nickey was very excited about it. Showed us how it worked, and stuck it up in all sorts of poses. They get those things up so well now, it was almost real.

'Presently there was a ring at the bell and Nickey went to the door himself. It was a parcel – left by some poor little wretch who'd been told to leave it on his way home and had lost his way, and was crying. You know how crazy Nickey is over children! He flung the parcel on the table – dashed about finding cake and fruit, gave the lad all his spare silver and some of mine, and sent him home in a taxi.

'When he came to look at the parcel, it wasn't for him at all. It was addressed to Hugh. In the dark the boy had mistaken the numbers.

'Nickey thought it a great joke. He pictured Hugh waiting patiently for bed socks or chest protectors. Hugh was such an ideal man to rag, with his frog's eyes behind those thick lenses. He'd not an atom of humour. Fancy a man setting out to be a surgeon and hating the sight of blood!

'Then Nickey had a brainwave. He suggested we should open the parcel and send Hugh some old boots and rubbish, and before we could stop him he'd cut the string. In the paper was an old book – a solemn-looking tome, musty and yellow with age. He turned the pages over in disgust – couldn't read a word of it – and passed it over to us. I thought it was Chinese, the characters looked so weird, but Somers, who is apparently an authority on dead languages, became quite interested, and took the book on his knee.

'"It's Sanskrit," he pronounced, "the ancient and sacred language of India. Lord! It's about Devil-Worship."

'"Devil-Worship," cried Nickey. "I didn't know there was such a thing."

'Somers said that when he was in Bombay some fakir told him

wonderful things were done in the heart of the Himalayas by the Devil-Worshippers. Meanwhile he was turning over the dog-eared pages.

'"I say," he blurted out suddenly. "This book is the very thing — definite instructions for the practice of Devil-Worship. It actually gives the formula for casting or projecting a man's soul out of his body."

'Nickey and I laughed. "You don't mean to say you believe such nonsense?" I asked.

'"I don't know," he replied guardedly. "Shouldn't like to say. If half the old man told me was true —" And he went on deciphering, with Nickey looking over his shoulder.

'"I say, Mason," exclaimed Nickey, "let's have a séance, or whatever they call it, and do a little devil-worshipping of our own. Call up the old boy — what d'you say, Charlie?"

'I thought Nickey was crazy, and told him so, but once he gets an idea into his head he is never satisfied until it's exploded.

'He began arranging the room, pushing the table back against the wall to give us plenty of working space, he explained. Then he went into his bedroom and came back with a bundle of joss-sticks which he lighted and stuck in vases round the room.

'You know what a curious effect that heavy scent has on the senses. It seems to unlock the gate of grotesque fancies or fears. Personally it sends me to sleep, and I wanted to be off, but Nickey wouldn't hear of it, practically bullied me into staying.

'Then the lights didn't suit him. "Devils like gloom," he said, and the next minute we were in the subdued light from a standard lamp, one of those red-shaded affairs you plug into the wainscoting with the end of a flex wire.

'Somers was taking the thing quite seriously, too. The book seemed to obsess him. He said we must have some definite line of action — some object upon which to focus our attention — somebody.

'And in the spirit of devilry, Nickey suggested Hugh. "He'll make a splendid medium, swotting up there. Won't he be mad when I tell him tomorrow he hasn't got a soul."

'"Yes, but where are we going to send his soul?" worried Somers.

'I could see what was on the tip of Nickey's tongue, but he didn't say it. His eyes were wandering round the room, searching for an idea, when he saw the lay figure, and he clutched Somers's arm excitedly.

'"The very thing — we'll command Hugh's soul to come out and enter that — wait a bit; I'll dress it up — make it more realistic — more like —" But he didn't finish what he was saying.

'A fierce enthusiasm caught him. I watched him feverishly bursting open drawers, dragging out trousers, waistcoat and jacket. He even buttoned a collar round the neck and knotted a black tie with flowing ends. Finally, he sat the figure up in a chair with its hands resting on its knees and stepped back to survey it, but Somers put the finishing touch to it by seizing my glasses and balancing them on the aquiline nose.

'The effect was uncanny. Nickey was like a child with a new toy in his glee.

'"Half-close your eyes, Mason; no, blink a little," he persisted. "Can't you imagine him?"

'There certainly was a suggestion of Hugh about it. Of course, the clothes helped – Hugh always looked as if he'd got out of a rag bag – and the subdued lamplight encouraged one to imagine the foxy look in his glassy eyes.

'"We must form a circle and link hands," directed Somers. "I'll recite the formula from the book – it's only a few sentences, and we must all concentrate on Hugh – visualizing his soul leaving his body and entering the dummy."

'I still didn't like the idea – it seemed so childish – so bizarre – but I hadn't the courage to quarrel with Nickey. He was so desperately set on it. He danced over to my chair and pulled me up by the arms.

'"Come on, Mason," he said, and in a sceptical frame of mind I took their hands and we made a ring round the chair where the figure sat, stiff and solemn, and the séance commenced.

'After a few seconds Somers began reciting something in a dreary monotone. I couldn't understand what he said, but it reminded me of the droning of native priests, while we glued our eyes on the figure.

'Every now and then Somers stopped, and we waited placidly for the chanting to go on again. Gradually, but unconsciously, we began to get serious. In spite of ourselves, our minds were fired with the idea. The atmosphere became mesmeric. In the pauses the silence seemed pregnant with possibilities. A feeling of waiting and watching for something crept over us. The expectancy was almost painful. As it became tenser I had a vague feeling of uneasiness; all sense of time and space had vanished.

'I stole a glance at Nickey. His face was flushed with excitement. Suddenly I felt him grip my hand tight. I turned sharply, and saw he had raised himself on his toes with his head half tilted upwards, as if he were straining to hear something.

'Somers had come to one of his pauses, when, without any warning, there was a peal of fierce maniacal laughter immediately above our heads. Just one peal – no more – then a pulsating, awful silence. An icy fear went down my spine. It was such an inhuman sound – bloodless – like a triumphant devil. I wanted to do something – make some physical movement. I wanted to shout – scream – anything – but I couldn't.

'And then something happened. Something we couldn't see, but felt – something that made us afraid with a sweating fear. *Somebody – something came into the room.* We became aware of another presence. We sensed it – that warning, creepy sensation all down your back, of being watched by somebody you couldn't see.

'Stealthily, afraid of being caught, I twisted my head and looked at Nickey. Then my blood froze. His face was distorted with horror and his lower lip quivered convulsively, but it was the terror – the dying hope in his eyes – that galvanized my sinking spirits.

'"Nickey! Nickey!" I shouted out. "Stop it – d'you hear me? Stop it!"

'He shivered and passed his hand across his forehead. Then he started giggling – laughing, shrieking, *in the same diabolical way we had heard above.* "It's Hugh," he raved. "Hugh, I tell you. He's here – there – look at him – he's grinning at me; he's –"

'The lay figure had fallen back in the chair, with its head resting on the back, but turned towards Nickey. The right arm was raised.

'Nickey was pugnacious with fear. "I'll stop his gibbering," he yelled; "you see." He darted back to the table, and snatching up a long steel paper-knife, sprang towards the chair, but he must have caught his foot in the flex from the lamp, for the next instant the room was in darkness.

'I heard a scuffle, then short gasps of men struggling for mastery, as I grovelled to find the switch. I was clumsy in locating it, but when I turned on the lights Nickey had his knee on the dummy's chest, and with blind savagery drove the paper-knife fiercely into its neck. Then he seized the figure, and with a passionate ferocity flung it to the floor.

'Even as it fell there was a second thud, of something falling heavily *on the floor above.* Whatever we were going to say – died in our throats. We made for the door, the three of us, but Nickey had previously locked it against intrusion.

'We flung it open and rushed up the stairs. We rang and hammered and kicked on the front door, but nobody came. Then Somers ran down again, and we knew he had gone for the porter. Neither Nickey nor I spoke while we waited, but, like frightened children, we felt for each other's hand.

'When they came back, and we got into the little hall, we went straight to Hugh's study, but the door was locked on the inside. Bending down, we could see the key in the lock, yet there wasn't a sound from within, so we put our shoulders against the door. It gave after the fifth attempt, and I fell into the room.

'The light was on, but everything was disarranged, as if there had been a struggle, and on the floor just about where Nickey had thrown down the figure, was Hugh – dead! Blood was slowly oozing from a wound in the neck, *in the identical spot where the paper-knife was sticking in the figure downstairs.* But there was no knife or implement of any sort that we could find.

'And we still hadn't said a word to each other – only Nickey whispered something to the porter, and he went away while we quietly sat down to wait for the police.'

# The Judge's House

## *Bram Stoker*

When the time for his examination drew near Malcolm Malcolmson made up his mind to go somewhere to read by himself. He feared the attractions of the seaside, and also he feared completely rural isolation, for of old he knew its charms, and so he determined to find some unpretentious little town where there would be nothing to distract him. He refrained from asking suggestions from any of his friends, for he argued that each would recommend some place of which he had knowledge, and where he had already acquaintances. As Malcolmson wished to avoid friends he had no wish to encumber himself with the attention of friends' friends, and so he determined to look out for a place for himself. He packed a portmanteau with some clothes and all the books he required, and then took a ticket for the first name on the local timetable which he did not know.

When at the end of three hours' journey he alighted at Benchurch, he felt satisfied that he had so far obliterated his tracks as to be sure of having a peaceful opportunity of pursuing his studies. He went straight to the one inn which the sleepy little place contained, and put up for the night. Benchurch was a market town, and once in three weeks was crowded to excess, but for the remainder of the twenty-one days it was as attractive as a desert. Malcolmson looked around the day after his arrival to try to find quarters more isolated than even so quiet an inn as 'The Good Traveller' afforded. There was only one place which took his fancy, and it certainly satisfied his wildest ideas regarding quiet; in fact, quiet was not the proper word to apply to it – desolation was the only term conveying any suitable idea of its isolation. It was an old rambling, heavy-built house of the Jacobean style, with heavy gables and windows, unusually small, and set higher than was customary in such houses, and was surrounded with a high brick wall massively built. Indeed, on examination, it looked more like a fortified house than an ordinary dwelling. But all these things pleased Malcolmson. 'Here,' he thought, 'is the very spot I have been looking for, and if I can only get opportunity of using it I shall be happy.' His joy was increased when he realized beyond doubt that it was not at present inhabited.

From the post office he got the name of the agent, who was rarely surprised at the application to rent a part of the old house. Mr Carnford, the local lawyer and agent, was a genial old gentleman, and frankly confessed his delight at anyone being willing to live in the house.

'To tell you the truth,' said he, 'I should be only too happy, on behalf of the owners, to let anyone have the house rent free for a term of years if only to accustom the people here to see it inhabited. It has been so long empty that some kind of absurd prejudice has grown up about it, and this can be best put down by its occupation – if only,' he added with a sly glance at Malcolmson, 'by a scholar like yourself, who wants its quiet for a time.'

Malcolmson thought it needless to ask the agent about the 'absurd prejudice'; he knew he would get more information, if he should require it, on that subject from other quarters. He paid his three months' rent, got a receipt, and the name of an old woman who would probably undertake to 'do' for him, and came away with the keys in his pocket. He then went to the landlady of the inn, who was a cheerful and most kindly person, and asked her advice as to such stores and provision as he would be likely to require. She threw up her hands in amazement when he told her where he was going to settle himself.

'Not in the Judge's House!' she said, and grew pale as she spoke. He explained the locality of the house, saying that he did not know its name. When he had finished she answered:

'Aye, sure enough – sure enough the very place! It is the Judge's House sure enough.' He asked her to tell him about the place, why so called, and what there was against it. She told him that it was so called locally because it had been many years before – how long she could not say, as she was herself from another part of the country, but she thought it must have been a hundred years or more – the abode of a judge who was held in great terror on account of his harsh sentences and his hostility to prisoners at Assizes. As to what there was against the house itself she could not tell. She had often asked, but no one could inform her; but there was a general feeling that there was *something*, and for her own part she would not take all the money in Drinkwater's Bank and stay in the house an hour by herself. Then she apologized to Malcolmson for her disturbing talk.

'It is too bad of me, sir, and you – and a young gentleman, too – if you will pardon me saying it, going to live there all alone. If you were my boy – and you'll excuse me for saying it – you wouldn't sleep there a night, not if I had to go there myself and pull the big alarm bell that's on the roof!' The good creature was so manifestly in earnest, and was so kindly in her intentions, that Malcolmson, although amused, was touched. He told her kindly how much he appreciated her interest in him, and added:

'But, my dear Mrs Witham, indeed you need not be concerned about me! A man who is reading for the Mathematical Tripos has too much to think of to be disturbed by any of these mysterious "somethings", and his work is of too exact and prosaic a kind to allow of his having any corner in his mind for mysteries of any kind. Harmonical Progression, Permutations and Combinations, and Elliptic Functions have sufficient mysteries for me!' Mrs Witham kindly undertook to see after his commissions, and he went himself to look for the old woman who had been recommended to him. When he returned to the Judge's House with her, after an interval of a couple of hours, he found Mrs Witham herself waiting with several men and boys carrying parcels, and an upholsterer's man with a bed in a cart, for she said, though tables and chairs might be all very well, a bed that hadn't been aired for mayhap fifty years was not proper for young bones to lie on. She was evidently curious to see the inside of the house; and though manifestly so afraid of the 'somethings' that at the slightest sound she clutched on to Malcolmson, whom she never left for a moment, went over the whole place.

After his examination of the house, Malcolmson decided to take up his abode in the great dining room, which was big enough to serve for all his requirements; amd Mrs Witham, with the aid of the charwoman, Mrs Dempster, proceeded to arrange matters. When the hampers were brought in and unpacked, Malcolmson saw that with much kind forethought she had sent from her own kitchen sufficient provisions to last for a few days. Before going she expressed all sorts of kind wishes; and at the door turned and said:

'And perhaps, sir, as the room is big and draughty it might be well to have one of those big screens put round your bed at night – though, truth to tell, I would die myself if I were to be so shut in with all kinds of – of "things", that put their heads round the sides, or over the top, and look on me!' The image which she had called up was too much for her nerves, and she fled incontinently.

Mrs Dempster sniffed in a superior manner as the landlady disappeared, and remarked that for her own part she wasn't afraid of all the bogies in the kingdom.

'I'll tell you what it is, sir,' she said; 'bogies is all kinds and sorts of things – except bogies! Rats and mice, and beetles; and creaky doors, and loose slates, and broken panes, and stiff drawer handles, that stay out when you pull them and then fall down in the middle of the night. Look at the wainscot of the room! It is old – hundreds of years old! Do you think there's no rats and beetles there! And do you imagine, sir, that you won't see none of them? Rats is bogies, I tell you, and bogies is rats; and don't you get to think anything else!'

'Mrs Dempster,' said Malcolmson gravely, making her a polite bow, 'you know more than a Senior Wrangler! And let me say, that, as a mark of esteem for your indubitable soundness of head and heart, I shall, when I go, give you possession of this house, and let you stay here by yourself for the last two months of my tenancy, for four weeks will serve my purpose.'

'Thank you kindly, sir!' she answered, 'but I couldn't sleep away from home a night. I am in Greenhow's Charity, and if I slept a night away from my rooms I should lose all I have got to live on. The rules is very strict; and there's too many watching for a vacancy for me to run any risks in the matter. Only for that, sir, I'd gladly come here and attend on you altogether during your stay.'

'My good woman,' said Malcolmson hastily, 'I have come here on purpose to obtain solitude; and believe me that I am grateful to the late Greenhow for having so organized his admirable charity – whatever it is – that I am perforce denied the opportunity of suffering from such a form of temptation! Saint Anthony himself could not be more rigid on the point!'

The old woman laughed harshly. 'Ah, you young gentlemen,' she said, 'you don't fear for naught; and belike you'll get all the solitude you want here.' She set to work with her cleaning; and by nightfall, when Malcolmson returned from his walk – he always had one of his books to study as he walked – he found the room swept and tidied, a fire burning in the old hearth, the lamp lit, and the table spread for supper with Mrs Witham's excellent fare. 'This is comfort, indeed,' he said, as he rubbed his hands.

When he had finished his supper, and lifted the tray to the other end of the great oak dining table, he got out his books again, put fresh wood on the fire, trimmed his lamp, and set himself down to a spell of real hard work. He went on without pause till about eleven o'clock, when he knocked off for a bit to fix his fire and lamp, and to make himself a cup of tea. He had always been a tea drinker, and during his college life had sat late at work and had taken tea late. The rest was a great luxury to him, and he enjoyed it with a sense of delicious, voluptuous ease. The renewed fire leaped and sparkled and threw quaint shadows through the great old room; and as he sipped his hot tea he revelled in the sense of isolation from his kind. Then it was that he began to notice for the first time what a noise the rats were making.

'Surely,' he thought, 'they cannot have been at it all the time I was reading. Had they been, I must have noticed it!' Presently, when the noise increased, he satisfied himself that it was really new. It was evident that at first the rats had been frightened at the presence of a stranger, and the light of fire and lamp; but that as the time went on they had grown bolder and were now disporting themselves as was their wont.

How busy they were! and hark to the strange noises! Up and down, behind the old wainscot, over the ceiling and under the floor they raced, and gnawed, and scratched! Malcolmson smiled to himself as he recalled to mind the saying of Mrs Dempster, 'Bogies is rats, and rats is bogies!' The tea began to have its effect of intellectual and nervous stimulus, he saw with joy another long spell of work to be done before the night was past, and in the sense of security which it gave him, he allowed himself the luxury of a good look round the room. He took his lamp in one hand, and went all around, wondering that so quaint and beautiful an old house had been so long neglected. The carving of the oak on the panels of the wainscot was fine, and on and round the doors and windows it was beautiful and of rare merit. There were some old pictures on the walls, but they were coated so thick with dust and dirt that he could not distinguish any detail of them, though he held his lamp as high as he could over his head. Here and there as he went round he saw some crack or hole blocked for a moment by the face of a rat with its bright eyes glittering in the light, but in an instant it was gone, and a squeak and a scamper followed. The thing that most struck him, however, was the rope of the great alarm bell on the roof, which hung down in a corner of the room on the right-hand side of the fireplace. He pulled up close to the hearth a great high-backed carved oak chair, and sat down to his last cup of tea. When this was done he made up the fire, and went back to his work sitting at the corner of the table, having the fire to his left. For a little while the rats disturbed him somewhat with their perpetual scampering, but he got accustomed to the noise as one does to the ticking of a clock or to the roar of moving water; and he became so immersed in his work that everything in the world, except the problem which he was trying to solve, passed away from him.

He suddenly looked up, his problem was still unsolved, and there was in the air that sense of the hour before the dawn, which is so dread to doubtful life. The noise of the rats had ceased. Indeed it seemed to him that it must have ceased but lately and that it was the sudden cessation which had disturbed him. The fire had fallen low, but still it threw out a deep red glow. As he looked he started in spite of his *sang froid*.

There on the great high-backed carved oak chair by the right side of the fireplace sat an enormous rat, steadily glaring at him with baleful eyes. He made a motion to it as though to hunt it away, but it did not stir. Then he made the motion of throwing something. Still it did not stir, but showed its great white teeth angrily, and its cruel eyes shone in the lamplight with an added vindictiveness.

Malcolmson felt amazed, and seizing the poker from the hearth ran at it to kill it. Before, however, he could strike it, the rat, with a squeak that sounded like the concentration of hate, jumped upon the floor, and, running up the rope of the alarm bell, disappeared in the darkness beyond the range of the green-shaded lamp. Instantly, strange to say, the noisy scampering of the rats in the wainscot began again.

By this time Malcolmson's mind was quite off the problem; and as a shrill cock crow outside told him of the approach of morning, he went to bed and to sleep.

He slept so soundly that he was not even wakened by Mrs Dempster coming in to make up his room. It was only when she had tidied up the place and got his breakfast ready and tapped on the screen which closed in his bed that he woke. He was a little tired still after his night's hard work, but a strong cup of tea soon freshened him up, and, taking his book, he went out for his morning walk, bringing with him a few sandwiches lest he should not care to return till dinner time. He found a quiet walk between high elms some way outside the town, and here he spent the greater part of the day studying his Laplace. On his return he looked in to see Mrs Witham and to thank her for her kindness. When she saw him coming through the diamond-paned bay window of her sanctum she came out to meet him and asked him in. She looked at him searchingly and shook her head as she said:

'You must not overdo it, sir. You are paler this morning than you should be. Too late hours and too hard work on the brain isn't good for any man! But tell me, sir, how did you pass the night? Well, I hope? But, my heart! sir, I was glad when Mrs Dempster told me this morning that you were all right and sleeping sound when she went in.'

'Oh, I was all right,' he answered smiling, 'the "somethings" didn't worry me, as yet. Only the rats; and they had a circus, I tell you, all over the place. There was one wicked-looking old devil that sat up on my own chair by the fire, and wouldn't go till I took the poker to him, and then he ran up the rope of the alarm bell and got to somewhere up the wall or the ceiling – I couldn't see where, it was so dark.'

'Mercy on us,' said Mrs Witham, 'an old devil, and sitting on a chair by the fireside! Take care, sir! take care! There's many a true word spoken in jest.'

'How do you mean? 'Pon my word I don't understand.'

'An old devil! The old devil, perhaps. There! sir, you needn't laugh,' for Malcolmson had broken into a hearty peal. 'You young folks thinks it easy to laugh at things that makes older ones shudder. Never mind, sir! never mind! Please God, you'll laugh all the time. It's what I wish you myself!' and the good lady beamed all over in sympathy with his enjoyment, her fears gone for a moment.

'Oh, forgive me!' said Malcolmson presently. 'Don't think me rude; but the idea was too much for me – that the old devil himself was on the chair last night!' And at the thought he laughed again. Then he went home to dinner.

This evening the scampering of the rats began earlier; indeed it had been going on before his arrival, and only ceased while his presence by its freshness disturbed them. After dinner he sat by the fire for a while and had a smoke; and then, having cleared his table, began to work as before. Tonight the rats disturbed him more than they had done on the previous night. How they scampered up and down and under and over! How they squeaked, and scratched, and gnawed! How they, getting bolder by degrees, came to the mouths of their holes and to the chinks and cracks and crannies in the wainscoting till their eyes shone like tiny lamps as the firelight rose and fell. But to him, now doubtless accustomed to them, their eyes were not wicked; only their playfulness touched him. Sometimes the boldest of them made sallies out on the floor or along the mouldings of the wainscot. Now and again as they disturbed him Malcolmson made a sound to frighten them, smiting the table with his hand or giving a fierce 'Hsh, hsh,' so that they fled straightway to their holes.

And so the early part of the night wore on; and despite the noise Malcolmson got more and more immersed in his work.

All at once he stopped, as on the previous night, being overcome by a sudden sense of silence. There was not the faintest sound of gnaw, or scratch, or squeak. The silence was as of the grave. He remembered the odd occurrence of the previous night, and instinctively he looked at the chair standing close by the fireside. And then a very odd sensation thrilled through him.

There, on the great old high-backed carved oak chair beside the fireplace sat the same enormous rat, steadily glaring at him with baleful eyes.

Instinctively he took the nearest thing to his hand, a book of logarithms, and flung it at it. The book was badly aimed and the rat did not stir, so again the poker performance of the previous night was repeated; and again the rat, being closely pursued, fled up the rope of the alarm bell. Strangely too, the departure of this rat was instantly followed by the renewal of the noise made by the general rat community. On this occasion, as on the previous one, Malcolmson could not see at what part of the room the rat disappeared, for the green shade of his lamp left the upper part of the room in darkness, and the fire had burned low.

On looking at his watch he found it was close on midnight; and, not sorry for the *divertissement*, he made up his fire and made himself his nightly pot of tea. He had got through a good spell of work, and thought himself entitled to a cigarette; and so he sat on the great carved oak chair before the fire and enjoyed it. While smoking he began to think that he would like to know where the rat disappeared to, for he had certain ideas for the morrow not entirely disconnected with a rat trap. Accordingly he lit another lamp and placed it so that it would shine well into the right-hand corner of the wall by the fireplace. Then he got all the books he had with him, and placed them handy to throw at the vermin. Finally he lifted the rope of the alarm bell and placed the end of it on the table, fixing the extreme end under the lamp. As he handled it he could not help noticing how pliable it was, especially for so strong a rope, and one not in use. 'You could hang a man with it,' he thought to himself. When his preparations were made he looked around, and said complacently:

'There now, my friend, I think we shall learn something of you this time!' He began his work again, and though as before somewhat disturbed at first by the noise of the rats, soon lost himself in his propositions and problems.

Again he was called to his immediate surroundings suddenly. This time it might not have been the sudden silence only which took his attention; there was a slight movement of the rope, and the lamp moved. Without stirring, he looked to see if his pile of books was within range, and then cast his eye along the rope. As he looked he saw the great rat drop from the rope on the oak armchair and sit there glaring at him. He raised a book in his right hand, and taking careful aim, flung it at the rat. The latter, with a quick movement, sprang aside and dodged the missile. He then took another book, and a third, and flung them one after another at the rat, but each time unsuccessfully. At last, as he stood with a book poised in his hand to throw, the rat squeaked and seemed afraid. This made Malcolmson more than ever eager to strike, and the book flew and struck the rat a resounding blow. It gave a terrified squeak, and turning on his pursuer a look of terrible malevolence, ran up the chair back and made a great jump to the rope of the alarm bell and ran up it like lightning. The lamp rocked under the sudden strain, but it was a heavy one and did not topple over. Malcolmson kept his eyes on the rat, and saw it by the light of the second lamp leap to a moulding of the wainscot and disappear through a hole in one of the great pictures which hung on the wall, obscured and invisible through its coating of dirt and dust.

'I shall look up my friend's habitation in the morning,' said the student, as he went over to collect his books. The third picture from the fireplace; I shall not forget.' He picked up the books one by one, commenting on them as he lifted them. '*Conic Sections* he does not mind, nor *Cycloidal Oscillations*, nor the *Principia*, nor *Quaternions*, nor *Thermodynamics*. Now for the book that fetched him!' Malcolmson took it up and looked at it. As he did so he started, and a sudden pallor overspread his face. He looked round uneasily and shivered slightly, as he murmured to himself:

'The Bible my mother gave me! What an odd coincidence.' He sat down to work again, and the rats in the wainscot renewed their gambols. They did not disturb him, however; somehow their presence gave him a sense of companionship. But he could not attend to his work, and after striving to master the subject on which he was engaged gave it up in despair, and went to bed as the first streak of dawn stole in through the eastern window.

He slept heavily but uneasily, and dreamed much; and when Mrs Dempster woke him late in the morning he seemed ill at ease, and for a few minutes did not seem to realize exactly where he was. His first request rather surprised the servant.

'Mrs Dempster, when I am out today I wish you would get the steps and dust or wash those pictures – especially that one the third from the fireplace – I want to see what they are.'

Late in the afternoon Malcolmson worked at his books in the shaded walk, and the cheerfulness of the previous day came back to him as the day wore on, and he found that his reading was progressing well. He had worked out to a satisfactory conclusion all the problems which had as yet baffled him, and it was in a state of jubilation that he paid a visit to Mrs Witham at 'The Good Traveller'. He found a stranger in the cosy sitting room with the landlady, who was introduced to him as Dr Thornhill. She was not quite at ease, and this, combined with the doctor's plunging at once into a series of questions, made Malcolmson come to the conclusion that his presence was not an accident, so without preliminary he said:

'Dr Thornhill, I shall with pleasure answer you any question you may choose to ask me if you will answer me one question first.'

The doctor seemed surprised, but he smiled and answered at once, 'Done! What is it?'

'Did Mrs Witham ask you to come here and see me and advise me?'

Dr Thornhill for a moment was taken aback, and Mrs Witham got fiery red and turned away; but the doctor was a frank and ready man, and he answered at once and openly:

'She did: but she didn't intend you to know it. I suppose it was my clumsy haste that made you suspect. She told me that she did not like the idea of your being in that house all by yourself and that she thought you took too much strong tea. In fact, she wants me to advise you if possible to give up the tea and the very late hours. I was a keen student in my time, so I suppose I may take the liberty of a college man and, without offence, advise you not quite as a stranger.'

Malcolmson with a bright smile held out his hand. 'Shake! as they say in America,' he said. 'I must thank you for your kindness and Mrs Witham too, and your kindness deserves a return on my part. I promise to take no more strong tea – no tea at all till you let me – and I shall go to bed tonight at one o'clock at latest. Will that do?'

'Capital,' said the doctor. 'Now tell us all that you noticed in the old house,' and so Malcolmson then and there told in minute detail all that had happened in the last two nights. He was interrupted every now and then by some exclamation from Mrs Witham, till finally when he told of the episode of the Bible the landlady's pent-up emotions found vent in a shriek; and it was not till a stiff glass of brandy and water had been administered that she grew composed again. Dr Thornhill listened with a face of growing gravity, and when the narrative was complete and Mrs Witham had been restored he asked:

'The rat always went up the rope of the alarm bell?'

'Always.'

'I suppose you know,' said the Doctor after a pause, 'what the rope is?'

'No!'

'It is,' said the doctor slowly, 'the very rope which the hangman used for all the victims of the Judge's judicial rancour!' Here he was interrupted by another scream from Mrs Witham, and steps had to be taken for her recovery. Malcolmson having looked at his watch, and found that it was close to his dinner hour, had gone home before her complete recovery.

When Mrs Witham was herself again she almost assailed the doctor with angry questions as to what he meant by putting such horrible ideas into the poor young man's mind. 'He has quite enough there already to upset him,' she added. Dr Thornhill replied:

'My dear madam, I had a distinct purpose in it! I wanted to draw his attention to the bell rope, and to fix it there. It may be that he is in a highly overwrought state, and has been studying too much, although I am bound to say that he seems as sound and healthy a young man, mentally and bodily, as ever I saw – but then the rats – and that suggestion of the devil.' The doctor shook his head and went on. 'I would have offered to go and stay the first night with him but that I felt sure it would have been a cause of offence. He may get in the night some strange fright or hallucination; and if he does I want him to pull that rope. All alone as he is it will give us warning, and we may reach him in time to be of service. I shall be sitting up pretty late tonight and shall keep my ears open. Do not be alarmed if Benchurch gets a surprise before morning.'

'Oh, Doctor, what do you mean? What do you mean?'

'I mean this; that possibly – nay, more probably – we shall hear the great alarm bell from the Judge's House tonight,' and the doctor made about as effective an exit as could be thought of.

When Malcolmson arrived home he found that it was a little after his usual time, and Mrs Dempster had gone away – the rules of Greenhow's Charity were not to be neglected. He was glad to see that the place was bright and tidy with a cheerful fire and a well-trimmed lamp. The evening was colder than might have been expected in April, and a heavy wind was blowing with such rapidly increasing strength that there was every promise of a storm during the night. For a few minutes after his entrance the noise of the rats ceased; but so soon as they became accustomed to his presence they began again. He was glad to hear them, for he felt once more the feeling of companionship in their noise, and his mind ran back to the strange fact that they only ceased to manifest themselves when that other – the great rat with the baleful eyes – came upon the scene. The reading lamp only was lit and its green shade kept the ceiling and the upper part of the room in darkness, so that the cheerful light from the hearth spreading over the floor and shining on the white cloth laid over the end of the table was warm and cheery. Malcolmson sat down to his dinner with a good appetite and a buoyant spirit. After his dinner and a cigarette he sat steadily down to work, determined not to let anything disturb him, for he remembered his promise to the doctor, and made up his mind to make the best of the time at his disposal.

For an hour or so he worked all right, and then his thoughts began to wander from his books. The actual circumstances around him, the calls on his physical attention, and his nervous susceptibility were not to be denied. By this time the wind had become a gale, and the gale a storm. The old house, solid though it was, seemed to shake to its foundations, and the storm roared and raged through its many chimneys and its queer old gables, producing strange, unearthly sounds in the empty rooms and corridors. Even the great alarm bell on the roof must have felt the force of the wind, for the rope rose and fell slightly, as though the bell were moved a little from time to time, and the limber rope fell on the oak floor with a hard and hollow sound.

As Malcolmson listened to it he bethought himself of the doctor's words, 'It is the rope which the hangman used for the victims of the Judge's judicial rancour,' and he went over to the corner of the fireplace and took it in his hand to look at it. There seemed a sort of deadly interest in it, and as he stood there he lost himself for a moment in speculation as to who these victims were, and the grim wish of the Judge to have such a ghastly relic ever under his eyes. As he stood there the swaying of the bell on the roof still lifted the rope now and again; but presently there came a new sensation – a sort of tremor in the rope, as though something was moving along it.

Looking up instinctively Malcolmson saw the great rat coming slowly down towards him, glaring at him steadily. He dropped the rope and started back with a muttered curse, and the rat turning ran up the rope again and disappeared, and at the same instant Malcolmson became conscious that the noise of the rats, which had ceased for a while, began again.

All this set him thinking, and it occurred to him that he had not investigated the lair of the rat or looked at the pictures, as he had intended. He lit the other lamp without the shade, and, holding it up, went and stood opposite the third picture from the fireplace on the right-hand side where he had seen the rat disappear on the previous night.

At the first glance he started back so suddenly that he almost dropped the lamp, and a deadly pallor overspread his face. His knees shook, and heavy drops of sweat came on his forehead, and he trembled like an aspen. But he was young and plucky, and pulled himself together, and after the pause of a few seconds stepped forward again, raised the lamp, and examined the picture which had been dusted and washed, and now stood out clearly.

It was of a judge dressed in his robes of scarlet and ermine. His face was strong and merciless, evil, crafty, and vindictive, with a sensual mouth, hooked nose of ruddy colour, and shaped like the beak of a bird of prey. The rest of the face was of a cadaverous colour. The eyes were of peculiar brilliance and with a terribly malignant expression. As he looked at them, Malcolmson grew cold, for he saw there the very counterpart of the eyes of the great rat. The lamp almost fell from his hand, he saw the rat with its baleful eyes peering out through the hole in the corner of the picture, and noted the sudden cessation of the noise of the other rats. However, he pulled himself together, and went on with his examination of the picture.

The Judge was seated in a great high-backed carved oak chair, on the right-hand side of a great stone fireplace where, in the corner, a rope hung down from the ceiling, its end lying coiled on the floor. With a feeling of something like horror, Malcolmson recognized the scene of the room as it stood, and gazed around him in an awestruck manner as though he expected to find some strange presence behind him. Then he looked over to the corner of the fireplace – and with a loud cry he let the lamp fall from his hand.

There, in the Judge's armchair, with the rope hanging behind, sat the rat with the Judge's baleful eyes, now intensified and with a fiendish leer. Save for the howling of the storm without there was silence.

The fallen lamp recalled Malcolmson to himself. Fortunately it was of metal, and so the oil was not spilt. However, the practical need of attending to it settled at once his nervous apprehensions. When he had turned it out, he wiped his brow and thought for a moment.

'This will not do,' he said to himself. 'If I go on like this I shall become a crazy fool. This must stop! I promised the doctor I would not take tea. Faith, he was pretty right! My nerves must have been getting into a queer state. Funny I did not notice it. I never felt better in my life. However, it is all right now, and I shall not be such a fool again.'

Then he mixed himself a good stiff glass of brandy and water and resolutely sat down to his work.

It was nearly an hour when he looked up from his book, disturbed by the sudden stillness. Without, the wind howled and roared louder than ever, and the rain drove in sheets against the windows, beating like hail on the glass; but within there was no sound whatever save the echo of the wind as it roared in the great chimney, and now and then a hiss as a few raindrops found their way down the chimney in a lull of the storm. The fire had fallen low and had ceased to flame, though it threw out a red glow. Malcolmson listened attentively, and presently heard a thin, squeaking noise, very faint. It came from the corner of the room where the rope hung down, and he thought it was the creaking of the rope on the floor as the swaying of the bell raised and lowered it. Looking up, however, he saw in the dim light the great rat clinging to the rope and gnawing it. The rope was already nearly gnawed through – he could see the lighter colour where the strands were laid bare. As he looked the job was completed, and the severed end of the rope fell clattering on the oaken floor, while for an instant the great rat remained like a knob or tassel at the end of the rope, which now began to sway to and fro. Malcolmson felt for a moment another pang of terror as he thought that now the possibility of calling the outer world to his assistance was cut off, but an intense anger took its place, and seizing the book he was reading he hurled it at the rat. The blow was well aimed, but before the missile could reach him the rat dropped off and struck the floor with a soft thud. Malcolmson instantly rushed over towards him, but it darted away and disappeared in the darkness of the shadows of the room. Malcolmson felt that his work was over for the night, and determined then and there to vary the monotony of the proceedings by a hunt for the rat, and took off the green shade of the lamp so as to insure a wider spreading light. As he did so the gloom of the upper part of the room was relieved, and in the new flood of light, great by comparison with the previous darkness, the pictures on the wall stood out boldly. From where he stood, Malcolmson saw right opposite to him the third picture on the wall from the right of the fireplace. He rubbed his eyes in surprise, and then a great fear began to come upon him.

In the centre of the picture was a great irregular patch of brown canvas, as fresh as when it was stretched on the frame. The background was as before, with chair and chimney-corner and rope, but the figure of the Judge had disappeared.

Malcolmson, almost in a chill of horror, turned slowly round, and then he began to shake and tremble like a man in a palsy. His strength seemed to have left him, and he was incapable of action or movement, hardly even of thought. He could only see and hear.

There, on the great high-backed carved oak chair sat the Judge in his robes of scarlet and ermine, with his baleful eyes glaring vindictively, and a smile of triumph on the resolute, cruel mouth, as he lifted with his hands a *black cap*. Malcolmson felt as if the blood was running from his heart, as one does in moments of prolonged suspense. There was a singing in his ears. Without, he could hear the roar and howl of the tempest, and through it, swept on the storm, came the striking of midnight by the great chimes in the market place. He stood for a space of time that seemed to him endless, still as a statue, and with wide-open, horror-struck eyes, breathless. As the clock struck, so the smile of triumph on the Judge's face intensified, and at the last stroke of midnight he placed the black cap on his head.

Slowly and deliberately the Judge rose from his chair and picked up the piece of the rope of the alarm bell which lay on the floor, drew it through his hands as if he enjoyed its touch, and then deliberately began to knot one end of it, fashioning it into a noose. This he tightened and tested with his foot, pulling hard at it till he was satisfied and then making a running noose of it, which he held in his hand. Then he began to move along the table on the opposite side to Malcolmson keeping his eyes on him until he had passed him, when with a quick movement he stood in front of the door. Malcolmson then began to feel that he was trapped, and tried to think of what he should do. There was some fascination in the Judge's eyes, which he never took off him, and he had, perforce to look. He saw the Judge approach – still keeping between him and the door – and raise the noose and throw it towards him as if to entangle him. With a great effort he made a quick movement to one side, and saw the rope fall beside him, and heard it strike the oaken floor. Again the Judge raised the noose and tried to ensnare him, ever keeping his baleful eyes fixed on him, and each time by a mighty effort the student just managed to evade it. So this went on for many times, the Judge seeming never discouraged nor discomposed at failure, but playing as a cat does with a mouse. At last in despair, which had reached its climax, Malcolmson cast a quick glance round him. The lamp seemed to have blazed up, and there was a fairly good light in the room. At the many rat holes and in the chinks and crannies of the wainscot he saw the rats' eyes; and this aspect, that was purely physical, gave him a gleam of comfort. He looked around and saw that the rope of the great alarm bell was laden with rats. Every inch of it was covered with them, and more and more were pouring through the small circular hole in the ceiling whence it emerged, so that with their weight the bell was beginning to sway.

Hark! it had swayed till the clapper had touched the bell. The sound was but a tiny one, but the bell was only beginning to sway, and it would increase.

At the sound the Judge, who had been keeping his eyes fixed on Malcolmson, looked up, and a scowl of diabolical anger overspread his face. His eyes fairly glowed like hot coals, and he stamped his foot with a sound that seemed to make the house shake. A dreadful peal of thunder broke overhead as he raised the rope again, while the rats kept running up and down the rope as though working against time. This time, instead of throwing it, he drew close to his victim, and held open the noose as he approached. As he came closer there seemed something paralysing in his very presence, and Malcolmson stood rigid as a corpse. He felt the Judge's icy fingers touch his throat as he adjusted the rope. The noose tightened – tightened. Then the Judge, taking the rigid form of the student in his arms, carried him over and placed him standing in the oak chair, and stepping up beside him, put his hand up and caught the end of the swaying rope of the alarm bell. As he raised his hand the rats fled squeaking, and disappeared through the hole in the ceiling. Taking the end of the noose which was round Malcolmson's neck he tied it to the hanging-bell rope, and then descending pulled away the chair.

When the alarm bell of the Judge's House began to sound a crowd soon assembled. Lights and torches of various kinds appeared, and soon a silent crowd was hurrying to the spot. They knocked loudly at the door, but there was no reply. Then they burst in the door, and poured into the great dining room, the doctor at the head.

There at the end of the rope of the great alarm bell hung the body of the student, and on the face of the Judge in the picture was a malignant smile.

# Polish the Lid

## *Terry Tapp*

Ian knew what was to come and he was dreading it. When the back door slammed he knew that his father was home, and he jumped up from his chair to find a book to hide behind.

Ernest Perryman kicked off his muddy boots at the door, placed his grub bag by the refrigerator and went through to the dining-room.

'Well, lad?'

'Fine, thanks, Dad,' said Ian.

'How did it go?'

'All right.'

'Is that all?'

'He doesn't want to talk about it,' Mary Perryman cut in as she came from the kitchen. 'Don't you go bothering the lad with your questions now, Ernest.'

'Bothering?' Ernest said. 'Is it bothering him to ask how he got on at work?' He frowned, groping along the mantelshelf for his briar pipe and tin of tobacco; he filled the pipe, pushing the thick, sticky strands deep, deep into the bowl, his face lined with disapproval. 'Am I not to know, then?'

'Don't press the lad,' Mary said. 'He's had a busy day.'

'And how would you be knowing that?' asked Ernest.

'He told me.'

'Yet he hasn't told me a thing,' said Ernest. 'Not a damned thing. Lad's first day at work and a father wants to know about it. Nothing wrong with that, is there?'

He sucked smoke from the pipe and snorted at out into the room so that it curled and billowed like a lilac-blue mist, choking and swirling, making Ian feel sick with its sweetness.

'I saw a dead person today,' Ian said, his face slick and grey with the memory of it.

'Aye, I reckoned you would,' said Ernest.

'An old woman.'

'Better than a young 'un. We've all got to pack our bags sometime. What else?'

'Pardon?'

'What else did you do? You can't have spent the whole day looking at one dead old woman.'

'Stop goading the lad!' Mary cried. 'Can you not see how upset he is? He doesn't want to talk about it.'

'Go to kitchen,' Ernest ordered, jerking his head at the door. 'I'm after hearing more of this.'

'You would be,' Mary said, barely concealing the disgust in her voice. 'Well, I certainly don't want to hear about it, and if young Ian has any sense at all he won't be talking to you about it. Look at you – your face is quite flushed with excitement.'

'Enough!' shouted Ernest. 'I will talk with the lad. Now get to the kitchen and leave us.'

Ian watched them arguing, the book held up before his face so that he could just see over the top, yet retreat quickly when the attention was focused upon him.

'Anyone would think the lad has done something to be proud of,' Mary said acidly.

'He has,' Ernest replied. 'He's got himself a good job, and that is something to be proud of in these days. It's not easy to get a job, you know.'

'A job?' Mary cried, slamming the door hard.

Ernest gave a rueful grin and pushed his spatula thumb over his pipe, sucking and blowing so that his cheeks hollowed and puffed like a frog. 'Take no account of your mother,' he advised. 'Women are daft things when it comes to death.' The smoke now coiled around him, enveloping him in thick, stifling layers.

'Not much to tell,' Ian said, looking up from his book and making a point of placing his finger on the text as if he were just about to return to reading.

'What was the place like?' asked Ernest.

Ian sighed. Damn you, he thought, you're going to squeeze and squeeze until the juice flows. Why did you have to get me the job in the first place? Now you have to hear all about it – you have to know every detail, every twist and turn. I can see it in your eyes.

'Answer me, then,' said Ernest.

'What?'

'I asked you what it was like over at Monmouth's,' said Ernest. 'You've got that thousand-mile stare in your eyes, laddie. Come on, snap out of it.'

'It was all right,' said Ian. 'Nothing much happened.'

'Nonetheless, I expect you have a few stories to tell,' Ernest encouraged. 'Come on. Tell me about it.'

'Mr Monmouth is a very sympathetic man,' Ian said.

'The hell with Monmouth,' snapped Ernest. 'Anyway, he has to be sympathetic, doesn't he. 'Tis hardly the trade where a man goes about laughing. What I want to know is what *happens*. I've heard tell that they take out the gold fillings. Can't say that I believe it, but I've heard it all the same.'

'I wouldn't know,' Ian said, allowing his eyes to drift back to the book again. For God's sake, switch on the television or something, he thought. Go out and look at your precious pigeons, or sweep the back yard, or do anything – anything rather than ask me about it. I don't want to talk about it. Can't you see that? Can't you see? Of course he could see. Ernest wasn't a silly man. He could see that his son was reluctant, and that is why he pressed him to answer. The reluctance indicated that something quite horrible had taken place, and the more Ian refused to talk about it, the more excited Ernest would become.

'Robert, my pal at the yard, tells me that they make noises sometimes,' said Ernest. 'The gas builds up inside their bodies as they lay there, and then it has to come out. Is that true, lad? Do dead people make noises?'

Pretending that he did not hear the question, Ian concentrated upon the book, his face placid, but inside his head there was a roaring of a mad giant. For God's sake, he cried out inside himself. For God's sake, don't ask me any more. Don't keep on and on about it. Stop pushing and prodding at me all the time. Stop goading me. Stop it . . .

'Stop it!' The words bubbled over his lips before he could prevent their escape.

'What?' Ernest said, somewhat taken aback by such behaviour in his usually placid son. 'What did you say?'

'I was just saying that I only saw the one dead woman,' Ian replied. 'Just one woman brought in as I was leaving. Mr Manders said he was going to take care of her tomorrow because he had an appointment tonight.'

'And is that all?'

'I did what every new boy does in any new job,' Ian explained. 'I swept the floor and dusted around and then made tea. Things like that. Nothing gruesome.'

'Oh,' said Ernest. 'Is that all you've done?'

'I did polish some wood as practice,' said Ian. 'I'll be allowed to polish a coffin tomorrow.'

'So you did learn a thing or two.'

'Just how to polish,' said Ian.

'Well, it will make a man of you,' said Ernest. 'You'll learn a thing or two at that job, and it won't do you no harm.'

'I suppose not,' Ian agreed.

'You don't seem keen on it.'

'Would you be?' Ian asked. 'It isn't exactly the sort of job I had in mind when I passed my examinations.'

'No, I don't suppose it is,' Ernest said. 'But we have to settle for what we can get nowadays. You're damned lucky I managed to fix it up for you. Some of your schoolmates are still on the dole, you know.'

'I know.'

'Then what's up wi' you, lad? Are you afraid or something?'

'Afraid?' Ian asked.

'Of the dead. Are you afraid of the dead?'

'No. They are dead, aren't they? What's to be afraid of in a dead person?'

Ernest looked away from his son's direct eyes. 'Don't know rightly,' he countered. 'I just thought you might be afraid of dead bodies. Ghosts, maybe?'

'Ghosts?' Ian laughed. 'Come off it, Dad, I'm not stupid.'

'You don't have to be stupid to be afraid,' Ernest said.

'But ghosts!' Ian grinned broadly. 'Whatever made you think of ghosts?'

For a moment Ernest looked rather shamefacedly at his son, then shifted his feet awkwardly. 'Don't know.'

'You watch too many late night films on television,' said Ian.

'Aye, perhaps so,' Ernest agreed. 'Only there seems to be something uncanny about a dead person.'

'I'm not scared,' Ian said. 'It's just like looking at a sleeping person, really.'

'Is it?' Ernest asked. 'I've never seen anyone – dead.'

'Just like sleeping.'

'And do they cross the hands over the chest like you see on the films?' Ernest asked. 'And what about the actual preparation of the body? Did you see any of that going on?'

'No. Don't forget I've only been there a day.'

'Yes, I know that, but you must have heard tales. What are the blokes like that you work with? I bet they could tell a tale or two.'

'I expect so,' Ian agreed.

'Bet they've seen some strange goings on.'

'I'll bet.'

Seeing that his son was not able to supply any entertaining anecdotes that evening, Ernest gave a sigh and picked up the paper to see what was on television. 'Ah, well,' he said. 'Early days yet. But I'll be bound you'll have a few yarns to spin come the weekend.'

Ian did not reply.

When the television set was turned on, and he thought his father was engrossed in the programme, he looked across the tiny room and studied his face. Even now he was sitting forward in the chair, ready to have his incredulity assaulted. Ernest Perryman was a man who lived in a state of permanent wonder. He was an avid reader of world records and achievements and was never happier than when marvelling at something.

Dinner was served and the family settled down to watch television for the evening. Ian breathed a sigh of relief.

Next morning, Ian was up early and dressed in his black suit and tie ready for another day. He caught the bus to the recreation ground and walked up the steep hill until he came to the door marked 'J. G. Monmouth. Undertaker'. Nervously making sure that his tie was not crooked (a defect which Mr Monmouth had noted yesterday), he curled his fingers around the brass doorknob. How many hands, he wondered, had held this very doorknob? And what grief had passed over the threshold into the parlour?

Wiping his feet on the mat, Ian closed the door, taking care not to make a sound.

'Good morning, Perryman,' a voice said.

'Good morning, Mr Monmouth.'

The undertaker was about to issue orders for the day when the door opened and a young woman entered the parlour, her eyes misted and red. Mr Monmouth's expression changed. His stern, disapproving look dissolved as his hands came together in an attitude of prayer.

'Good morning.'

She pulled a large handkerchief from her raincoat pocket and dabbed it against her face. 'Good morning. I would like to ... I want to ...'

'I can see that you are bereaved,' Monmouth said, the corners of his mouth twisting upwards just the right amount to indicate sympathy, yet not sufficiently to show his delight in obtaining a new client. Ian watched his employer's face with interest.

'I don't know what I have to do,' the woman said helplessly.

'Nothing,' said Monmouth. 'You may leave the arrangements in our hands. I presume you are a relation of Mr Carter?'

'You have heard, then?'

'Yes,' Monmouth told her. 'We usually hear of such things very quickly indeed. Now, if you would like to leave everything to me, I am sure we can arrange for a tasteful and expedient arrangement.'

'Thank you.' She shot him a grateful glance through tear-laden eyes.

But it did not end there. Ian watched closely as Monmouth pursued the stricken woman like a hunter. Would madam care to see the range of caskets and accessories? A catalogue of coffins? A host of handles? A flock of flowers? Most tasteful, I am sure. Leave it to Monmouth's. We are experts in the trade. We have been attending to – such matters – for many years. We even use our own services . . . couldn't possibly say more than that, could we? Satin? Purple? Of course. Purple looks so right for the occasion. Regal, yet tasteful. The cars? Leave it to Monmouth's. We were established in 1789, you know. Yes, really. Over two hundred years we have been setting dear ones to rest. Money? He was insured. Good . . . excellent. We shall consult about money later. Of course, no expense to be spared on an occasion like this. Sign of respect. Tribute to the dear departed.

We take care of absolutely everything. Burial? Oh, cremation, how sensible. Yes, much to be preferred. So sorry to see you in such a distressed state. Yes, I knew Mr Carter well. Who would have thought it? Well, it comes to all of us, and life must go on. Sudden . . . better than a lingering illness . . . And on and on and on until Ian felt his fingernails digging deep into the palms of his hands and the sweat dripping from his forehad.

When the woman was ushered to the front door, Monmouth's look of sympathy dissolved instantly. 'Hurry up, lad. Get Mr Manders to prepare a six hundred and fifty-seven coffin, satin-lined, number eight brass handles on a schedule five arrangement. Hurry up, now!'

Ian walked around the back yard until he came to the low door where Mr Manders worked. He knocked.

'Come!'

He opened the door.

'Come in, lad,' the voice said. 'She's dead. She won't bite you.'

'I know,' Ian said. 'Mr Monmouth wants a coffin prepared, satin-lined, number eight brass handles and on a schedule five arrangement.'

'What model coffin?' asked Manders.

'Six-five-seven,' Ian said.

'Right. You go over to the workroom and get polishing a lid for me.'

'Any lid?'

'Either of them. There are only two there.'

'Only two?'

Manders narrowed his eyes. 'Just do like you've been told, lad. Ask no questions.'

Ian went over to the workshop and opened the cupboard door where he had seen the coffin lids the day before. He pulled them both out and took them over to the window, where the sunlight slanted in, and examined them. Both were scratched, but the one in his right hand would need less work. He laid it on the bench and picked up the milk bottle of water and shook it over the floor to lay the dust. Then, taking great care, he applied the French polish and linseed oil with his rubber, making sure that he used the correct, figure-of-eight movement so that the rubber would not suddenly stick to the highly polished surface and ruin his handiwork.

It took nearly two hours to get the surface of the lid up to a flawless, mirrorlike finish, and when Ian had finished he reported to Mr Manders, who was working on the old woman who had been brought into the funeral parlour late the previous day.

'Waste of time,' Manders grunted. 'Some idiot wants to see the old girl before they burn her up, so I've got all this extra trouble. I have to get her into some sort of shape or we'll have tears and moaning and God knows what.'

The flat, masterful hands worked as Ian watched, kneading and pulling features into the desired shapes, combing and brushing and pushing and pulling; heaving and tugging and grunting and groaning – lifting and pushing an arm over there and an arm over here and laying and arranging and oiling and filling and washing and smoothing and fondling.

Ian felt the room spinning.

Stitching!

My God! He's sewing her!

Now make-up and padding and slapping and colouring and dressing and snapping until the body fitted the pattern which Manders had in mind. The mouth, the eyes, the lips and cheeks and hair and face.

Dear God! Ian felt the room spin faster and faster as the sweat dripped from Manders onto the face of the woman lying there. Rivulets of sweat running down Manders's face onto the old, grotesque face which had been moulded by the sweating, grunting, grinning man.

'Time for grub,' said Manders at once, sitting back on an upturned box. He took out his wrap of sandwiches and pushed thick, choking wedges into his slit, grinning mouth, masticating with awful relish. His rubber lips moved like mating snakes, sliding and slipping together, yet locked over his yellow teeth.

He had not even washed his hands.

Cheese, with Manders's dirty finger imprints upon it; yellow, sweating cheese and porous bread, infested with the smell of spirit.

'Feeling all right?' Manders laughed, opening his mouth wide like a hippo to reveal the chewed-up mess which clogged his red, glistening mouth.

'I'm all right,' said Ian.

'Then have a sandwich,' said Manders, 'a cheese sandwich.'

'I'm not hungry.'

'Not hungry?' Manders made a laughing noise in his belly. 'Go on,' he said, his eyes searching Ian's face. 'Have some of this tack, it'll put hairs on your chest.'

'No!' Ian felt the room start spinning again. 'No, thank you, Mr Manders. I really am not in the least bit hungry.'

'I really am not in the least bit hungry,' Manders mimicked. 'I think you're going to be sick.'

'I'm not,' Ian said.

Manders shrugged, poured some milk and tea into his flask cup and sipped noisily. 'That was a rush job,' he said. 'She's for the fire this afternoon, after some grasping relative has come to pay last respects, like. After that they don't give a damn what happens because they'll be back at the house sorting through all her possessions, trying to salvage what they can out of her pathetic life. I've seen it all before, you know. Sometimes I think I ought to leave the corpse just like it was when it came in, and that would really scare the hell out of them.'

Ian felt the walls of his stomach gather up like two gigantic hands inside him, squeezing out and out and out.

Manders poured his tea, ate more bread and watched and laughed.

'When you've finished making a mess, you can polish the other lid,' Manders said, his mouth full of stodgy, pulpy food.

Ian left the room instantly, glad to be able to return to the workshop, where the polishing of the lid would leave him little of the morning for other jobs. After lunch, which Ian could not face, he was told to attend the funeral of the old woman, and when that was over he returned, in the hearse, to the workshop. 'You can spend the rest of the day polishing this lid,' Manders said.

And when Ian looked at the lid closely, he saw that it was the one he had been polishing that very morning.

'Ask no questions,' said Manders with a huge wink.

When Ian arrived home that evening, Ernest Perryman was waiting. 'Evening, son,' he said. 'How did things go?'

'All right,' Ian replied.

'Leave the lad be,' said Mary. 'He's not well, I can tell by the look on his face. And he hasn't eaten his sandwiches, either. Oh, Ian, you should eat something, you know. I took special care over these, too. Ham isn't cheap, and I thought you would –'

'Ham?' Ernest cried out indignantly. 'You gave him ham and I only got cheese?'

'Just for the first few days,' said Mary. 'He needs the food, you know.'

'What time's dinner?' Ernest asked.

'About an hour,' Mary said.

'Then I'll eat the sandwiches,' Ernest decided. 'It won't hurt my appetite none. Give them over here.'

Ian sat in the armchair opposite his father, picked up a book and thumbed through the pages. He had no idea what the book was, or what the words said; he was using it as protection, to form a barrier between himself and his father. And as he looked at the pages, he heard Ernest's lips smacking at the sandwiches.

The mouth opened wide, the sandwich was pushed in and snuffled off. As Ernest pulled it away from his mouth, silver threads of saliva, still attached to the sandwich, drew out like thin, glistening cords. 'Fancy you having ham,' Ernest said. 'I only got cheese.'

'I wasn't hungry,' said Ian.

'Well, come on, then. Tell me all about it. You said you had an old woman in yesterday – tell me what happened to her.'

'She was cremated.'

'Did you go?'

Ian nodded.

'I've never been to a cremation,' Ernest said wistfully. 'What's it like? What do they do? Did you see the body being screwed down in the coffin?'

'I don't want to talk about it,' Ian snapped.

'Keep your shirt on,' Ernest said. 'Don't say I've got a winnow for a son. Ye gods, I believe I have, though. I only wanted to know what happened.'

'Yes, I know you do.'

'So what's wrong with telling me about it?'

'I don't like talking about what happened.'

'Scared?'

'No. I just don't like to talk about it.'

'Because it was a terrible thing to see?'

'Yes,' Ian said.

His curt reply was fuel to Ernest's curiosity. 'Best thing is to talk about it and get it off your chest,' Ernest said. 'The doctors always advise that. Talk about it before it becomes a repression and you have to go to the loony bin. People who don't talk about things like that eventually go round the twist, you know. If you bottle it up, one day it will explode out of you.'

'I can handle it,' Ian said.

Ernest tried another tack. 'After all, I did go out of my way to get that job for you. It took some doing.'

'I'd like to say I'm grateful, but I'm not,' said Ian.

'No, I can see that,' Ernest snapped irritably. 'I just wanted to know how you got on. That's all.'

'And I've told you. God knows how many times I've told you.'

'Keep your hair on.'

'All right!' Suddenly Ian stood up, eyes blazing. 'You want to hear about it, do you?'

'I'd have liked to know,' Ernest said uncomfortably.

'Oh, you shall,' Ian said, a thin, bitter smile stretching across his pale face. 'You want to drool over the horrific things which you imagine happening in an undertaker's.'

'I don't want to drool,' Ernest replied hotly. 'I'm just interested.'

'Too interested!' Ian cried. 'Well, you've asked for it. Remember that . . .'

'You don't have to say anything if you don't want,' Ernest said, shocked by the sudden change in his son's appearance.

'I want,' Ian said. 'I want to talk about it now. I want to see your face when I tell you what really happens.'

'Maybe another time,' Ernest parried. 'You're too upset now.'

'No,' Ian growled, 'I'll tell you now. You've been begging for it and I'll tell you. The first thing you have to know is that Monmouth's have only two coffin lids in the whole place.'

Not realizing the significance of such an observation, Ernest raised his eyebrows in query.

'You don't get it,' Ian said with a sneer. 'Just the two lids and over sixty coffin styles to choose from?'

'No, I still don't see what you're getting at,' Ernest said.

'They use the lids again,' Ian said.

'Get on. Do they?' Ernest swallowed hard.

'You asked for this, Dad, and I'm going to make your eyes pop out of your head. I'm going to enjoy telling you every single sordid detail so that you'll never, never ask me again.'

'No need to get heated about it,' said Ernest.

'If you're anything like me, I'll expect to see that ham sandwich again shortly.'

'I doubt that,' Ernest replied unconvincingly.

'So they put the lid upon the coffin,' said Ian, 'and then they took the woman to the crematorium.'

'Oh,' said Ernest. 'Didn't anything happen to her before they put the lid on?'

'You want it in detail? You want every grisly, greasy step?' Ian was shocked by the look of disappointment on his father's face. 'I'll tell you,' he said. 'I won't miss out a single detail.'

By now Ernest's face was high flushed with excitement, and his mouth sagged open, the ham and bread lying thick and pulpy on his tongue. Ian started to tell him about the process of death, telling him how Manders had abused the old woman's body with his hands and how, after he had finished his dreadful task, he had boasted of his skills.

'Do you want to know what he told me?' Ian asked, then he continued without waiting for a reply. 'Manders told me that the old woman was

so bent crooked that he had to break her back to get her in the coffin.
Do you understand me, Dad? He had to actually break her back.'

Ernest gave a flutter of a smile.

Disgusted by his father's obvious enjoyment, Ian determined to fill
him with as many gory details as he could remember.

'Mr Manders drained the blood from her and then he injected the
body with the preserving fluids. Do you know he had to seal the body to
make it watertight?'

'Seal it?'

'Oh yes. All bodies are sealed so that the fluids don't drain away. And
coffins are waterproofed, too. Mr Manders says he has carried many a
rush job to the crematorium where he can actually hear the fluids swilling
about inside the coffin.'

Ernest sat in silence, his eyes fixed upon Ian's face.

'You want more?' Ian asked. He was nauseated by his own memories,
yet still determined that his father would not press him to talk about his
job again.

'So when Mr Manders had broken the old woman's back, he forced
her body into the coffin. Then he pushed her about a bit to make her
look presentable. After that, we took her to the crematorium in the
hearse, and they held a short service. Then the purple curtains closed
and the people filed out and it was over.'

'And was that it?' Ernest asked, now chewing heartily on the sandwich
again.

With dismay, Ian realized that his father had recovered from the
shocking story and was still hungry for excitement.

'Wasn't that enough?' Ian cried. 'My God, what more do you want
to know?'

'I don't know,' said Ernest with a sly grin. 'What more is there to
know?'

It was like licking the plate at the dinner table . . . Ian felt sick, but he
had to continue.

'When they had drawn the curtains and we were alone, Mr Monmouth
signalled Mr Manders to begin his work. The flowers were removed and
taken outside and then Mr Manders started to unscrew the handles on
the coffin.'

'What for?' Ernest asked.

'The handles are made so that they melt, leaving no metallic traces,'
said Ian. 'But Mr Manders declared that it would be a waste to burn
them up. Then he unscrewed the coffin lid. I had to pack the handles in
tissue paper and put them back in the boxes so that they could be sold
again and, by the time I had finished, I noticed that the purple satin
lining had also been removed from the coffin.'

'Do they always do that?' asked Ernest.

'Monmouth's do,' Ian said.

'I never realized,' said Ernest, his face now pale and sweating lightly so that it glowed like the face of the dead woman Ian had seen in the coffin.

'Neither did I,' Ian said. 'Another thing which was unexpected was that she sat up.'

'Sat up?' Ernest almost shrieked.

'The lid of the coffin must have been restraining her,' said Ian. 'All I know is that she suddenly sat bolt upright, with her mouth open wide. I suppose there must have been a certain amount of gas in the body, because, as she sat up, she issued a terrible scream. It was a high, banshee sort of cry, and I couldn't help shrieking, too. But Mr Manders only laughed and pushed her roughly back. I tell you, that woman had a broken back, yet still she sat upright as if –' Ian swallowed.

'As if?' Ernest prompted.

'As if she was afraid of the flames.'

'And did you actually see her burn?' Ernest asked.

'I did,' said Ian. 'When she was in the incinerator I looked through the peephole, which was covered with heat-resistant glass.'

'So you actually saw her burn?'

'She sat up again as the flames roared at her. It was a terrible sight – like she was being burned alive. All I could hear was the roar of the flames, and all I could see was her white hair streaming out behind her, burning and sparkling. Her eyes opened as the heat increased and, almost instantly, she was burning.'

'Still sitting up?'

'Good God!' Ian cried. 'You do want every last detail, don't you!'

'I might as well hear all of it,' said Ernest defensively.

'Right! She was sitting up. She was screaming silently and her body was swelling up like a great, white blister. You should have seen it, Dad. You would have loved it. Now she had no hair, and her clothing was black-burned deep into her skin, which was blowing up like a balloon. I saw the flames reflected in her hopeless eyes and I heard Mr Manders chuckle as the body exploded. The skin peeled away as he watched, his face shoved up tight to mine so that he, too, could observe through the hole. Then she danced.'

'Danced?'

'The body burned and the sinews contracted, making her writhe and twist grotesquely. So intense was the heat, it made the bones snap and crack, and the body convulsed like a primitive dancer. It was a Hell dance. Then she dissolved, still dancing, into a faceless, hopeless mess of black.'

'I didn't realize . . .' Ernest said hoarsely.

'There's a lot you didn't realize,' replied Ian bitterly. 'I only hope to God that this story will teach you never to ask me about Monmouth's again.'

Ernest was breathing quickly now, his eyes searching Ian's face wildly, his hand clutching and unclutching his chest as he asked again and again, 'Is it true? Is it really true?'

And each time he asked, Ian nodded. 'Horror is always true,' he said. 'Have you had enough horror? Have you had your fill yet?'

Ernest looked away and became very still.

Next morning, Ian was up early and dressed in his black suit. He arrived punctually at Monmouth's and stood before his employer, listening to, but not hearing, the words which dripped endlessly from the older man's mouth.

'As you know, Monmouth's take care of everything,' he was saying. 'We care – and that's what really matters. We are experts in our field and masters of our trade. Leave it to Monmouth's, I always say. Just leave it to us.'

'I think the six-five-seven coffin with the six Florentine brass handles would be suitable. Purple satin lining would also be tasteful, in the circumstances. Of course, there will be a special discount rate, but then, as we have insurances to cover such things, I don't think the cost is at all relevant, do you?'

Ian shook his head.

'Tragic – quite tragic,' said Monmouth. 'Your father always struck me as a particularly healthy man. Always alive and bright and full of interest. Not the sort of man I could look forward to being of service to in my own lifetime, I would have thought, but then, God moves in such mysterious ways. Heart, you say? Had a bad heart, did he? Just shows how uncertain this life is. Perhaps he was overdoing it? Too many late nights? Worry, perhaps? A sudden shock can do it, you know. Bad news, or a terrible shock can cause the heart to fail.'

Monmouth tapped his fingers impatiently on the table.

'Ah well, life must go on. Perhaps you would be so good as to polish the lid for the coffin. Polish it until it shines like a mirror – as a tribute, of course. If you wish, when Mr Manders has finished his treatment, you may see your father for a few minutes in the Chapel of Rest.'

Ian turned abruptly on his heel and went out to polish the coffin lid until he could see his face in it.

# Evening Flight

*Alan Temperley*

Robert Trenchard and Mike Dickson emerged from the prefects' entrance of Friary Grammar School. It was Friday lunchtime, a brooding November day. Above them, mullioned windows rose to a featureless sky. Trees dripped along the curving drive. No breeze stirred the silver puddles in the school car park.

They had changed from prefects' blazers and dark flannels. In country corduroys and bulky waterproof jackets they went towards a rusting red Mini. Slung on one shoulder Mike carried an ancient rucksack; a neat holdall was in Robert's hand. Beneath their arms, casual but self-conscious, hung twelve-bore shotguns in canvas cases.

'Where are you off to, then?' An elderly chemistry master in stained and ragged gown greeted the boys amiably.

'Shooting, sir.' Mike smiled.

'Shooting, eh! Wish I was going with you. Got the head's permission, have you?'

'Yes.' Neat and dark, Robert regarded the old man coolly. Head boy of the school, he never addressed the masters as 'sir'.

'Where do you go, then?'

'My parents have got a bothy on the north shore of the Solway,' Mike said. He sneezed, for he had a cold, and sneezed again. 'Good shooting along the tide-line.'

'Wildfowling, eh! What will you get?'

'A few mallard, teal, that sort of thing. Widgeon if they've arrived yet.'

'Mike says the greylags are pretty thick this year,' Robert said. 'We might get a goose.'

'Very good.' The old man twitched his gown on to a shoulder. 'Well, a brace of mallard would do me fine. If you shoot more than you know what to do with, remember a poor old chemistry teacher. Eh!' He chuckled, a gap-toothed laugh. 'Good luck, boys. Take care.'

'Thanks. Cheerio, sir.'

The old man flapped on.

'Silly old fool,' Robert said savagely, as they continued towards the car. 'I can't stand people like that. Half-cracked old failures, hiding behind eccentricity and bonhomie.'

'He's all right,' Mike said. 'I quite like him.' Rough-headed and easy-going, a farmer's son, he swung his rucksack to the ground at the rear of the red Mini.

The car belonged to Robert. His father, a city solicitor, had bought it for him on his seventeenth birthday; a reward for athletic and academic honours. Already he had won a scholarship to Jesus College, Cambridge. On sports day, five months previously, he had broken the long-standing school 1500 metres record by eleven seconds. He was one of a small but select number of pupils who drove in to school each day.

Robert swung open the boot and they stowed away their gear and heavy jackets, then laid the shotguns carefully along the back seat. A sudden bout of coughing made Mike double up. Still wheezing, he climbed into the passenger seat.

'You sure you should be going?' Robert pulled the driver's door shut and reached for the safety belt.

'Yes, I'll be fine.' Mike rummaged in his pocket and pulled out a crumpled packet of throat lozenges. 'You want one?'

'No thanks.' Robert turned the key. At once the engine burst into life. He glanced sideways and drew out between the teachers' cars into the school drive. 'I'll stop at the wine shop in town. A half-bottle of whisky will keep out the bugs better than those disgusting sweets.'

He wound the window down. A bitter breeze swirled through the car. Mike's brow was damp with perspiration. He shivered and pulled the neck of his sweater close.

Robert drove well. Two hours later, at a quarter to three, he turned from the twisting and little-used coast road down a woodland track towards the shore. After several hundred metres it ran out into a deserted clearing and stopped. As the engine was switched off, silence closed about their ears. The two schoolboys climbed from the car and stretched their legs. At their backs the land rose steadily above the trees to a high and deserted crest of moors. Before them it dropped away through wintry branches to the dun and silver shore. Mud, still wet from the receding tide, glinted in the afternoon light. The sea itself was not to be seen. Channels, deeply etched in the mud-banks, wound in slow sweeps as far out as the eye could follow. It was very still; no twig moved. Only the occasional whistle of a wader pierced the silence. The unbroken ceiling of cloud pressed low overhead.

A ten-minute descent through the wood brought them to the bothy, a desolate farm cottage a hundred metres above the high-water mark. As they approached across sheep-nibbled grass, a scattering of gulls and crows rose from a tumbled dry-stone wall a little distance away. As they came closer Mike spotted a sheep caught by the wool in a tangle of thorns. It lay on its side and did not move. The boys set down their boxes of provisions and crossed to look closer. The animal was not long dead. It had died slowly, fleece tangled so tightly in the stems of bramble and wild-briar that only clippers or a knife could have released it. In its days-long struggle to get free it had trampled the grass to a circle of bare earth, thick with droppings. Now its mouth gaped horribly. With cruel beaks the birds had fed first from the sheep's eyes.

'Poor beggar,' Mike said. 'I'll cut it free tomorrow and lug it to the edge of the sea. Before it begins to stink.' He sneezed violently.

Robert moved the eyeless head with the toe of his boot. 'What sort of teeth have sheep got?' He crouched and turned back the lips with firm fingers, then rinsed them in a pool.

They returned to the boxes of provisions and continued towards the house. Half a dozen vigorous ewes, tails swirling, scattered from shelter beneath a rusty tin awning. A lanky hare made off at incredible speed.

Mike produced a large iron key from his pocket and let them into the house. It was clean and sparsely furnished, a little damp from standing empty throughout the autumn. They slung down their bags and boxes by the living-room wall and set about making the place comfortable.

In half an hour a grate of logs sent yellow flames leaping up the chimney. Mattresses were propped against the wall opposite. In sweaters and stocking feet the boys lounged back on settee and armchair, steaming cups of coffee alongside, a packet of biscuits passing from one to the other.

Mike sneezed for the hundredth time and wiped watery eyes with a wet handkerchief. 'Ohhh!' he sighed. 'I don't know if I'll go out with you tonight. I feel a bit rotten, frankly. What a stinking cold! Didn't it have to happen this weekend! A-choo!' Roughly he scrubbed his red nose. 'Sorry!'

'Can't be helped. Here!' Robert reached to the floor for the half-bottle of whisky. They had started it on the journey, wiping the neck and passing the bottle as the hedgerows sped past. Already it was a third gone. 'Have a drop in your coffee,' Robert said. 'Pull in by the fire, best thing in the world. Sweat it out of you.'

Mike did as he suggested and passed his mug across. Robert poured in a generous tot and took as much for himself. He had drunk more than Mike and was in excellent humour.

'I'll away by myself tonight, then,' he said. 'Ten more minutes by the fire and I'll start getting ready.' With relish he took a throatful of the spirituous coffee. 'All we need now is a couple of girls.' His dark eyes danced. 'Who do you fancy?'

Mike shook his head. 'At the minute I couldn't care less.'

'Couldn't care less! Heavens, you *are* sick!' Robert gazed thoughtfully into the flames. 'What about Jane and Angela? Or Maureen? Yes, Maureen Bates!' He stretched and wriggled his toes luxuriously. 'Oh! That pink woolly sweater! I reckon she fancies me already.'

Mike was looking out of the window. He changed the topic.

'It looks as if the mist's coming down. If you're going out you'd better not leave it too late.'

Robert crossed the room and gazed out on the puddled shore and glistening mud-flats. The horizon had disappeared. He glanced from side to side, assessing the afternoon light.

'No, it will be all right for a while yet.'

'I think you're wrong,' Mike said. 'Listen how still it is. Not a breath of wind.'

For a moment both boys listened intently. The fire crackled, far off a sea-bird called. No other sound broke the silence.

'My dad says, "Never go out on the mud-flats when there's a chance of mist."'

'It'll be all right.' Robert added another dash of whisky to the last of his coffee and drank it off. 'Anyway, it's perfectly safe. All you've got to do is keep your head and travel north.' He lifted the waist of his sweater and flipped the compass that hung from his belt. He laughed light-headedly and with a hint of arrogance. 'Simple as pie. The cold's making you soft in the head.'

He turned from the window and began making preparations. A pair of rubber waders engulfed his corduroys to the thigh. He pulled on the heavy shooting jacket and hung a scarf about his neck. A tweed hat with a tuft of feathers in the band covered his neat black hair. From a box of red cartridges he took two number six shot and thrust them into the breech of his twelve-bore, snapped the gun shut and pressed on the safety-catch. Carelessly he took two handfuls of the brass-ended cartridges, added a few number three shot for geese, and dropped them into a voluminous pocket. From a leather case he took a pair of 8 × 30 Zeiss binoculars and slung them round his neck.

'What will you do while I'm away?'

'Toast myself by the fire. I might do a bit of maths.'

Robert looked across. 'Maths!'

'Yes, I've got an exam on Monday.'

Mike was not clever. Though he worked hard and was popular – much more than the brilliant and intolerant Robert – his results were mediocre. His hope was to gain entrance to a good agricultural college the following summer.

Robert raised dark eyebrows. 'What is it? Do you want any help?'

Mike was used to his companion's easy arrogance; nevertheless he flushed slightly.

'I don't think so. Thanks all the same.'

'Well, just say if you do.' Robert slung a blood-stained khaki bag over his shoulder. Feathers clung to the inside. He picked up the whisky bottle and took another warming mouthful. The powerful spirit made him shudder. He held it out. Mike shook his head.

'I wonder if I should take it with me?' Robert thought for a moment. 'No, better not.' He took another quick swig, grimaced, and set the bottle on the window-ledge. 'Help yourself if you want any,' he said.

'Thanks.' Mike was looking down the shore. 'Look, you'll really have to be careful, very careful. You shouldn't go out alone – really, you shouldn't. Dad's made me promise.' He rose from the chair. 'I'd better come with you.'

Robert pushed him back. 'Rubbish. I've told you, if the mist does come down, all I've got to do is keep my head and travel due north. Straight as an arrow I'll come to the shore. Safe as my own back garden.'

Mike was unconvinced. 'Well, don't go too far out. If it does start to . . .'

'You're like an old woman.' Robert interrupted him. 'You stay here and keep the fire built up. Make the meal if you want something to do. OK? I'll be back about dark.'

Robert's preparations were soon complete. Mike followed his companion through the hall and out into the late afternoon. An hour and a half of gloomy daylight remained. The woods hung motionless at their backs; a brooding stillness lay over the shore. Business-like, Robert collected a pair of mud-pattens from the shed. Somehow, even in shooting jacket and waders, he contrived to look neat.

'Well, see you.' He hitched the gleaming gun comfortably beneath his arm and turned away towards the brown and silver levels of the mud-flats.

'Good luck!' Mike called after the retreating back. Aware that he sounded like his mother, he added, 'Remember, don't go too far.'

The chill air brought on a succession of explosive sneezes and he retreated indoors. Through watering blue eyes he watched from the window as Robert grew smaller down the shingle and rutted banks of shore grass. With an uneasy sigh he moved the whisky bottle aside and turned back into the kitchen to make another cup of coffee.

Robert dropped his pattens 'slap – slap' at the edge of the mud-flats. They were stout wooden boards about fifty centimetres long and thirty broad. Their purpose, rather like snow-shoes, was to aid walking on the mud. Wooden slats beneath stopped them from slipping, two rope loops attached them to the feet. Robert had made the pattens himself and soon they were secured over his rubber thigh-boots. With sticky, squelching steps he advanced from the shore.

The whisky made him light-headed. On every side the Solway mud spread into the dim afternoon light. Films of mist clung among branches above the cottage. The murky horizon had moved closer; visibility was a mile at most. Enjoying the freshness of the open air, imagining in his solitude and adventure the heroes of boyhood reading, Robert headed steadily out across the mud-flats.

Fifteen minutes brought him to the meandering channel which was his destination. Carefully he descended the mud-bank until his head was below the level of the surrounding flats. From his shooting bag he produced an empty polythene sack and spread it on a hard patch of mud. Laying the bag on top, he lowered himself upon it and took the shotgun across his knees. Before him shallow water, brown and pewter, rippled in the channel. The air was chill. He adjusted his scarf and pulled his collar close, accepting the discomfort without complaint.

Now all Robert had to do was wait. Soon the duck and geese, having spent all day by the edge of the tide, would fly inland to pass their nights in fields by river and loch. This was the evening flight. As the birds passed overhead, Robert was well positioned and as hidden as possible on that naked shore, to bring them down with his twelve-bore.

Slim fingers protruding from fingerless gloves, he broke open the shotgun to inspect the cartridges, snapped it shut and checked that the safety-catch was off. Through bright binoculars he surveyed up and down the channel.

His brain was muzzy, his thoughts confused with the unaccustomed whisky. Robert was annoyed, for he prided himself on the clarity of his mind. In the stillness of waiting he forced himself to concentrate. Beneath his breath he repeated passages of poetry, worked out a mathematical calculation, composed a description in French of the scene before him, practised a piece for piano on the cold steel of the gun-barrel.

A distant call of duck recalled him to the present. It grew louder. Robert rose to his feet, dark eyes scouring the grey sky for sign of the approaching birds. Soon he spotted them, a pair of mallard flying low. They would pass about thirty metres off. He swung the shotgun to his shoulder and sighted along the hollow between the twin barrels. In poor light the unsuspecting birds did not see him, clad in brown and dark green, motionless in the channel below. As they flew past, Robert's aim was just in front of the leading duck. His finger tightened on the trigger. Bang! The noise was deafening. The barrel kicked, the butt thudded into his shoulder. In mid-air the mallard crumpled up, fell in a brief curve, and disappeared somewhere on the gloomy mud-flat. Instantly the second bird circled away in alarm. Robert swung his gun to follow it, but by the time he was on target the bird was too far away. He let the barrel fall.

Pleased at his success, he climbed from the channel and searched for the mallard on the open mud. He soon found it. The bird's feathers were fouled with mire and blood. It was not dead, and regarded him with a bright eye. A firm twist and jerk and the head fell limp upon the glossy neck. Briefly Robert admired it, held out the patterned wings, stroked the shimmering neck feathers with the tip of one finger, then opened his bag and dropped it inside.

Now light was fading the birds came more quickly. In the space of half an hour Robert had added a teal and a widgeon.

But Mike had been right. The mist was closing in. The shore was dim, almost indistinguishable, though only half a mile distant.

Far out across the mud-flats the tide had turned. Slowly at first, films of water came whispering across the mud-banks. In the channel at Robert's feet the water stirred as if expectantly. Brown bubbles, checked in their outward flow, began to inch back in.

Robert lifted his jacket to check the compass. Even as he did so he heard the sound that quickens the pulse of all wildfowlers, the clear, fluting call of a flight of greylag geese. Eyes alert, he stared seawards. Quickly he broke open his shotgun and replaced the cartridges with a couple of the longer number three goose-shot. Expectantly he raised the gun to his shoulder. The crying was loud, but still nothing was to be seen in the dim light. Then suddenly, with a speed and rush of wings that caught Robert unawares, they were upon him, a straggling line of a dozen or fifteen geese with necks outstretched. At the same instant the birds spotted his dark figure, spinning to face them on the edge of the channel. Before he could aim they veered. Robert swung and found a great bird in his sights. Two fingers tightened. Bang! ... Bang! Visibly the goose lurched in mid-air, struggled on for a few more wing-beats, then suddenly dropped, all but lost in the closing walls of mist. With an audible thud it struck the mud.

His first goose! Robert's heart leaped. Exultantly, with awkward strides, pattens flapping on the ooze, he hurried down the bank, crossed the watery channel, and struggled up the far side.

On the brink he paused. All around him the thickening mist pressed closer. For the first time Robert felt a shadow of anxiety, but he cast it aside in the excitement of the moment. The goose should be somewhere over – there. He hurried forward.

In a minute he found the spot, a splash in the mud, a scattering of white and grey feathers. But of the goose there was no sign. A messy trail showed the direction in which it had struggled. Disappointed that he had not killed the bird outright, Robert ejected the spent cartridges, thrust two more into the breech, and set off in pursuit.

In the gathering darkness he followed the huge footprints and trench-like furrow of the bird's body. Tracks at either side showed where the wounded goose had helped itself along with its wings.

For seven or eight hundred metres the trail wound ahead, turning first this way and then that. In the clumsy pattens progress was slow. Several times Robert halted, certain he had lost the bird. Twice he almost turned back. He could no longer see the shore; his situation was becoming alarming. Then he recalled one of the first laws of hunting: 'Never leave an injured animal to die. Track it down and finish the job cleanly.' Perspiring in his heavy clothes, Robert pressed on through the mist.

At length his perseverance was rewarded. In a sprawled heap the greylag lay before him. Its wings were fouled, its pure breast clotted with mud. The beautiful goose-head lay twisted against the body. It was quite dead.

Excitement tempered by sudden regret that he had killed such a splendid creature, Robert lifted the goose by its downy neck. It was heavy. The wings hung limp. It was difficult to believe that all life was extinguished behind those brilliant black eyes. Opening the shooting bag wide, he folded the bird inside and settled the strap over his shoulder.

Three duck and a goose – it had been a splendid evening's sport! Now it was time to return to the bothy. Robert belched and grimaced. The remains of the whisky burned in his stomach. After the excitement of the chase he felt a little thick-headed. Judiciously he regarded the line of tracks winding back into the mist. The general direction of his pursuit had been parallel to the channel, he was sure of it. Instead of trailing them back, it would be much quicker simply to head due north, as he had told Mike. That would take him straight to the shore.

He unzipped the bottom of his jacket and pulled out the compass on its short lanyard. The direction of north surprised him. In following the goose he had apparently veered more to seaward than he realized. It was easy to be misled in the mist – Mike's father was right in that, at least. Still, a man had only to keep his head. The compass could not lie. Carefully Robert lined up the swinging needle and double-checked his direction, secured the safety-catch on his shotgun and started forward.

Back at the cottage, meanwhile, Mike was busy in the kitchen. The Calor gas stove flamed blue, a frying pan of sausages sizzled alongside a steaming saucepan of potatoes. He shivered and sipped yet another mug of scalding coffee. The window was steamed. He rubbed fingertips across a dewed pane and bent to look out.

From the lamplit room the shore seemed dark. Daylight was almost gone. The mist grew thicker by the minute. A solitary hawthorn, quite close at hand, was barely discernible. Checking that the food would not burn, he pulled a jacket over his thick jersey and stepped from the front door.

Soon his eyes adjusted themselves to the dusk. The mist muffled his ears. It was very lonely. Fifty paces down the shore the house was reduced to a dim shape. The lamplit window was a hazy glow, the only touch of colour in a bleak world.

At the edge of a small creek he paused.

'Robert! Ro-bert!'

In the silence his voice was shockingly loud, damped dead by the fog. Staring to left and right he strained his ears for a reply.

'Ro-bert! Ro-o-bert!'

The silence of the shore remained unbroken. Shouting and the wet night air brought on a racking spasm of coughing. Slowly Mike retraced his steps to the cottage.

The steamy scent of potatoes and sausages greeted him as he opened the door. The lamplight was golden, the house warm and welcoming. Mike dropped his jacket on the settee and returned to the kitchen. Robert should not have gone, he told himself; he should have been prevented. When his headstrong companion was not there it was easy to say. But there was no point in worrying, not yet. Robert of all people knew what he was doing; he knew how to look after himself. He would be back soon.

Mike tore two sheets from a roll of toilet paper and blew his nose loudly. He caught sight of himself in a peeling mirror above the sink. His nose was red, his eyes were swollen. With a misshapen fork he stabbed the blackening sausages and turned them in the pan. Then he turned off the gas and retreated to the yellow, spitting fire in the living-room.

'Slap – flap – slap – flap,' went Robert's pattens on the sticky mud. 'Slap – flap – slap – flap.' The mist had closed about him. Beyond thirty metres all was hidden in a shrouding blanket of fog, darkening now as the November daylight faded. Despite his confidence and determination the solitude was frightening; suddenly the dark and silver banks of mud were menacing. Robert refused to admit it. He pressed forward, forcing himself to think of the goose and three duck in the heavy bag at his side.

All at once, twenty paces ahead, he came upon the glinting channel. Robert smiled with relief. He had been right; all he had to do was head north. The tide was advancing more swiftly now. The bubbles flowed past as if borne on a muddy river – from left to right. All was as it should be. Carefully he descended the bank and waded across. The brown water swilled almost to the top of his thigh boots. In a minute he was on the opposite bank and climbing back to the level of the mud-flats.

Panting slightly, Robert eased the bag on his shoulder and tramped. 'Squelch – flap – squelch – flap.' How envious Mike would be, he thought. He had never shot a goose. Yet he was a good-hearted fellow, despite being a bit of a clod-hopper. Robert's stomach rumbled, and he grimaced again with indigestion. The whisky had not been a good idea. He was ravenous. He hoped Mike would have the meal ready when he reached the cottage. Afterwards they would put their feet up on either side of a roaring fire.

'Flap – squelch – flap – squelch.' The mist deadened all other sound. Nothing was to be heard but the noise of his own clumsy progress. It was as if his ears and face were padded with cotton-wool. Repeatedly he checked his direction with the compass at his belt.

Ten minutes passed. Robert began to look for sign of the grass and shingle shore, to seek the looming shadow of the steep wood beyond.

Abruptly he stopped. A shudder passed through him. A second channel lay before him, wetter and slimier than the one he had crossed previously, deeper in water. In the half-light the brown bubbles danced by.

Horrified, Robert seized the compass. It had become difficult to read at his waist. Quickly he unhooked the lanyard and wrapped it about his wrist. Holding the compass steady in both hands, he took the direction of north.

It lay straight across the deep channel. But how could that be? Robert pulled himself together. The current ran from right to left. He must have moved further along the coast than he realized, and the channel wound inshore. As quickly as the pattens allowed, he explored up and down the bank. No spot seemed better than another. The water was deepening all the time. Bracing himself, holding shotgun, compass and canvas bag on high, he descended the shortened bank into the water.

The mud was slippery; the current bore against his legs. As he lifted each foot it tore at the clumsy pattens. The water rose above the long boots and filled them, ice-cold and heavy. It reached to his waist, tugging at the heavy jacket, then to his chest. Robert gritted his teeth. His foot struck a solitary boulder. He stumbled, fighting the current, and nearly fell. Slowly the water became shallower. Suddenly, before he could stop it, one of the pattens tugged loose. He struggled to hold it in place, but the force of the current was too great. In an instant the patten was torn from his foot and went whirling away inshore in the rushing flood of brown water.

A minute later Robert was across. Clothes clinging, waders heavy as lead and slopping gouts of water, he struggled up the bank. One foot sank ankle-deep. Panting with exertion, he stared around the desolate spot, then looked down at his remaining patten. One was useless. With a vicious swear he kicked it off and caught up the rope loops in his hand. Clots of mud smeared his fingers. Gun, compass, bag, patten – it was too much to carry. In sudden anger he heaved the patten into the streaming current. Instantly it was twitched away, turning on the flood, and vanished into the gloom.

With a sigh Robert turned from the channel, checked his direction with the compass and trudged forward. There was only a short way to go now; the shore must be close at hand.

Five minutes passed. It had become quite dark. Though he could still see the compass needle, the luminous markings glowed white-green.

All at once Robert found that he was walking in water, a shallow film on the mud that splashed at each footfall. Surprised, he stopped and stared down. The water was flowing, a thin and steady flood that carried the silt from his footsteps behind him. His heart lurched. He looked more closely. The water moved to meet him. For all the world it looked as if he was walking into the advancing tide – walking out to sea. But that could not be. The compass did not lie.

Again he held out the precious instrument. The glowing needle wavered and settled as he was heading. That must be north. Yet something was wrong. Suddenly, to his horror, Robert saw that he held the compass right against the breech of his shotgun. The steel barrel pulled the magnetic needle sideways. Almost in a frenzy, he swung the shotgun far behind his back and looked at the compass again. At once the needle swung, a steady semi-circle, and pointed back the way he had come.

As if a map was drawn in his mind, Robert recalled the route he had taken: the journey from shore to the first channel; the half mile after he had shot the goose; then following the compass to the second channel, and the third. He was far out on the mud-flats, a mile at least, perhaps a mile and a half. The mist pressed close, darkness intensified. At his feet the water, now two centimetres deep, swirled past, parting round his boots. At that moment, if ever in his life, it was a time to keep calm. Yet Robert shivered. Bitterly he cursed his stupidity for drinking whisky before he set out on the mud-flats. For the first time in a dozen years he felt fear. Not a second was to be wasted. Clutching the shotgun firmly and attempting to hold his shooting bag steady, he started back the way he had come – running.

The binoculars bounced at his neck. His boots were still weighted with water, knee-deep and heavy as lead. Mud and the advancing tide splashed round him at every footfall. He began to count: one – two – three – four – the effort was exhausting. At fifty-eight his right leg sank deep and he sprawled headlong. Hands, face, jacket, shotgun, compass, were smeared with ooze. In wet gobbets, as he sat up and dragged the leg free, it slid down his cheek and neck. Panting, he lay back in the mud and lifted his legs. A gallon of seawater gushed from each boot.

Heavily, avoiding the soft patch, Robert pushed himself to his feet and ran on. One – two – three – four – five ... seventy-eight – seventy-nine – eighty ... one hundred and forty-three – one hundred and forty-four – one hundred and ...

. Suddenly there was no ground beneath his feet. The channel was brim-full. Before he knew it was there, Robert ran straight into deep water. The current twitched him away, the heavy boots dragged him down. He let go of his beautiful shotgun. Irrevocably, on the instant, it was gone. So were his binoculars. Down and down, over and over, the current bowled him in the soft ooze of the channel. But Robert was tough and fit, a fighter. Exerting all his strength, he clawed and kicked his way to the surface. In two minutes, sinking a dozen times in his progress, he struggled to the opposite bank and collapsed in the spilling tide.

It was long moments before he could lift his head and rise from the lap – lap – lapping water. His precious twelve-bore was gone. Darkness and the shrouding mist formed a cocoon about him. Mud and water streamed from his head and shoulders.

The struggle had drained Robert of strength. Lurching with fatigue he tried to run on. Again his boots were like lead. He collapsed on the mud and tugged them off. With a loud suck his legs were free. Leaving the boots where they lay, he stumbled on.

The greylag and wild duck bumped awkwardly against his side. He tugged the strap over his head and let his shooting bag fall in the mud.

Now he made better progress. His heavy socks tugged loose. Barefoot he squelched on. His jacket too was clumsy. He unzipped it as he ran and dropped it in the tide behind him. Reduced to trousers and jersey, Robert was now better equipped for running. A dozen times he tumbled headlong as a patch of softer mud seized his legs and dragged him to the ground. He tugged his legs free. Clawing at the ooze, he slithered clear of the dangerous spot like a turtle.

Luckily it was a good compass. Each time he fell he clutched it tight, the lanyard wound about his wrist. With filthy fingers he scraped clear the mud to see the luminous, life-saving needle beneath. North, ever north, he splashed on.

Abruptly, in the last pewter gleam of daylight that filtered through the mist, Robert saw that he had run clear of the advancing tide. He stopped, breathing heavily. A moment later, hissing and bubbling on the mud-flats, the scum-edged line of water emerged from the darkness at his back and whispered onward towards the shore.

Robert took a steadying breath and ran on, hampered by his clinging clothes. He passed the rim of the flooding tide. His feet sank ankle-deep; mud spurted between his toes. Five minutes later the second channel lay before him, only centimetres short of brim-full. Pausing briefly on the bank, he took a deep breath and flung himself full-length. It was a clumsy dive. The current plucked him sideways. He struck out boldly. The water was numbingly cold. Soon he was across. Shuddering, he checked the compass and rubbed the hair from his face with an icy hand.

Slowly, as he trotted on, as two hundred, three hundred sluggish metres unreeled behind him, Robert's panic receded. By sheer will-power, the steely determination that had won him athletic honours and a scholarship to Cambridge, he forced himself to rise above weariness and cold. He would not admit them. Steadily the old, lifelong confidence began to re-assert itself. He had been in a tricky spot and was far from out of it yet, but all he had to do was keep heading north. Soon he must reach the last deep stretch of channel where he had sat before shooting. After that there remained only the final straight half-mile to the Solway shore. He recalled the levels of silvery mud he had crossed in the afternoon light, and looked down at the treacherous mire underfoot.

'Suck! Splash! Plot! Squelch!' his feet went in the ooze. Another hundred metres passed. Robert looked up at the pressing cloud overhead, a gloomy blanket so close that it seemed he could reach up and touch it. As he did so, he failed to notice a small, glass-smooth circle of mud right in his path. In pattens, with difficulty, he might have crossed it. Now he ran straight in. The mud seized him by the ankles and calves. Already covered in mire from head to foot, Robert pitched full-length. He struggled to release his leg, but the bog held him fast. Each tug only made him sink deeper. Soon he was to his knees. Robert spread-eagled himself on the mud and heaved. Slowly, as he strained, his legs began to suck clear. He could not maintain the pressure. The instant it was released the bog dragged him deeper.

In a minute he was to his thighs. Robert called aloud, howled for help. His voice boomed about him in the fog, deadened in a hundred metres. 'Aaaaahhh! Aaaaahhh! He-e-e-lp!' The implacable mud sucked him waist-deep.

Soon it was to his chest. Suddenly Robert felt a firm surface beneath his foot. Hard mud – he had reached the bottom. The treacherous hollow was only about 120 centimetres deep. With fear and relief Robert sobbed aloud and called again. 'Mi-i-ike! Mi-i-i-ike! He-e-e-lp!'

He stopped, listening. All was silent.

This way and that he twisted, clawing at the mud. Throughout his life Robert had always been able to do anything he put his mind to. It was impossible to believe there was not some way to heave his slim frame out of that hole. But the mud held him tight. In fear and frustration he screamed and cried aloud for help. His ears rang with deafening shouts.

Again he stopped, listening, staring about into the silent mist. But not even a solitary sea-bird heard him on the desolate mud-flats. He was unutterably alone.

Then creeping, whispering bubbling, the rim of the tide advanced out of the darkness. A rippling film of water lapped about Robert's chest and spilled onward towards the shore. Slowly, infinitely slowly, the Solway tide deepened around him.

In the bothy above the shore, dinner had been ready for an hour. Potatoes and sausages grew cold in the saucepan. Beyond the windows darkness was absolute. Mike's fear and distress mounted. Repeatedly he pulled on his jacket, wound a scarf about his throat, and descended to the mud-flats. Loudly he called, coughing in the night air. By torchlight, beam dazzling on the shrouding mist, he explored east and west along the deserted shore. The woods loomed dark at his back, the incoming tide rocked in the creek. As he returned, praying that Robert would be back before him, he almost missed the bothy, squat and solitary as some ancient tower in the mist.

At nine o'clock he could wait no longer. Taking Robert's car keys from the shelf, he climbed the track through the wood. As he mounted above the shore one or two stars appeared overhead, and in the east the white halo of a gibbous moon. Ignoring the fact that he had only a provisional licence, he took the car and drove three miles to the nearest farmhouse. From there he telephoned the police and the coastguard.

It was fourteen hours later, and the fog had lifted when a young policeman, one of the searchers, spotted a cloud of gulls wheeling and settling about a tiny object far out on the mud-flats. He raised his binoculars. It looked like a brown stump uncovered by the ebbing tide, and yet . . .

'Hey, Sarge!' he called.

Mike, standing with Robert's parents, looked across and followed the young policeman's gaze. The cruel and excited cries of the birds rose faintly on the morning air.

# Dengué Fever

## *Paul Theroux*

There is a curious tree, native to Malaysia, called 'The Midnight Horror'. We had several in Ayer Hitam, one in an overgrown part of the Botanical Gardens, the other in the front garden of William Ladysmith's house. His house was huge, nearly as grand as mine, but I was the American Consul and Ladysmith was an English teacher on a short contract. I assumed it was the tree that had brought the value of his house down. The house itself had been built before the war – one of those great breezy places, a masterpiece of colonial carpentry, with cement walls two feet thick and window blinds the size of sails on a Chinese junk. It was said that it had been the centre of operations during the occupation. All this history diminished by a tree! In fact, no local person would go near the house; the Chinese members of the staff at Ladysmith's school chose to live in that row of low warrens near the bus depot.

During the day the tree looked comic, a tall simple pole like an enormous coat-rack with big leaves that looked like branches – but there were very few of them. It was covered with knobs, stark black things; and around the base of the trunk there were always fragments of leaves that looked like shattered bones, but not human bones.

At night the tree was different, not comic at all. It was Ladysmith who showed me the underlined passage in his copy of Professor Corner's *Wayside Trees of Malaya*. Below the entry for *Oroxylum indicum* it read, 'Botanically, it is the sole representative of its kind; aesthetically, it is monstrous . . . The corolla begins to open about 10 p.m., when the tumid, wrinkled lips part and the harsh odour escapes from them. By midnight, the lurid mouth gapes widely and is filled with stink . . . The flowers are pollinated by bats which are attracted by the smell and, holding to the fleshy corolla with the claws on their wings, thrust their noses into its throat; scratches, as of bats, can be seen on the fallen leaves the next morning . . .'

Smelly! Ugly! Pollinated by bats! I said, 'No wonder no one wants to live in this house.'

'It suits me fine,' said Ladysmith. He was a lanky fellow, very pleasant, one of our uncomplicated Americans, who thrives in bush postings. He cycled around in his bermuda shorts, organizing talent shows in *kampongs*. His description in my consulate file was 'Low risk, high gain'. Full of enthusiasm and blue-eyed belief; and open-hearted: he was forever having tea with tradesmen, whose status was raised as soon as he crossed the threshold.

Ladysmith didn't come to the Club much, although he was a member and had appeared in the Footlighters' production of Maugham's *The Letter*. I think he disapproved of us. He was young, one of the Vietnam generation with a punished conscience and muddled notions of colonialism. That war created drop-outs, but Ladysmith I took to be one of the more constructive ones, a volunteer teacher. After the cease-fire there were fewer; now there are none, neither hippies nor do-gooders. Ladysmith was delighted to take his guilt to Malaysia, and he once told me that Ayer Hitam was more lively than his home-town, which surprised me until he said he was from Caribou, Maine.

He was tremendously popular with his students. He had put up a backboard and basketball hoop in the playground and after school he taught them the fundamentals of the game. He was, for all his apparent awkwardness, an athletic fellow, though it didn't show until he was in action – jumping or dribbling a ball down the court. Perhaps it never does. He ate like a horse, and knowing he lived alone I made a point of inviting him often to dinners for visiting firemen from Kuala Lumpur or Singapore. He didn't have a cook; he said he would not have a servant, but I don't believe he would have got any local person to live in his house, so close to that grotesque tree.

I was sorry but not surprised, two months after he arrived, to hear that Ladysmith had a fever. Ayer Hitam was malarial, and the tablets we took every Sunday like communion were only suppressants. The Chinese headmaster at the school stopped in at the consulate and said that Ladysmith wanted to see me. I went that afternoon.

The house was empty; a few chairs in the sitting room, a shelf of paperbacks, a short-wave radio, and in the room beyond a table holding only a large bottle of ketchup. The kitchen smelled of peanut butter and stale bread. Bachelor's quarters. I climbed the stairs, but before I entered the bedroom I heard Ladysmith call out in an anxious voice, 'Who is it?'

'Boy, am I glad to see you,' he said, relaxing as I came through the door.

He looked thinner, his face was grey, his hair awry in bunches of standing hackles; and he lay in the rumpled bed as if he had been thrown there. His eyes were sunken and oddly coloured with the yellow light of fever.

'Malaria?'

'I think so – I've been taking chloroquine. But it doesn't seem to be working. I've got the most awful headache.' He closed his eyes. 'I can't sleep. I have these nightmares. I –'

'What does the doctor say?'

'I'm treating myself,' said Ladysmith.

'You'll kill yourself,' I said. 'I'll send Alec over tonight.'

We talked for a while, and eventually I convinced Ladysmith that he needed attention. Alec Stewart was a member of the Club Ladysmith particularly disliked. He wasn't a bad sort, but as he was married to a Chinese girl he felt he could call them 'Chinks' without blame. He had been a ship's surgeon in the Royal Navy and had come to Ayer Hitam after the war. With a young wife and all that sunshine he was able to reclaim some of his youth. Back at the office I sent Peeraswami over with a pot of soup and the latest issue of *Newsweek* from the consulate library.

Alec went that night. I saw him at the Club later. He said, 'Our friend's pretty rocky.'

'I had malaria myself,' I said. 'It wasn't much fun.'

Alec blew a cautionary snort. 'He's not got malaria. He's got dengué.'

'Are you sure?'

'All the symptoms are there.'

'What did you give him for it?'

'The only thing there is worth a docken – aspirin.'

'I suppose he'll have to sweat it out.'

'He'll do that all right.' Alec leaned over. 'The lad's having hallucinations.'

'I didn't know that was a symptom of dengué,' I said.

'Dengué's a curse.'

He described it to me. It is a virus, carried by a mosquito, and begins as a headache of such voltage that you tremble and can't stand or sit. You're knocked flat; your muscles ache, you're doubled up with cramp and your temperature stays over a hundred. Then your skin becomes paper-thin, sensitive to the slightest touch – the weight of a sheet can cause pain. And your hair falls out – not all of it, but enough to fill a comb. These severe irritations produce another agony, a depression so black the dengué sufferer continually sobs. All the while your bones ache, as if every inch of you has been smashed with a hammer. This sensation of bruising gives dengué its colloquial name, 'break-bone fever'. I pitied Ladysmith.

Although it was after eleven when Alec left the Club, I went straight over to Ladysmith's house. I was walking up the gravel drive when I heard the most ungodly shriek – frightening in its intensity and full of alarm. I did not recognize it as Ladysmith's – indeed, it scarcely sounded human. But it was coming from his room. It was so loud and charged in pitch with such suddenness it might easily have been two or three people screaming, or a dozen doomed cats. The Midnight Horror tree was in full bloom and filled the night with stink.

Ladysmith lay in bed whimpering. The magazine I'd sent him was tossed against the wall, and the effect of disorder was heightened by the overhead fan which was lifting and ruffling the pages.

He was propped on one arm, but seeing me he sighed and fell back. His face was slick with perspiration and tearstreaks. He was short of breath.

'Are you all right?'

'My skin is burning,' he said. I noticed his lips were swollen and cracked with fever, and I saw then how dengué was like a species of grief.

'I thought I heard a scream,' I said. Screaming takes energy; Ladysmith was beyond screaming, I thought.

'Massacre,' he said. 'Soldiers – killing women and children. Horrible. Over there –' he pointed to a perfectly ordinary table with a jug of water on it, and he breathed, 'War. You should see their faces all covered with blood. Some have arms missing. I've never –' He broke off and began to sob.

'Alec says you have dengué fever,' I said.

'Two of them – women. They look the same,' said Ladysmith lifting his head. 'They scream at me, and it's so loud! They have no teeth!'

'Are you taking the aspirin?' I saw the amber jar was full.

'Aspirin! For this!' He lay quietly, then said, 'I'll be all right. Sometimes it's nothing – just a high temperature. Then these Chinese . . . then I get these dreams.'

'About war?'

'Yes. Flashes.'

As gently as I could I said, 'You didn't want to go to Vietnam, did you?'

'No. Nobody wanted to go. I registered as a c.o.'

Hallucinations are replies. Peeraswami was always seeing Tamil ghosts on his way home. They leapt from those green fountains by the road the Malays call *daun pontianak* – 'ghost leaf' – surprising him with plates of hot samosas or tureens of curry; not so much ghosts as ghostesses. I told him to eat something before setting out from home in the dark and he stopped seeing them. I took Ladysmith's vision of massacre to be replies to his conscientious objection. It is the draft-dodger who speaks most graphically of war, not the soldier. Pacifists know all the atrocity stories.

But Ladysmith's hallucinations had odd highlights: the soldiers he saw weren't American. They were dark orientals in dirty undershirts, probably Vietcong, and mingled with the screams of the people with bloody faces was another sound, the creaking of bicycle seats. So there were two horrors – the massacre and these phantom cyclists. He was especially frightened by the two women with no teeth, who opened their mouths wide and screamed at him.

I said, 'Give it a few days.'

'I don't think I can take much more of this.'

'Listen,' I said. 'Dengué can depress you. You'll feel like giving up and going home – you might feel like hanging yourself. But take these aspirin and keep telling yourself – whenever you get these nightmares – it's dengué fever.'

'No teeth, and their gums are dripping with blood –'

His head dropped to the pillow, his eyes closed, and I remember thinking: everyone is fighting this war, everyone in the world. Poor Ladysmith was fighting hardest of all. Lying there he could have been bivouacked in the Central Highlands, haggard from a siege, his dengué a version of battle fatigue.

I left him sleeping and walked again through the echoing house. But the smell had penetrated to the house itself, the high thick stink of rotting corpses. It stung my eyes and I almost fainted with the force of it until, against the moon, I saw the blossoming coat-rack and the wheeling bats – The Midnight Horror.

'Rotting flesh,' Ladysmith said late the next afternoon. I tried not to smile. I had brought Alec along for a second look. Ladysmith began describing the smell, the mutilated people, the sound of bicycles and those Chinese women, the toothless ones. The victims had pleaded with him. Ladysmith looked wretched.

Alec said, 'How's your head?'

'It feels like it's going to explode.'

Alec nodded. 'Joints a bit stiff?'

'I can't move.'

'Dengué's a curse.' Alec smiled: doctors so often do when their grim diagnosis is proved right.

'*I can't –*' Ladysmith started, then grimaced and continued in a softer tone. 'I can't sleep. If I could only sleep I'd be all right. For God's sake give me something to make me sleep.'

Alec considered this.

'Can't you give him anything?' I asked.

'I've never prescribed a sleeping pill in my life,' said Alec, 'and I'm not going to do so now. Young man, take my advice. Drink lots of liquid – you're dehydrating. You've got a severe fever. Don't underestimate it.

It can be a killer. But I guarantee if you follow my instructions, get lots of bed-rest, take aspirin every four hours, you'll be right as ninepence.'

'My hair is falling out.'

Alec smiled – right again. 'Dengué,' he said. 'But you've still got plenty. When you've as little hair as I have you'll have something to complain about.'

Outside the house I said, 'That tree is the most malignant thing I've ever seen.'

Alec said, 'You're talking like a Chink.'

'Sure, it looks innocent enough now, with the sun shining on it. But have you smelled it at night?'

'I agree. A wee aromatic. Like a Bengali's fart.'

'If we cut it down I think Ladysmith would stop having his night-mares.'

'Don't be a fool. That tree's medicinal. The Malays use it for potions. It works – I use it myself.'

'Well, if it's so harmless why don't the Malays want to live in this house?'

'It's not been offered to a Malay. How many Malay teachers do you know? It's the Chinks won't live here – I don't have a clue why that's so, but I won't have you running down that tree. It's going to cure our friend.'

I stopped walking. 'What do you mean by that?'

Alec said, 'The aspirin – or rather, not the aspirin. I'm using native medicine. Those tablets are made from the bark of that tree – I wish it didn't have that shocking name.'

'You're giving him *that*?'

'Calm down, it'll do him a world of good,' Alec said brightly. 'Ask any witch-doctor.'

I slept badly that night, thinking of Alec's ridiculous cure – he had truly gone bush – but I was tied up all day with visa inquiries and it was not until the following evening that I got back to Ladysmith's. I was determined to take him away. I had aspirin at my house; I'd keep him away from Alec.

Downstairs, I called out and knocked as usual to warn him I'd come, and as usual there was no response from him. I entered the bedroom and saw him asleep, but uncovered. Perhaps the fever had passed: his face was dry. He did not look well, but then few people do when they're sound asleep – most take on the ghastly colour of illness. Then I saw that the amber bottle was empty – the 'aspirin' bottle.

I tried to feel his pulse. Impossible: I've never been able to feel a person's pulse, but his hand was cool, almost cold. I put my ear against his mouth and I thought I could detect a faint purr of respiration.

It was dusk when I arrived, but darkness in Ayer Hitam fell quickly, the blanket of night dropped and the only warning was the sound of insects tuning up, the chirrup of geckoes and those squeaking bats making for the tree. I switched on the lamp and as I did so heard a low cry, as of someone dying in dreadful pain. And there by the window – just as Ladysmith had described – I saw the moonlit faces of two Chinese women, smeared with blood. They opened their mouths and howled: they were toothless and their screeches seemed to gain volume from that emptiness.

'Stop!' I shouted.

The two faces in those black rags hung there, and I caught the whiff of the tree which was the whiff of wounds. It should have scared me, but it only surprised me. Ladysmith had prepared me, and felt certain that he had passed that horror on. I stepped forward, caught the cord and dropped the window blinds. The two faces were gone.

This took seconds, but an after-image remained, like a lamp switched rapidly on and off. I gathered up Ladysmith. Having lost weight he was very light, pathetically so. I carried him downstairs and through the garden to the road.

Behind me, in the darkness, was the rattle of pedals, the squeak of a bicycle seat. The phantom cyclists! It gave me a shock, and I tried to run, but carrying Ladysmith I could not move quickly. The cycling noises approached, frantic squeakings at my back. I spun round.

It was a trishaw, cruising for fares. I put Ladysmith on the seat, and running alongside it we made our way to the mission hospital.

A stomach pump is little more than a slender rubber tube pushed into one nostril and down the back of the throat. A primitive device: I couldn't watch. I stayed until Ladysmith regained consciousness. But it was useless to talk to him. His stomach was empty and he was coughing up bile, spewing into a bucket. I told the nursing sister to keep an eye on him.

I said, 'He's got dengué.'

The succeeding days showed such an improvement in Ladysmith that the doctors insisted he be discharged to make room for more serious cases. And indeed everyone said he'd made a rapid recovery. Alec was astonished, but told him rather sternly, 'You should be ashamed of yourself for taking that overdose.'

Ladysmith was well, but I didn't have the heart to send him back to that empty house. I put him up at my own place. Normally, I hate house-guests – they interfered with my reading and never seemed to have much to do themselves except punish my gin bottle. But Ladysmith was unobtrusive. He drank milk, he wrote letters home. He made no mention of his hallucinations, and I didn't tell him what I'd thought I'd seen. In my own case I believed his suggestions had been so strong that I had imagined what he had seen – somehow shared his own terror of the toothless women.

One day at lunch Ladysmith said, 'How about eating out tonight? On me. A little celebration. After all, you saved my life.'

'Do you feel well enough to face the Club buffet?'

He made a face. 'I hate the Club – no offence. But I was thinking of a meal in town. What about that *kedai* – City Bar? I had a terrific meal there the week I arrived. I've been meaning to go back.'

'You're the boss.'

It was a hot night. The verandah tables were taken, so we had to sit inside, jammed against a wall. We ordered: mee-hoon soup, spring rolls, pork strips, fried kway-teow and a bowl of laksa that seemed to blister the lining of my mouth.

'One thing's for sure,' said Ladysmith, 'I won't get dengué fever again for a while. The sister said I'm immune for a year.'

'Thank God for that,' I said. 'By then you'll be back in Caribou, Maine.'

'I don't know,' he said. 'I like it here.'

He was smiling, glancing around the room, poking noodles into his mouth. Then I saw him lose control of his chopsticks. His jaw dropped, he turned pale, and I thought for a moment that he was going to cry.

'Is anything wrong?'

He shook his head, but he looked stricken.

'It's this food,' I said. 'You shouldn't be eating such strong –'

'No,' he said. 'It's those pictures.'

On the white-washed wall of the *kedai* was a series of framed photographs, old hand-coloured ones, lozenge-shaped, like huge lockets. Two women and some children. Not so unusual; the Chinese always have photographs of relations around – a casual reverence. One could hardly call them a pious people, their brand of religion is ancestor worship, the simple display of the family album. But I had not realized until then that Woo Boh Swee's relations had had money. The evidence was in the pictures: both women were smiling, showing large sets of gold dentures.

'That's them,' said Ladysmith.

'Who?' I said. Staring at them I noticed certain wrinkles of familiarity, but the Chinese are very hard to tell apart. The cliché is annoyingly true.

Ladysmith put his chopsticks down and began to whisper: 'The women in my room – that's *them*. That one had blood on her hair, and the other one –'

'Dengué fever,' I said. 'You said they didn't have any teeth. Now I ask you – look at those teeth. You've got the wrong ladies, my boy.'

'No!'

His pallor had returned, and the face I saw across the table was the one I had seen on that pillow. I felt sorry for him, as helpless as I had before.

Woo Boh Swee, the owner of the City Bar, went by the table. He was brisk, snapping a towel. 'Okay? Anything? More beer? What you want?'

'We're fine, Mr Woo,' I said. 'But I wonder if you can tell us something. We were wondering who those women are in the pictures – over there.'

He looked at the wall, grunted, lowered his head and simply walked away, muttering.

'I don't get it,' I said. I left the table and went to the back of the bar, where Boh Swee's son Reggie – the 'English' son – was playing mah-jongg. I asked Reggie the same question: who are they?

'I'm glad you asked me,' said Reggie. 'Don't mention them to my father. One's his auntie, the other one's his sister. It's a sad story. They were cut up during the war by the dwarf bandits. That's what my old man called them in Hokkien. The Japanese. It happened over at the head-quarters – what they used for head-quarters when they occupied the town. My old man was in Singapore.'

'But the Japanese were only here for a few months,' I said.

'Bunch of thieves,' said Reggie. 'They took anything they could lay their hands on. They used those old ladies for house-girls, at the headquarters, that big house, where the tree is. Then they killed them, just like that, and hid the bodies – we never found the graves. But that was before they captured Singapore. The British couldn't stop them, you know. The dwarf bandits were clever – they pretended they were Chinese and rode all the way to the Causeway on bicycles.'

I looked back at the table. Ladysmith was staring, his eyes again bright with fever; staring at those gold teeth.

# Message for Margie

*Christine Campbell Thomson*

The fair girl in the pale-blue coat twisted her gloves in her hands and seemed unwilling to leave the room. The others filed out into the linoleum-covered hall, but she still lingered, half in and half out of the doorway.

Blocking any attempt to return to the séance room, the medium, a stout woman in black with a lace stole over her shoulders, raised her eyebrows a trifle.

'There was no message for me,' the girl said, diffidently.

Half-suspiciously, half-kindly, the medium looked at her. She knew the type; it didn't do to let them think themselves neglected, but it wasn't always easy to get a contact for a newcomer; generally the delay paid off: it brought them again and again.

'Wasn't there?'

The girl shook her head. Her young, childlike face was framed in a blue hood that matched her coat, and both were one shade deeper than her very blue eyes. She looked rather like a harebell, thought the medium, who was not entirely without poetry in her soul. 'A breath of wind would puff her away.' She forgot, or did not know, that the harebell bends to the fiercest gale or the heaviest foot and rises triumphant when all is over.

'Were you expecting someone special?' she said, tentatively. Her sharp experienced eyes took in the probable cost of the blue outfit, the gold charm bracelet on one slender wrist, and the good-quality handbag that looked likely to contain a wallet stuffed with notes.

'Yes . . .'

'Why not come again next week? Sometimes they can't get through the first time – not expecting you, you see. Most of the circle are regulars. Mrs Burrage recommended you, didn't she? It is your first time?'

A sharper note had crept into her voice. A faint suspicion showed in her eyes. Hadn't she seen this girl before somewhere? There was a familiar suggestion about her – but not in those clothes – not quite like that. Some of those young policewomen were quite attractive when they were properly made up. . . .

'My very first time at any séance,' replied the girl, and the quality of her tone left no doubt as to the truth of the words.

'Ah . . . and who were you expecting?'

Fishing in very shallow water, but inexperience coupled with emotion will sometimes betray a great deal, and nothing is too small grist for the mill of a South London medium trying to earn an honest living and by no means always able to make contact with her guides. When they failed, it was necessary to fall back on the known and the inferred, and, at worst, on the complete guess.

'Just – just my brother. . . . He passed over – last year. . . .'

'I see.'

Lie number one, thought the medium. Or perhaps hardly a lie. They all called them brothers or sisters. Wouldn't admit to having lovers. Got her into trouble perhaps . . . the medium sniffed a little. She estimated the girl's age at around twenty.

'An accident . . . ?'

'Ye-es.' The girl evidently assumed the sniff to be contempt for her lack of even a semblance of mourning. 'He – he didn't like black. . . .'

'Well, that's right enough, dearie.' She was on firm ground now and regaining control of the situation. 'The spirits always tell us they can't abide sad colours and sad faces. After all, they say they're in a beautiful land where it is always sunshine and blue skies – and – and . . .' She caught herself up sharply.

No need to use up material that rightly belonged to those who'd paid for it. All that could come next time – and very nicely, too. It was the regular form of the first-contact chat – reassuring, that's what they all found it. And the others in the group expected it for a newcomer; gave her the freedom of the circle, so to speak – a kind of admission ticket to the play. Worst of being so regular with those reports from the Other Side; they crept into the everyday speech until before you knew where you were you'd ruined the work for the next sitting.

A clock struck four and she turned sharply.

'You'll have to go now, dearie. There's another group coming in shortly, and I've got to have my cuppa and a bit of a rest. I need something to keep up my strength with all these sittings . . . they're a terrible strain. . . .'

'Of course. I must go. Thank you.'

'Come again next week. You're booked into that group now at two-thirty, so don't mix it. I can't take more than a certain number at a time. The spirits don't like it. They can't cope. See how you were left out this afternoon! But I'll have a word with them and see if we can't get you a message right at the beginning of the sitting next time. See you Saturday. Ta-ta for now. . . .'

She turned on her heel, appearing even larger than life, as befitted one who could summon spirits from the vast deep and instruct them in what order to deliver their communications, and swayed through the sitting-room into the kitchenette, which was so small it could barely contain her and the necessary fixtures. Forgetting to shut the sitting-room door behind her, she stood like a giant bat outlined against the light.

The girl in blue fumbled her way along the hall to the front door. As she reached it, it was pushed open from the outside by a faded-looking woman in black who edged against the wall as though afraid of being seen and recognized. Behind her came a round-faced, red-cheeked dumpling of a woman who cried brightly:

'Look, there's still someone from the last sitting. We aren't late after all. I told you Robinson's clock was fast.'

She pushed her way through, nearly crushing both her companion and the girl in blue, who were on opposite sides of the hall. As she went by, the medium switched on the light from a control inside the sitting-room and both the newcomers' faces were illuminated. With a gasp, the girl lowered her own so that her features were masked by her hat. She slipped quickly and silently down the steps into the late afternoon.

'And that,' she remarked to herself, 'was, believe it or not, Ada and Lucy ... fancy them going there! School Welfare workers! Lucky they didn't recognize me, though I don't suppose they'd mention it. Still, you never know, and that medium was bent on finding out all she could about me. Wonder whose message they're hoping to get! Lucky I'm not in their group.' She chuckled to herself. 'That would have torn it!'

The following Saturday afternoon the girl was back at the séance. The medium recognized her at once, although this time she was wearing dark glasses and a pull-on hat. The chance of meeting Ada and Lucy either on the doorstep or in the street was one she was not prepared to risk unprotected.

'I expect there'll be a message for you today, dearie,' she said comfortingly as the ill-assorted group took their places in a rough circle. Hands were linked, a gramophone wheezed out 'Abide with Me' and someone switched off the lights. The séance had begun.

Messages came as usual, but in spite of the medium's assurance of her personal intervention, nothing and no one contacted the girl. A silence fell; the medium breathed even more stertorously; the circle, feeling that they had had their money's worth, began to fidget; someone was on the point of breaking the link when the voice came – a voice they had never heard before. It was harsh, as though it were coming from a distance and with considerable effort; it was young, and, as everyone was prepared to swear later, it had an urgency, a vitality usually painfully lacking in the supposed voices of their own dead.

'Margie!' it called. 'Margie!'

The girl in blue raised her head at once. Her neighbour swore long afterwards that the hand she was holding turned as cold as ice – like the hand of a corpse, as she dramatically described it – it felt like no living hand.

'Margie!' the voice repeated, and the medium groaned.

'I'm here, Tom.' The words were distinctly uttered and there was no tremor in the tone.

'Good – not easy – to speak – come again. . . .'

The medium stirred and sat up, and the circle automatically broke its contact. There was excitement on most faces; this was something like! A novelty. Every one of them, and some had been half-hearted, determined to come without fail on the next Saturday.

'So you got a message, dearie?' the medium wheezed as she said a careful farewell to her clients; every word was weighed, every indication of pleasure or displeasure or disappointment carefully noted, so that there might be good and fruitful results at the next sitting. Mrs Goldstine seemed to think her husband ought to have stayed longer – greedy, some of these foreign women, thought the medium. Miss Alsopp was in tears; she had had a wonderful message of love and hope from her mother; another one would do no harm.

'Yes – thank you. . . .'

'What you wanted?'

'Well . . .' The word was drawn out, hesitant.

'I know.' The woman spoke quickly to forestall criticism. 'The first time they come through it's difficult – for them, I mean. They can't always make contact easily; have to practise, just like you have to practise to talk a foreign language. Next time there'll be a real message, I expect. . . .' Her eyes were greedily devouring the girl's face. Yes, she was a certainty for two or three more sittings. Played carefully, maybe even longer.

'Tiresome little thing,' the medium said to herself when the door had been finally closed. 'Doesn't give away much. How'm I supposed to find out what sort of message she wants? Tom . . . I heard that meself, coming round. But who is he? Brother? Not likely. She's a deep one, she is. Cagey. And died young, too. Car smash – torn up boy, maybe? P'raps I could risk something about speeding. . . .'

She felt justifiably annoyed. After all, she couldn't be expected to do it all herself with the help of her Guide from time to time. This year he was a Chinese – he called himself a Mandarin – not that the medium was very clear what they meant, connecting it, as did most of her circles, with a type of orange; still, it sounded classy. Last year he'd been a Red Indian. One had to keep up with the fashions, and it wasn't as if the same crowd came year after year. Three months was about their limit, as a rule, and that meant hard work starting new circles each quarter or thereabouts.

'I'd like a nice regular group once a week at three guineas a time and a crystal ball,' she muttered, putting the kettle on. 'Posh place in the West End and real ladies. . . .' Not for nothing did she study the columns of the journals carrying advertisements of her own trade and the allied professions.

Margie dutifully turned up at the next two sittings, but Tom was a disappointment. He identified himself badly. Told Margie that he was always thinking of her and that she was to do her stuff – but what that stuff was and his own relationship still remained a mystery. A passing hopeful reference to motor-bikes brought no response – in fact there seemed something perilously like a guffaw.

Margie knew, but she wasn't telling. She went about her daily life, all through the week, teaching in an infants' school, 'mothering' the babies, occasionally exchanging words with Ada and Lucy, blowing noses, counting heads, superintending milk and biscuits and lunches, handing over her charges to mothers at the gate, all in her usual unperturbed way. But that was the outward form. Inwardly she was in a turmoil.

Tom had communicated; he wanted her to do her stuff; Margie guessed what it meant but the means to the end was still uncertain. She brooded over it, planning, discarding, wondering. She brooded so much that, with the extra stimulation of the weekly contacts, she began to believe him present with her at home. She started to talk to him as if he were there; little short simple sentences. And she was certain that she got replies – and without the help of any medium. She found that it was easiest to contact him after school, when the light was fading; she sat beside her open window in the dusk and could have vowed she saw him coming up the garden path – looking just as he had done that September of last year when he left the house to meet his friends and never came back. Once his presence was so real that she got up and opened the french window to let him in, but there was no one – just the gentle patter of autumn leaves falling on the stones.

She sat back again, disappointed, but with a smile on her lips.

'I know what you want me to do, Tom,' she said, half-aloud. 'I've always known – but I didn't know how. Now tell me how. . . .' And she sat there in the gloaming with her head a little on one side, listening – to something?

Every Saturday afternoon she went to the séance and joined in the circle; the composition changed slightly with the weeks, but the newcomers were much of the same stamp as those who left it. Mrs Goldstine went off, complaining bitterly; Miss Alsopp had become so lachrymose that the medium suggested she was disturbing her mother's rest; she was certainly disturbing the circle. Mr Wesson, who took her place, was anxiously waiting to make contact with his wife; he wanted her advice about the future of the house: should he redecorate or sell as it stood? Mrs Essbridge longed to talk with an uncle whose will was missing and believed to be in her favour.

There was seldom a message for Margie. The contact was there, but that was all. The medium knew no more of her than she had done before. But she did know that she was sitting with another whose powers were equal to if not greater than her own. Now Margie sat at her left hand and the Guide seemed more familiar and the voices and the messages seemed stronger. Like called to like.

'D'j ever think of doing this yourself? Séances – circles, I mean?' she asked one afternoon, keeping Margie back when the others had gone.

'No-o. . . .'

'You'd be a success. You've got the gift. I can see it, watching you; I can feel it when you take my hand. You'd need to learn the ropes. I could put you wise. We might make a do of it together. It's a lot of work for one. You'd get a Guide if you asked ... I could speak for you.'

There was something alarming in the girl's quiet appraisal as she looked the older woman over. The medium stirred restlessly.

'Seems a shame to waste a gift like yours. Wants cultivating – training. There's money in it. Look how these old girls come week after week – so do you, for that matter. But you ain't had your message yet?'

'No. . . .' Margie seemed to be considering. 'Not yet. But I think it's coming soon.'

'Who's Tom?' the medium blurted out, unable to contain her curiosity.

'I told you – long ago. My brother.'

Still the same fiction. Well, if she liked to play it that way. . . . Suddenly the medium felt exhausted. It was, as she said, a tiring job, and a lot of people didn't appreciate what you did for them. Sometimes you were genuinely under control and sometimes you weren't, and when you weren't you had to make something up. Couldn't let the clients down, or they'd never come back. That's why it was so necessary to know something about them – know what they wanted. That young woman could be useful – anyone would confide in her; she'd got that look –

daughterly, sort of – you'd trust her, confide in her. She could get the inside dope without trouble.

When she turned to speak again, she found that Margie had left.

That night Tom came as Margie sat by the window. As a rule she did not expect him on a Saturday after the séance; she knew that it was an effort to contact her there. But that night he arrived. The weather was turning colder and it grew dark earlier; his time was directly after tea instead of just before supper. He seemed to have gained solidity; she could almost see him with her physical eye. And there seemed something urgent about him. With a start, Margie remembered that next Saturday would be the first anniversary of his passing over.

'What do you want me to do?' she asked.

And this time there was a voice that answered: Tom's voice, stronger than at the séances, but not yet quite of this world. Gravely she listened, nodded, and promised to obey.

She arrived at the next circle meeting in the same unobtrusive manner as usual; her suppressed excitement did not show in her gentle greeting and she took her place at the medium's left hand without comment. The sitting began like all the others. A hymn, greetings from the Other Side, platitudes and trivial messages. Quite suddenly the tension increased and grew almost unbearable. The medium slumped down in her chair, her head thrown back, her mouth open, and her breathing loud and deep; she would have been an unlovely sight had it been possible to see more than her outline.

One of the women in the circle gasped and another hushed her peremptorily. A voice was coming through from the Other Side – but not the pleasant, soothing voice of Kung Foo, the Chinese, with his measured cadences and flow of philosophical axioms. This was a young, stronger voice, a rougher one – and it had a horrible quality to it – a quality combined of urgency, pleasure, and revenge.

'Margie! Margie! Now – do it now!'

There was a slight scuffle; no one saw the girl in blue detach her hand from that of the medium but they all felt the circle break and they all heard the strangled scream. Someone switched on the lights. And then every woman in the room screamed in unison.

The medium's head still lolled back on the chair, but now there was a scarlet band across the greying, flabby flesh of her throat – a band which was spreading and dripping as they looked.

And beside her, laughing softly and continuously, was Margie, the gentle little girl in blue. At first they thought she was suffering from hysteria, but then they saw the razor blade in its crude handle still grasped between her fingers. . . .

When the police searched her handbag, there was nothing there but a cutting from a newspaper a year and a day out of date; it reported the capital punishment of a young man and beside the report it showed a picture of the woman whose evidence had been instrumental in convict-ing him. Even in the blurred reproduction of the popular press it was impossible not to identify the medium.

# Harry

## *Rosemary Timperley*

Such ordinary things make me afraid. Sunshine. Sharp shadows on
grass. White roses. Children with red hair. And the name – Harry. Such
an ordinary name.

Yet the first time Christine mentioned the name, I felt a premonition
of fear.

She was five years old, due to start school in three months' time. It
was a hot, beautiful day and she was playing alone in the garden, as she
often did. I saw her lying on her stomach in the grass, picking daisies
and making daisy-chains with laborious pleasure. The sun burned on
her pale red hair and made her skin look very white. Her big blue eyes
were wide with concentration.

Suddenly she looked towards the bush of white roses, which cast its
shadow over the grass, and smiled.

'Yes, I'm Christine,' she said. She rose and walked slowly towards the
bush, her little plump legs defenceless and endearing beneath the too
short blue cotton skirt. She was growing fast.

'With my mummy and daddy,' she said clearly. Then, after a pause,
'Oh, but they *are* my mummy and daddy.'

She walked in the shadow of the bush now. It was as if she'd walked
out of the world of light into darkness. Uneasy, without quite knowing
why, I called her:

'Chris, what are you doing?'

'Nothing.' The voice sounded too far away.

'Come indoors now. It's too hot for you out there.'

'Not too hot.'

'Come indoors, Chris.'

She said: 'I must go in now. Goodbye,' then walked slowly towards
the house.

'Chris, who were you talking to?'

'Harry,' she said.

'Who's Harry?'

'Harry.'

I couldn't get anything else out of her, so I just gave her some cake and milk and read to her until bedtime. As she listened, she stared out at the garden. Once she smiled and waved. It was a relief finally to tuck her up in bed and feel she was safe.

When Jim, my husband, came home I told him about the mysterious 'Harry'. He laughed.

'Oh, she's started that lark, has she?'

'What do you mean, Jim?'

'It's not so very rare for only children to have an imaginary companion. Some kids talk to their dolls. Chris has never been keen on her dolls. She hasn't any brothers or sisters. She hasn't any friends her own age. So she imagines someone.'

'But why has she picked that particular name?'

He shrugged. 'You know how kids pick things up. I don't know what you're worrying about, honestly I don't.'

'Nor do I really. It's just that I feel extra responsible for her. More so than if I were her real mother.'

'I know, but she's all right. Chris is fine. She's a pretty, healthy, intelligent little girl. A credit to you.'

'And to you.'

'In fact, we're thoroughly nice parents!'

'And so modest!'

We laughed together and he kissed me. I felt consoled.

Until next morning.

Again the sun shone brilliantly on the small, bright lawn and white roses. Christine was sitting on the grass, cross-legged, staring towards the rose bush, smiling.

'Hello,' she said. 'I hoped you'd come ... Because I like you. How old are you? ... I'm only five and a piece ... I'm *not* a baby! I'm going to school soon and I shall have a new dress. A green one. Do you go to school? ... What do you do then?' She was silent for a while, nodding, listening, absorbed.

I felt myself going cold as I stood there in the kitchen. 'Don't be silly. Lots of children have an imaginary companion,' I told myself desperately. 'Just carry on as if nothing were happening. Don't listen. Don't be a fool.'

But I called Chris in earlier than usual for her mid-morning milk.

'Your milk's ready, Chris. Come along.'

'In a minute.' This was a strange reply. Usually she rushed in eagerly for her milk and the special sandwich cream biscuits, over which she was a little gourmande.

'Come now, darling,' I said.

'Can Harry come too?'

'No!' The cry burst from me harshly, surprising me.

'Goodbye, Harry. I'm sorry you can't come in but I've got to have my milk,' Chris said, then ran towards the house.

'Why can't Harry have some milk too?' She challenged me.

'Who *is* Harry, darling?'

'Harry's my brother.'

'But Chris, you haven't got a brother. Daddy and mummy have only got one child, one little girl, that's you. Harry can't be your brother.'

'Harry's my brother. He says so.' She bent over the glass of milk and emerged with a smeary top lip. Then she grabbed at the biscuits. At least 'Harry' hadn't spoilt her appetite!

After she'd had her milk, I said, 'We'll go shopping now, Chris. You'd like to come to the shops with me, wouldn't you?'

'I want to stay with Harry.'

'Well you can't. You're coming with me.'

'Can Harry come too?'

'No.'

My hands were trembling as I put on my hat and gloves. It was chilly in the house nowadays, as if there were a cold shadow over it in spite of the sun outside. Chris came with me meekly enough, but as we walked down the street, she turned and waved.

I didn't mention any of this to Jim that night. I knew he'd only scoff as he'd done before. But when Christine's 'Harry' fantasy went on day after day, it got more and more on my nerves. I came to hate and dread those long summer days. I longed for grey skies and rain. I longed for the white roses to wither and die. I trembled when I heard Christine's voice prattling away in the garden. She talked quite unrestrainedly to 'Harry' now.

One Sunday, when Jim heard her at it, he said:

'I'll say one thing for imaginary companions, they help a child on with her talking. Chris is talking much more freely than she used to.'

'With an accent,' I blurted out.

'An accent?'

'A slight cockney accent.'

'My dearest, every London child gets a slight cockney accent. It'll be much worse when she goes to school and meets lots of other kids.'

'We don't talk cockney. Where does she get it from? Who can she be getting it from except Ha . . .' I couldn't say the name.

'The baker, the milkman, the dustman, the coalman, the window cleaner – want any more?'

'I suppose not.' I laughed ruefully. Jim made me feel foolish.

'Anyway,' said Jim, '*I* haven't noticed any cockney in her voice.'

'There isn't when she talks to us. It's only when she's talking to – to him.'

'To Harry. You know, I'm getting quite attached to young Harry. Wouldn't it be fun if one day we looked out and saw him?'

'Don't!' I cried. 'Don't say that! It's my nightmare. My waking nightmare. Oh, Jim, I can't bear it much longer.'

He looked astonished. 'This Harry business is really getting you down, isn't it?'

'Of course it is! Day in, day out, I hear nothing but "Harry this," "Harry that," "Harry says," "Harry thinks," "Can Harry have some?", "Can Harry come too?" – it's all right for you out at the office all day, but I have to live with it: I'm – I'm afraid of it, Jim. It's so queer.'

'Do you know what I think you should do to put your mind at rest?'

'What?'

'Take Chris along to see Dr Webster tomorrow. Let me have a little talk with her.'

'Do you think she's ill – in her mind?'

'Good heavens, no! But when we come across something that's a bit beyond us, it's as well to take professional advice.'

Next day I took Chris to see Dr Webster. I left her in the waiting-room while I told him briefly about Harry. He nodded sympathetically, then said:

'It's a fairly unusual case, Mrs James, but by no means unique. I've had several cases of children's imaginary companions becoming so real to them that the parents get the jitters. I expect she's rather a lonely little girl, isn't she?'

'She doesn't know any other children. We're new in the neighbourhood, you see. But that will be put right when she starts school.'

'And I think you'll find that when she goes to school and meets other children, these fantasies will disappear. You see, every child needs company of her own age, and if she doesn't get it, she invents it. Older people who are lonely talk to themselves. That doesn't mean that they're crazy, just that they need to talk to someone. A child is more practical. Seems silly to talk to oneself, she thinks, so she invents someone to talk to. I honestly don't think you've anything to worry about.'

'That's what my husband says.'

'I'm sure he does. Still, I'll have a chat with Christine as you've brought her. Leave us alone together.'

I went to the waiting-room to fetch Chris. She was at the window. She said: 'Harry's waiting.'

'Where, Chris?' I said quietly, wanting suddenly to see with her eyes.

'There. By the rose bush.'

The doctor had a bush of white roses in his garden.

'There's no one there,' I said. Chris gave me a glance of unchildlike scorn. 'Dr Webster wants to see you now, darling,' I said shakily. 'You remember him, don't you? He gave you sweets when you were getting better from chicken pox.'

'Yes,' she said and went willingly enough to the doctor's surgery. I waited restlessly. Faintly I heard their voices through the wall, heard the doctor's chuckle, Christine's high peal of laughter. She was talking away to the doctor in a way she didn't talk to me.

When they came out, he said: 'Nothing wrong with her whatever. She's just an imaginative little monkey. A word of advice, Mrs James. Let her talk about Harry. Let her become accustomed to confiding in you. I gather you've shown some disapproval of this "brother" of hers so she doesn't talk much to you about him. He makes wooden toys, doesn't he, Chris?'

'Yes, Harry makes wooden toys.'

'And he can read and write, can't he?'

'And swim and climb trees and paint pictures. Harry can do everything. He's a wonderful brother.' Her little face flushed with adoration.

The doctor patted me on the shoulder and said: 'Harry sounds a very nice brother for her. He's even got red hair like you, Chris, hasn't he?'

'Harry's got red hair,' said Chris proudly, 'Redder than my hair. And he's nearly as tall as daddy only thinner. He's as tall as you, mummy. He's fourteen. He says he's tall for his age. What *is* tall for his age?'

'Mummy will tell you about that as you walk home,' said Dr Webster. 'Now, goodbye, Mrs James. Don't worry. Just let her prattle. Goodbye, Chris. Give my love to Harry.'

'He's there,' said Chris, pointing to the doctor's garden. 'He's been waiting for me.'

Dr Webster laughed. 'They're incorrigible, aren't they?' he said. 'I knew one poor mother whose children invented a whole tribe of imaginary natives whose rituals and taboos ruled the household. Perhaps you're lucky, Mrs James!'

I tried to feel comforted by all this, but I wasn't. I hoped sincerely that when Chris started school this wretched Harry business would finish.

Chris ran ahead of me. She looked up as if at someone beside her. For a brief, dreadful second, I saw a shadow on the pavement alongside her own – a long, thin shadow – like a boy's shadow. Then it was gone. I ran to catch her up and held her hand tightly all the way home. Even in the comparative security of the house – the house so strangely cold in this hot weather – I never let her out of my sight. On the face of it she behaved no differently towards me, but in reality she was drifting away. The child in my house was becoming a stranger.

For the first time since Jim and I had adopted Chris, I wondered seriously: Who is she? Where does she come from? Who were her real parents? Who is this little loved stranger I've taken as a daughter? Who *is* Christine?

Another week passed. It was Harry, Harry all the time. The day before she was to start school, Chris said:

'Not going to school.'

'You're going to school tomorrow, Chris. You're looking forward to it. You know you are. There'll be lots of other little girls and boys.'

'Harry says he can't come too.'

'You won't want Harry at school. He'll –' I tried hard to follow the doctor's advice and appear to believe in Harry – 'He'll be too old. He'd feel silly among little boys and girls, a great lad of fourteen.'

'I won't go to school without Harry. I want to be with Harry.' She began to weep, loudly, painfully.

'Chris, stop this nonsense! Stop it!' I struck her sharply on the arm. Her crying ceased immediately. She stared at me, her blue eyes wide open and frighteningly cold. She gave me an adult stare that made me tremble. Then she said:

'You don't love me. Harry loves me. Harry wants me. He says I can go with him.'

'I will not hear any more of this!' I shouted, hating the anger in my voice, hating myself for being angry at all with a little girl – *my* little girl – mine –

I went down on one knee and held out my arms.

'Chris, darling, come here.'

She came, slowly. 'I love you,' I said. 'I love you, Chris, and I'm real. School is real. Go to school to please me.'

'Harry will go away if I do.'

'You'll have other friends.'

'I want Harry.' Again the tears, wet against my shoulder now. I held her closely.

'You're tired, baby. Come to bed.'

She slept with the tear stains still on her face.

It was still daylight. I went to the window to draw her curtains. Golden shadows and long strips of sunshine in the garden. Then, again like a dream, the long thin clear-cut shadow of a boy near the white roses. Like a mad woman I opened the window and shouted:

'Harry! Harry!'

I thought I saw a glimmer of red among the roses, like close red curls on a boy's head. Then there was nothing.

When I told Jim about Christine's emotional outburst he said: 'Poor little kid. It's always a nervy business, starting school. She'll be all right once she gets there. You'll be hearing less about Harry too, as time goes on.'

'Harry doesn't want her to go to school.'

'Hey! You sound as if you believe in Harry yourself!'

'Sometimes I do.'

'Believing in evil spirits in your old age?' he teased me. But his eyes were concerned. He thought I was going 'round the bend' and small blame to him!

'I don't think Harry's evil,' I said. 'He's just a boy. A boy who doesn't exist, except for Christine. And who *is* Christine?'

'None of that!' said Jim sharply. 'When we adopted Chris we decided she was to be our own child. No probing into the past. No wondering and worrying. No mysteries. Chris is as much ours as if she'd been born of our flesh. Who is Christine indeed! She's our daughter – and just you remember that!'

'Yes, Jim, you're right. Of course you're right.'

He'd been so fierce about it that I didn't tell him what I planned to do the next day while Chris was at school.

Next morning Chris was silent and sulky. Jim joked with her and tried to cheer her, but all she would do was look out of the window and say: 'Harry's gone.'

'You won't need Harry now. You're going to school,' said Jim.

Chris gave him that look of grown-up contempt she'd given me sometimes.

She and I didn't speak as I took her to school. I was almost in tears. Although I was glad for her to start school, I felt a sense of loss at parting with her. I suppose every mother feels that when she takes her ewe-lamb to school for the first time. It's the end of babyhood for the child, the beginning of life in reality, life with its cruelty, its strangeness, its barbarity. I kissed her goodbye at the gate and said:

'You'll be having dinner at school with the other children, Chris, and I'll call for you when school is over, at three o'clock.'

'Yes, mummy.' She held my hand tightly. Other nervous little children were arriving with equally nervous parents. A pleasant young teacher with fair hair and a white linen dress appeared at the gate. She gathered the new children towards her and led them away. She gave me a sympathetic smile as she passed and said: 'We'll take good care of her.'

I felt quite light-hearted as I walked away, knowing that Chris was safe and I didn't have to worry.

Now I started on my secret mission. I took a bus to town and went to the big, gaunt building I hadn't visited for over five years. Then, Jim and I had gone together. The top floor of the building belonged to the Greythorne Adoption Society. I climbed the four flights and knocked on the familiar door with its scratched paint. A secretary whose face I didn't know let me in.

'May I see Miss Cleaver? My name is Mrs James.'

'Have you an appointment?'

'No, but it's very important.'

'I'll see.' The girl went out and returned a second later. 'Miss Cleaver will see you, Mrs James.'

Miss Cleaver, a tall, thin, grey haired woman with a charming smile, a plain, kindly face and a very wrinkled brow, rose to meet me. 'Mrs James. How nice to see you again. How's Christine?'

'She's very well. Miss Cleaver, I'd better get straight to the point. I know you don't normally divulge the origin of a child to its adopters and vice versa, but I must know who Christine is.'

'Sorry, Mrs James,' she began, 'our rules . . .'

'Please let me tell you the whole story, then you'll see I'm not just suffering from vulgar curiosity.'

I told her about Harry.

When I'd finished, she said: 'It's very queer. Very queer indeed. Mrs James, I'm going to break my rule for once. I'm going to tell you in strict confidence where Christine came from.

'She was born in a very poor part of London. There were four in the family, father, mother, son and Christine herself.'

'Son?'

'Yes. He was fourteen when – when it happened.'

'When what happened?'

'Let me start at the beginning. The parents hadn't really wanted Christine. The family lived in one room at the top of an old house which should have been condemned by the Sanitary Inspector in my opinion. It was difficult enough when there were only three of them, but with a baby as well life became a nightmare. The mother was a neurotic creature, slatternly, unhappy, too fat. After she'd had the baby she took no interest in it. The brother, however, adored the little girl from the start. He got into trouble for cutting school so he could look after her.

'The father had a steady job in a warehouse, not much money, but enough to keep them alive. Then he was sick for several weeks and lost his job. He was laid up in that messy room, ill, worrying, nagged by his wife, irked by the baby's crying and his son's eternal fussing over the child – I got all these details from the neighbours afterwards, by the way. I was also told that he'd had a particularly bad time in the war and had been in a nerve hospital for several months before he was fit to come home at all after his demob. Suddenly it all proved too much for him.

'One morning, in the small hours, a woman in the ground floor room saw something fall past her window and heard a thud on the ground. She went out to look. The son of the family was there on the ground.

Christine was in his arms. The boy's neck was broken. He was dead. Christine was blue in the face but still breathing faintly.

'The women woke the household, sent for the police and the doctor, then they went to the top room. They had to break down the door, which was locked and sealed inside. An overpowering smell of gas greeted them, in spite of the open window.

'They found husband and wife dead in bed with a note from the husband saying:

"I can't go on. I am going to kill them all.
It's the only way."

'The police concluded that he'd sealed up door and windows and turned on the gas when his family were asleep, then lain beside his wife until he drifted into unconsciousness, and death. But the son must have wakened. Perhaps he struggled with the door but couldn't open it. He'd be too weak to shout. All he could do was pluck away the seals from the window, open it, and fling himself out, holding his adored little sister tightly in his arms.

'Why Christine herself wasn't gassed is rather a mystery. Perhaps her head was right under the bedclothes, pressed against her brother's chest — they always slept together. Anyway, the child was taken to hospital, then to the home where you and Mr James first saw her ... and a lucky day that was for little Christine!'

'So her brother saved her life and died himself?' I said.

'Yes. He was a very brave young man.'

'Perhaps he thought not so much of saving her as of keeping her with him. Oh dear! That sounds ungenerous. I didn't mean to be. Miss Cleaver, what was his name?'

'I'll have to look that up for you.' She referred to one of her many files and said at last: 'The family's name was Jones and the fourteen-year-old brother was called "Harold".'

'And did he have red hair?' I murmured.

'That I don't know, Mrs James.'

'But it's Harry. The boy was Harry. What does it mean? I can't understand it.'

'It's not easy, but I think perhaps deep in her unconscious mind Christine has always remembered Harry, the companion of her baby-hood. We don't think of children as having much memory, but there must be images of the past tucked away somewhere in their little heads. Christine doesn't *invent* this Harry. She *remembers* him. So clearly that she's almost brought him to life again. I know it sounds far-fetched, but the whole story is so odd that I can't think of any other explanation.'

'May I have the address of the house where they lived?'

She was reluctant to give me this information, but I persuaded her and set out at last to find No. 13 Canver Row, where the man Jones had tried to kill himself and his whole family and almost succeeded.

The house seemed deserted. It was filthy and derelict. But one thing made me stare and stare. There was a tiny garden. A scatter of bright uneven grass splashed the bald brown patches of earth. But the little garden had one strange glory that none of the other houses in the poor sad street possessed – a bush of white roses. They bloomed gloriously. Their scent was overpowering.

I stood by the bush and stared up at the top window.

A voice startled me: 'What are you doing here?'

It was an old woman, peering from the ground floor window.

'I thought the house was empty,' I said.

'Should be. Been condemned. But they can't get me out. Nowhere else to go. Won't go. The others went quickly enough after it happened. No one else wants to come. They say the place is haunted. So it is. But what's the fuss about? Life and death. They're very close. You get to know that when you're old. Alive or dead. What's the difference?'

She looked at me with yellowish, bloodshot eyes and said: 'I saw him fall past my window. That's where he fell. Among the roses. He still comes back. I see him. He won't go away until he gets her.'

'Who – who are you talking about?'

'Harry Jones. Nice boy he was. Red hair. Very thin. Too determined, though. Always got his own way. Loved Christine too much I thought. Died among the roses. Used to sit down here with her for hours, by the roses. Then died there. Or do people die? The church ought to give us an answer, but it doesn't. Not one you can believe. Go away, will you? This place isn't for you. It's for the dead who aren't dead, and the living who aren't alive. Am I alive or dead? You tell me. I don't know.'

The crazy eyes staring at me beneath the matted white fringe of hair frightened me. Mad people are terrifying. One can pity them, but one is still afraid. I murmured:

'I'll go now. Goodbye,' and tried to hurry across the hard hot pavements although my legs felt heavy and half-paralysed, as in a nightmare.

The sun blazed down on my head, but I was hardly aware of it. I lost all sense of time or place as I stumbled on.

Then I heard something that chilled my blood.

A clock struck three.

At three o'clock I was supposed to be at the school gates, waiting for Christine.

Where was I now? How near the school? What bus should I take?

I made frantic inquiries of passers-by, who looked at me fearfully, as I had looked at the old woman. They must have thought I was crazy.

At last I caught the right bus and, sick with dust, petrol fumes and fear, reached the school. I ran across the hot, empty playground. In a classroom, the young teacher in white was gathering her books together.

'I've come for Christine James. I'm her mother. I'm so sorry I'm late. Where is she?' I gasped.

'Christine James?' The girl frowned, then said brightly: 'Oh, yes, I remember, the pretty little red-haired girl. That's all right, Mrs James. Her brother called for her. How alike they are, aren't they? And so devoted. It's rather sweet to see a boy of that age so fond of his baby sister. Has your husband got red hair, like the two children?'

'What did – her brother – say?' I asked faintly.

'He didn't say anything. When I spoke to him, he just smiled. They'll be home by now, I should think. I say, do you feel all right?'

'Yes, thank you. I must go home.'

I ran all the way home through the burning streets.

'Chris! Christine, where are you? Chris! Chris!' Sometimes even now I hear my own voice of the past screaming through the cold house. 'Christine! Chris! Where are you? Answer me! Chrrriiiiiss!' 'Harry! Don't take her away! Come back! Harry! Harry!'

Demented, I rushed out into the garden. The sun struck me like a hot blade. The roses glared whitely. The air was so still I seemed to stand in timelessness, placelessness. For a moment, I seemed very near to Christine, although I couldn't see her. Then the roses danced before my eyes and turned red. The world turned red. Blood red. Wet red. I fell through redness to blackness to nothingness – to almost death.

For weeks I was in bed with sunstroke which turned to brain fever. During that time Jim and the police searched for Christine in vain. The futile search continued for months. The papers were full of the strange disappearance of the red-haired child. The teacher described the 'brother' who had called for her. There were newspaper stories of kidnapping, baby-snatching, child-murders.

Then the sensation died down. Just another unsolved mystery in police files.

And only two people knew what had happened. An old crazed woman living in a derelict house, and myself.

Years have passed. But I walk in fear.

Such ordinary things make me afraid. Sunshine. Sharp shadows on grass. White roses. Children with red hair. And the name – Harry. Such an ordinary name!

# Lucky's Grove

## H. R. Wakefield

*And Loki begat Hel, Goddess of the Grave, Fenris, the Great Wolf, and the Serpent, Nidnogg, who lives beneath The Tree.*

Mr Braxton strolled with his land-agent, Curtis, into the Great Barn.

'There you are,' said Curtis, in a satisfied tone, 'the finest little larch I ever saw, and the kiddies will never set eyes on a lovelier Christmas tree.'

Mr Braxton examined it; it stood twenty feet from huge green pot to crisp, straight peak, and was exquisitely sturdy, fresh and symmetrical.

'Yes, it's a beauty,' he agreed. 'Where did you find it?'

'In that odd little spinney they call Lucky's Grove in the long meadow near the river boundary.'

'Oh!' remarked Mr Braxton uncertainly. To himself he was saying vaguely, 'He shouldn't have got it from there, of course he wouldn't realize it, but he shouldn't have got it from there.'

'Of course we'll replant it,' said Curtis, noticing his employer's diminished enthusiasm. 'It's a curious thing, but it isn't a young tree; it's apparently full-grown. Must be a dwarf variety, but I don't know as much about trees as I should like.'

Mr Braxton was surprised to find there was one branch of country lore on which Curtis was not an expert; for he was about the best-known man at his job in the British Isles. Pigs, bees, chickens, cattle, crops, running a shoot, he had mastered them one and all. He paid him two thousand a year with house and car. He was worth treble.

'I expect it's all right,' said Mr Braxton; 'it's just that Lucky's Grove is – is – well, "sacred" is perhaps too strong a word. Maybe I should have told you, but I expect it's all right.'

'That accounts for it then,' laughed Curtis. 'I thought there seemed some reluctance on the part of the men while we were yanking it up and getting it on the lorry. They handled it a bit gingerly; on the part of the older men, I mean; the youngsters didn't worry.'

'Yes, there would be,' said Mr Braxton. 'But never mind, it'll be back in a few days and it's a superb little tree. I'll bring Mrs Braxton along to see it after lunch,' and he strolled back into Abingdale Hall.

Fifty-five years ago Mr Braxton's father had been a labourer on this very estate, and in that year young Percy, aged eight, had got an errand boy's job in Oxford. Twenty years later he'd owned one small shop. Twenty-five years after that fifty big shops. Now, though he had finally retired, he owned two hundred and eighty vast shops and was a millionaire whichever way you added it up. How had this happened? No one can quite answer such questions. Certainly he'd worked like a brigade of Trojans, but midnight oil has to burn in Aladdin's lamp before it can transform ninepence into one million pounds. It was just that he asked no quarter from the unforgiving minute, but squeezed from it the fruit of others' many hours. Those like Mr Braxton seem to have their own time-scale; they just say the word and up springs a fine castle of commerce, but the knowledge of that word cannot be imparted; it is as mysterious as the Logos. But all through his great labours he had been moved by one fixed resolve – to avenge his father – that fettered spirit – for he had been an able, intelligent man who had had no earthly chance of revealing the fact to the world. Always the categorical determination had blazed in his son's brain, 'I will own Abingdale Hall, and, where my father sweated, I will rule and be lord.' And of course it happened. Fate accepts the dictates of such men as Mr Braxton, shrugs its shoulders, and leaves its revenge to Death. The Hall had come on the market just when he was about to retire, and with an odd delight, an obscure sense of home-coming, the native returned, and his riding boots, shooting boots, golf shoes, and all the many glittering guineas' worth, stamped in and obliterated the prints of his father's hob-nails.

That was the picture he often re-visualized, the way it amused him to 'put it to himself', as he roamed his broad acres and surveyed the many glowing triumphs of his model husbandry.

Some credit was due to buxom, blithe and debonair Mrs Braxton, kindly, competent and innately adaptable. She was awaiting him in the morning-room and they went in solitary state, to luncheon. But it was the last peaceful lunch they would have for a spell – 'the Families' were pouring in on the morrow.

As a footman was helping them to Sole Meunière Mr Braxton said, 'Curtis has found a very fine Christmas tree. It's in the barn. You must come and look at it after lunch.'

'That *is* good,' replied his wife. 'Where did he get it from?'

Mr Braxton hesitated for a moment.

'From Lucky's Grove.'

Mrs Braxton looked up sharply.

'From the grove!' she said, surprised.

'Yes, of course he didn't realize – anyway it'll be all right, it's all rather ridiculous, and it'll be replanted before the New Year.'

'Oh, yes,' agreed Mrs Braxton. 'After all it's only just a clump of trees.'

'Quite. And it's just the right height for the ballroom. It'll be taken in there to-morrow morning and the electricians will work on it in the afternoon.'

'I heard from Lady Pounser just now,' said Mrs Braxton. 'She's bringing six over, that'll make seventy-four; only two refusals. The presents are arriving this afternoon.'

They discussed the party discursively over the cutlets and Peach Melba and soon after lunch walked across to the barn. Mr Braxton waved to Curtis, who was examining a new tractor in the garage fifty yards away, and he came over.

Mrs Braxton looked the tree over and was graciously delighted with it, but remarked that the pot could have done with another coat of paint. She pointed to several streaks, rust-coloured, running through the green. 'Of course it won't show when it's wrapped, but they didn't do a very good job.'

Curtis leant down. 'They certainly didn't,' he answered irritably. 'I'll see to it. I think it's spilled over from the soil; that copse is on a curious patch of red sand – there are some at Frilford too. When we pulled it up I noticed the roots were stained a dark crimson.' He put his hand down and scraped at the stains with his thumb. He seemed a shade puzzled.

'It shall have another coat at once,' he said. 'What did you think of Lampson and Colletts' scheme for the barn?'

'Quite good,' replied Mrs Braxton, 'but the sketches for the chains are too fancy.'

'I agree,' said Curtis, who usually did so in the case of unessentials; reserving his tactful vetoes for the others.

The Great Barn was by far the most aesthetically satisfying, as it was the oldest feature of the Hall buildings; it was vast, exquisitely proportioned, and mellow. That could hardly be said of the house itself, which the 4th Baron of Abingdale had rebuilt on the cinders of its predecessors in 1752.

This nobleman had travelled abroad extensively and returned with most enthusiastic, grandiose and indigestible ideas of architecture. The result was a gargantuan piece of rococo-jocoso which only an entirely humourless pedant could condemn. It contained forty-two bedrooms and eighteen reception rooms – so Mrs Braxton had made it at the last recount. But Mr Braxton had not repeated with the interiors the errors of the 4th Baron. He'd briefed the greatest expert in Europe, with the result that the interior was quite tasteful and sublimely confortable.

'Ugh!' he exclaimed, as they stepped out into the air, 'it *is* getting nippy!'

'Yes,' said Curtis, 'there's a nor'-easter blowing up – may be snow for Christmas.'

On getting back to the house Mrs Braxton went into a huddle with butler and housekeeper and Mr Braxton returned to his study for a doze. But instead his mind settled on Lucky's Grove. When he'd first seen it again after buying the estate, it seemed as if fifty years had rolled away, and he realized that Abingdale was far more summed up to him in the little copse than in the gigantic barracks two miles away. At once he felt at home again. Yet, just as when he'd been a small boy, the emotion the Grove had aroused in him had been sharply tinged with awe, so it had been now, half a century later. He still had a sneaking dread of it. How precisely he could see it, glowing darkly in the womb of the fire before him, standing starkly there in the centre of the big, fallow field, a perfect circle; and first, a ring of holm-oaks and, facing east, a breach therein to the larches and past them on the west a gap to the yews. It had always required a tug at his courage – not always forthcoming – to pass through them and face the mighty Scotch fir, rearing up its great bole from the grass mound. And when he stood before it, he'd always known an odd longing to fling himself down and – well, worship – it was the only word – the towering tree. His father had told him his forebears had done that very thing, but always when alone and at certain seasons of the year; and that no bird or beast was ever seen there. A lot of traditional nonsense, no doubt, but he himself had absorbed the spirit of the place and knew it would be always so.

One afternoon in late November, a few weeks after they had moved in, he'd gone off alone in the drowsing misty dusk; and when he'd reached the holm-oak bastion and seen the great tree surrounded by its sentinels, he'd known again that quick turmoil of confused emotions. As he'd walked slowly towards it, it had seemed to quicken and be aware of his coming. As he passed the shallow grassy fosse and entered the oak ring he felt there was something he ought to say, some greeting, password or prayer. It was the most aloof, silent little place under the sun, and oh, so old. He'd tiptoed past the larches and faced the barrier of yews. He'd stood there for a long musing minute, tingling with the sensation that he was being watched and regarded. At length he stepped forward and stood before the God – that mighty word came abruptly and unforeseen – and he felt a wild desire to fling himself down on the mound and do obeisance. And then he'd hurried home. As he recalled all this most vividly and minutely, he was seized with a sudden gust of uncontrollable anger at the thought of the desecration of the Grove. He knew now that if he'd had the slightest idea of Curtis's purpose he'd have resisted and opposed it. It was too late now. He realized he'd 'worked himself up' rather absurdly. What could it matter! He was still a superstitious bumpkin at heart. Anyway it was no fault of Curtis. It was the finest Christmas tree anyone could hope for, and the whole thing was too nonsensical for words. The general tone of these cadentic conclusions did not quite accurately represent his thoughts – a very rare failing with Mr Braxton.

About dinner-time the blizzard set furiously in, and the snow was lying.

'Chains on the cars to-morrow,' Mrs Braxton told the head chauffeur.

'Boar's Hill'll be a beggar,' thought that person.

Mr and Mrs Braxton dined early, casually examined the presents, and went to bed. Mr Braxton was asleep at once as usual, but was awakened by the beating of a blind which had slipped its moorings. Reluctantly he got out of bed and went to fix it. As he was doing so he became conscious of the frenzied hysterical barking of a dog. The sound, muffled by the gale, came, he judged, from the barn. He believed the underkeeper kept his whippet there. Scared by the storm, he supposed, and returned to bed.

The morning was brilliantly fine and cold, but the snowfall had been heavy.

'I heard a dog howling in the night, Perkins,' said Mr Braxton to the butler at breakfast; 'Drake's, I imagine. What's the matter with it?'

'I will ascertain, sir,' replied Perkins.

'It *was* Drake's dog,' he announced a little later. 'Apparently something alarmed the animal, for when Drake went to let it out this morning, it appeared to be extremely frightened. When the barn door was opened, it took to its heels and, although Drake pursued it, it jumped into the river and Drake fears it was drowned.'

'Um,' said Mr Braxton, 'must have been the storm; whippets are nervous dogs.'

'So I understand, sir.'

'Drake was so fond of it,' said Mrs Braxton, 'though it always looked so naked and shivering to me.'

'Yes, madam,' agreed Perkins, 'it had that appearance.'

Soon after, Mr Braxton sauntered out into the blinding glitter. Curtis came over from the garage. He was heavily muffled up.

'They've got chains on all the cars,' he said. 'Very seasonable and all that, but farmers have another word for it.' His voice was thick and hoarse.

'Yes,' said Mr Braxton. 'You're not looking very fit.'

'Not feeling it. Had to get up in the night. Thought I heard someone trying to break into the house; thought I saw him, too.'

'Indeed,' said Mr Braxton. 'Did you see what he was like?'

'No,' replied Curtis uncertainly. 'It was snowing like the devil. Anyway, I got properly chilled to the marrow, skipping around in my nightie.'

'You'd better get to bed,' said Mr Braxton solicitously. He had affection and a great respect for Curtis.

'I'll stick it out today and see how I feel to-morrow. We're going to get the tree across in a few minutes. Can I borrow the two footmen? I want another couple of pullers and haulers.'

Mr Braxton consented, and went off on his favourite little stroll across the sparkling meadows to the river and the pool where the big trout set their cunning noses to the stream.

Half an hour later Curtis had mobilized his scratch team of sleeve-rolled assistants and, with Perkins steering and himself braking, they got to grips with the tree and bore it like a camouflaged battering ram towards the ballroom, which occupied the left centre of the frenetic frontage on the ground floor. There was a good deal of bumping and boring and genial blasphemy before the tree was manoeuvred into the middle of the room and levered by rope and muscle into position. As it came up its pinnacle just cleared the ceiling. Sam, a cow-man, whose ginger mop had been buried in the foliage for some time, exclaimed tartly as he slapped the trunk, 'There ye are, ye old sod! Thanks for the scratches on me mug, ye old –'

The next moment he was lying on his back, a livid weal across his right cheek.

This caused general merriment, and even Perkins permitted himself a spectral smile. There was more astonishment than pain on the face of Sam. He stared at the tree in a humble way for a moment, like a chastised and guilty dog, and then slunk from the room. The merriment of the others died away.

'More spring in these branches than you'd think,' said Curtis to Perkins.

'No doubt, sir, that is due to the abrupt release of the tension,' replied Perkins scientifically.

The 'Families' met at Paddington and travelled down together, so at five o'clock three car-loads drew up at the Hall. There was Jack and Mary with Paddy aged eight, Walter and Pamela with Jane and Peter, seven and five respectively, and George and Gloria with Gregory and Phyllis, ten and eight.

Jack and Walter were sons of the house. They were much of a muchness, burly, handsome and as dominating as their sire; a fine pair of commercial kings, entirely capable rulers, but just lacking that something which founds dynasties. Their wives conformed equally to the social type to which they belonged, good-lookers, smart dressers, excellent wives and mothers; but rather coolly colourless, spiritually. Their offspring were 'charming children', flawless products of the English matrix, though Paddy showed signs of some obstreperous originality. 'George' was the Honourable George, Calvin, Roderick, etcetera Penables, and Gloria was Mr and Mrs Braxton's only daughter. George had inherited half a million and had started off at twenty-four to be something big in the City. In a sense he achieved his ambition, for two years later he was generally reckoned the biggest 'Something' in the City, from which he then withdrew, desperately clutching his last hundred thousand and vowing lachrymose repentance. He had kept his word and his wad, hunted and shot six days a week in the winter, and spent most of the summer wrestling with the two dozen devils in his golf bag. According to current jargon he was the complete extrovert, but what a relief are such, in spite of the pitying shrugs of those who for ever are peering into the septic recesses of their souls.

Gloria had inherited some of her father's force. She was rather overwhelmingly primed with energy and pep for her opportunities of releasing it. So she was always rather pent up and explosive, though maternity had kept the pressure down. She was dispassionately fond of George who had presented her with a nice little title and aristocratic background and two 'charming children'. Phyllis gave promise of such extreme beauty that, beyond being the cynosure of every press-camera's eye, and making a resounding match, no more was to be expected of her. Gregory, however, on the strength of some artistic precocity and a violent temper, was already somewhat prematurely marked down as a genius to be.

Such were the 'Families'.

During the afternoon four engineers arrived from one of the Braxton factories to fix up the lighting of the tree. The fairy lamps for this had been specially designed and executed for the occasion. Disney figures had been grafted upon them and made to revolve by an ingenious mechanism; the effect being to give the tree, when illuminated, an aspect of whirling life meant to be very cheerful and pleasing.

Mr Braxton happened to see these electricians departing in their lorry and noticed one of them had a bandaged arm and a rather white face. He asked Perkins what had happened.

'A slight accident, sir. A bulb burst and burnt him in some manner. But the injury is, I understand, not of a very serious nature.'

'He looked a bit white.'

'Apparently, sir, he got a fright, a shock of some kind, when the bulb exploded.'

After dinner the grown-ups went to the ballroom. Mr Braxton

switched on the mechanism and great enthusiasm was shown. 'Won't the kiddies love it,' said George, grinning at the kaleidoscope. 'Look at the Big Bad Wolf. He looks so darn realistic I'm not sure I'd give him a "U" certificate.'

'It's almost frightening,' said Pamela, 'they look incredibly real. Daddie, you really are rather bright, darling.'

It was arranged that the work of decoration should be tackled on the morrow and finished on Christmas Eve.

'All the presents have arrived,' said Mrs Braxton, 'and are being unpacked. But I'll explain about them to-morrow.'

They went back to the drawing-room. Presently Gloria puffed and remarked: 'Papa, aren't you keeping the house rather too hot?'

'I noticed the same thing,' said Mrs Braxton.

Mr Braxton walked over to a thermometer on the wall. 'You're right,' he remarked, 'seventy.' He rang the bell.

'Perkins,' he asked, 'who's on the furnace?'

'Churchill, sir.'

'Well, he's overdoing it. It's seventy. Tell him to get it back to fifty-seven.'

Perkins departed and returned shortly after.

'Churchill informs me he has damped down and cannot account for the increasing warmth, sir.'

'Tell him to get it back to fifty-seven at once,' rapped Mr Braxton.

'Very good, sir.'

'Open a window,' said Mrs Braxton.

'It's snowing again, madam.'

'Never mind.'

'My God,' exclaimed Mary, when she and Jack went up to bed. 'That furnace man is certainly stepping on it. Open all the windows.'

A wild flurry of snow beat against the curtains.

Mr Braxton did what he very seldom did, woke up in the early hours. He awoke sweating from a furtive and demoralizing dream. It had seemed to him that he had been crouching down in the fosse round Lucky's Grove and peering beneath the holm-oaks, and that there had been activity of a sort vaguely to be discerned therein, some quick, shadowy business. He knew a very tight terror at the thought of being detected at this spying, but he could not wrench himself away. That was all, and he awoke still trembling and troubled. No wonder he'd had such a nightmare, the room seemed like a stokehold. He went to the windows and flung another open, and as he did so glanced out. His room looked over the rock garden and down the path to the maze. Something moving just outside it caught his eye. He thought he knew what it was, that big Alsatian which had been sheep-worrying in the neighbourhood. What an enormous brute! Or was it just because it was outlined against the snow? It vanished suddenly, apparently into the maze. He'd organize a hunt for it after Christmas; if the snow lay, it should be easy to track.

The first thing he did after breakfast was to send for Churchill, severely reprimand him and threaten him with dismissal from his ship. That person was almost tearfully insistent that he had obeyed orders and kept his jets low. 'I can't make it out, sir. It's got no right to be as 'ot as what it is.'

'That's nonsense!' said Mr Braxton. 'The system has been perfected and cannot take charge, as you suggest. See to it. You don't want me to get an engineer down, do you?'

'No, sir.'

'That's enough. Get it to fifty-seven and keep it there.'

Shortly after, Mrs Curtis rang up to say her husband was quite ill with a temperature and that the doctor was coming. Mr Braxton asked her to ring him again after he'd been.

During the morning the children played in the snow. After a pitched battle in which the girls lost their tempers, Gregory organized the erection of a snow-man. He designed, the others fetched the material. He knew he had a reputation for brilliance to maintain, and he produced something Epsteinish, huge and squat. The other children regarded it with little enthusiasm, but, being Gregory, they supposed it must be admired. When it was finished Gregory wandered off by himself while the others went in to dry. He came in a little late for lunch, during which he was silent and preoccupied. Afterwards the grown-ups sallied forth.

'Let's see your snow-man, Greg,' said Gloria, in a mother-of-genius tone.

'It isn't all his, we helped,' said Phyllis, voicing a point of view which was to have many echoes in the coming years.

'Why, he's changed it!' exclaimed a chorus two minutes later.

'What an ugly thing!' exclaimed Mary, rather pleased at being able to say so with conviction.

Gregory had certainly given his imagination its head, for now the squat, inert trunk was topped by a big wolf's head with open jaw and ears snarlingly laid back, surprisingly well modelled. Trailing behind it was a coiled, serpentine tail.

'Whatever gave you the idea for that?' asked Jack.

Usually Gregory was facile and eloquent in explaining his inspiration, but this time he refused to be drawn, bit his lip and turned away.

There was a moment's silence and then Gloria said with convincing emphasis, 'I think it's wonderful, Greg!'

And then they all strolled off to examine the pigs and the poultry and the Suffolk punches.

They had just got back for tea when the telephone rang in Mr Braxton's study. It was Mrs Curtis. The patient was no better and Dr Knowles had seemed rather worried, and so on. So Mr Braxton rang up the doctor.

'I haven't diagnosed his trouble yet,' he said. 'And I'm going to watch him carefully and take a blood-test if he's not better to-morrow. He has a temperature of a hundred and two, but no other superficial symptoms, which is rather peculiar. By the way, one of your cow-men, Sam Colley, got a nasty wound on the face yesterday and shows signs of blood poisoning. I'm considering sending him to hospital. Some of your other men have been in to see me – quite a little outbreak of illness since Tuesday. However, I hope we'll have a clean bill again soon. I'll keep you informed about Curtis.'

Mr Braxton was one of those incredible people who never have a day's illness – till their first and last. Consequently his conception of disease was unimaginative and mechanical. If one of his more essential human machines was running unsatisfactorily, there was a machine-mender called a doctor whose business it was to ensure that all the plug leads were attached firmly and that the manifold drainpipe was not blocked. But he found himself beginning to worry about Curtis, and this little epidemic amongst his henchmen affected him disagreeably – there was something disturbing to his spirit about it. But just what and why, he couldn't analyse and decide.

After dinner, with the children out of the way, the business of decorating the tree was begun. The general scheme had been sketched out and coloured by one of the Braxton display experts and the company consulted this as they worked, which they did rather silently; possibly Mr Braxton's palpable anxiety somewhat affected them.

Pamela stayed behind after the others had left the ballroom to put some finishing touches to her section of the tree. When she rejoined the others she was looking rather white and tight-lipped. She said good-night a shade abruptly and went to her room. Walter, a very, very good husband, quickly joined her.

'Anything the matter, old girl?' he asked anxiously.

'Yes,' replied Pamela. 'I'm frightened.'

'Frightened! What d'you mean?'

'You'll think it's all rot, but I'll tell you. When you'd all left the ballroom, I suddenly felt very uneasy – you know the sort of feeling when one keeps on looking round and can't concentrate. However, I stuck at it. I was a little way up the steps when I heard a sharp hiss from above me in the tree. I jumped back to the floor and looked up; now, of course, you won't believe me, but the trunk of the tree was moving – it was like the coils of a snake writhing upward, and there was something at the top of the tree, horrid-looking, peering at me. I know you won't believe me.'

Walter didn't, but he also didn't know what to make of it. 'I know what happened!' he improvised lightly. 'You'd been staring in at that trunk for nearly two hours and you got dizzy – like staring at the sun on the sea; and that snow dazzle this afternoon helped it. You've heard of snow-blindness – something like that, it still echoes from the retina or whatever . . .'

'You think it might have been that?'

'I'm sure of it.'

'And that horrible head?'

'Well, as George put it rather brightly, I don't think some of those figures on the lamps should get a "U" certificate. There's the wolf to which he referred, and the witch.'

'Which witch?' laughed Pamela a little hysterically. 'I didn't notice one.'

'I did. I was working just near it, at least, I suppose it's meant to be a witch. A figure in black squinting round from behind a tree. As a matter of fact fairies never seemed all fun and frolic to me, there's often something diabolical about them – or rather casually cruel. Disney knows that.'

'Yes, there is,' agreed Pamela. 'So you think that's all there was to it?'

'I'm certain. One's eyes can play tricks on one.'

'Yes,' said Pamela, 'I know what you mean, as if they saw what one knew wasn't there or was different. Though who would "one" be then?'

'Oh, don't ask me that sort of question!' laughed Walter. 'Probably Master Gregory will be able to tell you in a year or two.'

'He's a nice little boy, really,' protested Pamela. 'Gloria just spoils him and it's natural.'

'I know he is, it's not his fault, but they will *force* him. Look at that snow-man – and staying behind to do it. A foul-looking thing!'

'Perhaps his eyes played funny tricks with him,' said Pamela.

'What d'you mean by that?'

'I don't know why I said it,' said Pamela, frowning. 'Sort of echo, I suppose. Let's go to bed.'

Walter kissed her gently but fervently, as he loved her. He was a one-lady's-man and had felt a bit nervous about her for a moment or two.

Was the house a little cooler? wondered Mr Braxton, as he was undressing, or was it that he was getting more used to it? He was now convinced there was something wrong with the installation; he'd get an expert down. Meanwhile they must stick it. He yawned, wondered how Curtis was, and switched off the light.

Soon all the occupants were at rest and the great house swinging silently against the stars. Should have been at rest, rather, for one and all recalled that night with reluctance and dread. Their dreams were harsh and unhallowed, yet oddly enough related, being concerned with dim, uncertain and yet somehow urgent happenings in and around the house, as though some thing or things were stirring while they slept and communicated their motions to their dreaming consciousness. They awoke tired with a sense of unaccountable malaise.

Mrs Curtis rang up during breakfast and her voice revealed her distress. Timothy was delirious and much worse. The doctor was coming at ten-thirty.

Mr and Mrs Braxton decided to go over there, and sent for the car. Knowles was waiting just outside the house when they arrived.

'He's very bad,' he said quietly. 'I've sent for two nurses and Sir Arthur Galley; I want another opinion. Has he had some trouble with a tree?'

'Trouble with a tree!' said Mr Braxton, his nerves giving a flick.

'Yes, it's probably just a haphazard, irrational idea of delirium, but he continually fusses about some tree.'

'How bad is he?' asked Mrs Braxton.

The doctor frowned. 'I wish I knew. I'm fairly out of my depth. He's keeping up his strength fairly well, but he can't go on like this.'

'As bad as that!' exclaimed Mr Braxton.

'I'm very much afraid so. I'm anxiously awaiting Sir Arthur's verdict. By the way, that cow-man is very ill indeed; I'm sending him into hospital.'

'What happened to him?' asked Mr Braxton, absently, his mind on Curtis.

'Apparently a branch of your Christmas tree snapped back at him and struck his face. Blood-poisoning set in almost at once.'

Mr Braxton felt that tremor again, but merely nodded.

'I was just wondering if there might be some connection between the two, that Curtis is blaming himself for the accident. Seems an absurd idea, but judging from his ravings he appears to think he is lashed to some tree and that the great heat he feels comes from it.'

They went into the house and did their best to comfort and reassure Mrs Curtis, instructed Knowles to ring up as soon as Sir Arthur's verdict was known, and then drove home.

The children had just come in from playing in the snow.

'Grandpa, the snow-man's melted,' said Paddy, 'did it thaw in the night?'

'Must have done,' replied Mr Braxton, forcing a smile.

'Come and look, Grandpa,' persisted Paddy, 'there's nothing left of it.'

'Grandpa doesn't want to be bothered,' said Mary, noticing his troubled face.

'I'll come,' said Mr Braxton. When he reached the site of the snow-man his thoughts were still elsewhere, but his mind quickly refocused itself, for he was faced with something a little strange. Not a vestige of the statue remained, though the snow was frozen crisp and crunched hard beneath their feet; and yet that snow-man was completely obliterated and where it had stood was a circle of bare, brown grass.

'It must have thawed in the night and then frozen again,' he said uncertainly.

'Then why —' began Paddy.

'Don't bother Grandpa,' said Mary sharply. 'He's told you what happened.'

They wandered off towards the heavy, hurrying river.

'Are those dog-paw marks?' asked Phyllis.

That reminded Mr Braxton. He peered down. 'Yes,' he replied. 'And I bet they're those of that brute of an Alsatian; it must be a colossal beast.'

'And it must have paws like a young bear,' laughed Mary. 'They're funny dogs, sort of Jekyll-and-Hydes. I rather adore them.'

'You wouldn't adore this devil. He's all Hyde.' (I'm in the wrong mood for these festivities, he thought irritably.)

During the afternoon George and Walter took the kids to a cinema in Oxford; the others finished the decoration of the tree.

The presents, labelled with the names of their recipients, were arranged on tables round the room and the huge cracker, ten feet long and forty inches in circumference, was placed on its gaily decorated trestle near the tree. Just as the job was finished, Mary did a three-quarters faint, but was quickly revived with brandy.

'It's the simply ghastly heat in the house!' exclaimed Gloria, who was not looking too grand herself. 'The installation must be completely diseased. Ours always works perfectly.' Mary had her dinner in bed and Jack came up to her immediately he had finished his.

'How are you feeling, darling?' he asked.

'Oh, I'm all right.'

'It *was* the heat, of course?'

'Oh, yes,' replied Mary with rather forced emphasis.

'Scared you a bit, going off like that?' suggested Jack, regarding her rather sharply.

'I'm quite all right, thank you,' said Mary in the tone she always adopted when she'd had enough of a subject. 'I'd like to rest. Switch off the light.'

But when Jack had gone, she didn't close her eyes, but lay on her back staring up at the faint outline of the ceiling. She frowned and lightly chewed the little finger of her left hand, a habit of hers when unpleasantly puzzled. Mary, like most people of strong character and limited imagination, hated to be puzzled. Everything, she considered, ought to have a simple explanation if one tried hard enough to find it. But how could one explain this odd thing that had happened to her? Besides the grandiose gifts on the tables which bore a number, as well as the recipient's name, a small present for everyone was hung on the tree. This also bore a number, the same one as the lordly gift, so easing the Braxtons' task of handing these out to the right people. Mary had just fixed Curtis's label to a cigarette lighter and tied it on the tree when it swung on its silk thread, so that the back of the card was visible; and on it was this inscription: 'Died, December 25th, 1928.' It spun away again and back and the inscription was no longer there.

Now Mary came of a family which rather prided itself on being unimaginative. Her father had confined his flights of fancy to the Annual Meeting of his Shareholders, while, to her mother, imagination and mendacity were at least first cousins. So Mary could hardly credit the explanation, that, being remotely worried about Mr Curtis, she had subconsciously concocted that sinister sentence. On the other hand she knew poor Mr Curtis was very ill and, therefore, perhaps, if her brain had played that malign little trick on her, it might have done so in 'tombstone writing'.

This was a considerable logical exercise for Mary, the effort tired her, the impression began to fade and she started wondering how much longer Jack was going to sit up. She dozed off and there, as if flashed on the screen 'inside her head', was 'Died, December 25th, 1938.' This, oddly enough, completely reassured her. There was 'nothing there' this time. There had been nothing that other time. She'd been very weak and imaginative even to think otherwise.

While she was deciding this, Dr Knowles rang up. 'Sir Arthur has just been,' he said. 'And I'm sorry to say he's pessimistic. He says Curtis is very weak.'

'But what's the matter with him?' asked Mr Braxton urgently.

'He doesn't know. He calls it P.U.O., which really means nothing.'

'But what's it stand for?'

'Pyrexia unknown origin. There are some fevers which cannot be described more precisely.'

'How ill is he really?'

'All I can say is, we must hope for the best.'

'My God!' exclaimed Mr Braxton. 'When's Sir Arthur coming again?'

'At eleven to-morrow. I'll ring you up after he's been.'

Mr Braxton excused himself and went to his room. Like many men of his dominating, sometimes ruthless type, he was capable of an intensity of feeling, anger, resolution, desire for revenge, but also affection and sympathy, unknown to more superficially Christian and kindly souls. He was genuinely attached to Curtis and his wife and very harshly and poignantly moved by this news which, he realized, could hardly have been worse. He would have to exercise all his will power if he was to sleep.

If on the preceding night the rest of the sleepers had been broken by influences which had insinuated themselves into their dreams, that which caused the night of that Christmas Eve to be unforgettable was the demoniacal violence of the elements. The north-easter had been waxing steadily all the evening and by midnight reached hurricane force, driving before it an almost impenetrable wall of snow. Not only so, but continually all through the night the wall was enflamed, and the roar of the hurricane silenced, by fearful flashes of lightning and raffales of thunder. The combination was almost intolerably menacing. As the great house shook from the gale and trembled at the blasts and the windows blazed with strange polychromatic balls of flame, all were tense and troubled. The children fought or succumbed to their terror according to their natures; their parents soothed and reassured them.

Mr Braxton was convinced the lightning conductors were struck three times within ten minutes, and he could imagine them recoiling from the mighty impacts and seething from the terrific charges. Not till a dilatory, chaotic dawn staggered up the sky did the storm temporarily lull. For a time the sky cleared and the frost came hard. It was a yawning and haggard company which assembled at breakfast. But determined efforts were made to engender a communal cheerfulness. Mr Braxton did his best to contribute his quota of seasonable bonhomie, but his mind was plagued by thoughts of Curtis. Before the meal was finished the vicar rang up to say the church tower had been struck and almost demolished, so there could be no services. It rang again to say that Brent's farmhouse had been burnt to the ground.

While the others went off to inspect the church Mr Braxton remained in the study. Presently Knowles rang to say Sir Arthur had been and pronounced Curtis weaker, but his condition was not quite hopeless. One of the most ominous symptoms was the violence of the delirium. Curtis appeared to be in great terror and sedatives had no effect.

'How's that cow-man?' asked Mr Braxton.

'He died in the night, I'm sorry to say.'

Whereupon Mr Braxton broke one of his strictest rules by drinking a very stiff whisky with very little soda.

Christmas dinner was tolerably hilarious, and after it, the children, bulging and incipiently bilious, slept some of it off, while their elders put the final touches to the preparations for the party.

In spite of the weather, not a single 'cry-off' was telephoned. There was a good reason for this; Mr Braxton's entertainments were justly famous.

So from four-thirty onwards the 'Cream of North Berkshire Society' came ploughing through the snow to the Hall; Lady Pounser and party bringing up the rear in her heirloom Rolls which was dribbling steam from its ancient and aristocratic beak. A tea of teas, not merely a high-tea, an Everest tea, towering, sky-scraping, was then attacked by the already stuffed juveniles, who, by the end of it, were almost livid with repletion, finding even the efforts of cracker-pulling almost beyond them.

They were then propelled into the library where rows of chairs had been provided for them. There was a screen at one end of the room, a projector at the other. Mr Braxton had provided one of his famous surprises! The room was darkened and on the screen was flashed the sentence: '*The North Berks News Reel.*'

During the last few weeks Mr Braxton had had a sharpwitted and discreetly furtive camera-man at work shooting some of the guests while busy about their more or less lawful occasions.

For example, there was a sentence from a speech by Lord Gallen, the Socialist Peer: 'It is a damnable and calculated lie for our opponents to suggest we aim at a preposterous and essentially *inequitable* equalization on income –' And then there was His Lordship just entering his limousine, and an obsequious footman, rug in hand, holding the door open for him.

His Lordship's laughter was raucous and vehement, though he *would* have liked to have said a few words in rebuttal.

And there was Lady Pounser's Rolls, locally known as 'the hippogriffe', stuck in a snow-drift and enveloped in steam, with the caption, 'Oh, Mr Mercury, *do* give me a start!' And other kindly, slightly sardonic japes at the expense of the North Berks Cream.

The last scene was meant as an appropriate prelude to the climax of the festivities. It showed Curtis and his crew digging up the tree from Lucky's Grove. Out they came from the holm-oaks straining under their load, but close observers noticed there was one who remained behind, standing menacing and motionless, a very tall, dark, brooding figure. There came a blinding lightning flash which seemed to blaze sparking round the room, and a fearsome metallic bang. The storm had returned with rasping and imperious salute.

The lights immediately came on and the children were marshalled to the ballroom. As they entered and saw the high tree shining there and the little people so lively upon its branches a prolonged 'O—h!' of astonishment was extorted from the blasé brats. But there was another wave of flame against the windows which rattled wildly at the ensuing roar, and the cries of delight were tinged with terror. And, indeed, the hard, blue glare flung a sinister glow on the tree and its whirling throng.

The grown-ups hastened to restore equanimity and, forming rings of children, circled round the tree.

Presently Mrs Braxton exclaimed: 'Now then, look for your names on the cards and see what Father Christmas has brought you.'

Though hardly one of the disillusioned infants retained any belief in that superannuated Deliverer of Goods, the response was immediate. For they had sharp ears which had eagerly absorbed the tales of Braxton munificence. At the same time it was noticeable that some approached the tree with diffidence, almost reluctance, and started back as a livid flare broke against the window-blinds and the dread peals shook the streaming snow from the eaves.

Mary had just picked up little Angela Rayner so that she could reach her card, when the child screamed and pulled away her hand.

'The worm!' she cried, and a thick, black-grey squirming maggot fell from her fingers to the floor and writhed away. George, who was near, put his shoe on it with a squish.

One of the Pounser tribe, whose card was just below the Big Bad Wolf, refused to approach it. No wonder, thought Walter, for it looked horribly hunting and alive. There were other mischances too. The witch behind the sombre tree seemed to pounce out at Clarissa Balder, so she tearfully complained, and Gloria had to pull off her card for her. Of course Gregory was temperamental, seeming to stare at a spot just below the taut peak of the tree, as if mazed and entranced. But the presents were wonderful and more than worth the small ordeal of finding one's card and pretending not to be frightened when the whole room seemed full of fiery hands and the thunder cracked against one's ear-drums and shook one's teeth. Easy to be afraid!

At length the last present had been bestowed and it was time for the *pièce de résistance*, the pulling of the great cracker. Long, silken cords streamed from each end with room among them for fifty chubby fists, and a great surprise inside, for sure. The languid, uneasy troops were lined up at each end and took a grip on the silken cords.

At that moment a footman came in and told Mr Braxton he was wanted on the telephone.

Filled with foreboding he went to his study. He heard the voice of Knowles –

'I'm afraid I have very bad news for you. . .'

The chubby fists gripped the silken cords.

'Now pull!' cried Mrs Braxton.

The opposing teams took the strain.

A leaping flash and a blasting roar. The children were hurled, writhing and screaming, over each other.

Up from the middle of the cracker leapt a rosy shaft of flame which, as it reached the ceiling, seemed to flatten its peak so that it resembled a great snake of fire which turned and hurled itself against the tree in a blinding embrace. There was a fierce sustained 'Hiss', the tree flamed like a torch, and all the fairy globes upon it burst and splintered. And then the roaring torch cast itself down amongst the screaming chaos. For a moment the great pot, swathed in green, was a carmine cauldron and its paint streamed like blood upon the floor. Then the big room was a dream of fire and those within it driven wildly from its heat.

Phil Tangler, whose farmhouse, on the early slopes of Missen Rise, overlooked both Lucky's Grove and the Hall, solemnly declared that at seven-thirty on Christmas Day, 1938, he was watching from a window and marvelling at the dense and boiling race of snow, the bitter gale, and the wicked flame and fury of the storm, when he saw a huge fist of fire form a rift in the cloud-rack, a fist with two huge blazing fingers, one of which speared down on the Hall, another touched and kindled the towering fir in Lucky's Grove, as though saluting it. Five minutes later he was racing through the hurricane to join in a vain night-long fight to save the Hall, already blazing from stem to stern.

# Tarnhelm

## or

# The Death of My Uncle Robert

*Hugh Walpole*

### I

I was, I suppose, at that time a peculiar child, peculiar a little by nature, but also because I had spent so much of my young life in the company of people very much older than myself.

After the events that I am now going to relate, some quite indelible mark was set on me. I became then, and have always been since, one of those persons, otherwise insignificant, who have decided, without possibility of change, about certain questions.

Some things, doubted by most of the world, are for these people true and beyond argument; this certainty of theirs gives them a kind of stamp, as though they lived so much in their imagination as to have very little assurance as to what is fact and what fiction. This 'oddness' of theirs puts them apart. If now, at the age of fifty, I am a man with very few friends, very much alone, it is because, if you like, my Uncle Robert died in a strange manner forty years ago and I was a witness of his death.

I have never until now given any account of the strange proceedings that occurred at Faildyke Hall on the evening of Christmas Eve in the year 1890. The incidents of that evening are still remembered very clearly by one or two people, and a kind of legend of my Uncle Robert's death has been carried on into the younger generation. But no one still alive was a witness of them as I was, and I feel it is time that I set them down upon paper.

I write them down without comment. I extenuate nothing; I disguise nothing. I am not, I hope, in any way a vindictive man, but my brief meeting with my Uncle Robert and the circumstances of his death gave my life, even at that early age, a twist difficult for me very readily to forgive.

As to the so-called supernatural element in my story, everyone must judge for himself about that. We deride or we accept according to our natures. If we are built of a certain solid practical material the probability is that no evidence, however definite, however first-hand, will convince us. If dreams are our daily portion, our dream more or less will scarcely shake our sense of reality.

However, to my story.

My father and mother were in India from my eighth to my thirteenth years. I did not see them, except on two occasions when they visited England. I was an only child, loved dearly by both my parents, who, however, loved one another yet more. They were an exceedingly senti-mental couple of the old-fashioned kind. My father was in the Indian Civil Service, and wrote poetry. He even had his epic, *Tantalus: A Poem in Four Cantos*, published at his own expense.

This, added to the fact that my mother had been considered an invalid before he married her, made my parents feel that they bore a very close resemblance to the Brownings, and my father even had a pet name for my mother that sounded curiously like the famous and hideous 'Ba'.

I was a delicate child, was sent to Mr Ferguson's Private Academy at the tender age of eight, and spent my holidays as the rather unwanted guest of various relations.

'Unwanted' because I was, I imagine, a difficult child to understand. I had an old grandmother who lived at Folkestone, two aunts who shared a little house in Kensington, an aunt, uncle and a brood of cousins inhabiting Cheltenham, and two uncles who lived in Cumberland. All these relations, except the two uncles, had their proper share of me and for none of them had I any great affection.

Children were not studied in those days as they are now. I was thin, pale and bespectacled, aching for affection but not knowing at all how to obtain it; outwardly undemonstrative but inwardly emotional and sensitive, playing games, because of my poor sight, very badly, reading a great deal more than was good for me, and telling myself stories all day and part of every night.

All of my relations tired of me, I fancy, in turn, and at last it was decided that my uncles in Cumberland must do their share. These two were my father's brothers, the eldest of a long family of which he was the youngest. My Uncle Robert, I understood, was nearly seventy, my Uncle Constance some five years younger. I remember always thinking that Constance was a funny name for a man.

My Uncle Robert was the owner of Faildyke Hall, a country house between the lake of Wastwater and the little town of Seascale on the sea coast. Uncle Constance had lived with Uncle Robert for many years. It was decided, after some family correspondence, that the Christmas of this year, 1890, should be spent by me at Faildyke Hall.

I was at this time just eleven years old, thin and skinny, with a bulging forehead, large spectacles and a nervous, shy manner. I always set out, I remember, on any new adventures with mingled emotions of terror and anticipation. Maybe *this* time the miracle would occur: I should discover a friend or a fortune, should cover myself with glory in some unexpected way; be at last what I always longed to be, a hero.

I was glad that I was not going to any of my other relations for Christmas, and especially not to my cousins at Cheltenham, who teased and persecuted me and were never free of ear-splitting noises. What I wanted most in life was to be allowed to read in peace. I understood that at Faildyke there was a glorious library.

My aunt saw me into the train. I had been presented by my uncle with one of the most gory of Harrison Ainsworth's romances, *The Lancashire Witches*, and I had five bars of chocolate cream, so that that journey was as blissfully happy as any experience could be to me at that time. I was permitted to read in peace, and I had just then little more to ask of life.

Nevertheless, as the train puffed its way north, this new country began to force itself on my attention. I had never before been in the North of England, and I was not prepared for the sudden sense of space and freshness that I received.

The naked, unsystematic hills, the freshness of the wind on which the birds seemed to be carried with especial glee, the stone walls that ran like grey ribbons about the moors, and, above all, the vast expanse of sky upon whose surface clouds swam, raced, eddied and extended as I had never anywhere witnessed...

I sat, lost and absorbed, at my carriage window, and when at last, long after dark had fallen, I heard 'Seascale' called by the porter, I was still staring in a sort of romantic dream. When I stepped out onto the little narrow platform and was greeted by the salt tang of the sea wind my first real introduction to the North Country may be said to have been completed. I am writing now in another part of that same Cumberland country, and beyond my window the line of the fell runs strong and bare against the sky, while below it the Lake lies, a fragment of silver glass at the feet of Skiddaw.

It may be that my sense of the deep mystery of this country had its origin in this same strange story that I am now relating. But again perhaps not, for I believe that that first evening arrival at Seascale worked some change in me, so that since then none of the world's beauties – from the crimson waters of Kashmir to the rough glories of our own Cornish coast – can rival for me the sharp, peaty winds and strong, resilient turf of the Cumberland hills.

That was a magical drive in the pony-trap to Faildyke that evening. It was bitterly cold, but I did not seem to mind it. Everything was magical to me.

From the first I could see the great slow hump of Black Combe jet against the frothy clouds of the winter night, and I could hear the sea breaking and the soft rustle of the bare twigs in the hedgerows.

I made, too, the friend of my life that night, for it was Bob Armstrong who was driving the trap. He has often told me since (for although he is a slow man of few words he likes to repeat the things that seem to him worth while) that I struck him as 'pitifully lost' that evening on the Seascale platform. I looked, I don't doubt, pinched and cold enough. In any case it was a lucky appearance for me, for I won Armstrong's heart there and then, and he, once he gave it, could never bear to take it back again.

He, on his side, seemed to me gigantic that night. He had, I believe, one of the broadest chests in the world: it was a curse to him, he said, because no ready-made shirts would ever suit him.

I sat in close to him because of the cold; he was very warm, and I could feel his heart beating like a steady clock inside his rough coat. It beat for me that night, and it has beaten for me, I'm glad to say, ever since.

In truth, as things turned out, I needed a friend. I was nearly asleep and stiff all over my little body when I was handed down from the trap and at once led into what seemed to me an immense hall crowded with the staring heads of slaughtered animals and smelling of straw.

I was so sadly weary that my uncles, when I met them in a vast billiard-room in which a great fire roared in a stone fireplace like a demon, seemed to me to be double.

In any case, what an odd pair they were! My Uncle Robert was a little man with grey untidy hair and little sharp eyes hooded by two of the bushiest eyebrows known to humanity. He wore (I remember as though it were yesterday) shabby country clothes of a faded green colour, and he had on one finger a ring with a thick red stone.

Another thing that I noticed at once when he kissed me (I detested being kissed by anybody) was a faint scent that he had, connected at once in my mind with the caraway-seeds that there are in seed-cake. I noticed, too, that his teeth were discoloured and yellow.

My Uncle Constance I liked at once. He was fat, round, friendly and clean. Rather a dandy was Uncle Constance. He wore a flower in his buttonhole, and his linen was snowy white in contrast with his brother's.

I noticed one thing, though, at that very first meeting, and that was that before he spoke to me and put his fat arm around my shoulder he seemed to look towards his brother as though for permission. You may say that it was unusual for a boy of my age to notice so much, but in fact I noticed everything at that time. Years and laziness, alas! have slackened my observation.

2

I had a horrible dream that night; it woke me screaming, and brought Bob Armstrong in to quiet me.

My room was large, like all the other rooms that I had seen, and empty, with a great expanse of floor and a stone fireplace like the one in the billiard-room. It was, I afterwards found, next to the servants' quarters. Armstrong's room was next to mine, and Mrs Spender's, the housekeeper's, beyond his.

Armstrong was then, and is yet, a bachelor. He used to tell me that he loved so many women that he never could bring his mind to choose any one of them. And now he has been too long my personal bodyguard and is too lazily used to my ways to change his condition. He is, moreover, seventy years of age.

Well, what I saw in my dream was this. They had lit a fire for me (and it was necessary; the room was of an icy coldness) and I dreamt that I awoke to see the flames rise to a last vigour before they died away. In the brilliance of that illumination I was conscious that something was moving in the room. I heard the movement for some little while before I saw anything.

I sat up, my heart hammering, and then to my horror discerned, slinking against the farther wall, the evillest-looking yellow mongrel of a dog that you can fancy.

I find it difficult, I have always found it difficult, to describe exactly the horror of that yellow dog. It lay partly in its colour, which was vile, partly in its mean and bony body, but for the most part in its evil head – flat, with sharp little eyes and jagged yellow teeth.

As I looked at it, it bared those teeth at me and then began to creep, with an indescribably loathsome action, in the direction of my bed. I was at first stiffened with terror. Then, as it neared the bed, its little eyes fixed upon me and its teeth bared, I screamed again and again.

The next I knew was that Armstrong was sitting on my bed, his strong arm about my trembling little body. All I could say over and over was, 'The Dog! the Dog! the Dog!'

He soothed me as though he had been my mother.

'See, there's no dog there! There's no one but me! There's no one but me!'

I continued to tremble, so he got into bed with me, held me close to him, and it was in his comforting arms that I fell asleep.

## 3

In the morning I woke to a fresh breeze and a shining sun and the chrysanthemums, orange, crimson and dun, blowing against the grey stone wall beyond the sloping lawns. So I forgot about my dream. I only knew that I loved Bob Armstrong better than anyone else on earth.

Everyone during the next days was very kind to me. I was so deeply excited by this country, so new to me, that at first I could think of nothing else. Bob Armstrong was Cumbrian from the top of his flaxen head to the thick nails under his boots, and, in grunts and monosyllables, as was his way, he gave me the colour of the ground.

There was romance everywhere: smugglers stealing in and out of Drigg and Seascale, the ancient Cross in Gosforth churchyard, Ravenglass, with all its seabirds, once a port of splendour.

Muncaster Castle and Broughton and black Wastwater with the grim Screes, Black Combe, upon whose broad back the shadows were always dancing – even the little station at Seascale, naked to the sea-winds, at whose bookstalls I bought a publication entitled the *Weekly Telegraph* that contained, week by week, instalments of the most thrilling story in the world.

Everywhere romance – the cows moving along the sandy lanes, the sea thundering along the Drigg beach, Gable and Scafell pulling their cloud-caps about their heads, the slow voices of the Cumbrian farmers calling their animals, the little tinkling bell of the Gosforth church – everywhere romance and beauty.

Soon, though, as I became better accustomed to the country, the people immediately around me began to occupy my attention, stimulate my restless curiosity, and especially my two uncles. They were, in fact, queer enough.

Faildyke Hall itself was not queer, only very ugly. It had been built about 1830, I should imagine, a square white building, like a thick-set, rather conceited woman with a very plain face. The rooms were large, the passages innumerable, and everything covered with a very hideous whitewash. Against this whitewash hung old photographs yellowed with age, and faded, bad water-colours. The furniture was strong and ugly.

One romantic feature, though, there was – and that was the little Grey Tower where my Uncle Robert lived. This Tower was at the end of the garden and looked out over a sloping field to the Scafell group beyond Wastwater. It had been built hundreds of years ago as a defence against the Scots. Robert had had his study and bedroom there for many years and it was his domain; no one was allowed to enter it save his old servant Hucking, a bent, wizened, grubby little man who spoke to no one and, so they said in the kitchen, managed to go through life without sleeping. He looked after my Uncle Robert, cleaned his rooms, and was supposed to clean his clothes.

I, being both an inquisitive and romantic-minded boy, was soon as eagerly excited about this Tower as was Bluebeard's wife about the forbidden room. Bob told me that whatever I did I was never to set foot inside.

And then I discovered another thing – that Bob Armstrong hated, feared and was proud of my Uncle Robert. He was proud of him because he was head of the family, and because, so he said, he was the cleverest old man in the world.

'Nothing he can't seemingly do,' said Bob, 'but he don't like you to watch him at it.'

All this only increased my longing to see the inside of the Tower, although I couldn't be said to be fond of my Uncle Robert either.

It would be hard to say that I disliked him during those first days. He was quite kindly to me when he met me, and at meal-times, when I sat with my two uncles at the long table in the big, bare, whitewashed dining-room, he was always anxious to see that I had plenty to eat. But I never liked him; it was perhaps because he wasn't clean. Children are sensitive to those things. Perhaps I didn't like the fusty, seed-caky smell that he carried about with him.

Then there came the day when he invited me into the Grey Tower and told me about Tarnhelm.

Pale slanting shadows of sunlight fell across the chrysanthemums and the grey stone walls, the long fields and the dusky hills. I was playing by myself by the little stream that ran beyond the rose garden, when Uncle Robert came up behind me in the soundless way he had, and, tweaking me by the ear, asked me whether I would like to come with him inside the Tower. I was, of course, eager enough; but I was frightened too, especially when I saw Hucking's moth-eaten old countenance peering at us from one of the narrow slits that pretended to be windows.

However, in we went, my hand in Uncle Robert's hot dry one. There wasn't in reality, so very much to see when you were inside – all untidy and musty, with cobwebs over the doorways and old pieces of rusty iron and empty boxes in the corners, and the long table in Uncle Robert's study covered with a thousand things – books with the covers hanging on them, sticky green bottles, a looking-glass, a pair of scales, a globe, a cage with mice in it, a statue of a naked woman, an hour-glass – everything old and stained and dusty.

However, Uncle Robert made me sit down close to him, and told me many interesting stories. Among others the story about Tarnhelm.

Tarnhelm was something that you put over your head, and its magic turned you into any animal that you wished to be. Uncle Robert told me the story of a god called Wotan, and how he teased the dwarf who possessed Tarnhelm by saying that he couldn't turn himself into a mouse or some such animal; and the dwarf, his pride wounded, turned himself into a mouse, which the god easily captured and so stole Tarnhelm.

On the table, among all the litter, was a grey skull-cap.

'That's my Tarnhelm,' said Uncle Robert, laughing. 'Like to see me put it on?'

But I was suddenly frightened, terribly frightened. The sight of Uncle Robert made me feel quite ill. The room began to run round and round. The white mice in the cage twittered. It was stuffy in that room, enough to turn any boy sick.

<h1 style="text-align:center">4</h1>

That was the moment, I think, when Uncle Robert stretched out his hand towards his grey skull-cap – after that I was never happy again in Faildyke Hall. That action of his, simple and apparently friendly though it was, seemed to open my eyes to a number of things.

We were now within ten days of Christmas. The thought of Christmas had then – and, to tell the truth, still has – a most happy effect on me. There is the beautiful story, the geniality and kindliness, still, in spite of modern pessimists, much happiness and goodwill. Even now I yet enjoy giving presents and receiving them – then it was an ecstasy to me, the look of the parcel, the paper, the string, the exquisite surprise.

Therefore I had been anticipating Christmas eagerly. I had been promised a trip into Whitehaven for present-buying, and there was to be a tree and a dance for the Gosforth villagers. Then after my visit to Uncle Robert's Tower, all my happiness of anticipation vanished. As the days went on and my observation of one thing and another developed, I would, I think, have run away back to my aunts in Kensington, had it not been for Bob Armstrong.

It was, in fact, Armstrong who started me on that voyage of observation that ended so horribly, for when he had heard that Uncle Robert had taken me inside his Tower his anger was fearful. I had never before seen him angry; now his great body shook, and he caught me and held me until I cried out.

He wanted me to promise that I would never go inside there again. What? Not even with Uncle Robert? No, most especially not with Uncle Robert; and then, dropping his voice and looking around him to be sure that there was no one listening, he began to curse Uncle Robert. This amazed me, because loyalty to his masters was one of Bob's great laws. I can see us now, standing on the stable cobbles in the falling white dusk while the horses stamped in their stalls, and the little sharp stars appeared one after another glittering between the driving clouds.

'I'll not stay,' I heard him say to himself. 'I'll be like the rest. I'll not be staying. To bring a child into it. . .'

From that moment he seemed to have me very specially in his charge. Even when I could not see him I felt that his kindly eye was upon me, and this sense of the necessity that I should be guarded made me yet more uneasy and distressed.

The next thing that I observed was that the servants were all fresh, had been there not more than a month or two. Then, only a week before Christmas, the housekeeper departed. Uncle Constance seemed greatly upset at these occurrences; Uncle Robert did not seem in the least affected by them.

I come now to my Uncle Constance. At this distance of time it is strange with what clarity I still can see him – his stoutness, his shining cleanliness, his dandyism, the flower in his buttonhole, his little brilliantly shod feet, his thin, rather feminine voice. He would have been kind to me, I think, had he dared, but something kept him back. And what that something was I soon discovered; it was fear of my Uncle Robert.

It did not take me a day to discover that he was utterly subject to his brother. He said nothing without looking to see how Uncle Robert took it; suggested no plan until he first had assurance from his brother; was terrified beyond anything that I had before witnessed in a human being at any sign of irritation in my uncle.

I discovered after this that Uncle Robert enjoyed greatly to play on his brother's fears. I did not understand enough of their life to realize what were the weapons that Robert used, but that they were sharp and piercing I was neither too young nor too ignorant to perceive.

Such was our situation, then, a week before Christmas. The weather had become very wild, with a great wind. All nature seemed in an uproar. I could fancy when I lay in my bed at night and heard the shouting in my chimney that I could catch the crash of the waves upon the beach, see the black waters of Wastwater cream and curdle under the Screes. I would lie awake and long for Bob Armstrong – the strength of his arm and the warmth of his breath – but I considered myself too grown a boy to make any appeal.

I remember that now almost minute by minute my fears increased. What gave them force and power who can say? I was much alone, I had now a great terror of my uncle, the weather was wild, the rooms of the house large and desolate, the servants mysterious, the walls of the passages lit always with an unnatural glimmer because of their white colour, and although Armstrong had watch over me he was busy in his affairs and could not always be with me.

I grew to fear and dislike my Uncle Robert more and more. Hatred and fear of him seemed to be everywhere and yet he was always soft-voiced and kindly. Then, a few days before Christmas, occurred the event that was to turn my terror into panic.

I had been reading in the library Mrs Radcliffe's *Romance of the Forest*, an old book long forgotten, worthy of revival. The library was a fine room run to seed, bookcases from floor to ceiling, the windows small and dark, holes in the old faded carpet. A lamp burnt at a distant table. One stood on a little shelf at my side.

Something, I know not what, made me look up. What I saw then can even now stamp my heart in its recollection. By the library door, not moving, staring across the room's length at me, was a yellow dog.

I will not attempt to describe all the pitiful fear and mad freezing terror that caught and held me. My main thought, I fancy, was that that other vision on my first night in the place had not been a dream. I was not asleep now; the book in which I had been reading had fallen to the floor, the lamps shed their glow, I could hear the ivy tapping on the pane. No, this was reality.

The dog lifted a long, horrible leg and scratched itself. Then very slowly and silently across the carpet it came towards me.

I could not scream; I could not move; I waited. The animal was even more evil than it had seemed before, with its flat head, its narrow eyes, its yellow fangs. It came steadily in my direction, stopped once to scratch itself again, then was almost at my chair.

It looked at me, bared its fangs, but now as though it grinned at me, then passed on. After it was gone there was a thick foetid scent in the air – the scent of caraway-seed.

## 5

I think now on looking back that it was remarkable enough that I, a pale, nervous child who trembled at every sound, should have met the situation as I did. I said nothing about the dog to any living soul, not even to Bob Armstrong. I hid my fears – and fears of a beastly and sickening kind they were, too – within my breast. I had the intelligence to perceive – and *how* I caught in the air the awareness of this I can't, at this distance, understand – that I was playing my little part in the climax to something that had been piling up, for many a month, like the clouds over Gable.

Understand that I offer from first to last in this no kind of explanation. There is possibly – and to this day I cannot quite be sure – nothing to explain. My Uncle Robert died simply – but you shall hear.

What was beyond any doubt or question was that it was after my seeing the dog in the library that Uncle Robert changed so strangely in his behaviour to me. That may have been the merest coincidence. I only know that as one grows older one calls things coincidence more and more seldom.

In any case, that same night at dinner, Uncle Robert seemed twenty years older. He was bent, shrivelled, would not eat, snarled at anyone who spoke to him and especially avoided even looking at me. It was a painful meal, and it was after it, when Uncle Constance and I were sitting alone in the old yellow-papered drawing-room – a room with two ticking clocks for ever racing one another – that the most extraordinary thing occurred. Uncle Constance and I were playing draughts. The only sounds were the roaring of the wind down the chimney, the hiss and splutter of the fire, the silly ticking of the clocks. Suddenly Uncle Constance put down the piece that he was about to move and began to cry.

To a child it is always a terrible thing to see a grown-up person cry, and even to this day to hear a man cry is very distressing to me. I was moved desperately by poor Uncle Constance, who sat there, his head in his white plump hands, all his stout body shaking. I ran over to him and he clutched me and held me as though he would never let me go. He sobbed incoherent words about protecting me, caring for me . . . seeing that that monster. . .

At the word I remember that I too began to tremble. I asked my uncle what monster, but he could only continue to murmur incoherently about hate and not having the pluck, and if only he had the courage. . .

Then, recovering a little, he began to ask me questions. Where had I been? Had I been into his brother's Tower? Had I seen anything that frightened me? If I did would I at once tell him? And then he muttered that he would never have allowed me to come had he known that it would go as far as this, that it would be better if I went away that night, and that if he were not afraid. . . Then he began to tremble again and to look at the door, and I trembled too. He held me in his arms; then we thought that there was a sound and we listened, our heads up, our two hearts hammering. But it was only the clocks ticking and the wind shrieking as though it would tear the house to pieces.

That night, however, when Bob Armstrong came up to bed he found me sheltering there. I whispered to him that I was frightened; I put my arms around his neck and begged him not to send me away; he promised me that I should not leave him and I slept all night in the protection of his strength.

How, though, can I give any true picture of the fear that pursued me now? For I knew from what both Armstrong and Uncle Constance had said that there was real danger, that it was no hysterical fancy of mine or ill-digested dream. It made it worse that Uncle Robert was now no more seen. He was sick; he kept within his Tower, cared for by his wizened manservant. And so, being nowhere, he was everywhere. I stayed with Armstrong when I could, but a kind of pride prevented me from clinging like a girl to his coat.

A deathly silence seemed to fall about the place. No one laughed or sang, no dog barked, no bird sang. Two days before Christmas an iron frost came to grip the land. The fields were rigid, the sky itself seemed to be frozen grey, and under the olive cloud Scafell and Gable were black.

Christmas Eve came.

On that morning, I remember, I was trying to draw – some childish picture of one of Mrs Radcliffe's scenes – when the double doors unfolded and Uncle Robert stood there. He stood there, bent, shrivelled, his long, grey locks falling over his collar, his bushy eyebrows thrust forward. He wore his old green suit and on his finger gleamed his heavy red ring. I was frightened, of course, but also I was touched with pity. He looked so old, so frail, so small in this large empty house.

I sprang up. 'Uncle Robert,' I asked timidly, 'are you better?'

He bent still lower until he was almost on his hands and feet; then he looked up at me, and his yellow teeth were bared, almost as an animal snarls. Then the doors closed again.

The slow, stealthy, grey afternoon came at last. I walked with Armstrong to Gosforth village on some business that he had. We said no word of any matter at the Hall. I told him, he has reminded me, of how fond I was of him and that I wanted to be with him always, and he answered that perhaps it might be so, little knowing how true that prophecy was to stand. Like all children I had a great capacity for forgetting the atmosphere that I was not at that moment in, and I walked beside Bob along the frozen roads, with some of my fears surrendered.

But not for long. It was dark when I came into the long, yellow drawing-room. I could hear the bells of Gosforth church pealing as I passed from the ante-room.

A moment later there came a shrill, terrified cry: 'Who's that? Who is it?'

It was Uncle Constance, who was standing in front of the yellow silk window curtains, staring at the dusk. I went over to him and he held me close to him.

'Listen!' he whispered. 'What can you hear?'

The double doors through which I had come were half open. At first I could hear nothing but the clocks, the very faint rumble of a cart on the frozen road. There was no wind.

My uncle's fingers gripped my shoulder. 'Listen!' he said again. And now I heard. On the stone passage beyond the drawing-room was the patter of an animal's feet. Uncle Constance and I looked at one another. In that exchanged glance we confessed that our secret was the same. We knew what we should see.

A moment later it was there, standing in the double doorway, crouching a little and staring at us with a hatred that was mad and sick – the hatred of a sick animal crazy with unhappiness, but loathing us more than its own misery.

Slowly it came towards us, and to my reeling fancy all the room seemed to stink of caraway-seed.

'Keep back! Keep away!' my uncle screamed.

I became oddly in my turn the protector.

'It shan't touch you! It shan't touch you, Uncle!' I called.

But the animal came on.

It stayed for a moment near a little round table that contained a composition of dead waxen fruit under a glass dome. It stayed here, its nose down, smelling the ground. Then, looking up at us, it came on again.

Oh God! – even now as I write after all these years it is with me again, the flat skull, the cringing body in its evil colour and that loathsome smell. It slobbered a little at its jaw. It bared its fangs.

Then I screamed, hid my face in my uncle's breast and saw that he held, in his trembling hand, a thick, heavy, old-fashioned revolver.

Then he cried out:

'Go back, Robert. . . Go back!'

The animal came on. He fired. The detonation shook the room. The dog turned and, blood dripping from its throat, crawled across the floor.

By the door it halted, turned and looked at us. Then it disappeared into the other room.

My uncle had flung down his revolver; he was crying, sniffling; he kept stroking my forehead, murmuring words.

At last, clinging to one another, we followed the splotches of blood, across the carpet, beside the door, through the doorway.

Huddled against a chair in the outer sitting-room, one leg twisted under him, was my Uncle Robert, shot through the throat.

On the floor, by his side, was a grey skull-cap.

# The Tibetan Box

*Elizabeth Walter*

It was during tea that the Tibetan box was first mentioned. As soon as she noticed it, incongruously perched on the rosewood work-table in the window, Alice Norrington wondered how she could possibly have overlooked it till then. In the same instant she asked in her most authoritarian manner, 'Mary, where did you get that box?'

From her sofa Mary Norrington followed the direction of her sister's gaze. She was not yet used to being a semi-invalid, and the excitement of her only sister's return after a three-year tour of duty in the mission field had tired her more than she wanted to admit. As if that were not enough, there was the strain of a third person's presence. She had somehow never suspected that her sister would be accompanied by her friend and colleague Ellen Whittaker. Equally, it had obviously never occurred to Alice that Miss Whittaker was not included in the invitation. An extra room had had to be made ready as unobtrusively as possible. Mrs Forrest, who 'did', had not been pleased. Moreover, since the moment of her arrival Alice had kept up a ceaseless catechism on Mary's health, finances, future plans and wishes. Now she had started on the box.

'I bought it in a jumble sale,' Mary said tiredly. 'It's rather unusual, isn't it?'

'It's unusual to find anything worth buying in a jumble sale,' Miss Whittaker observed.

Alice was already on her feet. 'May I look at it?' she asked, moving briskly across the room at a rate that Mary now envied, (remembering that she could have equalled it a mere six months ago. A moment later she was calling from the window: 'I say! This is magnificent. Ellen, come here and have a look at this.'

'Why don't you bring it nearer the fire?' Miss Whittaker asked placidly, continuing to sip her tea. The visit to Alice's sister was proving even more difficult than she had expected, and she had never expected very much. She had expressed her doubts about accompanying Alice, but Alice in her autocratic way had insisted that she should, and since Miss Whittaker had no friends or relatives in England, she had allowed her scruples to be overborne. Now, of course, she was regretting it. Her presence was too obviously neither anticipated nor desired. Moreover, as is often the way with sisters, Mary and Alice were too much alike to get on. The same imprudence, arrogance and self-confidence – a 'strong personality', in short – were evident in both the Misses Norrington. They had never forgotten that they were the squire's daughters, and that it was for them to be liberal with advice, lofty in example, and inalienably right at all times. Alice, at least, possessed considerable administrative ability; the African mission field was pock-marked by her vigorous descents upon it; but neither sister possessed what Miss Whittaker would have described as humility. Mary, for all her weakened state, was the less humble of the two.

She was sitting up now with something of her old decisive manner. It was all very well for Alice to invade her home, even though that home was no more than four-bedroomed Throstle Cottage when once they had been used to living at The Hall. Times (and servants) might not be what they had been; incomes remain fixed in a world where all else rose; but an Englishwoman's home was still her castle and only one woman was in control.

'Bring the box over here, Alice,' she commanded, superimposing her orders on Miss Whittaker's request. 'And please draw the curtains while you're at the window. It's already beginning to get dark.'

She was right. The garden was filling with shadows. The trees, still in leaf for it was only October as yet, were bowing to one another in a gently rising wind. This will bring the leaves down, Alice Norrington reflected. We must sweep the garden and have a bonfire soon.

As though she had communicated her thoughts in some way, Mary said: 'We need another log on this fire, Alice dear. I wonder if you would be good enough to put one on.'

Her sister complied with some annoyance, placing the box on her chair. Mary's severe heart attack had in no way softened that organ. She was as autocratic as she had ever been. More so, in fact, for her invalid state gave her certain rights and privileges which she was not slow to abuse. Nevertheless, it seemed odd and unnatural to see Mary so much shrunken and aged. Her face had a greyness, despite a discreet use of make-up; the excitement of their arrival had made her pant. The doctor said bluntly it had been touch and go with her. It was doubtful if she would ever lead a normally active life again. And the attack had come without the slightest sign or warning. Since childhood, Mary had never had a day's illness in her life. If it came to that, Alice thought, she hadn't either. The Norringtons were what one might call healthy stock.

She smiled grimly and stood up, brushing her tweed skirt as she did so. Ellen Whittaker had picked up the box. It was on her lap, and from where she stood Alice could see it clearly. It reaffirmed her impression that it was a magnificent piece of work. Made of some unknown dark hardwood, its carvings burnished by age and care to a subtle sheen, it measured some 13 by 9 by $3\frac{1}{2}$ inches, and was fitted with a hinged lid and a lock. The key was missing, but this could hardly count as a defect, and the lid and sides of the box were so ornately and intricately carved that it would have been well worth snapping up at a jumble sale even if it had been in far worse condition. But who ever would give a box like that to a jumble sale?

'Major Murphy,' Mary said when asked, adding: 'I don't think you would know him, Alice. They only came here since you were last home on leave. They took the Red House on a seven-year renewable tenancy. We all liked them so much. Stella Murphy was a great gardener; she had that garden looking lovely. Such a pity the new people have let it go.'

'New people? Didn't the Murphys finish their tenancy?'

'My dear, the most dreadful thing! Stella died.'

'Good gracious,' Alice exclaimed, 'how tragic!'

'Tragic it certainly was. She jabbed the fork into her finger while bedding out some rock-plants. Such a little cut it was – I saw it. Within forty-eight hours she was dead. Tetanus. I never heard anything so dreadful.'

Alice duly echoed her sister, but Ellen Whittaker, who had seen and heard many dreadful things, did not. Instead, she asked, examining the box intently: 'Did the Major tell you where this came from?'

'I don't think he knew,' Mary said. 'It actually belonged to Stella. I thought it rather unfeeling, putting something of hers in the sale. But perhaps he only wanted to help the church – he was leaving the district – and it was such an obvious snip. I asked him what he estimated it was worth and he said he thought a pound would be plenty. So I put in thirty shillings and took it home myself. I never thought to ask him where it came from, but it looks Chinese to me.'

Miss Whittaker shook her heal decidedly. 'It's not Chinese. I can tell you that for sure. I'd say it was Tibetan.'

The sisters looked at her inquiringly. 'Ellen, how do you know?' Alice asked.

'I was in India before I came to Africa,' Miss Whittaker answered. 'I spent some time in Nepal. It's on the Tibetan border. I've seen a good deal of Tibetan work.'

'If you can read their writing,' Mary suggested, 'there's an inscription underneath that might help. I asked Major Murphy about it and he said he didn't know what it meant. I'm sure he was lying, somehow. It's probably something not quite nice.'

'The carvings don't look particularly erotic,' Alice observed with interest. 'Offhand, I'd have said they were threatening in some way.'

The adjective was a disturbingly apt one. The surface of the lid was filled by a rampant dragon, his face surrounded by a curious beard or frill. His eyes must originally have been jewels, but now only the empty sockets remained. From these flared two long whiskers, like a mandarin's moustache. Face and body were covered with fish-like scales, and a ridge of spines ran down the centre of the back. One forefoot was raised as if to lash out, and every foot had four wicked-looking claws. The body writhed and coiled in undulation, this way and that across the lid. The tail, with a final upward flick towards the vertical, was finished with a vicious little barb. Round the sides of the box were lesser dragons, carved in profile but equally aroused. Two dragons faced each other on the long side; on the short, a single dragon glared outward at the world.

'There seems no reason why the Major shouldn't have translated the inscription,' Alice continued. 'Do you think he knew what it said?'

'He very well may have done. I understand he was in the Indian Army.'

'And how long ago did all this take place?' Alice questioned.

'It's seven months today since I bought the box,' Mary said. Seeing her sister look startled, she elaborated. 'The jumble sale was on a Saturday. Contributions were brought in on Thursday to leave us Friday for marking and pricing the stuff. So I bought the box on a Thursday, and three weeks later I had my heart attack. I remember when that was without trying, so that makes it seven months to the day. It's a pity there wasn't a longer interval,' she added. 'I was going to have the dragon's missing eyes restored. I thought rubies, perhaps – very small and deep and glowing.'

She was interrupted by a cry from Ellen Whittaker, who was gazing intently at the underside of the box.

'What is it?' Alice asked. 'A protruding nail?'

'No, oh no. It's nothing like that. It's this – this inscription.'

'Do you mean to say you can read it?'

'I'm afraid I can.'

Mary clapped her hands in childlike triumph. 'I'm so glad. I've been longing to know what it says.'

'You won't be so glad when you hear it.'

'Is it really something obscene?'

'I wish it were,' Ellen Whittaker said grimly. She put the box on the floor and drew imperceptibly away. 'It's Tibetan all right,' she informed them. 'A Tibetan magician's box. In it would have been kept all the tools of his art or profession, closely guarded from curious eyes.'

'A sort of conjuror's box,' Alice suggested.

'No, something more sinister than that. There is no accounting for the power of these magicians. No rational explanation will suffice. They can bless or curse with equal efficaciousness, and the inscription on the box is a curse.'

'What a terrible hold superstition has on these people!' Alice Norrington was already planning a crusade.

Miss Whittaker answered her sharply. 'Superstition's hardly the word. You don't have to believe in their magic to be affected.'

'Even in England?' Mary inquired.

Miss Whittaker did not trouble to answer. She had seen Tibetan magic at work. But the Misses Norrington, younger and less experienced, were clamorous to know details.

'Why the curse?' Alice Norrington demanded.

'In case the box was stolen,' her friend replied. 'The magician's is a hereditary calling. The box would be handed down from father to son. It could only fall into unauthorized hands because it was stolen – in the first instance, at any rate. Hence the curse on all those who possess it. They have no right to it, you see.'

'I like that!' Mary Norrington exclaimed angrily. 'I paid a perfectly fair price for that box.' Her anger was the greater because it was not strictly ethical to buy items before the jumble sale had started. She remembered Major Murphy had looked at her oddly at the time. 'There was nothing dishonest about my acquiring it,' she said defensively.

'How did Major Murphy get hold of it, do you know?'

'I told you, it belonged to Stella.'

'The woman who died of tetanus. Ah yes.'

Miss Whittaker stood up abruptly, clasping her hands behind her, feet astride. She looked oddly out of place among the chintz and afternoon tea-things of Throstle Cottage – too gaunt, too sallow, too much an archetype.

'Mary,' she announced, putting all the urgency into her words of which she was capable, 'you must get rid of that accursed box.'

'Certainly not. It's one of my favourite possessions.'

'If you don't you'll be dead in six months.'

'What ever are you talking about, Ellen? What has the box to do with me?'

'Merely that it promises death within a twelvemonth to all unlawful possessors. You've already had half your time.'

There was a moment's horrified silence. Then Mary Norrington gave a shaky laugh. 'You're not going to tell me you believe this nonsense, Ellen? You, a worker in the Christian mission field!'

'Christianity has nothing to do with it,' Miss Whittaker answered firmly. 'These magicians have a curious control over natural forces, to which the human body is as much subject as anything else. I needn't point out the coincidence of your having a heart attack three weeks after you first acquired the box. I beg you to get rid of it before further mischief comes upon you – as most assuredly it will.'

Her sincerity was so obvious that Mary Norrington began to hesitate. The heart attack that had so sorely reduced her had come like a bolt from the blue. There was no history of cardiac disorder in the family, and she herself had seemed as strong as an ox. Her doctor had been quite unable to account for it, although he assured her there was nothing unique about her case. What was even more disturbing was her failure to make a good recovery. Six months later she was still as weak as a kitten, and this had been preying on her mind.

None the less, she had no intention of yielding to Ellen Whittaker's superstition. Such a show of respect for heathen practice should receive no condonation from her.

'I hardly see how I can give the box away,' she said sweetly, 'now that you have acquainted me with the nature of the curse. It would be tantamount, surely, to murder. I do not think I could bring myself to commit it.'

'The best thing would be to return it to Tibet,' Miss Whittaker suggested, 'and hope that it falls into good hands.'

'There might be difficulties with the Customs declaration. Besides, can one send things to Tibet?'

'I have a friend in India who might help us.'

'Why go to so much trouble?' Alice Norrington asked. She had been listening uneasily to the argument, which reflected her own divided state of mind. On the one hand, her faith and reason were against it; on the other, was the fact that Mary was ill. And there was not only Mary, but also the previous owner, the late Mrs Murphy. Of course, both could be coincidence merely. All the same, it was unpleasantly odd.

But Alice's was a direct, uncomplicated nature. The devious was foreign to her mind. She was accustomed to going to the root of any problem, and her solutions were effective, if extreme. 'Why bother to return the box to Tibet?' she repeated. 'Why not simply destroy it here and now?'

Mary smiled at her with sisterly approval. 'An excellent notion, my dear.'

With Alice, thought was quickly succeeded by action. 'If you have no objection, I will attend to it straightaway. There is no doubt a hatchet in the cellar. I will chop it up for firewood at once.'

'I wouldn't, if I were you, Alice.' Miss Whittaker had gone very pale.

Both sisters regarded her in amazement. 'Ellen, what is it? Are you ill?'

'No, no. But you must not touch that box. It is dangerous.'

'I really must ask you to explain.'

'There is another line in the inscription,' Miss Whittaker whispered. 'It promises destruction to anyone attempting to destroy.'

'So one can neither keep the box nor destroy it. What can one do with it, may I ask?'

Miss Whittaker shook her head helplessly. 'You can only send it back.'

'Nonsense, Ellen.' Alice Norrington spoke very firmly. 'You must not allow these superstitious thoughts to get a hold. You will soon be little better than the heathen you are supposed to be converting. This error must be rooted out at once. I shall go to the cellar now and dispose of this ridiculous Tibetan magic box for ever. No –' as her friend put out a restraining hand – 'don't try to stop me. I have quite made up my mind.'

'You will regret it,' Ellen Whittaker murmured. 'You will regret it all your life, or what is left.'

Alice Norrington did not bother to answer, and a moment later they heard her going down the cellar stairs. The cellar was directly under the sitting-room, and they could hear her moving about, shifting the chopping-block into position and then a clatter as she dropped the axe. Mary Norrington jumped as though the blade had bitten her, but Miss Whittaker showed all the calmness of despair. A moment later they heard the first ringing blows of the hatchet, and perceptibly they both relaxed.

'When one is ill,' Mary said apologetically, 'one so easily becomes overwrought.'

'When one has spent long years on the Tibetan border,' Miss Whittaker responded bravely, 'one forgets that in England its standards do not apply.'

Before she had finished speaking, both women were paralysed by a hoarse and terrible cry. It rose out of the depths of the cellarage beneath them, an animal cry of anguish and pain and fear. The voice was recognizably Alice Norrington's. A moment later they heard her stumbling up the stairs.

Both listeners were on their feet in an instant, but Miss Whittaker was first through the door. The cellar door opened into the hall of Throstle Cottage. Alice Norrington had almost reached the top of the cellar stairs. She had been silent since that first inexplicable scream of terror, but they could hear the rasping of her breath. Mary was leaning, white-faced, upon the hall table. It fell to Miss Whittaker to move towards the cellar door.

She was half-way across the hall when Alice entered. Her features were still rigid from the shock she had undergone, blood was spurting from a hand on which three fingers were now missing, her protruding eyes were fixed unseeingly in space.

Mary hid her face in her hands with a little cry of horror, but it was not the first time Ellen Whittaker had faced emergency. She had seen violent death and bodies torn and broke, and her common sense and energy, as usual, did not fail to respond. Almost before her senses had recovered, her brain was active, propelling her body forwards, uttering commands.

'It's all right, Alice, don't be frightened. Mary, the doctor – quick! No, give me the table-napkins before you telephone. We must put a tourniquet on at once. Keep your head down, Alice, it may help you to feel better. I promise you, we'll not let you die of this.'

Half carrying, half dragging, she got the fainting Alice to a chair. Mary was already dialling the doctor's number as she applied pressure to the artery in the wrist. To her relief, the blood-spurts slackened and slowed to nothing, although the blood continued to well out copiously. Alice moaned and stirred and endeavoured to sit upright.

'It's all right,' Miss Whittaker reassured her. 'It's better you shouldn't look.'

Alice took no notice of the injunction. Her eyes were still staring and wild. From the sitting-room Mary's voice on the telephone came faintly: '. . . my sister . . . an accident . . . come at once . . .'

Suddenly Alice gripped her friend's arm with unexpected intensity. Her fingertips were cold on Miss Whittaker's flesh.

'It was the box,' she whispered hoarsely. 'It moved as I was about to strike it and dragged my fingers under the axe. Otherwise it would never have happened. But the box moved and I couldn't stop it. I tell you, Ellen, the Tibetan box moved!'

While Alice Norrington was in hospital, Miss Whittaker remained at Throstle Cottage in a position which she rapidly recognized as that of unpaid companion-drudge. There was no doubt that Mary Norrington had been shaken by her sister's accident. There was equally no doubt that with her heart condition shock and distress were liable to bring on another attack, which attack might possibly prove fatal; but this was problematical. Miss Whittaker could not feel that it warranted the day-in, day-out attendance she was obviously expected to provide. By the end of the first week she had enough not only of Mary's tyranny, but of Mary's patronage, which was worse.

It began with Miss Whittaker's appearance. Mary had no scruples about making personal remarks. Indeed, it amused Miss Whittaker to note the resemblance between the sisters, except that, whereas Alice spent her energies in the mission field, Mary Norrington pursued lesser ends nearer home. But she adopted the same bludgeoning tactics as her sister, with possibly comparable results, for while there was no doubt that Alice was effective in securing conversions, Miss Whittaker wondered to what extent they represented change of heart. She was half amused, half horrified to find herself giving way to Mary, putting cold cream on her face for the first time in twenty years, and treating her dry hair to an oil bath before a special shampoo. She consoled herself that she was doing it for Alice, but she was too honest to accept such glazing for long. She was doing it for the sake of peace and quietness. Alice's converts presumably did the same.

The thought of Alice as a colleague brought back to her the tragic aspect of the affair, for with her maimed hand it seemed unlikely that Alice would ever be passed fit for service in the mission field again. Moreover, her nervous system had suffered a severe shock, and the tense, fevered woman who laid her sound hand like a claw on Miss Whittaker's arm whenever they were alone together and besought her to get rid of the Tibetan box was someone very different from the active, no-nonsense colleague whom Ellen Whittaker had always known. By common consent they did not mention the matter to Mary, who knew nothing of her sister's allegation about the box.

Mary tended, indeed, to dismiss the element of superstition in the accident. 'Alice has always considered herself too practical,' she claimed. 'It was inevitable that she should some day have to recognize her limitations. Why, she could not even thinly slice a loaf of bread! To attempt to chop up hardwood was sheer folly.'

Miss Whittaker thought she did not exaggerate, though of course it had not been Mary who had had to venture into the cellar, blood-bespattered like a slaughter-house, and retrieve the box to which Alice Norrington's fingers were adhering, glued into place by sticky, congealing blood. If it had been, Miss Whittaker thought grimly, she could not have borne to restore the box to its accustomed place in the sitting-room, where its incongruous presence was now emphasized by a gash from the axe along the edge of the lid. She wondered if Mary would be insensitive enough to leave the box there when her sister came out of hospital. She was rather afraid that she would.

Her surprise and relief were therefore considerable when, returning from a visit to Alice one afternoon, she saw that the box had gone from the rosewood work-table in the window. Before she could inquire the reason, Mrs Forrest came in to say that Miss Mary was lying down in her room.

'Is she worse?' Miss Whittaker demanded, fearing some fresh disaster.

'The Vicar called and then she was took poorly. She said I was to ask you to go in.'

The Vicar's visits were not usually distressing. Miss Whittaker hastened to ascertain the facts. Tapping at the door of the bedroom (the former dining-room, since Mary was now unable to manage stairs), she found her sitting up in bed with the same tense and twitching anxiety that her injured sister habitually displayed.

'What's the matter?' Miss Whittaker asked non-committally.

'I have had a very serious shock. It means that you are right about the box, Ellen. We must certainly dispose of it at once.'

Miss Whittaker wondered what the Vicar could have had to do with this development. She was not left long in doubt.

'We had been speaking of Alice's accident,' Mary Norrington said faintly, 'and I remembered what you said about the box – how it must have been stolen in the first place because such objects were always handed down. It occurred to me to ask the Vicar if he had any idea how Stella had acquired it, and to my surprise he had. He said she inherited it from her father only six months before she died.'

'An old family treasure?' Miss Whittaker inquired softly, though the sinking of her heart already told her this was not going to prove to be the case.

'Not at all. The old man had bought it at an auction without even knowing what it was. He was something of an antique collector, and had bid for a mahogany roll-top desk. When the desk was delivered, the box was discovered in a drawer. The auctioneer said he could reckon it as part of the lot. He had no interest in it and stored it away in an attic, where it was found only after his death. Because he too died, Ellen, within a year of acquiring it. He caught pneumonia and it proved too much for his heart. So it begins to look as if you're right about the curse, doesn't it? Especially when I tell you this last bit.

'You remember I told you Stella's father bought the box accidentally at an auction? Well, do you know why that auction was taking place?'

'I can guess,' Miss Whittaker murmured *sotto voce*. Mary Norrington seemed not to hear.

'The owner of the house had been killed in a car crash,' she whispered. 'His widow put everything up for sale. I don't know how long he'd had the box or who'd had it before him, but I am certain the box was to blame. So many deaths cannot be coincidence. I was foolish not to have believed you before. There is clearly something noxious about the object. I have had Mrs Forrest put it in the garden shed.'

'That won't save you,' Miss Whittaker said automatically.

Mary Norrington gripped her arm. 'Then what will? We cannot give it away because it will bring destruction upon others, and we know what happened when Alice tried to chop it up. Of course she is, as I say, rather clumsy, but I should not wish anyone else to try. How, then, are we to rid ourselves of this evil object? Or must I, like its previous owners, die?'

'We could burn it,' Miss Whittaker said slowly. 'Magic is supposed to have no power against fire.'

'Like burning a witch in the old days?'

'Yes,' Ellen Whittaker answered. 'A little like that.'

'And would you be prepared to burn it? Do you think it would be safe for you to try?'

Miss Whittaker looked thoughtful. 'Yes, I think so. At any rate, I am prepared to make the attempt. Only not in the house – in the garden. I will do it tomorrow if it is fine.'

Mary Norrington relaxed against her pillows. 'Dear Ellen, what should I do without you? You are such a tower of strength. And I believe your hair is looking better for that oil treatment. We must remember to try another one quite soon.'

Miss Whittaker was for once glad to take up the subject of her appearance in preference to the burning of the box. She was reluctant to admit to Mary Norrington that her knowledge of magic was greater than she had disclosed. For Ellen Whittaker was intellectually adventurous, and by no means prepared to stop short at the limits of Christian belief when there was something outside it that seemed worth her exploration. In Nepal, she had made friends with a magician, who, besides much else, had taught her a secret sign, which would, he claimed, protect her from all danger should anyone ever lay a spell on her. Miss Whittaker had been suitably grateful, having witnessed Tibetan magic at work, but she had shortly afterwards been posted to Africa and had never needed to make use of the sign. She was relieved about this for several different reasons, not the least being that she felt it incompatible with her faith. To inquire into native magic was one thing; to resort to its ritual, something else. For this reason she had never mentioned her knowledge; in fact, she had half forgotten it herself, until the destruction of the Tibetan box became imperative and she realized that the task must fall to her. For she alone had the power to overcome its magic, provided she used the chosen agent, fire.

The next day was fine and almost windless. Miss Whittaker resolved to have her bonfire after lunch. The morning was spent in preparation, for she was anxious that nothing should go wrong. She had amassed a pile of leaves and withered branches, chrysanthemum stalks and rotting flower-heads, and to these she added firewood from the cellar, old newspapers and a paraffin-impregnated briquette. The pyre was built by the angle of the wall which at this point was bare of fruit trees, so that no living thing should suffer any harm.

Nevertheless, Miss Whittaker knew a certain uneasiness which common sense was unable to dispel. Perhaps it was this that made her place two buckets of water within easy reach of her prospective blaze. She was taking no chances with magic, and that included her own untried magic power. She was relieved when Mary Norrington announced that she would not be present at the incineration; she would not even watch from the sitting-room. This meant that there would be no one to witness the operation, for the nearest house was some little distance away. Mrs Forrest went home at two-thirty. Whatever happened, there would be no one there to see. If it became necessary to resort to the use of magic, Miss Whittaker could do so in secret and alone.

All the same, she sincerely hoped it would not be necessary and took all scientific precautions first. In addition to the two buckets of water, she equipped herself with tongs and a rake. Stout Oxfords and thick socks protected feet and ankles, and her hands were shielded by heavy gauntlet gloves. Her tweed skirt would have smothered fire sooner than kindle; the same went for her cardigan of Shetland wool. Her head was muffled in a scarf tied turban-fashion; not a single lock poked forth from underneath. Miss Whittaker was particularly careful with the turban, which was doing double duty that afternoon. Not only did it serve to protect her hair from ash-fragments, but it also concealed its unappetizingly greasy state, Miss Whittaker having submitted that morning to another of Mary Norrington's oil treatments, to be followed that evening by another special shampoo.

But between the morning and the evening came the afternoon, and Mary had retired for her rest. Clutching the box to her like a living creature, Miss Whittaker made a conspiratorial exit from the garden shed. The sun was shining with almost the warmth of summer. She felt herself sweating under her wool and tweed. The thought of fire-heat as well was intolerable. She had a sudden impulse to go back. The sharp contours of the box recalled her to a sense of duty. To leave it intact would mean that Mary Norrington must die; or if not Mary, some other innocent possessor. There was nothing for it; the box must be destroyed. And the burning of wood was an entirely natural process. There was no reason why she should feel this growing fear. Besides, if the worst happened and there were unnatural manifestations, she had only to make the sign. The magician had assured her it was infallible; whatsoever saw it must withdraw at once. She was probably the one person in England who could burn the box in safety. With trembling hands, she knelt and lighted the pyre.

The paraffin briquette caught at once and so did the paper; then the sticks kindled into a lively blaze. The twigs caught, and some of the drier dead leaves crackled. The smell of autumn burning filled the air. The bonfire was built high in the centre to support a level platform of sticks. Miss Whittaker approached and placed the Tibetan box upon it, then stepped backwards with a nervous little gasp.

The fire continued to burn brightly, with much crackling and showering of sparks. Then, as it spread to the damp leaves, stalks and flowerheads, it began to give off smoke. Miss Whittaker drew back, coughing. She had not supposed there would be so pungent a small. The fire, too, was burning less brightly. The afternoon seemed suddenly overcast. Looking up, she was astonished to see the smoke reeling in dense black clouds overhead, forming a tented ceiling above her, shutting out the sky and the sun. Meanwhile, its columns continued to wreathe upwards with a curious serpentine twine, so black they appeared to have substance and to move in response to some directional control.

The box had remained untouched in the centre of the bonfire, which was subsiding now into ash. So far as Miss Whittaker could see, the flames had not even touched it. She poked nervously with the rake, causing the platform of sticks to collapse with a sputter, tilting the box onto its side. The smoke was growing momently more acrid. It was becoming difficult to breathe. Miss Whittaker's eyes were watering. She clapped a handkerchief to her nose.

No doubt it was blurred vision that first made her perceive in the smoke-coils a vaguely remembered design. The double curve folding back on itself with a foot uplifted – was it not the dragon of the box? She wiped her eyes, blaming an overstrained nervous system, and looked again. But surely those were scales! Black and sinuous and almost stationary, the dragon reared up from the pyre. The terrible four-clawed feet were extended, groping. The head, in profile now, moved lightly from side to side. Miss Whittaker could see clearly the protective frill surrounding jaw and throat. The mandarin whiskers, even longer and thinner than she remembered them, trailed off into wisps of smoke. Now and again a puff exuded from the wide-spaced, flaring nostrils. Each time the cavernous mouth opened, there was a rolling belch of smoke.

The dragon seemed to be searching for something. Its body made sudden lurches in the air. It was for all the world as if it were playing blind man's buff with an imaginary opponent, who, fortunately for him, was never there. For there was no doubt of the dragon's hostile intentions. The groping claws were poised to seize and tear, and the size of the creature was such that a full-grown buffalo could have been dismembered as easily as a rat.

Miss Whittaker watched in horrified fascination. She had never seen anything to equal this. This was Tibetan magic with a vengeance – which was what the dragon appeared to desire. And she herself was its immediate object! Instinctively she drew a little further back. It was one thing to know the sign which would invalidate Tibetan magic, but quite another to have to put it into use. She flexed her fingers into the required position. At least she had not forgotten what to do. It was comforting to realize that she had power over this dragon, who looked so terrible and black.

A twig snapped sharply behind her. As if it had heard, the dragon turned its head. The long neck undulated gently. At the other end of the beast the barbed tail lashed. The smoke which composed the dragon had now completely blotted out the sky. The brightness of the flames had sunk to the dull glow of ashes. A wind seemed suddenly to have sprung up. It lifted the frill about the dragon's jaw-line. The mandarin whiskers streamed wide. The distended nostrils were a-quiver, as the dragon sought to scent its prey.

Suddenly the head poised in its veering peregrinations. Despite the smoke, it had caught Miss Whittaker's scent. With a tremendous writhe of all its coils and convolutions, it reared up to its full height. The claws were fully extended. Some four feet above her the bearded face looked down. It held an indescribable weight of menace. For all her confidence, Miss Whittaker began to be afraid. She raised her hand in the required ritual gesture, and looked up to meet the dragon's gaze. It peered down at her, evil and impassive, from the orbless sockets of its eyes.

With a little scream, Miss Whittaker flung herself sideways as the dragon's claws lashed down. They missed her, but she felt the wind of their passing. The dragon reared itself again. Now that it seemed to have her scent in its nostrils, it proved impossible for her to evade. Whichever way she darted in the smoke-pall, the blind monster's claws were just behind. There was a clatter as she knocked over the buckets. The water spread round her, soaking her socks and shoes. She was already exhausted and panting, the acrid fumes from the pyre were making her choke and cough. The house, the garden, seemed suddenly to have receded. There was only darkness and smoke.

On the fire which gave the dragon its being, the Tibetan box lay up-ended, still untouched. If only the flames would consume it, the dragon would surely cease to exist. Seizing the rake, Miss Whittaker made one last desperate assault upon it and thrust it into the heart of the fire, while the dragon reared itself above her, preparing to nail her to the ground. At the last moment, by a dexterous twist and feint, she escaped it. A shower of sparks rained down. They smouldered for a moment on her heavy woollen garments. Gasping, Miss Whittaker beat them out.

One corner of the box had taken; the wood was beginning to char. The dragon, though still dangerous, appeared to be shrinking. The clouds of smoke were less voluminous, less dense. Yet the heat seemed all at once to have become quite insupportable. Miss Whittaker had a sudden glimpse of the sun. She saw the house, the garden, the chrysanthemums and the apple-trees, the peaceful normality of it all. Then as an unquenched spark ignited her oil-soaked hair into combustion, she ran screaming towards the house.

She did not see her bonfire fall apart and burn itself out in isolated patches. She did not see the Tibetan box roll free. She saw only the horrified face of Mary Norrington, as she emerged from her room into the hall.

'Mary, help me! Help me!' Miss Whittaker screamed in terror, endeavouring to beat out the flames.

But Mary only stood white-faced and clutching the doorpost, unable either to move or speak. She saw before her Ellen Whittaker's body, on her head a strange corona of flame, the skin of the scalp already blackening and peeling, the face distorted beyond belief. The apparition from Hell was advancing towards her. The Tibetan box's curse was coming true. With a cry, Mary Norrington doubled up in the doorway. She was dead before her body reached the ground.

The 'Double Tragedy at Throstle Cottage', as the newspapers called it, did nothing to reassure Miss Alice Norrington as to the innocuous nature of the box. Nor did her convictions regarding this fire- and axe-scarred object and her insistence on returning it (via the late Miss Whittaker's friend in India) to Tibet do anything to reassure her superiors at evangelical headquarters as to her suitability for return to the mission field. She was compulsorily retired from service (without too much protesting on her part) and now lives on the south coast near Worthing and attends psychometry readings once a week.

# The Sea Raiders

## *H. G. Wells*

### I

Until the extraordinary affair at Sidmouth, the peculiar species *Haploteuthis ferox* was known to science only generically, on the strength of a half-digested tentacle obtained near the Azores, and a decaying body pecked by birds and nibbled by fish, found early in 1896 by Mr Jennings, near Land's End.

In no department of zoological science, indeed, are we quite so much in the dark as with regard to the deep-sea cephalopods. A mere accident, for instance, it was that led to the Prince of Monaco's discovery of nearly a dozen new forms in the summer of 1895; a discovery in which the before-mentioned tentacle was included. It chanced that a cachalot was killed off Terceira by some sperm whalers, and in its last struggles charged almost to the Prince's yacht, missed it, rolled under, and died within twenty yards of his rudder. And in its agony it threw up a number of large objects, which the Prince, dimly perceiving they were strange and important, was, by a happy expedient, able to secure before they sank. He set his screws in motion, and kept them circling in the vortices thus created, until a boat could be lowered. And these specimens were whole cephalopods and fragments of cephalopods, some of gigantic proportions, and almost all of them unknown to science!

It would seem, indeed, that these large and agile creatures, living in the middle depths of the sea, must, to a large extent, for ever remain unknown to us, since under water they are too nimble for nets, and it is only by such rare unlooked-for accidents that specimens can be obtained. In the case of *Haploteuthis ferox*, for instance, we are still altogether ignorant of its habitat, as ignorant as we are of the breeding-ground of the herring or the sea-ways of the salmon. And zoologists are altogether at a loss to account for its sudden appearance on our coast. Possibly it was the stress of a hunger migration that drove it hither out of the deep. But it will be, perhaps, better to avoid necessarily inconclusive discussion, and to proceed at once with our narrative.

The first human being to set eyes upon a living *Haploteuthis* – the first human being to survive, that is, for there can be little doubt now that the wave of bathing fatalities and boating accidents that travelled along

the coast of Cornwall and Devon in early May was due to this cause –
was a retired tea-dealer of the name of Fison, who was stopping at a
Sidmouth boarding-house. It was in the afternoon, and he was walking
along the cliff path between Sidmouth and Ladram Bay. The cliffs in
this direction are very high, but down the red face of them in one place
a kind of ladder staircase has been made. He was near this when his
attention was attracted by what at first he thought to be a cluster of
birds struggling over a fragment of food that caught the sunlight, and
glistened pinkish-white. The tide was right out, and this object was not
only far below him, but remote across a broad waste of rock reefs covered
with dark seaweed and interspersed with silvery shining tidal pools. And
he was, moreover, dazzled by the brightness of the further water.

In a minute, regarding this again, he perceived that his judgement
was in fault, for over this struggle circled a number of birds, jackdaws
and gulls for the most part, the latter gleaming blindingly when the
sunlight smote their wings, and they seemed minute in comparison with
it. And his curiosity was, perhaps, aroused all the more strongly because
of his first insufficient explanations.

As he had nothing better to do than amuse himself, he decided to
make this object, whatever it was, the goal of his afternoon walk, instead
of Ladram Bay, conceiving it might perhaps be a great fish of some sort,
stranded by some chance, and flapping about in its distress. And so he
hurried down the long steep ladder, stopping at intervals of thirty feet
or so to take breath and scan the mysterious movement.

At the foot of the cliff he was, of course, nearer his object than he had
been; but, on the other hand, it now came up against the incandescent
sky, beneath the sun, so as to seem dark and indistinct. Whatever was
pinkish of it was now hidden by a skerry of weedy boulders. But he
perceived that it was made up of seven rounded bodies, distinct or
connected, and that the birds kept up a constant croaking and screaming,
but seemed afraid to approach it too closely.

Mr Fison, torn by curiosity, began picking his way across the wave-
worn rocks, and, finding the wet seaweed that covered them thickly
rendered them extremely slippery, he stopped, removed his shoes and
socks, and coiled his trousers above his knees. His object was, of course,
merely to avoid stumbling into the rocky pools about him, and perhaps
he was rather glad, as all men are, of an excuse to resume, even for a
moment, the sensations of his boyhood. At any rate, it is to this, no doubt,
that he owes his life.

He approached his mark with all the assurance which the absolute
security of this country against all forms of animal life gives its inhabitants. The round bodies moved to and fro, but it was only when he

surmounted the skerry of boulders I have mentioned that he realized the horrible nature of the discovery. It came upon him with some suddenness.

The rounded bodies fell apart as he came into sight over the ridge, and displayed the pinkish object to be the partially devoured body of a human being, but whether of a man or woman he was unable to say. And the rounded bodies were new and ghastly-looking creatures, in shape somewhat resembling an octopus, and with huge and very long and flexible tentacles, coiled copiously on the ground. The skin had a glistening texture, unpleasant to see, like shiny leather. The downward bend of the tentacle-surrounded mouth, the curious excrescence at the bend, the tentacles, and the large intelligent eyes, gave the creatures a grotesque suggestion of a face. They were the size of a fair-sized swine about the body, and the tentacles seemed to him to be many feet in length. There were, he thinks, seven or eight at least of the creatures. Twenty yards beyond them, amid the surf of the now returning tide, two others were emerging from the sea.

Their bodies lay flatly on the rocks, and their eyes regarded him with evil interest; but it does not appear that Mr Fison was afraid, or that he realized that he was in any danger. Possibly his confidence is to be ascribed to the limpness of their attitudes. But he was horrified, of course, and intensely excited and indignant at such revolting creatures preying upon human flesh. He thought they had chanced upon a drowned body. He shouted to them, with the idea of driving them off, and, finding they did not budge, cast about him, picked up a big rounded lump of rock, and flung it at one.

And then, slowly uncoiling their tentacles, they all began moving towards him – creeping at first deliberately, and making a soft purring sound to each other.

In a moment, Mr Fison realized that he was in danger. He shouted again, threw both his boots and started off, with a leap, forthwith. Twenty yards off he stopped and faced about, judging them slow, and behold! the tentacles of their leader were already pouring over the rocky ridge on which he had just been standing!

At that he shouted again, but this time not threatening, but a cry of dismay, and began jumping, striding, slipping, wading across the uneven expanse between him and the beach. The tall red cliffs seemed suddenly at a vast distance, and he saw, as though they were creatures in another world, two minute workmen engaged in the repair of the ladder-way, and little suspecting the race for life that was beginning below them. At one time he could hear the creatures splashing in the pools not a dozen feet behind him, and once he slipped and almost fell.

They chased him to the very foot of the cliffs, and desisted only when he had been joined by the workmen at the foot of the ladder-way up the cliff. All three of the men pelted them with stones for a time, and then hurried to the cliff top and along the path towards Sidmouth, to secure assistance and a boat, and to rescue the desecrated body from the clutches of these abominable creatures.

2

And, as if he had not already been in sufficient peril that day, Mr Fison went with the boat to point out the exact spot of his adventure.

As the tide was down, it required a considerable detour to reach the spot, and when at last they came off the ladder-way, the mangled body had disappeared. The water was now running in, submerging first one slab of slimy rock and then another, and the four men in the boat – the workmen, that is, the boatman, and Mr Fison – now turned their attention from the bearings off shore to the water beneath the keel.

At first they could see little below them, save a dark jungle of laminaria, with an occasional darting fish. Their minds were set on adventure, and they expressed their disappointment freely. But presently they saw one of the monsters swimming through the water seaward, with a curious rolling motion that suggested to Mr Fison the spinning roll of a captive balloon. Almost immediately after, the waving streamers of laminaria were extraordinarily perturbed, parted for a moment, and three of these beasts became darkly visible, struggling for what was probably some fragment of the drowned man. In a moment the copious olive-green ribbons had poured again over this writhing group.

At that all four men, greatly excited, began beating the water with oars and shouting, and immediately they saw a tumultuous movement among the weeds. They desisted to see more clearly, and as soon as the water was smooth, they saw, as it seemed to them, the whole sea bottom among the weeds set with eyes.

'Ugly swine!' cried one of the men. 'Why, there's dozens!'

And forthwith the things began to rise through the water about them. Mr Fison has since described to the writer this startling eruption out of the waving laminaria meadows. To him it seemed to occupy a considerable time, but it is probable that really it was an affair of a few seconds only. For a time nothing but eyes, and then he speaks of tentacles streaming out and parting the weed fronds this way and that. Then these things, growing larger, until at last the bottom was hidden by their intercoiling forms, and the tips of tentacles rose darkly here and there into the air above the swell of the waters.

One came up boldly to the side of the boat, and, clinging to this with three of its sucker-set tentacles, threw four others over the gunwale, as if with an intention either of oversetting the boat or of clambering into it.

Mr Fison at once caught up the boathook, and, jabbing furiously at the soft tentacles, forced it to desist. He was struck in the back and almost pitched overboard by the boatman, who was using his oar to resist a similar attack on the other side of the boat. But the tentacles on either side at once relaxed their hold at this, slid out of sight, and splashed into the water.

'We'd better get out of this,' said Mr Fison, who was trembling violently. He went to the tiller, while the boatman and one of the workmen seated themselves and began rowing. The other workman stood up in the fore part of the boat, with the boathook, ready to strike any more tentacles that might appear. Nothing else seems to have been said. Mr Fison had expressed the common feeling beyond amendment. In a hushed, scared mood, with faces white and drawn, they set about escaping from the position into which they had so recklessly blundered.

But the oars had scarcely dropped into the water before dark, tapering, serpentine ropes had bound them, and were about the rudder, and creeping up the sides of the boat with a looping motion came the suckers again. The men gripped their oars and pulled, but it was like trying to move a boat in a floating raft of weeds. 'Help here!' cried the boatman, and Mr Fison and the second workman rushed to help lug at the oar.

Then the man with the boathook – his name was Ewan, or Ewen – sprang up with a curse, and began striking downward over the side, as far as he could reach, at the bank of tentacles that now clustered along the boat's bottom. And, at the same time, the two rowers stood up to get a better purchase for the recovery of their oars. The boatman handed his to Mr Fison, who lugged desperately, and, meanwhile, the boatman opened a big clasp-knife, and, leaning over the side of the boat, began hacking at the spiring arms upon the oar shaft.

Mr Fison, staggering with the quivering rocking of the boat, his teeth set, his breath coming short, and the veins starting on his hands as he pulled at his oar, suddenly cast his eyes seaward. And there, not fifty yards off, across the long rollers of the incoming tide, was a large boat standing in towards them, with three women and a little child in it. A boatman was rowing, and a little man in a pink-ribboned straw hat and whites stood in the stern, hailing them. For a moment, of course, Mr Fison thought of help, and then he thought of the child. He abandoned his oar forthwith, threw up his arms in a frantic gesture, and screamed to the party in the boat to keep away 'for God's sake!' It says much for the modesty and courage of Mr Fison that he does not seem to be aware that there was any quality of heroism in his action at this juncture. The oar he had abandoned was at once drawn under, and presently reappeared floating about twenty yards away.

At the same moment Mr Fison felt the boat under him lurch violently, and a hoarse scream, a prolonged cry of terror from Hill, the boatman, caused him to forget the party of excursionists altogether. He turned, and saw Hill crouching by the forward rowlock, his face convulsed with terror, and his right arm over the side and drawn tightly down. He gave now a succession of short, sharp cries, 'Oh! oh! oh!' Mr Fison believes that he must have been hacking at the tentacles below the water-line, and have been grasped by them, but, of course, it is quite impossible to say now certainly what had happened. The boat was heeling over, so that the gunwale was within ten inches of the water, and both Ewan and the other labourer were striking down into the water, with oar and boathook, on either side of Hill's arm. Mr Fison instinctively placed himself to counterpose them.

Then Hill, who was a burly, powerful man, made a strenuous effort, and rose almost to a standing position. He lifted his arm, indeed, clean out of the water. Hanging to it was a complicated tangle of brown ropes; and the eyes of one of the brutes that had hold of him, glaring straight and resolute, showed momentarily above the surface. The boat heeled more and more, and the green-brown water came pouring in a cascade over the side. Then Hill slipped and fell with his ribs across the side, and his arm and the mass of tentacles about it splashed back into the water. He rolled over; his boot kicked Mr Fison's knee as that gentleman rushed forward to seize him, and in another moment fresh tentacles had whipped about his waist and neck, and after a brief, convulsive struggle, in which the boat was nearly capsized, Hill was lugged overboard. The boat righted with a violent jerk that all but sent Mr Fison over the other side, and hid the struggle in the water from his eyes.

He stood staggering to recover his balance for a moment, and as he did so, he became aware that the struggle and the inflowing tide had carried them close upon the weedy rocks again. Not four yards off a table of rock still rose in rhythmic movements above the inwash of the tide. In a moment Mr Fison seized the oar from Ewan, gave one vigorous stroke, then, dropping it, ran to the bows and leapt. He felt his feet slide over the rock, and, by a frantic effort, leapt again towards a further mass. He stumbled over this, came to his knees, and rose again.

'Look out!' cried someone, and a large drab body struck him. He was knocked flat into a tidal pool by one of the workmen, and as he went down he heard smothered, choking cries, that he believed at the time came from Hill. Then he found himself marvelling at the shrillness and variety of Hill's voice. Someone jumped over him, and a curving rush of foamy water poured over him, and passed. He scrambled to his feet dripping, and, without looking seaward, ran as fast as his terror would let him shoreward. Before him, over the flat space of scattered rocks, stumbled the two workmen – one a dozen yards in front of the other.

He looked over his shoulder at last, and, seeing that he was not pursued, faced about. He was astonished. From the moment of the rising of the cephalopods out of the water, he had been acting too swiftly to fully comprehend his actions. Now it seemed to him as if he had suddenly jumped out of an evil dream.

For there were the sky, cloudless and blazing with the afternoon sun, the sea weltering under its pitiless brightness, the soft creamy foam of the breaking water, and the low, long, dark ridges of rock. The righted boat floated, rising and falling gently on the swell about a dozen yards from shore. Hill and the monsters, all the stress and tumult of that fierce fight for life, had vanished as though they had never been.

Mr Fison's heart was beating violently; he was throbbing to the finger-tips, and his breath came deep.

There was something missing. For some seconds he could not think clearly enough what this might be. Sun, sky, sea, rocks – what was it? Then he remembered the boatload of excursionists. It had vanished. He wondered whether he had imagined it. He turned, and saw the two workmen standing side by side under the projecting masses of the tall pink cliffs. He hesitated whether he should make one last attempt to save the man Hill. His physical excitement seemed to desert him suddenly, and leave him aimless and helpless. He turned shoreward, stumbling and wading towards his two companions.

He looked back again, and there were now two boats floating, and the one farthest out at sea pitched clumsily, bottom upward.

# 3

So it was *Haploteuthis ferox* made its appearance upon the Devonshire coast. So far, this has been its most serious aggression. Mr Fison's account, taken together with the wave of boating and bathing casualties to which I have already alluded, and the absence of fish from the Cornish coasts that year, points clearly to a shoal of these voracious deep-sea monsters prowling slowly along the sub-tidal coastline. Hunger migration has, I know, been suggested as the force that drove them hither; but, for my own part, I prefer to believe the alternative theory of Hemsley. Hemsley holds that a pack or shoal of these creatures may have become enamoured of human flesh by the accident of a foundered ship sinking among them, and have wandered in search of it out of their accustomed zone; first waylaying and following ships, and so coming to our shores in the wake of the Atlantic traffic. But to discuss Hemsley's cogent and admirably stated arguments would be out of place here.

It would seem that the appetites of the shoal were satisfied by the catch of eleven people – for so far as can be ascertained, there were ten

772        Realms of Darkness

people in the second boat, and certainly these creatures gave no further signs of their presence off Sidmouth that day. The coast between Seaton and Budleigh Salterton was patrolled all that evening and night by four Preventive Service boats, the men in which were armed with harpoons and cutlasses, and as the evening advanced, a number of more or less similarly equipped expeditions, organized by private individuals, joined in. Mr Fison took no part in any of these expeditions.

About midnight excited hails were heard from a boat about a couple of miles out at sea to the south-east of Sidmouth, and a lantern was seen waving in a strange manner to and fro and up and down. The nearer boats at once hurried towards the alarm. The venturesome occupants of the boat, a seaman, a curate, and two schoolboys, had actually seen the monsters passing under their boat. The creatures, it seems, like most deep-sea organisms, were phosphorescent, and they had been floating five fathoms deep or so, like creatures of moonshine through the blackness of the water, their tentacles retracted and as if asleep, rolling over and over, and moving slowly in a wedge-like formation towards the south-east.

These people told their story in gesticulated fragments, as first one boat drew alongside and then another. At last there was a little fleet of eight or nine boats collected together, and from them a tumult, like the chatter of a market-place, rose into the stillness of the night. There was little or no disposition to pursue the shoal, the people had neither weapons nor experience for such a dubious chase, and presently – even with a certain relief, it may be – the boats turned shoreward.

And now to tell what is perhaps the most astonishing fact in this whole astonishing raid. We have not the slightest knowledge of the subsequent movements of the shoal, although the whole south-west coast was now alert for it. But it may, perhaps, be significant that a cachalot was stranded off Sark on 3rd June. Two weeks and three days after this Sidmouth affair, a living *Haploteuthis* came ashore on Calais sands. It was alive, because several witnesses saw its tentacles moving in a convulsive way. But it is probable that it was dying. A gentleman named Pouchet obtained a rifle and shot it.

That was the last appearance of a living *Haploteuthis*. No others were seen on the French coast. On the 15th of June a dead body, almost complete, was washed ashore near Torquay, and a few days later a boat from the Marine Biological station, engaged in dredging off Plymouth, picked up a rotting specimen, slashed deeply with a cutlass wound. How the former specimen had come by its death it is impossible to say. And on the last day of June, Mr Egbert Caine, an artist, bathing near Newlyn, threw up his arms, shrieked, and was drawn under. A friend bathing with him made no attempt to save him, but swam at once for the shore.

This is the last fact to tell of this extraordinary raid from the deeper sea. Whether it is really the last of these horrible creatures it is, as yet, premature to say. But it is believed, and certainly it is to be hoped, that they have returned now, and returned for good, to the sunless depths of the middle seas, out of which they have so strangely and so mysteriously arisen.

# A Thin Gentleman with Gloves

*Simon West*

At first glance you would have thought Corbin Bellaman an old duffer who had long ago run to seed. At second, you might have considered him a benign and harmless fellow who was somebody's grandfather. As a matter of fact, Bellaman was distinctly on the shady side; he was a crafty barrister in his late fifties who had for better than twenty years been the last resort of fences, petty thieves, murderers, embezzlers, and eccentrics – like Alonzo Potter. Bellaman had done very well for himself in those two decades plus, but Alonzo Potter was his downfall. Not at all in the way one might suspect, however. He got along very well with Alonzo alive; but Alonzo dead was a different matter entirely.

Alonzo Potter, almost alone among Bellaman's clients, was not a criminal. That is to say, he was not obviously one; the fact is, no one knew very much about him, except that he had once written a book which a great many people had burned with a lot of public and private to-do, since it was a book purporting to tell the secrets of black magic, necromancy, sorcery, and the like. At the time Bellaman first knew his client, Potter was already an old man, a wizened, stooped figure of a man who got around with the aid of a cane, and was never without a tall, gangling companion, who walked a little behind him and to one side, like a mendicant, holding his head bowed and saying nothing. This might have occasioned considerable comment if Potter had gone out much; but he did not; he kept to his out-of-the-way house in Soho, living quietly, despite the queer stories that got around about strange happenings in his house, and eventually dying quietly, leaving Bellaman to execute his will, which revealed that there was a little matter of fifty thousand pounds to be bestowed upon Miss Clarice Tregardis, an old flame of Potter's.

Despite his dealings with the underworld, Bellaman had never in his life seen fifty thousand pounds all in one lump, and the prospects of having so much money under his control was an exciting one. However, it was not until he had seen Miss Clarice Tregardis that any thought of appropriating the money entered his head. He had supposed that Miss Tregardis was most likely a chorus girl with a dubious past and a questionable present; but when she came to his office in response to his request, she turned out to be a pleasant old lady who was rather vague about the reason she had been sent for, and remembered Potter as an unsuccessful suitor – 'A nice boy, to be sure, Mr Bellaman, and for a long time we were very dear friends, *very dear* – but, time and events! Well, you know how it is, I'm sure, Mr Bellaman.'

'Well, he's left you all his money, Miss Tregardis,' said Bellaman.

'Dear me! How surprising! But then, he always used to do such queer things! Is it very much?'

It was then that the idea of appropriating some of Potter's money for his own use occurred to Bellaman; he had been telling himself all along that he would charge a nice fat fee for acting as executor of the will; but now he realized that Miss Tregardis had no idea at all how much Potter might have left, and, since she was obviously in poor circumstances, virtually any sum at all would be satisfactory. A chorus girl might have raised an immediate outcry and demanded to see the papers, but this old lady would be only too happy to leave it all in Bellaman's hands and take whatever he cared to hand out to her.

'The exact sum hasn't been computed as yet, Miss Tregardis,' said Bellaman cautiously, 'but when the tax to the Crown has been deducted, I have no doubt it will leave your fairly comfortable for a while.'

That was putting it nicely, he thought.

'Oh, really!' she said. 'Then perhaps I could buy myself a few new dresses, and a coat, and perhaps I could even have my apartment refurnished. Yes, perhaps I could!'

'I think you could,' agreed Bellaman – she might as well be assured of that much; it would not take a large percentage of the total sum left in his predatory hands. 'Would you care to retain legal representation, Miss Tregardis, or are you content to leave the matter in my hands?'

'Oh, if Alonzo trusted you, I'm sure I can, too,' she said naïvely, and departed.

Bellaman had not expected it to be that easy.

He set about laying his plans at once. Of course, he did not intend to take any unnecessary chances; the old lady might, like as not, have some inquisitive relative who might poke his nose into the affair and demand a full accounting; so, to take care of any such contingency, Bellaman determined to rig up dummy papers and a plausible account of doctored expenses in connection with the disposal of the money for anyone to see on demand. He toyed with the idea of just decamping with the entire sum, but then there would be the tax collectors for the Crown, and besides, he was comfortable where he was, and there was no need of leaving his routine or his business, which was drawn largely from

Whitechapel, Limehouse, Soho, and Wapping along the Thames; more unsavoury areas of London could hardly be imagined.

His plans were laid, with the care of an old master.

He began by abstracting a modest sum – a thousand pounds – with which to play the races; he did this with the idea that if he could make a goodly sum by so doing, he need not deduct as much as he had planned from Potter's hoard. Gambling was Bellaman's weakness; he might have been the owner of a comfortable nest-egg if he had not insisted upon trying to double or triple every fee he took in, with the result that he was constantly living from hand to mouth.

He lost the thousand pounds.

Moreover, he had a most disagreeable experience at the races. Just after he had placed his money, he fancied that someone tapped him on the shoulder, and, turning around to look, he did not immediately see anyone he knew; but then saw, standing a little distance away, a tall, thin gentleman wearing a bowler hat not unlike that Alonzo Potter had worn, and with a certain familiarity about him. He turned away, wondering where he could have seen him before; but in a flash he remembered. It was the silent companion who had always appeared with Potter, and who had vanished completely on the day that Potter was found dead. He looked back, but the fellow had gone. The disagreeable aspect of this trivial event lay not in the event itself but in the uncomfortable twinge it gave to his vestigial conscience, particularly after he had lost the money.

Before he dipped further into Potter's funds, he determined to conduct an inquiry into the identity of Potter's one-time companion, to discover for himself whether he might have any knowledge which would be brought to the attention of Clarice Tregardis.

He worked at it for a week, utilizing every source of underworld information that was his.

At the end of that time he was not one whit better informed than he had been before. No one knew anything whatever about Potter's companion save that he was never known to speak, no one had ever seen his face, the fellow habitually wore gloves, he was thin to emaciation, and he shuffled along after Potter more like a dog than a fellow human being. That he had disappeared completely after Potter's death, everyone was agreed. While the lack of information annoyed Bellaman, nevertheless, the unanimity of opinion about the fellow's disappearance was reassuring.

He closed the incident by coming to the conclusion that he had mistaken someone else for the cadaverous companion of Alonzo Potter.

After the lapse of a week, he tried the races once more, this time with two thousand pounds, in that sublime confidence which always obsesses the gambler and leads him to believe that he can recoup previous losses as if by a magic windfall, convincing him each time he ventures anew that his luck must turn by that mythical law of chance, and that this is the time.

But this was not Bellaman's time. Far from it.

He lost not only Potter's two thousand, but also ten and six of his own. Moreover, all the way back to his office he could not shake himself of the conviction that he was being followed. Naturally, being guilty of such peccadilloes, he imagined that the police might be keeping an eye on him, and kept looking for anything resembling an officer; but of course, the ludicrousness of this presently impressed him, and his range of vision became more general. It was then that he saw the thin man, with his gangling arms and his gloved fingers, shuffling along as unobtrusively as possible half a block behind him.

He stopped the first passer-by to whom he came, caught him by the arm, and said, 'Pardon me. I've lost my glasses, and I've been expecting a friend. He's a tall, thin fellow, who shuffles along, wears gloves, holds his head down so that his face is prectically invisible. I thought I heard him behind me, but I can't see well enough to be sure. Is there anyone fitting that description walking along behind me?'

After a moment of careful scrutiny, the passer-by, looking askance at Bellaman, as if the barrister had been drinking, assured him that there was no one even remotely answering that description in sight.

His forehead beaded with cold perspiration, Bellaman went directly to his office and took out Potter's will, thinking that perhaps he might have missed some reference to that mysterious companion in it, and hoping against hope that he would discover it without delay.

He did.

'As for Simeon Brown, who has been my constant companion for several years, he shall be considered released from the bondage I have put upon him, when the terms of this will shall have been carried out.'

That was all, nothing more. After he had read it a dozen times, Bellaman was more mystified than ever. No matter how one looked it it, it did not make sense. What bondage? How could the dead Potter exercise any choice in the matter of 'releasing' Simeon Brown – the thin gentleman with gloves who had manifested himself so curiously on these two occasions? No, the whole thing was fantastic.

All except the thin gentleman with gloves – Simeon Brown. Bellaman might have made a mistake the first time, but not the second. Bellaman was no fool. Clearly, there was more to this than met the eye. With a vague sense of uneasiness, the barrister laid his plans to go away for a while – in the company of as much of Miss Tregardis's legacy as he could make away with.

He paid the tax to the Crown, made out a preposterous bill, and converted certain of his own securities into more cash – just in case he should take it into his head not to come back at all. Then he prepared, when the time was ripe, to send a cheque for a thousand pounds to Miss Tregardis, supremely confident that she would be completely satisfied with this amount in lieu of what, unknown to her, she had coming.

However, he reasoned, before he did anything rash, there would be no harm in looking into the matter of Simeon Brown. Since that last disturbing glimpse of him hurrying down the street in his wake, Bellaman had seen nothing more of him; he did not connect with this fact the incident that he had kept his hands off Potter's money throughout this time.

He pursued a careful inquiry, investigating Potter's papers to the last of them. He came upon a great many extremely strange references to subjects which Bellaman thought properly belonged in the Middle Ages, when people still had a healthy respect and fear for witches, warlocks, and the like, and when spells and enchantments and potions were the order of the day. Curious, how old recluses, male and female, seemed to go in for spiritualism, table-rappings, ouija, and the like.

The late Mr Potter's activities, however, did not come under any one of these heads.

He had been a warlock; in his modest way, he had been a good warlock. He knew how to adapt even the most difficult of the old spells to his own uses; and he had left behind him a great many of these old spells, most of them in Latin, so that Bellaman did not take the trouble to decipher them. However, it was among them that Bellaman caught sight of the name of Simeon Brown, and after it, what appeared to be an address: *37, 213 Upper Leshaway*. At least, that is what it appeared to be; Bellaman could not be sure, for Potter's writing was spidery and small and not very certain. There was nothing else.

And even this turned out to be a false lead, Bellaman thought, when he tracked down the address, for 213 Upper Leshaway was not a house address at all, but the number of the gate post of a cemetery. Obviously Potter's script had been beyond Bellaman. There was a Latterby Lane, and there was also a Leshly Street – it might have been one of those; but both were at such a distance from his office that Bellaman was loath to go there.

However, before taking his final drastic step, he made careful note of his findings, together with his suppositions as to where he had made a mistake, and set out for a meeting with three of his old cronies, two of whom were medical men of a sort and had known the late Potter. With a directness singular for him, he told them about his experiences with Simeon Brown.

Peter Benfield, who was the oldest among them, opined that this may have been the same Brown with whom Potter had once had so much trouble.

'No, Sim died years ago,' offered Pearson.

Benfield smiled oddly, and turned to Bellaman. 'You know, Bellaman – you might be dealing with Potter's familiar.'

The others took up the theme at once, making sport of the barrister. There was no doubt of it, they averred, with many a wink and sly joke, Bellaman was being hounded by Potter's familiar. Stung, Bellaman suggested that someone might explain the meaning of the jest which was amusing them at his expense.

Oh, said Benfield, a familiar was just halfpenny magic for an old wizard like Potter. A familiar was a companion summoned from outside somewhere, to attend the wizard and obey his commands. A spell was put upon him by the wizard – if you went in for that sort of thing.

'A ghost?' asked Bellaman, with a poor attempt at concealing his ire at his companions.

'Well, I don't think I'd call it a ghost exactly,' conceded Benfield. 'But then, it might be that – or a skeleton, an imp, maybe even a corpse.'

He cackled mirthfully, much to Bellaman's disgust, so that the barrister did not know whether Benfield was joking or not. Wouldn't it have been just like old Potter, Benfield went on, to command Simeon Brown? It certainly would. But Pearson, who had a literal mind, reflected again that poor Brown had passed on some years ago.

Instead of clarifying the matter, it seemed that Bellaman only got himself more perplexed. This was annoying to a man of his calibre, and it was inevitable that he should chuck the whole thing and go ahead with his plans.

The tax to the Crown had been straightforward enough.

The carefully doctored bill, preposterous as it was, Bellaman put into his files, for any curious person to see if any kind of investigation should follow in the wake of his absence from his usual haunts.

Then he dispatched the cheque by the late post, and that evening he set out for Paddington to entrain for Aldershot, from whence he would cross the channel and lose himself somewhere in France or Switzerland.

Alas! for plans of mice and men!

Bellaman had scarcely stepped from the building which housed his office when he was conscious of someone walking along behind him. It was a dark night, and he was not at first listening, being busy with a reconsideration of his plans; only when he had passed the street light did he become aware of the fact that the sounds coming along behind him were rather a steadily mounting shuffling than orthodox footsteps. He looked back.

It was the thin gentleman with gloves!

A kind of panic seized Bellaman. He did not for an instant believe anything of the conversation he had had with Benfield and Pearson, but there was undeniably something uncanny about the appearance of old Potter's companion at moments such as this. He felt frantically for the money which he carried in a stout wallet in the inside pocket of his coat; it was safe, for it bulked large there and filled his questing hand. He increased his pace, his agile mind concerned now with some way of escape from Potter's companion.

There was an alley which led out into a brightly lit street where he might take the underground to the Praed Street station; it was a short cut, and by vanishing into its dark maw, Bellaman's chance of outdistancing his pursuer was much greater. Accordingly, he slipped across the street, keeping to the shadows, and, at the appropriate moment, he darted skilfully into the alley.

If he had had the proper kind of imagination, he would have thought twice about doing what he did. His foresight, however, was limited, and when first he heard the shuffling sound behind him, he was only annoyed that the fellow had seen him enter the alley. Then he was conscious of the increased pace of his pursuer; indeed, all within an instant, it seemed, the fellow was directly behind him.

Could it be?

He turned startled, and looked back.

Out of the alley's darkness came a pair of long thin arms reaching for him with gloved fingers, and behind it came an utterly horrible, soul-searing travesty of a face, whose eyeless sockets seemed to gleam with a hellish light, whose lipless mouth seemed to work in drooling ecstasy.

Bellaman did not have time even to scream.

In the morning Miss Clarice Tregardis received Mr Bellaman's cheque for a thousand pounds; there was also in her mailbox a well-filled wallet, the contents of which, added to the cheque, made up the precise sum which Miss Regardis was legally entitled to receive from Mr Potter's fifty-thousand pound legacy, minus the tax to the Crown.

Bellaman's disappearance was more than a nine day wonder.

The police ultimately got around to discovering that address he had written down and went out to investigate. Being possessed of far more imagination than the late Mr Bellaman, they proceeded at once to the Upper Leshaway cemetery, and went directly to lot thirty-seven, which presumably had been meant.

So it had. Lot thirty-seven held the grave of one Simeon Brown. Moreover, there was every evidence that the grave had been recently disturbed; so an exhumation order was got and the grave opened.

The grave contained the body of Corbin Bellaman, who had been strangled and otherwise badly mauled, together with the remains of the said Brown, badly decayed and partly skeletal, a tall, thin gentleman apparently, whose bony black-gloved fingers were curiously closed about Bellaman's neck.

It was a ghastly business, even for Scotland Yard. They issued a strongly worded statement in regard to the shocking vandalism accompanying the murder of the late Corbin Bellaman and hinted ominously that the entire mystery would soon be completely explained by the master minds behind the walls of that sacrosanct sanctuary of mysteries.

But, of course, it never was.

# The Case of the Haunted Château

## Dennis Wheatley

'France!' Bruce Hemmingway raised his eyebrows and looked inquiringly across the table at his curious little host. 'Would I like to go on a visit to the front? I'll say I would; but as an American and a neutral, I'd never get a pass.'

Neils Orsen smiled and scrutinized one of his long slender hands. 'I'm a neutral, too, but I've been invited to go over there to investigate a little matter. It won't actually be the Maginot Line, but it's in the *Zone des Armées* and I have permission to take an assistant, so I'm sure a pass for you could be arranged.'

'My dear Neils, I'd love to go,' the young international lawyer declared with rising excitement. 'Tell me all about it.'

'Two days ago General Hayes, who is an old friend of mine, came to see me,' Orsen began, his cool voice only slightly tinged with a Swedish accent. 'He has always been interested in psychical research and is now on leave from France. It seems that an old château which had been taken over by the British had to be abandoned as a billet because it is so badly haunted that even the officers refuse to stay in it.'

The big American lit a cigarette. 'Then it must be the grandfather of all hauntings. What form does it take?'

'As usual, it does not affect everyone, but at least one or two out of each group of men that has been stationed there have felt its influence, and the manifestations always occur at night. The wretched victim is apparently always taken by surprise, lets out a piercing yell, and throws some sort of fit. Afterwards they state that they heard nothing, saw nothing, but were stabbed through the hands or feet and paralysed, rooted to the spot, transfixed by an agonizing pain which racked their whole bodies. The curious thing is that these attacks have taken place in nearly every room in the house. However, the worst cases have occurred in the one and only bathroom and it was there, about ten days ago, that one victim died – presumably as the result of a heart attack. It was that which finally decided the authorities to evacuate the château.'

'How long has the haunting been going on?'

The Swede blinked his large pale-blue eyes, so curiously like those of his Siamese cat, Pāst, 'I'm not sure. You see, the château was empty and in a very dilapidated condition when the Army took over. I gather that it was untenanted for some considerable time before war started.'

'Was your friend able to find out the history of the place from the villagers?'

'Yes, and a most unpleasant story it is. But they seemed vague as to when the haunting began.'

'What was the story?'

'Before the French Revolution the château was owned by a really bad example of the French aristocracy of that time. Cruel, avaricious, and inordinately proud, the Victomte de Cheterau treated his serfs worse than animals, beating, imprisoning, and torturing them at his pleasure. One day he devised the sadistic idea of adding yet another thong to his whip by placing a local tax on nails. As you know, it's practically impossible to build anything without them, so the poorest peasants had to revert to the ancient, laborious practice of carving their own from the odd pieces of wood they could gather from the hedge-rows.'

'He must have been a swine.'

'Perhaps,' Neils agreed. 'But no man, however cruel, deserved such a frightful death.'

'How did he die?'

Orsen stared at his reflection in the polished table. 'One dark night, soon after the Revolution broke loose, his serfs crept into the château and pulled him out of bed. They dragged him to his business room and there they crucified him with their wooden nails. It took him three days to die; and they came each night to mock him in his agony with tantalizing jars of water and bowls of food.'

Bruce shuddered. 'Horrible – did anyone ever live in the château again?'

'I believe so; but no tenant has ever stayed for long in recent years. Of course, the villagers won't go near it. They are convinced that it's haunted, as the story of the Vicomte de Cheterau has been handed down from father to son for generations.'

Hemmingway leaned forward. 'Do you think these stabs the victims feel in their hands and feet are some sort of psychic repetition of the pains the Vicomte felt when the mob drove their wooden nails through his palms and insteps?'

'Quite possibly,' replied Orsen slowly. 'There are many well-authenticated cases of monks and nuns who have developed stigmata from too intensive a contemplation of the agony suffered by Jesus Christ at His crucifixion.'

'It sounds a pretty tough proposition, then. When do we leave?'

'The day after tomorrow.' Neils gently stroked the back of his Siamese cat and his big pale eyes were glowing. 'I may be able to show you a real Saati manifestation this time, Bruce; but we must take nothing for granted. You can leave all arrangements to me.'

A watery sun was shining through the avenue of lime trees, throwing chequered patterns on the wet gravel below, as the two friends were driven towards the château by a cheerful young captain into whose charge they had been given at the local HQ.

'General Hayes told me about you, Mr Orsen,' he was saying. 'I find it difficult to believe in spooks myself, but there's certainly something devilish going on in the old place, and we shall be jolly grateful if you can find it for us. Those cottages in the village are damned uncomfortable.'

Neils leaned forwards to peer through the window at the rearing pile of grey stone just ahead of them, and the captain added: 'Gloomy sort of place, isn't it?'

As Bruce stepped out of the car he thoroughly agreed. The silence was eerie, broken only by a monotonous sound of water dripping from the rain-sodden trees that surrounded the château and almost shut out the sky. A dank, musty smell greeted them as they entered; a rat scurried away into the dark shadows of the hall.

'Well, Neils, old man,' he said with a wry grin. 'This place certainly seems to have the right atmosphere.'

The little Swede did not appear to hear him. He was standing quite still, his large head thrown back and his eyes closed as if he were listening. Their guide gave an embarrassed cough. Unlike Bruce, he was not accustomed to Orsen's peculiarities, and he felt that ghost-hunting was at the best an unhealthy form of amusement.

'Shall we get a move on?' he asked abruptly. 'I mean, if you want me to show you round; it's quite a big place, and the light will be gone in less than an hour.'

Neils blinked, then fluttered one slender hand apologetically. 'Forgive me; please lead the way.'

They mounted the twisting stairs and as they passed the windows the evening light threw their shadows, elongated and grotesque, against the damp-sodden walls; no one spoke and the emptiness seemed to close in on them like a fog. As they wandered from room to room Neils followed behind the other two men humming a quiet old-fashioned tune to himself.

After an hour they made their way back to the hall and as they walked out towards the car their guide turned towards Orsen. 'Well, now you've seen it. Are you really going to spend the night here?'

The little man smiled. 'Certainly we are.'

Mentally shrugging his shoulders the captain helped Bruce to carry the luggage upstairs, then ironically wished them goodnight. When the sound of the car was lost in the distance Bruce returned to the ballroom and found Neils standing by one of the long bow-windows.

'Can you hear the sh-sh-sh of panniered dresses, the brittle laughter of powered ladies with their gallants, and the tapping of their heels as they dance a minuet to the tinkle of the harpsichord?' he said softly. His eyes stared blindly, and their pupils contracted. 'Or do you hear the hoarse cries of those ragged, half-starved creatures as they stumble through these rooms smashing everything in sight, their mouths slobbering with frantic desire for revenge? Can you hear the shrieks, hardly human in their terror, of the wretched Vicomte as he is dragged to his death by those who were once his slaves?'

'No,' said Bruce uneasily, 'but I'll believe you that these walls would have a tale to tell if they could only talk.'

'My friend, they have no need when the seventh child of a seventh child is listening.'

Bruce shivered, as an icy chill seemed to rise up from the bare floor. 'I'm hungry,' he said as brightly as he could. 'What about unpacking and having a little light on the scene?'

Neils smiled. 'Yes, we will eat and sleep here. We shall have to shade the candles though, as there aren't any blackout precautions. I suppose the Army thought this room too big to bother about. I see they've done the bedrooms and everywhere else downstairs.'

'What made you choose the ballroom?'

'Because Hayes told that it is one of the few rooms in which no one has yet been attacked; so we shall be able to see if the Force possesses harmful powers against humans anywhere in the house, or whether it can only become an evil manifestation in certain spots.'

While Bruce set out an appetizing array of food from the hamper on the floor, Neils unpacked his cameras. The American had seen them keep him company on more than one thrilling adventure, but their process, Orsen's invention, was a mystery to him. Neils explained them only by saying that their plates were abnormally sensitive. He said the same thing of his sound-recorder, an instrument like a miniature dictaphone.

Having finished their dinner with some excellent coffee, cooked on a primus stove, they went along to the big, old-fashioned bathroom to fix Orsen's first camera and his sound machine. As they entered the room Bruce wrinkled his nose. 'What a filthy smell! The drainage must be terrible.'

Neils agreed as he placed one instrument on the window-sill and one on the broad mahogany ledge that surrounded the old-fashioned bath.

He sealed the windows with fine silken threads and did the same to the door. Then, with their footsteps echoing behind them, they made a tour of the silent château, leaving the Swede's cameras in carefully selected places, till they came to the front hall, where Orsen left his last camera, and sealed the door leading to the back stairs with the remains of the reel of silk. Their job done they returned to the ballroom, and having made themselves as comfortable as possible with the rugs and cushions, settled down for the night.

Bruce could not sleep. They had lit a fire with some dry logs found in the kitchen and its dying flames sent a cavalcade of writhing shapes racing across the walls and ceiling.

Presently a moon shone through the uncertained windows; propping himself on his elbow Bruce started at the unfamiliar lines it etched on Neil's face as he lay on his back, breathing gently. Orsen's enormous domed forehead shone like some beautiful Chinese ivory as the cold white light glanced across it, and his heavy blue-veined lids and sensitive mouth were curiously like those of a woman. He was sound asleep, yet Bruce knew that if there were the slightest sound or if an evil presence approached, he would be alert and fully in command of all his faculties in a fraction of a second.

Bruce lay back reassured. He could hear the muffled scuffling of rats behind the wainscoting. At length he dozed off.

Suddenly a shrill scream rent the silence, tearing it apart with devastating hands of terror. Bruce sprang to his feet and rushed to the window. The driveway was brilliantly illuminated by the glare of the moon, but he could see nothing. Orsen sat up slowly. 'It's all right,' he murmured; 'only an owl.'

Nodding dumbly, Bruce returned to his couch, his heart thudding against his ribs.

Morning came at last, and after breakfast Orsen went off to examine his cameras. He found their plates negative and his seals all undisturbed, while the sound-machine recorded only the scrambling noise of rats. Resetting his apparatus, he returned to the ballroom. Bruce was staring gloomily out of the window at the steady downpour of rain now falling from a leaden sky. He wheeled round as Neils came in. 'Well?'

'Nothing. I think we'll go down to the village now. We might get a hot bath and you can have a drink. You look pretty done in.'

'Yes,' Bruce agreed laconically.

After lunch in the officers' Mess, Neils arranged with his friend to bring their provisions up to the château before dark and left him in the genial company of the officers. As the rain had ceased he had decided to go for a walk and wandered off, a queer little figure in the misty yellow light of the afternoon.

The woods that almost covered the estate were full of a quiet beauty as the dusty sunlight filtered through their branches onto the sharply scented earth below and their calm, ageless indifference to the travails of men filled Orsen with a delightful sense of being in another world. The evening passed slowly. Bruce played patience, while Orsen paced up and down like a small caged animal. He would never have admitted it, but his nerves were badly on edge, for, although they had lit a fire, the cold was intense, a thing that always made him feel ill. After dinner, having made a final inspection of his cameras, he boiled some water on the primus for a hot water bottle, and settled down in his improvised bed. Bruce followed suit.

The black moonless night dragged by on crippled feet, its silence disturbed only by the rats and the faint boom of gunfire in the distance. Morning found the two men pale and haggard. They fried themselves eggs and bacon, then went along to the bathroom, where the stench was now so appalling that they had to hold their noses.

Once again the camera plates proved negative and the seals were untouched; but on the record of the sound-machine there was a new noise. It came at intervals above the scuffling of the rats and was like that of someone beating with his fingernails irregularly against a pane of glass.

'What do you think it is?' Bruce asked excitedly.

Neils went over to the window and peered out. 'It's possible that it was caused by this branch of creeper,' he said, opening the window and breaking off the branch. 'If it was; the noise won't recur tonight.'

The day passed uneventfully and both men were curiously relieved when darkness fell once more.

Close on midnight Orsen slid out of bed noiselessly and crept along to the bathroom. On reaching it he stood motionless for a second. In the queer half-green light of his torch he resembled a ghost himself.

Not a sound disturbed the silence; even the rats seemed to have disappeared. Putting his ear to the key-hole he listened, but could hear nothing. He hesitated, then, grasping the door-handle, he twisted it sharply and with a vicious kick sent the door flying open, at the same instant flattening himself back against the wall.

Breathlessly, he waited, the unearthly quiet singing in his head. Still nothing happened. Making the sign of the Cross he muttered four words of power and, easing himself forward, peered into the bathroom. Only the horrible stench of decaying life and the heavy tomb-like atmosphere greeted him. He flashed his torch across the ceiling and sent its beam piercing into every corner, but his cameras were all unviolated. With a sigh of disappointment he closed the door swiftly behind him and retraced his steps.

After breakfast the next morning they developed the plates from those in the bathroom last, having found all the others blank. Those of the one on the window-sill showed the door open and Neils's head and shoulders. On the other was only the flash of his torch. They tried the sound-machine and a puzzled frown crossed Orsen's brow as once again they heard the faint noise like fingernails beating against the window.

'This is most peculiar,' he murmured, as the record ceased. 'I tore off that branch and I'll swear there was no sound perceptible to human ears when I was in the room ten hours ago.'

'Perhaps it had started before – or afterwards,' Bruce hazarded.

'No; the sound-machine does not start recording until the cameras operate. On our first night I set them to function automatically at midnight; but last night I fixed them so that they should not operate at all unless someone or something broke the threads across the window or the door. I set them off myself by entering the room, so that noise must have been going on.' He paused. 'I shall spend the coming night there myself.'

'Not on your own!' Bruce declared quickly. 'Remember, a man died in that room from – well, from unknown causes little more than a fortnight ago.'

A gentle smile illuminated Neil's face. 'I was hoping you would offer to keep me company; but I wouldn't agree to you doing so unless I felt confident I could protect you. I intend to make a pentacle; one of the oldest forms of protection against evil manifestations, and, fortunately, I brought all the things necessary for it in my luggage. But we must get a change of clothes in the village.'

That afternoon they began their preparations with handkerchiefs soaked in eau-de-Cologne tied over the lower part of their faces to counteract the appalling smell. First, they spring-cleaned the whole room with infinite care, Bruce scrubbing the floor and bath with carbolic soap, while Orsen went over the walls and ceiling with a mop which he dipped constantly in a pail of disinfected water.

'There must not be a speck of dust anywhere, particularly on the floor,' the Swede explained, 'since evil entities can fasten on any form of dirt to assist their materialization. That is why I asked the captain to lend us blankets, battle-dresses, and issue underclothes straight from new stocks in the quartermaster's stores. And now,' he went on, 'I want two glasses and a jug of water, also fruit and biscuits. We must have no material needs to tempt us from our astral stronghold should any dark force try to corrupt our will-power through our sub-conscious minds.'

When Bruce returned, Neils had opened a suit-case and taken from it a piece of chalk, a length of string, and a footrule. Marking a spot approximately in the centre of the room, he asked Bruce to hold the end of the string to it and, using him as a pivot, drew a large circle in chalk.

Next the string was lengthened and an outer circle drawn. Then the most difficult part of the operation began. A five-rayed star had to be made with its points touching the outer circle and its valleys resting upon the inner. But, as Neils pointed out, while such a defence could be highly potent if constructed with geometrical accuracy, should any of the angles vary to any marked degree or the distance of the apexes from the central point differ more than a fraction, the pentacle would prove not only useless, but even dangerous. 'This may all be completely unnecessary,' he added. We have no actual proof yet that an evil power is active here, but I have always thought that it was better not to spill the milk than to have to cry when it was done.'

Bruce smiled at the Swede's slightly muddled version of the old English proverb, but at the same time he heartily concurred with his friend's sentiments.

For an hour they measured and checked till eventually the broad white lines were drawn to Neils's satisfaction, forming the magical star in which it was his intention they should remain while darkness lasted. He then drew certain ancient symbols in its valleys and mounts, and when he had finished Bruce laid the blankets, glasses, water jug, and food in its centre. Meanwhile, Orsen was producing further impedimenta from his case. With lengths of asafoetida grass and blue wax he sealed the windows and bath-waste, making the Sign of the Cross over each seal as he completed it.

'That'll do for now. I must leave the door till we're settled in,' he said. 'I think we might as well go out and get some fresh air while we can.'

It was then nearly six o'clock. an hour later they returned to the château for an early supper. Almost before they had finished eating, dusk began to fall and Orsen glanced anxiously at the lengthening shadows. 'We'd better go now,' he said, gulping down the remains of his coffee.

Shivering with cold they undressed and reclothed themselves outside the bathroom. Once inside, the Swede sealed the door; then turning to Bruce gave him a long wreath of garlic flowers and a gold crucifix on a chain which he told him to hang round his neck. Unquestioningly the American obeyed and watched the little man follow suit. As they stepped into the pentacle, Neils gripped his friend by the hand, and said urgently:

'Now, whatever happens and whatever ideas you get about all this being nonsense, you must on no account leave the circle. The evil force, if there is one, is almost certain to try to undermine our defences through you, owing to your spiritual inexperience. *Please* remember what I've said.' Having huddled into their blankets and tied the handkerchiefs newly soaked in eau-de-Cologne over their faces, they settled down to wait.

Time plodded wearily by and as they had left their watches outside with their clothes they had no means of checking it. Conversation soon flagged owing to the difficulty of speaking through the wet masks, so the two men crouched in silence, each longing desperately for the coming of dawn. Outside, the trees sighed quietly and darkness held the château in its thrall.

'It's very odd, I can't sense any evil presence here; and if there were one I should have by now,' Orsen whispered after a long silence.

Bruce stiffened and peered through the darkness at the white blob that was Neils's face. 'Now, don't *you* start talking like that. Remember what you told *me*. It looks as though those things you mentioned a while ago are having a dig at you.'

'No,' Orsen muttered after a moment, 'no, it's not that. Will you give me some water, please, it's over on your side.'

Bruce put out his hand to feel for the jug. Without the least warning his strangled yell shattered the deep quiet of the night and he collapsed in a limp tangle over the Swede's legs.

Orsen stumbled to his feet, his mind reeling – the Thing was in the pentacle. *Inside it!* There, *with* them; at their elbows, instead of beyond the barrier which should have kept it out. Why had he felt no warning – no indication of evil?

Shouting aloud a Latin exorcism which would keep the evil at bay for a space of eleven human heart-beats, he stopped, grabbed Bruce under the armpits, and dragged him from the circle.

Once outside it he allowed himself a pause to get back his breath; knowing that since the Thing was *in* the pentacle the magic barrier would act like the bars of a cage and keep it from getting *out*. But would it? Even Neils was scared by such an unusual and extraordinary potent phenomenon.

Wrenching the door open he seized Bruce's unconscious form again and, exerting all his frail physical strength, hauled it along the passage. When at last he reached the ballroom sweat was pouring down his face and he was gasping as though his lungs would burst. Feverishly he searched for his torch and finding it threw its beam on Bruce's face. It was deathly pale, but with a sob of relief Neils felt the faintly beating heart beneath his hand.

A few minutes later Bruce came out of his faint, but he could remember nothing, save that when he had put out his hand for the water-jug it seemed as though a thousand knives had pierced his body; then everything had gone black.

Neils nodded as his friend finished. 'It's a good thing we left our blankets here. we'll try and get some sleep!' But he himself did not attempt to sleep. Puzzled and anxious, he remained on watch all night, and as the first rays of dawn crept through the windows he returned to the bathroom.

Two hours later he told Bruce: 'I think I've found the root of the evil, and I'm going down the village to borrow the largest electric battery I can find.'

'Whatever for?'

'Electric force can be used for many purposes,' was all Neils would say.

It was not until they had completed their evening meal that Neils undid a parcel and produced four bottles of champagne.

'Hullo! What's this?' Bruce exclaimed.

'I got them from the local *estaminet* this morning as I thought it was time we returned hospitality to some of the officers in the Mess. They're coming in about ten o'clock.'

'That's fine,' Bruce grinned. 'I reckon I deserve a party after last night.'

Soon after ten their friend the captain, a colonel, and three other officers arrived and they immediately began to make half-humorous inquiries about the ghost.

'Gentlemen,' replied Neils, 'I asked you up here because I hope to lay the ghost tonight; but we can't start work for an hour or two, and in the meantime, as I am a teetotaller, I hope you'll join Bruce Hemmingway in a glass of wine.'

For two hours Neils kept them enthralled with stories of Saati manifestations he had encountered, so that even the most sceptical was secretly glad that the party numbered seven resolute men; but he would say nothing of his discoveries in the château until, glancing at his watch, he saw that it was half-past twelve. Then he began to recount the experiences of Bruce and himself since their arrival.

Turning to Bruce, he went on: 'My suspicions were aroused last night when you were attacked in the pentacle. Mentally you were unharmed, but your hand was red and inflamed, as though it had been burnt. Early this morning I returned to the bathroom and pulled up the boards upon which the water-jug was resting, taking care not to touch the floor anywhere near it. Underneath there were the decaying bodies of two rats and three electric wires, the naked leads of which were inserted in the plank to look from above like nails. You remember that curious sound of tapping fingers on the recording machine, which is so much more sensitive than our ears. When I saw those wires I suddenly realized what it meant. Somewhere in the château a person was working a morse transmitter.'

'By Jove!' The Colonel jumped to his feet. 'A spy!'

Neils nodded. 'Yes. Long before the war, no doubt, the Germans laid a secret cable from their own lines to the château, reckoning that their agent here would be able to work undisturbed because no one would come to the place on account of its sinister reputation. But to make quite certain of being able to scare away any intruders they ran electric wires to a dozen different points in the building, mainly to door-knobs; but the lavatory seats and bathroom also particularly lent themselves to such purpose.'

'But we've searched every room in the place,' Bruce exclaimed, 'so where does the spy conceal himself?'

The officers were now all on their feet. 'Grand work, Mr Orsen!' cried the Colonel. 'He may even be sending a message now. Let's go and get him.'

It was after one o'clock when Orsen led the way out of the château. They stumbled through tangled undergrowth, barking their shins on unseen obstacles for nearly twenty minutes until Neils halted in a clearing among the trees which was almost filled by a large grassy mound.

'What's this?' the captain asked, flashing his torch.

'It's an ice-house,' the little man replied as he pulled open a thick, slanting wooden trap almost hidden by moss and ivy. 'In the old days, before refrigerators were invented, people used to cut blocks of ice out of their lakes when they were frozen in the winter and store them in these places. The temperature remained constant owing to the fact that they were underground and invariably in woods, which always retain moisture, so the ice was preserved right through the summer.'

A dank musty smell filled their nostrils as, almost bent double, they followed Neils inside. Ahead of them in the far corner of the cellar loomed a dark cavity. 'This is the way the ghost comes,' Orsen murmured. 'Mind how you go; there'll be one or two holes, I expect.'

The silence seemed to bear down on them as they crept forward through a dark tunnel and the deathly chill penetrated their thick overcoats. No one spoke. On and on they went. The passage seemed to wind interminably before them; occasionally a rat scurried across their path. Suddenly, as they rounded a bend, a bright shaft of light struck their eyes. For a second they stood practically blinded and two of the officers produced revolvers.

Neils let them precede him into the secret cellar, but they did not need their weapons. At its far end, sprawled over the table which held a big telegraphic transmitting-set, was the body of a man.

'There, gentlemen, is your ghost,' Orsen announced quietly. 'No, don't touch him, you fool!' he snapped, as the captain stretched out a hand towards the corpse. 'He's been electrocuted and the current isn't switched off yet.'

'Electrocuted?' the captain gasped. 'But how did that happen?'

'The powerful battery you borrowed for me this morning from the Air Force people,' Neils said. 'I attached it to the leads in the bathroom, then came down here and fixed the other end of the wires to the side of the transmitter key.'

'Good God!' exclaimed the colonel. 'But this is most irregular.'

'Quite,' Neils agreed, 'and, of course, I'm neutral in this war, but I'm not neutral in the greater war that is always going on between good and evil. This man murdered that poor fellow who died in the bathroom. So I decided to save you a shooting party.'

# Acknowledgements

*The Editor gratefully acknowledges permission to reprint copyright material to the following: Martin Amis and A. D. Peters & Co. Ltd for* Denton's Death. *Denys Val Baker and William Kimber & Co. Ltd for* The Potter's Art *from 'The Secret Place' (pub. 1977); copyright © Jess Val Baker 1977. The Executors of the Estate of K. S. P. McDowall and A. P. Watt Ltd for* The Thing in the Hall *by E. F. Benson, from 'The Horror Hour and Other Stories'. Robert Bloch and the Scott Meredith Literary Agency Inc., 845 Third Avenue, New York, N.Y. 10022, U.S.A., for* The Mannikin. *The Author and Curtis Brown Ltd, New York, N.Y., for* They Bite; *copyright © Anthony Boucher 1943. The Estate of Elizabeth Bowen, Jonathan Cape Ltd, and Alfred A. Knopf Inc. for* The Demon Lover *from 'The Demon Lover' and 'The Collected Stories of Elizabeth Bowen'; copyright 1946 and renewed 1974 by Elizabeth Bowen. Hilary Long for* The Crown Derby Plate *by Marjorie Bowen, from 'The Last Bouquet'; copyright © Hilary Long 1952. The Author, A. M. Heath & Co. Ltd and Nat Sobel Literary Agency, New York, for* The Kite *by Christianna Brand (first published in the U.S.A. under the title 'King of the Air'). David Higham Associates Ltd for* Blind Man's Hood *by John Dickson Carr. The Author for* The Door *from 'Cold Terror'; copyright © R. Chetwynd-Hayes 1973. Hughes Massie Ltd and Dodd, Mead & Co., Inc. for* The Strange Case of Sir Arthur Carmichael, *from 'The Hound of Death'; copyright © Agatha Christie 1933; also from 'The Golden Ball and Other Stories' by Agatha Christie; copyright © 1933 by Christie Copyrights Trust; copyright © 1971 by Christie Copyrights Trust. The Author and Murray Pollinger for* Blackberries; *copyright © Roger Clarke 1983. The Author for* The Moon Web; *copyright © Adrian Cole 1978. Mrs. Doris M. Cowles for* The Horror of Abbot's Grange *by Frederick Cowles. Roald Dahl, Murray Pollinger and Alfred A. Knopf Inc. for* Pig, *from 'Kiss Kiss', published by Michael Joseph and Penguin Books in the U.K., and Alfred A. Knopf Inc. in the U.S.A. copyright © 1959 by Roald Dahl.* Robbie *is copyright © Mary Danby 1982. Arkham House Publishers Inc., Sauk City, Wisconsin 53583, U.S.A., for* The Extra Passenger *by August Derleth. John Goodchild for* The Witch's Bone *by William Croft Dickinson from 'Dark Encounters', copyright © William Croft Dickinson 1963.* The Haunted Haven *is copyright © A. E. Ellis 1982. The Author for* Friends; *copyright © Catherine Gleason 1976. The Author and A. M. Heath & Co. for* The Circus *by Winston Graham. Harold Matson Co., Inc. for* Where the Woodbine Twineth *by Davis Grubb; copyright © Davis Grubb 1964. The Author and London Management for* Waking or Sleeping, *reprinted from 'The Midnight Ghost Book' edited by James Hale; copyright © Willis Hall 1978. Hamish Hamilton Ltd for* Someone in the Lift *from 'The Complete Short Stories of L. P. Hartley'; copyright © The Executors of the Estate of L. P. Hartley 1973. The Author for* The Peculiar Case of Mrs. Grimmond; *copyright © Dorothy K. Haynes 1973. Patricia Highsmith, Wm. Heinemann Ltd and Gotham Art and Literary Agency, New York, for* The Day of Reckoning *from 'The Animal-Lovers Book of Beastly Murder'. A. M. Heath & Co. Ltd for* Taboo *by Geoffrey Household, from*